Praise for Larry Bond and *Cold Choices*

"Nobody alive knows more about submarines and submarine tactics than Larry Bond, the designer of *Harpoon*. In addition, he's one hell of a writer, which he proves once again in *Cold Choices*."

—Stephen Coonts,
New York Times bestselling author of *The Assassin*

"Larry Bond's new submarine thriller, *Cold Choices*, sends *The Hunt for Red October*, *Das Boot*, and *Run Silent, Run Deep* straight to the bottom of the sea!"

—Douglas Preston,
New York Times bestselling author of *Blasphemy*

"Forget everything you've ever heard about submarine novels! The sub battles in *Cold Choices* will have you biting your nails, shaking in your shoes, and gasping for breath. The king of the twenty-first-century sub thrillers is back."

—David Hagberg,
New York Times bestselling author of *The Expediter*

FORGE BOOKS BY LARRY BOND

Dangerous Ground
Cold Choices
Crash Dive (editor)

FORGE BOOKS BY LARRY BOND AND JIM DEFELICE

Larry Bond's First Team
Larry Bond's First Team: Angels of Wrath
Larry Bond's First Team: Fires of War
Larry Bond's First Team: Soul of the Assassin

LARRY BOND

COLD CHOICES

A TOM DOHERTY ASSOCIATES BOOK
NEW YORK

NOTE: If you purchased this book without a cover, you should be aware that this book is stolen property. It was reported as "unsold and destroyed" to the publisher, and neither the author nor the publisher has received any payment for this "stripped book."

This is a work of fiction. All of the characters, organizations, and events portrayed in this novel are either products of the author's imagination or are used fictitiously.

COLD CHOICES

A Forge Book
Published by Tom Doherty Associates, LLC
175 Fifth Avenue
New York, NY 10010

www.tor-forge.com

ISBN 978-0-7653-5846-2

First Edition: May 2009
First Mass Market Edition: March 2010

Printed in the United States of America

0 9 8 7 6 5 4 3 2 1

Dedicated to our former comrades aboard USS *McKean* (DD-784) and USS *Lafayette* (SSBN-616). The ships are both gone, but we will always be shipmates.

Thanks to Mike and Angela Pelke for your friendship as well as your sharp eyes.

AUTHOR'S NOTE

I like writing, and the experience is only improved when you have someone to bounce ideas off of, to find a way through the twists and turns of a plot, and to cheer you on when inspiration is lagging. It's better still when the coauthor is someone whose judgment you trust as much or even more than your own.

I've known Chris Carlson for twenty-seven years, and we've worked together on a dozen projects of our own creation. His ability to process facts is only matched by his ability to tolerate my own fuzzy understanding of technology.

Each of us approached this story from a different angle, but instead of creating conflict, it made our combined work a richer story. It's impossible to look at the text and say, "Chris wrote this," or "I wrote that." And why would I want to? This work is equally Chris's and mine. By respecting and understanding what each of us brings to the task, we can do things together that would be impossible alone.

I'm already looking forward to the next one.

COLD CHOICES

PROLOGUE

ALL THE WATER IN THE WORLD

20 August 2008
Groton, Connecticut

Jerry Mitchell braced himself. There was no sensation of a hit, but the force of the inrushing water almost knocked two sailors off their feet. The liquid roar fought with the loudspeaker. "FLOODING IN ENGINE ROOM LOWER LEVEL!" The mechanical voice echoed off the metal bulkheads. He felt the air temperature drop, which gave only the briefest warning when the cold spray reached where he stood.

Jerry fought the urge to rush in and help. Like all submariners, he was trained to run toward the sound of rushing water, but he was also supposed to lead these men. They struggled against the multiple fire-hose jets, but there were enough guys to get the job done. That was one of the first things he looked for, then whether they had the right equipment to plug each leak. But as he watched them work, he relaxed, as much as any submariner could with water lapping around his ankles. His men were on top of it. They knew what to do, and they were working together.

He watched and waited. He suspected they were in for a beating. Sure enough, a rattling BOOM echoed through the space, and the loudspeaker blared "DEPTH CHARGE ATTACK! CLOSE ABOARD!" The reverberation hadn't even died down when Jerry was drenched by a new jet of water as a pipe behind him cracked. He got out of the way as Petty Officer Robinson ran over with a bandit patch and began fitting it over the pipe. Two other pipe joints had also ruptured, and Jerry heard ETC Hudson, the leading chief petty officer, quickly order people to deal with those new leaks. Turning toward Lieutenant Chandler, his phone talker, Jerry passed on the disheartening news to control.

Engine room lower level was a crowded collection of machinery, piping, and tanks, with catwalks and ladders passing through the tangled compartment. People filled most of the open space—very active people, as they struggled with tools and materials to plug or patch the holes in the pipes. Water continued gushing in, with some of the jets packing enough punch to knock a man over if he wasn't careful. The solid streams splashed and ricocheted off the jumbled surfaces, throwing spray up in everyone's face. Even when Jerry could keep the water out of his eyes, the white spray made it difficult to see more than a couple of feet away. And there was the incredible noise. The extra leaks raised the sound to levels reserved for the back end of a jet engine.

In spite of the cold and the wet, the operations department was doing a great job. They worked as a team, looking to Hudson or one of the other senior petty officers for direction. Jerry occasionally heard shouting, of course. They had to raise their voices to be heard over the roaring water, but the tone was calm, reports and directions deliberate.

The water was up to his knees when the auxiliary seawater flange broke. A three-quarter-inch gap opened up where two pipe flanges joined near the overhead. If anyone in the space had been bone dry, this alone would have drenched them. Jerry could see the water level begin to rise more quickly.

Hudson, shaking the water off his face, immediately detailed two men to deal with the flange. Jerry watched them try to bring the pieces back together and his eyes continued upward to a glass-covered booth. Inside, a master chief petty officer, his arms folded, looked down on the chaos and smiled.

Of course, they'd lose in the end. It was impossible to keep USS *Buttercup* afloat. No matter how many leaks the crew patched, new ones would appear, more water would flood in, and eventually the trainer would "sink." The real question was, how would his team perform before the inevitable?

It was one thing to sit through damage-control lectures, study diagrams, and practice in a dry, quiet space. The "wet trainer" made it real. You learned how to handle wet tools, how to hold a mattress over a torrent of inrushing water, and how to keep working as water battered your body and the water temperature made your internal organs cluster around your spine, huddling together for warmth.

Most wet trainers looked like the inside of a surface ship's berthing or engineering spaces. This one, in Groton, Connecticut, was built to look like the inside of a submarine. From the outside, it was just another anonymous concrete brick building on the base, identified by a blue and yellow building number. Inside the two-story building, a mass of catwalks and piping surrounded the incongruous-looking hull section. An 80,000-gallon tank supplied the facility with enough water to fill it to the overhead.

The trainers sat above the space in comfort, controlling which leaks occurred and the water pressure behind them. Although the control booth sat well above the simulated compartment, the windows were fitted with windshield wipers—in use, Jerry noted.

Lieutenant Jerry Mitchell was the navigator/operations officer aboard USS *Seawolf* (SSN 21), one of the U.S. Navy's most capable nuclear attack submarines. He still couldn't believe his luck in landing an assignment on *Seawolf,* but didn't trust to luck in doing his job.

Jerry was in charge of the operations department, with enlisted rates like quartermasters, electronics technicians, and information systems technicians working for him. They were not engineering specialists, but all submariners were sensibly required to be experts in fighting flooding and fire, and all other types of "casualties." That was the less threatening navy term for an accident or equipment failure. Jerry drilled his men hard, maybe even a little harder than they wanted. Now it was paying big dividends.

He'd been aboard for almost six months, and he knew these men well. Like all submariners, they were volunteers: screened, tested, and trained. But that didn't mean they couldn't screw up.

Or make poor choices. The broken flange really had dramatically increased the rate the water was rising, and the level was approaching Jerry's chest. Poor Bishop, the shortest guy in the department, was already treading water. Chief Hudson was trying to cover every leak, but there were just not enough people anymore.

"Chief Hudson!" Jerry was only a few feet away, but in the soggy pandemonium, Hudson couldn't hear. He was absorbed in wedging a shoring timber properly. He was too close to the problem. Jerry fought the urge to give the orders himself. Instead, he put his hand on Hudson's shoulder, gently pulling him back from the action. He spoke slowly, forcing calm into the situation. "Worry about the big ones! You can't plug them all! The drain pumps can handle the smaller leaks!"

He swung his arm around the space, encouraging Hudson to take in the "big picture." Hudson quickly nodded, droplets of water flying as he did. The electronics technician paused for a moment, considering, before calling out to his team and reassigning some men to the larger leaks.

Jerry knew the simulation would be over soon, but it was never too late to do the right thing. Sure enough, no sooner had Hudson's men started their new tasks than an amazingly loud klaxon jolted them to a stop. The rush of water faded, taking the urgency with it. It left Jerry and his department standing in neck-deep water. A new sound, a low-pitched whirring, took over as pumps began dewatering the space.

"Well done, *Seawolf* ops department." The chief trainer's voice boomed over the loudspeaker. "Debrief in fifteen minutes." The trainer's compliment let a part of Jerry relax as well. *Seawolf* had a reputation in her squadron and the Atlantic Fleet. This might have been just an exercise, but it was also a chance for *Seawolf* to shine. Neither Jerry nor his men had any intention of letting their boat down.

As the water level fell, his men stowed the tools and materials they'd used, then filed out, dripping and shivering.

They toweled off as the trainers conferred, then started their debrief. The master chief was matter-of-fact, but merciless. Jerry's men knew the basics—that was expected—but they had to be better than just good. The master chief reviewed how they used their tools, how to quickly set up a shoring timber, even how to hammer wedges into a hole that was underwater. "You may think you're wet now. But if your boat takes a hit, you'll be a long way from help, and all the water in the world is on the other side of that hole. If you can't deal with it, you'll lose the boat, the mission, and your lives."

Jerry watched as his men listened attentively to the critique. A deep sense of pride welled up within him; each one was a professional. He felt particularly blessed, as Chief Hudson and the other senior enlisted men in the department were all strong performers. The "plankowners" that had brought *Seawolf* into service had long ago rotated off, and theoretically the submariners now assigned to her were no better than the rest of the fleet, but Jerry felt and thought they were a cut above the rest. And yes, they were "his" guys . . .

"All things considered, gentlemen, you did very well," concluded the master chief with a grin. "I'll inform your XO that you all died valiantly trying to save your boat. Any questions?"

A collective groan, plus a volley of wet towels, was the operations department's response. Jerry laughed as the master chief expertly dodged the assault. The skipper and the XO were going to be pleased with his department's grade. His men had taken everything the training team had to give before they lost the fight. In a way, it was almost a compliment, if a damp one.

Jerry didn't mind. The more you trained for something, the less likely it was that you'd ever actually have to use it.

1

BEWARE THE WOLF

7 September 2008
Pier 8, New London Submarine Base

"Petty Officer Gibson, front and center," barked Jerry as he and the communications officer, Lieutenant Chandler, stood in front of the operations department, assembled in *Seawolf*'s navigation equipment room. *Seawolf* was one of the biggest attack submarines in the U.S. Navy, but the ops department was just barely able to squeeze everyone in.

When Jerry called out his name, Gibson stepped up smartly and took the clipboard. IT2 Paul Gibson had been aboard the boat longer than Jerry. He was a little on the pudgy side, a common problem on subs where great food and few opportunities for exercise left their mark. He was twenty-seven, with a wife and a one-year-old son. He took position in front of the assembled sailors and began reading the plan of the day.

"Our underway is now in eight days. Supply chits have to be turned in by tomorrow if Mr. Constantino is supposed to fill them . . ."

Jerry already knew what the PoD said, and Gibson had everything under control. As he stood, half-listening, Jerry looked over the operations department—*his* department.

That still sounded strange, even after six months on board. Ops department was eighteen men, including Jerry and Lieutenant Chandler.

As the commo, Chandler was in charge of six "information systems technicians," or "ITs," although most of the crew still called them radiomen. And he was responsible for all the boat's communications equipment and encryption gear.

And as operations officer, Jerry was responsible for everyone in the department, including Chandler. Jerry was also *Seawolf*'s navigator, in direct charge of the four quartermasters and six electronics technicians who ran the boat's navigation systems.

His sailors were neatly lined up in three groups, wearing clean working uniforms. Civilians would be impressed by their military bearing and discipline. But Jerry knew he faced a band of rugged individualists who worked together only by choice. And while they worked together well, that didn't come automatically, or even easily.

"Family day is Saturday, with a cookout at the ball field. We're still looking for some people to help with the kids' games, so contact MM2 Stone if you're interested. The ship's ombudsman and the family support network still need email addresses . . ."

Jerry's mind wandered to his own personal "to do" list. However, since he was navigator, operations officer, and senior watch officer, technically it was "lists." Oh. And he was one of three qualified divers on board.

As he mentally went down his tally, he looked down at his watch to check the time. No sweat, he still had fifteen minutes before his meeting with Lieutenant Commander Shimko, the executive officer. He had to go over the voyage plan—again. The crew wouldn't be briefed about their destination until they were under way, but Jerry not only knew where they were going, he had planned out their entire trip in detail.

It was to *Seawolf*'s benefit that the XO was a detail freak, but it didn't make Jerry's life any easier. He was pretty sure he'd dreamed about the north Barents Sea again last night. He'd been cold when he woke up.

Gibson finished reading the PoD and looked expectantly at Jerry. Sensing his cue, Mitchell stepped forward and asked, "Do the chiefs or leading petty officers have anything further to add?" All four men responded in the negative.

"All right, then. Turn to and commence ship's work. Dismissed." As the members of the department queued up to exit through the narrow door into the control room, Jerry saw QM1 Peters waiting for his turn, and caught the quartermaster's eye. He pointed to his watch and then held up five fingers. Peters nodded, understanding. The ship's leading quartermaster would be at the briefing with the XO as well.

Jerry waited patiently to exit the nav equipment space and quickly headed aft to his stateroom. Even though the wardroom was on the same deck, and near his quarters, he'd have to hurry a little if he wanted to be punctual. To save time, he'd already organized the materials he needed to bring the night before, but as he approached his stateroom he saw Lieutenant Chandler waiting with a sheaf of papers in his hand and an earnest expression on his face. "Jerry, here are the last of our school requests, but I need to ask you a few questions . . ."

Jerry cut him off as he stepped into his stateroom. "Sorry, Matt. I'm wearing my navigator hat right now. I've got a voyage planning review in the wardroom with the XO." He dialed his safe and began removing his notes.

"I know, but this will only take a moment, and I have to turn them in this morning," the comms officer pleaded.

"It'll be morning for some time yet, and I do not want to keep the XO waiting." Closing the safe should have added a note of finality to Jerry's statement.

Chandler wouldn't give up. "I'll just turn them in as is. They're probably fine."

"Not without me seeing them first," Jerry insisted. That was standard procedure for any paperwork going up the chain of command. And Chandler knew better. When the commo smiled and started to offer Jerry the documents, Jerry repeated, "After the meeting. Find me then," he said firmly, letting some irritation show. Jerry didn't like mind games. Chandler seemed to think it was the only way to get things done.

Hurrying the few steps to the wardroom, Jerry entered and found QM1 Peters already inside, laying out the charts. Jerry checked them over one last time, carefully comparing them to his own notes. Only after everything appeared in order did he allow himself to get a cup of coffee.

ETC Hudson and Lieutenant Commander Shimko appeared in the door as Jerry was pouring. He offered a cup to the XO, who gratefully accepted one. Peters also had some, but Hudson declined.

Marcus Shimko was second-generation American, born to Andrei and Natalia six years after they'd emigrated from what was then the Soviet Union and now Belarus. He was short, about Jerry's height, but stocky where Jerry was slim. Shimko had already lost a lot of his hair, but what was left was sandy and cut very short. He was all business, an exceptional organizer and a detail hound—the perfect executive officer.

Jerry teased Hudson about "not stooping to drink wardroom coffee" but kept one eye on the XO. When the executive officer sat down, ship's business took over. Jerry picked up his notes while Hudson double-checked the wardroom door, making sure it was locked.

With his laser pointer, Jerry highlighted individual sections of the entire mission on the nautical chart taped to the table. The bright blue and yellow chart was overlaid with black lines showing *Seawolf*'s plotted course, and red TOP SECRET labels rubber-stamped on each corner.

"Our projected track takes us out of the Block Island Sound, east, and then northeast. I've recommended passing to the west of Iceland, using the Denmark Strait. Once past Iceland, we follow the east coast of Greenland, using shallow water and biologics wherever possible to mask our approach. Assuming an on-time departure on the fifteenth and a speed of advance of sixteen knots, we should arrive at Point Alpha at 1200 Zulu time on the twenty-third." Jerry pointed to the first of a series of x's on the chart.

He'd rehearsed the speech several times, and gotten it off smoothly. Shimko just nodded, inviting Jerry to continue. So far, so good.

"I've marked the known Russian exercise areas and traffic lanes on the chart. They've used these same areas for six years, and there's no indication that they plan to change them. We have two areas to survey, and a total of eighteen sorties with the three UUVs. Based on what little information we have about this part of the Barents, I've chosen sites within each area with potentially good bottom topography and reasonable acoustic conditions, but also a safe route in and out during the survey."

Shimko and Hudson studied the chart closely. Jerry and Peters, having laid out the courses and knowing them by heart, stayed out of the way to give the XO and chief some room.

"How long for each survey?" Shimko asked.

"I'm planning on forty-five hours. The UUVs have a fifty-hour operational endurance with a ten-hour emergency reserve. That gives us about a twenty-five-percent safety margin."

"How many UUVs will we have out at any one time?"

"Technically, XO, there are times during the mission, for about an hour, when all three UUVs will be out. One will be deployed surveying sites, while a second unit is launched and the third waits to be recovered."

"During which *Seawolf* is tied to one area."

"Yessir. We're only constrained in our ability to maneuver when we're launching or recovering a UUV, which takes no more than half an hour. Once that's done we can maneuver freely, we just have to stay relatively close to the rendezvous point so the UUV can find us again . . ."

"Never mind," Shimko interrupted. "The critical issue is being committed to one spot while a UUV is deployed. What if we have to abort a rendezvous to evade a transiting vessel?"

Jerry had an answer. "Sea ice will be starting to form in the area by the time we arrive, so there is little risk of running into fishing traffic or even other merchant ships. The only likely problem would be from Russian warships or submarines, and according to the intel weenies, their training cycle is largely over for the year. There may be some small-scale operations before the ports freeze up, but they just concluded a major exercise period. Our mission plan is to get in, do the surveys, and then get out before they start any last-minute training evolutions."

Shimko was not deflected. "If we have to bug out, we need a plan to rendezvous with the UUV somewhere else." He pointed to an exercise area, outlined in blue and neatly labeled "R-Two."

"Overall, you've got a good approach route into the area, and the route leading from one survey site to the next is along a good path. You also have an emergency recovery location for each site, but it's too close to the site itself. I want two alternate rendezvous locations for each survey site, well away from the box."

"Yessir," Jerry responded. "For unmanned vehicles, they are pretty smart. If a survey is interrupted, we can give it a new location and tell it to loiter there until we arrive."

"That's fine, but I don't want you hunting all over the chart for a spot when the air is filled with flying excrement. I want it already picked and plotted in calmer times." Jerry nodded his understanding.

Shimko pushed his point. "This is the Russian Navy's playground, even if it is international waters. They're normally touchy about visitors, but since they lost *Gepard,* they've reached new heights of paranoia—even for Slavs.

"You know, they blame us for *Gepard*'s loss." Shimko gave Jerry a look that seemed much longer and more intense than a simple glance. Jerry's last boat, *Memphis,* had been very involved with the Russian sub's demise, but the entire event had been classified, sealed, and was withheld even from the rest of the submarine service. Jerry tried to look innocent.

"We can't assume they won't change their routine," Shimko continued. "Maybe they'll patrol in the thickening sea ice for a longer period than we think. The hulls on their surface ships are ice-strengthened." He shrugged, then ordered, "Also, find and plot more than one exit route from each site, and make sure the routes lead to areas with lots of maneuvering room."

"Yessir." Jerry acknowledged the order and checked to make sure that Peters was taking notes.

"Now walk me through it," Shimko ordered, and Jerry began with *Seawolf*'s careful entrance to the Barents Sea. Framed as it was by the Russian coast to the south and Novaya Zemlya on the east, it was easy to understand why the Russians considered it home waters, the same way Americans might view the Gulf of Mexico.

Seawolf would cross the gap from Greenland to Svalbard, under broken sea ice and hopefully bad weather. Svalbard was a cluster of islands under Norwegian control. It usually hugged the southern edge of the North Pole's permanent ice cap. The sub would pass south of the islands, then turn southeast to conceal her approach as much as possible.

Once in the Barents Sea, *Seawolf* would slow, creeping into areas used by the Russians for fleet training and exercises. These were no more than rectangular shapes drawn on a Russian chart, but they were used by the Russian Navy to manage their at-sea training during the Arctic summer.

The U.S. didn't have those charts, of course. Careful observation of Russian exercises by satellites and submarines and other methods had given U.S. intelligence a pretty good idea of where they were.

American and other Western submarines had prowled those waters for years, watching the Russian Fleet practice their craft, recording signals, sometimes even recovering expended weapons. The Russians watched for outsiders, sometimes finding them, often not. Although the training areas were in international waters and thus theoretically open to anyone, the Russians could make eavesdroppers feel very unwelcome.

Lately Russian antisurveillance measures had become so stringent that it was not only difficult to get close enough to gather any useful intelligence, it had become downright hazardous to anyone making the attempt. And with a shrinking submarine fleet, the U.S. Navy was experiencing difficulties providing comprehensive coverage during the exercise cycle.

So it was time for a new plan. The U.S. would plant acoustic recording devices on the seabed to monitor Russian activity. The information could be recovered later by another submarine when the area was quiet. These sensors would gather some of the raw intelligence data that a submarine would normally be tasked to collect. There would be other Western assets that would still be watching, but their observations would be from a safe distance.

Obviously, secrecy was paramount. If the Russians discovered the sensors' existence, they could be easily destroyed or recovered. Besides the embarrassment, and loss of valuable intelligence, the devices used some very sophisticated technology—not the sort the U.S. wanted to share.

Jerry showed the XO how *Seawolf* would approach each survey site and launch a UUV, an automated underwater robot, to check out the bottom topography and to measure the ambient acoustic conditions. Several sites would be examined in each exercise area. The collected data would be used by the bright boys back home to compute the exact sensor locations, which would be planted later.

After examining every yard of their planned path, the XO quizzed Jerry about GPS satellite coverage, deviation from standard sonar conditions, marine life in the area, and the effects of the aurora borealis on communications. Jerry's ready answers pleased Shimko, but earned him a crack about "smartass know-it-all."

"Make those changes I mentioned and we'll brief the Skipper tomorrow at nineteen hundred."

"Aye, aye, XO," Jerry replied. Shimko finished, "That's all, then."

Jerry turned to help his chief gather up the maps and notes, but Shimko called him aside.

"How's the watch bill coming?" the XO asked.

"It's done," Jerry answered, "I'll have a smooth copy on your desk this afternoon."

"Fine." Having watched Jerry mentally shift gears,

Shimko hit him with the real question. "Who's taking her out?" he asked, in a voice slightly softer than normal conversation.

As senior watch officer, Jerry not only made up the underway watch bill, he managed the junior officers' training. Conning *Seawolf* when she got under way was an important learning opportunity for a junior member of the wardroom.

"Hayes," Jerry replied followed by a short pause, "and Palmer. With your permission, sir."

Shimko frowned. "Palmer," he repeated, working through the idea and not enjoying the implications. "After the hash he made of his last underway, why should I give him another chance?"

Jerry hoped the question was rhetorical. "Because he can't qualify without it," he replied earnestly. "Because he learns from his mistakes."

"And if he flubs, it's too late to replace him," Shimko replied acidly. "*Seawolf* is not just a training aid, and I'm not inclined to risk the boat as we leave for an important mission."

"Lieutenant Palmer would be pleased to answer any questions about underway procedures you wish to ask," Jerry replied positively.

"Fine. I'll see both of you right after lunch tomorrow."

"Day after tomorrow?" Jerry replied hopefully. "They'll be loading weapons all day today and most of tomorrow."

Shimko sighed. "All right. Day after tomorrow, then." He paused, then said, "You can't carry him forever, Jerry."

"He'll find his feet, sir. He just needs a little more time."

"I hope so, for everyone's sake," the XO answered as he left the wardroom.

Peters and Hudson had finished collecting all the charts, and Jerry double-checked them as they left to make sure nothing was left behind. Everyone on a nuclear submarine had some sort of security clearance, but it didn't pay to get sloppy with sensitive documents. Although he might have more room in a jail cell, the food was worse.

CHANDLER WAS not in his stateroom, or in the comms shack. Jerry hadn't expected the man to be waiting outside the wardroom, but he begrudged the time it would take to find the commo, and he couldn't trust Chandler to find him.

Matthew Lloyd Chandler III was a good officer. The son of a successful submarine admiral, he'd just made lieutenant and seemed destined for higher rank. But as communications officer and Jerry's subordinate on the ship's organizational chart, Chandler seemed to be a drain on his time, not an asset.

He finally found Chandler in the ship's office. When he saw Jerry, the lieutenant spoke first. "I got those questions answered, sir. I should have looked in the manual," he said humbly, gesturing to a fat notebook on a rack over the yeoman's desk.

Chandler's formality irked Jerry. He did work for Jerry, and it was of course proper to address officers senior to oneself as "sir," but naval custom allowed officers who worked together and were separated by one pay grade to use first names. The submarine service was even more informal. And any pretext for formality had been removed two months ago, when Chandler had been promoted from lieutenant j.g. to full lieutenant, the same rank as Jerry.

"Petty Officer Wallace helped me find what I needed." Chandler nodded toward the yeoman, sounding grateful.

Then why didn't you ask him in the first place? Jerry thought, but suppressed the urge to say it. He simply said, "Good. Then are they ready for me?"

"Yessir." Chandler handed over the forms.

Jerry reviewed them on the spot, since their next stop was the ship's office. They were neatly filled out. He took his time, but couldn't decide if he was pleased or irritated to find everything in order.

As Jerry read, the phone in the ship's office buzzed, and Wallace answered. He listened for a moment, then replied, "I'll tell him." Wallace turned to Jerry. "Chief Hudson's looking for you. He's in officers' country."

"I'll meet him there," Jerry answered. He initialed the forms and handed them to the yeoman.

Chief Hudson was waiting by Jerry's stateroom with a third-class petty officer Jerry didn't recognize. The young sailor nervously came to attention when he saw Jerry, and Mitchell let him stay that way for the moment.

"Lieutenant Mitchell, this is Petty Officer Dennis Rountree," Hudson reported. "He's just come aboard, fresh from school. Here's his service jacket."

Jerry opened the file and skimmed it quickly. Twenty years old, although he looked about fourteen. Good scores, no disciplinary problems. He'd expected that, but it never hurt to check. "At ease, Petty Officer Rountree." Jerry smiled as he said it, trying to really put the young man at ease. "Welcome aboard. You're coming to a great boat with a handpicked crew. Since you've just been picked as well, you're allowed a few moments to feel proud, before Chief Hudson starts working your tail off. We're getting under way in eight days, and we'll be gone for a while. Are you ready for that? Everything squared away ashore?"

"Yes, sir. I can't wait," Rountree replied enthusiastically.

Jerry's smile matched the chief's. "Keep that attitude, and you'll do well." Turning to Hudson, he asked, "Did you phone the XO?"

"Yessir, he said to see him when we're done."

It was only a few steps from Jerry's stateroom to the XO's. Jerry knocked twice, lightly, and waited to hear "Come" before turning the knob.

Lieutenant Commander Shimko had the neatest stateroom Jerry had ever seen. Of course, when you live in a space the size of a walk-in closet, neatness is more than just a virtue, but the XO's room was almost pathologically spotless. Shimko's stateroom had two bunks on one side, separated from the opposite bulkhead by a three-foot-wide patch of linoleum deck. That bulkhead held a sink and mirror. Next to that was a closet, and next to that a fold-down desk. A chair in front of the desk took up about a third of the available floor space.

Any open wall space was covered with clipboards or papers taped to the bulkhead. All the papers were taped in exactly the same way, at exactly the same height. The clipboards all hung at the same height as the papers.

Although the stateroom could accommodate two officers, the XO customarily had the stateroom to himself, unless a guest was aboard. Shimko had converted the upper bunk into additional file space, piles of folders and papers arranged with mathematical precision. Even the in and out baskets, full almost to overflowing, managed to look organized.

"XO, sir, this is Electronics Technician Third Class Rountree." Jerry offered the XO his file.

Shimko took it and then offered his hand to the sailor. "Welcome aboard. Any issues or questions so far?"

"No, sir," Rountree replied quickly.

"Good, let me see if the Captain's free." He stepped down the passageway to a door with *Seawolf*'s seal on it. It showed a snarling wolf's head rising from the blue ocean against a black background. A black banner across the top held the boat's name in red. Another banner under the seal read, "*Cave Lupum*"—"Beware the Wolf." Underneath the seal, a gleaming brass plaque read "Captain." Jerry could hear music from the captain's stateroom; it was the bugle solo from the skipper's favorite song, "Boogie Woogie Bugle Boy." For some strange reason, their captain loved

1930s–1940s-era music. Shimko sighed, rapped once, then cracked the door. "Petty Officer Rountree, sir."

Jerry heard the music stop, and then the captain say, "Good. Show him in, XO," and then the door opened the rest of the way. The XO stepped back and motioned for the young sailor to step forward. Jerry and Chief Hudson remained at ease, but Rountree snapped to attention.

Commander Thomas Rudel looked more like a bank teller than a sea captain. He wasn't tall, didn't have a barrel chest, and didn't even have a bellowing voice. Jerry had seldom ever heard him raise it, or even speak sharply.

He didn't need to raise it. The crew had learned that Rudel was incredibly smart, eminently practical, and at times very funny. The XO tended toward the more satirical "phortune cookie filosophy," but Rudel's humor was subtle and dry—you had to listen for it, but it was worth the effort.

"Welcome aboard, Petty Officer Rountree." Rudel sounded genuinely glad to have the young man aboard. "You're joining a great boat with a great crew. 'Great' means getting the job done, and it means taking care of each other. You can't do one without the other. Everyone in the chain of command, which now includes you, watches out above, below, and to either side for his shipmates . . ."

Jerry didn't mean to tune out the captain's welcome-aboard speech, but he'd heard it several times, including on his own arrival aboard. And he couldn't listen to Rudel's speech without flashing back to his first boat, and his first captain.

JERRY'S TOUR aboard USS *Memphis* had turned out well, but that was in spite of Commander Lowell Hardy, *Memphis*'s skipper. Where Rudel called on nobler motives, Hardy had ruled by fear. Jerry's first meeting with his first captain was a preemptive ass-chewing that had left Jerry questioning his career choice.

Hardy had compensated for his intimidating manner by micromanaging the entire boat. Any good submariner was detail-oriented, but focused on his own job. Hardy didn't trust anyone's skills or motivation—and the crew had felt it, both the officers and the enlisted men.

Hardy ruled by fear because that's what he felt. His fear of someone else's error ruining his record was transformed by the crew into fear of doing anything without first checking with the captain. It was no way to run any naval vessel, much less a submarine. A fire on board had caused serious damage to *Memphis*, and the crew's response showed Hardy that there were better ways to lead men.

He'd just started to trust Jerry when they'd been attacked by Russian forces . . .

MITCHELL SNAPPED back to the present when Commander Rudel finished his speech with his trademark line: "Now go work your tail off." Jerry realized he'd used the same phrase when he welcomed Rountree aboard, but he wasn't worried about copying Rudel's command style.

Hudson and Rountree headed aft. Jerry noted the smile on Rountree's face. The skipper had that effect on people. Excusing himself, Jerry headed forward and down one deck to the torpedo room. He had to find Palmer, and check on the UUVs.

Lieutenant (j.g.) Jeff Palmer was a weak link in *Seawolf*'s chain of command. It wasn't enough to have intelligence or determination or even a good attitude. Nobody got through the nuclear pipeline and sub school without those abilities, but they weren't enough to get Jeff Palmer qualified.

Every submariner had to "qualify" aboard his boat. It meant knowing every system aboard in detail, not just the equipment you worked with in your own job. In an emergency, if the boat suffered some sort of accident or was damaged in a fight, everyone aboard had to know what to do. The candidate had to be able to draw the air, hydraulic, electrical, and other vital systems from memory. He had to find valves and damage-control equipment while blindfolded. In a real emergency, with the lights out, or the air filled with thick smoke, conditions could be much worse. In addition, the initial response to any casualty also had to be memorized, and understood. And it didn't hurt to have the secondary procedures committed to memory as well.

Both officers and enlisted went through the process. When they qualified, the captain awarded them their "dolphins," an insignia worn on their shirt. Officers had gold dolphins, enlisted men silver. Like an aviator's wings, they represented a lot of work, and were worn with pride.

Jerry's first qualification, aboard *Memphis,* had been an ordeal, for many reasons. Still, he'd done it in record time, in a single patrol. Normally, an officer new to subs would take about a year and a half to qualify. Palmer had been at it now for seventeen months, and had run into trouble from the very start.

Part of the qualification process were "murder boards," oral quizzes by a group of officers on a particular topic. Palmer could study the manuals and practice the procedures until they were second nature, but he seized up under any sort of pressure. Too many questions in rapid succession caused him to freeze, or give answers that were obviously wrong. Men who couldn't handle pressure did not belong on a sub.

Palmer was in the torpedo room, along with Torpedoman Chief Johnson, his division chief, and several of the torpedomen. They were loading weapons for the upcoming mission, which on a *Seawolf*-class sub took quite a while.

The torpedo room on modern U.S. nuclear subs is located aft of the bow, not in it like the old-style WWII boats. The bow on *Seawolf* was completely taken up by three large sonar arrays, including a monstrously huge sonar "ball," covered with passive hydrophones. The eight torpedo tubes, four to a side, were mounted in port and starboard nests complete with individual launching system, and angled outward. Modern guided torpedoes were smart enough to turn after they were launched and head for their prey.

Jerry had been torpedo officer on *Memphis,* and was still impressed by the scale of *Seawolf*'s torpedo armament. His old boat could carry a warload of twenty-six torpedoes and missiles. *Seawolf* could load fifty, and the racks for them filled a two-story compartment. *Seawolf*'s tubes were bigger as well, thirty inches in diameter instead of twenty-one inches. Unfortunately, the U.S. Navy never developed thirty-inch torpedoes, so the tubes were sleeved to accept the standard twenty-one-inch weapons. The space was crowded with weapons and the machinery to move them, but to Jerry it was as large as a cathedral.

Unusually, daylight and sounds from outside filtered into the space. A loading ramp angled from *Seawolf*'s deck, just aft of the sail, down through two decks into the torpedo room. Because Mark 48 torpedoes are twenty and a half feet long and weigh almost two tons, a special loading tray had been rigged to control their downward journey. Torpedomen handled the massive weapons as if they were made of glass, while Chief Johnson watched their every move. One torpedoman wore a set of sound-powered phones, communicating with the rest of the loading detail above.

Jerry paused in the doorway, taking in the division's progress and deciding if this was a good time to talk to Palmer. He was reluctant to distract men loading explosives, but the jaygee saw him and walked over.

"What's up, Nav?" Palmer's good mood almost gave

Jerry another excuse to delay telling him, but it had to be done.

"You're going to conn the boat out when we leave on the fifteenth," Jerry said simply.

Palmer acted like he'd been shot. "Oh, no." If he hadn't been leaning on a fitting, he might have fallen down. He was obviously remembering his last attempt, which had cost the navy a splintered piling and nearly a crushed sonar dome.

"You need this ticket punched, Jeff." Jerry's tone was firm, but positive.

Jeff Palmer was taller than Jerry, though slim. He seemed to shrink as he reluctantly nodded agreement. "You're right, I have to do this."

"And you'll have to answer questions about underway procedures for the XO day after tomorrow. He'll see you in his stateroom right after lunch."

A pale redhead, Palmer turned white. "He'll grind me up like hamburger! I'll never be able to satisfy him."

"Do you think the XO's going to deliberately trip you up?"

"No, but you know what will happen."

Jerry sighed, but managed to do it on the inside. Palmer had developed a real confidence problem, but Jerry wasn't going to blow sunshine at him. That wasn't his job, and it didn't really help the guy. Still, he needed to be positive.

"Jeff, you know the material, you've proven that to me. If you want to stay in subs, you've got to show the XO you know it, then use it to get *Seawolf* under way safely."

"What if I can't get past the XO?"

"Then I'll have Santana take her out," Jerry answered flatly. Ensign Santana was the electrical officer, and was also working on his qualification. To himself, Jerry added,

"And you'll be off the boat and out of subs the day we get back from patrol."

"Who will be the OOD?" asked Palmer hesitantly.

"Mr. Hayes," Jerry replied, and then with a slight grin, "And yes, he knows what he's getting into."

"Thanks, Nav. I'm not too popular with my department head right now. And I don't think I could be up on the bridge with him again. At least not right away."

"You're right, he's not happy with your progress," said Jerry frankly. "And yes, he was upset about your earlier attempt, and not just because he was the OOD. It's his *job* to push you, Jeff. If Greg Wolfe had given you up as a lost cause, would he have spent all those hours working with you?"

"No, sir," answered Palmer quietly.

"All right then. Get your act together and show him you are capable of conning a boat on the surface. You know what to do. You just need to muster the intestinal fortitude and do it. Okay?"

"Yes, sir. I will, sir."

"Correct answer, Mr. Palmer," remarked Jerry. "Now you'd better get back to supervising the weapons loading evolution."

"Aye, aye, sir," Palmer replied with a little more confidence. "And Nav . . . thanks."

Tuesday afternoon
USS *Seawolf*, executive officer's stateroom

When Jeff Palmer knocked on the XO's door and went inside, Jerry stayed in the passageway. The XO had required Jerry to be here, but Palmer would have to answer Shimko's questions alone.

Which was as it should be, Jerry mused. So why was he here at all, he asked himself. Not moral support. The XO had left the door cracked, so Jerry could hear Palmer's performance.

"Mr. Palmer. What will the tides be when we get under way?"

"Ebb tide, sir. Two feet above mean low water, with a two-knot current."

"And the weather?"

"High scattered clouds, light winds from the south, about sixty-five degrees. That's as of this morning according to the NOAA website. I'll check . . ."

"What rudder and bells will you start with?"

"Well, sir, last time I used back one-third and twenty—"

The XO interrupted Palmer. "I didn't ask for a history lesson, mister. What rudder and bells would you use this time, *if* I let you take her out?"

There was a pause, a little longer than Jerry would have liked, and then Palmer said, "The same. Back one-third and twenty-five degrees right rudder." Jerry started to worry. He thought Palmer would last longer before getting rattled, but the XO knew where to apply pressure. Which might be what he wanted Jerry to see.

"What orders are you giving the tug?"

"None yet, sir. I have to get our stern swung out . . ."

"Won't that smash our bow into the pier?" The XO's tone was neutral, with just a tinge of concern. He was challenging Palmer's answers now.

Palmer stammered, but he knew the answer. "I have to limit the swing to no more than thirty degrees. There's a tower on the north shore you can use as a mark. As the rudder swings past that point, I tell the tug to start backing . . ."

"The tug's suffered an engineering casualty." Shimko's tone was still flat, but he spoke quickly.

"Sir?"

"The tug captain tells you he's suffered a breakdown. His engines are dead. He can't give you any help."

Jerry didn't hear an answer right away, and counted the seconds. He imagined the wheels spinning in Palmer's head, and hoped they were finding traction.

"Put number three line back over, then shift to ahead one-third. Use side force from the screw and pivot on number three to push the bow away from the pier." Palmer sounded tentative. If Jerry heard it, so did the XO.

"But you're using ahead engines. Won't that drive our bow into the pier?" More concern in the XO's tone, mixed with skepticism. He was really leaning on Palmer. Shimko remembered Palmer's first underway as well. He knew Palmer would be worried about the bow.

"I'd only leave it on for a moment, sir. We have some sternway. As soon as our sternway was off . . ."

"But what about the tug? As the bow swings around, won't we hit the tug? We're big enough to cave in his hull."

That was a sucker question. Since the tug was up against *Seawolf*'s side, with fenders rigged, there was no chance of damage. Jerry waited for Palmer's reply. And waited.

"Sir, I'm not sure . . ." Palmer's voice was more than unsure.

"The tug skipper's on the radio, yelling that he's holding you personally responsible for any damage to his vessel."

"Sir . . ."

Jerry was waiting for Palmer to implode when the door to the captain's stateroom opened and Rudel stepped into the passageway. Jerry stepped back out of the way, and the skipper politely nodded to him as he walked to the XO's stateroom. Knocking on the half-open door, he walked in without waiting for a reply.

Jerry heard him ask lightly, "So XO, what's the situation?" Shimko quickly summarized the scenario and pointedly remarked, "I'm still waiting for Mr. Palmer's answer." After a short pause, he added, "Mr. Palmer is liable for any damage to the tug."

Jerry was tempted to peek inside, but he didn't really need to, and certainly didn't want to be seen. He listened to Rudel ask softly, "Mr. Palmer, do you know the answer to the XO's question?" His question demanded an answer, but at the same time had a positive tone.

After a short pause, Jerry heard Palmer say, "Yes, sir. I do." After another pause, he answered, "There can't be any damage, because he's tight alongside us."

Rudel asked, "But won't he keep our bow from moving out from the pier?"

"No sir, we're so much bigger than the tug, with a much deeper draft, and he's at our pivot point anyway. Then, as soon as our headway's off and we've swung more parallel to the pier, I'd send the lines back over and get us moored again."

"Why would you do that, mister?" The XO's voice was still level. "I thought the idea was to get under way."

"Not with the tug in the way. Besides, he's broken down and we can't leave him adrift in the channel."

"Very good, Mr. Palmer, never abandon a mariner in distress." The captain's praise was followed by a quick "Carry on," and he stepped out of the XO's stateroom and back to his own. As he passed Jerry, the skipper winked at him, smiling. Jerry felt himself smiling as well. He was sure now Palmer would pass.

Rudel's kind words were the only praise Palmer received. The XO grilled him for another twenty minutes, and there were more trick questions as well as hard ones. Jerry knew the XO wasn't really testing Palmer's knowledge, but his presence of mind, his ability to think under pressure.

Finally, he said, "All right, Mr. Palmer, I'm satisfied

that you're able to properly get *Seawolf* under way next Monday. Continue your preparations. The Navigator and I will review them Monday after quarters."

Jeff Palmer stepped out of the XO's stateroom, pale but smiling. Jerry and Palmer walked some distance away from the XO's stateroom before either spoke. "Compared to that, the underway will be a breeze." Palmer sounded stressed but pleased.

"Just hope you're right, Jeff. Things can get past you before you know you're in trouble." Jerry gestured back toward the XO's stateroom. "In there, you knew you were being asked a question. On the bridge, you'll have to ask yourself the questions, as well as answer them."

Palmer's expression became more serious, but his smile didn't go away completely. "Believe me, sir, I get it. My first underway taught me that. We live in a boat designed to sink, filled with explosives and a nuclear reactor. If we don't stay on our toes, we're screwed."

"Learning from your mistakes is a good thing. But dwelling on them is not," advised Jerry sternly. "You lost the bubble last time and it's been holding you back. This time you need to stay in control, which means you have to think ahead. We may move slowly, but a submarine on the surface reacts to your helm orders just as slowly—so keep your wits about you and plan accordingly."

"I will, Nav. And this time, I won't screw up."

"Sounds good, Jeff. Let's plan to meet on Friday, you and Mr. Hayes, to do a final review, okay?"

"Yes, sir. I'll inform Will."

"Very well, Mr. Palmer, carry on."

2

PROTECTIVE RESPONSE

8 September 2008
Northern Fleet Headquarters, Severomorsk, Russia

The four men marched down the main hall of the Northern Fleet Headquarters building in perfect, if unintentional, unison. The echoes of their footsteps reverberated sharply off the ornate walls, giving the illusion of a much larger contingent. The mood was somber, the air formal, the countenance of the men stern and determined. "How perfectly Russian," mused Captain First Rank Aleksey Igorevich Petrov. Flanked by his *eskadra* and *diviziya* commanders, Petrov followed the staff functionary as he led the way to the fleet commander's conference room. "Finally," thought the young captain, "we will finish this godforsaken fleet acceptance process and I will be able to take my boat to sea." Frustrated and irritated by the unceasing paperwork, inspections, and constant bickering with the shipyard, Petrov longed for the peace and serenity that only the sea could provide.

He was born in Severodvinsk on the Kola Peninsula, the son of a senior shipyard engineer, and submarines were in his blood. He remembered many visits to the shipyard with his father to watch those underwater behemoths as they were rolled out of the great construction halls.

As a boy, he'd dreamed of commanding one, and that dream had never changed. And it was with great pride that he bid his parents farewell to join the Soviet Navy to pursue his dream. He graduated first in his class from the Lenin Komsomol Higher Naval Submarine School in

Leningrad, and everything seemed to be going according to plan when disaster struck in December 1991.

The fall of the Soviet Union brought nothing but chaos and poverty to the "new" Russian Navy, whose members lost the respect of their countrymen along with their paychecks. Petrov didn't care about the fate of the Communist Party. They had brought this on themselves. He was deeply concerned, however, about the effects their sudden collapse had on the navy in general, and his career prospects in particular.

Good fortune smiled on him, however, as he was assigned to a fairly new Project 671RTM attack submarine in the Northern Fleet. Known as an Improved Victor III class SSN in the West, they were some of the quietest and most capable boats in the Russian order of battle. Being relatively new, it was fully functional and not suffering from the neglect that was all too common with the older boats, brought on by the decaying Soviet maintenance infrastructure.

Petrov also considered himself to be doubly blessed, as his commanding officer was the master tactician Captain First Rank Dmitriy Makeyev, a brilliant and cunning hunter who handed numerous NATO submarine skippers their heads on a silver platter. Even some of the vaunted American 688-class submarines fell victim to the "Dark Lord," as he was called. According to the waterfront gossip, Makeyev had never been caught unawares. He always maintained tactical control, only revealing himself when he wished and usually by a vicious lashing with his main active sonar.

"To be victorious in submarine combat," he preached, "one has to be aggressive. If you are not aggressive, you lose. If you lose, then you die. It is that simple."

Aleksey Igorevich accepted, believed, and lived by this tactical philosophy, so eloquently coined by his first captain, throughout his career. And it had served him well; very well indeed, as it enabled him to chalk up an impressive history of success in whatever he did. Now Petrov was the commanding officer of the newest and most advanced attack submarine in the Russian Navy—*Severodvinsk.* The very thought of being in command of his home's namesake filled him with immense pride. Now if only the damned bureaucrats would release their icy grip and allow him to command his boat, then the dream that he had worked so hard for would finally become a reality.

Petrov's half-musing, half-stewing daydreaming was brought to an abrupt end when the staff officer opened the large double doors to the conference room. Inside the spacious hall were over a dozen flag officers milling about, drinking tea or coffee and chatting in small groups. As soon as Petrov and his commanders entered, a large man at the far end quickly made his way over toward them. Although Petrov had met him only once before, it was hard to forget the commander of the Northern Fleet, Vice Admiral Sergey Mikhailovich Kokurin. Rounding the corner of the table, Kokurin grasped Petrov's eskadra commander's hand and shook it heartily. It was well known within the fleet that the fleet commander and Vice Admiral Pavel Borisov were close friends.

"It is good to see you again, Pavel," boomed Kokurin as he slapped Borisov's shoulder. "How is Irina? Well, I trust?"

"She is quite well, sir," replied Borisov as a devilish grin appeared on his face. "But, I regret to inform you that she is *most* displeased with you. Twice now, you have been to Gadzhiyevo without stopping by to visit and she is very disappointed that . . ."

Kokurin interrupted, waving his hands in mock surrender, a pained expression sweeping across his brow. "I know. I know. I . . . I am guilty as charged." Sighing heavily, and placing his large hands on Borisov's shoulders, he said, "Please tell Her Highness, the tzarina, that I will pay my respects the next time I must travel to the submarine base at Sayda Guba. You have my word!"

"I will gladly inform her of your most wise decision," jabbed Borisov. Both men burst into laughter.

Composing himself, Borisov then gestured toward his two officers. "Sir, this is my new Commander of the Twenty-fourth Submarine Diviziya, Rear Admiral Vasiliy Vitalyevich Vidchenko."

"Pleased to meet you, sir," replied Vidchenko stiffly.

"Ah, yes. Welcome to the Northern Fleet, Admiral. I hope your transfer has gone smoothly. You came to us from the Baltic Fleet, did you not?"

"Yes sir. The trip north was uneventful, and I am getting acquainted with my new duties."

"Excellent. I look forward to working with you and the submarine commanders in your division," responded Kokurin as he mentally took stock of the junior admiral.

Vidchenko acknowledged the fleet commander's comments with a slight bow and stepped out of the way as VADM Borisov brought Petrov forward. "And you know Captain Petrov, of course."

"Good day, sir," Petrov said politely.

Kokurin took a slow deliberate step toward Petrov and offered his hand. "Welcome to Northern Fleet Headquarters, Captain. And today is a very good day indeed. It has been far too long since we took acceptance of a new *podvodnaya lodka atomnaya* and I have been looking forward to this day with great anticipation." Petrov was surprised by the old admiral's sentimental tone and the intense emotion in his eyes. This man truly cares for the fleet, thought Petrov, and receiving a new atomic submarine after nearly eight years was, in this fleet commander's mind, a cause for celebration.

In the old days of the Soviet Union, shipyards turned out three or four nuclear submarines each year. New classes followed each other in quick succession, each improvement closing the quality gap with their Western adversaries. Now it was years between commissionings, and Kokurin's celebratory mood was well justified. Petrov's pride was all the greater. He'd had many rivals for *Severodvinsk.*

"I have read every inspection and evaluation report with great interest," continued Kokurin sincerely, "and I am very impressed with your crew's performance. You have done well, Captain Petrov."

"Thank you . . . sir," replied Petrov uneasily. "I will convey your compliments to the crew." It had been a very long time since he had received a favorable comment from a flag officer. Petrov was far more accustomed to the lectures and stern criticism that had been the staple of his crew's training diet throughout the long certification process.

"I must also ask for your patience today, Captain."

"Sir? I, ah, I don't understand." Petrov was now completely confused and it showed.

Amused by the young captain's response, Kokurin's face broke out into a broad smile. "You and your crew have gone through a lengthy, trying, and difficult certification process. One that I demanded to be more rigorous than usual. Now that the end is in sight, I know you just want to get this over with so you can take your boat to sea." Petrov felt his face flush, like a schoolboy caught by the headmaster with his hand in the cookie jar. Can this man also read minds?

The fleet commander chuckled loudly and said, "I was once a young new submarine commander itching to be set free from the fleet's bureaucratic clutches. So I know exactly how you feel. But today, many of us old men, some with more ballast than we need," Kokurin patted his protruding abdomen as he spoke, "are reliving those memories through you. So please, be patient with us today. I promise the proceedings will end this afternoon."

"Of course, sir," responded Petrov confidently. And then with heartfelt sincerity, "It *is* an honor to be here today, Admiral."

"Excellent!" exclaimed Kokurin happily. But as the elderly submariner looked up, the smile quickly vanished from his face. For over at the head table was his chief of staff pointing in an exasperated fashion at his watch.

"Bah," sneered the fleet commander with a curt dismissing wave.

"Is something wrong, sir?" inquired Borisov after seeing his friend's abrupt mood change.

"It's just my personal nag, Pavel. He's complaining that I haven't started the conference on time."

"Pardon me, sir, but I do believe that is his job," replied Borisov with a hint of sarcasm.

With a deep sigh and resigned nod, Kokurin said, "You are correct, as always, Pavel Dmitriyevich. But I just wish he wouldn't take such joy in exercising his duties. There are times when I wonder who really is the Commander of the Northern Fleet!" Turning back to his chief of staff, Kokurin politely gestured for him to call the conference attendants to order.

"Comrades," announced VADM Radetskiy, "please take your seats so we may begin."

As the various admirals and captains shuffled about getting to their assigned chairs, Kokurin turned one last time toward Borisov and said, "Admiral Borisov, I want you, Admiral Vidchenko, and Captain Petrov to remain once the conference is completed. I have another issue, of a more operational nature, to discuss with you afterward."

Sensing the shift from friend to superior, and recognizing when an order had just been given, Borisov drew himself to attention and answered with a militarily appropriate "Yes, sir."

As Kokurin walked back toward the head of the table, Vidchenko and Petrov both looked at Borisov with bewilderment. With a mild shaking of his head, and a puzzled expression, Borisov signaled to his subordinates that he didn't know what the fleet commander meant either, and motioned for them to take their seats.

Petrov moved quickly to his chair and looked around the conference room as the flag officers slowly sat down. He recognized many of them, since they headed numerous inspection teams during the various stages of the certification process.

The chiefs of navigation, armaments, communications, and the technical directorate had been tough judges of his boat's capabilities. Petrov respected their findings and accepted their recommendations, even though it hurt his pride a little. But the chief of combat training, VADM Vlasov, was the devil incarnate. Nothing Petrov or his crew did seemed to ever satisfy this man and he was particularly acidic in delivering his critiques during the combat training exercises. If there was one member of the certification board who could hold up *Severodvinsk*'s acceptance into the fleet, it was him. Realizing that he was staring intently at Vlasov and that his resentment was growing, Petrov shifted his gaze back to Kokurin, who had taken his place at the head table.

"Greetings, comrades," boomed Kokurin as he rose, "and welcome to the fleet acceptance board for PLA K-329 *Severodvinsk*. I do not believe it would be inappropriate for me to remind everyone that this is the first new atomic submarine in nearly a decade to join the ranks of the Russian Navy. Because of this unfortunate hiatus, I have been doubly hard on the inspection teams, as well as the commanding officer and crew of the *Severodvinsk*. To this I make no apologies. I had to be certain that with all the problems the shipyard encountered during this submarine's construction that we are accepting delivery of a fully functional combatant, and not a floating Potemkin village. Therefore, I must stress that these proceedings are no mere formality. And I expect everyone to be truthful with his findings, opinions, and recommendations. Our goal is, and must remain focused on, ensuring the proper certification of the crew of the *Severodvinsk* for independent operations."

Petrov heard earnestness in the admiral's voice, and understood its source. *Kursk*, their newest and best guided-missile submarine, the pride of the Northern Fleet, had been lost in 2000 with all hands during an exercise. The investigation that followed had found many instances of training requirements ignored, certifications lapsed, procedures not followed. Sloppy maintenance by poorly trained personnel didn't mix well with explosive torpedoes and volatile oxidizers. In the wake of the disaster, the entire Northern Fleet command structure had been relieved. There were rumors that similar problems were behind the loss of *Gepard* in 2005, although there were an equal number of rumors that claimed she had been sunk by an American submarine. Regardless, the results were the same and most of the senior officers in the Northern Fleet were relieved for cause. Kokurin was the "new broom." He meant every word he said.

The fleet commander paused momentarily, which gave Petrov the opportunity to glance over at VADM Vlasov. The chief of combat training was slowly nodding his head, a fully developed frown on his face. Not a good omen, Petrov thought. But at least now he knew why the inspections and training exercises had been so intense, and so difficult. He had always suspected it was due to the ridiculous length of time it took to build *Severodvinsk,* fifteen years instead of the normal four under the Soviet Union, but no one would ever tell him this outright. All he was told was that his crew displayed deficiencies that were noted in the crews of the *Kursk* and *Gepard.* In his heart Petrov didn't believe this line of reasoning; it seemed too convenient and didn't square with what he saw on a daily basis. Admittedly he was biased toward his crew, but he knew without a doubt that they were better than what they were being given credit for. And as much as it pained Petrov to sit and listen to the unceasing criticism, arguing with a flag-level inspection team is at best an unwise tactic—even if you're convinced that their findings are full of shit. As Kokurin continued with his opening remarks, Petrov's attention was yanked back to the head table.

"Now, there is much material to cover today during our deliberations. And I did promise the young captain that we would get through all of it by the end of the afternoon. However, before I turn this board over to my Chief of Staff, I wish to issue a special welcome to Vice Admiral Borisov, Commander of the Twelfth Submarine Eskadra, Rear Admiral Vidchenko, Commander of the Twenty-fourth Atomic Submarine Diviziya, and Captain First Rank Petrov, Commanding Officer of submarine K-329 *Severodvinsk.* Gentlemen, I am very pleased that you are here with us today. Over the past year you have worked hard; all of you have worked very hard," stated Kokurin as he gestured toward everyone present, "to bring us to this point. You have my thanks, and that of the Russian people. Today is truly a great day for the Russian Navy and the Northern Fleet. Rear Admiral Radetskiy, if you please."

As the fleet commander lowered his bulky figure into his chair, still beaming with pride, Petrov suddenly realized that the board was in reality a formality, despite what the admiral had just said. And while there would probably be some unpleasant moments, ultimately the decision had already been made—his crew would get their certification and *Severodvinsk* would be accepted into the fleet's combat-ready force. He would finally be able to take his boat to sea without a division babysitter. Confident that his lifelong dream was about to be fulfilled, Petrov felt as if a huge weight had been lifted off his shoulders. It took all his discipline to maintain a proper military composure. He'd celebrate later with his crew.

"Gentlemen," announced the chief of staff, "the binders before you contain all the final inspection reports and training exercise evaluations. They are state secrets and you are to handle them accordingly. We will now commence with the formal boarding process. Each directorate is to read a brief summary of the technical or tactical readiness of K-329 *Severodvinsk,* along with your final evaluation and certification recommendation. I would ask Rear Admiral Smelkov, Chief of the Technical Directorate, to get us started."

"Good morning, comrade Admiral," began Smelkov, looking over at Kokurin. "Over the last year, my directorate has conducted numerous inspections during the state acceptance trials to evaluate the technical readiness of Project 885 PLA *Severodvinsk,* hull number 160, pennant number K-329. Our findings are as follows."

What followed was anything but brief as the chief of the technical directorate went through the whole boat, compartment by compartment and system by system, describing how each system met the design specifications established by the Russian Navy and the Ministry of Shipbuilding. He then went on to provide detailed results of the propulsion plant tests, deep diving trials, sonar calibration trials, hydroacoustic and magnetic field measurements, and on and on. Most of the discrepancies noted in technical directorate's report were minor and had, in fact, already been taken care of. This annoyed Petrov a little, but he understood that it was all part of the game. After a little over an hour, Smelkov finally managed to get around to announcing his directorate's verdict.

"In conclusion, it is our professional judgment that PLA K-329 *Severodvinsk* is in compliance with all tactical technical requirements, as well as all submarine design specifications as promulgated by state organs. We therefore recommend that the submarine and crew be certified for independent operations and accepted into the fleet."

"Thank you, Rear Admiral Smelkov. Your recommendation is noted," replied Radetskiy nonchalantly. "Next we will hear from the Chief of the Navigation Directorate."

If there were any hope that the other directorates would heed the "brief summary" instruction, it was soon dashed upon the rocky shoals of administration and self-promotion. Each of the directorate chiefs for navigation, armaments, communications, medical services, and chemical services took their requisite hour or so to deliver a recommendation that could have been done in fifteen minutes or less. Petrov knew that this kind of posturing was common among junior admirals, particularly in front of a fleet commander. He also understood that even admirals had to "wave his flag," as it were, to gain the kind of senior attention that would benefit their promotion potential. Still, Petrov held this practice of self-centered showmanship in contempt.

By the time the chief of the armaments directorate had finished his report, Petrov's mind was numb with boredom. He had heard all of this before, many times before. Nothing new was presented in the final reports, and the overwhelming majority of the adverse comments were on nitpicky items that had already been dealt with by his crew or the shipyard. Of course, there was no mention of that fact. To keep up with the schedule, lunch was shortened and hurried. Breaks were few and far between. More than once Petrov cursed his excessive coffee-drinking habit. Just when Petrov thought he would either go mad or fall asleep, he would remember the fleet commander's specific request for patience. Quietly, he sat and endured one monologue after another.

It was well into the afternoon before the chief of staff made the announcement that Petrov was longing for, and dreading at the same time.

"Our last report will be from the Chief of the Combat Training Directorate. Vice Admiral Vlasov, will you please present your findings."

"Good afternoon, comrade Admiral," spoke Vlasov with a severe and deliberate tone. "In accordance with your instructions, my staff exercised the crew of *Severodvinsk* in as thorough a manner as was humanly possible. We drove them near to the point of breaking, and then we pushed even harder."

"No shit, you damned Cossack," muttered Petrov under his breath. The clearing of Borisov's throat, and a stern look, informed Petrov that the comment had been heard and was not appreciated. Chastened, he turned his attention back to Vlasov as he continued his report.

"As most of you are aware, my directorate is responsible for evaluating a crew's performance in the execution of combat training tasks. Although we assist the other directorates with phase one and two exercises, it is the phase three at sea exercises that concern us the most. Captain Petrov and the crew of *Severodvinsk* completed all prescribed combat training tasks as required in the Russian Navy manual on Combat Readiness Training for Nuclear Submarines. The detailed reports are in your binders but in the interest of brevity, we found the crew to be satisfactory in carrying out their combat-readiness requirements."

We are much better than that, you miserly bastard, thought Petrov, fuming. Many of the older boats, some that were not even able to go to sea, had crews that had earned a satisfactory rating in their combat training tasks. By contrast, his crew had worked infinitely harder, and to get the same rating was way beyond insulting. Striving valiantly to contain his anger, Petrov stewed while Vlasov droned on.

"Therefore, we assign the crew of *Severodvinsk* a collective grade of 4.5 for all combat training tasks, and it is our judgment that the crew is ready for independent operations. We further recommend that the submarine be accepted in to the fleet's combat-ready force."

Petrov sat in stunned silence and stark disbelief. The grading scheme for Russian naval readiness exercises is based on a five-point scale with 3.0 being "Satisfactory." A collective grade of 4.5 was in the "Superior" to "Excellent" range and reflected a crew that was on top of their game. Both Borisov and Vidchenko were clearly pleased with such a good score and there were murmurs of approval from around the conference room.

"Quiet please," barked the chief of staff. "Do you have anything further to offer, Vice Admiral Vlasov?"

"Sir, I have a personal observation that is not in the final report that I would like to bring to this board's attention."

A still-shocked Petrov looked at Vlasov with a mix of confusion and concern. Raising issues that were not documented in a final report was definitely not the norm for the Russian Navy.

Kokurin leaned forward, a serious expression materialized on his face as he looked intently at his chief of training, "Please continue, Admiral."

"During the final antisubmarine exercise, Captain Petrov displayed *unusual* aggressiveness in prosecuting his attack against PLA K-157 *Vepr.* On at least two occasions he knowingly violated the one-kilometer safety zone as he executed his maneuvers. And while I believe Captain Petrov retained a firm grasp of the tactical situation, such aggressiveness has brought this fleet no small degree of suffering in the recent past." The allusion to the loss of *Gepard* as a result of Admiral Yuriy Kirichenko's unbridled aggressiveness was not lost on all those present. Even Petrov bristled at the implied comparison, especially since the after-action analysis of the engagement had proven he had correctly assessed *Vepr*'s exact location and intended movement. Once again there was murmuring as several side discussions started up.

Thumping the table loudly with his fingers to gain everyone's attention, Kokurin stood up and said, "Thank you, Yuriy Vasilyevich, for your candid statements. All of you would do well to remember that this is exactly what I asked for at the beginning of this board."

The fleet commander paused, rose, and began to slowly pace around the room, a well-known habit of his that he displayed only when considering how to respond to an important issue. It was said that he'd worn a groove in his office carpet while thinking.

"Admiral, while I value your observation, we will have to disagree. In my opinion, there is a marked difference between my predecessor and Captain Petrov. I say this for two reasons. Firstly, by your own admission in the evaluation report Captain Petrov exhibited a calm composure during the antisubmarine exercise and seemed to weigh all considerations before issuing a maneuver order that brought him within 850 meters of *Vepr*. To me this is not undisciplined aggressiveness unleashed in the heat of the moment, but rather an example of rational decision-making skills and a well-honed ability to consider the risks before taking action."

Realizing that the tenor and volume of his voice was

rising, Kokurin stopped momentarily and straightened his uniform jacket before resuming.

"Secondly, most of you are aware of Captain Petrov's upbringing in the submarine force. His teacher, Dmitriy Ivanovich Makeyev, was the best submarine tactician that Russia has ever produced and he spoke very favorably of our young captain's abilities. And while Captain Petrov's record speaks highly of him, I cannot think of a better judge of an officer's tactical qualities than Makeyev. So, no, Admiral Vlasov, I do not agree that Captain Petrov's aggressiveness is excessive. I will agree that it is unusual, and that is a shame. Right now Russia needs a few more wolfhounds; not another tethered mongrel whose best defense is that it barks loudly."

As the fleet commander walked back toward his chair, Petrov scanned the room and saw that everyone was looking straight at him. Uncomfortable with this degree of attention, the young captain occupied himself by straightening the papers and binders in front of him.

"Gentlemen," Kokurin said as he sat down. "Unless there are any more issues to discuss, I will now read the judgment of this board." The silence assured everyone that the time for discussion was over. Clearing his throat, Kokurin proceeded with the formal announcement.

"Captain First Rank Aleksey Igorevich Petrov, it is the judgment of this board that the crew of the *Severodvinsk* has met all combat training requirements and tasks, and that the submarine is at one hundred percent technical readiness. We therefore certify the submarine and crew as qualified for independent combat duty. We further decree that the Russian Federation submarine K-329 *Severodvinsk* is hereby accepted into the Northern Fleet and is assigned to the Twenty-fourth Atomic Submarine Diviziya of the Twelfth Submarine Eskadra. Congratulations, Captain."

A hearty applause broke out from all corners of the conference room; Petrov rose and thanked the collective audience for their kind sentiments. He then spent the next half hour receiving individual congratulations and wishes of success from the directorate chiefs and their staffs.

As the last of the participants slowly departed, Petrov and his commanders were ushered back to the conference table by the chief of staff. As they headed toward their original seats, Kokurin motioned for them to move down, closer to his end of the table.

"Pavel, please join us."

"Of course, sir."

In stark contrast to the packed room earlier, there were only eight men at the table now, including Petrov and his immediate superiors. Of the five fleet officers present, Petrov had met the majority of them, including the deputy fleet commander and the deputy chief of staff for operations. He didn't know, however, who the rear admiral was that sat next to his eskadra commander. A large map board with a chart of the Barents Sea was brought forward and placed to the left of the fleet commander's chair. The entire scene filled Petrov with an immense sense of curiosity as he recalled the admiral's earlier cryptic comment.

"Now that the bureaucratic requirements have been met," said Kokurin, eyeing his chief of staff, "we can get on to more important business."

Pointing to the unidentified admiral, he added, "This is Rear Admiral Litenkov, my Chief of the Intelligence Directorate. He will brief you on the operational background. Afterward, we'll discuss what I intend to do about the situation. Admiral."

"Thank you, sir. Comrades, you may or may not know that we have indirect evidence that a U.S. submarine was involved in the loss of *Gepard* several years ago. I say indirect evidence because there was no positive proof other than several hydroacoustic detections. I say again, nothing definite. Unfortunately, we do have direct evidence of Russian torpedoes exploding either in or on contact with *Gepard*. To compound the uncertainty, the prosecuting antisubmarine forces recorded up to half a dozen simultaneous 'confirmed' submarine contacts over an area that spanned several hundreds of square nautical miles. This lack of precision in reporting significantly weakened any case we had against the Americans, and the president determined that our only option was to issue a diplomatic demarche to the American ambassador. Since then, there have been a growing number of contact reports of foreign submarines in our operational areas."

Litenkov rose and walked toward the map board. "During the latest exercise period last month, there were eight such reports. But only one led to a follow-on prosecution by fleet antisubmarine assets, the rest were inconclusive and could have been false alarms. Unfortunately, contact was held only briefly before the submarine escaped to deeper water. We were, however, able to identify the submarine's nationality. It was an American *Los Angeles*–class submarine."

Picking up a pointer, Litenkov traced out an area on the chart just west of Novaya Zemlya. "This latest contact was in Operations Areas 21 and 22, which are the fleet's northernmost combat training ranges. In addition, there is some evidence that certain U.S. attack submarines are fitted with tethered remote operating vehicles that are used for intelligence-gathering purposes. One such attack submarine, USS *Alexandria,* was at sea during the time frame in question. *Alexandria* is an Improved *Los Angeles*–class PLA."

As Litenkov put the pointer down and returned to his seat, Kokurin suddenly leapt to his feet, reached over, and slapped the chart with his burly hand. "Since the loss of

Gepard we have been wallowing in despair, and we have been very timid. Such attributes do not command respect. Without question, Kirichenko was out of control. He may have been blinded more by frustration than the political motives that were claimed, but his intentions were valid! I will not tolerate the Americans strolling merrily through my training ranges as if they were a park! Something must be done!"

Petrov was impressed and taken aback by the fierceness of Kokurin's outburst. As Kokurin sat down, he gestured sharply to his chief of staff for operations. "Aleksandr, explain the plan to our comrades."

"We plan to set a trap along the border of Operations Areas 21 and 22 using fixed acoustic sensors and *Severodvinsk.* We have one more small exercise period in October, before the ice gets too bad, and we intend to use Operations Areas 18 and 19 to the south. It is our belief that if the Americans attempt to send a submarine on a reconnaissance mission, they will approach from the north and use the broken ice as cover."

Petrov watched as the operations officer flipped the large-scale chart over to reveal a smaller-scale one with greater detail of the operating areas.

"This chart shows where we've laid thirty-six of the new Amga autonomous submarine detection buoys in a single line barrier. The buoys are four nautical miles apart, which gives us a ninety percent probability of detection should a submarine attempt to traverse the barrier. You, Captain Petrov, will take *Severodvinsk* and patrol along the south side of the barrier. Fleet headquarters will relay any contact reports from the buoys. You will be close by, ready to pounce. Any questions?"

"What kind of sensors are on these new buoys?" asked Borisov.

"They use passive acoustic hydrophones with broadband

and narrowband processing. The technical specifications are included in your orders packet."

"I'm concerned about false alarms," injected Vidchenko. "How does the buoy's processor determine if a contact is valid?"

"The buoy's onboard processor will compare any signal it detects to an extensive library of submarine signatures and other sounds. The false-alarm rate is much lower than previous systems. But your point is still valid and that is why we are going to use *Severodvinsk*. A nuclear-powered submarine is a much better platform to do the follow-up detection and prosecution. Anything else?"

Both Borisov and Vidchenko signaled they were satisfied for the moment. Somewhat hesitantly, Petrov raised his hand and asked, "Sir, what are my orders if I find an American?"

"Drive him away with his tail between his legs," answered Kokurin firmly. "This is where Kirichenko failed us all. He wanted a trophy to demonstrate our prowess to the world. I'm not interested in convincing the world of our greatness, that's the job of the foreign and economic ministries. All I care is that the United States, Great Britain, and the rest of NATO knows that my fleet has the ability to protect our homeland and its contiguous waters. They must learn to respect us!"

"You are," continued the operations officer, "not authorized to fire any weapons unless fired upon first, and then only if you cannot evade and report. You are authorized to use decoys and countermeasures at your discretion to achieve the mission's objective. Are there any other questions?"

Petrov shook his head indicating he had nothing more to ask.

"Excellent!" cried Kokurin as he rose. "This mission is very similar to your phase three antisubmarine exercise,

Captain Petrov, only this time with an unfriendly and uncooperative opponent. I expect you to embarrass the Americans, should they show up, as badly as you did poor *Vepr* and Captain Zubov."

"I will strive to not disappoint you, sir."

"I know you will, Captain. But may I offer you one piece of fatherly advice?"

"Yes, sir. Anything."

"Admiral Vlasov is partially correct. You must be mindful of your own warrior spirit." Kokurin advanced slowly, deliberately toward Petrov as he spoke. "Aggressiveness can be a blessing or a curse. If it is not tempered by wisdom, it will lead to recklessness. And that can have unfortunate consequences. Be my wolfhound, but don't be a rabid one."

Bursting with pride and overwhelmed by the fleet commander's gentle admonition, Petrov could only nod his understanding.

Extending his hand, Kokurin said, "Good luck, Captain, and good hunting."

Grasping the old submariner's hand firmly, and looking him straight in the eye, Petrov replied, "Thank you, sir."

As he departed, Petrov could not believe his good fortune. Receiving an unexpectedly good evaluation score, full certification and acceptance into the fleet, and his first mission all in one day was just too much to comprehend. The stars, as his mother used to say, were aligning in his favor.

3

PRIDE OF THE FLEET

Sayda Guba Submarine Base, Russia

The hour-long drive from Severomorsk to Gadzhiyevo seemed unnaturally short, almost as if Petrov were dreaming. And yet, he clearly remembered discussing several aspects of his upcoming mission with Vice Admiral Borisov and Rear Admiral Vidchenko during the return trip. Still feeling a little giddy from the conference, Petrov stared out at the rocky terrain along the ill-kept road and tried to figure out just how he was going to get his boat to sea in only three weeks. There were still some minor adjustments to be made to the navigation, sonar, and combat systems. The torpedo bays and missile complex needed a full ordnance load, and then provisions and spare parts would have to be brought aboard.

As fatigue started to set in, Petrov found it hard to concentrate on the growing list of things that needed to be done before *Severodvinsk* could slip free from her earthly bonds. Slumping back into his seat, yawning, he thought to himself, I shouldn't worry so much. Vasiliy will see to everything.

A sinister amusement rose in Petrov as he tried to imagine how his poor *starpom* would take the news of the radical change in their plans. As the ship's executive officer, Captain Second Rank Vasiliy Sergeyevich Kalinin would have to oversee all of the preparations. A master planner with a hyperactive sense of responsibility, Kalinin was an indispensable asset to Petrov and the boat. Unfortunately, his regimented personality didn't take change very well. No, Vasiliy will not be amused by his captain's news.

Petrov was gently pushed back in his seat as the car started climbing up the hilly approaches to the coast. As the vehicle crested the top of the ridge, he could see the submarine base below with its piers arrayed in a rough semicircle and a number of large bluish black objects nestled alongside. The sun was already well down on the horizon and the bright red and orange twilight made the submarines look even more spectral. The sheer beauty of the moment was soon shattered as the run-down and dilapidated gray buildings of the base came into view. Most of the buildings along the main road were apartments for the submarine crews and their families. It angered Petrov to see some of the finest men in the navy and their families live in such squalor. But there was nothing he could do but suppress the image. Dwelling on the unpleasantness of living on the Kola Peninsula only led one to drink. This was the escape of choice in Russia, especially for those who lived above the Arctic Circle, where there was no sunlight for months during the frigid winters.

The car slowly rolled to a stop at the head of the far right-hand pier. A large gantry crane from the missile-loading wharf nearby loomed in the background like a giant arm reaching out from the shadows into the evening sky. On the left-hand side of the pier lay *Severodvinsk,* her sleek form barely discernible in the fading light. Petrov exited the car and bid his commanders a good evening. Borisov and Vidchenko congratulated him once again and then sped off toward home.

Walking slowly down the pier, Petrov savored the cool evening air and mentally prepared himself for the task ahead. All doubts were instantly banished as he approached *his* boat. He was the captain and he had to be the living embodiment of conviction and confidence, or at least appear that way. Acknowledging the sentry's salute and greeting, Petrov bounded up the brow onto the submarine and quickly made his way toward the open hatch on the port side of the sail. Maneuvering around the forest of masts and antennas, he squeezed his way to the bridge access trunk hatch and climbed down the ladder.

Instead of jumping past the last few rungs, as was his habit, Petrov quietly finished his descent, turned around, and came face-to-face with a wall of men. There must have been over two dozen crewmen packed into the central command post, and in the very front were his starpom and his battle department commanders. All of them stared at him with an intense visage of anxious expectation. For a brief moment they just stood there, nobody moved or spoke—the only detectable sound being the sharp ticking of the mechanical clock on the bulkhead. The eerie silence was finally broken by the starpom with a single word.

"Well?"

"It must be bad news," injected the engineering commander, Captain Second Rank Sergey Vladimirovich Lyachin, "otherwise he wouldn't have tried to sneak back on board."

"Shhh, give the Captain a chance to speak," said someone in the back.

Recovering his composure, Petrov threw his cover on to the watch commander's desk and slowly started to unbutton his uniform coat.

"What is the meaning of this mutinous congregation, Starpom?" growled Petrov with feigned sternness. "I feel like a dying animal facing a flock of ravenous vultures."

"Nothing quite so sinister, my dear Captain," replied Kalinin reassuringly. "But I do believe it would be unwise, sir, to further delay in telling these desperate men the judgment of the fleet acceptance board."

"Hmmm, I see."

With deliberate slowness, Petrov put his coat on the chair and reached for the main announcing system microphone. Pulling it toward him, he tried to project an image of fatigue and disappointment. The former wasn't difficult but the latter took some doing; he wasn't the best of actors. Hesitating, he let out an exasperated sigh and said, "Well, I guess it would be best if I got this unpleasant duty over with.

"Attention all hands, this is the Captain." Petrov shifted about in an agitated manner as he spoke. "I have just recently returned from Northern Fleet Headquarters. As you know, the Fleet Commander held the formal acceptance board for our boat today. And as expected, the testimony by the inspecting officials labored long and hard on our deficiencies. I know you gave your all in trying to meet the considerable expectations placed upon you, but the weight of evidence against us was overwhelming." Pausing, he looked around the room as pained expressions started to emerge on his men's faces. Kalinin was frowning, eyeing his commander suspiciously.

"So, it is my reluctant duty to inform you that we barely squeaked by with a final grade of . . ." Yet another pause as he sucked the crew in for the kill. ". . . 4.5, a superior to excellent rating! Well done to you all!"

The shock-induced delayed reaction to the captain's prank was priceless. Within the blink of an eye, the men in the central post went from complete dejection to absolute elation as the meaning of his words sank in. And then the cheering started.

Petrov watched with amusement as grown men, professional seamen, cheered and hollered as they jumped up and down, hugging each other and slapping one another's backs. Kalinin leapt forward and eagerly grasped his captain's hand. Shaking it vigorously he exclaimed, "Congratulations, sir! I knew we wouldn't let you down."

Releasing Petrov's hand, the starpom then wagged his finger at him in an accusatory way, "With respect, sir, you are a cunning bastard! That was cruel to lead the crew on like that."

"A last-minute inspiration, I can assure you. But that's not what you're objecting to, you're just jealous that you didn't get to do it yourself."

"True," replied Kalinin soberly, and then suddenly burst into laughter. Petrov, unable to maintain the casual façade any longer, also started laughing. Pointing toward the ladder that led down to the second deck the starpom added, "Come, the rest of the crew will want to join in the festivities on the mess deck. The cooks have been slaving away since you left this morning and they have prepared a small celebration for everyone."

"Excellent! I could use a little snack, and a drink. I wasn't lying when I said the inspectors labored long and hard on our deficiencies."

As Petrov meandered through the tightly packed mob toward the ladder, he was bombarded with words of congratulations and thanks, as well as the occasional pat on the back. Every few steps he would stop to shake someone's hand, and a sea of humanity would begin to surround him. Impatiently, Kalinin literally towed his captain to the ladder well. One by one they filed down the constricted companionway and headed forward to the first compartment, where the majority of the living spaces were located.

Even though *Severodvinsk* was one of the largest nuclear-powered attack submarines in the world, displacing 11,500 tons when submerged, open space was still hard to come by. The passageways were very narrow. Only one man could walk down one comfortably, and they were flanked on both sides by yellow-painted electrical panels, electronic cabinets, fans, pumps, and other miscellaneous equipment. Occasionally a piece of machinery intruded into the walking area, often at the ankle or head level, and would painfully announce its presence to the unwary traveler. The procession to the mess deck was by necessity one long single-file line. As he approached the circular watertight door between the two compartments, Petrov heard someone yell, "Stand by!" The incredible smell of fresh baked goods wafted in the air.

With his stomach growling in response to the delicious aroma, Petrov expertly ducked through the hatch and eagerly strode into the crew's mess. As he entered, he saw that the space was literally packed with the rest of his men. Immediately the crew came to attention and yelled out in unison, "Hoorah, Petrov!"

Momentarily stunned by their cheer, Petrov staggered a little as he walked over and shook hands with his most junior crew members. Before he could completely regain his bearings, Kalinin delivered the coup de grâce by gently turning him around. The sight made Petrov gasp audibly.

Before him lay an incredible array of food. Stuffed chebureki, a Crimean lamb pie; roast suckling pig; baked codfish in aspic; pelmeni, stuffed dumplings in a beef broth; radish salad; pickled mushrooms; caviar; and an assortment of breads, cakes, and cookies adorned two tables. The banquet was worthy of a tzar and must have cost a small fortune.

"As I mentioned earlier," gloated Kalinin, "the cooks have been slaving away all day."

"My God, Vasiliy," Petrov whispered. "Do I even want to know where . . ."

"No sir, you do not. But I can assure you that *most* of it was obtained legally." The mischievous twinkle in the starpom's eyes eliminated any possible doubts his words might have raised. Then with a far more serious tone he said, "Everyone contributed to this little celebration. It's our way of showing gratitude for the miraculous way you held this boat, and us, together during the certification process."

"I . . . I don't know what to say."

"Well, a normal human being would say thank you. But it would appear your throat requires some lubrication to utter such a simple phrase," taunted Kalinin as he handed Petrov a shot glass full of vodka. Turning back toward the crew, Kalinin raised his glass and said, "A toast to the Captain and crew of the *Severodvinsk*. May the Americans rue the day they run into us! *Nostrovia!*"

"*Nostrovia!*" shouted all in response, clinked glasses with his neighbor and threw the fiery liquid down their throats. A large number of "ahh"s signaled the crew's approval.

"Comrades," Petrov announced using his best command voice. "I cannot begin to express my appreciation for your dedicated service to this boat, the fleet, and the motherland. You have, from the very beginning, always performed above and beyond what was demanded of you. And, much has been demanded." Petrov paused momentarily as he fought to maintain his composure. "I could not have asked for a better crew and I am honored and proud to be your Captain. As a team, we have done wonders and I thank you all for your efforts. I also want to pass on Vice Admiral Kokurin's personal compliments for a job well done. He was most impressed with your performance."

As Petrov spoke, several of the mess stewards had quickly moved about and refilled everyone's glasses. Raising his toward his shipmates, Petrov offered another toast. "To the officers and crew of this fine submarine. To your continued good health and success in all your future endeavors. *Nostrovia!*"

Once again the men collectively replied, "*Nostrovia!*"

Finishing his drink, Kalinin set his glass down on a nearby table. Then lifting his arms to the assembly, he declared, "And now my comrades-in-arms, let the feast begin!"

The enthusiastic cheer reverberated sharply off the bulkheads. And as quickly as it came, it was replaced by the clinking of china plates and silverware as the crew helped themselves to the delectable morsels. Kalinin handed his captain a plate piled high with chebureki, mushrooms, caviar, and bread smothered in butter. Petrov thanked him as he reached eagerly for the loaded dish and began to devour the lamb pie. The taste was incredible.

After forty-five minutes, and more food than he should have eaten, Petrov snatched a cup of hot tea and motioned for Kalinin to follow him. Even though the party was technically in Petrov's honor, it was hard for a crew to really celebrate with the two senior officers in close company. And the sooner he broke the news to his starpom about their orders, the sooner Kalinin would get over his tantrum and get to work. Quietly, the two slipped their way out of the crew's mess and headed for the captain's stateroom one deck up.

"Thank you again, Vasiliy. That was a very pleasant surprise," said Petrov as he entered his stateroom and offered Kalinin a chair at the small worktable.

"Actually, it really was the crew's idea," remarked Kalinin as he plopped himself down in the seat. "They just didn't know how to covertly organize such an event. Fortunately, that happens to be my specialty."

"So I have noticed. Remind me to forward your resume to the FSB. You'd fit right in with that secretive state organ," teased Petrov as he opened the locked briefcase and took out his orders.

"Please, sir, bite your tongue," Kalinin shot back vehemently as the smile vanished from his face. The mere mention of the Federal Security Service, the heir to the KGB, even in jest, was enough to make the starpom a little edgy. During the submarine's fitting out, deals had been struck with certain shipyard personnel to keep things moving along. While trivial in nature, some were less than legal. The FSB had never met a minor charge that couldn't be constructed into a heinous crime if it suited them. During Vladimir Putin's presidency, the FSB had grown considerably in power and prestige.

Sensing that he had stepped over the line with his attempted humor, Petrov quickly apologized. "I'm sorry, Vasiliy. That was a bad joke."

"Actually, sir," replied Kalinin with a renewed grin, "it was a dreadful one. But I'm assuming you didn't drag me away from the party just to threaten me. I take it there was some discussions after the acceptance board that will affect us, yes?"

"Correct," said Petrov as he sat down opposite Kalinin. "Vice Admiral Kokurin asked the eskadra and diviziya commanders and myself to stay behind after the formal board to discuss some changes to our schedule."

"Awwww," wailed Kalinin as he ran his fingers through his hair. "How long of a delay this time?"

"No, Vasiliy. There won't be another delay," countered Petrov calmly. "Quite the opposite in fact, they want us to accelerate our schedule."

The confused expression on the starpom's face almost made Petrov smile. It wasn't often that he caught this man by surprise. But in his defense, the claim that they were going to increase the tempo of their preparations would be incredible to any officer in the Russian Navy given the slothlike pace of the last ten years.

"Accelerate?" repeated Kalinin as he wrestled with the idea. "By how much?"

"We have three weeks," responded Petrov matter-of-factly.

With a sigh of relief, Kalinin sat up and appeared relaxed. "Three weeks, eh? I think we can we can do that." He paused momentarily, mentally going over the predeployment checklist.

The unexpectedly calm response by his second-in-command left Petrov somewhat disappointed. Where was the more colorful reaction that *should* have occurred? They hadn't drunk that much vodka at the party to tranquilize his starpom's legendary temper.

"Yes, sir, we can do it," said Kalinin with confidence. "I can trim three weeks off our schedule with only minor inconvenience."

The naïveté of the remark, coupled with an ill-timed sip, almost caused Petrov to choke. Half coughing, half laughing, with tea dripping on the table, Petrov urgently reached for a napkin and wiped his mouth and nose.

"Are you all right, sir?" asked Kalinin, a combination of surprise and concern on his face.

"I will be fine, Vasiliy," rasped Petrov hoarsely as he cleared the last of the tea from his windpipe. "But I'm afraid you misunderstood me. We aren't cutting our schedule by three weeks, we only *have* three weeks."

"What?" whispered Kalinin in utter disbelief.

"The Fleet Commander has issued orders for us to sail on the twenty-ninth of this month. We have twenty-one days to get ready." If anyone had been walking outside of the captain's stateroom at that moment, they would have sworn a polar bear was inside.

"Three weeks! What do those self-serving bureaucratic jackasses think we are? Magicians? How in God's name do they expect me to compress all of this into three weeks?" Kalinin picked up the copy of the schedule he had given Petrov and waved it about wildly as he ranted. "Those damned fools don't have the faintest clue as to what it takes to bring a submarine into service!"

Petrov sat there quietly as the starpom vented his frustrations. Even though Kalinin's words were insubordinate, his statements were accurate and showed an excellent grasp of fleet procedures and politics.

Petrov knew the trick to handling men like Kalinin was to allow them to say what they needed to, without fear of retribution, and let them get it out of their system. Afterward, they would move heaven and earth to accomplish an impossible task. Trust and an understanding ear went a long way toward harnessing the dedication and boundless energy of these men. It also encouraged a fierce loyalty that was infectious throughout the crew. Properly managed, such a crew could do unbelievable things.

The tirade lasted for only a few minutes. As Kalinin began to wind down, Petrov gestured for him to take his seat and said, "Calm yourself, Vasiliy. It's not quite as bad as it sounds."

"Not quite as bad!?!" replied Kalinin incredulously. "Sir, you know just as well as I that we are nowhere near ready to go on combat patrol. There are just too many things that have to be done. Three weeks is simply not enough."

"Then we defer those tasks that are irrelevant to this particular mission," Petrov responded firmly. "I also have both Borisov's and Vidchenko's assurances that we will have the highest priority to assist us in our preparations."

"Sir, with all due respect, we have been the navy's top priority for the last several years and I don't think I need to remind you of what we had to do to just get out of the shipyard, or how long it took us!"

"I thought the same as you originally, but there is an important distinction that we both have missed."

"What is that?"

"While in the shipyard, we were under the fleet's jurisdiction but only peripherally. Remember, any request we made was sent to the Main Navy Staff via the manufacturing representative at the shipyard. The Northern Fleet staff was only informed of our requirements. They never approved them."

Kalinin leaned forward as he listened to his captain's explanation with focused attention. Petrov knew that the quickest way to get his starpom to engage his mind instead of his heart was to throw a well-reasoned argument at him.

"On top of this, we have Rear Admiral Vidchenko, our new diviziya commander. He undoubtedly wants to prove himself to both Borisov and Kokurin, and I should think he'd be rather motivated to assist us in any way possible. So you see, Vasiliy, I don't think we'll get the same response as we did before."

Standing slowly, Kalinin looked his commander straight in the eyes, and with a slight nod acknowledged his orders, "Very well, sir. I will recalculate our schedule based on your intuition."

"You are the best planner and organizer in the diviziya, and very likely the eskadra as well, Vasiliy. If anyone can compress three months of effort into three weeks, it is you."

"I shall try not to disappoint you, my Captain," answered Kalinin, still uneasy with Petrov's news.

"I know you won't, Vasiliy. You have never given me cause to doubt your abilities and I'm not about to start now. But before you begin working your magic, I want you to read our orders," said Petrov as he handed the folder to his starpom. "Focus our efforts on those items that are absolutely essential to carry out this assignment. If you decide something isn't mission-critical, you have my authority to defer it until we return."

Buoyed by Petrov's confidence in him, Kalinin said, "We will be ready to sail on time. We will not miss this opportunity, comrade Captain."

"Very good, Starpom," replied Petrov smartly. "Carry out your duties."

"Aye, aye, sir."

4

MISSION BRIEFING

15 September 2008
Atlantic Ocean—100 nm SE of Subase New London
(39°55'N, 070°45'W)

The lookout was the first man down, followed soon after by Palmer and Hayes. "Chief of the Watch," announced Palmer, "the bridge is rigged for dive, last man down, hatch secured."

Jerry winced a little as he listened to the report. Technically, it was accurate. But Palmer's voice still had a note of uncertainty to it. The chief of the watch acknowledged the report and then relayed it to LTJG Shawn McClelland, *Seawolf*'s sonar officer. McClelland had temporarily taken over as the officer of the deck, or OOD, while Hayes and Palmer prepared the bridge to submerge. This transfer of command ensured the safety of the ship while the men in the cockpit topside focused their attention on removing flat panel displays and other pieces of equipment that preferred not to get soaked. After a brief turnover, Hayes resumed his role as OOD and Palmer his as the junior officer of the deck (JOOD).

Looking down at the plotting table, Jerry saw the quartermaster of the watch point to a colorfully labeled position on the navigation chart and hold up two fingers. Nodding, Jerry turned and exclaimed, "Officer of the Deck, two minutes to the dive point."

"Very well, Nav," answered Hayes. "Mark the sounding."

"Two nine eight fathoms," replied the quartermaster.

IT HAD been raining topside, and the discarded foul-weather gear added to the crowding and bustle as *Seawolf* prepared to submerge. Filled with control panels, mechanical and electrical equipment, the control room had about the same floor space as a large suburban kitchen.

The layout of the control room was similar to the older *Los Angeles* class, with the ship control panel and ballast control panel in the forward left-hand corner. To the forward and right was the entrance to the sonar room, and the five fire-control consoles directly aft of the entrance. The two periscopes were in the center of the space, flanked by two plotting tables, one on each side, and a series of command displays directly in front. While the normal watch in the control room was eleven or twelve men, additional watchstanders were required for the maneuvering watch. With the wet foul-weather gear taking up prime deck space, there was little room left for the captain and the XO. And nobody wanted to crowd the captain.

Rudel stood off to the side with Shimko and waited patiently for his cue. Upon hearing the sounding report, he maneuvered around the extra obstacles and stepped up to the periscope stand. "OOD, report."

Although Rudel had said "OOD," his gaze was firmly fixed on Palmer. Understanding his captain's desire, Hayes said, "Mr. Palmer, make the report."

"Aye, aye, sir," Palmer responded nervously. Then, after taking a deep breath, he began his lengthy report on the ship's status. "Captain, the ship is on course one six five at all ahead flank, making two four knots. The ship is rigged for dive. We are about one minute from the dive point and the ship's inertial navigation system is tracking with GPS. We hold one contact on radar; bearing 180 degrees, range two five thousand yards. Contact is past CPA and opening. Sounding is two nine eight fathoms beneath the keel. Request permission to submerge the ship, sir."

The captain took in the report while maintaining full eye contact with Palmer, who fidgeted under his CO's scrutiny. Although Rudel already knew everything that his JOOD had just told him, it was navy procedure to go over it again to ensure that everyone in the ship's control party was operating with the same information—especially the junior members. He then glanced over at the ballast and ship control panels to verify the boat's readiness to submerge. Satisfied, he turned and looked toward Jerry.

"Navigator?"

Jerry answered, "Mark the dive point, sir."

"Very well, Mr. Palmer. Submerge the ship to one five zero feet." In spite of the bustle, Rudel spoke in a conversational tone. Palmer echoed the captain's order, "Submerge the ship to one five zero feet, aye." Reflexively, Jerry checked the ordered depth against their plotted position and the fathometer. Plenty of room—now over three hundred fathoms, or eighteen hundred feet, beneath them.

Palmer then passed the order on to the diving officer, who in turn leaned forward and repeated it to the planesman and the chief of the watch. The three men echoed it back in unison. Six back-and-forth repetitions of the exact same simple order might seem a little tedious, but well-drilled procedures weighed lightly compared with the price of a mistake.

"Dive! Dive!" announced the chief of the watch over the 1MC, the ship's main announcing circuit, followed immediately by two blasts of the diving alarm. *WREEEEEE, WREEEEEE.*

"Dive! Dive!" he announced a second time.

Once the word had been passed that boat was about to submerge, the diving officer paused momentarily, waiting. After about ten seconds, he looked over at Palmer, who was at the number two periscope looking forward. "Off'sa'deck, request ahead two-thirds."

"What?" responded Palmer, puzzled.

Hayes quickly came beside him and whispered, "We need to slow down, Mr. Palmer. It won't do to bend a periscope on our way out now, would it?"

"Yes, sir. I mean, no sir," Palmer replied. Then, struggling to regain his composure, he said, "Helm, all ahead two-thirds."

"All ahead two-thirds, helm aye." Reaching down to the engine order telegraph, the petty officer rotated the handle that shifted an arrow from "Flank" to "⅔." A second arrow on the dial soon followed suit. "Maneuvering answers ahead two-thirds."

"Very well," said Palmer, followed immediately with, "Thanks, Dive."

Acknowledging the comment with a nod, the diving officer proceeded with the business at hand. "Chief of the Watch, open the forward main ballast tank vents."

"Open the forward main ballast tank vents, aye." A few toggle switches later, the green bars shifted to red open circles on the ballast control panel or BCP. "Diving Officer, forward main ballast tank vents indicate open."

Palmer trained the periscope forward and rotated the

optics downward. Six towering geysers of air and water vapor leapt from openings on *Seawolf*'s bow as seawater rushed into the ballast tanks from below and pushed the air out through the vents. "Venting forward," he reported.

"Venting forward, aye," responded the diving officer. "Open aft main ballast tank vents."

"Open the aft main ballast tank vents, aye."

Rotating the periscope around toward the stern, Palmer saw a similar eruption from the four after vents. "Venting aft."

Unlike World War II fleet boats that were designed to quickly flood their ballast tanks and "crash dive" under the waves in less than a minute, *Seawolf* took her sweet time getting under. Like all nuclear-powered submarines, she was designed to stay submerged for long periods of time and wasn't burdened with the need to surface often like the older diesel boats. The requirement for rapid submergence had been replaced by virtually unlimited underwater endurance and high speed. Furthermore, *Seawolf* was four times the size of a fleet boat and the increased tankage just took longer to fill. When the time came to submerge, *Seawolf* sort of waddled her way down, but once all the way under she transformed into a graceful sea creature, completely at ease in her element.

"Rig out the bow planes," ordered the diving officer.

As the ship control party continued with the diving procedures, Jerry watched Palmer supervising the evolution. One of Jerry's duties as the senior watch officer was to provide the XO with an evaluation of Palmer's performance, and he wanted the report to be based on factual observations, not fantasy. So far, Palmer seemed to be doing okay. Not great, but okay.

A couple of mechanical clunks told Jerry that the bow planes had been extended and locked. After a quick test, the helmsman was ordered to put ten-degree dive on the bow planes. The effect was immediate as the planes forced *Seawolf*'s bow downward, driving her under the waves. The video monitor showed the forward part of the hull burrowing deeper into the ocean; the venting geysers becoming more of a bubbling mass.

While the view was spectacular, it was also unnerving. Palmer should be doing 360-degree scans as the boat dove. Once again he had allowed himself to become fixated on a single aspect of this highly complex process. Jerry wasn't concerned for the safety of the ship, as Hayes was on number-one scope and was keeping a vigilant circle search, but the lack of attention on Palmer's part didn't encourage confidence in his abilities. And if the captain didn't have confidence in a JO, he wouldn't get qualified. Fortunately, Hayes quickly recognized what was not happening and coaxed Palmer to resume a proper search.

Jerry's brooding was interrupted by the diving officer's next report: "Off'sa'deck, stern planes tested sat. I have the bubble, sir. Stern planes to ten-degree dive. Proceeding to ten-degree down bubble."

"Very well, Dive," replied Palmer.

With the stern planes in the act, the deck started to dip toward the bow. The force of the water on the depressed stern planes quickly caused the boat's hull to rotate downward, driving her under the sea. The diving officer watched both the gauge on the ship control panel and the inclinometer attached to the bulkhead. Like a carpenter's level, a gas bubble indicated the amount of the ship's tilt as it approached the ordered ten-degree down angle. The reference to the ship's angle by the position of the "bubble" was firmly rooted in submarine tradition, if somewhat antiquated.

"Depth five five feet," called out the diving officer.

Palmer acknowledged the report as he kept up his circle search. Going around and around on the periscope, while necessary, was also tedious and somewhat tiring, even with a power assist to help turn the scope. "Dancing with the fat lady," as the periscope watch was called, could give a person a good workout.

"Depth six zero feet."

"Decks awash," Palmer reported.

The diving officer kept on announcing the increasing depth, and after the seventy-foot mark, Palmer announced, "Scopes under. Lowering number-two scope."

Simultaneously, Hayes lowered the number-one periscope. From start to finish it had taken *Seawolf* almost eight minutes to dive. Pretty much par for the course, thought Jerry as the quartermaster noted the time in the ship's log.

Ten minutes later, *Seawolf* was at 150 feet and with a satisfactory slow speed trim. All balanced out and in her natural environment, she could now truly begin their journey north.

Jerry listened as the captain set *Seawolf*'s course and speed in a northeasterly direction at sixteen knots. By reflex, he double-checked the plotted course against the captain's orders. Open water lay before them for hundreds of miles. He noted that the time of the next course change was several days away.

Captain Rudel stayed in control until after the watch had turned over, then headed aft toward his stateroom. The XO followed, announcing "Briefing at 1300" before he left. It was only a reminder. Not only had the briefing been part of the plan of the day, but out of the 130 men aboard, only a handful, Jerry included, knew the details of the boat's destination and mission. There was more than a little curiosity.

With the maneuvering watch secured, Jerry returned to his stateroom and got busy collecting his briefing materials. He was providing the visual aids, as the XO put it, for the briefing to the CO and the rest of the wardroom.

Wardroom, USS *Seawolf*

Lieutenant Commander Shimko finished presenting *Seawolf*'s planned track. "And here's the part we all like. Course two seven zero, then two two five. West and southwest to home. Total voyage time seven weeks, two days, and change. All things considered, a fairly short northern run."

The packed wardroom held thirteen of *Seawolf*'s fifteen officers, along with Master Chief Hess, the chief of the boat. Lieutenant Commander Lavoie, the sub's engineer, had the watch in control while Lieutenant (j.g.) Todd Williams, the ship's damage control assistant, was back in maneuvering. When the wardroom was used for meals, the officers would eat in two shifts, and it was still a tight fit. With the space this full, everyone kept their elbows pulled in. Jerry had a little more space up front, because he had to handle the charts.

It had taken only fifteen minutes for the XO to lay out their planned course and describe their mission. Shimko didn't waste words. He expected a routine transit, a smooth mission, and a speedy return home.

"Mr. Mitchell." He turned to Jerry. "This is a very packed mission plan. Can you keep us on schedule?"

Jerry caught the XO's tone. "Well, sir, there's construction on the turnpike. If we take the bypass . . ."

Everyone laughed, a comfortable joke among officers comfortable with each other and pleased with their new assignment.

Shimko announced, "Our torpedo officer will now describe exactly how the UUVs will be used on this op."

Lieutenant (j.g.) Palmer, standing near the doorway, pulled some notes out of his shirt pocket. He didn't try to move from where he stood.

He unfolded the notes and paused for a moment. "The vehicles we are carrying are prototypes of the Advanced Development UUVs. They have high-frequency imaging sonars and precision underwater mapping software. The high-resolution imaging sonar will allow us to collect precise bottom bathymetric data. There is also a special camera module that can take seven-megapixel digital photos of the bottom or anything interesting that it comes across.

"Each UUV is fitted with a GPS and inertial navigation system, and they're smart enough to follow complex instructions. *Seawolf* will get in range of an 'area of interest,' typically about five nautical miles. We will launch one of the three vehicles—Maxine, Patty, or LaVerne." Those who hadn't heard the three names before, but understood the reference, smiled or chuckled; Palmer didn't pause. "Each has an endurance of about sixty hours, but we expect each mission to take no more than forty-five, allowing a fifteen-hour margin.

"We can communicate with one acoustically within seven nautical miles, or by SATCOM, which gives us the flexibility to be much farther away. We can preset times when a UUV will come up to a shallow depth, find a safe hole in the sea ice, and listen for instructions. It can also use the same procedure to take its own GPS fixes.

"We won't be able to see what a UUV has found until it returns to the boat. The imaging sonar returns almost photographic-quality images, but the acoustic modem would choke on that much data. We'll download the detailed bottom data after the UUV is recovered. Instead, we'll get basic data—a usable picture of the bottom, position, course and speed, and so on, as long as we're within that seven-mile acoustic comms range.

"When a UUV completes a mission and returns to the boat, it will need about two hours' maintenance. Basically, while we're sending one out, one will be running a survey, and we'll be servicing or recovering the third. We don't charge the lithium-thionyl-chloride batteries on these UUVs. The energy sections are completely replaced. That shortens our turnaround time."

The XO asked, "Questions?"

"Sir, what if we have problems with the UUVs?" Lieutenant Will Hayes was main propulsion assistant. The engineering department would not be directly concerned with survey operations, but it was an honest question.

Shimko looked to Palmer. The torpedo officer only paused for a moment. "Losing a vehicle would be bad, but would only cost us one or two sorties at the very most. And those could be made up if we stayed on station a little longer. The consumables can be used by any of the three vehicles. We've loaded the top starboard torpedo tube with the mechanical arm that recovers the UUVs. We can use any of the three other starboard tubes for actually launching or recovering them. I've laid in extra repair parts for the arm, the control console, and the handling equipment. Barring a catastrophe, we can fix all the gear underway."

Hayes and everyone else seemed satisfied by Palmer's answer.

Chandler then raised his hand. "Sir, if we're doing this after the Russian training exercises are done for the year, why did we embark CTs and the ACINT riders?" The cryptological techs were enlisted men who were experts in electronic eavesdropping and would be spending a lot of time in the radio room and the ESM bay. Most could speak Russian, several were fluent in a couple of languages. Given their skill level, they were dramatically underpaid. The acoustic intelligence riders were hypertrained sonar technicians who would assist *Seawolf*'s own sonar shop.

Boats on intelligence-collection missions near foreign waters routinely carried CTs and ACINT specialists to actually gather signals and acoustic intelligence data and advise the captain on procedures and the conduct of the mission. They usually kept to themselves, and submariners had learned that "the riders" never talked shop.

The XO answered this question. "They're aboard because we can't be sure the Russians will do what they've done in the past. We will be monitoring their transmissions, if there are any. And since we're looking at the seabed, we may find expended weapons or other matériel and if there are any markings, I'd like to know what they say." He paused for a moment. "Although our ordered mission is to conduct precise bottom surveys, we will always use every opportunity to gather useful intelligence. Confucius says, 'Man who search at night better use long candle.' "

While everyone laughed, the captain stood up. He nodded toward Ensign Santana, who turned on the ship's announcing circuit and handed the microphone to Rudel.

"Attention, all hands. This is the Captain. Before we sailed, you were all told our mission would be up north, and would last just over seven weeks. Here's the rest of it. After transiting to the Barents Sea, we will be surveying parts of the seabed there. We will also aggressively collect any intelligence we can on Russian naval operations. In the course of your work, you may learn more details about our mission. Do not discuss what you learn with other members of the crew or anyone off the boat without my express permission.

"Our work will involve using the three prototype UUVs we are carrying. As it is early fall up there, we will spend most of our time under sea ice. None of this will be any more unusual or hazardous than our typical hair-raising exploits. All we have to do is work our tails off, get the job done, and then we'll return home quickly and safely. That is all."

As soon as the briefing broke up, Jerry headed forward to control. As navigator, he'd made it his business to look at the chart table at least twice each watch. Yes, they were still in the Atlantic Ocean, with hundreds of miles of water hundreds of fathoms deep below them. Then Jerry imagined how embarrassed he'd be if they ran aground.

QM2 Keith Dunn had the watch. His folks were Georgia farmers, Jerry remembered, and he had five-year-old twins, a boy and a girl. The petty officer was leaning on the chart table, quietly talking with another member of the watch, when Jerry came into control. Dunn quickly turned to the chart table.

"Afternoon, sir." He pointed to a spot in the chart. The quartermaster reeled off his report with practiced formality. "As of 1330 we're ninety miles south of Martha's Vineyard, which is also the closest land. Still on course zero eight zero at sixteen knots, depth two hundred feet. Next planned course change isn't for two days until after we clear the Grand Banks. It's going to be a bit dull for us quartermasters, sir."

Dunn's report was routine, and Jerry double-checked to make sure he was updating the chart properly. Jerry had watched QM1 Peters take the last GPS fix, just before they submerged, which raised Jerry's confidence about their location. As long as they were underway, Jerry would be responsible for making sure that *Seawolf* was where she needed to be, and knowing where she was supposed to go next.

DRIVING A submarine was very different from what he'd expected to do in the Navy. Jerry had been selected for aviation and trained as a pilot, and he'd done well. He was short and athletic, with the reflexes and eyesight that flying a fighter demanded. But a tire had blown on takeoff one day, forcing him to eject. He'd made it out of the jet alive, but landed badly, shattering his right wrist. While the doctors had been able to repair the damage, his right hand had "a limited range of motion."

Those hated words had washed him out of aviation, at least as a pilot. Years of training had been wasted, and the Navy had wanted Jerry to settle for an assignment to surface ships. Jerry was too much a competitor to settle for something offered to him. He'd asked for submarines, another elite branch with a long and difficult entry. The Navy had initially refused. He'd made it, though, using every trick in the book to get the transfer. And he'd made it through nuclear power school and the rest of the submarine training pipeline.

He'd had to adjust. Instead of a single man controlling an agile fighter, he was part of team that controlled a massive underwater machine—a creature of the sea instead of the sky. And while a plane would fly as part of a squadron, a sub always operated alone.

There were similarities, though. Technology made it possible to live and work underwater, just as it let him fly. It let him find and fight an enemy, if he needed to, and the hardware could also kill him if he didn't stay on top of it. Submariners and aviators both tended to be detail freaks. It was the little stuff that made the difference.

AND PRACTICE made perfect. The ship's 1MC system announced, "SIMULATE UUV LAUNCH OPERATIONS." Launching and operating a UUV involved only control and the torpedo room watchstanders, but getting the vehicles launched and recovered was going to be critical to the mission. The torpedo division held loading drills every day.

Jerry watched Dunn hook up his sound-powered phones and check communications with the torpedo room. For a real launch, *Seawolf* had to slow to five knots, and the captain would authorize the UUV's launch and recovery. And the vehicle's position had to be plotted, so Dunn monitored the control circuit. For the drill, Dunn would provide control's responses, but *Seawolf* wouldn't actually maneuver.

Jerry wasn't involved with the loading drill, so he headed aft. There was a mountain of paperwork that he'd put off, and it was all due to the XO before they returned to port. He'd been working only about twenty minutes when the phone buzzed. "Jerry, it's Greg. Can you come down to the torpedo room?"

Lieutenant Greg Wolfe was *Seawolf*'s weapons officer. He was responsible for the UUVs as well as the sub's torpedoes and cruise missiles. The two department heads had worked closely on the UUV operational plan for this mission. Jerry's extensive experience with UUVs aboard *Memphis* had been very useful during the planning phase. He could tell from Wolfe's voice that something was seriously wrong.

JERRY STOPPED outside the door to the torpedo room. He could hear urgent voices inside, and wondered for half a moment if there was a genuine emergency. Logic answered that question immediately, though. If there had been a real problem, alarms would have sounded minutes ago.

Instead, as he stepped in, alarms went off inside him. Enlisted ratings clustered around the starboard tube nest. The recovery arm, used to bring the UUVs back aboard the sub, was pulled halfway out of its tube back inside the torpedo room.

Cables and equipment clustered around a thick steel beam. Painted a bright green, the recovery arm was designed to fit in a twenty-one-inch-diameter torpedo tube, but just barely. Even though *Seawolf*'s tubes were larger, they had been sleeved to take the smaller weapons in the U.S. submarine inventory. While the tube was a little over twenty-three feet long, the arm actually expanded out to sixty feet when it was deployed outside the hull.

When a UUV returned to the sub, the recovery arm telescoped out of the uppermost starboard torpedo tube. It had a short-range acoustic homing beacon on the end that guided the underwater robot to within a few feet. Then the arm automatically grabbed the vehicle and lined it up with the torpedo tube below. Finally, it guided the UUV into the tube and retracted back into its own tube. It was as complicated as a Chinese puzzle and as easy to work on as a tax form.

Chief Johnson was directing some sort of activity while Palmer and Wolfe stood in one corner, flipping through tech manuals. Both officers looked up at the same time and saw Jerry. He hurried over to join them, but Wolfe started talking while Jerry was still a few steps away.

"It's jammed halfway in." Jerry's heart sank. He didn't bother asking how. Wolfe was already explaining.

"We interrupted the loading drill when the recovery arm showed a hydraulic leak. We found the problem and corrected it simply enough, but when we tried to re-stow the mechanism, it only slid part of the way in.

"As we pushed it back into the tube, it made a scraping noise—the kind of sound you don't want precision machinery to make. When we tried to back it out and look for the cause, it made the same noise, only louder."

"Did you ever see this on *Memphis*?" Palmer asked.

Jerry answered quickly, "No. Whenever we worked on the arm, it always went back in smoothly. But the retrieval system and procedures were a lot different since we used a tethered vehicle."

"It's like I said, it's gotta be the tracks." Palmer was insistent, but then added, "We're screwed."

"No we're not," Wolfe said firmly. "We'll sort this out." He turned to Jerry. "I've got Chief Johnson and the division locking it in place so it doesn't move until we figure out what's wrong."

"Losing a vehicle would be bad enough, but losing the arm kills the entire mission. It's the one thing we can't replace or work around. We aren't out even one day and this happens." Palmer sounded like he was ready to go back to his stateroom and start packing his bags. Jerry thought he sounded frightened, worried more about his career than the jammed arm. Jerry was grateful that they were speaking softly.

"I said we'll sort this out, and we will," Wolfe repeated. "Now go make sure the arm can't shift if we have to maneuver."

While Palmer checked on the division's progress, Wolfe said, "I was hoping you might have seen something like this on your last boat. We routinely pull it out for servicing, and the arm seems to work well. In the sea trials last week, we launched a vehicle and everything worked perfectly."

Wolfe sighed, then asked Jerry, "Would you brief the XO? I know it's my job, but I want to stay on top of this, and," jerking his thumb in Palmer's direction, "I've got to keep a lid on Palmer."

"Okay." Jerry nodded, and glanced at his watch to mark the time. "It's been what, five minutes?"

Wolfe checked the clipboard. "Ten since we tried to restow the arm."

"Yeah, it's time to put the XO in the loop." Jerry headed forward. He climbed the ladders between the two decks without even thinking about it, his mind trying to process the implications of a jammed recovery arm. He knocked on the XO's door and heard, "Come."

Lieutenant Commander Shimko was examining two forms, one in each hand, as if comparing signatures. As Jerry started to tell the XO about the problem, he methodically laid them back into a folder and placed the folder precisely on the corner of his desk.

He frowned as he heard the news, but nodded agreement when he heard Wolfe's apology for not making the report personally. Jerry expected the XO to hurry down to the torpedo room, but instead he asked Jerry, "Is there any hazard to the boat?"

"No, sir."

"Is there any need to change our course or depth?"

"Not at this time, sir."

"And Mr. Wolfe and Mr. Palmer are both on task?"

"Yessir."

"Then tell Mr. Wolfe I'll be down there in a while. I'll report to the Captain in the meantime. Thank you, Jerry."

"Aye, aye, sir."

JERRY SHOWED up in control at 1730 hours, half an hour before his watch started. He'd eaten an early dinner, in the first sitting. Not only did his rank allow him his pick of which sitting to use, a pending watch preempted everybody except the captain. It was a good meal—stuffed pork chops. Jerry savored the salad. The fresh vegetables would disappear after two weeks.

The captain or the XO couldn't be in control all the time, so qualified officers stood watches as "officer of the deck" or "OOD." Responsible for the operation of the sub when the captain wasn't there, the OOD acted in the captain's name. Any aspect of the ship that affected its operations was his responsibility. An OOD was expected to keep the sub out of trouble, deal quickly with any casualty, and if necessary, fight the boat until battle stations were manned. If there was time, he would notify the captain of developments, but he didn't need the captain's permission to act.

Lieutenant Commander Stan Lavoie had stood the noon-to-six watch in control, along with two chief petty officers and five enlisted men. Other officers and enlisted men stood watch elsewhere in the boat. The sonar displays were always manned, as was engineering, with almost twelve men tending the nuclear reactor and the engines. Others took care of the auxiliary machinery, located throughout the sub. About one-quarter of *Seawolf*'s 130-man crew was on watch at any one time. While the working day technically ended at dinnertime, the boat never slept.

Lavoie was waiting for Jerry, and had his briefing ready. While Jerry reviewed the ship's course, speed, depth, and other information, the enlisted men on watch each passed information on to their reliefs, and then traded places, reporting to the chief of the watch, who also briefed his relief. Although somewhat crowded with twice the number of men it normally held, control remained quiet, the men speaking in low voices.

The chief of the watch reported to Lieutenant Commander Lavoie, "Sir, the watch has been relieved."

"Very well, Chief. Thank you."

Lavioie turned to Jerry. "I am ready to be relieved."

Jerry responded formally, "I relieve you sir," then said, "This is Lieutenant Mitchell, I have the deck and the conn." Each of the enlisted operators acknowledged Jerry's announcement that he was now in charge.

Jerry toured each of the enlisted men's stations—conn, sonar, fire control, the chart table, and the rest. Everything was in order, as it should be when *Seawolf* was simply moving from Point A to Point B.

The captain had even suspended any drills until the

UUV arm was unstuck. Normally after a boat went to sea, the XO ordered a flurry of emergency drills: fires, equipment failures, flooding, a simulated radiation leak. Those drills would still happen, but not until the weapons department solved their "little problem." In the meantime, Jerry periodically updated the heading they'd need and the time it would take to reach New London, just in case the captain asked.

The quiet and lack of change wore away at Jerry's alertness. He'd developed and enforced a routine, checking important displays every five minutes, and every display on the half hour. He paced the limited space, and thought up questions to ask himself.

Robinson did show up with the two junior electronics technicians. Although the extra bodies crowded everyone, he was glad for the activity, and to watch some of his men at work.

Halfway through the watch, Lieutenant Wolfe appeared, grinning widely. "War's over," he announced, almost euphoric. "The arm moves freely and appears undamaged."

Jerry felt several bricks fall from his shoulders. The mission could continue. "How'd you fix it?"

"All it took was a bucket of bear grease, a crowbar, and Chief Johnson cursing a blue streak." Wolfe grinned and Jerry could see the strain falling away. He felt it himself, and he wasn't even responsible for the retrieval arm.

"We found some debris on two of the wheels. It's gummy, and there was some solid material in it, either grit or metal. Anyway, the chief thinks it may have been lurking, stuck to the underside of the mechanism. The division's inspecting the entire arm now—top, bottom, and sides—for any piece of gunk big enough to see or feel."

The XO walked into control and saw Wolfe. "I've briefed the Captain. He says well done, and he wants your report when you're finished with your inspection."

"Aye, aye," Wolfe answered brightly.

"OOD, call away a fire drill. Make it in the auxiliary machinery room, third level."

Jerry smiled. It was going to be a good watch.

5

TRIALS

20 September 2008
Atlantic Ocean, Lat 58°25'N, Long 035°50'W
Course 015° true, speed 16 knots

Jerry's alarm clock went off at 0530. The recorded bird songs and the wind rustling through trees gradually grew louder, drawing him gently from his semicomatose state. He'd spent quite a bit of money on it, and it was worth every penny. Not only did it show the day and date, but it could display multiple time zones and it gave him a choice of "gentle environmental noises" designed to wake him slowly. He'd bypassed the "ocean surf" in favor of forest sounds.

Jerry spent a moment looking at the clock's digital display, fixing the day and date in his mind; like the ship's ordered course and speed, it helped him to orient himself. It was Saturday, the 20th of September. They'd been at sea five days. *Seawolf* would reach the op area in the Barents in four more days.

Jerry needed the clock. The unchanging hum of machinery gave no clue to time of day or season. On top of that was the submarine force's unorthodox watch rotation of six hours on and twelve hours off, which threw any normal human being's circadian rhythm into chaos. In the berthing spaces, the lights were turned to red at night, but in the control room and other working spaces, the white lights were almost always on. There were no windows, and even if there had been one, it would have showed only dark water.

One clue to the time of day was the sound of quiet movement in the passageway outside his stateroom. And Jerry could smell breakfast in the wardroom, just a few feet down the passageway.

Jerry shared his stateroom with Lieutenant Chandler, who occupied the lower bunk, and Ensign Tim Miller, who had the top rack. Being a department head, Jerry had the middle bunk—the easiest one to get in and out of. Still, Jerry was always careful to make sure of Chandler's location before getting out of his bunk. He remembered the perils of being in the lower bunk during his tour on *Memphis* when Lenny Berg nearly jumped on him once or twice. Space management becomes very important when three people occupy the floor space of a walk-in closet—a small closet.

Chandler and Miller were gone, already risen and dressed, much to Jerry's relief. It wasn't just the extra floor space. Ever since Jeff Chandler's promotion, there'd been friction.

There used to be four lieutenants aboard *Seawolf*, and then there were five. Jerry was competitive. He understood the natural drive, not to reach some goal, but to beat someone or something.

But he didn't understand Chandler. His roommate, subordinate officer, and shipmate was doing everything he could to get ranked as the best lieutenant aboard *Seawolf*, and that "everything" went far beyond just doing a stellar job.

Every officer was evaluated annually on a standard fitness report form. It was filed in his jacket and used to decide if he merited promotion. It was also used by the Bureau of Personnel to see if an officer was a good fit for their next duty station. A "bad" fitness report, even as a junior officer, could haunt someone throughout their entire career. And bad, in the highly competitive, small-town community of submarine officers, could be interpreted as anything less than perfection.

Shortly after Chandler's promotion, they'd both been doing paperwork in their stateroom. Chandler had to leave and offered to take a stack of Jerry's finished paperwork to the XO on his way. Jerry had of course agreed, but later the XO asked him about some of the documents. Several were missing, and had to be redone. Jerry was sure he'd done them—pretty sure, at any rate.

And Chandler had started finding reasons to talk to the XO and the skipper. A division officer like Chandler was supposed to check with his department head, Jerry, before seeing the XO, and then he was supposed to check with the XO before seeing the captain. It was part of the chain of command. Your juniors weren't supposed to deal directly with a senior officer without your knowledge and permission. Sure there were social occasions, even while at sea, when the CO would spend time with his junior officers to watch a movie, play games, or just talk. That helped to build camaraderie and a tight wardroom.

But Jerry had recently seen Chandler speaking with the XO and even the captain—never for long, and about trivial matters, as far as Jerry knew, but what was he after? More face time? You couldn't help but get face time on a submarine, but that seemed to be his goal.

Jerry detested politics, especially petty office politics. It was a drain, a distraction, and it destroyed trust. He'd seen a lot of this self-promoting posturing in his career already, and had hoped to avoid it on *Seawolf.* Chandler's shenanigans could also affect Jerry's fitness report, simply because part of Jerry's evaluation covered his ability to lead those under him in the chain of command.

By 0545, Jerry was dressed. He stopped in the wardroom just long enough to grab some coffee, then headed for control. The watch was changing as he reviewed the charts and the planned course for the day. As usual, *Seawolf* was where she should be and on schedule. He inspected the chart and the logs and found them being properly maintained. He hadn't expected anything else, but he couldn't sit down to breakfast until he'd satisfied himself that everything was in order.

The weather report showed a storm overhead. Winds gusted to forty knots, with waves up to twenty-five feet high. It was an early winter storm, but not too early. The weather would get worse as they sailed farther north, but *Seawolf* might as well be on blocks for all the motion Jerry felt. His sensitive stomach appreciated their isolation from the surface. Submarines were not designed to ride the waves, and Jerry turned a pale gray-green every time *Seawolf* ran on the surface in a rough sea.

And Jerry hated to lose his appetite. Food on a sub was always good. The cooks regularly served pancakes or French toast, eggs and hot and cold cereal, along with bacon, sausage, and lots of fruit. And then there were the hot, fresh cinnamon sticky buns—the bane of every waistline on board. Jerry could easily make breakfast a big meal, but he'd disciplined himself early on to eat lightly. There was almost no room to exercise aboard a sub, although there was an exercise bike and some free weights crammed into one of the auxiliary machinery rooms. A lot of submariners joined the jogging circuit after they returned from patrol.

A stack of angled-in boxes on the bulkhead held each officer's message traffic, and Jerry picked at his fruit salad as he read a mix of news summaries and administrative traffic.

At sea, the XO never held morning officers' call. There was little room in the cramped spaces, and too many of the officers were on duty throughout the ship. Besides, it really wasn't necessary; Jerry and the other department heads spoke with Shimko at breakfast or immediately after the meal, trading information about the day's activities.

When Jerry found the XO this morning, his greeting was "On track, sir. No adjustment required until the next course change at 0700 tomorrow."

Finishing a bite of eggs, Shimko nodded, unsmiling. Swallowing, he asked, "And the other checkpoint?" He managed to sound conversational.

"Also on schedule, sir."

"Good. See me later."

"Aye, aye, sir."

JERRY TOURED his spaces quickly, finding everything in order. The ITs were dealing with a bad display in the radio room, but they expected to have it up in an hour, "no prob." Chandler was in radio as well, working with Chief Morrison on the rate training schedule for the next advancement exam. Jerry headed back to officers' country, pleased to find the passageway empty.

Shimko answered Jerry's soft knock, and urged him inside. "Shut the door." Jerry eased the door closed, and held the knob so it wouldn't make a noise.

"Sir, I recommend a small speed change when we change course tomorrow so that we'll cross the Arctic Circle at 1400 hours tomorrow afternoon," Jerry reported.

"Do it. Then it's still tomorrow after lunch, eh? Excellent. You'll be secretary," Shimko informed Jerry.

"Aye, sir. Who's going to be Boreas?"

Shimko grinned broadly.

"Uh, XO, weren't you Boreas last year?" Jerry's tone was mildly accusatory.

"Yeah," replied Shimko defensively. "Do you have a problem with that, Mr. Mitchell?"

"No sir! Absolutely not!" Jerry exclaimed, wisely recognizing the right answer when told. "But from the rumors I heard, you had way too much fun last time."

"And that's why I want to do it again. XO's prerogative." Shimko was still smiling. "COB still has the props from last time."

"Aye, aye, sir. I mean, Your Majesty. I'll need the list of candidates."

Shimko handed him a single sheet with a list of names. "There are thirty-seven unrepentant warm bodies for you to keep track of."

Jerry took the paper, read it, and whistled. "This is over a quarter of the crew."

"It'll take a while," Shimko agreed. "But it will be fun. That I promise."

Jerry winced, remembering his own trials and tribulations during the initiation into the Royal Order of the Bluenose. He was grateful he wouldn't have to do that again.

OVER THAT day and the next, Jerry watched the plot as *Seawolf* drove steadily north beneath dark gray waves. The seawater turned colder, there were few surface contacts, and the sound of clinking ice floes appeared on the sonar displays. *Seawolf* was crossing into the Marginal Ice Zone, an area where sea ice covered the ocean's surface. This was to be their cover for the rest of the approach north.

Jerry could visualize the northern wilderness in front of them, civilization and all it offered falling away behind.

Electrician's Mate Master Chief Hess was chief of the boat, the senior enlisted man on board. He was also one of the key conspirators, having crossed the Arctic Circle so often he'd worn a bare spot on the chart. Immediately after lunch, he and Jerry met by one of the auxilary machinery spaces, midships fourth deck.

The storage room's door was locked, but the master chief had a key. No one saw the COB and Jerry quickly slip inside. The space held racks of spare electronic equipment and other supplies. It also contained the ship's small stock of holiday decorations. A narrow strip of linoleum-covered deck provided the only room to pull out the well-organized boxes. Hess, taller than Jerry, hunched over, since the overhead was not only low, but covered with brackets and cables.

A gray-painted metal box, labeled "D. Jones," sat at one end of the space. The master chief unlocked it and began passing bizarre items back to Jerry: a quill pen, a green eyeshade, a leather-bound book, and a silver cloak covered with gold-colored paper letters.

Jerry couldn't help grinning. This was only his second Bluenose ceremony, and his first as a member of the Royal Court. His first had been aboard *Memphis*. When she had crossed the Arctic Circle, the vessel had been visited by King Boreas, Lord of the Northern Waters, and his Royal Court. They had sensed the presence of warm-blooded intruders to their icy realm, and demanded they be transformed into proper Bluenoses.

The navy took this seriously. At the end of a Bluenose ceremony, each initiate received a Bluenose certificate, and an entry was made in his service record so that on future voyages, he could prove to future King Boreases that he was cold-blooded enough to safely enter his realm.

. . .

BESIDES HIS own regalia as Royal Secretary, Jerry collected a garish crown dotted with snowflakes, a barber pole-striped scepter, and a rather nice fur-trimmed purple cloak. This was the XO's costume as Boreas. The COB also dug out a sheaf of blank certificates. Part of Jerry's job as Royal Secretary was to fill them out. More paperwork.

AT 1345 on Sunday afternoon, as soon as lunch had been cleared away, the 1MC came to life. It was not routinely used under way, and the sound boomed down the narrow passageways. "NOW HEAR THIS. ALL WARM BODIES AND ALL THOSE SEEKING AUDIENCE BEFORE KING BOREAS, LORD OF THE NORTHERN REALM, MUSTER IN THE CREW'S MESS. HONOR GUARD, MUSTER BY THE FORWARD ESCAPE TRUNK."

While the initiates, forewarned and dressed in swim trunks, gathered in the mess, Boreas and his Royal Court assembled in the forward passageway. There was a strict order for the procession.

Davy Jones was played by MM1 Bryan. He carried an oversized scroll that had been colorfully lettered with Magic Marker. A costume made of fake seaweed and plastic fish covered him from head to toe. Davy was the herald, preceding and announcing the king's arrival.

Shimko came next as King Boreas. In addition to his crown, cape, and battery-powered scepter, the XO had fashioned a beard from string, or possibly a mop. Jerry couldn't decide.

His consort, Aurora, Queen of the Snows, looked extremely uncomfortable, since the one dress in the costume locker was a little tight for Petty Officer Hoague. He was the right height, at least, but didn't dare bend over. A blond wing and makeup that looked more like war paint completed his ensemble.

Behind "her" came the Royal Baby. The bulk of Chief McCord's attire consisted of an extremely large, baggy diaper. He had been allowed to keep his socks on, but the oversized bonnet and bib weren't keeping him warm. He shivered, not for the first time.

As Royal Secretary, Jerry was next. He was loaded with paper, some of it props, most of it not. Chandler was the Master-at-Arms and brought up the rear.

A line of chief petty officers in their dress blues filled up the ladder from the chief's quarters. They took position behind Davy Jones as the King's honor guard. Master Chief Hess, at the head of the line and looking back at the XO, asked, "Are we ready, sir?"

Captain Rudel had already gone up to the mess decks. He would welcome the Royal Court to *Seawolf,* and it was not a good thing to make the captain wait. Shimko paused and looked back down the crowded corridor, counting noses. All the players were present and patiently waiting to make their grand entrance. "We're good to go, COB. Royal Court, forward march."

Proceeding at a stately pace, the procession threaded its way aft and up to the crew's mess on the second deck. Davy Jones ran ahead to fulfill his heraldic duties, and as the Royal Court reached the galley passageway, the 1MC boomed again. First came eight bells, which signaled the arrival of a person of high rank, then, "ALL HAIL HIS MAJESTY KING BOREAS, LORD OF THE NORTH-ERN REALMS, AND HIS ROYAL COURT!"

The XO timed it perfectly, arriving at the door to the mess as the announcement ended. Davy Jones called "Attention on deck!" and thirty-seven members of the crew snapped straight and tall. They were formed in ranks, but their military bearing was adversely affected by the swimsuits. Others of the crew, already having "experienced" the ritual, crowded into the rear of the mess to watch.

Shimko laid it on with a trowel. "Captain Rudel, I am delighted to have such an excellent sub as *Seawolf* enter my realm. Surely it is a smart and well-found vessel. But Captain, I am disappointed. Did you think you could sneak these unworthy warm-blooded wretches across my border without notice?"

Rudel played his part as well, placating the august monarch. "Of course not, Your Highness. These supplicants for admission are assembled here to plead their case. They are ready for your examination."

Boreas appeared to be mollified. "In truth, Captain, we had observed your coming for some time, and noted these hot-blooded sailors. They have much to answer for before they can be admitted to my kingdom. Royal Secretary!"

That was Jerry's cue. He stepped forward and opened up his ornate ledger book. He made a production of going through the book, as if sorting though a great number of documents, then handed Boreas a large sheet of parchment. "Here it is, Your Majesty, the *list of charges*." Jerry made the last three words sound ominous.

Boreas made a great affair of studying the document, saying "Tsk, tsk," and "I can't believe it!" as he examined the charges. Finally he handed the list back to Jerry. "Seaman John Inglis, front and center!"

Inglis was one of those pale-skinned, freckle-ladened redheads, with hair that almost glowed in the dark. He nervously approached the king, with a little assist from the Master-at-Arms.

"Seaman Inglis, you are accused of having red hair. Is this true?"

Inglis was but the first victim. Each penitent that was called before Boreas faced similarly absurd charges, such as "having overly large feet," or "having too pretty a girlfriend." Boreas then meted out punishment, with the assistance of the court. It could be ridiculous, humiliating, and possibly uncomfortable. Sometimes it was all three.

Jerry had drawn up the list of charges the day before, with some assistance from others in the wardroom and the chief's mess. Shimko and the COB had devised most of the punishment themselves.

Living and working in such close quarters, the crew knew each other well. Jerry had easily figured out most of the "charges." In fact, the only difficult candidate was one of Jerry's own men—Rountree, who'd reported to the sub just days before sailing. They'd learned a great deal about him, but not the kind of quirks one could poke fun at. Jerry had puzzled for some time before finding an appropriate offense.

Rountree was the last one called, and allowed himself to be marched by the Master-at-Arms to face the King. Even after watching the fates of the others, there was a hint of a smile on his face. Boreas laid into the young sailor. "Petty Officer Rountree, your constant complaints and grumbling have echoed through the ocean, sinking icebergs, corroding ship's hulls, and driving an entire school of tuna to seek an early death."

Since Rountree was eternally, unperturbedly cheerful, this brought laughter from everyone, including the victim.

Boreas ignored Rountree's laughter. "For the crime of extreme glumness, you are hereby condemned to wear this sign." Jerry pulled a piece of card stock out of his ledger book with a cord attached. Decorated with multicolored happy faces, it read, "Please cheer me up."

Then the Baby stepped forward with paint and a brush. "And since you refuse to smile," Boreas continued, "for your shipmates' sake we will give you one to wear." Gurgling happily, the Baby painted a clown smile and rosy cheeks on Rountree, even angling the eyebrows to improve his expression. As Jerry expected, the sailor took his ridiculous accusation and punishment with the same good humor he took everything else.

Following their individual punishments, the inductees had to undergo several "tests." The first involved running from the galley to the bow and back with an ice cube in each armpit. Next came bobbing for icebergs, a fish-identification drill, and as a final ordeal, each initiate had to crawl the length of the torpedo tube and touch his nose to the outer door. Since the metal of the tube, the door, and indeed the sub's hull were in direct contact with the arctic water, it was just barely above freezing. After emerging into the relative warmth of the torpedo room, each shivering sailor was baptized with ice-cold seawater and his nose was painted a dark Prussian blue.

When the last warm body had been appropriately blessed, they all enjoyed a "celebratory feast" of cold mashed potatoes shaped into "snowballs," mashed sardines, and "seaweed salad" made of cold boiled spinach and asparagus.

After the proceedings, Jerry retreated to his stateroom and quickly climbed into his coveralls. As he put his props away, he thought about how childish such a ceremony would seem to an outsider. And truth be told, it was pretty childish. But it helped to build camaraderie among the crew, solidified them as a team. Now the new intitiates would proudly display their deep-blue noses, fully vested members of a select club. No Ivy League leadership or management course could do as much.

Severodvinsk
Sayda Guba Submarine Base

Petrov felt the jolt from a door being slammed shut. He then heard a muffled voice through the bulkhead. It was Vasiliy's, and he wasn't happy—again. Sighing, he got up to go see what had caused his starpom to lose his temper this time. The last twelve days had been extraordinarily frustrating, and his second-in-command had been angry for most of them. Not without cause, as the submarine base personnel were being as uncooperative as they feared. And with only nine days left, the carefully orchestrated schedule to get *Severodvinsk* under way on time was in complete chaos.

As Petrov approached Kalinin's stateroom, he could clearly hear his starpom's raised voice. He was shouting to himself more than anything else, a method he often used to vent his anger before he hurt someone. Petrov knocked on the door and waited for a response.

"WHAT!?!" screamed Kalinin.

Cracking the door ajar, Petrov asked, "May I come in? Or do you still need time to calm down?"

"No, sir. Please, come in." Kalinin's response, while civil, still had fury in it. Petrov entered the stateroom to find his starpom breathing heavily, his face a deep crimson. After shutting the door, Petrov walked over to the small work desk and motioned toward the chair. Kalinin gave a curt nod, his rigidly clenched jaw yet another indicator of his displeasure.

Petrov pulled the chair away from the desk, slowly sat down, and took a deep breath. "All right, Vasiliy, what did they do this time?"

Struggling to restrain his temper, Kalinin blurted out only two words, "Ballast canisters."

"What about the ballast canisters?" coached Petrov.

"I had Captain Third Rank Kirichenko place a requisition for the ballast canisters over a week ago, and we hadn't heard anything so I sent him to the armaments section to find out what was going on." Kalinin started to pace as he described the sequence of events.

Kirichenko was the commander of Battle Department 2,

the weapons department, in charge of *Severodvinsk*'s missile weaponry. Unlike Western navies, the Russians separated naval armaments into two battle departments, one for torpedoes and mines and all other weapons in another.

The Russian Navy's standardized shipboard organization consists of seven battle departments, *Boevya Chast* or BCh in Russian, along with several supporting services, such as medical and supply. With the exception of BCh-6, the aviation battle department, *Severodvinsk*'s organization mirrored the rest of the fleet.

Petrov nodded his understanding and said, "Please continue."

"Yes, sir," Kalinin replied a little more calmly. "Well, Boris came back and reported that they didn't have our requisition. So I took a copy down to them and asked them to fill it as soon as possible. Then this petty bureaucratic asshole tells me he can't do it because the paperwork wasn't completed properly. After a brief *discussion,* he finally told me what he wanted and we submitted the revised requisition on Wednesday."

Judging from his starpom's facial features and tone the requisition had been correctly filled out in the first place, but the administrator was probably holding out for an incentive of some sort. Such behavior would irritate Kalinin to no end, and Petrov could only imagine the kind of discussion they had.

"So yesterday this stupid bastard shows up with ballistic-missile ballast canisters! Can you believe that? I told him that we required 3M-55 missile canisters, not something ten times their size! And to be absolutely clear, I told him, *again,* that we need twenty-four of them."

Severodvinsk was fitted with eight large vertical launch tubes aft of the sail, containing three 3M-55 Onyx antiship missiles per tube. With each missile and its launch canister weighing close to 8,600 pounds, a loadout of twenty-four missiles meant a little over one hundred tons of weight. Without the missiles on board, or specially constructed concrete ballast canisters in their place, *Severodvinsk* would not have the proper weight needed to submerge.

"I take it he still hasn't delivered the canisters," injected Petrov.

"Of course not!" cried Kalinin angrily. "In fact, this fool's supervisor came down today and told me they didn't know where they put the canisters we need. I'm afraid at that point I lost my temper and started screaming at them."

"Really? Losing your temper like that, how uncharacteristic of you, Vasiliy," joked Petrov. And then in a more serious tone, "Do you need me to get involved?"

A slight smile flashed across Kalinin's face, and then rubbing his forehead with his hand, he said, "I think you may have to, sir. Although I was pretty loud out there, I wouldn't be surprised if half the base heard me, I don't think my message penetrated their skulls."

"I'll bring the matter up with the diviziya commander when I meet with him this afternoon. How are we doing otherwise?"

Kalinin reached down and picked up his notebook and started going down the list of the items that were done and those yet to be completed.

"The repairs to the fire-control and navigation systems are complete. Tests have been conducted and they are fully functional. Specialists will arrive on Wednesday to effect repairs on the sonar suite. We have minimum levels of diesel fuel, fresh water, and provisions, but these aren't scheduled for delivery until Friday." He paused briefly as he flipped the page and ran his finger down the list.

"We have twelve USET-80 torpedoes and two 83RN antisubmarine missiles in both the port and starboard torpedo bays. I'd like some more weapons, if at all possible, but we can live with these if necessary.

"Finally, we have a significant deficiency in some damage-control equipment, particularly RP-6 air generation canisters for the fire-fighting rebreathers and V-64 emergency air regeneration cassettes. Of the latter, we have only a fifty percent loadout." As if to emphasize the finality of his report, he flipped the notebook shut and threw it on the desk.

"Fifty percent, eh?" repeated Petrov, concerned. "That won't do, Starpom. We have to have more. What have you done thus far?"

"Sir, I have used every contact at my disposal to find more. And while I have a line on some additional RP-6 canisters, there don't appear to be any spare regeneration cassettes available in our diviziya or eskadra."

Petrov sighed heavily, combing his hair with his hand. With disbelief he pressed Kalinin, "You're sure about that? You're absolutely sure that there are no spare cassettes available at all?"

"Yes, sir. I have exhausted all my options as of this morning. The very few regeneration cassettes that I have found were five years past their service life, and you know how unstable the chemicals in them can become with age. I didn't think they were safe to bring aboard."

Petrov was silent as he considered his possible options, and there weren't many. If Kalinin with all his considerable talents had run into a brick wall, then they were in serious trouble.

"You're right, or course. I'll bring this up with Rear Admiral Vidchenko as well. Perhaps I can convince him to allow us to borrow some air regeneration cassettes from one or two of the Project 971 PLAs. I know Captain Sokolov's boat, *Leopard,* has serious engineering problems and can't go to sea. Anything else, Vasiliy?"

"No sir, that is all the depressing news I have for you at the moment." Kalinin's broad smile told Petrov that he was over his tiff with the supply personnel.

"Well, don't trouble yourself by digging up any more," Petrov responded whimsically. "I don't think your heart could handle another episode like the one today."

"Why thank you, sir. Your genuine concern for my welfare is much appreciated." Kalinin then grabbed his coat and cover and politely gestured toward the door. "And now, by your leave, sir. I still have much to do to get this boat ready and I have only a scant nine days to do it in."

Shaking his head, Petrov could only reply, "Carry on, Starpom. Carry on."

6

EXPLORATION

29 September 2008
Barents Sea, Search Area One, 130 nm west of Novaya Zemlya

"Conn, sonar. Sierra two seven bears three three zero, still drifting slowly to the left."

The volume on the intercom circuit was turned down almost all the way, but sonar's report could still be heard clearly.

"Sonar, conn, aye," replied Greg Wolfe.

Jerry watched as the tracking party added another bearing line to their geoplot. The automated fire-control system paralleled their manual actions, and both agreed, more or less: Steady course and speed, closing, from the northeast.

They'd picked up the sub's sounds almost an hour earlier. It was usually dangerous to make assumptions, but under the sea ice, in this part of the world, it was almost certainly a sub. Sonar had detected the rhythmic pulsing of machinery, mixed in with the white noise of ice floes and the howls and burping of sea life—"biologics."

Their assumption had been quickly confirmed, and then reconfirmed as its sounds were sorted, processed, and analyzed. It was a boomer—a Delta IV–class ballistic-missile submarine. Based on intel reports, it was hull 2, *Yekaterineburg,* which had left her port of Sayda Guba about the same time *Seawolf* left New London. The current target motion analysis held her as being quite far away; about twenty thousand yards, maybe more.

Jerry shook his head in disbelief. These detection ranges are absurdly long, he thought. And yet, all the data pointed toward that conclusion. *Seawolf*'s design was driven by the requirement to fight the Soviet Union's most advanced attack submarines. No expense had been spared to make the *Seawolf* class one of the quietest boats in the world. Even at eight knots, *Seawolf* was, as Lieutenant (j.g.) Shawn McClelland, the sonar officer, put it, "doing her best to imitate a water molecule."

Along with her extremely quiet nature, *Seawolf* had the most capable sonar suite ever built, which included the TB-29A towed array. With almost 2,700 feet of passive hydrophone modules, the TB-29 arrays were also specifically designed to detect first-line nuclear subs. In this case, against an older "second-generation" submarine, even an improved design like the Delta IV, it was no contest. *Yekaterineburg* was simply not in the same league. The situation would be quite different if a late-model Akula, or even a fourth-generation sub like *Severodvinsk,* were out. But according to the latest reports, all of the Northern Fleet's SSNs were in port.

CAPTAIN RUDEL had already congratulated the sonar watch on spotting the sub; now he listened carefully as Shimko reported on the tracking party's efforts. "Contact's course is two two zero, speed five knots. Closest point of approach is estimated to be ten thousand yards in a little over two hours, if we maintain present course and speed." The Delta IV was on a converging course with *Seawolf,* and would pass astern of her at around five nautical miles.

Jerry had been plotting the Delta's progress on his chart. It was headed southwest. He added, "Course is consistent with a route back to her home port in Sayda Guba." Jerry used the same conversational tone as the XO. There would be no sign of buck fever in Tom Rudel's boat. "He should be home in a couple days, assuming he cranks up his speed to a standard bell."

"If he was outbound, I'd be sorely tempted to trail him," Rudel remarked wistfully.

"It's too bad we can't play with him a little," Shimko said. "We could steal their lunch and those poor dumb bastards wouldn't even know we were here."

"Agreed, XO, but our mission orders don't include playing with Russian boats, regardless of how attractive the prospects may be." Rudel smiled as he poked a little fun at Shimko.

"I curse the general irony of it all, sir," replied Shimko with a slight pompous air. "Man who walks away from free meal needs many forks."

Rudel stepped away from the periscope stand and went over to the geoplot. Despite all the high-tech displays available with the BYG-1 combat system, he still favored looking at a paper plot as he mulled over tactical problems. Picking up the dividers, he measured out the Delta IV's speed of advance and compared it to *Seawolf*'s projected course.

"I don't like this CPA," muttered Rudel to himself. Placing the dividers on the plotting table, he turned back toward the stand. "Mr. Wolfe, given the current situation, what do you think our chances of being counterdetected are?"

Greg Wolfe was the OOD. Captain Rudel had not relieved him of the conn, something other skippers might do when in contact with a Russian boomer. Wolfe had his answer ready. "Unlikely, sir. Even at five knots, he's significantly noisier than we are. And his towed array is not as good as ours."

"But there is still a chance he could get a whiff of us. Particularly if he doesn't do what we think he's going to. What can we do to lower his chance of detecting us even more?"

"Well sir, slowing down won't help; we are already limited by our narrowband signature. Rigging the ship for ultraquiet would do the trick, but then there would be some system issues since we'd have to secure air-conditioning. We could open the range . . ." Wolfe trailed off as he tried to think of other tactical possibilities, but remained silent for only a moment. "Sir, I recommend altering course to the south. This would put us on a divergent course from the contact and place us well outside his detection range while allowing us to continue tracking him."

"Very good, Greg. Do it."

"Aye, aye, sir. Helm, left standard rudder. Steady on course one eight zero."

As the helmsman repeated the conning orders, Jerry watched his quartermasters update *Seawolf*'s track. Once the Delta IV was gone, they'd need a new course to get them back to the next survey area to launch Patty.

Severodvinsk
Sayda Guba Inlet

"Helmsman, come left to course three five five," ordered Petrov.

It was a glorious day. The wind was howling from the northwest, the skies were covered with thick clouds, and it was raining—perfect weather for a covert departure. No radios were used as the tug pulled *Severodvinsk* from her pier. All communications were made with hand signals or flashing light, just in case those pesky American spy satellites were trying to listen in. With a little luck, the Americans wouldn't notice their absence until after the storms blew over; and that should take almost a week, according to the weather prognosticators.

Up ahead a rusted, dilapidated-looking tug, her stern lights burning brightly, showed the way out. Again for security reasons, *Severodvinsk* was not using her radar, and she would need a little help getting out of the bay in these foul conditions. Visibility was not good, but Petrov could still see the rocky shoreline of the submarine base to starboard and the pine-tree-covered island in the middle of the bay to port. The glowing lights from the city of Gadzhiyevo silhouetted the barren hills with a greenish gray hue.

The wind-driven rain stung his face, but Petrov hardly felt it. He was finally going to sea, on his own, no babysitters, and nothing Mother Nature could throw at him would dampen his spirits. A short toot and the flashing of the tug's stern lights was the prearranged indication that the turning point was getting close.

"Attention navigation watch, five hundred meters until the turn," squawked the loudspeaker. Petrov smiled, pleased that his commander of the navigation battle department, Captain-Lieutenant Dimitry Borisovich Ivanov, was on top of things. His announcement was right on time, and given the difference in distance perfectly matched that of the old and very cranky veteran tug captain.

Three minutes later, the tug sounded a long blast on her whistle and flashed her stern lights again—she was beginning her turn.

"Mark the turn," announced Ivanov.

"Helmsman, rudder right full. Steady on course zero nine zero," shouted Petrov down into the sail. Unlike Western submarines, Russian boats actually had a helmsman's position in the sail, right below the cockpit, for surface running. That made it easier for the conning officer and the helmsman to talk to each other without using an intercom.

"My rudder is right full, coming to course zero nine zero, Captain."

"Very well, helmsman. Just keep our nose on the tug's stern and he'll guide us through the channel."

"Aye, Captain," replied the sailor as he adjusted the rudder angle by pushing forward or pulling backward on the joystick control.

Petrov continued to scan from the left shoreline, to the tug, to the right shoreline and back again so as to keep *Severodvinsk* squarely in the middle of the channel. This was the most dangerous part of egress route. The channel between Sayda Guba and the Murmansk Fjord was very narrow. There would be little time to correct a mistake.

Because of the security concerns and the poor weather, it took *Severodvinsk* almost two hours to finally clear land and enter into the Barents Sea. After dismissing the tug, Petrov increased speed and barreled his way through the large swells. The wind picked up once they were outside the lee of the coast, and sea spray joined the rain in pelting the bridge watch. Every now and then Petrov would laugh, like a schoolboy on a carnival ride, as the boat fell into a deep trough. It was an exciting ride.

An hour and a half later, *Severodvinsk* dove beneath the stormy seas and proceeded on course to the buoy field.

3 October 2008
USS *Seawolf*

Jerry kept one eye on the fathometer. So far, readings matched the charts. "Seventeen fathoms under the keel. Point India bears zero nine five at seven hundred yards." Jerry's report put *Seawolf* within minutes of their next launch point. Number nine. "Present course is good."

Although Lieutenant Commander Lavoie was OOD, Jerry was essentially conning the boat. His recommendations guided *Seawolf* to the right spot. Theoretically, anywhere nearby would do, but Rudel had insisted on places with a smooth bottom. It would be bad luck to launch a UUV and have it strike one of the rolling hills or some sort of projection; a definite possibility in this neck of the Barents, which was shallower than usual.

"Maneuvering, conn. Make turns for three knots," spoke Lavoie into the intercom. The engineering officer of the watch, or EOOW, was back in the bowels of the engine room and supervised the operation of the reactor and main propulsion system. He controlled the ship's speed and responded to the OOD's orders.

"Make turns for three knots. Conn, maneuvering, aye."

"Watch your depth, Dive." Lavoie's second instruction was to the diving officer. As *Seawolf* slowed, she became slightly negatively buoyant, because the water flowing over her dive planes worked like air over a plane's wing and helped to keep the boat up. Less speed meant less lift. Chief Petersen needed a delicate touch to keep the sub at neutral buoyancy, where she would neither sink or rise.

Peterson moved water out of *Seawolf*'s variable ballast tanks. She used her main ballast tanks to get underwater, but variable ballast tanks were used to compensate for small changes in the boat's weight and to adjust her trim fore and aft. Peterson ordered a small amount of water to be pumped to sea to account for the excess weight.

The OOD waited another minute, then ordered, "Helm, all stop."

"All stop, aye. Maneuvering answers all stop."

Jerry watched the quartermasters update the chart. It was all by dead reckoning at this point, but the chart was still a check on the mental mathematics in Lavoie's head. The nav plot showed them slightly past their intended position, but only by a hundred yards or so, the length of the boat. Stan Lavoie had the right touch. "Plot shows us on station," Jerry reported softly. "Distance from planned position is within navigational error."

"Nicely done, Mr. Lavoie." Rudel's praise was always public. Reaching up, he pressed the talk button on the intercom and said, "Sonar, conn, report all contacts."

"Conn, sonar, only white noise from the ice, sir. Not even biologics." Sonar would have reported anything, of course, but Rudel's check was the last step. Since the encounter with the Delta IV, the only other Russian vessels they'd detected had been two distant icebreakers.

Picking up the Dialex handset, Rudel called the torpedo room. "Mr. Palmer, are you ready?" Jerry knew that the captain's question was also pro forma. Palmer and the torpedo gang had been ready since six that morning, when Jerry had visited the torpedo room before breakfast.

"LaVerne's loaded in tube four and is ready in all respects, sir."

"Very well." Hanging up, Rudel looked at Lavoie and said, "Stan, you have my permission to prepare the tube and launch the UUV when ready."

"Prep the tube and launch the UUV when ready, aye sir." Executing a rough facsimile of a pirouette, Lavoie crossed over to the right-hand side of the periscope stand by the fire-control consoles.

"FT of the Watch, flood down, equalize, and open the outer door on tube four."

While the fire-control tech prepared the tube, Jerry started leafing through a file folder until he found a sheet of tracing paper labeled "LaVerne #3."

"Sir, tube four is flooded, equalized, and the outer door is open."

"Stand by . . . Launch," Lavoie ordered.

The fire-control technician pressed the firing button and reported, "Tube four fired electrically."

A moment later, Palmer's voice reported, "LaVerne's away. No problems." There had been no detectable sound in control and only a slight pressure change as compressed air spun up the turbine pump and ejected the vehicle out of the tube.

"Conn, sonar," called out the sonar supervisor. "We have the UUV's motor running normally, bearing one two five." That matched Jerry's planned course for the first leg of her journey. He laid the tracing paper down on the chart. It showed a back-and-forth lattice of lines, spotted with colored symbols. Timed waypoints marked the end of each path of the search pattern. A faithful robot, LaVerne would follow these lines, programmed into her memory, until she reached the point marked "end," in a little over forty hours from now.

Captain Rudel walked over to the chart table and watched Jerry lay the plotted track over the chart. "We'll remain here for another half hour. I want LaVerne well away before we start moving on. I want to make sure the UUV hasn't been detected."

Jerry checked the chart. "Understood, sir. Recommended course to Point Hotel recovery position is two eight seven."

"Mr. Lavoie, you heard the Navigator." Rudel glanced at the clock. "Get us under way at zero one thirty-five hours on that course. Maintain normal patrol quiet, but have sonar keep a sharp watch to the southeast. I want to know if there's any reaction at all to the UUV."

Lavoie nodded, "Understood, sir." Comfortable with the situation, Rudel left control smiling.

Jerry looked around the quiet, smoothly running control room. "We're halfway there. I hope the rest of the surveys go as well as the first nine."

LAVERNE SWAM away from her launch point at three knots, her slowest and quietest speed. An hour and twenty minutes later, she reached her first nav point. Rising steadily, she quickly reached the surface, raised a small antenna, and listened for the GPS satellites. There were four above the horizon, and LaVerne fixed her geographic position within twenty feet. This would ensure an accurate survey.

She dove back into her element, heading for the start of her search grid. The UUV's most important sensors for this mission were its high-resolution side-looking sonars. They used very high-frequency sound beams to map the seabed. As well as mapping the depth and shape of the bottom, the type of return could hint at the bottom type—rock, sand, mud, whatever. She would store the information until she returned to *Seawolf,* where the data would be downloaded.

LaVerne skimmed over the seabed at a height of one hundred feet and at a speed of five knots. She had to be high enough off the ocean floor to get the desired swath width. The idea now was to cover as much ground as possible, sweeping an area over a thousand yards wide and fifteen miles long. Each survey zone was a fifteen-by-fifteen-nautical-mile box, and LaVerne would diligently scan almost eighty-five percent of it before returning to *Seawolf.*

The UUV's mission was to find places on the seabed suitable for automated acoustic sensors. She had to do it covertly, of course, to avoid alerting the Russians. The Russians, however, had long ago mapped this part of the Barents and more. It had been a simple matter to choose where their buoys would be emplaced.

The Amga autonomous submarine detection system was a heavily modified version of an earlier acoustic warning buoy. The cylindrical body was three feet in diameter and five feet long. The buoy was moored to the bottom, floating about sixteen feet off the seabed. Its only distinctive features were twenty-four three-foot metallic tubes running around the circumference of the cylinder. These were the passive hydrophones, the parts that actually received the sounds. The rest of the cylinder, top and bottom, and even the anchor that held it to the bottom, was coated with rubberized foam that hid it from any active sonar searching the area.

Inside the Amga buoy, a sophisticated computer listened to the ocean around it. Because the Russians were familiar with the area, they knew what sounds were typical: the sounds of ice, the sounds of sea life, even wave slap were stored in the computer's memory. They also stored the sounds made by a submarine, both Russian subs and other countries'.

The designers had worked hard on the automated signal processing. They didn't want the buoy sounding the alarm every time it heard something it didn't understand. In engineering terms, it had to have a "low false-alarm rate." So it used an intricate series of algorithms to assess the sounds it was hearing. For a contact to be valid, its noise pattern had to meet a majority of the preset conditions.

When LaVerne passed by one of the Russian buoys, it was two thousand yards away. That was close enough for the Russian buoy to hear the noise made by the UUV's motor, but it wasn't enough noise to trigger a response. According to the buoy's electronic brain, this contact didn't sound right. A submarine would make many different kinds of noises, from the many pumps, motors, and other equipment inside the sub's hull to the flow of water around the hull, and they would be louder.

On the next pass, LaVerne was on the other side of the buoy, and even closer, but the Russian computer still ignored the UUV. Her mapping sonar swept across the buoy, but LaVerne was programmed to search the bottom. It noted the location of an anomalous fuzzy echo, but took no other action. That wasn't part of its assigned task.

The two robots, both designed to search, studiously ignored each other as LaVerne worked its way past and away from her stationary Russian cousin.

JERRY WASN'T the only one watching the fathometer. In these waters, with the charts they had, the OOD, the quartermaster of the watch, even the sonar supervisor kept one eye on the display.

They'd had a bad scare earlier when they watched a seamount appear from out of the depths. In a little over three minutes, the bottom went from 128 fathoms beneath the keel to 47 fathoms. Fortunately, the seamount was right where it was supposed to be. *Seawolf* came up to 150 feet, 25 fathoms, to clear the obstacle.

Everyone on board remembered the vivid photos of USS *San Francisco* in the drydock after her high-speed interaction with an undersea mountain. Jerry was pleased that they weren't taken by surprise. And then it happened.

The depth under the keel changed from twenty-two fathoms to ten in less than a minute, and that was with *Seawolf* creeping at five knots. There was nothing on the chart to indicate a rapid change in the bottom contour. In fact, there was no depth marking near their position at all—*mare incognita.*

"Yellow sounding!" shouted QM2 Dunn.

The warning call, "yellow sounding," alerted the OOD that the ship was entering potentially dangerous depths and required immediate action. A red sounding meant you were at the limit of the captain's comfort zone and the OOD needed to call him immediately, in addition to any other actions. The actual warning depths themselves were chosen by the commanding officer. Given the uncertainty in their charts, Rudel had chosen a healthy ten fathoms for the yellow sounding and eight fathoms for the red sounding.

Jerry's "Recommend we slow to three knots" was matched by the OOD's order. They spoke at the same moment, then looked at each other and smiled, but only briefly. The OOD also changed *Seawolf*'s depth to 125 feet, just to be safe.

In another time, another place, Jerry had used UUVs to scout the bottom in front of an advancing sub, but there were none to spare here. Patty and LaVerne were both out, and *Seawolf* was headed for Patty's recovery point. Maxine was in the torpedo room being prepped for her next run.

"Recommend turn to port, new course zero five zero." That was at right angles to their old course. There was little on the chart to recommend port over starboard, but the coast lay some distance to starboard.

"Left standard rudder, steady on course zero five zero." Greg Wolfe was OOD again, and followed Jerry's recommendation almost before he finished. As *Seawolf* swung onto her new heading, Wolfe asked simply, "Depth?"

"I dunno, Greg. You've pretty much run out of our

allowed depth band. We've only got twenty-five more feet left to play with. We've still got twelve fathoms under our keel. We can afford to wait a beat."

At speed, *Seawolf* could turn almost like an aircraft, but creeping at three knots, her bow took almost a minute to swing ninety degrees. Jerry watched as the fathometer showed twelve fathoms as they finished the turn; then suddenly it read sixteen, then twenty-two fathoms.

"Steep slope, especially considering our speed," remarked Wolfe. Jerry nodded agreement. "If it's that steep, we'll only need a few minutes on this course . . ."

Jerry lost his thought as the numbers on the fathometer changed again. They dropped to thirty fathoms, but then spiked upward, to twenty, fifteen, ten, then eight almost too fast to read.

"Red sounding!" exclaimed Dunn.

"Helm, back one-third! Captain to control! Diving officer prepare to hover." Wolfe's order cut their speed quickly to zero. A slight shudder could be felt on the deck.

The chief of the watch had passed the OOD's call back to Rudel's stateroom almost as soon as he had said it. The captain appeared dressed in gray sweatpants and a dark sweatshirt as Wolfe and Jerry considered their options over the navigation plot. Surprised by the captain's dress, Jerry remembered it was past three in the morning.

Rudel joined Wolf and Jerry at the chart table.

"Sudden shallowing on two sides, sir," explained Wolfe, and Jerry showed their course changes and the depths. Aside from *Seawolf*'s annotated track, there were only the barest hydrographic data.

Rudel ratified Wolfe's actions. "Nice job, mister." He paused. "To both of you"—including Jerry. "The bow sonar cannot double as a bumper." It was just an offhand remark, but all three knew exactly what would happen if *Seawolf* struck a submerged obstruction, even at three knots.

They all studied the chart for a few moments, then Wolfe sighed. "Same drill as last time, sir?"

Rudel nodded, frowning. "Yes. Backtrack five miles, and then make a ten-mile detour to port, then a new course to the retrieval point. What will that do to our arrival at rendezvous?"

Jerry did the math in his head while Dunn laid in the new course. "It adds an hour and a half to the transit at five knots. It eats into our margin, but we'll still be waiting when Patty arrives."

"That's fine, Mr. Mitchell. Now use the rest of the transit, including that extra hour, to get some sleep. You don't look so good, and I want you alert when we recover Patty."

Reluctantly, Jerry headed for his stateroom. He knew Dunn was up to navigating for Wolfe, but if they hit something, it wouldn't matter who was on watch, and what Jerry thought of their abilities. It was always the navigator's responsibility, whoever was in control. Jerry still had to force himself to delegate.

IT SEEMED only seconds later when Chief Hudson was shaking his shoulder. "Mr. Mitchell, can you hear me?"

Jerry's initial response was a cross between "I'm awake" and "What time is it?"

Hudson ignored his confused mumble. "We've been buzzing your phone, but you didn't pick up. Patty's being recovered."

Jerry's head cleared a little. Good news, but he needed to be there. Should have been there half an hour ago. How long had they been buzzing him?

HE WAS in the torpedo room moments later. They'd already brought the UUV into the torpedo room. Only after she was secured did TM1 Yarborough and the chief begin their work. Unfastening access panels, they opened up the vehicle from just aft of the nose to where the motor compartment filled the last quarter of its length.

Once the all-important disk drive had been removed, the rest of the torpedo gang started servicing Patty. They wiped her down with a little fresh water, started a long inspection checklist, and began replacing her battery packs. The UUV's high-power lithium-thionyl-chloride batteries filled half her length. They could not be recharged. They had to be replaced by a fresh energy section for each run. This was the main limit on how many surveys *Seawolf*'s UUVs could make.

IT WAS Will Hayes's OOD watch when they retrieved Patty, and then Jeff Chandler's. Near the end of Jeff Chandler's watch, the XO came into control.

Lieutenant Chandler almost snapped to attention, "Afternoon, sir. Current course two two five at five knots at one hundred fifty feet. En route to retrieve LaVerne at . . ."

Shimko waved him off. "Very well, Mr. Chandler." The XO headed for the chart table. Jerry and most of his quartermasters clustered around several charts of the Barents Sea. One petty officer sifted through a stack of computer printouts while two others annotated a chart. Another was compiling a table of distances under Jerry's direction, while one petty officer plotted *Seawolf*'s position and watched the fathometer.

"What do you have for me?" asked the XO.

Jerry stepped away from the chart table, picking up a small map of the area. "Patty found four spots that match the criteria we were given—bottom type and contours, depth, and the rest. We can take a closer look at them after the two-day midpatrol break. I've roughed out a plan to cover them all."

He showed Shimko the small map. "I'm still working the numbers to make sure we can still reach the remaining UUV launch and recovery points as planned. Until we actually start the second set of surveys, all I can do is estimate how long each one will take."

Shimko agreed, reluctantly. "Just give me your best guesstimate. I'll brief the Skipper, but I need your recommendations ASAP."

Jerry glanced at the chart table behind him. "Twenty minutes, sir?"

"All right. Did Patty find anything unusual?"

Jerry gestured to the chart table behind him. "A gold mine of hydrographic data. I've got my guys working through it for obstructions, shoals, anything not on the charts." He paused. "She also marked over thirty man-made objects. I've compared their locations with ones we knew about on the charts. Only a handful match. Most are new or uncharted."

"Good. The same vessel that plants the sensors can examine those items."

"Should we use the UUVs to classify some of the bigger ones? We can tell the vehicle to take photos and sonar images when it detects one."

"No. A lot of that stuff is going to be old—leftovers from World War II or maybe just junk dumped out here. Besides, we have over two hundred new bottom contacts right now. We'd lose way too much time finding out which ones were worth exploiting." Shimko smiled. "Wise man says, 'Man who looks for noodle in haystack will be very hungry.' "

Jerry looked disappointed. Shimko reminded him, "We've got our own mission to finish, and I'd prefer not to poke around up here any more than we absolutely have to."

"Yessir, I understand. I'll have my course recommendations to you in a few minutes."

***SEAWOLF* GLIDED** confidently over the seabed at a stately five knots. As they doubled back to the rendezvous location to pick up LaVerne, the bottom crested within five fathoms of her keel, but they were following in Patty's path now. Jerry was confident of the data from the UUV, and his quartermasters were already adding Patty's bottom topography data to their charts. They would leave the Barents with better charts than the Russians, at least where the UUVs had been.

The first of eight detail surveys had gone as planned. Lieutenant (j.g.) McClelland, the sonar officer, and Jerry had worked out a procedure to gather additional hydroacoustic information that they needed, while Jerry plotted their precise position. He now had almost every quartermaster aboard working in control. Either they were updating charts or plotting the detailed survey data. Jerry had to fight the urge to use the quartermaster assigned to the control room watch. Their activities took over the fire-control plotting table as well as the chart table in control. And the extra bodies made the space both crowded and stuffy.

Jerry noted and reported the proximity of several newly plotted man-made objects along their course. Patty's navigational accuracy was precise enough to reassure the entire ship control team that they were well clear of any of them. According to his plot, the nearest object approached no closer than two thousand yards on *Seawolf*'s port side.

THE RUSSIAN sensor buoy listened carefully as the sound from *Seawolf* grew louder. Its sound receivers covered a wide range of frequencies, and now it isolated tones, pulses, rhythmic sounds that were not only man-made, but fit its detection criteria. It still waited, though. It detected and classified the sounds from the intruder within minutes, but would they persist? Would they change?

They didn't change, but grew steadily louder at a constant rate. The sounds made by *Seawolf* were no louder than a household appliance, but the buoy had more than enough to work with.

The buoy's computer was smart enough to recognize this as an approaching vessel, so waited, gathering and recording sounds. Finally, the intensity began to fade, at the same rate it had increased, and the bearing rate changed dramatically. The buoy realized that the submarine was moving away. It had gotten all the information that it was going to get, and it was time to report to its masters.

It uploaded its recordings and all target data, along with a message, into a small float, one of three located at the top of the buoy. The computer verified that the surface was clear of large ice chunks, and then released a catch. The float silently shot up toward the surface.

Seawolf was several miles away when the Russian sensor buoy broke the surface and broadcasted her presence.

7

INCIDENT

4 October 2008
Severodvinsk
Barents Sea, five nm south of the Amga Buoy Line

Petrov was in the aft auxiliary machinery compartment when the summons came over the intercom: "CAPTAIN TO CENTRAL POST." There was an urgency in the speaker's tone, and Petrov wondered what new disaster had befallen them. There was no sign of anything amiss in the engineering plant. Chief Engineer Lyachin had just been showing him the improvised repairs to one of the motor generators, and Petrov had praised his resourcefulness.

Heading forward from the sixth compartment, Petrov used the process of elimination to try and bound the problem. The reactor and propulsion plant were both functioning within safe limits. If not engineering, then weapons? Unlikely, since they weren't exercising those systems. Sailors saw him coming and flattened themselves against the passageway bulkheads, or ducked into doorways. The captain was in a hurry.

Sensors? Possible, he thought. Communications? Also a possibility. Each new suggestion made him increase his pace. As he leapt through the watertight doors, Petrov clutched the red case containing his IDA-59M close to his chest. The self-contained breathing apparatus was issued to everyone on board a Russian submarine and was designed to provide fifteen minutes of breathable air. That was long enough for a person to evacuate a compartment filled with thick, choking smoke.

In the central post, Kalinin started his report as soon as Petrov came into view. "It's an alert, sir—an Urgent message from Northern Fleet Headquarters. I've ordered the boat to communications depth. Sonar reports no contacts."

Petrov's anxiety quickly changed to curiosity, mixed with impatience. He thought, "I hope it's something other than a drill this time."

There were several levels of importance or precedence used in fleet messages. "Routine" messages were the administrative trash that he and the rest of his officers plowed through every day. "Priority" messages concerned fleet operations, and were handled quickly, if the communications commander wanted to keep his job. "Urgent" messages had to be passed instantly. If America attacked, the fleet would be warned by an Urgent alert message.

The cautious Kalinin, like any good starpom, would not

usually have maneuvered the boat without permission from his captain, but this was an exception. With an alert message, there could be no delay. Minutes might count. Petrov nodded his approval of Kalinin's actions and asked, "Is Mitrov ready?"

"Yes, comrade Captain. He's in the communications post and will keep us appraised."

Petrov watched the depth gauge rise. They'd been loitering near the edge of the sea ice, a hundred meters down. At that depth, *Severodvinsk* had to trail a long wire antenna to receive any signals at all, and they were limited to simple one-word codes—like "Alert!" That was the tradeoff with extremely-low-frequency communications. A submarine could receive messages at deeper depths, but they were incredibly short owing to the low bandwidth—little more than a "bell ringer" telling a boat to make contact. They'd received just such a message, calling them toward the surface where they could receive a more detailed message using a faster system.

"Slow to three knots." Petrov's order was echoed by the deck officer and the watch section engineer. It went against his grain to slow the boat, but it was necessary. As they ascended, they'd start bumping into ice floes on the surface. *Severodvinsk*'s sail was strengthened, but she wasn't an icebreaker.

"Deck Officer, make your depth twenty meters."

Once the top of her sail was close to the surface, they could receive the very-low-frequency transmission through the sail-mounted antenna assembly. Designed for use by submarines under the Arctic ice pack, where raising an antenna was not always possible, this specially designed system used four flat antennas that were flush with the top of the sail.

They'd have to come shallower than twenty meters to get a good signal, but Petrov wanted to make sure there was no one up there first, by raising a periscope and having a look around. He wasn't too worried about exposing his position. These were Russian waters. Any aircraft overhead would have a red star on the side, and with the ice, it was unlikely there were any surface vessels.

But prudence demanded he know for certain. And then there was always the possibility of a large and virtually silent iceberg. He'd see one of these frozen monsters long before they could detect it with their collision-avoidance sonar. Mikhail Shubin, the deck officer, announced "Twenty-five meters," and Petrov moved to the periscope. When Shubin announced, "Twenty-two meters, leveling off," Petrov ordered "Up periscope" almost before Shubin finished his report.

Petrov held his face against the eyepiece and rode the scope up. At twenty meters, the optics barely cleared the surface. The idea was to expose as little of the scope as possible. In a calm sea, a few centimeters above the water was plenty. Waves made it harder. Today there were large swells and it was still raining.

He quickly turned the scope in a circle, first searching on the horizon and the surface of the water, then a second rotation to search above the horizon. The periscope was extended to its full height, and with most of the barrel still underwater the rocking of the boat didn't make it easy to finish the safety search quickly. Long practice had taught him how to make a fast scan.

As Petrov ordered "Down periscope!" Kalinin checked his watch and said, "Thirty-two seconds."

The captain reported, "No contacts. Make your depth sixteen meters." He frowned, an artist rating his latest performance. "That was too long, I had to slow down because of the chop. There must be a gale blowing. There are good-sized waves up there, in spite of the ice."

The periscope image was recorded on a hard drive and then displayed on a TV monitor in the central post. Kalinin and Petrov reviewed it together, looking for any contacts that might have been missed on the first quick viewing—all standard procedure.

Although a color image, it was nothing but grays, with a dark mottled sky and darker gray water that occasionally lapped over and smeared the periscope lens. This close to the edge of the ice pack, the ice floes were different shapes and sizes, dancing on the waves as they were tossed about by the wind. Under a clear sky, Petrov had seen them splashed with blues and greens. Now they were dirty, almost greasy, uneven lumps.

He'd been born in the north, and he'd served in the Northern Fleet his entire career, but that only allowed him to cope with the environment better than men from the south. No amount of acclimatization would allow a wise man to become complacent when out on the Barents Sea. It was still a cold and hostile place.

"We're receiving the message." Mitrov's voice on the intercom sounded almost triumphant. Communications officers lived for such times. A few moments later, the intercom announced, "Message complete. Decoding."

Petrov ordered Kalinin, "Get us back down to one hundred meters, but stay at three knots. I'll be in my cabin. Join me there once we're at depth."

He'd barely reached his cabin before the communications commander knocked and almost broke the door down. Mitrov thrust the page at him. "Contact report, sir."

DTG: 0735 04/10/2008
TO: PLA *Severodvinsk*, K-329
FROM: Operations Directorate. Northern Fleet Headquarters

Amga warning buoy 11 reports acoustic contact on 04/10/08 from 0231–0240 hours local, probable Western submarine. Location 70° 40' 15" North Latitude, 046° 48' 50" East Longitude. Contact moving northeasterly at slow speed. Locate, identify, and report. Trail and disrupt operations if possible. More contact information to follow as obtained.

Petrov looked at his watch as he bolted from his cabin. Mitrov scrambled out of the way. It was 0747. Fleet headquarters had just told him the location of a Western submarine as of five hours ago. He spotted Kalinin en route to his cabin. The starpom saw his captain at the same time, got out of the way, and then fell in behind Petrov.

"We've got one, Vasiliy! Those damn things actually work!"

"The warning buoys?"

"Yes!" replied Petrov excitedly as he shot up the ladder.

Seconds later, they both raced into the central post. Eagerly looking around for the deck officer among the watch section, Petrov spotted the red and white armband with the gold star over by the combat information and control or BIUS consoles.

"Deck Officer, make our depth one hundred fifty meters, change course to zero six zero, and increase speed to fifteen knots." Over his shoulder, Petrov explained, "That will get us started in the right direction while we compute a proper intercept course."

As Shubin issued the conning orders to swing *Severodvinsk* around, Petrov headed straight for the chart table. He threw the message at the quartermaster. "Plot this location." With the speed of a veteran, the navigation warrant officer found and marked the spot. Petrov compared it with their current position, then ordered, "Change course to zero four five."

He laid a ruler along their new path, studying the chart, then said, "Just our luck. We are not in the best of positions. The contact's location is a little over five hours old. Theoretically, he could be right on top of us even if he were doing five knots. Odds are he isn't quite so close, but we can't make that assumption."

Pausing briefly to weigh his options, Petrov tapped his fingers on the chart table. He measured the distance for a second time, frowned, and then tossed the dividers down onto the chart. "No, we can't afford to make rash assumptions right now. Deck Officer, slow to ten knots."

As he ordered the speed change, Petrov walked over to the ship's announcing system. Flipping a switch, he picked up the microphone. "This is the Captain. Fleet headquarters has provided us with the location of a Western nuclear submarine. We are going to find this intruder and show him what the Motherland's newest attack submarine can do. All hands stand by to assume combat alert status."

Petrov switched off the microphone and hung it up. He paused again, and forced himself to draw a slow breath, then another. Excitement filled him; his former worries about the boat's material state were no longer of primary concern. There were minor mechanical problems, and they were to be expected, but they could be overcome. Coming back to port with something more than just a list of needed repairs—that would make this a real shakedown!

The entire central post watch section waited expectantly in absolute silence. He'd flown in, spitting orders and energizing the boat. Petrov stood for a moment, considering his options, then walked back over to the chart table.

"At 0230 hours, a little over five hours ago, a nuclear submarine, probably an American attack boat, was here." He stabbed at the mark on the chart. "We are going to find him and make his life hell.

"Starpom, have Mitrov construct a sonar search pattern based on our best arrival time in the area and the American's reported movements to the northeast at slow speed—assume eight knots. And see if we can do better than ten knots without them hearing our approach. Every minute we shave off narrows our search.

"As soon as you've calculated our arrival time, put it in a signal buoy along with our current position. Tell fleet headquarters we are en route. We'll send another message once we've obtained his hull number." Petrov smiled grimly, and he was pleased to see every man in the central post smiling as well.

USS *Seawolf*

Jerry and his men finished compiling the survey data from the eighth run in good order. *Seawolf* was now headed for the next rendezvous site. It was time to pick up LaVerne. Jerry felt a deep sense of satisfaction that the work was going so well, but frustrated that so much still needed to be done. The extensive data collection would have to be analyzed when they returned, and then another unit would have to come back and actually place the sensors. It would have been much more satisfying to finish the job, but *Seawolf* couldn't do the detailed analysis, and she wasn't equipped to work on the seabed.

It was 0810, and he hadn't seen his stateroom since yesterday evening. The survey work would continue around the clock, both because there was so much to do, and to minimize their time in these waters. Jerry was tired, but forced himself to properly organize their notes and survey results before stepping away from the chart table. It was only fair to the watchstanders, and he'd be glad, later, when they were handing it in for analysis. The CO had scheduled a short midpatrol break to give the crew time to rest, clean up, and conduct the necessary maintenance that had been put on hold while doing the surveys. Jerry looked forward to catching up on his department's administrative issues, which were slowly piling up while he and his QMs put the data package together. Once LaVerne was back on board, they could all slow down a little.

Jerry yawned; one of those deep yawns that cracks a jaw joint. He had a couple of hours before they recovered LaVerne, and he planned to spend all of it horizontal.

Severodvinsk

As they closed on the unknown sub's reported position, Petrov kept his crew busy preparing for their first encounter. They were all eager to think about something other than the sub's mechanical problems, and there was much to be done. His men were barely used to working together, and he set up drill after drill for the sonar and fire-control teams.

Captain Third Rank Vladimir Mitrov, in charge of the sonar personnel as well as communications and radar, was tasked with computing detection ranges against different classes of Western submarines. Petrov reminded him that the advantage lay with *Severodvinsk*. She was not only an advanced design, she'd never been heard by the West. They were an unknown, and it would take time for them to decide who they were and how to react—time Petrov would use to his advantage.

Just to be on the safe side, Petrov also drilled the torpedo room crews. He did not expect to fire on the intruder. These were international waters, and he had no intention of starting a war.

But what were the Americans' intentions? Petrov ran scenarios through his own mind, testing and preparing his own reactions. The first part was easy, at least in theory: Find the boat. Then, collect enough hydroacoustic information to identify its type and nation of origin. Beyond that, it really depended on what the intruder was doing.

Western boats often probed Russian waters, gathering information, even practicing mock attacks against live targets. They usually kept out of the way, given the covert nature of their mission, but they had occasionally interfered with exercises in the past, either deliberately or accidentally. Simply discovering the intruder's presence could end his mission, since his presence was no longer secret.

It was really a test, for both sides. The West baited the Russian bear, teasing him right in front of his own den. Was the bear fast enough and strong enough to catch him or drive him off? If Russia couldn't keep the waters in front of her home bases clear of intruders, why have a navy at all?

And this was not just a game. A few years ago, *Gepard* had also been Russia's newest and best when she left Sayda Guba to find an American submarine discovered in the Kara Sea. Nobody Petrov had ever talked to had the complete story, or the same one; the only consistent fact was *Gepard* had been lost with all hands. She had been ordered to intercept the American sub in international waters. What happened was known only by the two submarines involved, and *Gepard* had taken all her knowledge to the bottom.

So what were the intruders doing there? According to the fleet operational schedule, there was nothing of interest scheduled in that area. Was it something on the seabed? NATO subs often attempted to recover Russian matériel.

Could they be investigating the Amga buoys themselves? That was an unwelcome and disturbing possibility. As soon as it occurred to him, Petrov hoped it wasn't true. According to the briefing he'd received, the warning buoys had been laid in complete secrecy, and were totally passive in operation. Knowledge of their existence would mean security had been severely compromised.

The central post alerted him to another urgent transmission, and Petrov brought *Severodvinsk* near the surface again, taking as little time as possible to receive the message before racing southwest again. Mitrov hurried into the command center with the message printout.

Petrov scanned it quickly, then briefed the starpom and his tracking team. "They think it's an American, a first-rank boat at that. It has almost no discernible narrowband components, and what little they heard was detected at close range, very close to the buoy. They were moving slowly as well, possibly less than five knots."

"That's not an effective search speed. Could they be loitering in the area? Waiting for something?" Kalinin was thinking out loud.

Petrov was dismissive. "Possible, but pure speculation. We can't guess at his activities from this. The bad news is, we're looking for a very quiet boat, of advanced design, at very low speed. The good news is, at slow speed, he's still close to the position we were given.

"Starpom, assume that he's making no more than five knots and adjust our search pattern to look for an extremely quiet vessel. If he's increased speed and we miss him, we'll need a second, wider search plan."

Kalinin nodded, acknowledging Petrov's instructions but busy with a calculator. "Recommend slowing to eight knots in twenty minutes, and to five knots another half an hour later. That should allow us to enter the area with a minimum probability of detection by a first-rank boat at creep speed."

"How much margin in your calculations?" Petrov asked.

"Twenty-five percent."

Petrov looked down at the chart, silently weighing Kalinin's recommendation with his own assessment of the situation. A slight frown developed. After a brief moment, he turned toward his starpom, shaking his head.

"Take it out, Vasiliy. No margin. Time is our enemy. We'll depend on surprise. I'm willing to make the assumption that he doesn't know about the buoys, so he can't know he's been detected."

Looking dubious, the starpom recalculated. "In that case, hold this speed for another half an hour, then slow to eight knots, and go to five knots forty minutes later. We will reach the edge of the search area in eighty-five minutes."

"Agreed, and set silence mode when we slow to five knots. Pass the word that all compartments will be personally inspected by me to make sure it's properly set."

"Aye, Captain."

As the watch section hurried about to carry out his orders, Petrov forced himself to walk away and let his men do their work. He had to pour some of his excitement back into the bottle. Splash it around too much and his crew would start making mistakes. But it was so hard to just stand there and wait. Surprisingly, it didn't take very long.

A LITTLE over thirty minutes after setting silence mode, Petrov was summoned yet again to the central post. As he entered the command center, he found the normally bustling central command post as quiet as a morgue. Shubin was hunched over one of the BIUS consoles, staring intently at the display.

"Report," order Petrov curtly.

"Hydroacoustic contact, Captain. Bearing red zero seven three."

A quick glance at the BIUS display told Petrov what he needed to know. "Helmsman, rudder left full. New course three four zero. Deck Officer, quietly, I repeat quietly, set readiness condition one, combat alert. And be quick about it, Mikhail Olegovich."

"Yes, Captain."

While Shubin brought *Severodvinsk* to battle stations, Petrov quickly ducked into the sonar post where Mitrov and a senior warrant officer were busily adjusting the passive sonar settings on the control consoles, desperately trying to find the contact they had heard just moments ago.

Speaking softly Petrov asked, "What do you have for me, comrades?"

"A short sequence of transients, Captain, bearing red zero seven three. Definitely mechanical in nature," replied Mitrov.

"Show me," demanded Petrov.

The warrant officer handed his captain a set of headphones and called up the historical display and replayed the signal. Sure enough, there was a faint series of mechanical-sounding clunks to the north. His men had done well to pick up the weak signal with all the ice noise around them.

"Captain . . ." whispered Mitrov as he pointed toward his display. There on the screen, amid the interfering speckles from the ice, appeared a faint coherent trace, and then another.

As the three men watched the trace lines slowly get longer, Kalinin stuck his head into the small room. "Captain, combat alert has . . ." A sharp wave of Petrov's hand cut his starpom off.

In total silence, Petrov watched as the first trace got a little stronger, showing a slight left-bearing drift. The second contact was much weaker and had no discernible bearing rate at all. Mitrov hit a few buttons and an automatic tracker locked on to each of the contacts and started sending data to the fire-control system. With a wicked grin on his face, Petrov turned toward Kalinin and said, "We have him, Vasiliy. We have him!"

USS *Seawolf*

ETC Hudson had expected to find his department head fast asleep. He didn't monitor Lieutenant Mitchell's every move, but by his reckoning, the young officer was running about half empty, and that will catch up with a body after a while. Nobody wanted a cranky lieutenant.

But Mr. Mitchell was up and half buried in paperwork. The door was open, but Hudson still rapped politely on the doorframe. Jerry looked up and smiled. "Chief, excellent, come in. Here are the draft E-6 evaluations you gave me last week. I've made some changes . . ."

Hudson glanced at the forms, marked with a red pen, then reported. "They're preparing to recover LaVerne, sir."

Jerry sighed and pushed himself back from the desk. "So soon?"

"They've already deployed the recovery arm."

"Thanks, Chief, I'll be along . . ."

Suddenly the *BONG, BONG, BONG* of the general alarm filled the passageway, and both men dashed for the control room. The captain had promised that once UUV operations started, there would be no drills. Something was very wrong.

JERRY HELD in his questions as he hurried over to the plotting table by the fire-control consoles. He listened as Will Hayes quickly turned the deck over to Stan Lavoie, the General Quarters OOD. "New sonar contact, Sierra three zero, is on our port quarter, bearing one six five. The computer says it's a submerged contact, close by at slow speed, with a zero bearing rate. Tracking party's still getting set up, so they can't confirm."

Then Captain Rudel showed up and Hayes had to repeat himself. He'd barely finished when Rudel asked, "And the UUV?"

Hayes shook his head. "Still approaching the basket. About five hundred yards to port . . ."

Hayes's report was cut short when the WLR-9 acoustic intercept receiver started wailing.

"Conn, sonar, Mouse Squeak transmissions in the direction of Sierra three zero. Bearing one six five."

Rudel quickly looked at the WLR-9 display and saw that the transmission frequency and pulse type matched the collision-avoidance/mine-hunting sonar on Russian submarines. "Mr. Mitchell, get the arm back inside, and send the UUV away."

Jerry acknowledged the order and checked the chart. There was a likely spot over deep water a few miles from here, and it was already programmed . . .

"Conn, sonar! Sierra three zero is increasing speed!" There was concern in the sonar supervisor's voice. A few seconds later, the intercom announced, "Sierra three zero is cavitating! Near zero bearing rate!" The last word was almost shouted over the intercom. Jerry recognized ST1 Stapp's voice. He wasn't easily rattled.

"Captain, recovery arm is stowed and the outer door is shut on tube two," reported Shimko as he took his battle-stations position by the fire-control consoles.

"Very well, XO. I want a TMA solution on Sierra three zero immediately. Engineer, get us moving."

Both men responded with, "Aye, aye, sir."

"Conn, sonar. Sierra three zero's speed is thirty-plus

knots. Blade rate does not match any known Russian submarine."

Rudel and Shimko looked at each other, both confused by the sonar supervisor's report. Rudel reached up to the intercom. "Sonar, conn. Please confirm your last."

"Conn, sonar. Sierra three zero's acoustic signature does not match any, repeat any, known Russian submarine."

"Who the hell are we dealing with?" asked Shimko.

"We'll worry about that later, XO. For now, let's concern ourselves with getting out of here."

"Yessir!" Shimko replied enthusiastically. Then ten seconds later, "Captain, WAA range is . . . is seven hundred yards and closing!"

"Conn, sonar. Sierra three zero is closing rapidly. Bearing rate is slightly to the left."

"He's passing down our port side!" exclaimed Shimko.

"Helm, hard right rudder!" shouted Rudel.

"Captain has the conn," announced Lavoie. While this statement would appear trivial to an outside observer, particularly given the circumstance, its importance was crucial. From this point on, until Rudel decided otherwise, he was giving the conning orders and everyone in control needed to know this.

A moment later Jerry heard the noise himself, right though the hull. It started as a soft rush, like a ventilation fan in high speed, but a few seconds later it was a solid rumble, and then a loud swishing that could be felt as well as heard.

A few more seconds and the sound was past them. Just as it started to fade, Jerry felt a vibration in the deck and then the whole boat was rocked first to starboard and then to port. Jerry had been leaning against the chart table and had reflexively grabbed at it. The watch stared at each other, wide-eyed.

Severodvinsk

"Sonar officer reports closest point of approach was four hundred meters," said Kalinin.

"That will make them think twice!" laughed Petrov. "Make turns for ten knots. Shubin, do you still see their remote vehicle?"

"Yes, sir. Bearing red zero six five, range seventy-four meters, speed about three knots. It's still heading toward the American sub." Shubin was tracking the American UUV with *Severodvinsk*'s MG-519M mine-hunting sonar. It was no good as a general search set, but its high-resolution range and bearing data made it perfect for finding small objects nearby. "Recommend slow turn to port, or it will pass into our blind spot aft."

"Agreed. Helm, left standard rudder, reverse our course, steady one five five. Starpom, don't lose that thing's position. If we've cut its tether, it should slow down and stop now. With luck, it will sink to the bottom, and we can mark the spot. What's the American sub doing?"

"Passive sonar's still limited from our high-speed pass, sir, but he was just starting to turn to starboard as we went by."

The American was being slow to react. After surprising him so completely, Petrov had expected a more violent reaction.

The high-frequency active sonar display showed two objects: the larger American sub, and a much smaller blip, no larger than a torpedo. The U.S. boat had been stationary, hovering, and it was obvious they were up to something that involved a remotely operated vehicle. Planting something? Recovering something? Whatever they were doing, it was not in Russia's interests.

The obvious move was to break the tether on their ROV.

The Americans would be forced to abandon it, and *Severodvinsk* would guard the device until it was salvaged. The U.S. would not be able to deny the physical evidence, and the clues it provided would tell what the Americans had been up to.

"Sonar, report." Petrov was impatient. He'd made his move and was waiting for the Americans to react. Part of his impatience was because they had no good moves to make. This was his field, his game.

Mitrov responded, but he sounded puzzled. "The American sub is moving away slowly. Last good bearing before he went into our baffles was green one four five. The remote has turned sharply and is now heading away from the U.S. sub at a higher speed."

"Toward us?" Petrov's question held concern. It could still be a weapon.

"No sir, it's going northwest at about five knots."

"Then it's still under control," Petrov remarked, thinking aloud. "Apparently, we missed the tether."

By now, *Severodvinsk* had reversed course and was heading to the rear of the slow-moving U.S. submarine. "Position us for another pass, closer to the American. Closer this time."

USS *Seawolf*

"All hands, this is the Captain." Rudel's voice was calm. "We are not under attack. Nothing has collided with us. A Russian attack boat just made a fast, close-aboard pass down our port side. They're not happy about us being here. He seems upset, so we are not going to do anything to provoke him."

Rudel put the microphone down and asked Jerry, "Is the UUV heading away from us?"

Jerry nodded. "Just finished sending the instructions, sir. LaVerne's been ordered to loiter at point Romeo One, about ten miles from here."

"And the quickest course away from the Russian coast?"

Jerry didn't have to look at the chart. "Toward Romeo One, recommend three zero zero."

"Very well. Make turns for five knots, right fifteen degrees rudder, come to course three zero zero." That would take them through almost three-quarters of a full circle, but the quicker turn to the left would take *Seawolf* directly in front of their maneuvering adversary.

"Conn, sonar. Sierra three zero has zigged. Looks like he's turning. His blade rate is also increasing again. Rapidly."

"Sonar, conn, aye. Any classification yet? Who is he?"

"Hard to tell, sir." Snapp's voice was apologetic. "It's a first-line attack boat given its speed, but it doesn't match anything in the database. She's very quiet, though. I've had somebody reviewing the recordings when she was on top . . ."

Then Snapp interrupted his report. "Blade rate's still increasing, and the bearing drift's changed from left to right. I think he's going to make another run."

"Helm, increase your rudder, right full. Get us some more separation to starboard."

"Increase my rudder to right full, helm aye."

"Should we use our HF sonar? There's no point in staying covert," said Lavoie.

Jerry thought that sounded like a good idea. It would be nice to have a better idea of where the Russian was.

Rudel paused before answering Lavoie, but shook his head. "No. I don't know how he'd react to it. He might interpret it as a prelude to hostile action. Some Russians like to use HF sonars for fire-control ranging." The captain spoke quickly, and Lavoie nodded his understanding as they watched the command displays and tried to fathom the Russian's intention.

"Conn, sonar. Sierra three zero is closing, zero bearing rate, signal strength all increasing. I'm starting to get separate bearings on different parts of the boat!" Jerry felt a lump of ice forming in his chest. The Russian was closer this time.

Rudel looked over toward the BCP and yelled, "Chief of the Watch, sound collision. All hands brace for impact." As the collision alarm screeched, Jerry imagined men in spaces throughout the sub, with little idea of what was happening, being told to brace. Expecting what? A crushing blow, icy water, and a sudden death?

"Eventually we'll have to break contact and sort out how he found us, but right now my only goal is to not make a bad situation worse."

The Russian sub thundered by again, closer. This time the sound was stronger, more intense. Jerry could distinguish the beating of the sub's propeller blades.

As it reached a peak, another sound, an even louder solid bang, resonated in the control room. It stopped, then came again, and again, in fast rhythmic pulses. The Russian had turned on his main active sonar and focused its energy into a tight narrow beam, pointed straight at *Seawolf.*

A nuclear sub's main active sonar could send out a sound pulse that could be heard hundreds of miles away. It would kill a diver nearby. Almost in pain, Jerry tried to cover his ears, but by the time he could react, the Russian was gone, and welcome quiet returned.

Then *Seawolf,* all nine thousand two hundred tons, tilted to the right, pushed aside by the wake of the harassing Russian sub. Jerry was glad for the captain's warning, but he'd lost his grip raising his hands. He almost fell, and several in control did stumble.

Shaken, Jerry saw his face mirrored in the rest of the watch, pale and wide-eyed, some picking themselves up.

Lavoie, compelled to state the obvious, said, "That was too close."

"Conn, sonar. Sierra three zero is not, repeat not, transmitting known Shark Gill waveforms." Shark Gill was the NATO nickname for the SKAT family of sonars on all current Russian nuclear-powered attack submarines.

Jerry watched Captain Rudel, waiting for a reaction, or new orders, but the captain was as pale as the rest. Jerry watched him scan the displays, even glancing toward the plotting table. He was a man in desperate need of information. What boat was this? What did the Russian captain want? Would his next pass be even closer?

"Skipper, who are we dealing with?" asked Shimko, clearly shaken as well.

Rudel initially looked just as confused as the others; then abruptly, his demeanor changed as an idea popped into his head.

"Navigator, check the intel traffic and see if a Russian boat has left Sayda Guba in the last few days."

"Aye, aye, sir," replied Jerry, still puzzled.

"You've got that look, sir," quipped Shimko.

"I have a theory, XO. Nothing more."

"Would you mind sharing this theory with the rest of us ignorant peasants?"

"I think it's *Severodvinsk,* Marcus."

Shimko took his captain's theory and compared it to the available data. A nuclear-powered attack submarine with an unknown acoustic signature and unknown active sonar in the Northern Fleet led to but one conclusion—*Severodvinsk.*

"Ooh shit."

"Yeah, that's about it," said Rudel. "Hopefully, Jerry will be able to confirm it once he gets done searching the message traffic."

Lieutenant Commander Lavoie was searching as well. "Whoever he is, he's real unhappy we're here. Maybe he's trying to drive us away."

Rudel nodded, still thinking, but answering, "It's a possibility. Maybe we aren't moving fast enough for him. But then why block our path out?"

Lavoie continued. "If he'd wanted to hit us, he could have. He isn't that crazy."

"I sure as hell think he's nucking futs to get as close as he has," remarked Shimko.

"Concur, XO. He's crazy enough for me as well. Helm, all ahead two-thirds, steady on three zero zero."

Severodvinsk

"What about the remote vehicle?" Petrov's attention was almost entirely fixed on its progress. He'd let Kalinin take *Severodvinsk* in a right turn this time, paralleling the American's turn on the outside.

He might have been unconsciously acknowledging the starpom's concern. The last pass had been only two hundred meters to port of the American, at an unbelievable thirty-three knots. Even their mine-hunting sonar had been blind at that speed.

Mitrov answered, "It's still heading northwest at a steady speed. And we've identified the sub's class. It's an American *Seawolf*-class." Petrov barely acknowledged the report.

"Even if the tether's cut, it may have an inertial guidance and its own power supply. Assuming it's a tethered vehicle to begin with." Kalinin's suggestion was certainly possible. It would explain the vehicle's behavior, but it was unsatisfying. His evidence was slipping away. "We could follow it," the starpom suggested.

"And leave the perpetrator?" Petrov retorted. "The remote vehicle can lead us on a wild-goose chase while the American escapes. And we have no way to stop or recover the device. No," he concluded, "we will stay with the American sub."

Petrov studied the tactical display. The American lay ahead of him, to the north. He'd increased speed to fifteen knots and was headed northwest, away from Russian waters. *Severodvinsk* was in a slow right turn, swinging past south.

For one moment, he contemplated letting the American go. He had confirmed its existence, identified it, and disrupted whatever they were trying to do. He had met all his mission objectives.

Even as this thought flashed through Petrov's mind, he rejected it. He could trail them. He could follow them out of this area, watch them recover their remote, and then leave Russian waters, virtually unscathed. They could deny ever being there, and Russia would have only the word of *Severodvinsk* and her crew. And they still didn't know what the Americans' mission was.

They needed more proof. "Increase our speed to twenty-five knots and set up an intercept. I want to pass directly in front of the American. I'm not letting him leave the area."

As Kalinin acknowledged and turned toward the helmsman, Petrov added, "And Vasiliy—no margin."

USS *Seawolf*

"Conn, sonar. Sierra three zero's blade rate is increasing again. Possible target zig to starboard. He may be getting ready to make another pass."

"That's it," Rudel announced defiantly. "I'm not betting

our lives on his seamanship. Increase speed to twenty knots. XO, prepare a spread of countermeasures. Two ADC Mk 5s, an NAE, and a mobile decoy." He didn't wait for a reply. "Sonar, conn. We're speeding up. Stand by to go active on the HF set, but try and keep tracking him passively. Regular reports."

Sonar's first report put the Russian at two thousand yards, off their port quarter. "Blade rate is increasing. Contact has steadied up on a new course."

"Sonar, conn. Good job, Stapp, you're our eyes. Keep the reports coming." Rudel released the intercom key and looked at the control-room watch. They were silent, expectant.

"There's no point in only maneuvering. He can follow our movements and it just increases the chance of a collision. I intend to wait until he's committed to his run, release a mobile decoy and some countermeasures, then break hard left away at speed. We will then head southwest and break contact. Comments?"

Jerry felt some of the ice in his chest start to melt. The skipper had a plan. It was reassuring to know the captain could still think clearly with a nuclear sub buzzing them.

"Captain, Sierra three zero now bears one seven five at fourteen hundred yards. Estimated speed twenty-three knots and increasing," reported Shimko.

Rudel watched the display. "Very well, XO. What's the status of the decoy?"

"CSA launcher ready, where do you want the mobile decoy to go?"

"Preset base course three five zero, maximum speed. Jamming function enabled."

"Aye, aye, sir."

"Conn, sonar. Sierra three zero's bearing is unchanged! Repeat, constant bearing, decreasing range. Speed now twenty-five knots." If a contact didn't change his bearing and the range decreased, there was only one possible result. Jerry wondered if the Russian planned to swerve at the last minute. Or did he really intend to ram them?

"Sound collision!" Rudel ordered. Once again, the collision alarm's scream echoed in the boat.

"Course change, sir?" Lavoie asked to ease his own nervousness, but Jerry knew what the answer would be.

"Hold this course, Mr. Lavoie. We don't know his plans, and if we zig while he zags . . ."

Severodvinsk

"Captain, the American's speed increase has slowed our overtake." Petrov could hear the relief in Kalinin's report. A slower closure rate would reduce the chance of a collision.

"Increase speed to ahead flank. Continue the intercept, Vasiliy."

"Aye, sir. Adjusting for the new speed. We should pass no more than a boat length in front of him. I've even factored in the amount of time it will take for us to cross his intended track." Petrov knew the starpom was nervous, maybe afraid, but he still followed Petrov's orders exactly.

"Our speed is now twenty-seven knots."

USS *Seawolf*

"Range is eight hundred yards, Captain. Speed is now twenty-seven knots, still building, slight left bearing drift," said Shimko nervously.

"Which he would have if he was overtaking," Rudel mused aloud. "Chief of the Watch, pass the word, all hands stand by for hard maneuvers."

"Conn, sonar, Sierra three zero's speed is still increasing."

"Sonar, conn, aye."

"XO, tell me when he's at five hundred yards."

"Yessir."

That was cutting things awfully close. Jerry wondered exactly what spot on the Russian boat the hull array was measuring its bearing from. And if the skipper ordered a turn, the sub's pivot point was amidships, with the stern swinging wide . . .

"Mark, five hundred yards!" shouted Shimko.

Rudel spit out the orders quickly, as if he'd rehearsed them for days. "Launch NAE and ADC Mk 5s! Helm, all back emergency, left full rudder, steady on course two eight zero. XO, launch the mobile decoy."

Severodvinsk

Shubin's voice overflowed with panic! "Captain, we've lost contact with the mine-hunting sonar!"

"Equipment failure?" Petrov cursed inside. That would be their luck.

"No sir, it's flooded with white noise."

"A decoy, then. Say so and save us the trouble." Petrov's rebuke was deserved, but he checked himself. He was letting his frustration show. His people were excited enough already. "Mitrov, go active on the main sonar. Find them!"

Petrov could feel *Severodvinsk* still surging through the water. His boat wasn't waiting, but he forced himself to wait for the echoes. He needed information to act.

"Two weak contacts, one to port, bearing red one three zero, and one to starboard, bearing green one two zero. Range to both contacts seven hundred meters."

"Ahh, he's trying to break away." Petrov glanced at the BIUS display.

Kalinin looked up to his commander. "Which one do we pursue, Captain? The American could be either contact."

"He's the one to left, Vasiliy! Toward the remote vehicle! Helmsman, rudder hard left. Steady on two three zero. We'll make a larger circle and head him off. I will not let him leave."

"Captain, I recommend we slow down. With all this interference we no longer have an accurate tracking solution on the American."

"No, Starpom! I will not give up the tactical advantage. We know where he was when he deployed the decoys. Maintain speed."

Like everyone else, Petrov held on as *Severodvinsk* heeled over to port. With the combination of maximum rudder and flank speed, her turning circle would be a bit wide. They hadn't even done this during sea trials, Petrov remembered. He watched Kalinin trying to calculate the separation between the two boats, but there was no way to know.

USS *Seawolf*

"Conn, sonar. Contact has passed into our baffles and there is interference from our countermeasures. He went active just before entered the baffles." Stapp's report was matter-of-fact, and expected. *Seawolf*'s stern, and the blind spot for her hull arrays, was now pointed directly at the Russian, while, hopefully, he headed north, chasing the simulator. For a short time, it would move like a submarine, and mimic the noises and sonar signature of one.

But if *Seawolf* moved too fast, it would be a dead give-away.

"Helm, all ahead one-third. Mr. Mitchell, can you find us a shallow spot along our course?"

Jerry only had to glance at the chart. The shallow area where Jerry and Hayes had experienced some trouble was nearby. "That shallow spot is close by, bears two six five, extends for"—he paused to measure—"twelve miles. Current sounding is seventy fathoms."

"Helm, come left to two six five, make our depth three hundred feet." Jerry saw what the skipper was trying to do. Slow to reduce their noise and to make it harder to distinguish *Seawolf* from the decoy, and hug the bottom to hide from active sonar. If *Seawolf* could break contact for a moment, Rudel would turn that into a minute, and then ten minutes, and . . .

Stapp kept up a running commentary. "Conn, sonar. Sierra three zero is coming out of our baffles to starboard." As expected, Jerry thought. "He's still at high speed—very high speed." Jerry thought he should slow down. Even the Russian's active sonar would have problems seeing anything, and the countermeasures and decoy would only make things more confusing.

"Captain, I'm getting a slight left-bearing drift," said Shimko as he watched the fire-control display. That was wrong, Jerry thought. He should be drawing right if he's chasing the simulator. Jerry tried to piece together the discordant facts. Once again, the strong pounding from the Russian's powerful active sonar could be heard through the hull.

"Sir, I now show constant bearing. He is closing on us! I can't get a range on the WAA—nearfield effect!" Shimko shouted.

Jerry's mental picture flashed into clarity. The Russian hadn't taken the bait. He was turning with *Seawolf*, not heading away to the north. And he was very, very close.

"Helm, hard left rudder, increase speed to . . ."

Something struck the hull, a monstrous hammerblow that rolled *Seawolf* hard to port. Jerry struggled to maintain his balance as the deck fell away beneath him. Pencils, books, and every other object on the tables were catapulted into the air. Jerry managed to hang on, but several members of the fire-control party were thrown by the massive shock. One sailor rose and struck the overhead, and another actually flew across the control room at waist level.

Just as *Seawolf* started to right herself, a series of smaller but still powerful rapid shocks pushed her even further to port and downward, accompanied by a sound that mixed splitting metal with a horrible grinding noise. Jerry felt his feet go out from under him as the deck seemed to cartwheel. It was impossible to tell up from down. The sledgehammer-like blows and intense sound went on forever, changing from a clanging anvil to a wailing screech.

The shouted reports of the control party were almost drowned out by the noise. What he heard wasn't encouraging. Jerry was desperately trying to find his footing when he heard Rudel yell for an emergency surface. Before they could execute the order, *Seawolf*'s bow again pitched down sharply and Jerry lost his grip. No longer supported, he slid headfirst into one of the plotting tables and all thought ended.

8

RECOVERY

Jerry came to lying on the deck, his head and shoulder throbbing with pain. QM1 Peters was kneeling over him, pressing something on his head and calling for the corpsman. The deck was pitched upward and vibrating badly as the main engines drove them toward the surface. It was dark in control. The lights were out and the emergency battle lanterns were providing the only illumination. Most of the flat-panel displays were blank; the few that were alive displayed reddish fuzz. The air smelled of smoke and burnt insulation. A lot of men were down, crumpled on the deck where they fell.

The XO was on the sound-powered phones taking in reports from all over the ship. "Personnel casualties in engineering! Sonar reports all systems are down." As he spoke, the lights flickered, then failed. "Engineering reports there are numerous shorts in the forward compartment. They are trying to isolate the affected circuits."

As Jerry's eyes started to adapt to the low light, he could see that every face in control held the same horrified look. *Seawolf* had collided with the Russian and they were now fighting for their lives.

MM1 Bryan, the GQ chief of the watch, had hit the "chicken switches" for the emergency blow system as soon as the captain had ordered "Emergency surface!" High-pressure air blasted into every ballast tank on the boat, giving her an immediate boost of buoyancy. The diving officer, Master Chief Hess, had ordered, "All ahead full," and then, "Full rise on bow and stern planes." Jerry could hear Hess controlling the fear in his voice as the ship's control party executed the well-drilled routine.

The helmsman repeated the order automatically, "Planes to full rise, aye," but a moment later reported, "Bow planes are not responding."

Hess glanced at the repeater, then the helm controls. Both were down and the bow planes had shifted into emergency, but nothing was happening. The helmsman had the wheel pulled all the way back, but the mechanical angle indicator still read zero.

The XO cut in again. "Chief Gallant has reached the engine room and is tending to the injured." *Seawolf* didn't carry a doctor, and Jerry prayed there was nothing that required skills beyond that of a chief hospital corpsman.

The sternplanes were still working, and Jerry felt the deck tilt even more as the boat clawed her way toward the surface. Just as *Seawolf* had driven herself under, she'd come up using her powerful engines. Normally they wouldn't even bother blowing the ballast tanks completely dry with compressed air, they'd just drive on up and use the low-pressure blower. But this wasn't a normal surfacing by any stretch of the imagination.

Jerry slowly climbed to his feet, despite his leading quartermaster urging him to stay down. He took the cloth and held it to the side of his head. It was warm, wet, and stung like crazy. Jerry could feel enough through the fabric to know he had an ugly cut. He wished for a mirror. On second thought, maybe he didn't want to know. He motioned for the QM1 to go and assist the XO with the damage reports.

"Main Ballast Tank One Alpha is not holding pressure," Chief McCord reported. That meant a leak, more likely a rip, in the forwardmost ballast tanks. "One Bravo is mushy, it's holding pressure a little better. It probably has a leak as well."

The diving officer acknowledged the report, but there was nothing they could do right now. There was no easy way to isolate the air to the leaking tanks; they'd have to rely on the two remaining forward ballast tanks to get them up.

Jerry looked for the speed and depth displays on the command console. Both were out. The backup mechanical depth gauge reassuringly showed they were going up. *Seawolf* had been hit forward. What else had she lost besides bowplanes and ballast tanks? The deck vibration was intensifying with the acceleration, and Jerry tried to analyze the unfamiliar sensation. Was *Seawolf* responding properly?

Suddenly, the boat started shaking more violently. A series of loud bangs and a grinding noise startled them all, even Rudel, and Jerry imagined pieces of the hull breaking off. He glanced again at the mechanical depth gauge. They were very close to the surface.

"It's the ice," Shimko announced with relief, and Jerry felt himself breathe again. He tightened his grip as the deck surged below him, then abruptly fell forward. For half a minute *Seawolf* bobbed up and down and rolled from side to side as their upward inertia dissipated. And then there was nothing but a gentle roll and silence. They were on the roof. They'd reached the surface.

Rudel slowed the sub to five knots, and the control-room watch busied themselves closing ballast blow valves and balancing *Seawolf* so she would stay afloat on an even keel.

A subtler banging and grinding started, and Jerry imagined ice floes, some weighing tons, rubbing against *Seawolf*'s sides. He also felt the deck rolling under his feet, and wondered what the sea state was. Normally, he took antiseasickness medicine if they planned to operate on the surface, but this had caught him unprepared.

Jerry was still holding the cloth to his forehead and, experimentally, he gently dabbed the wound. It still hurt, and he could feel a good-sized lump forming. Peters had a first-aid kit, and after treating another sailor who'd gashed his hand, he treated Jerry's cut with antibiotic. Jerry had only thought the cut stung, but it did feel better once Peters had taped a gauze bandage over it.

The overhead lights came back on, and Lavoie reflexively checked the breaker panels in the control room. Many of the displays were still dark, and he asked IC2 Keiler, the General Quarters auxiliary electrician forward, to reset the panel. He did, but the breaker popped almost immediately.

"Head up to the electronics equipment space and find out what's wrong," Lavoie ordered. Keiler left in a hurry. Jerry knew that much of the boat's electronics were in two rooms one deck above control—directly overhead. The control room had the displays, but the number-crunching guts of the gear were in those spaces.

Rudel turned to the XO. Jerry never heard what the captain intended to say, because Keiler reappeared at the forward door. He'd barely had time to climb the ladder to the deck above. Keiler took a breath, and Jerry could see him fighting for control. He swallowed, almost a gulp, and said, "Fire in the electronic equipment spaces! I opened the door and everything's wet! There's smoke and sparks everywhere!"

"I'm on it," yelled Shimko.

The XO headed forward at speed, with Keiler behind him. Oddly, Rudel was silent, almost immobile.

Lavoie shouted, "Tell engineering to secure power to the electronic equipment spaces. And pass the word of fire in the forward compartment. All hands don EABs."

The chief of the watch attempted to use the 1MC announcing system, but it was dead, not surprisingly. All the interior communications circuits were housed in the electronics rooms above. Grabbing the sound-powered phone, he spoke carefully into the mouthpiece. "Fire in the electronics equipment space, forward compartment first level. Away the casualty assistance team! All hands don EABs!"

Jerry scrambled over to the fire-control consoles and started pulling the bags with the emergency air breathing masks from the overhead. His head began throbbing again as the rapid motions aggravated his wound.

Fighting the dizziness that welled up every time he turned his head, Jerry and others worked feverishly to get all the bags down. Rapidly and efficiently, they yanked the masks from their bags, checked to see that the regulators worked, and then slipped the masks over the faces of their unconscious shipmates. A slight gray haze started to roll into control and Jerry could smell the acrid scent of burning rubber insulation.

Peters tossed Jerry an EAB mask and he pulled it quickly over his face. Immediately, he felt an intense stabbing pain that almost caused him to lose his balance. Just my luck, thought Jerry, as he felt the edge of the mask run right over his wound. Gingerly, he tried to adjust the face mask. But after a few more stabs he decided it was best just to leave it alone. Synching down the straps to get a good seal brought tears to his eyes.

Seawolf was still rocking in the swells. If anything, they had grown stronger, and Lavoie, thinking of the casualty team and the water sloshing about in the spaces above, shouted, "CAPTAIN, WE NEED TO GET ON A SMOOTHER COURSE."

Rudel nodded silently, and Jerry tried to remember what the weather was supposed to be. Blowing up to a storm, winds from the northwest? In any case, their course would be westerly. Jerry took a deep breath and yanked his hose from the air manifold. He walked over to the plotting table on the other side of control, plugged his hose into another manifold, and started working the charts with QM1 Peters.

The chief of the watch had taken over as the phone talker and he kept up a running commentary. "CHIEF GALLANT IS SETTING UP THE EMERGENCY AID STATION IN THE WARDROOM." *Seawolf*'s sickbay was barely large enough to treat a single minor injury. The standard procedure when there were more casualties was to take over the wardroom, as it had been designed to serve as an emergency operating room.

"THE XO REPORTS THE FIRE IS OUT AND THE REFLASH WATCH IS SET. RECOMMENDS THAT THE FORWARD COMPARTMENT BE EVACUATED WITH THE DIESEL."

Lavoie looked at his captain. By rights, Rudel had the conn and should be taking action. The last thing a sub needed was two men giving orders. But the CO remained silent. The engineer knew what needed to be done.

"CHIEF, PASS THE WORD TO PREPARE TO EMERGENCY VENTILATE THE FORWARD COMPARTMENT WITH THE DIESEL. NAV, I NEED A GOOD COURSE TO REDUCE THE ROLL."

As Chief McCord passed on Lavoie's orders, Jerry walked over and said, "LAST KNOWN WIND DIRECTION WAS FROM THE NORTHWEST, RECOMMEND STEERING THREE TWO ZERO UNTIL WE CAN GET A BETTER ESTIMATE."

There was one way, right in control, to see what the weather was like. Lavoie walked over to the pedestal for periscope number one and yelled, "UP SCOPE." Grabbing the ring, he rotated it but the periscope didn't move at all. Lavoie looked over at the chief of the watch, who was checking the hydraulic power plant section on the BCP. McCord started a hydraulic pump and glanced at the breaker panel. "THE EXTERNAL HYDRAULICS SYSTEM HAS POWER." Lavoie tried periscope number two, but its hoist didn't work either.

Nor did the snorkel mast. The snorkel was the intake for fresh air to the emergency diesel. More problems. Reacting quickly, Lavoie ordered that the emergency ventilation be switched to the low-pressure blower, and a half hour later the air was breathable, if unpleasant.

Shimko came back into control, his uniform spattered with water, grease, sweat, and soot. "The packing glands around the masts started leaking after the collision. There was spray under pressure from some of them onto the cabinets. It's stopped now that we're on the surface. The drains in the space can handle the accumulated water, but I can't guess what will happen if we submerge."

Rudel managed to look concerned and relieved at the same time. Jerry felt the same. It was bad, but it could have been worse.

The XO walked over to where Rudel and Lavoie stood together. "All the gear in there is soaked with salt water. A lot of it's shorted out. There was a class-C electrical fire, but the casualty team made short work of it once the power was turned off."

Jerry tried to remember which systems were in the electronic equipment space. They'd lost radio, certainly, and also the radar and ESM . . .

"There's worse news," Shimko added sadly. "Rountree was in there. They pulled him out of the space, but he's unconscious. He took a couple of good whacks judging from the bruises, and he's got electrical burns. He probably took a bad jolt when the equipment started arcing."

Jerry had stopped working as he overheard the XO's report, but now he couldn't remember what he'd been doing. He took two steps toward the forward control room door, intending to go up and help. Rountree was one of his guys. But then he checked himself. The boat was still at General Quarters; Chief Gallant would take care of him. On top of that, they were still recovering form a nasty collision and a fire. There was nothing Jerry could do to help Rountree, and he'd probably just get in the way. Duty demanded that he stay at his post, but he wanted to go nonetheless.

Lavoie, the XO, and the captain turned back to the problem with the masts. None of them could be raised. Jerry wondered how many others of the crew had been hurt. Was Dennis Rountree the only serious one? Rudel only listened.

The XO pulled Lavoie aside and softly told him to take over in control and get some eyes up on the bridge. Lavoie nodded silently and then turned to Chief McCord. "We need to set the surface bridge watch. Get some foul-weather gear up here." McCord acknowledged the order and sent the messenger of the watch and the stern planesman off to fetch the necessary apparel.

Jerry spoke up. "I'll take the bridge. Peters can handle the nav plot."

Lavoie nodded. "Fine, Jerry. I'll keep the deck here. You'll have the conn." Suddenly, Jerry could hardly wait to get topside.

It took McCord a few minutes to break out the cold-weather clothing. When it arrived, Shimko grabbed a set as well. "As soon as you're set up, I'll join you."

Jerry automatically answered "Yessir," half-expecting the captain to come up as well, but Rudel simply watched the preparations.

When they opened the lower hatch to the bridge access trunk, the water pouring down the ladder was so cold that at first Jerry thought they had a leak up there as well. After a moment, the rush of water ended. He quickly climbed up the ladder, grabbed the hand wheel, and undogged the hatch. Ready for the next blast, with gloves on and every zipper the parka had closed and buttoned, Jerry pushed the hatch open and locked it. He then released the bolt on the clamshell and tried to lower it—it didn't budge. After a second failed attempt, Jerry had the lookout grab hold of the handle and they pulled hard together. With a sharp pop the clamshell fell away, opening the cockpit to the elements. Making sure that his lookout was also ready, the two crawled out into the open.

The hard-driven icy air tore at his hood. There was more than just a strong wind blowing. Looking windward, Jerry could see a dark, uneven line of clouds. Remembering where he was, Jerry used his binoculars to scan the area.

For the first time since the collision, Jerry wondered about the other boat. Was it surfaced nearby? The uneven sea was almost completely covered with ice floes, but he saw no sign of it. Occasionally, one of the larger ice chunks would thud into *Seawolf*'s bow, but most were pushed away by her bow wave.

"Horizon's clear," Seaman Boster reported.

"I concur," Jerry replied. "With this ice, there won't be a lot of surface traffic, but there's a good chance of aircraft—and watch out for the other submarine. Report anything that isn't an ice floe." Jerry had to shout to be heard over the wind. Boster nodded. "Permission to come up to the bridge," came a voice from below.

"Granted," replied Jerry. "But I'd advise you to be properly dressed. It's cold up here."

"No problem, sir," said IT3 Fisher. "We ain't stayin' up here long! We're just here to install the bridge suitcase."

Two enlisted ratings hurried up, bringing the "suitcase" with the compass and other instruments. The navaids needed to conn the boat on the surface would never survive extended submergence, so they were designed as a removable package that could be quickly plugged in whenever *Seawolf* operated on the surface. It only took a few minutes for them to install and test the instruments.

"That looks a little different," remarked Jerry sarcastically as he gazed at their handiwork.

"Well sir, it's what we call an unauthorized shipalt. Since the network is still down, we can't use the flat-panel displays. At least this way the older mechanical dials can tell you which direction the bow is pointing."

"I'll take whatever I can get. But what about comms?"

"Here you go, sir," answered Fisher while handing Jerry a headphone set. "Your own sound-powered phone line. Now, sir, with your permission, we're out of here."

Jerry chuckled as his two guys bolted for the warm interior of the submarine. With the suitcase installed and the surface clear, Jerry used his improvised comms circuit to report his status below. "This is Lieutenant Mitchell, I have the conn. XO, sir, all clear."

Shimko must have been waiting on the ladder, because Jerry had hardly started speaking when the XO appeared from the access trunk below. He was holding a digital camera.

Together, they studied *Seawolf*. Her bow was half hidden by the waves, but the way the water flowed told the ugly story. Normally, *Seawolf*'s round nose pushed a bow wave up onto her forward casing in a smooth, clear sheet, which fell off to the sides and turned into white foam. Now, the bow itself was covered in uneven froth, making whitewater rapids as the bow pitched in the sea. It was clear that a large chunk of the sonar dome was missing.

Shimko took photos, then said, "Slow to three knots."

Jerry passed the order down. Three knots was bare steerageway, enough to give the rudder control so *Seawolf* could stay on a straight course. The speed change did reduce the turbulence a little, and Jerry spotted an angular shape poking up from the foam. Steel or fiberglass, it had been torn and bent several feet out of its proper position. There were also huge gashes in the hull around main ballast tank 1A. But as bad as it looked, there was clearly much more damage still out of view.

"I don't think the sonar techs will be able to get any of the bow arrays working again," Jerry observed.

"If we still have them at all," Shimko remarked darkly. Jerry wondered if the XO was being pessimistic, but the bow wave made sense if you imagined *Seawolf*'s nose as a twisted and raggedly torn beer can.

They could also see damage on the sail, a large grooved dent running up the starboard side all the way to the top. Shimko took more photos, cursing the damage but praising their luck. "At that speed, if he'd hit us dead-on, we'd be on the bottom right now."

It was harder to see the aft part of the casing from the sail, but Shimko managed to spot damage back there as well, an angled scar in the boat's anechoic tiles. The pressure hull underneath was made of HY100 steel two inches thick. It didn't appear to be dented, so if the Russian had hit them there, the two boats must have bounced, hard.

Jerry occasionally checked the gyrocompass and scanned the horizon. There were no navigational hazards, except for the ice, for miles in any direction, but they were under way, and he had the conn. The roll of the deck reminded him of unfinished business.

"XO, I recommend two eight zero to smooth out the ride." That would take them into the wind, and also toward where the UUV was waiting for them.

Shimko, still taking photos, agreed, and Jerry ordered them onto the westerly course. Toward the line of clouds.

He felt the wind swing around as they slowly turned,

and found what shelter he could from the wind. Almost unwillingly, Jerry focused on the pitch and roll of the hull. It was a little better. And so far, his stomach was behaving itself. Too much other stuff to think about.

"We'll stay surfaced until they've finished plugging the leaks around the masts. Stay at three knots." Shimko finished taking pictures, but continued to stare at the bow. "I'll move it along as quickly as I can, but figure on being surfaced for at least a couple of hours."

"Yessir. If you get any information on the casualties, sir, could you please pass it up?"

Shimko nodded. "It's first on my list."

The XO left and Jerry began his regular bridge watch routine. Scan all the dials, sweep the horizon with binoculars, check on the lookout. Poor Boster was just as exposed to the elements as he was; there was really nowhere to hide from the wind. Seeing no reason to freeze lookouts, Jerry recommended that they be relieved every hour. Lavoie agreed, and said he'd arrange it.

The dark radar repeater reminded Jerry of their damage, as well as their location. Normally, when *Seawolf* ran on the surface, she extended a radar mast, but none of their masts would function. Even if the mast had worked, the transmitter module in the electronics equipment space was fried. And even if everything did work, broadcasting a U.S. military radar here, practically on the Russians' doorstep, was a great way to attract unwelcome attention.

They'd lost their bow sonars, their periscopes and all their other masts, the radar, and their radios. Most of that gear, except the sonar, was his responsibility, maintained by his electronics techs and ITs. It was too soon to think about all the repairs, not while they were still at General Quarters, but the instant they secured, he'd have to find Chandler and Hudson and put them to work.

Jerry shivered as the wind gusted. But it wasn't only the

cold chilling his bones. They were virtually blind, close to the Russian coast, with a leaky boat and no way to call for help. And that storm was coming right at them and it didn't look friendly.

Shimko was good as his word. He'd been gone only a few minutes when his voice came over the sound-powered phones. "Jerry, you asked about the casualties. We've got nine total, besides the bumps and bruises on just about everyone. Most are minor injuries, but they also include two fractures—and Rountree. The doc's working on him, but that's all I can say."

Jerry thanked the XO, and returned his attention to his bridge watch duties. The boat's slow speed and the bleak horizon belied the urgency of the situation. A Russian aircraft could appear at any time, and without their sensors, they'd have no warning until it basically flew overhead. He wasn't afraid of being attacked, but it would be best for everyone if they could leave the Barents undetected.

Shuffling about in an attempt to keep warm, Jerry found his mind constantly going back to the events that led to the collision. He knew he'd have to write a report, possibly testify at a board of inquiry, so he tried to fix details while they were clear in his mind. It would be important later.

He wasn't worried about the outcome of any investigation. American and Russian subs had collided before on operations like this, although it wasn't common. The entire incident would be reviewed, but as far as he could see, Rudel's actions had been correct and the Russian had acted with incredible aggressiveness.

The cold wind swirled around him in the sub's cockpit, and Jerry busied himself to pass the time. With Lavoie's concurrence, he tried several different courses to smooth out the boat's ride. Jerry wasn't the only submariner vulnerable to seasickness.

An hour after he'd started his bridge watch, they

secured from General Quarters. A moment later, a relief lookout appeared, ET2 Lamberth. Bundled up as the enlisted man was, Jerry didn't recognize one of his own petty officers until Lamberth spoke, relieving Boster, who gratefully hurried below.

"I don't remember you being on the watch bill as a lookout," Jerry remarked.

"I'm taking Stone's place. He banged up his knee, and can't climb a ladder too well. Besides, I wanted to tell you about Rountree."

Jerry's heart sank when he heard Lamberth's foreboding tone. "Are his injuries that bad?" Jerry prompted.

"Yeah." Lamberth paused, swallowed hard, and then just spat it out. "He's gone, Mr. Mitchell. He died."

The news hit Jerry like a freight train. Stunned, silent, he turned away from Lamberth, desperately trying to maintain his composure. A young sailor entrusted to his care had died. Rountree was his responsibility, and now he was gone.

Helpless, angry, Jerry slammed his fist on the coaming. "Shit!" He couldn't think of anything else to say.

"Yeah, sir. You got that right. It was his heart, sir. Chief Gallant said it was probably the electrical shock. It damaged the muscles in his heart, and they kept on wanting to stop. It did stop, twice, and the chief zapped him and brought him back. Everybody was rooting for him, even Brann with his broken leg, half drugged up.

"But it stopped again, and the chief ran out of things to do. They've got him bundled up in a blanket off to one side in the wardroom. Guys keep coming over to it and patting it, saying good-bye. Robinson's sitting with him right now. He and Blocker are taking it pretty hard. I mean, we all are, it's just bugging them more . . . I guess."

They aren't the only ones, thought Jerry as he wiped the

stinging salt water from his face. "Thanks for coming up to tell me."

Lamberth nodded sadly and moved over to the lookout position. Jerry turned back to check the bridge instruments, but then the petty officer spoke again.

"He's got family in Florida, I think." He had to raise his voice to be heard.

Jerry searched his memory of Rountree's service record. "Parents and a younger sister," Jerry answered. He'd never met them. Rountree hadn't been aboard long enough for his family to visit.

Lamberth nodded and raised the binoculars again. Conscious of their exposed position, Jerry kept searching the sky, hoping he wouldn't see anything. If something did appear, they couldn't escape quickly. Nuclear subs couldn't crash-dive the way the old fleet boats did in WWII. Come to think of it, he didn't want to dive at all. Not with all those leaks, and the depleted air banks . . .

"Will we bury him at sea?" Lamberth asked. It took a moment for Jerry to realize he'd asked a question, and the petty officer had to repeat it.

Jerry paused before answering. Finally, he shook his head.

"I don't think so." Then more definitely, "No. We should bring him back to his family."

"But where will we keep him?"

It surprised Jerry that they would have to think of such things, but there was hardly a spare inch of space on *Seawolf,* in spite of her size.

"They'll have to put him in the freezer."

Lamberth considered Jerry's answer for a moment, then shrugged. It made sense. What else could they do?

There'd be a death investigation, Jerry realized. And how would they explain this to Rountree's parents? The navy couldn't tell them what really happened. They'd have to make up a cover story about something. Shoot, the navy would need a cover story for everyone on the boat. They couldn't pull into port with this kind of damage without some plausible explanation.

A voice from the sound-powered phones broke Jerry's train of thought. "Bridge, control. Lieutenant Wolfe wants to come up and take a look at the bow."

"Control, bridge. Send him up."

Greg Wolfe came through the access hatch as quickly as possible. He didn't even greet Jerry, his attention fully taken up by *Seawolf*'s damaged bow. "Oh, migod. I was hoping the XO was wrong. It's trashed!"

"He thinks the sphere, the low-frequency bow array, and the medium-frequency active array are all gone," Jerry suggested.

"I think he's right," Wolfe answered in awe. Then more apologetically, "Oh. Sorry to hear about Denny Rountree."

"Yeah. Thanks, I guess." His division was the closest thing to family Rountree had aboard, and that made Jerry the head of the family.

"The whole boat's taking it pretty hard. Everybody liked the kid."

Jerry felt something sting his cheek and automatically turned in that direction, into the wind. He was rewarded with particles of wind-driven snow pelting his face. Or ice. Whatever it was, he turned to avoid the stuff, then half-turned back to study the advancing front more closely.

He'd been an aviator in an earlier life, and had developed a good sense for weather. This oncoming storm was going to be a bad one. The front had advanced in the past hour, and Jerry could see a dark gray haze living under the cloud line.

"Greg, are you done?"

Wolfe had been looking at the storm front as well. "I'm gone," and he was through the hatch.

Jerry pressed the intercom. "Control, bridge. What the status of the repairs?"

Lieutenant Constantino, the ship's supply officer, was in control as the contact coordinator after *Seawolf* had secured from General Quarters. His answer was not helpful. "Feeling the cold, Jerry?"

"Everyone's going to feel it when this storm reaches us." Jerry then described the advancing weather.

"Those ice floes will beat us to death," Constatino agreed. Some of *Seawolf*'s sonar arrays were mounted on her sides. They weren't designed to be hammered by multi-ton hunks of ice.

"And the ride's going to get a lot worse," Jerry added from the bridge.

"Understood, Mr. Mitchell." The XO's voice surprised Jerry. "There are new issues. The collision may have cracked the pressure hull forward. We were stripping some wet insulation from the bulkhead and found out that one of the frames is bent."

Jerry took a moment to take that in. The frames were steel ribs that reinforced the pressure hull. The force involved when the two subs came together must have been massive . . .

"We could change course, sir, run before the storm. Just five knots would buy us more time."

"Negative, mister. That would mean heading east and closing on the Russian coast. We keep heading west."

"Aye, aye, sir. Can you ask the chief to pass us up some safety harnesses?"

The harnesses came up a few minutes later, along with some hot cocoa for Jerry and Lamberth. Never did anything taste and feel so good to the two men.

The nylon webbing went on like a parachute harness, with some difficulty, over their parkas. It had a line that could be clipped to different spots on the hull. There were several such places in the bridge cockpit and up on the top of the sail when the flying bridge was erected. After Jerry double-checked Lamberth's line, he made sure his own was secure and tried to guess how long it would be until they needed them.

Jerry had matter-of-factly accepted their need to stay on the surface. Until they figured out how badly the pressure hull was damaged, they dare not submerge.

He tried to visualize the impact. Two subs, each over three hundred feet long and displacing nearly ten thousand tons, slamming into each other at high speed. The hull had been weakened at more than just one small point. He imagined an area the size of a window, or a door, or the side of a house, laced through with invisible cracks. Under pressure, it might give way. In fact, it definitely would give way, at some depth. He wondered if they could submerge at all. But if they did, how deep could they go?

The roughness of the sea changed suddenly, well before the clouds reached them. Sea state three with four-foot waves became sea state five with peaks two or three times as high. The wind tore the tops off, adding their spray to the snow already flying into their faces. Small pieces of ice were picked up and hurled against the hull. And it was going to get worse.

Seawolf rolled violently in the swells, a fast combined pitching and rolling motion that threatened to knock Jerry off his feet. He looked up at Lamberth, who was hanging on to the cockpit's handrails, his face pale. "Get below! You can't do any more good up here!"

With careful timing, Lamberth unhooked his harness and almost dove into the bridge access trunk. Jerry steadied him as he went down. A sudden loud clang told him the larger ice chucks were starting to get thrown about. The wind's intensity was picking up even more and had shifted toward the south. They were facing a full-blown winter gale. Jerry called down a course correction, a little more southwesterly.

Constantino acknowledged the course change, and added, "We're ballasting her down a little as well. I know it gives you less freeboard up there, but it should help reduce the rolls." After a moment, he added, "They'll be done soon."

Jerry held on tightly to the coaming with one hand and the binoculars with the other. Facing directly into the wind, he was glad to have the binoculars. At least his eyes were protected from the spray. He hoped someone down in control was watching their heading, because he couldn't spare the time.

It started getting really bad when the waves began breaking halfway up the sail. Sheets of ice-cold water leapt over the top of the cockpit, drenching Jerry. Every once in a while he had to literally dodge a chunk of ice that was thrown by the waves. But as long as they were on the surface, somebody had to be up here.

He was getting ready to change the ship's course again when Fisher appeared from the hatchway below. "We're ready to submerge. I'll get the suitcase."

The console was caked with ice, but they finally knocked enough off to detach and close the lid, after which it was hurriedly manhandled below. With one last scan of the horizon, Jerry unclipped his safety harness and dropped through the hatch. He gratefully dogged it shut, double-checking to make sure it had sealed properly.

By the time he dropped into the control room, they were already heading down. He heard Lieutenant Wolfe, the new OOD, order "One hundred feet" and began to worry. That was shallow for a submarine of *Seawolf*'s size.

Jerry's face must have shown his concern, because Wolfe reassured him. "The XO wants us to take it slowly. We'll work our way down to three hundred feet, but in baby steps."

"Well, it's got to be better than riding it out on the surface. It's way beyond nasty up there," Jerry replied as he struggled to unzip his parka with half-frozen hands. And then more lightly, "I guess someone really pissed off King Boreas, because he's hopping mad right now."

"Wasn't me; honest," cried Wolfe defensively.

Jerry chuckled and then groaned as he gratefully stripped off the icy foul-weather gear. He hadn't realized just how sore he was. Somebody handed him a towel, and he stepped to one side, blotting the seawater from his face, while another sailor mopped up the puddle he'd left on the deck.

"The XO wants a status on all the gear ASAP." Jerry acknowledged Wolfe's message as he stepped over to the chart table. QM3 Bishop was tending the nav plot, and Jerry studied their track, the twists and turns of their encounter with the Russian, their slow northwest crawl since. Their submerged speed was still just five knots.

He took a quick bearing to LaVerne's programmed location. Wolfe already had them on course to the rendezvous with the UUV. At five knots, they'd reach her in an hour or so.

Sighing, he asked the chief of the watch to please send the messenger of the watch to find Mr. Chandler, Chief Hudson, and QM1 Peters. "Tell them to meet me in the wardroom immediately." He headed aft, straight to the wardroom, half-expecting to find injured sailors, but the corpsman had finished his work. The space was clean.

QM1 Peters showed up first, then Chandler and finally Chief Hudson. The chief's clothes were stained and wet.

With all three of his divisions' leadership present, Jerry got straight to business. "All right. Who else was hurt?" He didn't need to mention Rountree.

Peters spoke first. "Gosnell slammed his shoulder, but that's all."

Hudson said, "Troy Kearney landed wrong on the deck and broke his wrist. The doc's already put a splint on it."

Chandler added, "Minor bumps and bruises, but nobody's reported anything serious."

"Chief?" Jerry dreaded Hudson's reply, but they had to know. "Does anything work?"

"We're still trying to get power to the racks. Between finding shorts and replacing charred cables, that's been hard enough. We've restored power to the ship control circuits, internal comms, and the WAA. I can tell you right now that the radar and ESM are a total loss."

"Matt, what about the radios?"

"Without power, we couldn't test the gear."

Jerry waited a moment, expecting to hear more, but Chandler seemed to be finished. "Fine. QM1, see what your people can do to help the ETs and the ITs. I know you're not techs, but they're shorthanded. Hourly reports. That's all."

They all turned to leave, but Jerry asked, "Matt, stay a minute." As soon as Peters and Hudson were gone, Jerry said, "I need to know more about our radios."

"I'll get right on it, sir. I've been busy with other things."

That "sir" thing again. Jerry fought to control his irritation. "What could be more important than fixing the radios, Matt?"

"Documenting the collision. I've been working on my account of events. I wanted to do it while they were still fresh in my mind." He reminded Jerry, "You know, we're all going to have to provide them."

Between Chandler's self-serving response and his own grief over Rountree's death, Jerry snapped. His anger flashed into full bloom. "Lieutenant, we're in the middle of the Barents on a boat that's deaf, dumb, and blind. Now is not the time to cover your ass."

"Sir, I resent the implication that I've neglected my duties." Chandler's injured demeanor increased Jerry's anger.

"I'm not implying it, I'm saying it. Drop the damn paperwork and get to work on those radios."

"Sir, are you ordering me to not work on recording my account of the collision?"

Jerry pulled himself up short. His irritation changed to caution. Chandler was looking for Jerry to say the wrong thing, something angry while he was cold and tired and strung out. It would go right into his report, part of an official record.

Jerry adopted a formal tone. "I am informing you of what our priorities are in this critical situation, and reminding you, as always, to spend your time wisely and to do your duty accordingly."

After a moment, Jerry added, "This is no time for mind games. Report to me in control in five minutes. I need to know exactly how quickly we can get one HF transmitter and receiver on line. And don't *ever* tell me that 'nobody's reported anything' to you. It's your job to find out. Is that clear?"

"Yes sir." Chandler's tone and expression didn't change, but Matt was no fool. The message had been received, for now.

Cursing Chandler, Jerry quickly changed into some drier clothing and headed for the electronic equipment space. He needed to know just how bad it was.

Standing outside the door, Jerry could smell burnt paint and rubber. Inside the cramped compartment, illuminated by work lights, three enlisted men struggled to pull blackened electronics modules from their racks. Every module had been sprayed with salt water, and would have to be thoroughly cleaned before anyone dared to run power through it.

Their movements were hampered by a wooden framework that had been roughly braced to the deck. Several beams angled up to an area of gray metal on the forward bulkhead. The insulation that normally covered it had been torn away, and Jerry could see the ribs that lined the inside and strengthened the pressure hull, spaced a few feet apart. Three ribs were exposed, and the center one was deformed inward—not a lot, but Jerry could see where it was no longer a perfect circle.

The wooden braces would shore up the weakened rib, although there was no way of knowing how much strain the area could take. He was enough of an engineer to know what their vulnerabilities were. He just couldn't calculate how much trouble they were in.

One enlisted man from auxiliary division, wearing sound-powered phones, had been posted in the space. His only job was to watch for signs of stress in the hull or the shoring, and for any new leaks.

One of the technicians, ET1 Kearney, looked up from his work and asked, "Need something, Mr. Mitchell?"

"No, Kearney. That's what I was going to ask you. How's your wrist?"

Kearney held out his right arm for Jerry to inspect. A metal splint surrounded his arm from below the elbow to his palm. "The chief did a good job. He says it's hardly more than a greenstick fracture."

Jerry flashed back to his own injury, a shattered right wrist that had ended his aviation career. "Now you'll always be able to tell when we change depth. How's the pain?"

Kearney shrugged. "It hurt like hell when he examined it, but since then it's just a dull ache."

"It's going to swell some. Keep taking the ibuprofen that the doc prescribed."

"How'd you know he'd told me that?"

Jerry held out his own wrist, showing him the scars. "Been there, done that, bought the pharmacy."

Jerry headed for control. He found the XO there, watching as Greg Wolfe cautiously took *Seawolf* deeper. They'd worked their way to two hundred and fifty feet and seven knots. Reflexively, Jerry checked their sea room on the chart and found no issues. They would reach the rendezvous with LaVerne in half an hour.

Lieutenant Chandler showed up, but as Jerry asked for his report, the XO appeared. "Department head meeting in the wardroom. Pass the word."

Chandler followed Jerry and the XO to the wardroom, with Lavoie and Wolf arriving moments later. Shimko sat down tiredly and the others did the same. Sonar Technician Senior Chief Mike Carpenter, one of the intelligence riders, knocked on the door and then took a seat at the XO's invitation.

"I asked the Senior Chief to tell us what he can about the Russian submarine—as much as he can, anyway," Shimko added. Jerry hadn't seen much of the acoustic intelligence, or ACINT, riders. There were three of them aboard, but they kept to themselves.

Carpenter's sandy hair made him look younger than his early forties would suggest. As a senior chief, Jerry guessed that he had at least twenty years' experience listening to Russian submarines. "In this case, sir, it's pretty much everything we know. We've got twenty-eight minutes of recordings that covers the time from our first detection until the collision. She was running at high speed, and using her sonars freely, so we got plenty to work with. In fact, we haven't gotten through all of it, but we've seen enough."

Carpenter stopped, and the XO waited for a moment before asking him, "For what?" He was impatient, but curious.

"We didn't get a positive match to anything in our database. That was the funny part. With so much recorded, we figured it would be simple to match his acoustic signature to one of the Northern Fleet's boats, but it's definitely not a match, which means it's *Severodvinsk* by default, their newest boat. She's been running trials, but we haven't heard her before."

"Given that it was *Severodvinsk,* does that explain how she found us or what she was doing?"

Carpenter frowned. "No sir, not at all. No transients, no unusual acoustic transmissions. Her sonar suite is the best the Russians have, but nothing exotic, as far as we know. We were a little noisier during the UUV recovery, mostly short mechanical transients, but nothing more than what's normal for that evolution."

"Then keep sorting though those recordings. I want to know everything you know." Carpenter nodded his understanding.

"Mr. Mitchell, what about the electronics?"

"We've lost radar and ESM. I was just about to get Mr. Chandler's report on the radios." Jerry didn't need to share his problems with the XO.

Chandler didn't wait to be asked. "We should be able to get an HF receiver circuit on line by the end of the day, an LF receiver will take a little more time. Chief Morrison said it would take at least six hours, maybe longer. He's got his people working on a transmitter, but they're in considerably worse shape." He shrugged. "The bridge-to-bridge radio works, so if we get in line of sight with another vessel on the surface, we can talk to them."

Jerry almost laughed. The bridge-to-bridge radio was no bigger than a good-sized walkie-talkie, and would not reach farther than the horizon. Still, they'd need it to communicate when they got back to a friendly port.

"Mr. Wolfe, what abut weapons department?"

"All bow arrays are officially gone. As is the TB-16 towed array. Its stowage tube was crushed during the collision. The TB-29, WAA, and HF sonar are on line, torpedo division is ready. Mr. Palmer is preparing to recover LaVerne."

The XO asked Lavoie, "Engineering?"

"Everything's on line, sir. The plant took a heckuva shock, but no equipment failures. We're watching everything very closely."

The XO absorbed the reports for a moment. "We've been hurt, but we are not in danger of losing the boat. We're ending the mission, of course. As soon as we recover the UUV we're turning southwest and heading for Faslane."

Jerry knew the place. On the western coast of Scotland, Faslane was a British submarine base. It was the closest friendly port that could take their injured and make emergency repairs.

"Mr. Mitchell, I'll need a recommended course as soon as possible."

"Aye, sir."

"Mr. Wolfe, you'll do the death investigation for Petty Officer Rountree."

"Yes, sir."

"Mr. Mitchell, start reconstructing the incident, beginning with our initial detection, up to the moment of the collision. You are not writing the incident report—that's my job—but I want a chronology that may help explain how he found us and what he was trying to do. And I will use it in my report." Shimko motioned toward Carpenter. "Use whatever the Senior Chief can give you about the Russian's movements and activities.

"That's all," Shimko said, dismissing them.

Jerry hurried back to control. It only took a few minutes to work out the course changes and times for Faslane, Scotland. He arrived at the XO's cabin just as Shimko was returning.

After Shimko reviewed and approved the route, Jerry said, "Thank you, sir. Should I go brief the Skipper now?" That was standard procedure.

"No, Jerry, I'll brief him." That was unusual. Rudel always wanted to be briefed by the officer involved. And it was unnecessary. Rudel's cabin was right there, a few steps away. And Shimko's tone was off. He was trying too hard to sound casual.

"Is everything all right, sir? Was the Captain hurt? I noticed he wasn't at the meeting." Jerry was deeply concerned. Rudel was more than a commanding officer. Everyone in the crew liked and admired Rudel, and thought of him as a friend, a father, or a favorite teacher.

"He's fine." But Shimko said it too quickly, and seemed uncomfortable. Finally, he added, "He's taken Rountree's death pretty hard."

"We all have," Jerry agreed. But then he added, "He doesn't think it's his fault, does he?"

"It's always the Captain's responsibility, you know that," Shimko answered. It was a mantra in the navy, but it didn't tell Jerry what was wrong with the captain.

9

DISASTER

A coughing fit yanked Petrov back to consciousness, an acrid scent that made his mouth taste of old tires. Disoriented, he fought to remember where he was. It was dark, but he didn't recall turning off the reading light in his bunk . . .

No. That wasn't right. This wasn't his cabin. He felt himself lying on the deck, propped up against the command console. His head and right shoulder burned with pain, which became sharper when he tried to pull himself up. As he struggled to stand, he saw the dim glow of the emergency lights.

Everything was wrong. What had happened to the power? The central post was dark, really dark, in the worst possible way. Not only were the lights out, but most of the console displays were dead as well. As his confusion subsided, he felt the sudden loss of information. What was happening throughout the rest of the boat?

He took a cautious first step, but nearly fell anyway. The deck was tilted, down by the bow and sharply to port. They must be resting on the bottom. He coughed again, and smelled what had to be smoke. Fear poured into him, and he searched for other signs of fire. By the time he'd scanned the entire central command post his head was clearing. Thankfully, there didn't seem to be any flames. But he still had to figure out where that smoke was coming from.

A number of the men were just getting up themselves, some with effort, a sure sign of injury. Others lay crumpled on the deck, unmoving. As Petrov started inching toward the nearest man, he asked himself two questions. How many of my crew are injured? What is the material condition of my boat? He needed answers, and he needed them now.

Chief Engineer Lyachin was just getting up as Petrov climbed over to the ship's systems-control station. Steadying the wobbly engineer, Petrov was relieved that he did not appear to be seriously hurt. "Sergey Vladimirovich, I need you to go back to the aft compartments and inspect them for damage. Can you walk?"

"Yes, Captain. I think so."

"Good, Chief. Report on casualties and the status of the engineering plant. Use messengers. The internal communications aren't working."

"I suspect that's not the only system that isn't functioning," remarked Lyachin with a slight grin. The engineer coughed and then sniffed the air, a look of concern flashed on his face. "Smoke?"

"Yes, Chief. I don't know if it's from some electrical equipment that shorted out or if we have an actual fire on board, so be careful."

"Understood, comrade Captain." Lyachin then pointed at a still-groggy Shubin and ordered, "You. With me. Let's see how badly we are hurt."

As the two men worked their way aft, Petrov's eyes reflexively went back to the darkened status displays. Their blank features mocked his ignorance, but he remembered that the mechanical depth gauge didn't need power. Grabbing the emergency flashlight attached to the commander's console, he crawled over to the maneuvering-control station and shined the light on the depth gauge. It showed 197 meters. That was well above collapse depth, but too deep for a free ascent if they had to abandon the submarine. It was clear that they were on the bottom, and it hadn't been a soft landing.

He scanned the rest of the central post with the flashlight, its bright beam highlighting the smoke that hung in the air. It didn't appear to be getting worse, but it was thick enough to sting any soft tissue exposed to it, including the lungs. Petrov saw that most of the watch section was on their feet, checking on each other and their equipment. He watched as they made their reports to Kalinin and cared for two men who had sustained more than just bruises.

Kalinin waddled over, favoring his left ankle. He spoke softly. "Two serious injuries, Seaman Naletov and Warrant Officer Kotkov. Kotkov is hurt very badly. He gashed an artery in his leg. They're putting a tourniquet on him now, but we really need Dr. Balanov. I've sent a runner to go look for him. As for the ship's systems, everything's nonoperational, even the backup power systems." The starpom paused to cough, then added, "I felt us collide with the American boat, Captain. We hit and slid along its hull before something pitched us nose down and drove us into the mud."

"That's more than I remember, Vasiliy."

"Yes, sir. You were thrown into the command console when we first collided. You were knocked out . . ."

"We'll piece our memories together later, Vasiliy. Right now we need to figure out how bad off we are. I already sent the Chief Engineer aft to check on the propulsion plant. Send some more runners forward and aft. Pass the word for each compartment to report their status via messenger, since the comms systems aren't functional."

"Already done, sir," replied Kalinin.

"Very good, Starpom." Petrov took a little comfort in the fact that his first officer was already dealing with the situation. "I presume you fired the emergency gas generators after we struck the American, yes?" Petrov was referring to a set of chemical generators in the main ballast tanks. They could be triggered to send a one-time blast of high-pressure gas that would push the water out of the ballast tanks, hopefully causing the sub to ascend. The system was designed to get a submarine on the surface quickly during an emergency.

"Yes, sir, but it didn't seem to help very much. Something was driving us down. Given that we are still on the bottom, I'm sure several ballast tanks were crushed on impact."

Abruptly, the high-pitched shrieking of a panic-stricken man interrupted their discussion. "Captain! Captain! Seawater is entering compartment one! There is water coming into compartment one!" A young seaman scrambled into the dim light. He was visibly shaking; his eyes were wide with fear. It was the junior rating the starpom had sent forward.

"Calm yourself, Seaman Kessler," Kalinin said reassuringly as he grabbed the young man's shoulders, steadying him. "Now, give us your report."

Kessler settled down a little. His shaking had subsided but he continued to gasp for air. Facing his captain, he struggled to speak clearly.

"Captain, the forward bulkhead in compartment one has been breached. There are numerous geysers pouring seawater into the compartment. The hull is . . . is starting to groan, sir!"

Petrov took the devastating report with a stoic expression, as if it were just part of a routine drill. He had to maintain control even though his own sense of fear was rising. If he panicked, the crew would soon follow suit and they all would perish. He was the rock on which they clung and he had to stand firm.

"Seaman, listen to me. Tell your compartment commander to . . ."

Kessler shook his head violently and cut his captain off in midsentence: "Senior-Lieutenant Geletin is dead, sir! And most of the remaining crew members are badly injured!"

With his frustration growing, Petrov pulled on the seaman's coveralls and looked at the billet number on the left breast pocket. The five-digit number told him what battle department the seaman belonged to, as well as his duty location and watch section. The first number was a "1," indicating that he belonged to the navigation battle department. Scanning the room with his flashlight, Petrov spotted his commander of navigation, Captain-Lieutenant Ivanov, tending Seaman Naletov.

"Dimitry, take command of compartment one. Assess the situation and report back immediately. Take Starshini Michman Zubov with you."

Senior Warrant Officer Vitaly Zubov was the senior and most experienced enlisted man on board *Severodvinsk.* His position *starshini michman* was roughly analogous to the American chief of the boat.

"Aye, Captain," replied Ivanov as he and Zubov dashed for the ladder well.

Stepping out of the way, Petrov moved closer to Kalinin, who leaned over and whispered, "Sir, that bulkhead took the brunt of two impacts. Should it fail . . ."

"Yes, Starpom," replied Petrov testily. "I am well aware of the implications. But I need an accurate report before I consign those injured crewmen to their deaths."

Kalinin nodded as Petrov shouted, "Captain Mitrov!"

"Yes sir," came the reply from the entrance to the sonar post.

Turning toward the voice, he ordered, "Get as many men as you can and evacuate the injured from compartment one. Then gather as many air-regeneration cassettes and emergency rations as possible. Post an able-bodied, clear-minded man at the watertight hatch. Seaman Kessler will take you to the injured men."

"Yes, comrade Captain." As Mitrov walked past Petrov, the captain grasped his arm, stopping him. Quietly, he said, "Move quickly, Vladimir Vasil'evich. If that bulkhead starts to go, I'll have to order the hatch closed, regardless of who is in compartment one."

"I understand, sir," responded Mitrov. Then turning to Kessler, he said, "Come, seaman, we need to go rescue our comrades."

For a brief moment, the room was still. Only slight murmurs could be heard as the remaining men tended to the wounded. But then a moving shadow at the rear of the central post caught Petrov's attention. It was Shubin. He was pale and sweaty, his breathing labored. An IDA-59M emergency respirator hung around his neck.

"Captain, Chief Engineer Lyachin reports that there is extensive damage aft. Compartment eight is flooding from the stern tube. The compartment is over half full of water and . . . and the level is rising quickly." The junior officer stopped as he tried to catch his breath. He was obviously fatigued and frightened.

"Please continue your report, Mikhail," coached Petrov calmly. He didn't need to rattle the young senior-lieutenant any more than he already was. Petrov and Kalinin needed an accurate account of the situation in the engineering spaces, not the incoherent babblings of an overly stressed and terrified man.

"Yes, sir. The shaft bearings are badly distorted and Chief Engineer Lyachin says we cannot use the main propulsion turbines. He also regrets to report that the bulkhead between compartments seven and eight has been compromised. He doesn't exactly know how bad, but water is welling up in the bilges in compartment seven. It's already up to the deck plates in the below decks. He doesn't think we can isolate it."

The last sentence struck both Petrov and Kalinin like a knife through the heart. Kalinin groaned audibly as he leaned up against the command console for support. Stunned by the additional dark news, Petrov stood speechless. *Severodvinsk* was crippled and slowly dying, and there was virtually no chance of them getting off the bottom. They'd have to abandon ship, if they could.

"I see," replied Petrov woodenly. "Anything else?"

"Yes, sir. Damage Control Chief Kolesnikov reports that there was a small electric fire in compartment three. It was put out with a portable chemical extinguisher. There was a far more serious fire in compartment six that required the application of the LOKh to extinguish." The LOKh was a compartment-level fire-fighting system that used Freon gas to smother a fire by depriving it of oxygen. Unfortunately, it would also kill anyone trapped in the compartment.

"Casualties?" asked Kalinin quietly.

"There are numerous casualties, Starpom. We haven't been able to compile a list just yet. Dr. Balanov is treating the wounded in compartment four."

"Where is Captain Kolesnikov now?" Petrov's voice was deadpan, but his face reflected the pain he felt.

"Captain Kolesnikov is on the line of defense established at the aft bulkhead of compartment five. He is assisting the Chief Engineer in evacuating compartments six and seven."

"Very well, tell the Chief Engineer . . ."

Suddenly the central post reverberated with the sound of mechanical popping and a low creaking groan that seemed to come from the hull itself. The unnatural noise grated on their already frayed nerves.

A puzzled Petrov looked toward Kalinin. His face was ashen; he understood. "My God! The forward bulkhead!"

Petrov took off running, while Kalinin hopped as best he could toward the ladder. The captain grabbed the handrails and sailed down the ladder well, the pain in his shoulder deadened by the adrenaline in his blood. It took him no more than ten seconds to reach the watertight door, despite having to jump over injured men lying on the deck. Mitrov was shoving Kessler through the hatch as Petrov arrived; both men were carrying two air-regeneration cassettes each.

"The bulkhead is failing, Captain!" shouted Mitrov as he stumbled through the door.

At the far end of the passageway, Petrov saw three men in orange rubber damage-control suits attempting to put up mechanical braces against the bulkhead. Heavy streams of water shot out of numerous small cracks in the steel hull.

"Are they the last ones in the compartment?" yelled Petrov.

"Yes, sir! All the injured are out and the belowdecks hatch is shut and dogged!"

As Kalinin hobbled up to the door, his face ablaze with pain, he found Petrov shouting and waving at the men to get away from the forward bulkhead. The hull groaned again, and new streams of high-pressure water shot out from the metal. A jet of water hit one of the men in the shoulder, spinning him violently into the wall; he bounced and fell into the pooling water on the deck. At this depth, the water had the force of a bullet, and it left its victim unconscious.

The larger man, seeing his unmoving comrade in the water, scooped him up and started retreating toward the watertight door. With the water level up to his knees, he waded at an agonizingly slow pace. He kept looking over his shoulder, motioning for the third man to follow, but the man remaining behind waved them on as he struggled to tighten up a brace.

Petrov watched in horror as the bulkhead visibly distorted even more—the low groaning became a high-pitched screech. Reaching through the doorway, he grabbed the injured man, pulled him through, and dumped his limp body on the deck. The larger man leapt through the door just as the forward bulkhead started to fail catastrophically. Petrov slammed the door shut and braced it with his body while Kalinin lunged on the locking mechanism handle, dogging the hatch. Less than a second later, the hull finally collapsed, and the resulting water hammer blasted the bulkhead between the two compartments. The transmitted force sent both Petrov and Kalinin flying, but the bulkhead held.

After a few seconds, the din of rushing water was replaced by the moaning and cries of injured men. Struggling to his feet, wet and in shock, Petrov stared at the watertight door. He'd just lost another man. How many was it now?

"Captain," Zubov's voice came from behind him. It was unsteady, broken, but grateful. "Thank you, sir."

Petrov looked up at the large man clad in the damage-control suit, his face now exposed, and nodded. Turning back toward the secured watertight door, he asked, "Who did we lose?"

Zubov swallowed hard, there were tears welling in his eyes. Fighting his emotions, it took him a few seconds to answer his captain. "Captain-Lieutenant Ivanov, sir."

Just then, several men came pouring down the ladder, their flashlight beams twitching wildly about as they descended. Chief Engineer Lyachin was in the lead.

"Dear God," he said as he maneuvered his way to Petrov. "We felt the hull collapse. I was afraid we were all doomed. We were fortunate this time."

"Some of us were, Chief," responded Petrov as he helped Kalinin to his feet. His words were heavy with weariness and remorse. "Some of us were spared. At least for the moment."

With one arm supporting Kalinin, he gestured to the injured men on the deck with the others. "Chief, get these men to compartment three. Set up the engineers' living quarters as a hospital and alert Dr. Balanov that he has more patients waiting. Then meet me and the Starpom in the central command post; we have much to discuss."

"Aye, Captain."

HALF AN hour later, Petrov and Kalinin met with the surviving battle department commanders and the service chiefs. Petrov needed to hear their reports so that he could understand the full extent of the damage, and to determine what options they had. Chief Engineer Lyachin started off with an assessment of the ship's overall status. As expected, the news was not good.

"Based on my direct observations, compartments one, seven, and eight are completely flooded. Compartment six is probably flooding slowly, since I heard water flowing as I left. The atmosphere in compartment six is toxic, as is compartment five, from the byproducts of the fire as well as the LOKh suppression system. The watertight bulkheads in compartments two and five appear to be holding. For now, our situation has stabilized."

Kalinin shook his head and chuckled, "You have an unusual definition of stable, Sergey Vladimirovich."

"I suppose so, Starpom, but we are in a rather unusual situation," quipped Lyachin with a weary smile.

"Please continue, Chief," commanded Petrov tersely.

"Yes, sir. The reactor is secure. The shutdown rods have been inserted and I initiated the emergency cooling system. This means we only have the reserve storage battery for electrical power. Used judiciously, it can last for several days."

"Thank you, Chief. Captain Fonarin, what is the status of our atmosphere?"

"It is breathable, Captain. Oxygen is at nineteen percent and carbon dioxide is at half a percent. That's a little high, but tolerable. The existing smoke particulates are annoying but not life-threatening. Pressure in the boat is a little over a standard atmosphere."

Petrov nodded as he scribbled down the facts in his notepad. "Now for the crucial question, Igor. How long before the air will no longer sustain life?"

"I believe we have several days before carbon dioxide becomes a critical concern. We have plenty of oxygen in the storage tanks, but without the air-purification system, we have limited means of removing the carbon dioxide. I will have a better estimate once I know how many air-regeneration cassettes we recovered and how many . . . how many of the crew are still alive." Fonarin's last sentence trailed off suddenly. Embarrassed at the implication that the deaths they'd suffered thus far were of benefit to the rest.

"Thank you, Igor. Gather your data and make your calculations quickly."

"Captain," interrupted Dr. Balanov. "Forgive my ignorance, but why are we even discussing this? Shouldn't we move the surviving crew members into the rescue chamber and abandon ship?"

An eerie silence filled the central post, as most of the senior officers looked down or away from the doctor and declined to speak. Sensing that he was missing an important point, he asked, "Why are you looking that way? What is it I do not understand?"

It was Kalinin who finally took pity on poor Balanov. "The reason why we haven't used the VSK, Doctor, is that our port list is too great. The locking mechanism that secures the chamber to the boat is friction-bound. There is no way for us to detach."

"I see," said Balanov nervously. "Thank you for the explanation, Starpom."

"Your report, Doctor," ordered Petrov.

"We have suffered at least six dead and we have over a dozen moderate to serious injuries. At least eight men are missing and are presumed dead. We are compiling a comprehensive list of the deceased, missing, and injured and you will have it within thirty minutes. We also have one psychological casualty."

"Psychological casualty?" inquired Petrov curiously. "Explain."

"I was forced to sedate Captain-Lieutenant Sadilenko.

He suffered a total loss of control and he was becoming a danger to his men."

Both Petrov and Kalinin were now even more confused. Yakov Sadilenko was a most promising young officer with nerves of steel. His performance during the certification trials had been exemplary and he clearly knew his duties. What could have caused him to crack?

Kolesnikov, the chief of damage control, spoke up. "As the commander of compartment five, Sadilenko personally initiated the delivery of the LOKh into compartment six when it appeared that the fire would fully engulf the space. We didn't know if everyone in compartment six had escaped. We couldn't see because of the thick smoke and we couldn't communicate with compartment seven." There was a pause in the narration as Kolesnikov fought to keep his emotions in check. He too was clearly affected.

"There were tears streaming down his face, sir, as I watched him turn the wheel and flood compartment six with Freon gas. After the fire was out, we went into the compartment and found two bodies. Both men had been suffocated by the gas. One of them was Captain Third Rank Aryapov, the commander of compartment six."

Kalinin closed his eyes and turned away, hiding the pain he felt. Petrov felt another blow. Aryapov and Sadilenko were exceptionally close. The joke was that they were twin sons born of different mothers. They worked together, played together, and drank together.

"He fulfilled his duty, comrade Captain," continued Kolesnikov. "But I fear it will cost him his sanity. As soon as he saw Aryapov's contorted face, Yakov knew he had killed him and his mind snapped. It took four of us to pin him down while the doctor administered the sedative."

An uncomfortable, haunting quiet fell upon the participants of the meeting. The grief and stress they all felt was palpable.

"Comrades," spoke Petrov softly, breaking the uneasy silence. "I know we all want to grieve the loss of our friends and shipmates. But unless we are willing to grieve much more, I need you to be focused on securing our survival. We have to fulfill our duty to the living first, then to the dead."

The shallow nodding of heads by all present told Petrov that his gentle admonishment had gotten through. "All right, then. Doctor, what are our biggest challenges, in priority order?"

"We have three major issues to deal with, comrade Captain." Dr. Balanov counted on his fingers as he ran down the list. "Number one. Captain Fonarin is absolutely correct, hypercapnia, carbon dioxide poisoning, is our greatest obstacle. A human being can function with oxygen as low as fourteen percent, and live down to about twelve percent with reduced mental capacities. But if carbon dioxide concentration gets above two percent, there are immediate and significant negative effects. Most prevalent are severe headaches, fatigue, and an increase in the rate of breathing. At five percent, an individual experiences hyperventilation, convulsions, and unconsciousness. Above six percent, death occurs.

"Second is atmospheric pressure. The more gas we release into the compartments, the higher the pressure. If the pressure gets sufficiently high to drive enough atmospheric gasses into our bloodstream, the crew could experience decompression sickness during the rescue operation." Decompression sickness, or the bends, results when an individual breathing compressed air is suddenly moved to an environment with a lower pressure. The gases in the blood form small bubbles that can cause significant pain, and even death if not treated promptly.

"In addition, higher atmospheric pressure will increase the effects of carbon dioxide poisoning. So this must be monitored carefully. Finally, the third issue is hypothermia. Without power for the heating system, the temperature inside the submarine will be down to about two or three degrees Centigrade in a few hours. Every possible effort needs to be taken to try and keep the crew as warm as possible. Excessive cold for long periods, while bad in and of itself, will also exacerbate the carbon dioxide problem."

"Understood, Doctor," Petrov responded, feeling a little more like his old self. Instead of merely reacting to circumstances, he was working with his men to come up with a plan of action to deal with a significant problem. "Starpom, make up a duty roster and limit the number of watchstanders to three: a deck officer, an engineer to keep watch on the reserve battery, and a sonar technician to monitor the underwater communications system."

"Aye, Captain," replied Kalinin. "Do you want a chemical service watchstander to monitor the atmosphere?"

"Fonarin will conduct an air sample once every four hours and report the results to the deck officer and Dr. Balanov. Beyond that, I don't think we need a dedicated watchstander. Everyone else not on watch is to lie down, no unnecessary physical activity. This should reduce the amount of carbon dioxide we produce."

"Captain," said Kolesnikov, "I recommend that we get as many men into survival suits as we can. They were designed for immersion in water and so they should work just as well, if not better, in air. This will help to reduce the chance of hypothermia."

"Good suggestion, Yury. Please, see to the distribution of the suits. Anything else? Anyone?" No one offered a response to the captain's questions.

As the officers collected their notes, Petrov spoke again. "One last item. Tell your men that the situation is not hopeless. We are not just waiting to die. The V-600 emergency distress information buoy was automatically deployed when we hit the ocean floor.

"Northern Fleet Headquarters is aware of our plight and will send all available resources to find us and rescue us. We are taking these measures to give the fleet time to get here, ascertain the situation, and effect a rescue. Emphasize that we need their help if we are to succeed.

"All right, then. You have your assigned duties, comrades, please carry them out with all due diligence. I will await your reports. Dismissed."

Petrov escorted the now-splinted Kalinin up to the central post, where his starpom started to put the watch rotation schedule into effect. Tired and very sore, Petrov walked over to the sonar post and sat down in one of the chairs. It would take his officers a little time to compile the detailed reports, and he just wanted to be off his feet for a minute or two.

An hour later, Kalinin woke him up with the reports in his hands. His demeanor spoke of more bad news. Petrov thanked his first officer and started to read the reports in the dim light.

Dr. Balanov's report was first. Seven crewmen were known dead, with nine missing and presumed to be dead. There were eighteen men with moderate or serious injuries; two were in critical condition, and in the doctor's professional opinion probably would not survive another day. And then there was Sadilenko's mental state. Virtually everyone else had some minor injuries of one form or another.

Petrov did the math in his head. Thirty-five men, well over a third of his crew, were dead or badly hurt. A stiff price to pay for his folly.

Fonarin's report was worse. They only had fifty-eight V-64 cassettes for the chemical air-regeneration units. They'd left port with only an eighty percent loadout and many cassettes had been lost in compartments one, seven, and eight. With sixty-nine men still alive, they only had three days' worth of chemicals. The only good news was that there was adequate electrical power in the reserve battery to run the blowers in the regeneration units for up to six days.

Given their resources and the number of men, Fonarin and Balanov recommended maintaining oxygen at seventeen percent and carbon dioxide at one percent. Dr. Balanov articulated the medical effects of this atmospheric composition, and it was clear they would all be suffering from nasty headaches and fatigue.

Petrov placed the reports on the dead sonar console, his head already throbbing. His thoughts were drawn back to the list of the dead and missing. Sixteen men gone because of him.

No wait, it was likely more than that. He hadn't even thought about the American submarine. Were they on the bottom, struggling to survive? Or were they already dead? He remembered that U.S. submarine designers didn't emphasize survivability like the Russian Navy.

And then he thought of the half-truth he had told his officers. It was true the emergency distress buoy had deployed, but he didn't know if it reached the surface, or that its message actually was sent and received by the Northern Fleet Headquarters. Could all of the measures they were preparing to take be pointless? Were they all doomed to die a slow and painful death from carbon dioxide poisoning?

And why? Just because he couldn't let go of the American after he had beaten him. Suddenly, the words of advice from Vice Admiral Kokurin jumped up from his memory: "Aggressiveness can be a blessing or a curse. If it is not tempered by wisdom, it will lead to recklessness.

And that can have unfortunate consequences. Be my wolfhound, but don't be a rabid one."

A cold sweat broke out on Petrov's brow as he realized he had become rabid during the heat of the hunt. He'd lost control and let emotion replace reason. The loss of sixteen men, and perhaps as many as two hundred, weighed heavily on Petrov's conscience. And there in the dark, cold and alone, Petrov wept.

10

EXIT

While the storm raged above them, *Seawolf* crept westward at the stately speed of four knots. With the bow ripped apart, they really couldn't go faster without something loose banging away. If they were going to leave quietly, this was the best they could do. Unfortunately, at this rate it would take them nearly five days just to get out of the Barents Sea. It was going to be a very long trip to Faslane.

Anxious to reestablish a routine underway schedule, Shimko encouraged his department heads to gently push a sense of normalcy. Jerry wholeheartedly agreed with the XO's plan, but he had reservations. Without the skipper, it wasn't going to fly with the rest of the crew.

Like a symphony conductor, a commanding officer sets the tone and tempo for his command. A good one can meld the various personalities of his crew into a cohesive group that works together in harmony. Without proper direction, the well-meaning efforts of individuals can work at cross-purposes with each other, generating a fair number of sour notes.

Commander Thomas Rudel was a master conductor. He had shaped the crew of *Seawolf* into such a well-oiled machine that they believed there was nothing they couldn't do. He was the quiet motivating force behind the scenes. Without his direct personal involvement, it would be nearly impossible to reestablish anything close to normal on board the boat.

Jerry usually ate dinner at the first sitting, along with the rest of the senior officers. It wasn't so much a class prerogative as a chance for *Seawolf*'s leadership to sit down together. It was amazing how hard it could be to find time for a simple meeting on such a small vessel.

He had heard the supply officer tell the cooks to put on a really good dinner. Constantino knew how important food was to the crew's morale, and he was playing that card for all it was worth. Besides, *Seawolf* would be going into the yards as soon as they returned home. Anything they didn't eat would have to be offloaded. Knowing it was a way they could help, the cooks had worked flat-out, creating a meal that was memorable without being celebratory: fried chicken, mashed potatoes and gravy, greens, fresh biscuits, and three kinds of pie for dessert, including Dutch apple pie, the skipper's favorite.

But Captain Rudel wasn't there. The XO sat in his place, and diverted any questions about the captain by asking his own questions—about the crew or the boat. After a few exchanges of question and counterquestion, they figured out that Shimko wasn't going to budge. The officers shifted their thoughts toward sharing their experiences during the collision. Stories almost bubbled out of the diners, but the discussion quickly turned to the most important topic: the Russian's identity and purpose.

Shimko didn't have to tell the others about Senior Chief Carpenter's information. It's very hard to keep a secret on a submarine, and the identity of the Russian attack sub had spread like wildfire throughout the crew. *Seawolf*'s own sonar techs had come to the same conclusion on the sub's identity. It was a Russian nuclear attack boat, but one that didn't match anything in the database—Q.E.D. *Severodvinsk.* The name *Severodvinsk* now echoed off the bulkheads in discussions all over *Seawolf,* as if it were some mystical creature.

"But what was he doing?" Greg Wolfe was the third to ask the question, but nobody had an answer. Lieutenant Commander Stan Lavoie described the Russian's movements, and the XO confirmed his account. Lieutenant (j.g.) McClelland told the others what the sonar gang knew about the Russian's sonar lashing, and there was general consensus that the Russian was "certifiable."

But the Russians didn't put lunatics in command of nuclear submarines. He'd certainly disrupted their survey. "Could he have been trying to ram the UUV?" asked Wolfe.

Shimko quickly shook his head, chewing. He swallowed and said, "His aim couldn't have been that bad. His mine-hunting sonar would see it. That's a precision set, accurate to within a couple of yards. He was a lot closer to us than to LaVerne."

Everyone at the table agreed that the Russian had "conclusively won" the encounter by disrupting their survey. "But he disrupted our operations the instant he announced his presence," Jerry said. "He didn't need to run circles around us."

"Is that what you call it?" Lavoie grumbled. "'Announcing his presence,' he says. Might as well have used a torpedo."

"He was trying to herd us," Constantino observed. "He cut across our path as we headed northwest."

"That was on his third run," Jerry countered. "On the first two, he passed down our port side, west of us. Was he telling us to sail east, toward the Russian coast?" Even as he said it, Jerry knew that was wrong. Russia was a hundred-plus miles away. Way too far.

"Was he herding us away from something else, then?" Wolfe asked.

"What's out here?" Constantino asked. But they all knew the answer. Nothing but them.

"The UUV. He was trying to herd us away from LaVerne," Wolfe said.

"So he could capture it?" Lavoie asked. "We had it under control the whole time. We could have kept it away from him."

"He didn't know that," Jerry realized. "He must have assumed we had a wire to it. Break the wire, and it goes dead. Then he sits on it until someone arrives to salvage it."

"And the Russians have an intelligence coup," Shimko concluded. "It might have worked, if LaVerne had a tether." He looked around the table. "Anybody see any holes in his theory?"

Jerry couldn't. The Russian captain didn't know that LaVerne was controlled by an acoustic modem. It explained a lot, and Jerry kicked himself mentally. He should have thought of that. It would have been simple to deceive them . . .

"I'll take it to the Captain," Shimko concluded, and stood. Everyone else turned to finishing dinner. There was still a second seating, and the discussion seemed to be finished.

It was Will Hayes who finally asked the one question that had eluded everyone. "What about the Russian? What do you think happened to him?"

Jerry's first thought was reflexive: He didn't want to know about him, and he didn't want to think about him.

But the question demanded an answer. He'd been damaged, certainly, but Russian subs were double-hulled, with internal compartmentalization that U.S. boats lacked. Their design philosophy had a significant emphasis on survivability, while U.S. designers focused predominantly on stealth. All other things being equal, the Russian sub was probably in better shape than they were.

"He wasn't waiting for us when we submerged," Lavoie reported. "If he headed south, toward home, while we were headed west, then we'll never see him again."

"Fine with me. He'll be back in his home port before we get to Faslane," Wolfe concluded.

"He found us easily enough out here," Jerry remarked pessimistically. "I hope none of his friends know how to do that trick."

"Which is why we're headed westward at our best speed," Shimko remarked, standing at the door to the wardroom. "Mr. Mitchell, the Captain has some questions for you." He didn't ask whether Jerry was finished with his meal.

Jerry followed the XO back up to the captain's cabin. The door was closed, and Shimko knocked, but hardly waited before opening it.

For a moment, Jerry thought the XO was waking Rudel, because the only light was from the lamp over his desk. But that didn't make sense. The captain had just asked to see him.

Rudel was sitting in his chair, tipped back against the bulkhead, a pad of paper in his lap. Jerry could see a few lines scrawled at the top, but the pen lay on the table next to him. He didn't speak, or even look up when Shimko opened the door.

"Sir, here's Mr. Mitchell. You wanted to ask him about tethered vehicles," Shimko prompted.

Rudel raised his head without moving the chair. It was

hard to see in the dark, but from what Jerry could tell, Captain Rudel looked terrible. His face was drawn, and there were dark areas under his eyes. He saw Jerry and the XO, then straightened up in the chair but didn't stand. "Mr. Mitchell, do you think the Russian sub was trying to cut a line between the UUV and *Seawolf*?"

"Yes, sir, I do." Admitting it made Jerry feel more guilty. Understanding that one fact could have changed everything. Rountree might still be alive.

The captain leaned back, seemingly satisfied, but the XO spoke up. "You've been to school on these ROVs, haven't you?"

"Yessir, before I reported to *Memphis*."

"Do most of our vehicles use a tether?"

"Many do, sir. Only the LMRS and our UUVs are untethered."

"What about the Russians? Did you learn anything about their ROVs?"

"We spent some time reviewing their technology in class."

"Is their stuff tethered?"

"Yes, sir. What little they have."

The XO's questions occupied Rudel's attention but the captain didn't ask or say anything else until the XO said, "That's all, then."

As Jerry started to turn, Rudel called him by name. "Jerry. I was sorry to hear about Dennis Rountree."

"Yes, sir."

"I want to have a short service when we pull into Faslane. They'll take the body off then, and it will give the crew a chance to say good-bye. Please set it up."

"Yes, sir."

"I'll make a few remarks, and some of his friends may want to say good-bye. But keep it short. This isn't a funeral. That will come later, after we're back."

"I understand, sir. I'll take care of everything."

"Very good. Dismissed."

Jerry left the captain's cabin confused. Rudel had been more interested in Rountree's memorial service than the UUV issue, and he hadn't asked one question about the down equipment, which was his responsibility. And he looked like hell.

Jerry had watched Rudel in control during the encounter. Shoot, everybody had watched the skipper for orders, for guidance. He'd been in control, and he'd asked all the right questions, done all the right things. At least, Jerry thought so. But *Seawolf* was hurt and someone was dead.

Jerry made his rounds, visiting all his department's spaces. He always did this before the eight o'clock reports. Chief Hudson was overseeing the work in the electronics equipment space. Electronics modules and test equipment were stacked against the bulkhead, almost blocking movement.

And there was a lot of movement. Jerry saw his ETs and ITs, and one of his off-watch quartermasters, but also sonar techs and even auxiliarymen. "Everybody's helping," Hudson explained. "We'll work through the night, and with this many people, we can take it in shifts."

Hudson's cheerful attitude drove out some of Jerry's gloom. He was able to give Shimko an upbeat report at eight that evening. It looked very good for one HF receiver to be up by early tomorrow morning. They weren't sure about any of the transmitters yet. They were in worse condition, but Hudson and Morrison hadn't given up.

The XO wasn't as cheerful. "So we can get a weather report. Wonderful." Then he remembered himself and added, "Tell your guys that they're doing a great job. Keep me apprised. And I need the encounter timeline."

"Yessir. I'll start on it tonight."

"Good, but don't pull an all-nighter. Nobody's life is at stake anymore. We're on our way home. And this needs to be done right."

"Understood."

Jerry headed for control. That was where all the data was—logs, navigation and geo plots, fire-control chits, sonar tapes. It took some time just to gather it all. It was the quartermasters' responsibility to maintain the logs, and Jerry called QM1 Peters to properly label all the documents. At this point, they were legal records. Evidence to be used in an investigation.

By the time he'd assembled everything, it was late, and Jerry decided to make a fresh start in the morning. He made one more visit to the electronics space, then headed for his stateroom. Lieutenant Chandler was working at his desk, but they ignored each other as Jerry set his alarm for five and gratefully hit the rack.

IT WAS bright, the sunlight from a clear sky doubled as it reflected off a concrete runway. His helmet visor was down, reducing the glare. Jerry watched the instruments as he advanced the throttle. He felt the engines pushing hard, fighting the brakes, but he counted carefully, waiting. The engine temperatures stayed in the green, and he released the brakes.

Jerry recognized the dream. He'd been here many times before. He watched the speed on the heads-up display shoot up, the numbers quickly passing one hundred knots, then one-twenty, one-forty, changing as quickly as he could read them. The runway became a white blur in front of the nose. He'd have takeoff speed any second.

There he felt the whole airframe shudder, and the nose swerved right. He'd blown a tire. Used to making featherlight corrections, he was slow correcting, but even full left on the controller didn't stop the swerve. He'd chopped the throttles, but that didn't help either. He was almost crossways on the runway, still moving, and he felt the right wing lift up. He was going to roll.

He reached for the loops at the top of the ejection seat, but they weren't there, and instead of sitting in the cockpit of his Hornet, he was standing now, in the bridge cockpit of *Seawolf,* but they were submerged, and he could see the Russian sub. It was to his right, bow-on.

It was huge, and he could see every detail of the boat—the pattern of the anechoic tiles on the hull, the silver patch of the bow sonar window, the intake scoops back by engineering. In spite of the props furiously churning the water, it was almost motionless, pointing straight at him. Jerry frantically tried to avoid the oncoming vessel, but no matter which way he turned *Seawolf,* the Russian's bearing never changed.

He never saw the collision, but suddenly he was hanging in the air from his chute over the twisted wreckage of *Seawolf* and the Russian submarine, lying together across the runway. Rescuers and emergency vehicles crowded around the two crushed hulls, reminding him of a train wreck.

Then he was standing next to an ambulance, and they were loading Dennis Rountree into it. He was looking at Jerry, and Jerry kept saying, "I'm sorry," louder and louder, but Rountree kept shaking his head, as if he couldn't hear. Then they started loading the rest of the crew into the ambulance, first Rudel, then Shimko, and then some of the chiefs, then . . .

The alarm woke him, shivering and disoriented. He lay in his bunk for several minutes, reaching out to touch the bulkheads and familiar objects around him. Jerry read and reread the time on the alarm clock. He recited the name of his boat, his billet, where they were. The images from the dream lingered, and he had to work to shake them off.

Jerry got up and silently dressed and washed. Chandler was asleep, but the red light in the stateroom was enough for his purposes.

His first stop was control. They were on course, on track for Faslane. QM2 Dunn seemed barely awake, but he'd tended the chart properly.

The electronics equipment space looked cleaner, but red danger tags hung from a lot of the gear, and two ratings were at work. He didn't bother them. He'd get a report from Chief Hudson before breakfast. Instead, he headed back to control.

It was quiet at that hour, and he took over one of the plotting tables, used only when they were tracking a target. Will Hayes was the OOD, and after making sure that he couldn't be of any help, left Jerry to his work.

He started building a timeline on his laptop, first working with the deck log. That recorded all the course and speed changes along with all the reports from other stations. The sonar logs told him when the other boat was detected, its bearing, and gave hints about its speed and direction.

Breakfast time came and went, but Jerry was on a roll. It felt good, satisfying, to patiently piece together the scraps of data into a coherent picture. Order from chaos, reason from insanity. And it drove out the unpleasant images from his dream.

He wasn't looking for patterns or meaning, not yet. He didn't have a lot of good information on the Russian's position, only his bearing and range from *Seawolf* when the wide aperture array had a good lock on him. He didn't know exactly when the Russian had changed course. That took time to compute, given the sparse range data to work with, and the Russian had maneuvered often and quickly.

STSC Carpenter showed up in control after breakfast. He brought Jerry coffee and one of the cook's sweet rolls, and more data. Carpenter's report was clearly an extract of their analysis, and Jerry wondered what they'd found out but couldn't share with him. He noticed that their Russian was described as probably a new "first line nuclear attack sub."

But what they'd shared with him was very helpful. Because they could see the narrowband tonals from the Russian's propulsion train, they'd been able to figure out when his speed had changed, and calculated what his speed was as he passed by them. Like an ambulance with its siren blaring, the sound changes as the ambulance approaches you and then drives by. At the closest point of approach, the noise from the Russian submarine was what he really sounded like. With this data, the sonar techs were able to map his propulsion train and thus, determine his speed.

Hudson came by with a progress report, and Jerry asked him to brief the XO as well.

Jerry was adding in speed changes from the engineering log when he realized that the XO was standing behind him.

"Good morning, sir."

"You've made a lot of progress, Jerry."

"It's incomplete, XO."

"And it will be, unless the Russian's deck log is in that pile somewhere," remarked Shimko with a broad grin. Then more seriously, "Still, it will be very useful."

He leaned closer, as if to examine the plot, and spoke softly. "I'm hoping it will convince the captain that the collision was not his fault."

Jerry had to fight to control his reaction. The encounter had been hashed over last night, and he heard it rehashed in the control room this morning. Most of the crew thought they were lucky to be alive, and that Rudel had been the only thing keeping them from an icy, wet end.

When Jerry didn't immediately reply, Shimko explained. "You know how much the Skipper cares about this crew and this boat. They're a part of him. He's hurting because *Seawolf* is hurting. I checked on him a couple times during the night, and he didn't sleep at all. He just sat there, writing draft after draft of a letter to Rountree's parents."

Jerry felt another pang of responsibility himself. In the back of his mind he'd been trying to see if he'd missed a chance to grasp the Russian's purpose. It was hard to second-guess a "failure of the imagination," but he kept thinking that he should have realized what was happening.

"I would like to show him, and anyone else, Jerry, that given the circumstances we were in, and the data we had on hand, Tom Rudel made the right calls."

Shimko straightened up and Jerry saw that he didn't look like he had slept much either. As if on cue, the XO stretched and stifled a deep yawn.

"Keep at it, Jerry. I need a logical, cogent analysis of the events leading up to the collision if I'm going to get through to the Skipper. Stay objective. I need an honest assessment based on facts, not sympathy. The Captain isn't about to let us blow sunshine up his skirt."

"Yes, sir. I'll do my best."

The XO nodded appreciatively. Then, reaching down and putting his hand on Jerry's shoulder, he said, "A wise man once said, 'The difficulties in life are intended to make us better, not bitter.' Well, right now, our Captain is slowly gnawing away at his stomach lining based on a belief that he made a mistake. We need to show him, if we can, that it wasn't his fault. We owe him that much, at least."

BY LUNCHTIME, Jerry had a draft master plot with all the data mixed together. He looked at the plot he'd been working on for hours. *Seawolf*'s track was a solid line; gently curving except for the hard turns Rudel had made to avoid the Russian. Lines radiated out from different points along the track, showing the bearing and range information to the Russian sub. Data tables along the margins listed other information. Unfortunately, no matter how neatly he arranged it, he still had squat.

Even with the data he had, the likely errors in the information made it difficult to make the conclusive case the XO wanted. This wasn't going to be enough to convince the captain. A gurgling sound from his stomach made it clear that the sticky bun he had early just wasn't enough. Jerry needed a break, and he needed some more eyes on the problem.

He took the plot and a printout of his timeline to lunch and showed it to the rest of the wardroom. They passed the diagram around, chewing over the dry facts, reviewing the collision again. The most concrete data that had come out of Jerry's work had been that their relative speed at the time of contact was eighteen knots, and that the angle between the two boats' bows at impact was about sixty-four degrees. Useful but unsatisfying.

Jeff Palmer traced the UUV's movements, looking for any relationship between them and the Russian. He didn't see any, but he did find a problem. "This track isn't right," he told Jerry. "Our data show a lot more maneuvers."

"The deck log shows all the commands we sent to LaVerne," Jerry said, a little defensively.

"And they were all brilliantly executed," Palmer agreed,

"but she also maneuvered on her own. When the Russian showed up, all big and noisy and closing fast, her collision-avoidance routines kicked in. If the UUV senses a potential collision risk, it locates the offending unit and moves to open the range."

"And she found out where the sub was . . ." Jerry started.

". . . by using her active sonar," Palmer completed. "We can get range and bearing readouts for both *Seawolf* and the Russian from LaVerne for most of the Russian's maneuvers."

Jerry kicked himself. The UUV's sonars were high-definition imaging sets, with wonderful resolution but very short range. They were not designed for general search, so he hadn't thought of using LaVerne's sensor logs.

Jerry and Palmer stood up from their seats at almost the same moment. "It'll take some time to print out the logs from LaVerne's memory," Palmer reminded him.

"Then I'll work off the console until you have them," Jerry answered. He left his lunch unfinished.

HE REPORTED to Shimko's cabin three hours later, beaming, with Palmer in tow. "It was better than we thought, sir," Jerry explained. "Not only did LaVerne track the Russian with her active sonar, but her imaging sonars also intercepted the Russian's mine-hunting set. They overlapped frequency bands."

Armed with this new data, Jerry had completely redrawn the plot. The fan of passive bearing lines with a range dot here and there was gone, and two dark lines ran across the paper. The black line, *Seawolf*'s, was curved in places, but was the straighter of the two by far. The red line spiraled and danced across *Seawolf*'s track. LaVerne's line was a dark green, like an innocent bystander. Her track now showed two arcing turns as she avoided the advancing Russian, before finally heading northwest.

Shimko took it eagerly, praising both of them. Then his face fell as he comprehended their maneuvers. "My God." He paused and looked up at the two officers. "I'm assuming you've double-checked these tracks—scales, bearings. That I'm reading these distances correctly."

Jerry quickly nodded. "Yes sir, the data from LaVerne is of better fidelity, but it closely matches our own. The distances are correct."

On the first pass, the Russian had approached to 372 yards, not a lot compared to *Seawolf*'s length of 360 feet. The second pass had been at only 186 yards, frighteningly close when combined with the Russians' speed of nearly thirty knots.

"Wise man says 'If dancing with crazy person, listen to crazy music.' There's no way we could have dodged this guy." He stood up abruptly, rolling up the plot, and began marching toward the door. Jerry and Palmer stepped back so Shimko could walk into the passageway. "Let's go brief the Skipper."

The lights were on in the captain's cabin this time, and Rudel was at his desk. He was pale, almost white, and his face was deeply lined. Jerry remembered a friend who looked that way after he'd broken an arm. He knew the captain hadn't slept.

Shimko handed Rudel the plot. "Please, look at this, sir."

The captain cleared a spot on his desk and laid the plot out carefully. All three officers watched as he studied the chart piece by piece. First the label and legend, then the supplementary tables, and then, finally, the tracks of the two submarines and the UUV.

"This is where I turned right to open the range on the first pass?" Rudel pointed to a mark on *Seawolf*'s track.

"Yes, sir," Jerry answered.

"And this is the second turn," Rudel observed, but this time he said it as a statement, not a question. He picked up a straightedge and laid it along *Seawolf*'s track. "If I hadn't opened the range, the closest point of approach would have been 250 yards the first time."

He moved the straightedge. "The second time it would have been"—he checked the scale—"less than a hundred yards."

"It reminds me of when I visited Naples. The Italians all drove like that." Jerry regretted the joke as soon as he'd said it, but even Rudel laughed.

"Maybe the Russians have been studying Italian submarine tactics," Rudel observed. Jerry knew Rudel had a good sense of humor. It was one of the reasons, and one of the ways, he'd connected so well with his crew.

Rudel looked at the three officers, then slowly paced in the small space allowed to a sub's commanding officer. "*Seawolf* was a dream assignment for me. A top-notch crew and a first-line sub in its prime. I've worked my whole life to be here.

"I realize why you wanted me to see this plot, and what you wanted me to know. I understand now that the collision was not my fault, or more properly, not the result of a bad decision by me. But Denny Rountree is still dead, and there could have been more, possibly many more. It has to make you stop and think. Question your choices, and your motives."

Jerry listened to the captain carefully, absorbing and trying to understand. He too had been walking down that same road of self-pity.

Nobody said anything for a moment. Then the XO said, "Dwelling on the negative simply contributes to its power."

"More fortune cookie philosophy, Marcus?" responded Rudel with a weary smile. "I hear what you're saying, but it's hard for me to admit that I couldn't get us out of that situation. That I had so little control."

Shimko shrugged his shoulders, "We like to think we are in control, but the truth is, we can't eliminate every risk."

Even as he nodded, Rudel said, "This was a stupid risk, one nobody should have had to take. Part of me wants to throttle the idiot Russian captain. He endangered his boat as well as ours, and he's back home, getting a pat on the back from the Commander of the Northern Fleet for chasing us off.

"Meanwhile, we go home with a crippled boat, a man dead, and many more injured, on what was supposed to have been a cakewalk. And we failed to complete our mission."

Jerry was almost glad the captain hadn't slept last night. He didn't even want to try and imagine the kind of dreams he would have had.

Jerry finally spoke. "Sir, we took those risks with you, and we'd do it again, the same way, if you asked us to. We're all behind you."

Rudel gave another small, tired smile. "That means a lot, Jerry. Thank you." He straightening up, and Jerry saw his "old" CO emerge from the ghost he had seen moments earlier. "So we go home, bury our dead, and heal. Simple enough."

Lieutenant Chandler appeared in the passageway, coming aft from control. Chiefs Hudson and Morrison were both with him, and all three were smiling.

11

SLOW REACTION

5 October 2008
Twenty-fourth Atomic Submarine Diviziya Headquarters, Sayda Guba Submarine Base

Rear Admiral Vidchenko stared out his office window, slowly sipping a steaming cup of coffee. The storm had descended with its full fury on the base, and gale-force winds pounded the office building with a wintry mix of snow, sleet, and rain. He glanced at the clock on the wall, 0845, over half an hour since the morning's main fleet support broadcast window had closed. His chief of staff was late in bringing him the morning's communiqués.

Vidchenko's mood matched the foul weather outside. He wondered again why he had accepted this posting in the first place. Sayda Guba was nothing but a primitive frontier outpost in comparison to the cosmopolitan air of Saint Petersburg, a fact his wife never tired of berating him with. Two years, he thought. In two years he could leave this godforsaken land for a comfortable staff position in Moscow, or even back in Saint Petersburg. For two years he could tolerate this cultural exile to the far north. He wasn't sure his marriage would, though. A knock at the door broke his brooding.

"Enter," he snapped.

"Good morning, sir," said Captain First Rank Boris Shepenetnov. "I apologize for being late, but there have been base-wide power problems because of the storm. The communications specialists just printed out your messages."

"Hrmph," growled Vidchenko as he sat. He was well aware there were power outages. He'd shaved by candlelight this morning in his quarters. Shepenetnov placed the folder on the desk in front of the admiral and stepped back. Vidchenko scanned the summary list of messages in the folder, and then shot a glaring look at his chief of staff. "Still no word from Petrov?"

"Er, no sir. Nothing was received from *Severodvinsk* this morning."

"I see," replied Vidchenko with growing displeasure. "Tell me, Captain, does every senior officer in this diviziya treat routine deadlines with such callous disregard?" He slapped the folder with his hand to emphasize his point.

"Not at all, comrade Admiral," answered Shepenetnov defensively. "Captain Petrov has been extremely punctual in maintaining his twice-daily communication schedule. In fact, this is the first time he has ever missed a routine communications period. Either the tactical situation or the elements preclude him from doing so."

"Nothing should preclude him from following orders, Captain!" Vidchenko bellowed as he jumped to his feet. "It has been my experience as a submarine captain that even in tactical contact with an enemy unit it was possible to report in without compromising my position."

"With all due respect, Admiral, this is not the Baltic Fleet." Shepenetnov paused as he forced himself to settle down. He couldn't afford to lose his temper, not with this admiral. If he continued down this road, it would only result in charges of insubordination. No, Rear Admiral Vidchenko could only be dealt with if one ignored his adversarial nature and focused on the topic at hand. One had to keep to the facts and pay no attention to his barbs.

The chief of staff appreciated Vidchenko's disciplined approach to running the diviziya. He had little tolerance for pomp and circumstance, thank God, but he lived for schedules and procedures. If schedules weren't kept and procedures not followed, he would lash out in rage at the offending individual. While not a bad trait in and of itself, Vidchenko's views were heavily biased by his experience in the Baltic Sea, a well-mannered duck pond in comparison to the Northern Fleet's operating area.

"Sir, Petrov's last report is just over twenty-five hours old and he was headed into an area with considerable sea ice. Given the high sea states over the past fourteen hours, it would be foolish to hoist a communications antenna in such an environment. It would be crushed in seconds."

"I am well versed on the limitations of our submarines' antenna complexes, Captain," Vidchenko said with a sneer. "The point is that Petrov has missed not one, but two regular communication periods, and by fleet procedures I need to report him as missing."

"Technically, sir," countered Shepenetnov patiently. "You have the discretion to wait until the first alternate period is missed, five hours from now."

"I intend to do so, but I will not tolerate any of my commanding officers failing to follow fleet protocols. I will deal with Petrov when he returns. Is there anything else of importance to report?"

Relieved that the subject of the discussion was changing, Shepenetnov opened his binder, skimmed down the list, and said, "Only one other matter, sir. PLAs *Vepr* and *Tigr* were required to conduct an emergency start-up of their reactors due to a loss of shore power. It appears that their pier lost its transmission station. Repairs won't be made until after the storm passes."

Vidchenko sat down as he listened to the additional bad news, a sour expression appearing on his face. "And when do the forecasters predict this storm will pass us by?"

"This is supposed to be the worst of it, sir. They expect conditions to slowly improve in the next two days."

"So for the next three or four days, precious reactor core life will have to be expended to keep those two submarines livable. What a waste!" Vidchenko almost spat as he spoke those last few words. He quickly scribbled down a note to have yet another discussion with the base commander about the shoddy support his submarines were getting.

"Will there be anything else, comrade Admiral?" inquired Shepenetnov, eager to leave.

"Yes, Captain. Instruct the commanding officers of *Vepr* and *Tigr* to institute rigorous electrical power consumption procedures. Only vital equipment and minimal environment support are to be used until repairs to the pier's transmission stations are made. And send out a message to Petrov ordering him to report his status on the prosecution of the American submarine. Perhaps we can jog his memory to follow routine procedures."

Severodvinsk

"Captain. Captain, time to wake up." The voice was faint at first, but grew steadily louder. Suddenly there was a bright white light; Petrov recoiled from its intensity. Instinctively he threw his hands up to block it while grumbling, "Turn the damn light off!"

"He appears to be in reasonable health, Starpom, given the circumstances. He's going to be a bit stiff, and he'll probably experience headaches, but I don't believe he has a concussion," reported Balanov.

"Thank you, Doctor," replied Kalinin, a note of relief in his voice.

Still a bit groggy, Petrov rubbed his face and eyes. He started to shiver, and he pulled the loose blanket around him for warmth. "Would someone please tell me what is going on?" he demanded testily.

"Certainly, sir," said Balanov. "You've been asleep for over twelve hours, and your Starpom here became worried when he couldn't wake you. Naturally, I was very concerned with this report. I was afraid that you might have suffered a concussion during the collision and had slipped into a coma. My examination, though belated, indicates that you are in relatively good condition; barring the minor injuries to your head and shoulder."

The tone of the doctor's voice revealed he was still a little irritated with his captain, but Petrov had insisted that the rest of the crew be tended to first. The delay could have been life-threatening, but fortunately that was not the case this time. Treating a patient with a serious concussion would have severely stressed the medical department's already meager resources. This false alarm only heightened the doctor's frustration that he lacked the proper means to deal with many of the more serious injuries.

"Your concern is noted, and appreciated, Doctor. Oomph," Petrov grunted as he pulled himself up. The doctor was right. He was very stiff and sore. "How is the rest of the crew?"

"Starpom Kalinin has my most recent report, he can repeat it as well as I. I must tend to my other patients. With your permission, sir?"

"Very well, Doctor, you are dismissed." Petrov watched as Balanov slowly made his way out of the sonar post. His movements were wooden, his demeanor weary. As he entered the central command post, Petrov called out to him, "Thank you again, Doctor, for looking after my crew and me."

The doctor nodded curtly, a faint smile on his face, and then resumed his walk back to the makeshift hospital.

After Balanov was out of sight, Petrov motioned with his head in the doctor's direction and asked, "How's he doing, Vasiliy? He doesn't look good."

"He hasn't slept a wink since the collision, Captain. He's simply exhausted. On top of that, he hasn't had the best of days."

Petrov was starting to get used to the steady stream of bad news, but his starpom's tone and expression made it clear this was on the bad side of bad. Intuitively, he knew another member of the crew had died.

"Who?"

"Warrant Officer Kotkov and Senior Lieutenant Annekov," said Kalinin quietly.

Petrov's face reflected the pain he felt. The doctor had warned him earlier that it was likely that they would lose two more, but that wasn't much help now that reality had reared its ugly head. Shaken by the news, he leaned heavily on the chair to steady himself. Kalinin sympathized with his commander; he had felt the same pain a few hours earlier. Without being prompted, he provided additional details. "Kotkov died from severe blood loss, while Annekov died from complications of smoke inhalation. I've had the bodies placed in one of the portside torpedo tubes."

With his jaw firmly clenched, Petrov nodded his understanding and approval. Fighting to hold himself together, he was barely able to ask his next question. "What is our status?"

"Oxygen is at seventeen and a half percent and carbon dioxide is at one percent. We brought six air-regeneration units online at 2100 hours last night. The second set of regeneration cassettes will be depleted within a couple of hours. The units are quite popular with the crew right now."

Each air-regeneration cassette contained a series of chemical plates coated with highly reactive potassium hyperoxide and sodium superoxide compounds. These chemicals reacted with the moisture in the air to absorb carbon dioxide and replace it with oxygen. A beneficial side effect of the chemical reaction was that it generated a lot of heat, which was exhausted into the compartment by a blower in each regeneration unit. It was noticeably warmer near one of these machines and the crew tended to congregate around them.

"We have conducted an inventory of our emergency food and water supplies," continued Kalinin, "and with proper rationing, we can make them last for six or seven days. Chief Engineer Lyachin, however, believes he can gain access to one of the potable water tanks, which would greatly extend our water reserves." At this point, Kalinin stopped, shook his head, and started to laugh. This abrupt change caught Petrov off guard, and it snapped him out of his dark mood. Watching Kalinin laugh, Petrov wondered whether his starpom was already suffering from oxygen deprivation.

"What's so funny, Vasiliy?"

"Ohhh, it's Sergey and his boys," chortled Kalinin. "For the last six hours they have been calculating and debating on the best way to allocate power from the reserve battery. Our Chief Engineer called it a practical exercise." The starpom clearly found the engineers' wording to be rather humorous, and he had to pause before he was able to speak clearly.

"Anyway, after much discussion and brandishing of calculators, the engineering department has come up with a plan to briefly turn off two regeneration units each day and use the power to heat up some water to make tea and coffee for the crew. Did you know that those sneaky engineers had their own stash of coffee and tea?"

Petrov shrugged. "I wouldn't be surprised. Submarine engineers are notorious for finding creative storage methods for just about anything. How many stills have you found in your career?"

"Too many. And their output always tasted the same—hideous." He grimaced at the very thought of the foul-tasting, clear liquid common to all illegal distilleries. "But Lyachin and company have enough coffee and tea for every man to have two cups a day! Of course, the doctor is an enthusiastic supporter of the idea."

"Have you checked their figures?"

"Yes, sir. I went over everything with the Chief Engineer. With the six devices drawing approximately the same amount of power, we should have sufficient battery capacity for seven, or even eight days if we are lucky."

"So, once again it gets back to the carbon dioxide issue," Petrov asserted. "We have enough food, water, oxygen, and power for about a week, a little more if we are very thrifty. But within five days we'll be at lethal concentrations for carbon dioxide."

"Fonarin's estimate gives us five and a half days," Kalinin replied soberly.

Both men fell silent, a little uncomfortable with the cold, callous direction their conversation had taken. While they both cared deeply about the crew, their training drove them to deal with the stark facts in an objective, if mechanical, manner. Acknowledging the reality of a particular situation, even if the process seems uncaring, is the foundation for sound decision-making. And given their circumstances, they couldn't afford to make any poor decisions. The uneasy quiet lasted for only a few moments before Petrov broke it with a question.

"How's the crew's morale?"

"All things considered, sir, surprisingly good. The men are convinced that we will be rescued."

Petrov looked closely at Kalinin as he spoke. His face didn't mirror the confidence of his statement. Something was bothering him. Petrov could sense it.

"But?" he asked.

Warily, Kalinin eyed the doorway, making sure that no one was close by. Once he was sure their conversation would stay private, he leaned forward and whispered.

"Captain, I have listened to the underwater communications system several times while you were sleeping. There is a bitch of a storm up there. Ice floes are being tossed about like children's toys. I don't believe the distress buoy can survive in that kind of environment. In fact, we don't know if it even reached the surface intact. How can we be certain that the Northern Fleet Headquarters knows we're missing? Or even if they do, where to look for us?"

It was Petrov's turn to chuckle, much to his starpom's surprise.

"Am I certain they know we are missing right now? No. Am I confident that they will know in about six hours? Yes."

Kalinin looked at his watch, it read 0918, and understood what his captain was referring to. Still unconvinced, he began to argue with Petrov.

"How can you be so sure? Even though we've missed two regular communications periods, any one of our senior commanders could easily rationalize that given our last known heading, and the weather conditions, that we simply couldn't check in. They'd wait until after the storm abated before they would recognize that we are really missing!"

"Vasiliy, Vasiliy, you don't understand our diviziya commander very well, do you?" replied Petrov patiently. "Rear Admiral Vidchenko's very existence is defined by procedures, protocols, and schedules. He is one of those, oh, how do you put it, one of those loathsome bureaucratic assholes."

Kalinin looked down, a sheepish grin on his face, and admitted his guilt. "Yes, I uh . . . I seem to recall saying something like that once or twice."

"Well, it's true! If the instructions required Vidchenko to swim to each pier in the performance of his duties, he would stoically dive in headfirst, dress uniform and all, and execute a flawless breaststroke. That is just how the man works.

"No, Vasiliy, I have already been reprimanded in absentia for my flagrant violation of fleet procedures. By 1505 this afternoon, he *will* call Vice Admiral Borisov and report us missing. After that, those very same procedures will start things in motion automatically. The fleet *will* come for us."

Petrov shifted his weight around, getting a solid footing on the canted deck, as he prepared to leave the sonar post, but before he started walking, he turned once more to Kalinin and said, "You are right about one thing, Vasiliy. That is a devil of a storm and it won't be easy for the fleet to find us in the middle of this mess. And even if they do, they certainly wouldn't be able to deploy a rescue submersible in those seas. Those huge chunks of ice would crush it in an instant. But all we can do about that, Vasiliy, is pray. Pray that the storm will pass soon and that the fleet will find us quickly. Before it's too late."

Northern Fleet Headquarters, Severomorsk

Vice Admiral Kokurin growled at the growing pile of messages from his eskadra and base commanders. All of them spoke of minor damage inflicted by the storm to the Northern Fleet's elderly infrastructure. Individually the damage was annoying, but collectively it was becoming more than just a nuisance. Finding the funds necessary to pay for the repairs was going to be difficult, particularly since the budget year was coming to a close and the fleet's operating accounts had been sorely depleted by the aggressive training schedule.

"Why are you being so inhospitable, Grandfather Winter?" whined Kokurin to himself. A storm of this magnitude, so early in the season, did not bode well for the rest of the winter. The fleet commander wrote down a reminder to speak with the chief of rear services about ensuring an adequate fuel oil supply for the bases. He finished and was about to pick up his cup of tea when the intercom buzzer rang.

"Yes," answered Kokurin.

"Sir, Vice Admiral Borisov is on line one. He says he needs to speak to you about an urgent matter."

"Thank you." Reaching over, he picked up the phone and hit the blinking line.

"Greetings, Pavel Dmitriyevich, how are things at Sayda Guba?"

There was only silence on the line, and Kokurin thought that he had lost his connection with Borisov. "Pavel, are you there?"

"Yes, sir, I am still here," Borisov replied with some hesitation. Kokurin could hear him taking a deep breath. Something terrible must have happened.

"Steady yourself, Pavel. Tell me, what is wrong?"

"Admiral, I regret to inform you that *Severodvinsk* hasn't been heard from for thirty hours. Since Petrov has uncharacteristically missed two fleet communications periods, I am requesting you declare an emergency alert."

Kokurin sat up straight in his chair; he couldn't believe what he was hearing. "Thirty hours?" he repeated. "Did you send out messages ordering him to make contact?"

"Yes, sir. We have sent out three messages within the

last six hours telling Petrov to break off pursuit and respond. There has been no reply."

"Do you think he is still under the sea ice? That would limit his ability to communicate."

"We looked into that possibility, sir," Borisov admitted. "Unfortunately, we don't have a good position for *Severodvinsk.* His last reported location was just on the edge of the ice zone, and the Amga buoy he was heading toward is only eight miles inside the zone. Even at a standard bell, Petrov could have cleared the sea ice within an hour or two, raised an antenna, and reported in. This kind of behavior is totally unlike Petrov, sir. We are very concerned that something dreadful has happened. Sir, I repeat my request for you to issue Signal Number Six."

"Very well, Pavel, I concur. I will issue the alert," said Kokurin. "Make sure my staff has all your data and analysis."

"Aye, aye, sir. Thank you, sir."

"Don't thank me yet. You can see what the weather outside is like just as well as I can. Rescue missions under the best of circumstances are a difficult undertaking. With this storm, it may be impossible. But, I will do what I can."

"I know, sir," replied a solemn Borisov.

"Keep me apprised of any new developments," ordered Kokurin.

"Understood, Admiral. Good-bye."

"Good-bye, Pavel."

As the old admiral hung up the phone, his mind started racing. A hundred questions sprung up, and he had answers for none of them. Rubbing his thinly covered head with his hands, he wondered if they had lost yet another submarine and a brave crew. Slamming the desk with his fist, he cursed the fear that was gripping him. There was no time for self-pity. Hitting the intercom button, Kokurin summoned his deputy.

"Boris, get in here immediately. Bring Georgy with you."

Within seconds, both men hurried through the door. They knew their boss well enough to know that something was wrong. As they approached the fleet commander's desk, he began firing off orders at them.

"Boris, I am declaring an emergency alert. Have the communications officer issue Signal Number Six. *Severodvinsk* is thirty hours overdue and is considered missing. I want the readiness status of every vessel in the Atlantic Squadron within the hour, and I want them to prepare to sail at a moment's notice. And get me the latest weather forecasts for the next week."

Vice Admiral Baybarin furiously wrote down his instructions. He was full of curiosity, but there would be time for questions later. He bolted from the room as soon as Kokurin barked, "Now go!"

Vice Admiral Radetskiy was next, and he anxiously awaited his orders.

"Georgy, contact the Chief of the Search and Rescue Services and have him prepare *Mikhail Rudnitskiy* for departure within six hours. Tell him to bring as many functional rescue and salvage submersibles as he can. Coordinate with the Commander, Twelfth Nuclear Submarine Eskadra for specific information on *Severodvinsk*'s last known position and their analysis of the sub's possible location. Move!"

As the chief of staff left, Kokurin looked at the clock on his desk. It read 1529. He should see the emergency message in about ten minutes. Turning to face the window, he watched as the snow was whipped about by the gale-force winds. The dreariness of the afternoon matched his mood. The real question now was whether or not a rescue force could actually leave in the middle of this accursed storm. God willing, the ships should be ready to get underway by the early evening hours. Now, if Grandfather Winter would only cooperate.

National Security Agency, Fort Meade, Maryland

Jack Ferguson was already bored. It was less than two hours into his shift, and there wasn't much going on in the Russian Northern Fleet AOR. The winter storm had really shut things down. It's going to be a very long day, he thought.

"Hey, Jack," called Paul Anderson, Ferguson's supervisor, "anything good on the Russia Northern Fleet channel?"

"Nope, they're getting the snot beaten out of them by that storm. Overall traffic volume is way down, and most of the stuff is administrative shit. I did have one message, though, about ten minutes ago that had an urgent precedence. Nothing much since."

"Well, it certainly makes sense to just hunker down in that kind of weather," responded Anderson. "You know what this place is like if we get even an inch of snow. Say, I'm going down to the cafeteria for some coffee. You want anything?"

Ferguson didn't respond; he seemed to be mesmerized by his computer screen. "Jack, I said do you want anything?"

"Holy shit! Paul, you'd better get over here. I'm seeing over two dozen urgent messages from just about every major ship in the Northern Fleet."

"What!? This couldn't possibly be an exercise. Not in that weather," stated Anderson incredulously.

"Look at these ships that are answering. That is *Petr*

Velikiy. And that is *Marshal Ustinov.* There is the *Admiral Kuznetsov.* Everybody and their brother is rogering up for something. And whatever it is, it's big."

"All right Jack, start writing this up. I want a FLASH precedence message reporting this activity in ten minutes. Do you have any theories as to what is going on?"

"I do now," Ferguson replied smugly. "I just saw the *Mikhail Rudnitskiy,* the submarine rescue ship, send its reply. I think we have a submarine emergency."

12

COLD CHOICE

Lieutenant Chandler knocked on the captain's doorframe, just as a formality. The captain, the XO, and Jerry had all stopped their conversation and waited expectantly.

"One LF and one HF receiver are up," Chandler reported. "I just came from radio and they're copying the broadcast off the floating wire."

Captain Rudel smiled. It was a tired smile, but it was one of the few Jerry had seen from him since the collision. "Good news. Well done, Chiefs, Mr. Chandler." Then, turning to Jerry, "And you too, Mr. Mitchell."

Rudel asked the chiefs, "Are your people still up there?"

Hudson nodded. "Yes, sir."

"Well, let's go see them." Rudel headed out of his cabin and up the ladder to the next deck. The officers and chiefs crowding the passageway melted against the bulkheads to make room, then Chandler and the chiefs followed. Jerry and the XO remained behind. Let Chandler get his face time with the captain, Jerry thought. He's earned it this time.

Shimko smiled, broader than the captain's. "That's good. Once he talks with some of the crew, he'll start to pull out of it. He loves his guys, and when he sees they're okay, he'll be okay."

RUDEL DID appear at dinner that evening, subdued, but he was there. Chief Morrison also appeared shortly after the meal started and handed out message traffic to a mixture of applause and a few boos.

"Couldn't you have left the receivers down for a few more days?" joked Al Constantino. The supply officer, as usual, had one of the thicker piles of message traffic.

"You could just ignore your traffic," Morrison suggested playfully. "Maybe nobody would notice."

"Oh, they'd notice," Constantino sighed.

Jerry's own message traffic was trivial, but he looked through them as if they were the first naval messages he'd ever read. A weather report, some All-Navy notices, school availabilities. It was all routine, but they were back in touch with the rest of the world.

Shimko gave everyone ten minutes with their message traffic before he started working through his own list. They were going to show up, unannounced, at Faslane in a little less than two weeks and there were literally dozens of things that had to be done, arrangements to be made. Jerry's task list grew rapidly, but his mood improved as his workload rose. They were moving forward; getting back into the swing of things. Navy business could deal with almost any circumstance—just wrap it in paper. As the XO so quaintly put it, "There is no greater cure for misery than hard work."

As the first seating finished up, Jerry saw one of the cryptological technicians in the passageway, waiting. He caught the XO's eye, and the two of them headed forward. Jerry followed. He usually checked the nav plot after dinner, and besides, he was curious.

Entering control, he saw Shimko disappear through the aft door, the CT behind him, heading for officers' country. He'd barely had time to look at the chart before the XO came back and told the chief of the watch, "Pass the word, department heads to the Captain's cabin." His tone was routine, but Shimko's expression said he'd heard bad news.

Lieutenant Commander Lavoie, the engineering officer, had the deck watch, and the XO added quickly, "And get a relief. You need to be there, too." Lavoie nodded and picked up the phone.

Jerry hurried forward to find Rudel seated, head resting on one hand, staring at a single sheet of paper. The XO and the CT stood in the cabin, taking up what little floor space there was. Jerry knocked quietly on the doorframe, and Shimko looked over. All he said was "Stand by." Jerry waited silently.

Constantino showed up a moment later, with Wolfe right behind him. Even with the operations, supply, and weapons department heads present, the XO still kept everyone waiting. Finally Stan Lavoie, temporarily relieved as the OOD, appeared.

Rudel saw Lavoie in the doorway and stood, his department heads clustered at the door, the XO and the CT standing behind him. He spoke softly, as was his habit.

"CT1 Sayers brought the XO this intercept a few minutes ago." The CTs, or cryptological technicians, were intelligence specialists who recorded and analyzed Russian radio transmissions. As soon as the HF receiver had been repaired, they'd been able to resume their jobs. Their first priority had been listening for any reaction by the Northern

Fleet to the collision, for example, looking for a sortie of an ASW vessel or aircraft to look for the offending U.S. boat.

Sayers was a big man, a blond crew cut already starting to thin as he entered his thirties. He seemed to shrink, uncomfortable among so many listeners. His work was rarely this public, or this immediate. At Rudel's prompting, he explained.

"Most of the stuff we just tape for later analysis. It's almost always encoded, and even the voice stuff usually uses code words or phrases." He pointed to the paper. "But this was broadcast in the clear. Someone on the submarine rescue ship *Mikhail Rudnitskiy* asked the Northern Fleet Headquarters to confirm the emergency alert and to verify the coordinates. The duty officer at fleet headquarters was none too happy about it too. Chewed the guy's ass off."

"An emergency alert?" asked Lavoie. "What kind of emergency?"

"The message that the guy on *Rudnitskiy* referred to was Signal Number Six, a coded alert the Russians send out for a submarine in distress. The location given was supposedly where the missing sub was last heard from. It was near where we had the collision."

"I don't understand." Stan Lavoie's reaction was automatic, uncomprehending. "They lost a submarine? That can't be the one we collided with. We lost that encounter. It left and went home."

"We assumed it went home," the XO corrected him.

Jerry tried to process the information. If the Russian Northern Fleet had declared an alert, then the boat had failed to communicate with its base. Had the other sub lost its radio, too? But they were close enough to be home by now, even if they had to crawl at five knots. And if they were adrift on the surface, they had rescue gear and emergency transmitters, short-range equipment that they could use to call for help.

And they had that big escape capsule. Every modern Russian attack sub had a built-in escape chamber, large enough to hold the entire crew. It included emergency radios as well. Had they been prevented from using even that last resort?

He listened to others list and then dismiss the same possibilities, and others besides. It wasn't impossible that another sub had gone down, but with so few Russian attack boats in operational service, the chances of two of them operating together, with one being lost and the other not sounding the alarm, were nil.

Rudel listened to the discussion silently, letting it run its course. "The only reasonable explanation is that the Russian boat is severely damaged, probably crippled. It's down, and we know where it was, where it may still be."

Jerry couldn't disagree. If it had gone down, it was going to be near where they had run into each other.

"We're turning around. Immediately. Mr. Mitchell, give me the quickest course back to the location of our collision. Plan for a UUV search of the area when we arrive. We need to find the sub, if it's there."

Jerry automatically responded "Aye, aye, sir" even as his mind raced ahead. What would they do when they got there? What could they do?

"As of right now, this is a rescue mission. I'll inform the crew in a few minutes. Dismissed."

Stan Lavoie and Jerry headed back to control. Jerry was still on automatic pilot, only half his attention on his task as he checked the chart. He laid a straightedge along their path, then waited until Lavoie had taken over as OOD. "First cut, new course is zero eight zero."

Everyone in control heard Jerry's recommendation, but nobody reacted until Lieutenant Commander Lavoie ordered the course change, turning *Seawolf* away from Scotland and back into the Barents Sea.

QM3 Gosnell was the quartermaster of the watch, and he leaned across the chart table. "Mr. Mitchell, sir. What the . . ." He paused, then asked, "Sir, why are we changing course?"

Jerry could see other watchstanders looking at each other, and at the officers. They had question marks for faces.

"We're going back to look for the Russian," Jerry explained to Gosnell. "Northern Fleet's . . ."

"This is the Captain." Jerry gratefully let Rudel do the talking.

"The Russian Navy's Northern Fleet has broadcast an emergency alert for a lost submarine. This is no secret—someone on a submarine rescue ship sent it in the clear to the entire Northern Fleet. The sub they are looking for is almost certainly the boat we collided with. It hasn't come back to port, and they can't reach it by radio.

"It's likely that the Russian boat was damaged more severely than we thought, and it's probably down. We're going back to find them if they're there, and then guide rescue forces to the correct location."

Rudel paused for a moment, letting the crew absorb the news, then continued. "We could continue on to Faslane and home, but I would never get a good night's sleep again knowing I'd left those men to their fate. We will stay long enough to make sure that Russians have found their sub, then we leave."

After the captain finished, nobody spoke. Gosnell watched as Jerry worked out the course back east and passed a small correction to Lavoie.

Jerry straightened up from the chart table to see the XO talking to Lavoie. "Have your engineers double-check the patch work on the hull in the electronics equipment space."

He saw Lavoie's expression and raised his hands, defending himself. The XO cut him off: "I'm not saying they did a sloppy job, but they were in a hurry. Now it's got to last for a while. And tell me if you can brace it further—no, wait. Just find a way to strengthen the bracing."

Shimko walked over to the chart table and inspected the new track. Jerry showed him the course and the time to reach the collision site.

"As soon as Stan's men have reinforced the shoring, the skipper wants to increase speed. He wants us up to at least seven knots by midnight, preferably ten if we can swing it."

Jerry suppressed his immediate response, but his worried expression said it for him. Shimko didn't have any sympathy. "The Captain's going to move heaven and earth to find that boat. Remember what he said. This is now a rescue mission."

A dozen thoughts were running loose in Jerry's mind. He snagged one in passing. "The storm. The Russians won't be able to get any units in there until it clears."

"And when it does, they'll need to make up lost time." Shimko's intensity impressed Jerry. He'd taken the captain's decision and made it his own. "We may be the only chance those guys have."

"What if we can't find them?"

"I already asked the Skipper how hard he wants to look. We can cover a lot of ground with the UUVs and do a thorough job of it. Here's a rough search plan."

He showed Jerry a sheet of graph paper with a rounded fan shape. It narrowed near the site of the collision, with the wide end pointing toward the Russian coast. "Get together with Wolfe and Palmer. Refine the search pattern and figure out when we can launch two UUVs, how long it will take them to double-cover this area. When they're done looking, and if we haven't found the Russian, we go home."

Shimko handed him the search plan. "And while you're

doing that, I'll figure out what to do when we do find him."

IN THE torpedo room, some of the torpedomen were servicing the UUVs. Wolfe and Palmer were having a quiet conversation in another corner, but Wolfe seemed eager to involve Jerry when he saw him.

Lieutenant (j.g.) Palmer asked, "Did the Skipper say anything more about what we'd do once we found the Russian?"

"You sound worried, Jeff."

"You'd better believe I'm worried. The last Russian we met wasn't too stable, and I'm wondering how the next batch will react. Imagine their situation: They've lost one of their subs, and when they go looking, they find us instead, camped out right over their lost boat. And how did we know where it was? We sank it."

"We didn't sink it, we collided," Jerry stated flatly.

"I don't think they'll see it that way. We're still afloat."

Wolfe shrugged helplessly. Jerry understood why the weapons officer had been so eager to have him join the conversation.

"With a leaky pressure hull and half our sensors gone," Jerry countered. Impatiently, he cut off Palmer's response. "Hand-waving isn't going to help anything. Let's focus on the job the Skipper gave us. First things first, we need to find the Russian boat. Here's the area we need to cover and the XO's first cut at a search plan."

It took them time to build an efficient search plan. They would use Patty and Maxine in the search, holding LaVerne in reserve. *Seawolf* would also cover part of the search area. The trick lay in making sure that every area was swept twice, each time by a different unit, and as quickly as possible.

It was after midnight when they finished, and they

finished without Wolfe, who left at 2330 to relieve Lavoie as the OOD. While they worked, Palmer tried twice more to raise the issue of the Russians' reaction, but Jerry kept them focused on their task.

Finally, when they finished, as Jerry turned to leave, Palmer tried again. "I don't see how the Captain's going to make contact with the Russians and get us out of there safely."

"You don't have to, Jeff. That's the Captain's job." Jerry paused, then asked flatly, "Do you trust the Skipper?"

"Of course I do," Palmer answered automatically.

"Then trust him to do the right thing when the time comes."

Jerry left before Palmer could raise any more objections; share more of his fears. The problem was, Jerry understood Palmer's concerns. He shared them, and more that Palmer hadn't even considered yet. Every so often, another one would pop up, distracting him, threatening to take over his thoughts. This time, just after midnight, was especially bad, with the boat quiet and his own mind tired and stressed after a long day.

Palmer was letting those worries take over his ability to think clearly. With fear in the driver's seat, one's thoughts would only take dark turns.

Jerry fought his fear with reason and faith. Palmer's concerns about the Russians? They'd be in international waters. Jerry's own guilt about Rountree's death because he didn't recognize the Russian's misconception about the UUV's lack of a tether? Turns out it wouldn't have made any difference.

And when he looked over the edge, into the darkness, there were other demons lying in wait, watching for weakness—his lack of confidence, his apparent helplessness whenever disaster struck. There were facts countering these demoralizing feelings as well, good ones.

But fear and guilt are emotions, and emotions don't need reasons to exist or even thrive. Jerry had found he needed other emotions to hold his own fear in check. His confidence in *Seawolf*'s crew, his own competitive nature, and now his desire to help the Russian submariners replaced the negative feelings. They gave him reasons to work, something worth taking risks for.

JERRY'S DREAMS that night were vivid and frightening. He was back in the Hornet's cockpit, skimming an ice-covered sea. The canopy was folded back, like a convertible, and icy rain stung his face. He flew over *Seawolf* on the surface, damaged and listing, smoke coming from her sail. A moment later, the Russian boat flashed by underneath. It was badly damaged as well, the ice-covered steel hull somehow on fire under the water.

He realized that instead of bombs or missiles, he was loaded with life rafts. Jerry tried to turn and make a pass over the crippled vessels, but every time he put the stick over, he turned sharply, but still ended up pointing directly away from the two subs. He tried an Immelman, pulling the nose back and watching the horizon fall away below him, but when he spun level and looked for the subs, they were still dead aft.

The subs were sinking, men jumping from the open hatches, when the alarm saved him.

JERRY WAS still washing up when the door popped open. The XO said quickly, "The Captain's cabin, as soon as you dry off." He left without waiting for a reply.

Hurrying, Jerry ran a towel over his face and grabbed his coveralls. He was still fastening his belt when he reached Rudel's cabin. A small crowd was gathered outside, including Lieutenant Commander Lavoie and an embarrassed-looking second-class, one of the engineers.

They made a hole for Jerry, who saw the XO and the captain examining what looked like an oversized cell phone.

The XO spoke the moment he saw Jerry. "Jerry, get an OPREP-3 Pinnacle message written. I need it five minutes ago."

Jerry answered "Yes, sir," automatically, but didn't understand why the XO wanted it. An OPREP-3 Pinnacle message was a special incident report that was sent to inform a senior authority that an incident of high national interest had occurred involving a U.S. Navy ship. Instead of being sent to just its immediate superior, in this case commander, Submarine Development Squadron Twelve, it was sent to the entire chain of command at once, to the chief of naval operations and all the steps in between. It was almost always bad news, but it was designed to get that news to everyone as quickly as possible.

By rights, *Seawolf* should have sent out a Pinnacle within minutes after she'd collided with the Russian sub, but with all her transmitters down, it had been impossible.

Trying to grasp the XO's reasoning, Jerry asked, "Did we get one of the transmitters on line?" He should have heard the news from Chandler, though, before the XO and the skipper.

Shimko pointed to the enlisted man, Petty Officer Moreau. "Thanks to Moreau here, we don't need to get a transmitter back on line. He's loaned us his personal satellite phone."

"And it will work out here." Jerry didn't state it as a question. He was just working through the implications. "I'll have it for you ASAP, sir."

Jerry didn't run back to his stateroom, but he didn't waste any time pulling out a message blank and the manual from his bookshelf. The manual had instructions for each part of the message. It even included an example report, a hypothetical collision. Jerry marched through the fields quickly.

Date and time of the message, sender and addressees.

"Except that he'll just dial someone," Jerry thought. "Probably the squadron commander."

He felt the deck angle up slightly. They weren't all that deep, and he realized they were going to surface. To use the phone, the caller would have to stand in the bridge cockpit.

Precedence.

"Flash, never mind the fact that it's overdue by about two days."

Classification.

"Secret, which is kind of silly because we're going to tell the Russians about it."

The deck was moving now, side to side. His stomach began moving in time with the deck, and Jerry was glad he hadn't had breakfast yet. Huddled in his cabin writing a message was not the best way to ward off seasickness. Focus, Jerry.

Subject.

"Collision. No," he corrected himself. "Submerged collision."

Narrative. The instruction said to "include all salient facts."

"Right," Jerry muttered. He started with the facts, the date and time, latitude and longitude, depth course, and speed and what they were doing when the unknown submarine appeared and . . .

Jerry looked up to find Shimko watching him work. If the XO wanted to read over your shoulder, you just nodded and kept writing.

The second paragraph was harder. He turned eleven minutes of confused maneuvers into an understandable narrative by stating only the broadest generalities. He looked back at the XO for approval, who nodded but also tapped his watch.

Jerry sighed. The next paragraph listed damage to the originating unit, including casualties. Jerry finally had to look up a fact: Denny Rountree's Social Security number and date of birth. The rest of it, the details of the collision, personally experienced and then hashed over for two days, might as well be encoded in his DNA.

The final paragraph was damage to the other unit. He paused only for a moment, but it was no time to mince words. "Heavily damaged, may be down."

"Add this at the end," Shimko dictated. "Performing search at location of collision, will coordinate with rescue forces when they arrive."

As Jerry wrote, he muttered, "Yeah, Russian rescue forces."

Shimko shrugged. "Wise man says, 'Man with burning mustache happy whoever shaves him.' "

Jerry handed him the message form. "Is the Captain going to send this?"

"Hell, no. He's on the horn with the squadron commander right now. As soon as he's finished, I'll show this to him and get his approval. Have one of your ITs standing by to go topside and read it over the phone."

"Aye, sir." Shimko disappeared, heading for ops first level. Jerry made a quick call to radio, then followed him.

Rudel was coming down the ladder from the bridge access trunk. His foul weather gear was dripping wet, and a blast of cold air swirled down with him.

The XO handed the skipper a towel, meanwhile yelling up the ladder for "you knuckleheads" to "shut the damn hatch." He was rewarded with a heavy clunk.

Rudel stripped off the wet gear and handed it to the watch, then accepted the message from the XO. He read it quickly, ignoring the sailor mopping the water around him.

Lieutenant Chandler showed up with IT2 Solomon, one of the radiomen, in tow. "I heard about the sat phone," Chandler told Jerry. "We'll send Solomon up whenever you're ready."

"The Skipper's reviewing the OPREP-3 message right now. I know we've got a pile of outgoing messages that haven't been sent, to include a detailed casualty report. Pull out any important ones and get them to Solomon."

"You mean like the list of repair parts for the SATCOM transmitters?" Chandler asked.

"That's the second message to go out." Shimko had listened to their conversation. "We'll keep the boat surfaced for ten minutes. Then we're pulling the plug."

Rudel had heard them as well. "And send another man up there with Solomon to keep the rain off, or he'll never be able to work."

Chandler and Jerry both said, "Understood," and Chandler disappeared. The captain, XO and Jerry waddled down to control; the rough seas made even walking an exercise. Jerry checked his watch and reassured his digestive system that it only had to hang on for another ten minutes.

Once in control, he braced himself against the chart table and listened as the XO asked Rudel about his conversation with the squadron commander. He wasn't eavesdropping. As one of the more senior officers on the boat, he was being included.

Shimko prompted Rudel by asking, "Did Captain Jackson have any orders for us?"

Rudel almost laughed, but he didn't sound happy. "Orders? By the time I'd finished briefing him, he could barely speak." He stopped briefly, then said, "Imagine your kid calls and tells you that he's been in an accident, that he's wrecked the car and hurt someone, and that it was his fault."

"It wasn't your fault, Skipper," Shimko stated softly.

Chandler and another radioman showed up with a plastic binder. Both enlisted men hurriedly pulled on their foul-weather gear, and armed with the phone number of the Atlantic Fleet Message Center, proceeded up to the first deck to the bridge access trunk.

"Jackson says he'll arrange to get us transmitter parts and anything else we need, possibly through the Russians."

"So they'll tell the Russians we're here?" Jerry spoke without thinking, out of habit. It felt weird, like the Navy was betraying their presence, but then they weren't covert now.

Rudel was understanding. "It goes against my grain, too, but the Navy's got almost a day to bring the Russians up to speed. Knowing that we're in the area will help prevent an incident." Then Rudel corrected himself, ". . . another incident."

"He's also endorsing my decision to return to the collision site. He agrees it's the right thing to do, but he also feels that it will open up the biggest can of worms since *Vincennes* shot down that Iranian airliner in 1988."

Jerry tried to imagine the reaction back home. Crippled U.S. sub. Missing Russian sub. CNN. State Department. International relations. Media feeding frenzy. His sister Clarice in Minnesota. His uncle the senator. What would they think?

The two ITs scrambled down the ladder, and one of Jerry's quartermasters went up to disconnect the suitcase. They were submerging; thank Neptune and all the other gods of the sea.

They'd found a way to report, to tell the Navy what was happening, and that was a good thing. But part of him was very sad, a strange feeling considering the circumstances. He thought about it for a while, and realized it was because of the special incident report. He remembered a half-formed thought pushed aside while he was writing the message, but now he had the time to consider it fully.

It would take a little time to go through channels, but sometime tomorrow, Denny Rountree's parents in Florida were going to get the terrible news that their son was dead.

13

HOME FRONT

6 October 2008
10:55 AM
OPNAV N77 Director, Submarine Warfare Division
Main Office,
Fourth Floor, A Ring, the Pentagon

"Yes, sir. I'm watching the news as well. No, sir. I have no idea how they found out so quickly. My staff and I only got the word late last night from Norfolk."

Captain William Richardson, USN, spun in his chair at a knock and waved the yeoman into his office. Petty Officer Second Class Michaels walked in and held up a binder with a colorful title page and CD in a plastic case, smiling.

Richardson smiled back and gave him a thumbs-up even as he continued the conversation. "Admiral Keller is due to land in about an hour and a half. We have a briefing scheduled for him at 1400. I understand, sir. I'm sure he would want you there as well. Yes, sir. Of course not, sir. Someone will meet your plane and bring you straight here. Thank you, sir."

Richardson slammed the phone down, stood and grabbed his service dress blue uniform blouse. "We'll need another car at Andrews in half an hour. SUBGRU Two will be landing at 1125 from New London and he will join the admiral for the brief."

Michaels handed over the combined package with one hand and reached for Richardson's phone with the other. "He didn't give us a lot of warning."

"We're lucky he called to complain about the television coverage. Someone in New London was supposed to phone ahead."

Michaels nodded as he punched the buttons.

Richardson finished buttoning his coat and quickly flipped through the hard copy of the presentation. "And this has the stuff from BUPERS, the shots of Rudel and his service record?"

"Third slide. This is OPNAV N77 at the Pentagon. The executive assistant needs a driver to meet Rear Admiral Jeffrey Sloan, Commander Submarine Group Two, at Andrews at 1125. No, I'm not kidding. Our extension is 4257, and it's room 4A720. Thank you."

While Michaels ordered the car, Richardson hurriedly stuffed the binder, a stack of papers, and a laptop into his briefcase. He finished as the YN2 hung up. "Hernandez is at the Mall Entrance waiting for you. And Lieutenant Meeks has already left to meet Rear Admiral Keller."

"Good." Richardson headed for the door. "And now we'll need two flag-rank reservations for tonight instead of one."

"I'll see to it, sir. Good luck at the White House."

Richardson stopped to check his uniform and reflexively glanced at the television mounted in the corner. It showed a black-and-white video image of a submarine plowing through the water. The legend below said "USS *Thresher.*" He shuddered, grabbed his uniform cover, and yanked on the doorknob.

He hadn't taken three steps down the hallway when a woman's voice behind him called out, "Captain Bill! I just heard the news."

He turned to see a tall woman walking quickly to catch up. Her expensive dark-colored suit made her ash-blond hair look all the brighter. Richardson waited the few moments it took for her to catch up. "Dr. Patterson, it's good to see you."

Richardson turned back and resumed walking. If he hurried, he'd make the briefing on time.

Patterson matched his stride easily. She was half an inch taller. "I just came from the CNO Intel Plot. They brought me up to speed on *Seawolf*'s mission and the incident."

"What? Oh, of course." Richardson corrected his initial reaction. *Seawolf*'s mission was highly classified, but Dr. Patterson certainly had the necessary clearances.

"Pardon me if I hurry, Doctor, but I have a briefing at the White House."

"Yes, the NSC meeting at 1130. I won't slow you down."

"Thank you. I've got to get there early. I'll be presenting . . ." Richardson actually stopped walking. "Are you going to be at the meeting?"

"I think the Navy would want me to be there," Patterson answered matter-of-factly.

Richardson started walking again, maybe a little faster than before, and thinking faster still. He was due to brief the National Security Council in less than an hour about the *Seawolf* crisis. He'd been invited as the navy's senior submarine representative, since the director and deputy director were both on travel. He'd reviewed *Seawolf*'s mission, what they knew of her damage, and what the Navy's options were for dealing with the crisis.

His audience would include the President's National Security Advisor, the Chairman of the Joint Chiefs of Staff, the Chief of Naval Operations, the Director of National

Intelligence, and half a dozen other luminaries. He would brief them on the situation and answer questions about submarines in general and *Seawolf* in particular.

There were two other briefs after his, one about the Russians and one about the weather. When they were over, the assembled national-level decision-makers would list possible options and recommend one or more to the President of the United States. This was the real deal.

His intention was to give a good brief, answer their questions to the best of his ability, and otherwise keep the hell out of the way. Richardson was a full Navy captain, a "four-striper." He'd commanded two nuke subs, one a boomer, but these people operated at a much higher level.

Dr. Joanna Patterson was angling for an invite. Could she bring anything useful to the party? She was President Huber's science and technology advisor for intelligence, which meant she looked at intelligence from a scientific viewpoint and told President Huber what she thought. It said a lot about Huber's opinion of her.

JOANNA PATTERSON watched Bill Richardson consider her request, and she knew that's all it was, a request. One simply did not show up at an NSC meeting because one had something useful to say. One was invited.

And she needed to be invited. Ever since her patrol aboard *Memphis,* she'd become friends with many submariners. She'd socialized with them, gone to special events, learned about submarine technology. She'd even married a submariner.

Along with her husband, she'd gone to the change of command ceremony in New London when Tom Rudel had become *Seawolf*'s captain. Her husband Lowell and Tom had served together, and Jerry Mitchell was aboard *Seawolf* as well. Once one of her contacts had called to tell her about *Seawolf,* she'd dropped everything else.

Everyone at the NSC meeting would want to resolve the crisis, but state, defense, intelligence, even the navy had their own goals. Her only agenda was the crew of USS *Seawolf.* She knew Washington, and what was politely called "politics." She had helped President Huber and had his ear. And she would use every trick she knew to make sure the men in that room moved heaven and earth to bring *Seawolf* home.

RICHARDSON ALSO knew she'd been a powerful friend to the Navy, and submarines in particular. Word in the Pentagon was that she'd been involved in several technology programs, basically grading other agencies' homework for the president. She also had a Bluenose certificate in her office, framed in a place of honor. She refused to say where or how she got it.

He'd first met her at a Submarine League gathering, along with her husband, a retired submariner and now a congressman. She had a sharp mind and did not suffer fools at all. Both had political connections, but hers were wider and higher. Much, much, higher.

Three steps after Patterson's request, Richardson answered, "Doctor, I'd be delighted if you'd join me. I can add you to our list as a 'submarine technology subject-matter expert.' "

"That's accurate enough for our purposes. They have all my information over there on file."

They'd reached the car, and as soon they were moving Richardson called and made the arrangements. It was a twenty-minute ride to the White House, and risking rudeness, Richardson took the time to review the hard copy of what he hoped were error-free slides.

PATTERSON BUSIED herself with her BlackBerry. Her first email was to Lowell, of course, and then a general call to several submariner friends. There was no way she'd get answers in time for the meeting, but she needed input, ideas, wisdom.

Lowell, bless his heart, did answer her note with a two-word text reply: BE GENTLE.

THE MEETING was actually being held in the basement of the Old Executive Office Building, across the street from the White House. Richardson and Patterson passed through the security screenings at the main entrance, again on the basement level when they came off the elevator, and one last time when they reached the secure area. Richardson gave up his cell phone and laptop, while Patterson gave up her BlackBerry, a second cell phone, iPod, and digital camera.

Patterson knew the names and faces of all the cabinet-level officials. She was a little surprised when she didn't see any of them here. While Richardson set up his presentation, she worked the room.

The secretary of state was missing. Instead, a stocky forty-something introduced himself as the Assistant Secretary of State for European affairs. "The Secretary hopes this can be dealt with quickly, without involving the cabinet." His name was Abrams.

He'd brought along another assistant secretary, a carefully groomed woman named Parker, in charge of public affairs. She looked ready to step in front of a TV camera, but Patterson thought she had too much makeup on for a meeting. "Getting our message out properly is key to resolving this crisis," she declared.

"I would think successfully rescuing the Russian submariners and getting our people home would be a better goal," Patterson observed.

The Joint Chiefs had sent the vice chairman, a four-star

Air Force general, with a Navy four-star admiral at his elbow. Patterson actually knew the admiral, the vice chief of naval operations, named Sotera. He was an aviator, not that she had anything against pilots.

Intelligence had sent a senior executive service-level political-military expert along with a junior Russian Navy specialist, while Defense was represented by their senior counsel, a silver-haired man in an untidy suit. She hadn't expected the Vice President, the official head of the NSC, to be here, but even the National Security Advisor, who chaired in the VP's absence, was also missing.

Instead, a middle-aged woman, looking tired and a little impatient, called the meeting to order at precisely eleven thirty. "My name is Adrienne Gosport, I'm the deputy to National Security Advisor Wright." Gosport looked over at a secretary to make sure she was recording the proceedings. "We are convening to discuss the incident involving USS *Seawolf,* to assess the situation and determine if any action needs to be taken at the national level." She glanced at her notes. "Captain Richardson has prepared a brief of the situation."

The captain walked them through the background: Russian exercises, *Seawolf*'s mission, then what Rudel had reported of the encounter, *Seawolf*'s material condition, and Rudel's intentions. Richardson was good. He kept it short, stuck to the slides, and then sat down.

Gosport saw members start to ask questions, but cut them off. "Let's hold our questions until the other briefs are finished. Let's have the weather next."

An Air Force staff sergeant, remarkably at ease in the presence of such high rank, didn't mince words. "This area has some of the worst weather in the world. Vicious storms like the one near Svalbard are not uncommon this time of year, but it is not the norm. Units on the surface will experience heavy seas, winds of gale force, and visibility of less than a quarter mile. I've passed around printouts with the exact details, but the simple answer is that in the area of interest, conditions have worsened since yesterday and are expected to peak tomorrow.

"Even large surface ships will be affected by these conditions. Nothing's flying. Search-and-rescue operations are out of the question until the winds and sea states moderate in two, possibly three more days. And then there is the sea ice, which is getting thicker in the area near the reported position."

Joanna Patterson shuddered, remembering the water temperature on her own trip north. The interior of the sub was comfortable enough, but brushing up against any metal in contact with the hull had reminded her of the frigid wilderness inches away.

The intelligence analyst was the most interesting, a fifty-ish academic named Russo, with thinning hair and a limp. A former submariner, he knew his topic. The problem was that he loved his topic. His opening slide told them that his three-part briefing would review past and present Soviet and Russian submarine rescue platforms, then Russian submarine incidents and their successes or failures in rescuing downed crews, and he planned to wind up with a review of Russian-Western cooperative agreements.

Gosport interrupted him. "Which of your slides covers their current capabilities?"

Disappointed, the analyst flipped forward to a slide titled "Northern Fleet Rescue Assets." It was brutally short. One slide showed a photo of the *Mikhail Rudnitskiy* salvage and rescue ship, and the second a picture of an AS-34 Priz-class rescue submersible, built in 1991, and in "doubtful" mechanical condition.

"That's it?" Gosport asked, incredulous.

"Russian submarines themselves are very survivable.

They use a double hull design with internal compartmentation, which gives them very large reserve buoyancy. All of the attack submarines also have an internal escape chamber big enough to hold the entire crew." He flipped to a cutaway of a Russian nuclear attack sub, then pointed to a cylinder embedded in the sail. "There it is, equipped with medical supplies, food and water, and emergency radio equipment."

"But they haven't used it," General Winters, the vice chairman, observed.

"We don't know for sure, sir. But it's likely they haven't." The analyst was on familiar ground, and confidence buttressed his arguments. "For the Russians to declare a missing submarine alert means that it has failed to report in during a routine communications window, that it has not signaled in some other way, and repeated attempts to contact it have all been unsuccessful."

Gosport took over again. "Thank you, Dr. Russo. Does anyone have other information to contribute?"

Sotera, the navy representative, volunteered, "We ordered *Mystic* to prep for movement two hours ago. She's on twenty-four-hour notice, so she can be flown from San Diego early tomorrow, if we want to use her. The two Super Scorpio ROVs are already loaded on C-17s and are on strip alert. We've also detached USS *Churchill* from Standing Naval Force Atlantic. They're near Norway. She'll steam north, and we'll fly the repair parts *Seawolf* requested out to her. When she delivers the parts to *Seawolf* she'll also take off her casualties."

"Was that wise?" Abrams, the State Department official, asked. "What if *Churchill* encounters Russian naval vessels while searching for the sub?"

"It's international waters," the admiral replied, "and we've 'encountered' Russian units before." He wanted to say more, but Gosport kept things moving.

"We have several questions to be answered. I'll address them in order of their urgency. First, do we pass *Seawolf*'s information on to the Russians?"

"We haven't?" exclaimed Sotera. Several at the table were more than surprised. "It's all over CNN."

"The news reports are vague," Abrams countered. "They confirm a Russian submarine emergency, but only hint that a U.S. sub may have been involved. To my knowledge, nobody at the State Department has had any official or unofficial communication with any Russian national in any capacity."

"Mr. Abrams is correct," Gosport added. "The United States has not officially provided the time and location of the collision to Russia. Until we do, the news reports can be dismissed as speculation. Once we do give Russia the data, we confirm our presence in the area and more importantly, our part in the collision."

"They'll blame us," Abrams stated.

"Of course. Nothing new there," Winters replied. "But from Rudel's report, it sounds like he was doing his level best to avoid a collision."

"Didn't do a very good job," muttered Bronson, the DoD counsel. "I'm assuming we don't put incompetents in command of nuclear submarines, but couldn't Rudel have simply moved away from the other submarine?"

Gosport looked to Richardson for an answer. The captain explained, "The Russian was trying to drive *Seawolf* out of the area by making passes very close to her. Both navies have used the tactic in different times and places to make the other side feel 'unwelcome.' It's a risky business. There have been collisions between U.S. and Russian boats before, although never one this severe. In none of those cases was the U.S. captain held culpable." The last sentence was directed straight at the counsel.

Bronson nodded and made a notation. "Still, what do

we know about this man? He's screwed up this mission. What if he makes a hash of finding the Russian sub?"

Richardson bristled. "He didn't fail at anything, sir. *Seawolf*'s survey was interrupted by the Russian. That's certainly not his fault."

"I've met Captain Rudel." Patterson spoke up. She had to make Tom Rudel real to these people. "My husband served with him when they were both lieutenants. He's an excellent officer, intelligent and a good leader."

"Dr. Patterson, did you have a *technological* insight into this situation?" Bronson's attitude was almost hostile.

Patterson wasn't deflected by his snide comment. "The two nuclear subs involved are over three hundred feet long and displace almost ten thousand tons. Depending on their speed, it can take three to four boat lengths to change course. Given a noncooperative partner, maneuvering in close proximity, collisions are more than likely."

Sotera, the vice CNO, reminded the group, "Rudel's competence, or responsibility for the collision, doesn't affect the basic fact that we know where the Russian sub is."

"Where it may be," corrected Abrams.

"Where it probably is," countered the admiral. "This is a search-and-rescue mission. Not sharing what we know borders on the criminal. Furthermore, need I remind everyone here that we supported the Russians in August 2005 when the AS-28 got tangled in fishing nets off the Kamchatka Peninsula. And they were participants in this year's NATO Bold Monarch submarine rescue exercise in May."

Gosport's expression showed that she wasn't pleased at the admiral's inference. "Until we know what the effects will be, sharing the information would seem unwise."

"There's no rush," Abrams suggested. "The weather's rotten and will be for two or three more days. Let *Seawolf* investigate and we can pass the information on if there's anyone to rescue."

"Unsatisfactory," Sotera answered firmly. "Just like us, the Russians need time to prepare assets and equipment, and knowing where to look means they can start moving it now. And what if the weather breaks sooner than predicted?"

Bronson added, "The legal implications are fairly clear. Even if the Russian was totally responsible for the collision, withholding the information would have a very adverse effect on our position. And the Admiral is correct: We have included the Russians in rescue exercises as well as participating in the international submarine rescue liaison office. The course of action the State Department is recommending is completely counter to the president's present policy."

Patterson smiled, but only on the inside. That "adverse effect" would be a firestorm of international condemnation.

Gosport was convinced. "Then the Secretary of State will pass the information immediately to the Russian ambassador here in Washington. After that has occurred, the Navy may relay the exact same data through the submarine liaison office." She turned and spoke to an aide, who quickly left the room.

"The second question is whether we recall *Seawolf* or let her assist in the rescue operation."

"*Seawolf* can't be recalled, Ms. Gosport," Admiral Sotera reminded her. "According to Rudel's message, she's submerged, so we can't communicate with her again until she decides to surface."

Richardson looked uncomfortable. He didn't like correcting the aviator. "Sir, that's not completely correct. She can still receive messages via the floating wire antenna. She just can't talk to us without surfacing and using the satellite phone."

Sotera nodded and smiled. "Thank you, Captain." He

turned to Gosport. "I still recommend letting Captain Rudel proceed with his search."

"But what can he find?" Abrams asked. "According to the message, his bow sonar is destroyed."

Patterson leaned over to Richardson. She whispered, "I can answer this one, if you want." The captain nodded, and she spoke to the group. "*Seawolf* has three unmanned underwater vehicles fitted with high-resolution bottom-scanning sonar. Each can search a swath hundreds of yards wide at five knots . . ."

Gosport interrupted. "Then it sounds like *Seawolf* is very well equipped to find a downed submarine. But physically involving her in the search concerns me."

Abrams agreed. "Informing the Russians of our role does not require her to be there. If *Seawolf* stays, they will have to work with the Russians. And questions will be raised about what we were doing there in the first place."

"Describing her mission as oceanographic survey is both accurate and publicly acceptable," Bronson stated. "*Seawolf*'s classified mission is not relevant and had nothing to do with the circumstances of the collision."

"That's simple, at least." Gosport sounded relieved. "Dr. Russo, what do you think the Russians' reaction will be?"

Russo didn't hesitate. "Before the *Kursk* disaster, they'd probably ignore anything we said and conduct their own search. That would cost them days, but they've got their pride and always want to go it alone.

"Now they're under a lot pressure from their own citizens to work with other nations. Most likely, they'll use the information but not give us any of the credit." After a pause, he added, "And they'll say the whole thing is our fault, of course."

"We'll deal with that," Parker stated. "After the meeting, I'd like to get copies of Captain Richardson's brief, along with any other material you have on Rudel. Also, on the crew member that was killed, Rountree. I assume his next-of-kin's been notified."

Concern flashed up in Patterson, but she suppressed her urge to speak when she saw that Richardson, Sotera, even Winters were equally worried. The three uniformed officers exchanged glances, then Winters carefully asked, "Why would the State Department want personal information on service members?"

Parker explained, "For the press releases, of course. Since this involves our relations with a foreign country, State will coordinate our media response."

Gosport shook her head. "No. Involving State moves this to a higher level. For the moment, we will let the Navy deal with the media." She deliberately looked over the assembled group, including everyone in her gaze. "It is my desire that this crisis be resolved with as little media attention as possible, and with that coverage favorable."

"The last question regards who is best suited to coordinate the United States' response. While I'm sure State is willing to take this on, I will again insist that this be handled at a lower level." She looked to Admiral Sotera. "How about within the Navy?"

Richardson and the admiral conferred, the captain spoke. "*Seawolf* is part of Submarine Group Two in New London. Admiral Sloan is Commander SUBGRU Two and is en route here. So is Admiral Keller, COMSUBFORLANT, his immediate superior."

"Then my recommendation will be that Admiral Sloan is designated the action officer for this incident." She glanced at the clock. "I'll be speaking with Dr. Wright immediately. Please inform your superiors that he may convene a full meeting this evening. Thank you." She stood up and quickly left, while an aide gathered her notes.

That's it? Patterson checked her watch. Twenty minutes

of briefings and fifteen minutes of discussion? They'd barely mentioned *Seawolf* and her casualties, or the crew of the Russian sub. Both of them deserved, no, demanded more.

As the meeting broke up, Patterson approached Dr. Russo and asked for a copy of his brief—the full version.

Russo smiled at her interest. "I'm not usually called on to brief. I apologize for sharing my enthusiasm." He handed her his hard copy of the slides. "You might as well take this one. It would just go into the shredder. At least someone will read it."

"Don't throw all that work away just yet, Doctor." She smiled warmly. "And please, call me Joanna. We may need your expertise. I wish I'd heard more about actually helping those subs."

"I wouldn't like to be in Captain Rudel's place right now. No nuclear sub has ever been as damaged as his and not headed straight for the barn. Once he finds the Russian, he'll have to stay on station until the Northern Fleet shows up with a rescue force. And I don't think this is going to be a simple handoff. *Seawolf*'s UUVs could be critical in saving the boat. The Russians have nothing like them, which means *Seawolf* could be there for the entire operation."

Patterson frowned, imagining just how many ways things could go wrong. Then she wondered how many more ways there were that she couldn't imagine.

CNN Report

"This is Jody Stevens in Moscow. A Russian Navy spokesman just released a report on the loss of the nuclear attack submarine *Severodvinsk*.

"The press release did not name the sub, but did describe the 'loss of a new first-rank nuclear submarine to mysterious and hostile actions.' The Russian naval officer would not elaborate on what might have caused the loss, but stated that 'Russian submarines are well built and not subject to accidental loss. Only deliberate actions by another vessel could have put our submarine in danger.'

"When asked about Russian search-and-rescue plans, the Russian captain said the search was proceeding according to plans drawn up long before in accordance with fleet procedures. Weather in the area is very bad, but the captain insisted that the Northern Fleet was used to such severe conditions and would not be hampered.

"He refused to say whether the submarine has been located, or when rescue units could expect to arrive on the scene."

Washington, DC

Patterson's office was also in the Old Executive Office Building. She might have access to the president, with an appointment, of course, but that did not rate a desk in the West Wing.

Still, it was on the third floor, facing east, toward the White House, and she'd paid for the decorator herself. Antiques, warm colors and fresh flowers not only made it a pleasant place to work, but a place to visit. She also made sure that she had the best coffee on the floor, and comfortable chairs.

Her assistant, Jane Matsui, looked up as Patterson almost burst through the door. Patterson saw her reach for a stack of message slips and waved her off. "Call Ben Castle and tell him I need to speak with the advisor as soon as he finishes getting briefed by Gosport. It's about *Seawolf.* Don't let him put you off." Matsui recognized her tone and dialed.

While her assistant spoke to the national security advisor's office, Patterson quickly checked her emails. Only one answer, so far, but it was one of Lowell's friends in the Pentagon. His only thoughts on the crisis were "Make sure Rudel's got a friend in the room."

Fifteen minutes later and one floor up, Patterson nodded to Wright's staff. Adrienne Gosport was just leaving the advisor's office, and she was more than a little surprised to see Patterson. She recovered quickly, though, and smiled thinly as she left for her own office next door.

Jeffrey Wright's doctorate was in political economics. He tended to see conflicts in those terms, and he wasn't an ideologue, which meant he tended toward the long view. Huber had appointed him as the national security advisor based on his raw intellect and the fact that without Wright he might not have carried the northeastern states.

Wright was a tall man, almost scrawny. Patterson often thought of a pile of sticks when she saw him in a chair with his legs crossed. His bushy hair was almost pure white, with only a few streaks of his original brown remaining. Although over seventy, he exercised frequently, de rigueur for anyone in the Huber administration.

"Jeffrey, the administration has to take a more active role in assisting *Seawolf*."

"Nice to see you, too, Joanna." Wright smiled and shook hands, then ushered her to a seat—not the one across his desk, but another, nearer and on the same side of the desk as his. He shrugged. "We're letting Rudel continue with his search."

"And doing not a single thing more," Patterson countered. "He's on a crippled sub in the middle of the Barents Sea and the only help he's getting from us are some new radio parts."

"That's all he's asked for."

She smiled. "And you can't think of another thing we

can do to help him." When Wright didn't respond immediately, she stood and paced quickly, trying to walk off her frustration. "I wish you had run that meeting. This wouldn't be happening. They were worried about everything except getting those men home safely.

"Their plan is for Jeff Sloan to manage the 'incident' from New London," she argued. "He can barely communicate with *Seawolf,* even when her radios are working, which they're not!"

Wright sighed. "I agree. He's working at arm's length."

"And he'll be working at arm's length with the Russians, too," she added.

"You sound like that's a bad idea."

Patterson shook her head. "I'm not going to say anything bad about Jeff Sloan to the President's National Security Advisor. He's a fine officer and very charismatic."

"But," Wright prompted.

"He's like ninety-five percent of the military men I know. He's not political. He doesn't think in those terms. In fact, he avoids thinking in those terms."

"While you live for it." Wright smiled.

"I'm a people person, Jeffrey." She smiled back.

"All right. You've convinced me that we need better communications, both with *Seawolf* and the Russians. Adrienne really didn't look very hard for an action officer. I'm certainly not obligated to follow her recommendation. I think it should be you. We'll send you to USS *Churchill* along with those radio parts."

Patterson stared at him.

Wright started ticking off items on an imaginary checklist. "You understand the technical and political issues. You know many of the people involved personally. President Huber trusts your judgment, and you've delivered for him in the past. You've even been on a submarine patrol up there."

"The Russians probably shouldn't know about that last bit," Patterson mused. Pausing, she half-smiled. "I didn't know I was so annoying. You know, I might find my way back."

Wright laughed out loud, but before he could say anything in reply, Patterson argued, "It won't work. I'm not in the chain of command. I'm an adviser to the President."

"President Huber will appoint you an 'on-scene coordinator' for the search-and-rescue operation. Under international law, Rudel is the on-scene commander, since he was or is the first unit there. Given his limited communications, supporting him with a surface ship makes sense."

Wright made some notes. "Now, once the Russians arrive, they will quite properly take over the rescue effort, but you will stay there until *Seawolf* comes home."

"Who do I report to?" Patterson asked. She wasn't going to say yes until she knew where the wires led.

Wright grinned. "That depends. SUBGRU Two on matters relating to *Seawolf,* the Russians for the rescue, me for everything else. I'll stay out of your hair as long as I feel informed, and I'll get you whatever you need."

"Can I take along someone? Dr. Russo. I met him at the brief. He's an expert on Russian submarine rescue."

"I'll arrange it. I'll also include a State Department rep, in case things with the Russians get intense, and a naval officer as your aide." Wright saw her expression and reassured her. "They will work for you, I promise."

"All right."

"Splendid." Wright's smile lit the room. "Ben will arrange the travel details, but expect to leave tomorrow—early."

TWO HOURS later, she skipped dinner to hit an outfitter's store on Seventh Street. They expressed interest in her destination when she told them she needed arctic gear, but

Patterson put them off with a story abut an environmental survey in Alaska, which she'd actually done, years ago.

She'd barely started when her phone beeped. It was a text from Lowell. CHECK CNN. She hit a key and checked a list of articles on the screen. It was obvious which one he was referring to.

The audio with such a small speaker was awful, and she had to keep the volume down in the store, but the anchor's voice was understandable.

"The Russian Interfax news agency has announced that the Americans have admitted their role in the loss of their submarine, now identified as *Severodvinsk.* A Russian naval ministry spokesman says that the U.S. government has provided both the location and time of the submarine's loss through a collision with an American nuclear attack submarine.

"The Russian statement did not name the U.S. submarine, and questioned its 'oceanographic survey' mission. The submarine will evidently remain in the area conducting its own search for the downed Russian vessel.

"The ministry claims that because the location is in international waters, the only way the Russian submarine could have been crippled is through 'hostile actions' by the American vessel. They are discounting the American claim of an accidental collision, on the grounds that there is no reason for two submarines to be operating in such close proximity, and also the need to conduct a search, since it and the American had collided. He hinted the U.S. actually knows the precise location of their missing submarine, and is withholding it.

"The ministry says it is continuing its rescue plans, but that the search vessels will be escorted by Northern Fleet warships to prevent any interference."

14

UPHILL

In the Barents Sea

It was a series of regular, violent motions. First the deck would pitch down and to starboard as *Seawolf* crested a wave. Then the entire boat would actually slide to the right, finally rolling back to port as she came down into the trough. As the wave's crest moved toward her stern, it sometimes lifted her propulsor partway out of the water. The vanes would thrash for just a moment, and then as the water covered them, ice chunks would strike the vanes and then the cowling. The shuddering vibration, like ice cubes in a disposal, ran though the hull and everything attached to it.

There was some yaw in the motion, too, a slight turn to starboard and then back to port as the rudder lost its bite. And because the bow wasn't a smooth, round, symmetrical shape anymore, all manner of vibrations and clunks found their way into the pattern.

Jerry had long ago ceased being seasick, if that meant losing the contents of one's stomach. His stomach muscles were exhausted and sore, thankfully fatigued to the point where they were unable to spasm. He still felt weak and almost dizzy from the boat's motion, but he could function—barely. He was still keeping death as a fallback option.

On *Seawolf,* all normal functions had been stripped down to bare bones, and then the extra bones had been discarded. Sea state six meant near gale-force winds and ten to twelve-foot seas, streaked with large tails of ice-laden spray. Submarines just weren't built for this weather. Movement had to be carefully planned, not only through the passageways, but even simply crossing to the opposite side of a compartment. Handholds here and there, wait for the right moment to step, or risk banging your head on that cabinet, pipe, panel, or whatever as you're thrown forward.

Shimko had passed the word as soon as they turned east. Rig the boat for heavy weather. Anything that could move, would. Anything that could be shaken loose, would move. Two thankfully minor injuries in the first six hours had shown the strength of the storm, and that the crew needed to use their imagination when securing for rough seas.

Jerry moved carefully, shuffling in concert with the deck's gyrations in a nautical zen that came from hours of practice and a deep need to conserve energy. He, Shimko, and the captain were taking turns touring the boat, visiting each deck in every compartment, checking up on the tormented occupants. It was tiring, but necessary.

His first stop was enlisted berthing, aft and high up in the hull. The motion of the ship was, unfortunately, quite pronounced and the men literally had to wedge themselves in their bunks to prevent from being thrown out. With everyone not on watch confined to their rack, it was crowded, and noisier than usual from the motion of the ship and the sound of water and ice pounding the rubber-coated hull. Jerry was reminded of the old-style Pullman sleeper cars; assuming the train was riding a roller coaster in a hailstorm.

Many of the men were surprisingly asleep, but a few saw him, and waved or greeted him weakly. Jerry wasn't the only one suffering the *mal de mer.* While only a few were as sensitive as he was, in seas like this, more than two-thirds of the crew were affected.

He noted two men in berthing that had sick chits taped to their bunks and IV bags hung over them. Dehydration was a real risk with severe seasickness. He asked to make sure the doc was looking in on them regularly.

Down lower, closer to the bottom of the boat, the torpedo room offered a smoother ride. With the boat moving so violently, all regular maintenance had been suspended, so it was quiet. The single watchstander, a pale olive hue, was seated, braced against the weapon launch console and one of the stowage racks. He was wearing his sound-powered phones and was alert enough to notice Jerry's arrival and carefully stood.

Several other enlisted members had sought refuge there against the motion. A few were even trying to eat—cold boxed meals had been prepared by the galley. The smell of food stirred Jerry's stomach, but he quickly left before it could wake up and remember how unhappy it was.

Aft of the torpedo room were the auxiliary machinery spaces, and then the forward reactor bulkhead. Like the torpedo room, these spaces were sparsely populated. He then climbed back up to the next deck, passing by the wardroom to radio. Actual work was being done in the radio room, as the ITs printed out message traffic and sorted it by department. With the floating wire stowed, they couldn't monitor the fleet broadcast while on the surface; the two multipurpose antennas were still down. They'd bolted several fans, blowing as hard as they could, to cabinets and shelves to help keep the air moving. Stray bits of paper flew through the small space, but the two men on watch looked almost comfortable.

Chandler was in there as well, hunched over one corner of a table, struggling to return a binder to a storage rack filled with hefty-looking manuals. He looked pale, but focused on his task. He saw Jerry and stood, made sure the binders and manuals were secure, then stepped out into the passageway. "No change in equipment status, sir," Chandler reported.

"I'm sure you would have told me if there was," Jerry said coolly.

"With your permission, I'm helping the XO with a crew training summary. It's a required report, and with most of the radio gear down I've got some free time, so I offered to help him with it."

"Since you're already doing it, I suppose you can have my permission," replied Jerry with a touch of irritation. He was in no mood for Chandler's brown-nosing. "I'm sure you won't let this interfere with your regular duties, and you'll of course keep me informed."

"Yes, sir. Of course, sir." He was almost standing at attention, and Jerry noted an intensity in his manner. "The XO said he might have some other things for me to do as well."

"What about that write-up you were working on? Your account of the collision?" Jerry asked.

"I'm, I'm still working on it," Chandler replied nervously. "The fire-control plot narratives are taking a little longer to do than I expected. There is just so much information that I need to cram into a clear, succinct report." The commo's cheery expression vanished as he spoke, replaced by the haunted look Jerry had seen earlier.

"I thought if I took a little break to help out the XO—you know, clear my mind a bit—it would get a little easier." His gaze drifted downward, toward the deck, as he finished. Jerry wasn't sure if Chandler was ashamed at getting caught jumping the chain of command again, or if he was still wrestling with the effects of the collision.

Before he could say anything, Chandler's head whipped back up, a slight smile on his ashen face. "But I've finished my eval inputs for next month. They're on your desk. Well, at least that's where I put them."

Genuinely surprised, Jerry said, "That's good work, Matt. Thank you," and then added, "As you were." If the SOB liked formality, he'd give it to him.

Chandler disappeared back into the radio room, looking almost eager to get back to his task.

Jerry left radio glad that Chandler couldn't see his puzzled expression. He'd never seen anyone that eager to push paper. It wasn't natural, but it did make sense given Chandler's cover-your-ass philosophy. He actually thought collecting all those brownie points mattered, that somehow if he got enough paperwork done, it would protect him from whatever loomed around the corner. Something must be eating at him, Jerry thought. He sure seemed to be afraid. But of what? Failure? Or not being recognized as exceptional?

Jerry got in and out of control as quickly as possible. The bridge watch was being rotated frequently, and the prebriefs and debriefs were held in control. Every watchstander came down dripping wet; some still had ice in their hair. The air was wet, a cold clammy humid feel, almost dripping, in spite of the nuclear-powered dehumidifiers. They didn't bother putting the swab and bucket away, but two well-placed bungee cords made sure they didn't move.

He briefly stopped to look over the navigation plot. Dunn had the duty and was carefully updating the track as he approached, one hand writing and the other locked to the edge of the table to steady himself. Dunn looked good—tired, but evidently not suffering from the sub's motion.

Once he'd checked the chart, Jerry headed aft again. He'd meant to just pass through officer's country on his way to the XO's stateroom, but Palmer's desk light was on and the curtain drawn back. Loose papers had slid from his desk and were scattered across the deck. Jerry stepped in to gather them up, but saw Palmer, lying in his bunk, one arm limp over the edge and dangling, moving like a pendulum with the ship's motion.

Jerry hurriedly stepped over the papers and bent down to check on the junior officer. He was awake, a little pale, but Jerry had seen far worse.

"Jeff, are you OK?" Jerry was concerned but puzzled.

With obvious effort, Palmer turned his head to look at Jerry. "I'm whipped. No, that's what I'd feel like if I got better. I came down from the bridge an hour ago, and I meant to work on the search plan for the UUVs, but I was so tired I had to lie down."

Carefully lowering himself to one knee, Jerry gathered up the papers. "Try to get something to eat and drink, if you can keep it down."

"Oh, I grabbed a box lunch from the galley," Palmer answered. "The doc's pills are helping with the seasickness. I'm just fracking tired. It's so easy to stop what I'm doing."

Jerry left without saying anything else. It would have been easy, almost reflexive, to either haul Palmer's butt out of the rack, or blow sunshine at him until he was motivated to get up. Neither approach dealt with the real problem, and Palmer's gas tank might actually be near "E." But Jerry didn't think so.

Seawolf's crew had suffered a major hit, both physical and mental, when they collided with the Russian. Everyone in the service knows submarining is dangerous. The potential for disaster is just one mistake away. But submariners compensate for that with detailed procedures for any imaginable situation. Near-obsessive training pushes the danger and the fear it brings into the back corners of one's mind, where driving a boat seems no riskier than riding a commuter train every morning. Sure, something might happen. But you're much more likely to read about it happening to the other guy.

But now it had happened to them, and instead of having a chance to recover, Rudel had turned them around, back toward an uncertain and potentially threatening future. And regardless of how things would turn out in the end, nobody on *Seawolf* would ever think of submarines in the same way.

There was little to do about it, except recognize that it was happening. Jerry had faith that *Seawolf*'s crew would react quickly and properly when the next crisis came. In the meantime, let them rest and heal.

Jerry was just about to make his report to the XO when he realized he had skipped the electronics equipment space up on the first deck. "Well, that was pretty stupid," though Jerry out loud. Now he would have to trudge back up and check in on the guys doing repair work. He was briefly tempted to just report everything status quo, but that wasn't how he operated. With a weary sigh, Jerry turned back around and made his way forward.

Climbing up to the electronics equipment space was a circus act. Wait for the bow to begin pitching forward and the first step would take you halfway up the ladder. Watch for the roll to starboard, then step up at the bottom of the trough, but hang on as the boat swings back to port.

Here, once again as high inside the sub as Jerry could get, the motion was constant and violent enough to bruise him on any of a dozen angles. Like a climber, he made sure of the next handhold before releasing the one he had as he worked his way from the top of the ladder to the door of electronics space.

The noise was constant and unnerving. Instead of the quiet hum of electronics, Jerry heard wind-driven ice floes slammed and ground against the hull. It unnerved him, forcing him to remember that nothing was being crushed or mangled in runaway machinery.

This is where the action was. The periscope and other

retractable masts passed through the electronics equipment space on their way down. Packing glands in the overhead sealed them against the outside water pressure where they entered the pressure hull, and those joints had been strained and even opened by the impact of the Russian's hull.

EN2 Gaynor, one of Lieutenant (j.g.) Williams's men, had wedged himself into a small gap between the periscope assembly and the bulkhead. It was uncomfortable, but it freed both hands to work on the seal overhead. Another petty officer, MM3 Day, alternately handed Gaynor tools and mopped up seawater around the gland so the second class could see to work.

Day's efforts hadn't kept Gaynor from getting repeatedly splashed in the face with icy water. His shirt and even his pants were spattered, and he occasionally stopped long enough to wipe his glasses. It was crude, rough work, pounding material into the gland to plug the gap. It wasn't the kind of thing one associated with nuclear submarines, but in some ways, a sailor's work never changed.

Todd Williams was there, looking miserable. Braced in a corner, he greeted Jerry tiredly. "Gaynor's making progress." A muttered imprecation from the petty officer made him pause, but only for a moment. "This is the third try. The first two leaked, but the stuff seems to be working, now that Gaynor's got the proper tools."

Two more engineers maneuvered their way into the space, laden with tools and more packing material. Their clothing was wet enough to show they'd been working on the leak as well.

There was only one question, and Williams didn't wait for Jerry to ask. "Give it another two hours and we'll be ready for a test."

"That's good news, Todd. Thanks."

His tour of the operations compartment now finally complete, Jerry headed for the XO's stateroom and reported. Shimko, pale but still seated and working at his desk, said, "Good. That matches what he told me earlier. I'm glad he's still on schedule."

The deck shuddered, an unusual motion. Both Jerry and Shimko grabbed for support and waited until it had passed.

"The storm's getting worse," Shimko announced. It wasn't news, but it started him talking about what was obviously an uncomfortable request. "I want you to go topside and look at the weather."

Jerry smiled, almost involuntarily, and laughed, but only for a moment. "It's hard not to look at the weather when you're up there."

"We're starting to get more injuries," the XO explained. "It's mostly scrapes and bruises, but Garcia was actually thrown from his rack when he was asleep. The doc just put seven stitches in his forehead."

Shimko spoke carefully, as if he'd rehearsed what he had to ask. "As long as we're forced to remain on the surface, the Captain's concerned about the boat's ability to weather the storm. It's bad enough that the storm's moving slowly to southeast, but we're heading northeasterly, almost perpendicular to its path. Read the latest weather reports, go up and look things over, then report back to me. Should we keep going, or slow and try to find a more comfortable course?"

The confusion must have shown in Jerry's expression. Shimko explained, "Yes, this is the Captain's decision to make. And yes, he and I both went up a little while ago. He used the sat phone to call Rountree's parents. We both looked at the weather, but now he wants to hear your opinion as well."

There was only one answer. "Aye, aye, sir. I'll report back as soon as I can."

Jerry went back to his stateroom, trying to work it through. The captain might be testing him, seeing what Jerry's answer would be, but Shimko hadn't acted like this was a training evolution. The XO also hadn't hinted at his own opinion.

Rudel was an expert sailor. Certainly nobody aboard *Seawolf* would question his decision, whatever he chose. So why was the skipper taking a poll? Was he second-guessing his own judgment?

After changing into his thermals and several layers of warm clothes, Jerry worked his way to control and told the chief of the watch he needed to go up. He hadn't been topside since he'd inspected the damage with Shimko after the collision. Since then, qualified conning officers had taken one-hour watches topside, while the deck was manned in control.

An auxiliaryman met him on the first deck with the foul-weather gear, boots, pants, and a heavy coat, and helped Jerry climb into them. Standing on one leg was impossible with the motion of the boat, and Jerry sat on the deck to get the pants on. Getting up was strangely easy, a matter of waiting, then simply pushing up as the deck fell away beneath you.

A parachute harness went over everything, and the chief of the boat, EMCM Hess, double-checked the clips, as if Jerry was planning to jump from a plane. Then he helped Jerry into a bright orange life vest. "Sir, use the first clip, right at the top of the ladder." Master Chief Hess's tone was earnest, dead serious. "I shouldn't tell you this, but we almost lost someone because he didn't clip up quickly enough. He wanted to close the hatch first." As he talked, the master chief checked the emergency flasher and waterproof radio attached to the vest.

"Who?" Jerry question's was automatic.

The COB shook his head. "I promised I wouldn't say if he promised not to be a knucklehead again." He grinned. "Besides, I could get in trouble speaking that way to an officer."

Jerry suppressed his own smile and answered solemnly, "Just like you said, COB. Right away, first one at the top of the ladder."

As he stated to climb, carefully moving with the motion of the ship, the master chief said, "Wait until we're at the top of a wave. Most of the water's drained out the cockpit by then."

Jerry nodded and climbed the few rungs. He grabbed the hatch, then waited, feeling the bow pitch down once, then twice. On the third wave he quickly worked the mechanism, then, helped by the downward motion, threw the hatch up.

He spotted the clip at the top of the ladder and hurriedly secured his harness. Jerry was out of the ladder and closing the hatch when the fist wave hit. Some of the water went down the access trunk, but Jerry slammed it as quickly as he could.

Tom Norris, the reactor officer, had the watch, along with Fireman Inglis as lookout. To their credit, both had their glasses up and were searching the ragged horizon. The sound of the wind and ice masked his arrival until the hatch clanged shut and Jerry yelled, "Permission to come up."

Norris turned, one hand braced on the bridge coaming, and shouted back, "Granted. Watch your footing!" He pointed to the deck, and Jerry could see patches of ice on the wet surface.

Remembering the COB's instructions, Jerry waited for a break in the waves before quickly switching his harness clip to an attachment point nearer the front of the bridge.

He had to carefully pick his footing on the slippery surface while he braced against the ship's motion and the wind tearing at him.

The wind came from the port side, trying to roll *Seawolf* over while it pulled them out of the cockpit, but the sail didn't have enough area for the wind to work on. It drove the snow and ice ahead of it, making Jerry pull his hood around to shield his face.

A wave broke over the coaming. Jerry tried to dodge it, but the other two didn't bother. After it passed, leaving half an inch of water splashing in the cockpit, Norris leaned over as far as his harness allowed and said, "It's too early for my relief, but if you insist . . ." He had to speak up to be heard over the wind.

"How is she handling the weather?"

Norris turned his back to the wind, and the two huddled side by side as they talked. "The wind's come a little to the right since I got up here. The bow is starting to pound, and I'm worried about what happens if we strike a large ice floe. I've steered us around some really big ones, but I don't know how big is too big."

Jerry deliberately reassured him. "We're okay since they welded the reinforcements in place. That's still HY-100 steel. We'd have to ram something bigger and harder than an ice floe to be in trouble."

Norris shrugged, a gesture barely visible under the heavy clothing. "I hope you're right, but once in a while we go deeper in the trough, or are slower coming up. That's when these harnesses pay off. I'd recommend finding a smoother course, maybe we can turn more toward the southeast so we're taking the waves from the stern quarter."

"Understood," Jerry answered, and backed up a little, ending the conversation. He stayed on the bridge for another twenty minutes, until the watch changed, watching the storm and how *Seawolf* rode it.

The pitch-down, the slide to the right, the shudder as the ice hit were all there, but more pronounced, the difference between a football game on a big-screen TV and seeing it live. Jerry saw the boat take a big wave. Instead of smashing over the bow it rolled up the hull, a gray-green wall that broke against the sail. All three ducked as the spray engulfed them. Some froze in midair, pelting them with wet ice.

Strangely, Jerry wasn't seasick. The cold and the work of staying on his feet occupied most of his attention. The rest was focused on how *Seawolf* behaved in the wind-driven sea. For the most part, the beat-up boat was holding her own.

Finally the watch changed, two new victims climbing up while Jerry and the two watchstanders almost slid down the ladder. Their eagerness to get below was matched by the watch's desire to get the hatch closed.

As Jerry took off his dripping gear, the smell hit him. Twenty minutes of fresh air had rebooted his nose, and the odors of one hundred men, ozone, oil, and vomit were thick enough to chew. His stomach flashed a warning, but was too tired and empty to react. By the time he'd climbed into dry coveralls, his sense of smell was numb again.

Jerry headed straight to the XO's cabin. "*Seawolf* can handle the storm. We can stay on this course."

"Good, let's tell the Skipper."

Rudel's door was closed, but he answered quickly and was working at his desk. "Trying to get it all down before my memory fades," he explained. Which he didn't need to do, of course.

Jerry reported, "*Seawolf* should handle the weather until we finish the repairs and can submerge."

Rudel nodded silently, acknowledging the report and considering. “It’s pretty rough on the watchstanders up there.”

Was Rudel playing devil’s advocate? “Norris seemed okay when he came down, sir. We can always shorten the interval, especially since they should finish the repairs in a few hours.”

“I’m concerned about additional injuries.”

“They’ve been minor so far, sir, and the crew is learning how to deal with the rolls,” Shimko observed.

Rudel sighed. “This crew has been through so much. I think I’m just reluctant to put them through anything they don’t absolutely need to.”

Jerry’s mind raced. Rudel could ask this crew to swim through acid and they’d do it. He should know that. Finally, Jerry answered, “Whatever direction we sail, Captain, we’re stuck on the surface. I believe it’s best to push ahead.”

The captain stood. “You’re right.” He looked at both of them. “Thank you both. We’ll continue on course.”

Shimko and Jerry left, with Jerry working his way toward control, habit driving him to check the chart. His mind was still circling around the captain’s state of mind. Rudel had always been close to his troops, but he’d crossed a line somewhere, feeling their pain, and nobody can bear the suffering of a hundred men, especially if you’re responsible for it. A captain needs to be detached, removed emotionally because of the orders he might, almost certainly will, have to give.

Jerry tried to, or pretended to study the chart. It was the captain’s problem, but if the captain had a problem then they all had a problem. It was also Rudel’s problem to solve, just as Jerry faced his own demons. In the meantime, Jerry was more than willing to back up the skipper and keep *Seawolf* on task.

He finally focused on their course. They were closing on the collision site, and once they submerged they'd be able to increase speed. He ran a calculation to see how much time they had until they could begin the search.

Then Jerry headed forward, to boot Palmer out of his rack. They would need a search plan soon.

***SEAWOLF* FINALLY** submerged an hour and fifteen minutes later, with the crew at battle stations and the COB's hands hovering over the chicken switches. Rudel seemed more his old self as he carefully managed the boat's submergence.

Once submerged and still dry, he took the boat deeper and deeper, in steady increments. No matter how excited the report, Rudel smiled and took it all aboard as the seals stayed dry down to four hundred feet. "There's no need to go deeper than that, not in the Barents." Rudel's tone was so casual he could have been talking about the menu for dinner. He settled on a depth of two hundred feet and a speed of ten knots.

He passed the news over the 1MC, and included Brann and the rest of Todd Williams's gang in his public praise. "They've worked their tails off and given us all a dry boat. Now that our stomachs are recovering, the cooks have started on a feast in their honor." Rudel paused to glance at the clock. "After that, we'll begin our search."

15

RUSH JOB

7 October 2008
5:30 AM
Georgetown, Washington, DC

The car picked her up just before dawn, with Lowell's advice still filling her ears. Joanna Patterson's husband had insisted on getting up with her and making breakfast while she finished packing. She appreciated the meal, but Lowell insisted on briefing her on Navy protocol—again.

"You know the ranks and organization aboard a ship, dear, but I can't emphasize enough, make sure all your requests go through either the captain or XO. Don't go bossing the crew." Lowell, six foot two in his bare feet and flannel pajamas, still thought like a Navy captain. His congressional staff joked about the clock in his office that chimed "eight bells" rather than striking twelve.

"Lowell, I've dealt with Navy captains before." She smiled smugly. "Quite recently, as a matter of fact."

"And you're very good at it," he replied, kissing her warmly, "but that better not be how you plan on dealing with *Churchill*'s Skipper."

"Whatever works," she teased, but then she continued, "I made my choice. One port, one sailor." She patted his temple. "Even with your thinning hair."

The phone rang and Lowell jumped to answer it. "Hardy." He listened for a moment, then turned to his wife. "The car's outside. Did you pack your charger?"

"Yes. And my spare computer glasses. And don't you forget about that meeting with Representative Acheson."

"The man's made of clay," he complained.

"You need him, and he's a lot smarter than he looks," she cautioned. "Wish me luck."

She hugged Lowell one last time and pecked him on the cheek as the doorbell rang. The government driver identified himself, then gathered her bags and took them to the car.

The chill lasted only until she was inside, where she allowed herself ten minutes with the newspapers before she pulled out her BlackBerry. There were emails to answer.

Traffic was light, and they made good time to the Old Executive Building, where they picked up Jane Matsui. Like Patterson, she looked like she'd overpacked, but Matsui explained that one suitcase contained nothing but warm clothing. Another bag, which she kept with her, was filled with work from Patterson's office.

The instant they started moving, Matsui was ready to work. There were a lot of people who still thought Patterson would be in her office this morning, and the two women worked through the twenty-minute car ride to Andrews.

They were heading east, out of the city, so they made good time, and since it was a government car, they were waved through the front gate at Andrews Air Force Base with a minimum of delay.

An airman in dress blues met the car as it pulled up in front of the VIP waiting area. The nondescript door led into one of the buildings that made up the operations center. The Eighty-ninth Airlift Wing was tasked with ferrying all manner of government officials of any rank, in any numbers, wherever they needed to go, often at a moment's notice.

"Welcome to Andrews Air Force Base, Dr. Patterson, Miss Matsui." The young airman didn't salute, but treated the ladies with deference appropriate for a general. While the driver dealt with the bags, he walked the two ladies inside. "Another member of your party is inside already. We're waiting for two more." He checked the clipboard. "You'll be leaving at 0800 aboard a C-20B. It's one of our smaller aircraft, but it has intercontinental range."

The VIP waiting area looked like any airport terminal, except for the Air Force decor. The airman led them over to a Navy commander, the only other person in the room. He rose, almost coming to attention.

"I'm Commander John Silas, ma'am, your Navy liaison." Silas was short, in his early forties, and already fighting a paunch. He was dressed in neatly pressed khakis.

After introductions, Patterson asked, "Where are you stationed? When you're not TDY, that is."

"I'm on Admiral Sloan's staff, at SUBGRU Two. With your permission, I'll file regular reports with him, so he's kept up to date."

The door opened again and the airman ushered Dr. Russo into the waiting area. He shook Patterson's hand warmly. "Thank you for asking for me, Dr. Patterson. Frankly, I don't get out a lot, and I miss it."

"You're welcome, Doctor, I think your expertise will be a great help." There were more introductions, and Patterson discovered that Silas and Russo knew each other.

"Al Russo has come up to see us several times, and we send information to his office as well." Since Russo was a CIA technical analyst, she presumed that Silas was talking about intelligence data gathered by SUBGRU Two boats.

Silas offered, "Doctor, I've got a few suggestions about how the investigation should proceed . . ."

Patterson cut him off. "This isn't an investigation, Commander. I'm acting as on-scene coordinator for Commander Rudel and *Seawolf.* This is a search-and-rescue operation, not some fact-finding junket."

"Given the success rate of Soviet and Russian submarine rescues, Doctor, it's likely there will be little for us to do." Silas looked over at Russo.

The analyst shrugged. "The Russians have never been able to pull a large portion of crew out of a bottomed sub. For that matter, neither have we, at least not since *Squalus* went down, and that was in 1939."

"I won't accept that, not with so many unknowns. We don't know how badly the Russian boat is damaged. Nothing can be decided until we know that. And if there's the slightest chance of the U.S. improving their chances of survival, I want us to find out what it is and then make it happen."

"Bravo, Dr. Patterson, I wish I'd had a microphone." It was a woman's voice, behind her, and Patterson turned to see the public affairs official from yesterday's meeting.

"Joyce Parker, Doctor. It's good to see you again." She offered her hand, and Patterson automatically shook it as she absorbed Parker's presence. "I'm delighted to be part of this adventure."

Silas pulled out a sheet of paper and consulted it, confusion growing in his expression. "I'm confused, Ms. Parker. I was given a list of people who were accompanying Dr. Patterson. You're not on it."

"I'm taking Art Lopez's place," she explained almost casually. "It was a last-minute change. He has a bad case of the flu, and State didn't find out until early this morning, which is when I got the call." She grinned. "I've been scrounging cold-weather gear everywhere I could. I had to wake some of my girlfriends. Am I late? Are we ready to go?"

Patterson eyed Parker with suspicion. "State was supposed to send a Russian specialist from the European desk."

"Undersecretary Abrams said I could take Art's place

with the group. And you need a media specialist," Parker countered. "Have you looked at the television coverage?" She offered a digital player with a news story about the collision. "The Russians are now claiming that they can't find their sub, which they still refuse to identify, because a 'mysterious' U.S. sub is interfering with their operations."

Silas snorted. "Their stuff is either still stuck at the pier or grounded."

"The Russians say the search is progressing in spite of the weather," she countered. "Of course, it helps when you're not handicapped by the truth."

An Air Force officer approached the group. "Dr. Patterson, we're ready for your party to board."

The C-20, engines idling, waited with a roll-up stairs at the fuselage door. Patterson, glad to be moving, set a fast pace and hurried aboard. It was supposed to be a rescue mission, after all.

An Air Force first lieutenant in olive coveralls greeted her. "I'm Lieutenant Neal, ma'am, the copilot. We'll taxi and take off as soon as your party's seated and the luggage is aboard. It's a seven-hour flight to Orland, Norway. We'll refuel there, then fly to Bardufoss, where you'll transfer to an MV-22 Osprey for the trip out to *Winston Churchill*."

Patterson was all business. "I'm assuming you're flying as fast as possible."

"Yes, ma'am. We have priority clearance, and we'll do everything we can to get you there quickly."

Patterson thanked him and he left for the cockpit. As the rest of her group quickly settled in for the flight, she looked over the plane. The C-20B was the military version of a Gulfstream III and was configured for VIP transport, with three rows of first-class-sized seats, four across. Behind them, a bulkhead and door led to a conference area, including a communications center and a galley. It was not lavish, but looked more like an executive boardroom than a passenger aircraft.

Once she was buckled, an Air Force staff sergeant gave them a familiar-sounding speech about oxygen masks and aircraft exits, then belted in himself for takeoff.

As they taxied, Patterson found her mind racing. She'd turned off her BlackBerry, cell phone, and laptop for the takeoff, but begrudged even those few minutes of enforced idleness. She was eager to attack the problem.

She pulled the hard copy of Russo's brief that Matsui had brought with her and looked through it again. Patterson had given up thirty minutes of sleep the night before to read everything she could find online about Russian submarine rescue equipment, but the classified brief had considerably more detail and she needed time to absorb the information.

Russo was sitting across the aisle from her and noticed what she was reading. He grinned. "That's the canned one-hour briefing I usually give. I really should have edited it down for the NSC meeting."

"I'm glad you didn't," Patterson replied. "I'd only heard about a fraction of the ones listed here." She paused, thinking. "I'm having trouble understanding why the Russians allowed so many accidents to happen."

"Well, it's not like they choose to have accidents, but their submarine production and maintenance philosophy makes them more prone to them. Remember, they've always played catch-up with our nuclear technology. They were desperate to field and operate their own nuclear boats. The losses were bad, but the alternative was American naval dominance. The guy in second place always has to take more risks to level the playing field. We'd do the same if our positions were reversed. In fact, we've done it, in other areas."

Russo insisted, "They are not casual about their crew's lives." He gestured to the printout. "Turn to slide thirty. Look at the escape capsule."

Patterson examined a cutaway drawing of a Russian sub, with a cylinder inside the sail circled in red.

"The capsule looks small in that drawing, but consider the size of the sub. The thing is bigger than a Greyhound bus. It can hold the entire crew—that's over a hundred men, and has survival supplies, and an emergency radio to use when they reach the surface. The Russians put a lot of thought and effort into those things."

"And it just floats to the surface?" asked Patterson.

"Yep, simple buoyancy. They close the hatch in the bottom, release the locking clamps, and up it comes."

"Has it ever been used?"

"Once, when the lone Mike-class SSN, *Komsomolets,* was lost to a fire in April 1989. Most of the crew abandoned the boat while she was still on the surface, but the captain and four others weren't able to get off in time as the boat suddenly foundered and sank. They managed to get into the capsule, but the sub's trim was too great and the capsule wouldn't release until it hit the bottom and she leveled out. Unfortunately, toxic gases from the fire leaked into the capsule and four of the five died."

Russo shuddered. "It's not foolproof, and they haven't used it this time, for whatever reason. Submarining is a dangerous business."

Patterson automatically agreed, maybe a little too strongly, remembering her own experience during the fire aboard *Memphis.* Russo's expression of curiosity made her think of a new question before he started asking ones of his own.

"How long can they live, if they are alive?"

He shrugged again. "That all depends on how badly damaged the sub is, and how many of the crew survived.

Ideally, they've got stored oxygen and power from their emergency batteries for some warmth. The problem is carbon dioxide poisoning. If the survivors aren't able to keep CO_2 down below five percent, the clock starts ticking.

"Assuming most of the crew made it through the collision, and their emergency air-regeneration system still works, I estimate that they may be able to last for up to a week. Given Rudel's initial report, the Russians have already been down for three days. Unfortunately, the weather isn't cooperating and this makes things really sticky."

"But *Seawolf* can ignore the weather," Patterson stated, "and use her UUVs to find the sub quickly."

"Exactly. But finding *Severodvinsk* won't be the hard part." His unspoken question went unanswered.

Their conversation had taken them through the takeoff and climb to altitude. The copilot's voice over the announcing system announced, "Dr. Patterson, your group can unbuckle now and move around, and safely use electronic devices. Staff Sergeant Monroe can organize some breakfast as well, if you'd like."

The moment Patterson stood, Joyce Parker, seated two rows behind her, stood as well. "Dr. Patterson, I must speak to you about the media response."

"Ms. Parker, my only concern is supporting *Seawolf* and helping rescue *Severodvinsk*'s crew." Patterson used a coldly formal tone that usually made others wilt.

Parker stood her ground. "I thought it was representing U.S. interests in an international crisis. Did you know that the Russians are claiming that the U.S. State Department deliberately fed them a bad location?"

"I'm not interested in fighting Russian propaganda."

Parker showed Patterson her laptop. "Look at these headlines. The rest of the world is already calling this 'the *Seawolf* attack.' Our international reputation is being ruined, and we're not doing anything about it." Parker sounded deeply concerned.

The rest of the group had listened silently, but Russo now spoke up. "After *Kursk* went down, the Russians claimed that their boat had collided with a foreign submarine in the area. Early in the incident, they also claimed that they were in communication with the crew, and were sending air and power to them. Both statements were wildly false. Later they accused us directly of attacking *Kursk*; again a false statement."

"What's your point?" Parker was impatient with Russo's observation, almost hostile.

"Nobody in the Russian Navy ever has gotten in trouble for lying to the media. It's like the weather. We can't control it."

"Which means we have to get the truth out there." Parker's intensity was unnerving. Patterson could see that she cared deeply about the image of the United States, but her concern didn't make it Patterson's problem. Parker wasn't even supposed to be here.

"Ms. Parker, we are going to have some breakfast, then I'd like Dr. Russo to run us all through his briefing." Parker looked like she was gong to say something, but Patterson just ran out of patience. "We're done for now. Who else wants to eat?"

STAFF SERGEANT Monroe served fruit and pastries and excellent coffee, thank goodness. Patterson studied her team as they ate. No, they're not a team, she thought. So far, it's just a bunch of people together on an airplane. Like one of those disaster movies, she thought, but quickly squelched the comparison.

She had an empire builder, an intel analyst, and a naval officer who thought the whole endeavor is a waste of time. She had to make them work together.

During Russo's brief, she listened and learned a little more, but also made up a list of action items, and watched her people. Silas and Russo had a running discussion during the brief. They were comfortable with each other, and seemed to respect each other's expertise. Parker appeared interested, and took notes, but that could have been her journalist's instincts.

Silas continued to be pessimistic about *Severodvinsk*'s chances. "Even with a good location, they've got very few rescue submersibles that can go down and save them."

"They've asked for help from the British and the Norwegians," Russo offered.

"But it will be days before they can get there," Silas argued.

"The Russians don't even want us there," Parker commented, and turned her laptop around so they could see the screen. The Internet headline read, "Russians demand U.S. submarine to leave."

"This article says they have proof that the U.S. is interfering with their rescue operations, and may be trying to destroy evidence of a U.S. attack."

Silas laughed. "They haven't even left port."

Patterson had enough. They could sit here and argue their way across the Atlantic. "Let's make sure of that. Commander Silas, please contact the Office of Naval Intelligence and ask them for an update on the Russian rescue operations."

"Yes, ma'am. I'll add a request for any Northern Fleet movements, if that's all right." She nodded, and Silas headed aft for the communications gear. Good. At least he could take orders.

"Dr. Russo, figure a timeline for a Russian rescue attempt, assuming that *Seawolf* is able to guide them to the spot, and a second one assuming they can't. I want to know what they must do, where they have choices, and where they might run into problems."

She turned to Joyce Parker, who volunteered, "I'd suggest a press release. We have to show everyone that we are taking action."

"The National Security Adviser wanted the Navy to handle the publicity for this incident. Contact the public affairs officer at OPNAV and get copies of whatever they are releasing." Parker looked ready to protest again, but Patterson added firmly, "This mission should remain out of the press as long as possible. We will have greater freedom if we stay below the radar."

Parker nodded her reluctant understanding and turned to her laptop.

PATTERSON WORKED them for several hours, finding answers, building plans, and testing alternatives. She also tried to keep up with her own email. Monroe brought by a box lunch about halfway through the flight, but after that, she found herself waking up, covered by a blanket. Almost everyone was asleep, except for Russo, reading a paperback.

THEY LANDED at Orland, Norway, seven hours and thirty-two hundred miles after takeoff. "It's a major NATO base, ma'am," Monroe explained. "We'll taxi over to the refueling area, pick up our passengers, and then head for Bardufoss. Total time on the ground, about thirty minutes, less if we can manage."

"Passengers?" Patterson asked.

"Yes, ma'am. We received word as we landed that a van will be meeting us with some people who are joining your party."

Patterson was surprised, but curious. "Do you know who they are?"

"No, ma'am, we don't even know how many. The tower just said 'additional personnel.'"

Monroe opened the forward passenger cabin door, and waited as the ground crew brought up a rolling stairway. Patterson could see a slice of the airbase through the opening: hangars, vehicles, and a low ceiling of slate gray overcast. We're under the southern edge of the storm, she thought.

The clouds were moving, she noticed, and cool wet air swirled through the opening. "Staff Sergeant, can you please get me an update on the weather?"

"Of course, ma'am, as soon as our passengers are aboard."

They waited another ten minutes for the dark blue Air Force van. It finally pulled up as the refueling crew finished. Whoever they were, Patterson was eager for them to be aboard so they could get moving.

The first person out the van and up the ladder was dressed in jeans and bright red and white parka. His beard and hair were streaked with gray, and his face was so weathered Patterson couldn't tell whether he was thirty-five or fifty-five.

"My name is Arne Lindstrom. I'm with Marine Diving and Salvage. The Russians have contracted with us to help with the rescue." As Lindstrom stepped aboard, he shook Patterson's hand, but was then almost mugged by Russo, who introduced himself and began pelting the man with questions.

Behind Lindstrom was a twenty-something man in a suit. "My name is Hugh Glasgow. The base commander gave me permission to join your group." He offered his hand.

Patterson took it, but alarm bells went off. "And why would you want to join us, Mr. Glasgow?"

"I'm with CNN, assigned here in Norway, Ms. Patterson. Colonel Ed Jenkins, the base commander, said you had space on the plane."

She dropped his hand as if it was red-hot. "It's 'Dr. Patterson,'" she said coldly. "How did you find out about this trip?" It wasn't classified, but Patterson was alarmed to hear that others were even aware of her mission.

"Sources, ma'am." He smiled. "It's my job. I promise I won't be in the way . . ."

"That's absolutely right, because you're leaving, right now. I'm not letting any press on this trip."

"Colonel Jenkins authorized it."

"Colonel Jenkins is not running this operation, I am." She turned to her assistant, quietly seated and working in the third row. "And Jane, please remind me later to thank Colonel Jenkins appropriately. Staff Sergeant Monroe, please escort this person off the aircraft, and make sure he gets his luggage back."

Parker spoke up. "Dr. Patterson, CNN could help us get a lot of good press."

"Which I appreciate, but I'm not willing to pay the price. I am willing to work with the press, but we have to keep them at arm's length."

Two more people waiting on the stairs to board had to turn around and go back while Glasgow went down.

Once the reporter had left, an Air Force enlisted man in fatigues came aboard. He almost saluted Patterson, and did come to attention. "Tech Sergeant Hayes, ma'am," he said in a west Texas drawl that seemed entirely appropriate to his six-foot-two height and long, angled looks. "I'm a weather specialist. I'm supposed to support you, the sub, and the ship we'll be aboard."

As he headed aft to sit down, the final passenger stepped inside. He was stout, in his fifties, and looked a little worried. "I'm from NAVSEA, Doctor. Ken Bover. I'm supposed to assist with the repairs to *Seawolf*."

"You're a technician?"

"No ma'am, a naval architect." As Bover answered,

Moore motioned urgently for them to sit, and then turned to close the door. Patterson buckled in, and Bover sat down in the next seat, continuing their conversation.

"I was on TDY at Haaksonvern, the Norwegian base at Bergen. I coordinate NAVSEA's support for the new *Nansen*-class guided-missile frigates. I was scheduled to conduct sea trials on *Thor Heyerdahl* when I got a call yesterday from my boss telling me to get here pronto and be ready to support repairs to USS *Seawolf*."

Patterson nodded. "We're carrying spare electronics parts for her."

Bover pulled out a printout. "I've got the list. That was the one thing I was able to get, and it's the Air Force cargo manifest. It's all very last-minute. I almost didn't make the flight."

By now the plane was taxiing, and Patterson said, "Once we're in the air, Commander Silas will help you contact NAVSEA and get you whatever you need. We have top priority on this mission."

"Excellent. Thank you, Doctor. The most important thing is to find out where *Seawolf* is heading, Vadsø or Tromsø. I don't remember whether either port can take a vessel with her draft . . ."

"Mr. Bover, *Seawolf* is in the middle of a search-and-rescue operation for a downed Russian submarine."

Bover nodded vigorously. "I understand that, Doctor. It's all over the media and the Internet. I promise, the instant *Seawolf* reaches port, my techs will be all over her. We'll turn her around in record time."

"She's not coming in to port. The plan is to send these parts out to her."

Bover's shocked expression surprised her. "Who thought that up? The weather is just getting better here. It's still very bad to the north. Even if we can get the parts to her, the reported damage is extensive. Temporary repairs would normally take a few weeks. I was going to move heaven and earth to get it done in two, maybe three days."

"Are you saying that these repairs can't be made at sea?"

Bover answered instantly. "I'd recommend against it. This is sophisticated equipment. The techs will have a lot of work to do just identifying all the damaged parts. If they don't get all the bad boards out, they could fry the replacement parts when the gear's turned on."

He paused for a moment, then added, "I'm amazed she isn't heading for port right now."

"Mr. Bover, this is literally a life and death situation. *Seawolf* can't leave."

He sighed. "Then I don't know what I can do."

Confusion swirled inside Patterson as she considered Bover's information. What if he was right? But he said he wasn't a technician and his expertise was in surface ships.

They reached altitude and unbuckled, and Patterson immediately found herself surrounded. Hayes was first in line. "Jeff Monroe says you need a weather update, ma'am. Current conditions?"

Patterson nodded, "Yes, that would be fine."

"For what location, please?" She looked confused, and Hayes added, "For Bardufoss, or *Churchill*'s position, or the Barents? And how far in advance?" Getting a tailor-made weather forecast meant giving the tailor your measurements.

She paused, adjusting, but only for a moment. "Please forecast the progress of the storm, and when it will clear the site of the collision and the Northern Fleet's ports. And make sure to give the information to Dr. Russo as well." Hayes nodded and went aft.

After that, Commander Silas wanted permission to send a message to *Churchill* and tell her CO about the extra personnel. Then Joyce Parker wanted to protest Patterson's refusal to let a reporter on board, and Monroe wanted to know if they wanted dinner.

There were more introductions during the meal, and while the atmosphere was cordial, almost jovial, Patterson felt control slipping away. Russo and the Norwegian were huddled with Hayes the weather sergeant, Silas and Bover were conferring, while Parker was typing furiously on her laptop in a corner.

Then she noticed Jane Matsui, standing at her elbow with a question about an upcoming bill. It was a trivial issue given the circumstances, but she welcomed Jane's question gladly.

The flight to Bardufoss was only two hours, and halfway through she called another conference to hear Russo's analysis.

He kept it brief. "If *Seawolf* can find the Russian sub, that makes the rescue possible. Without *Seawolf,* it's doubtful they can be found in time." He nodded toward Hayes. "If the storm stays on track, the Russians can leave port late tomorrow, which puts them on station late the next day based on the max speed of their rescue ship. That means *Severodvinsk* will have already been down five days."

Russo looked around the table, saw no disagreement. "Arne's people will leave port this evening, which puts them on station in sixty-two hours, at their best speed. That's the good news. The bad news is that Russian crew will be almost out of breathable air by the time the Norwegians arrive. They'll be hurting, at best." Lindstrom nodded grimly. "The morning of the tenth of October is the earliest rescue operations can begin, other factors permitting."

"The other factors being that we've found her, that the weather does indeed improve—and that they're still alive to begin with," Silas offered. Patterson noticed Bover nodding agreement.

"We can't control that," Russo agreed, "but we need information from the Russians so that Arne's people are ready to go when they get on station. Technical data on *Severodvinsk*'s escape hatches and internal layout. That's the first thing we'll need from them."

Bover snorted. "Their newest nuclear attack sub? They'd rather sell their mothers."

Russo ignored the comment. "Good charts of the area would also help a lot. More than hydrography, the area has been used and fought over for a hundred years. Knowing the location of wrecks or expended ordnance will help *Seawolf* with her search as well as warn us of any potential trouble spots."

Patterson asked, "What if we can't get the information on *Severodvinsk*?"

Russo looked to Lindstrom. The Norwegian said, "It's all about time. Depending on the depth, we may not have the luxury of deploying divers. That means everything may have to be done with submersibles and ROVs. Even if we could get divers into the water, they would probably have to use atmospheric diving suits, there is simply not enough time for a saturation dive."

"Conditions will be difficult. Visibility will be measured in single meters, and it is cold. The suit makes any movement an effort. If there's a current, that makes it worse." Lindstrom's voice carried experience.

"Did your company help with the *Kursk* disaster?"

"No, but I was one of the divers working for Stolt Offshore and I dove on the boat. I am getting too old now, but I may make one or two early dives, so that I can see conditions for myself."

Patterson made a note to listen carefully whenever Lindstrom spoke.

"Ladies and gentlemen, we're approaching Bardufoss. Please take your seats."

As they buckled in, Monroe listened on the plane's interphone, then announced, "As soon as we land and you deplane, vans will take you over to the MV-22. It's waiting for us to land, and actually, they would like to expedite their takeoff, so that they can be back at base before dark."

The plane began to shudder, and Monroe warned, "It's going to be bumpy coming in. Ceiling and visibility are at minimums, but Bardufoss has excellent instrument-landing facilities."

As he reassured them, the staff sergeant carefully checked each passenger's seat belt, snugging down Bover's, and re-stowed several personal items. He almost lost his footing a few times, but finished, then hurried to his own jump seat and belted in.

At first, Patterson tried to make notes, but in the end she put the pad away, gripped the handrests and closed her eyes. Imagining the plane was a bus on a bumpy road helped, if she imagined it was a very bumpy road.

The shock of the landing was startling, but also a relief. A few minutes' fast taxi put them near a hangar, and when Monroe opened the door, she could see Air Force vans waiting nearby. The wind pushed its way into the cabin with a sharp edge, and the clouds were so low Patterson wondered what the "minimums" were.

She let the others deplane first while she organized her things. Her BlackBerry beeped, and a message from Lowell appeared. She'd texted him about Bover's concerns, and her husband's answer was brief. SUBMARINERS CAN FIX ANYTHING. STAY SAFE.

Both pilots came out of the cockpit, and along with Monroe, shook her hand. The pilot, a tanned, stocky major, said, "Good luck, ma'am. Watch those Navy types. I don't know if they're trustworthy." He didn't smile for half a second, but finally did, and she grinned at the joke as well.

Patterson made sure she was the last one of her party

off the plane, with Monroe offering to take her things to the van. Hurrying ahead, he hustled everyone into one of the two vehicles, saving space for her in the front as she hurried through the swirling wind. She realized it was spitting rain, not enough to see, but she could feel the drops stinging her face.

Monroe reached in to shake her hand again as she belted in. "Good luck, ma'am. I've got a brother in submarines."

The instant she closed the door, the van's driver took off at speed. A base "follow me" car led the two vehicles around several hangars to another part of the flight line.

A Marine Corps MV-22 Osprey sat parked at one end of a line of helicopters. It was the only one not secured against the weather. Chains ran from the fuselages of the others to the concrete and the blade tips were tied down by ropes as well.

The gray-painted aircraft had a squarish, boxy fuselage and a rounded nose in front, and swept up at the rear for a cargo ramp that was down and open, waiting for them. The wings looked wrong, and she realized they were pointed straight up, as were the engines, like two helicopter rotors.

As she spotted the aircraft, figures around it suddenly burst into action, as if waiting for their arrival. Even as the vans came to a stop, the huge blades began to turn. A thin whine quickly built up to a bass roar that fought the wind for control and filled the air with an almost visible vibration.

As her group left the vehicles, they were led over to airmen standing by another van. They pulled olive one-piece coveralls out of the rear, and she realized they were lined and had hoods.

A noncom looked her up and down and called, "Pass me a Large." He helped her out of her own civilian parka, reassuring her. "This survival suit is just as warm and will protect you if there are problems enroute, or during the transfer to the destroyer."

Grateful she'd worn slacks for warmth, she let the enlisted man wrap the suit around her and efficiently zip her in. A part of her mind wanted to ask about what kind of "problems" he was referring to, but then decided she didn't want to know.

Her own gear was transferred to a duffel, and he instructed, "Stand right there, and don't move until the loadmaster says so." The intensity in his instruction made her reluctant to even shift her stance. He patted her on the shoulder and said "Good luck" in an unnervingly serious tone. Standing with the others, she fiddled with the suit's zippers and wondered which one of the men near the plane was the loadmaster.

Almost immediately, one of the figures, a staff sergeant, trotted over to the group and called, "Dr. Patterson!" She realized the caller, inside a hooded parka, was female. The name on the outside read "Dolan."

Shouting over the noise of the engines, Staff Sergeant Dolan read a list of names from a clipboard, and each of Patterson's group signaled in turn. Satisfied that everyone was accounted for, she approached Patterson, then motioned for everyone to surround her.

"We'll approach the aircraft in single file. Please follow me, Doctor. All the baggage is aboard."

Patterson had to ask. "What about the repair parts?"

Dolan nodded. "They are loaded, and I personally double-checked them. The rest of your party is already aboard, so as soon as you're on we take off."

"What? What 'rest of my party'?" Either Patterson's question was lost in the wind or Dolan was in a hurry, because she turned and started walking toward the aircraft. Patterson hurried to keep up and fell in behind her. It seemed a simple enough task to just follow someone else, but the buffeting air and enveloping noise in the unfamiliar surroundings interfered.

It took only a moment or two to reach the end of the ramp, and Dolan stepped to one side, urging Patterson and then the rest of the group up into the aircraft's interior.

Nobody would ever confuse the inside of an MV-22 with an executive transport. The large interior was littered with fittings and fixtures she couldn't begin to recognize. Canvas-covered jump seats lined each side, and a Marine corporal in a flight suit and helmet motioned her to move forward and buckle in.

There were about ten seats to a side, and three of the seats on one side were already occupied. A cargo net forward enclosed a pile of luggage, wooden crates, and boxes—the repair parts, the original reason for the trip.

The marine was urgently motioning for her to sit down on the opposite side, in the forward seat. As she did so, one of the figures on the other side unbelted and quickly moved over to her, buckling into the seat next to her.

As soon as he was secured, he turned and offered his hand. "Dr. Patterson, I'm Dwight Manning, your State Department liaison."

"But." She paused. "We . . ."

Her confusion showed, and Manning explained, "When State found out Art Lopez was sick, they called me and asked me to take his place. I'm from the Political Office in the embassy in Moscow. I've been traveling since late last night. We landed at Bardufoss an hour ago, and we've been aboard less than fifteen minutes, waiting for you to arrive."

By this time, the rest of Patterson's group was aboard and belted in. Staff Sergeant Dolan spoke into a headset, then pressed a control. The ramp came up with a whine and closed with a solid latching sound, the sudden quiet and darkness startling.

Dolan picked up a microphone. "The flight will take approximately an hour and fifteen minutes. Once we're closer to our destination I'll give you instructions for leaving the aircraft. Do not leave your seat or unbuckle without asking my permission. Just raise your hand and I'll come over."

She spoke into her headset again and then belted in. Patterson heard an alarming series of whines and thumps, but outside her window she saw the wing and engines tilting, moving from vertical to horizontal. As soon as the wing was fully down, she felt the aircraft move, and they taxied for a short while, then picked up speed. The Osprey quickly became airborne. It was a bumpy takeoff, and for a while all Patterson could think about was a thrill ride that properly belonged in an amusement park.

The light outside the window suddenly disappeared as they pushed into the angry overcast she'd seen from the ground. The bumps grew milder, and Patterson picked up the conversation with Manning.

"State said Joyce Parker was taking Lopez's place."

Manning looked surprised. "I know Joyce Parker. She's in public affairs."

Patterson nodded. "That's right." She gestured to Parker, further back in the aircraft.

Manning leaned forward a little to look, then sat back shaking his head. "State would never send a press hack to liaise with the Russians. I'm the number two in the Moscow embassy's political office. I've studied and dealt with the Russians for twenty-three years. I speak Russian, Ukrainian, and even a little Georgian."

Patterson made a promise to herself to deal with Parker once they reached the destroyer. She wondered if modern ships still had brigs. "What about the others?"

"The person on the left came with me from the embassy. Ron Phillips is a communications specialist. State said you had a large party, and you'd be generating a lot of message traffic. The other one showed up at the embassy late last night. He's the Skynews Moscow correspondent, Britt Adams."

Manning saw alarm in Patterson's eyes and tried to reassure her. "I've worked with Adams many times. He's good—experienced, and speaks Russian as well. He had a letter from State telling him about your mission and suggesting he join us. Get our side of the story out and counter some of this Russian trash they're flinging around."

"How would he have gotten that letter? Who would have sent it to him?" Even as Patterson asked Manning the question, she knew the answer, and looked at Parker again. This time Parker met her gaze, then quickly looked down, lest she be burned to a crisp. A brig was too good for her.

Manning raised his hands, as if to ward off Patterson's anger. "We need a reporter, and we can use Joyce Parker. She's aggressive . . ."

Patterson snorted.

". . . but the good ones always are. I'm here to help you. Let me deal with her." He gestured around the inside of the aircraft. "It's a little late to send her back."

Patterson sat back, fuming at her helplessness and Parker's duplicity at weaseling her way into the group, and then getting around her to get a reporter on board. But she forced herself to set it aside. Instead, she concentrated on learning all she could about Manning and his skills, and telling him what they'd determined so far.

Manning shared one piece of interesting information. Moscow was full of rumors, fueled by the families' demands for information and the complete lack of anything useful from the Navy Ministry. The only official release from the ministry had stated that search operations were under way, and more information "would be released when it was available." So far, none was available.

Very quickly, it seemed, the loadmaster stood again and used the public address system. "We're twenty-five minutes out. *Churchill*'s doing her best to steer a smooth course, but she says there are ten-foot waves and twenty-five-knot winds. The pilot's going to use a fast straight-in approach, and not go vertical until the last minute."

"It's going to get pretty bumpy," she warned, "and I'll come around and make sure your straps are snug. When we land, you'll feel the thump. Do not unbuckle! After the pilot lands, he'll reverse the prop's pitch to hold us on the deck. When he's satisfied, he'll tell me, and then, while I drop the ramp, you all unbuckle and move quickly off the plane. Sailors will guide you from that point."

After her instructions, they all sat waiting. It was still bumpy, worse than any commercial flight she'd ever had, and Patterson wondered how bumpy it was going to get. It got worse, and she kicked herself for asking. She found herself checking her watch every few minutes, but didn't fight the urge. It was something to do.

It happened in less time than Dolan's instruction had taken. The plane banked sharply left, leveled, and then suddenly slowed. Patterson saw the wing and engine out her window tilt toward the vertical, and the plane mixed a front-and-back movement into its uneven flight path. It was hard to tell, but she hoped they were descending. The WHAM startled her, and they were down.

Dolan, still strapped in her own seat, motioned with her arms and shouted, "Stay put!" She looked up toward the ceiling, and Patterson saw a pair of lights. One, a bright red, was lit. A moment later the engines' vibration changed, then intensified again, and the airframe shuddered.

The other light came on, a brilliant green, and Dolan shouted, "Unbuckle! Go! Go!" The ramp was opening, and Patterson was near the back of the group. The overcast daylight nearly blinded her, and a freezing wind pulled at her clothes. Behind her, Dolan and another marine were working with the cargo net. Patterson concentrated on standing right behind Manning and the others. Once again, she would be the last one off the aircraft, and she looked over her enlarged flock almost protectively.

Dolan was urging her forward, even though there was nowhere to go. Patterson shuffled uselessly, then took two steps and felt a rough-surfaced deck beneath her. The wind grew stronger, but a sailor grabbed her by the shoulders and steered away from the aircraft, toward a ladder.

She took three steps and then turned back to look, but the Osprey was already lifting off, the ramp closing as it climbed away from the deck. She stood still for a moment, silently wishing them luck and realizing she'd never said a word to anyone aboard the plane.

A voice behind her said, "Welcome aboard *Winston S. Churchill*."

16

SORTIE

7 October 2008
9:45 AM
Severomorsk Naval Base

Sleet streaked the air with pale gray lines and added a glittering white to the freshly fallen snow. The winds had subsided a little, but the force on the car was quite noticeable once it left the lee of a nearby building. Vidchenko's driver took extra care on the pier's icy concrete.

The small antisubmarine ship *Legkiy* lay alongside to the right, her angles and edges softened by the weather.

Crates and drums with ice collecting on their tops were piled everywhere, with busy sailors rigging slings and passing boxes hand to hand.

At least, until they spotted the approaching staff car. A sailor pointed and called out, and suddenly every man headed for the ship, piling aboard with petty officers shouting.

As they pulled up to the pier, Vidchenko saw more men boiling out of the ship. They formed ranks along the lifelines on the main deck, and on each level above the main deck running the length of the ship. Twenty-plus officers, in their best uniforms, stood in two ranks on either side of the aft gangplank.

Vidchenko almost rubbed his eyes in disbelief. They were manning the rails! Ships usually did this to honor a high-ranking officer, but this was a working visit, not some ceremonial occasion.

As the car half-slid to a stop by the after gangplank, Vidchenko fought the urge to shout at the idiot captain. Instead, he calmly stepped out of the car, saluted the sentries at the foot of the gangplank, and then the Russian naval ensign when he reached the top.

Legkiy's captain was tall, with short blond hair under his oversized white uniform cap. Particles of ice were collecting on his cap and greatcoat. He stood stiffly, nervously at attention. What was his age? Mid-thirties? Obviously he was capable. Vidchenko knew that with so few ships in commission, the Navy had its pick of men for each commanding officer's position. Unfortunately, imagination didn't seem to be one of the selection board's priorities.

As Vidchenko stepped onto the deck, the captain called his crew to attention and he saluted, along with the other officers arranged behind him. Vidchenko went through the motions as quickly as he could, suppressing his irritation.

"Captain Second Rank Yuri Alexandrovich Smirnov reports *Legkiy* is ready! Will you inspect the ship, sir?"

"No, Captain, you may dismiss the crew."

"Thank you, sir." Firing a crisp salute, the captain spun in place and called "Dismiss by battle departments! Continue ship's routine!"

The junior officers disappeared, but the senior ones remained, and the captain invited Vidchenko below. "We have some refreshments in the wardroom, sir. The . . ."

"No thank you, Captain, this is not a social visit." Vidchenko glanced back at the other officers, waiting and listening. "Let's speak in your cabin."

"Yes, sir, of course." Smirnov seemed puzzled, and a little disappointed. "This way." Dismissing the waiting officers, he led the admiral forward along the main deck port side, then into an interior passageway and up one set of stairs.

As they walked along the port side, Vidchenko looked at everything. *Legkiy* was an escort frigate, designed to fight submarines with her medium frequency sonar and 85RU Metel missiles. She also carried short-range antiaircraft missiles and guns for self-defense. While one of the older ships in the fleet, commissioned in 1977, she had undergone an overhaul and modernization in the late 1980s and was still rated as a capable, combat-ready unit.

She looked a little shabby. Rust showed through the paint on corners, and he could see improvised repairs in several places, work that should have been done during a refit. But funds were scarce and the Project 1135 class ships that *Legkiy* belonged to were being retired. There were only three left in the Northern Fleet and the other two were *hors de combat*. There was barely enough money for fuel and pay, so spare parts got less and paint was an afterthought. The lines and gear, the admiral saw, were properly stowed. *Legkiy* was a neat ship, if a little worn.

Inside, in Smirnov's stateroom, Vidchenko could still hear the wind-driven sleet striking the ship's sides. A family portrait on his desk and several scribbled drawings taped to the bulkhead were the only personal touches.

Vidchenko spoke as soon as the door closed. "Captain, that ceremonial welcome was a waste of my time and your crew's." While he spoke softly, the admiral's tone and expression matched his words.

Smirnov protested, "Protocol demands we render proper honors, Admiral, we . . ."

"We are preparing for a search and rescue mission, Captain. I don't want anything as trivial as manning the rails to delay your preparations." Vidchenko reached into his briefcase. "Which is why I'm here."

He showed *Legkiy*'s captain a stack of messages. "This first one was received at 0700 October sixth, yesterday, reporting that you were ready for sea." He handed it to Smirnov, who read it and nodded.

"Yes, sir, I approved it and gave it to Senior-Lieutenant Rostov yesterday before breakfast to transmit." He smiled proudly.

Vidchenko angrily demanded, "Then why did we receive requests for food and fuel at 0900, ammunition at 1010, and important spare parts for your sonar at 1130?" He shoved the offending messages at Smirnov, one by one.

The captain almost snapped to attention. "The food is being loaded now, the fuel is due to show up in about half an hour, and the ammunition will be here late this afternoon."

"And yet you reported you were ready to sail yesterday morning?"

"We were ready, sir."

"How can you report as being ready for sea when you were missing so many supplies?" Although phrased as a question, Vidchenko's hostile tone challenged the officer.

"We would have experienced some difficulties, sir, but my sailors are used to hard conditions. *Legkiy* was the first ship of the task force to report ready for sea, and we can sail this minute if you wish."

Vidchenko almost exploded. "What good would you do without ammunition or food or a functioning sonar?" He bore down on the captain. "You knew the weather would keep us in port for another day or two, so you took the opportunity to posture. A paper prize for a meaningless accomplishment."

Stiffly, still at attention, Smirnov repeated, "If ordered, we would have sailed, and I am sure my crew could have overcome any supply difficulties."

The man was impossible. Either he was a fool or chose to cling to his lie. "Summon your Starpom."

"Yes sir." Smirnov turned and spoke quickly into a phone near his desk.

Legkiy's first officer showed up almost instantly. He must have been waiting outside the captain's cabin. "Captain Third Rank Vasiliy Ivanovich Filippov reporting as ordered." A younger man than Smirnov, he smiled, eager to please the high-ranking visitor.

Vidchenko returned Filippov's salute, then turned back to Smirnov. "Captain Second Rank Smirnov, you are relieved of command. Report immediately to the Headquarters Northern Fleet for reassignment."

Smirnov was still processing Vidchenko's order as the admiral turned to the equally shocked Filippov. "Captain Third Rank Filippov, take command of *Legkiy*. By the time I return to my headquarters, I want a full and correct report on her readiness for sea on my desk." Vidchenko let his expression soften a little. "You have a little time. I have one or two other stops to make."

Smirnov was starting to react, realization passing across his face in a wave. As he opened his mouth to speak, Vidchenko cut him off. "Relieved for cause is much better than being court-martialed. Falsifying official reports and lying to one's superiors are serious charges."

Vidchenko turned back to Filippov. "And I intend to sortie the task group early tomorrow morning." It was Filippov's turn to look shocked, but he wisely said nothing, so Vidchenko added, "We will be moving northwesterly while the storm moves east. Time is our first enemy. There may be others."

Filippov gathered himself enough to respond. "Yes, comrade Admiral."

"I'll find my own way out," Vidchenko announced as he left the two officers. He hadn't even taken off his greatcoat.

Petty Officer Denisov had turned the car around, and was smoking in the lee of a storehouse. By the time Vidchenko reached the gangplank, the driver had ditched the cheap cigarette and had one hand on the door handle. In spite of the ice, Vidchenko hurried down the gangplank.

Once in the car and out of the weather, the admiral ordered, "Take me to the Supply Motor Transport Section." He looked at his notes. "It's building K-115." Denisov nodded and started moving.

Vidchenko checked his notes. According to Captain-Lieutenant Morsky, it was simply impossible for him to transport the supplies they'd requested to all the ships in the task group today.

He was sure he could change Morsky's mind.

Northern Fleet Headquarters, Severomorsk

Vice Admiral Sergey Mikhailovich Kokurin was a solid-looking man. He'd had a wrestler's physique as a young man, and while some of the sand had settled, he was still an imposing figure.

He liked being imposing. His office was finished in rich colors with dark wood and filled with overstuffed furniture. The walls were covered with paintings and large photographs of great moments in Russian naval history. A bust of Fyodor Ushakov watched everyone from one corner, while flags of the Russian Federation and the Navy stood in the other.

Kokurin was the commander of the Russian Northern Fleet, and while it was smaller and weaker than the force he'd known as a young man, he loved it with all the devotion and protectiveness of a father.

Some of his men were missing, and he'd directed the entire Northern Fleet to do everything in its power to find *Severodvinsk* and rescue the crew, if they were still alive. He'd said so a dozen times since the crisis began. Everything that could be done was being done. He had his people keeping track of the rescue mission. He received briefings on their progress twice a day.

So why was he sitting behind the desk that had belonged to Admiral Ushakov, cornered like an animal by a pack of angry babushkas?

No, that isn't true, he thought to himself. A babushka is an old woman, a Russian grandmother or a mother-in-law. They were a force to be reckoned with, as fierce and relentless as a Russian winter. But this group included some young women as well, wives and mothers, some barely out of their teens.

The seven women in his office, quietly seated in an assortment of chairs, calmly drinking tea, were causing more problems than a collision at sea, than a weapons accident. He'd dealt with those things in his naval career. They had been Navy matters, handled within the Navy, and whatever the resolution, the matter had stayed inside the Navy's haze-gray walls.

But these wives and mothers had taken *Severodvinsk*'s loss outside the Navy, demanding answers from the government.

Kokurin remembered all too well the loss of *Kursk*. That tragedy, as well as the debacle in Chechnya, had been the start. The families of that submarine had been able to organize and demand an investigation, and they'd gotten it. As far as he was concerned, the Navy had expended almost as much effort satisfying the families as it had in finding and raising the submarine.

It had been different when he joined the fleet. Families were expected to sacrifice along with their servicemen, and to do so in silence. Discussing operational details or flaws or problems in training or matériel revealed valuable information. An enemy, especially one with the resources of the USA or NATO, could exploit those flaws. The Navy had actually released the official report of the *Kursk* investigation to the families. Normally such a document would have been highly classified, and now there were copies of it on the Internet!

The defense minister had virtually ordered him to meet with the families. "Say whatever will make them happy. Remember to blame the Americans. This crisis is their fault."

Olga Sadilenko, the spokesperson for the group, was a hard case. The mother of *Severodvinsk*'s reactor officer, she was articulate and unimpressed by busts, flags, paintings or admirals. Her questions were maddeningly simple.

"Have you confirmed the Americans' information?"

"If you mean the location they provided, no, we haven't. A Navy spokesman has suggested that the Americans may have deliberately given us incorrect information," Kokurin answered.

"But that makes no sense," the woman responded.

"Why admit your involvement and then lead the searcher to the wrong place? What did the ships find there?"

"I'm sorry, Mrs. Sadilenko, I'm not at liberty to say. There have been indications that the American is deliberately interfering with the search."

"How is he doing this?" Sadilenko demanded. "Why have your ships not driven him from the area?"

"That information is classified."

Kokurin had tried to sound final, but Sadilenko wasn't deterred. "Why classify it? The Americans obviously know, our Navy knows, and"—she paused to look at her notes—"Captain-Lieutenant Rvanin made the accusation public yesterday morning."

She looked straight at Kokurin. "If the Americans' actions are harming our progress, shouldn't we share our evidence with the world? Make them explain themselves?"

"I'm sorry, madam, I cannot explain further."

Sadilenko looked unhappy, and the women broke into sudden discussion, everyone seeming to talk at the same time. It trailed off with Sadilenko nodding. She turned back to Kokurin.

"Did the search forces at least include the Americans' information in their plan?"

"I'm sorry, that is classified."

"Do you know where the American submarine is?"

"That is also classified."

"Have you attempted to communicate with the American submarine?"

"No, we have not. There is no way to know if the Americans will tell us the truth."

"You can learn much from a man's lies," Sadilenko countered, quoting an old proverb.

Kokurin paused, but decided to ignore the accusation. "*Severodvinsk* is a Russian Federation Navy submarine that was engaged in routine operations when it was lost. The Navy is searching for it now with every means at its disposal. We want our men back as much as you want them back, and we have the added task of finding the cause of the accident and bringing to account those responsible."

One of the women, young with a face puffy from crying, stood up in back. "My friend says her husband is still in port. Her youngest is sick and he called to see if the baby was better. But he can't do that unless he's in port, can he?"

"He shouldn't have called at all. He violated regulations. What is your friend's name?"

"I won't tell you. This isn't like the old days. You can't arrest anyone for that. She has a family."

Sadilenko asked, "How can they be searching if they're still in port? Is the storm keeping them there? The Navy spokesman said two days ago that the storm wasn't interfering with the rescue."

Kokurin felt impatience rising. He wasn't used to being argued with. They were only women, unused to naval discipline and prone to emotion. But enough was enough.

Kokurin stood. "Fleet movements are highly classified." He tried to look directly at the young woman, but the others leaned toward her protectively. "Your friend's husband serves on one ship, whichever ship it is. There are many ships involved in the search, and we do not tell *anyone* outside the chain of command the location of our warships."

Sadilenko ignored Kokurin's hint that it was time to leave. "We would like to have a liaison assigned to the search and rescue force. He is the father-in-law of one of the missing officers, and a retired submariner. He could monitor the rescue effort and send regular updates to us here."

Kokurin was horrified at the thought. Let an outsider watch their operations? He'd rather blow a hole in the side of the flagship. It didn't matter that the man they suggested was a retired naval officer. In fact, dealing with a civilian would be easier. A former Navy man might see and understand too much. It was a tailor-made security breach.

"Absolutely not. It's against regulations to have a civilian, even a retired naval officer, on a ship during possible combat operations."

"Then he could work here, at headquarters."

"No. He would see too much classified information."

"But he's been cleared."

Kokurin paced behind his desk. "That was while he was in active service. He can tell you that his clearances were taken away when he retired."

"But you can give them back."

"Impossible. He'd have to be investigated all over again, and that takes time. The rules are quite clear on this matter."

Frustrated, Sadilenko commented, "It's sad, Admiral. We are leaving here with no new information. I am disappointed that the commander of the Northern Fleet knows so little about our loved ones."

Another accusation, but Kokurin refused to be drawn out.

"Blame the Americans, who have admitted their role in causing this crisis. The Navy is doing everything it can. As sailors' mothers and wives, your role is hard, but there is little to do but wait." Kokurin tried to sound paternal. It might not have worked, but at least they were finally leaving.

The women filed out, grumbling. Once the door was shut, Kokurin let out a whoosh of air and slumped with fatigue. That was over, thank goodness. He was still coming to grips with *Severodvinsk*'s loss himself, and he found the mere mention of it created a storm of emotions.

Grief, certainly, if they were dead, but did he dare hope they were alive? All of them? And anger at Petrov. He'd congratulated the boy how many days ago? Was this his fault? He was bright, an able commander, but certainly inexperienced. Could they have picked the wrong man to be captain?

They'd given Petrov Russia's newest boat, the best in the fleet. Could it be a matériel failure? Subs were designed to resist that, but others had succumbed over the years and *Severodvinsk* had spent an insane amount of time on the building ways. What did her loss mean for the Navy, and its future? He didn't know how he was supposed to feel.

Finally, he pushed the questions back into the shadows. Nothing would be resolved soon. Endurance was the only answer. He turned back to his desk and to next year's budget submission.

OUTSIDE THE headquarters building, the women sheltered in a corner. Olga Sadilenko listened to their complaints and protests for a few minutes, making sure everyone had a chance to speak. When there was a lull, she was ready. "I didn't expect that walrus to tell us anything. Who are we to them? Nothing? We give them our sons, our husbands, but they don't believe they owe us a thing."

A cold wind eddied into the corner where they stood, as if to confirm her statement. "Yelena." She turned to the young woman who had asked Kokurin about the phone call. "I'm proud of you for standing up to the admiral like that. Can you do more?"

The young woman nodded, her unhappy expression carved from stone.

"You and your friends call as many other families as you can. Find out which ships are still in port, or when they left. Get me what you can by noon tomorrow."

"Galina, do you have the notes?"

A middle-aged woman held up a stenographer's pad. "I'll have these typed up by this evening." Her face started to fall. "With my Yuri gone, there's little to do."

A young woman reached out to hug her. "Then come and type them up with me. I'm alone, too. And when you're done, I'll add them to our web page."

The older woman dabbed at her eyes, "Thank you, Irina."

Sadilenko added, "And make sure everyone gives Irina a photo and information of your family member. Include as much biographical information as you want."

Irina, a pale woman with straw-colored hair, nodded emphatically. "There's plenty of room on the server, and it takes no time to add the text and images. We need photos of every crewman, and also photos from parties and other gatherings while *Severodvinsk* was under construction."

As the group acknowledged their instructions, Sadilenko added one more task. "Nadya, make a list of every news organization you can find on the Internet—from every country in the world, if you can. As soon as Irina's page is ready, I want to send them the link. They have to be hungry for news about our submarine. We'll give them what we have." She smiled grimly. "And we'll tell them why we don't have any more."

Severomorsk Naval Base
Mikhail Rudnitskiy

Captain Second Rank Yefim Gradev stood back a fair distance. Even in this obscene weather, sparks flew about wildly, and the language the petty officers were using would certainly be grounds for disciplinary action, if he could actually hear them. They'd rigged a makeshift canvas shelter as a windbreak, but the men welding were sandwiched between fire and ice.

Gradev was captain of *Mikhail Rudnitskiy,* one of the two submarine rescue vessels assigned to the Northern Fleet. An alert like this was something they planned and trained for, but dreaded at the same time. Nobody wanted submariners to be in danger. Sailors' lives were at stake, and his ship, neglected and undermanned, was a weak reed.

He'd hardly slept since the alert two days ago. There would have been much to do, even if they were in perfect order. But maintenance had been deferred, supply requests denied. Suddenly they had priority, but the supply system was slow to respond, and repairs took time.

Their sister ship, *Georgi Titov,* was down with a bad turbine, and Gradev had been given permission to raid her for supplies and spare parts and even crewmen. He knew the entire rescue depended on this one ship.

They needed at least one of the fifty-ton cranes working. The foundations were fatigued, and the only way to strengthen them in time was unsafe, unauthorized and uncomfortable for the men welding the supports in place.

But it would last until *Severodvinsk* was found. Combined with the motors they'd cannibalized from *Titov,* the portside crane would be back . . .

"Captain, we need you to look at AS-34." Alex Radimov, *Rudnitskiy*'s starpom, intruded on his thoughts.

"What, are the supports still giving us trouble?"

"No, sir, that work is proceeding. It's the batteries again."

Shaking his head, Gradev turned and headed for the forward hold. *Rudnitskiy* was a timber-carrier design adapted to carry two rescue submersibles in what had been cargo holds. Originally, the after hold had carried a larger rescue vehicle, AS-36 *Bester,* but that vessel had been taken out of service years ago. With AS-26 out of commission owing to a main thruster motor failure, there was only one rescue sub available, and any problem with AS-34 *Priz* was a potential showstopper.

She sat in the roofed-over hold, out of the weather, but still surrounded by a storm of activity. Sparks bathed her sides as sailors expanded and reinforced the cradle that held the vessel. Nobody had ever imagined *Rudnitskiy* venturing out in such heavy weather, and Gradev had ordered extra battens fitted to brace the rescue sub in place. The thought of her breaking loose in seven-meter seas invoked several nightmares.

From the deck of the hold, AS-34 didn't feel like a "minisub." It towered over Gradev, with its 13.5-meter-long white-and-orange-banded cylindrical hull taking up half of the storage bay. From afar she resembled a traditional submarine, but she seemed a bit odd, misshapen. The miniature sail that protected the main hatch from the sea was out of proportion to her hull, and her diminutive ducted propulsor aft could only make about three knots at full power.

But she wasn't built for speed. *Rudnitskiy* was supposed to lower AS-34 into the water as close to a downed sub as possible. *Priz* would then use high-frequency sonar to find the victim, maneuver over it and lock on to one of the emergency escape hatches. The trapped submariners could then climb into AS-34 for a ride to the surface. She could hold twenty passengers on each trip.

When she was working. One of the engineers climbed out of the access hatch and threw a tool away in disgust. It clanged loudly on the deck.

Gradev looked at his starpom. "The batteries?"

Radimov nodded. "The batteries. Remember how they wouldn't hold a charge, and we found those grounds and thought fixing them would solve the problem?" He nodded toward the cursing crewman. "Turov chased down the last of the shorts late last night, and the batteries still won't hold a full charge. We've been running three different generators on them all night. They should glow in the dark."

Priz's main thruster motor was a power hog, even though she wasn't supposed to leave the vicinity of the mother ship, they still had to maneuver to properly land and then mate with an escape hatch. Add to that power for the maneuvering thrusters, sonar, the interior lights, heat and atmosphere control; the energy requirements were far outstripping the batteries' capacity. With a fresh charge before each trip, the batteries were theoretically supposed to be sufficient for almost six or seven hours.

"Of the thirty-two cells, less than half will hold a decent charge, about eighty percent. Of the rest, most are around fifty percent, and a few are as low as twenty-five percent—essentially useless."

Gradev absorbed the report, calculated the implications. "Three hours?"

"At best, Captain," Radimov answered. "We've still got those twelve new cells coming from storage, but there's no guarantee they haven't exceeded their service lives just sitting on the shelf. What will we tell Northern Fleet?"

He didn't even have to think about it. "Nothing," Gradev answered. His starpom's expression was filled with surprise and concern. Gradev knew exactly what was going through Radimov's mind and he attempted to reassure him. "We're still working on the problem. We may yet find a solution. AS-34's endurance should improve once the new cells are installed."

Radimov was not convinced. "They don't arrive until just before we sail. It takes hours to install a single cell, and we'll be working in heavy weather."

"The work can still be done well before we reach *Severodvinsk*'s location, if they find it at all. And three hours is more than enough for one trip. *Priz* will just have to have her batteries recharged more often. And let's see what we can do about improving the individual cells' capacities, get them back up to their old levels."

The first officer looked confused. "They're sealed units. We're not supposed to tamper with their internal components."

"Unseal one of the bad ones. They stopped making those batteries ten years ago. If we can't find a way for them to hold more power, this will be AS-34's last cruise."

"And Northern Fleet doesn't need to know this?"

"We've had one visit by Vidchenko. We don't need another."

8 October 2008
0530/5:30 AM

Petr Velikiy was the fourth and last unit of the *Orlan*-class, or *Kirov*-class, as they were known by NATO. A nuclear-powered guided-missile cruiser, she was flagship of the Northern Fleet and would lead the rescue force.

On the bridge, Rear Admiral Vidchenko sat in one of the flag chairs and fidgeted. Now that he'd given the order to sortie, there was little to do.

The bridge was huge, especially for a submariner. A full fifteen meters across, the long row of windows in the front made Vidchenko think of a greenhouse more than a warship. The electronic consoles that displayed the ship's functions didn't begin to fill it up. Thinking of a submarine's cramped central command post, Vidchenko had a sudden urge to play racquetball.

There were several clusters of officers on the bridge.

Captain First Rank Chicherin actually commanded *"Petya."* It was a prestige appointment, and Chicherin was widely regarded as a climber. His competence as a commander would never really be an issue, not with two higher levels of command embarked.

Chicherin was moving around a lot, trying to look busy while *Rudnitskiy* got underway. He kept going out onto the bridge wings, and staring at the rescue ship, as if that could speed its progress. *Petr Velikiy* would be next to leave.

Rear Admiral Ivan Kurganov, Commander of the Forty-third Missile Ship Division, was in charge of the task group, and Vidchenko watched him quietly chat with several of his staff. There was little for Kurganov to do either, but he did nothing much better than Chicherin. He would let the captain run his ship, but as the center of the task group, it would only go where Kurganov ordered.

Kurganov's staff monitored the task group's operations in flag plot, located in a separate space behind the bridge. Although *Petr Velikiy* was still tied up at the pier, for the admirals, the battle had already started. Escort vessels were searching the harbor for unwelcome observers. Western subs had lurked outside Russian bases many times before. Officers and crewmen in flag plot tracked the searchers' progress as they scoured the water with their active sonar.

The storm would make acoustic searches almost futile, but Vidchenko and Kurganov agreed that it was worth the time and effort. The storm would also prevent Western satellites from watching the group's departure. The formation also departed under total emission control; no military radars or communications systems were transmitting. They would not give the Americans a free ride. Delaying news of their departure meant the Americans couldn't predict when the task group would arrive in the search area. Vidchenko thought that was good.

Vidchenko was in command of the entire search and

rescue effort. This included not only Kurganov's task group, but aircraft from shore bases and eventually the Norwegians, when they arrived. During this mission, he reported directly to Admiral Kokurin, commander of the Northern Fleet. And Vidchenko didn't give a fig who Kokurin talked to.

He'd first met Kurganov when each had been given their assignments as part of the rescue. They'd gotten little sleep, not only preparing the ships for sea, but designing a search plan.

Kurganov was a Muscovite, urban and a little too worldly for Vidchenko's tastes. He'd been born in the north, to a Navy family, but preferred Saint Petersburg to the nation's capital. In spite of their different backgrounds, they'd got on famously, because they shared an utter distrust of the Americans and harbored deep suspicions about the U.S. submarine's true role in the incident.

The surface admiral had drawn heavily on Vidchenko's submarine experience. Together they'd developed an airtight search plan. They were searching for two subs: one that could not move, another that could.

After much discussion, they'd decided to head straight for the location provided by the Americans. They felt like prize fools for having to act on it, but they'd be bigger fools if they didn't look there first.

They'd polished the plan now for two days, and if the tactics were slanted more toward ASW than search-and-rescue, it was hard to imagine that anyone on *Severodvinsk* was still alive. Part of Vidchenko wanted to believe that they were still alive, but that meant they were trapped, probably in the dark, certainly cold, breathing foul air and praying for help that might not come in time. He was a submariner, and you accepted that possibility every time you submerged, but it was a nightmare nobody wanted to think about. Part of him believed a quick end might be better.

And most of him just wanted to find the American submarine. What would happen after that depended on *Severodvinsk*'s fate.

Chicherin walked over to Kurganov and saluted. Vidchenko couldn't hear the words, but saw line handlers moving on the main deck. Kurganov returned the salute, then walked over to Vidchenko's chair. "We're underway," he reported. "And good luck to us all."

"I'll give it all to *Severodvinsk,* if it would help," Vidchenko answered. He felt a vibration in the deck. They were moving, and it felt good. He'd been eager to go, of course. The urgency had been overpowering. The storm had kept them bottled up, like a pressure cooker, tension and worry building up with no way to release it.

Let the American show himself. Vidchenko was ready for him.

17

CONTACT

7 October 2008
1830/6:30 PM
Severodvinsk

Petrov stretched his aching body as he climbed out of his command chair in the central post. While his engineers had rigged it so he could sit safely, the significant port list had the back of the chair carrying a lot of his weight. Of course, this wasn't part of the design specifications, and while it could easily carry the load, it did so at the expense of human physiology. As he worked the kinks out, Petrov looked around at his watchstanders. Anatoliy Rodionov, the torpedo and mine commander, had the deck watch, while Maksim Tylik was over at the engineer's post. Fonarin sat cross-legged against the BIUS console with his log sheets and a calculator. He punched away at the buttons with dogged determination, a pencil clenched between his teeth. Petrov smiled at his chief of chemical service's dedication.

A sudden crunch announced the relief of stress in his spine, and even though this reduced the pain in his back, he still felt tired and sore. The lingering headache was also still there, more noticeable now that the back pain had subsided. Unfortunately, there wasn't much he could do about that. Looking down at his watch, Petrov reminded himself that they had been on the bottom now for over three days. So far, the emergency measures they had taken were working. Besides being a little chilly, the crew was holding up very well. Morale was still quite good. But the "easy" part of this endeavor was about to end. The next three days would see things get steadily worse. And there was still no sign that the fleet had found them.

The sound of heavy footsteps drew Petrov's attention to the passageway behind him. Kalinin emerged from the dim light carrying a steaming cup in his hand. "Your evening tea ration, sir," he said as he offered the cup to his captain.

"Bless you, Vasiliy," Petrov replied gratefully. Slowly, he sipped the hot liquid and felt its warmth penetrate his body. Despite wearing the insulated green survival suit, he still felt chilled and the hot tea seemed to melt away the cold. "Hmmm, good tea. Thank you."

Kalinin smiled and said, "You'd probably say the same thing about hot piss right now, but I accept your compliment."

Petrov grimaced at his first officer's crudity and gestured for him to sit down. "I see that even in these adverse circumstances you've retained your belowdecks sense of humor, Vasiliy."

"You know what they say, sir. You can take the sailor out of the bilge, but you can't take the bilge out of the sailor," Kalinin quipped as he plopped down on the deck.

Shaking his head in mock despair, Petrov sat back down in his chair. Then in a more serious tone asked, "What's our status, Starpom?"

Pulling out his notes from his breast pocket, Kalinin started going through the now all-too-familiar list. "The reserve battery is at fifty-eight percent, but a number of the emergency battle lanterns have depleted their batteries. Per your orders, I've secured all nonessential lights to preserve them for use in critical locations and for when we abandon ship. We are okay on food and water, although we are down to the less tasty bits. We have plenty of stale hardtack and a couple more days of canned meat paste, at least that is what the label says."

Petrov grinned as he recalled the popular debate of the last two days as to whether or not the contents of the cans were indeed a meat product, and then as to what parts of what animal it came from. All concerned had decided in the end that, in this case, ignorance was not necessarily a bad thing.

"What about the tea and coffee?" inquired Petrov as he raised his cup. Under normal conditions, such a question would be considered trivial in the extreme. But given the powerful effect it had on his crew's morale, being the only real creature comfort they could offer, it was of considerable importance to Petrov.

"We have both in abundance," Kalinin replied. "We'll run out of power long before the engineer's cache is consumed."

"Very good. It's important to the men. It gives them something to look forward to. Please continue your report."

"There has been no change, good or bad, in the condition of the injured, although Captain-Lieutenant Sadilenko had to be sedated again. The doctor says there is little that he can do for Yakov, and that it is best to keep him unconscious until we can get him to a proper mental health specialist."

"Ever the optimist, our good Dr. Balanov," remarked Petrov.

Kalinin nodded his agreement as he turned the page in his pocket notebook. "The quality of the atmosphere has declined slightly; oxygen has dropped to sixteen point five percent and carbon dioxide is up to one point two percent. The increase is due to the fact that there are now only four air regeneration units online, using the last of the V-64 cassettes, I might add."

"How long before this last set's chemicals are depleted?"

"We have less than an hour. After that, the air will slowly get worse and worse."

"Has Fonarin revised his estimate on the amount of time we have?" Petrov asked as he jerked his thumb in chemical service chief's direction.

"Igor has triple-checked—no, correction, quadruple-checked his figures. Taking into account the number of survivors and our rate of breathing, which will increase as the carbon dioxide levels climb, he believes we have until around midday on the tenth before we reach a lethal concentration. By the evening of the eleventh, we'll all be dead, unless we're rescued, of course."

Both men fell silent as Kalinin concluded his report, put his notebook away, and pulled himself up. Petrov could tell his starpom was exhausted; he had slept very little since the incident.

"Anything else, sir?"

"Yes, Vasiliy. Have Lyachin start recycling the used V-64 cassettes in the air-regeneration units. I know they're probably next to useless, but at this point I'll take every molecule of carbon dioxide that they can remove from our atmosphere. After that, I want you to get some sleep."

"Aye, aye, sir," replied Kalinin wearily. "I will see to both requirements immediately."

As Kalinin started to hobble toward the ladder well, Petrov called out to him, "Vasiliy, just one more item. Please confer with Dr. Balanov on the possibility of administering sleeping drugs to the majority of the crew."

The starpom was both surprised and shocked by Petrov's order and his expression showed it.

"Think about it, Vasiliy," explained Petrov has he stood and walked over to Kalinin. "If we can't remove carbon dioxide from the air, then we have to reduce the rate at which it is produced. The only way I know how to do that is to get a large number of the crew to sleep more."

"Yes, sir. You are correct, we do need to consider what options we have in case . . . in case the fleet takes longer than we would like to find us."

"Let's pray that it is as drastic as we need to get, Starpom. But on the good side, it appears that the storm is finally waning. Within twenty-four hours we'll know if Kokurin has sent anyone out to look for us."

USS *Seawolf*

Jerry was one of the last ones to arrive in the torpedo room, trailing down the ladder behind a couple of sonar techs from control. The captain, the XO, and even the chief engineer clustered around the UUV console. Behind them, edging around the officers for their own peek, were the off-watch torpedomen and other stragglers. The crewmen saw Jerry and quickly made a hole, and the officers edged over just a little. It was enough to see.

The color display was designed to show detailed bathymetric sonar data, not a high-resolution photographic image. Palmer had selected a false-color mode that showed a strong sonar return as a brighter color than a softer echo. Thus, rocks on the seabed showed as yellow against a mottled brown and purple bottom, probably sand and mud. The false colors only threw off an observer for a moment. The UUV's primary sensors used high frequency sonars along with a precision underwater mapping algorithm, which gave the image the sharpness of a television camera. The observers could see patterns on the seabed where currents had scoured the bottom, a few clusters of rocks, but nothing more.

Rudel ordered, "Shift back to the long-range search."

Palmer hit a key and a few seconds later the image shrank into the foreground as the sonar shifted range scales. Ahead and slightly to the left, near the top of the screen, a yellow-green shape appeared. "Range is six hundred fifty yards," Palmer reported.

"Take your time," Shimko cautioned, needlessly. The display showed LaVerne at a speed of three knots. She couldn't go any slower and still be steered reliably.

It had to be *Severodvinsk.* It was in the right place, and after a day and a half of searching they were running out of places to look. The system had reported an anomalous contact at a range of over eight hundred yards, about half of maximum range for the vehicle's sonar. An indistinct echo at that range, and in multiple sonar beams had to be something big, maybe a sunken submarine or a large outcropping of rocks.

The closer the UUV got, the more the blip took on a recognizable shape. Jerry studied it, along with everyone else in the room. He was looking for something that would show it wasn't the sub as much as something that said it was. They'd had several false alarms in the past twenty-four hours, and he'd been delayed in the control room checking the updated charts for wrecks. There were none recorded by any of the UUVs in the area—a good sign. But this was no false alarm. It was just too big.

"It's the right size," Shimko observed cautiously.

"Could be, XO, but shouldn't we have seen it further out than eight hundred yards?" asked Lavoie.

"We're probably dealing with a new type of anechoic coating on *Severodvinsk*. Maybe its high frequency performance is better than we thought," replied Shawn McClelland.

"Two points for the sonar officer," remarked Shimko without taking his eyes off the display screen.

After another few minutes, Palmer reported, "Range is five hundred yards." The range readout was shown on the computer screen, but not everyone in the room could see the whole display.

The shape was definitely narrower at one end, which Jerry automatically labeled the stern. An irregular blob of canary yellow occupied a spot one-quarter of the way back from the other end. It was the proper location for *Severodvinsk's* sail.

Rudel studied the readouts, then turned to the intercom. "Sonar, torpedo room. Do you have anything on bearing two four seven?"

"Torpedo room, sonar. We can hear LaVerne's motor on the wide aperture array, bearing is two four six. Nothing else, sir."

"Sonar, torpedo room, very well. Keep a special watch for anything from the southwest. LaVerne may have found the Russian."

"Torpedo room, sonar, aye."

Jerry shrugged. It would have been nice to have heard some sign of life, but couldn't imagine what machinery could still be running aboard the downed sub. The object was quiet, inert.

"Hold at two hundred fifty yards and circle the contact."

Palmer acknowledged Rudel's order and typed in the commands. The "contact" now filled a quarter of the screen, and Jerry started to think of it as a sub. The perspective shifted and the shape resolved even more.

"It's the Russian boat," Shimko declared. "It's *Severodvinsk.*" He turned to the torpedo room watchstander, wearing his sound-powered phones. "Tell control we've found the Russian. Log the time and location."

An excited buzz broke out in the torpedo room, but Rudel and the other officers ignored it. Jerry noticed money changing hands in the back of the room.

"Tell me you're recording this," Shimko asked Palmer, and the junior officer nodded vigorously, his eyes still fixed on the display. "The instant we got a detection," he answered, then pointed to a red "R" in one corner of the display.

The image's outlines continued to shift as the aspect changed. The sail took shape at the appropriate spot along the hull, but foreshortened.

"She's listing," Palmer observed. "It's bad." Resting on the uneven bottom, the sub was tilted to port—a lot. The UUV continued its circle around toward the bow, looking down the length of the boat.

"I'd guess . . . what? Thirty degrees?" Shimko sounded as if he hated to be right.

"At least," Rudel answered. "This is not good. With the deck at that angle, it'll be really tough to dock a DSRV on an escape hatch. And they haven't launched their rescue chamber, so if they're alive, they're trapped."

LaVerne finished her circuit. The imaging sonar had

given them a clear picture of the Russian, resting on a rocky shelf, down a few degrees by the bow and tilted drunkenly to port, like a child's discarded toy. The shape of the sub matched what they knew of *Severodvinsk*.

"All right, let's recall Maxine. She doesn't have to search anymore. And get Patty ready for launch, just in case." Shimko looked behind him. "And anyone who doesn't have business in the torpedo room, back to your own spaces."

The room cleared out quickly, but was soon filled with activity as the torpedo gang prepared to recover one UUV and readied another one for launch.

While they worked, at Rudel's direction, Palmer steered LaVerne in a close pass down *Severodvinsk*'s length. This time, the sub's bow filled the screen, and they could see dark patches, hollows in the curve of the bow. There were also several spots that had a ragged look to them. Dents where she'd struck? The bow planes looked small for such a large vessel, but stood out clearly.

LaVerne continued down the port side. The resolution was good enough to make out the limber holes in the hull, designed to let air escape from the ballast tanks when it submerged. Rudel had chosen the port side so that the deck would be tilted toward them. The sail loomed three stories above the hull, and Palmer started to back the UUV out to get a distance.

"No, stay in close," ordered Rudel. "Look. There it is. The escape chamber is still in place. No masts extended, either."

"They either didn't have time to use the chamber or couldn't use it," Shimko answered.

"Hopefully, it's 'couldn't use it,' " Rudel observed.

Stan Lavoie watched the image. "I'm not seeing any obvious breaks in the hull. Their sonar dome is crushed, but that's made of GRP."

"I agree," said Rudel. "But the sonar image isn't good enough to make an accurate call. Mr. Palmer, I want you to make another three-sixty pass once we're done, and this time take digital pictures as you go. We can use them to get a better idea as to the damage."

"Yessir," responded Palmer.

Another minute passed as LaVerne moved further aft. Behind the sail, *Severodvinsk*'s hull was essentially a smooth cylinder. Except for the limber holes and small deck fittings that passed beneath them, it was hard to see the UUV's motion. As the vehicle moved along the hull, a bright circular section appeared on the display.

"Look at that cavity!" exclaimed Lavoie. "Is that a hole in the hull?"

"Don't think so, Eng," Jerry replied. "It's in the right location for their emergency distress buoy."

"Well, it doesn't look like it went too far," commented Shimko sarcastically. "Look at that line on the starboard sonar display. It comes out of the hull and then snakes off towards the southwest on the ocean floor. The buoy probably never made it to the surface."

"Then it's a fair bet that the Russians don't have clue as to where she is," added Rudel, a grim tone in his voice. "Keep moving aft, Jeff."

LaVerne resumed her slow trek down *Severodvinsk*. A short time later it came across the emergency escape hatch; closed but apparently in good condition. Then the hull tapered sharply near the stern, and the rudder and stern planes came into view.

"Migod." Shimko's reaction was automatic, unthinking. Jerry felt the same horror. The starboard side stern plane was crushed, a mass of tangled color on the display that didn't reveal its exact shape, but confirmed its destruction. Had it struck the bottom? Or *Seawolf*?

The lower rudder was also crushed, but it was impossible to tell if that was from being dragged on the bottom or from the collision. They were so focused on the condition of the stern planes and rudder that Palmer was the first to notice. "The screw's gone!"

"What? Have LaVerne get us a view from the starboard quarter," Rudel instructed.

According to intelligence, *Severodvinsk* was fitted with a seven-bladed "scimitar" screw. Instead of the older four or five broad leaf-shaped blades, seven thinner blades, sharply curved and skewed, sliced through the turbulent wake with less vibration, which meant less noise. Modern Western and Russian subs both used highly skewed seven-bladed screws, or even more exotic ducted propulsors.

But the image showed no blades at all, just a flat round circle with an occasional ragged edge where the propeller should be.

Palmer sounded like he was protesting. "We didn't see it on the bottom. It's some twenty-odd feet in diameter. We should have seen it when LaVerne circled the boat."

"If the screw is gone, it would mark the actual spot where we collided," Shimko said confidently. "She must have struck us with her stern. Her screw would have chewed up our bow, but the shock would have broken the blades off the propeller hub."

"They hit us at a fairly high speed," Lavoie remembered. "Without the water resistance from the blades on the propeller shaft, the propulsion plant would have run wild. We know he was running at high speed. Imagine it—fifty thousand horsepower with nowhere to go. The turbines would have torn themselves apart before the overspeed safeties tripped."

Jerry added, "The shaft seals would have failed, so you've got massive flooding. Even if . . ."

Shimko impatiently ended the discussion. "Okay guys, enough. This speculation is pointless. They're down, and without propulsion they're helpless. There's no sign of working machinery, but the hull appears to be intact. Based on what we've seen, there may be survivors on board." He said the last with a note of formality, as if making an official statement.

"I concur," Rudel stated, and the other officers nodded their agreement as well. "One last thing before we phone home. We'll try the Gertrude." Rudel quickly headed for the ladder. Over his shoulder, he ordered the phone talker, "Tell the chief of the watch to have Petty Officer Sayers report to control immediately." Sayers was one of the crypto techs assigned to provide intelligence support. He spoke fluent Russian.

Jerry and the other officers followed their captain. "Gertrude" was a nickname for their underwater communications system. Jerry was suddenly reluctant to use it. No response might indicate there was nobody alive, or they might be alive, but without power.

But what if they did answer?

Severodvinsk

Senior Seaman Fesak was cold, tired, and bored. He had been sitting for the last three hours listening on the MG-35 underwater communications station for any sign that someone was out there looking for him and his crewmates. But all he had heard thus far was the same he had heard over the last several days—nothing but waves and ice. He stifled a yawn and wrapped himself more tightly with his blanket. In one more hour he would be relieved and then he could find someplace to take a nap. It was rather difficult to listen to wave noise for long periods of time without being lulled to sleep.

Suddenly, the young sonar technician was jolted out of

his half-dozing state. He thought he had heard something. Adjusting the gain on the receiver, he sat motionless, listening intently.

"*Severodvinsk, Severodvinsk.* Do you hear me? Please respond."

Fesak couldn't believe his ears. The voice spoke clear Russian. The fleet had found them! Excitedly, he called out, "Captain-Lieutenant Rodionov! Someone is out there! They are calling us!"

Rodionov bolted from his chair and quickly made his way to the underwater communications station. "Let me hear," he ordered.

Grabbing the headset, he put it on and listened. A moment later, a smile appeared on his face. Turning to Fesak, he said, "Find the Captain. Hurry, lad!" The seaman moved off as fast as he could, adrenaline temporarily relieving his fatigue.

Rodionov grabbed the microphone and set the system to transmit. Pushing down on the mike, he said, "Hello. This is *Severodvinsk.* It is good to hear you. Please identify yourself."

The smile on his face melted away as fast as it appeared when he received the reply. "*Severodvinsk,* this is the United States submarine *Seawolf.* You have been reported as missing and we are here to render assistance. We wish to speak with your Captain."

Rodionov sat there stunned. An American, not the Northern Fleet, had found them. What was he supposed to do now? Where was the captain?

"*Severodvinsk,* this is *Seawolf.* Did you receive my last?"

Shocked out of his stupor, Rodionov reluctantly responded, "Yes, yes. I received your last transmission. I am waiting for my Captain. Please stand by."

"*Severodvinsk, Seawolf.* Understood. Standing by."

In less than a minute, Petrov, Kalinin, and most of the battle department commanders were in the central post, surrounding the underwater communications station. All were smiling, hope beaming from their faces.

"Have you responded to their hail, Anatoliy?" asked Petrov.

"Yes comrade Captain," Rodionov replied nervously.

Puzzled by his junior officer's answer, Petrov looked at him curiously and said, "Then what's wrong?"

"Captain, it's not the fleet. We have been found by an American submarine!"

"What!?!" exclaimed Petrov, alarmed. "You mean the one we collided with?"

"I don't know, sir. They said they were the *Seawolf*, that we have been reported missing, and that they are here to render assistance."

An unexplainable anger arose within Petrov as he wondered if this was the same boat that had had a hand in their disaster? If so, where had they been for the last three days? If they were truly here to help them, then why had it taken so long? And where the hell was the Northern Fleet? These questions only served to intensify his fury as he remembered the eighteen men he had lost.

Petrov struggled silently to maintain a professional demeanor, but his clenched jaw betrayed his true emotions. It didn't matter if this was the same sub that had collided with them. Despite their circumstances, he could not bring himself to speak with an American, any American, right now.

"Captain," Kalinin asserted softly. "We need to respond."

Petrov rebelled at his first officer's gentle admonition. "I am well aware of that, Starpom!" The sheer venom in his response surprised even Petrov.

He saw the reaction of his men, and some of the rage left him. Taking a deep breath, he forced himself to calm down and then added, "My apologies, Vasiliy. You are quite correct. I just find the irony of the situation to be highly . . . aggravating."

Kalinin's slight smile told Petrov that all was forgiven without a single word being spoken. After another deep breath, Petrov unplugged the headset, selected the loudspeaker, and picked up the microphone.

"United States submarine, this is Captain First Rank Aleksey Petrov, commanding officer of the Russian Federation submarine *Severodvinsk.* Do you read me?"

"*Severodvinsk,* this is *Seawolf.* We read you loud and clear. Your Navy has reported you as missing, we are here to render assistance." The reply sounded a little wobbly and tinny over the loudspeaker, typical of acoustic communications through seawater.

"To whom am I speaking?" asked Petrov. After a brief pause, the American replied.

"Sir, my name is Petty Officer Wayne Sayers."

"I must compliment you on your Russian, Petty Officer Sayers," responded Petrov with a tinge of sarcasm. "Who is *Seawolf*'s commanding officer?"

"Commander Thomas Rudel is in command of USS *Seawolf.*"

"May I please speak with him directly?"

"Sir, Captain Rudel regrets that he does not speak Russian. Do you speak English?"

"Yes, I do," Petrov answered clearly, with only a hint of an accent. "I was once an assistant naval attaché in your country. May I please speak to Captain Rudel?"

"*Severodvinsk,* this is Captain Rudel speaking. What is your situation?"

The man doesn't waste time getting down to business, thought Petrov. The mark of a professional. Still, there was one thing that he had to know before they could get started.

"Captain Rudel, I must know. Was it your submarine that collided with us?"

There was an uncomfortable pause while Petrov waited for Rudel's reply. It was a straightforward enough question, and he wondered why the American was taking this long to answer it. Finally, Rudel's voice came over the loudspeaker.

"Yes, Captain, our boats collided a little over three days ago."

"Why did you hit us?" demanded Petrov angrily.

There was another short pause, but when Rudel did answer his voice sounded tense and angry as well. "It was not my intention to collide with you, Captain. In fact, I was doing everything I thought necessary to avoid just such a situation. My intention was to disengage and evade, as I was concerned with your rather aggressive behavior."

"THESE ARE OUR WATERS," yelled Petrov. His face a bright crimson, his body shaking with fury. At that moment, Kalinin placed his hand on Petrov's shoulder and squeezed tightly. Turning to face his starpom, Petrov saw him shaking his head no. Quietly Kalinin whispered, "Sir, this is not the time to argue with the American."

Almost as if on cue, Rudel's response to Petrov's accusation rang out from the speaker, "Captain Petrov, I will not debate issues of territory or policy right now. I hope there will be time for that later. Right now, my only concern is to assist in the rescue of you and your men."

Between his starpom's comment and the American captain's measured words, a torrent of emotions completely engulfed Petrov. Anger, frustration, guilt, and even shame washed over him. He almost wished the American had been more belligerent. With his ego bruised and his feelings crushed, Petrov let loose a heavy sigh.

Lifting the microphone, he spoke calmly and deliberately. "Agreed, Captain. We will deal with how the collision occurred later. But if you are here to help, why did it take you so long to find us?" The last sentence sounded more like a plea for an explanation, rather than a demand.

"Honestly, we thought you had returned home. I believed that my boat had suffered more damage than you, and we were limping to a friendly port to effect repairs. Given your country's reputation for building sturdy submarines, we never dreamed you had had the worst of the encounter," answered Rudel frankly. "It wasn't until we heard that you were reported as missing that we knew otherwise. After that, it took time for us to get back here and begin searching. My bow is badly torn up and we can't move very fast."

Petrov translated Rudel's explanation for the delay to his subordinates who listened with rapt attention. Some were nodding as the story unfolded.

"Sounds plausible," said Chief Engineer Lyachin. "It seems consistent with what we know."

"Plausible?" Kalinin exclaimed. "It's more than plausible, Captain. It's believable. This American didn't have to come back. He could have passed on what he knew to his commander and kept on going to Norway or Great Britain. No one would have questioned such a decision if he has suffered even a fraction of the damage we have. But instead, he turned around and went looking for us; probably at some risk to themselves. I believe this captain is an honorable man, sir."

Coming from his starpom, a professional naval officer with unusually high standards, this was high praise indeed. Petrov, reluctantly, had to agree. With a weary grin on his face, Petrov raised the microphone once more and said, "Captain Rudel, I accept your explanation and your offer for assistance. Here is our current status."

USS *Seawolf*

"Do you hear that son of a bitch!?!" exclaimed Shimko with total disbelief. "That stupid asshole is blaming us for the collision!"

Rudel rapidly drew his right hand across his throat with a slashing motion and ordered, "Quiet!" Then, in a more normal tone, "I don't have time for posturing from Petrov or any of you. Let's stay focused on the task at hand. He's more than a bit pissed off and I can't say I'd feel any differently if our roles were reversed."

Jerry had seen Rudel's initial reaction, and it was clear he was upset with the Russian captain's accusation. Being the navigator, Petrov's words had a particular sting to them that once again raised the ugly specter of doubt in Jerry's mind. I don't have time for this, he said to himself, and proceeded to stuff his personal demons back into their box. Jerry then listened as his skipper calmly and carefully disarmed Petrov's accusations and successfully convinced him that *Seawolf* was really here to help them.

Suddenly, Rudel snapped his fingers at Jerry and motioned for him to start writing down the data that Petrov was providing. Nine dead, nine missing and presumed dead, seventeen crewmen with serious injuries. Three compartments completely flooded, reactor shut down, power provided by the reserve battery; Jerry winced as the list went on and on. Without a doubt, the Russians had drawn the short straw and had suffered accordingly. Even Shimko was shocked at the degree of damage that *Severodvinsk* had sustained. Whistling softly, he said, "It's a miracle any of them are still alive."

Finally, Petrov started to report on their atmosphere. Sixteen point four percent oxygen, one point four percent carbon dioxide. That's not too bad, Jerry thought hopefully. But the last part of Petrov's report filled everyone in *Seawolf*'s control room with dread. "All chemical air-regeneration cassettes are depleted. Repeat, all chemical air-regeneration cassettes are depleted. Estimated time to lethal carbon dioxide concentrations is two and a half days. End of report."

Rudel groaned at the significance of Petrov's last statement. Without aid of some sort, the survivors would be incapacitated in less than two days and dead soon after. And there was still no sign that the Russian Northern Fleet was anywhere near. As he slowly raised the mike to his face, Rudel took a number of deep breaths and tried to sound as "normal" as he could.

"Captain Petrov, we have your data and we will relay it to our government along with your exact location. However, I must surface to transmit. We will be out of touch for a couple hours, but we *will* be back."

"Understood; and Captain, thank you. *Severodvinsk* out."

"Skipper, those guys are screwed!" exclaimed Lavoie, who looked just as stunned as everyone else.

"Enough of that, Engineer, I won't tolerate a defeatist attitude. We'll just have to come up with something to help them," replied Rudel with a fierce determination. He then quickly turned about and began shooting out orders.

"Mr. Hayes, get us on the roof, ASAP! Nav, give your notes to Mister Chandler and have him prepare a report to be sent by the sat phone. I want this stuff out within ten minutes after we surface. The rest of you go with the XO to the wardroom and work this problem over. I want options, not excuses. We are not just going to let those men die. Understood?"

A chorus of "Aye, aye, sir," rang out as people turned to and began to execute their skipper's instructions.

As Shimko and the other officers went to the wardroom, Jerry made a quick detour into the radio room. He found Chandler already putting together the initial draft of the phone message. "Here you go, Matt," said Jerry as he tossed his notes on the worktable. "This is all the information we got from the Russian skipper. Have it ready for transmission in fifteen minutes."

"Right, I'll have Chief Morrison put it together immediately."

Jerry looked around the room, there was no sign of the ITC. Confused, he turned back to find Chandler pushing the notes Jerry gave him to the opposite side of the table. He then started writing furiously in a standard navy-issue green logbook. "Excuse me, Matt. But what are you doing? The Skipper wants this message drafted ASAP."

"The chief will be here momentarily. I was going to finish up my report on the collision," replied Chandler with an air of innocence.

Red flashed before Jerry's eyes; he had had enough of Chandler's cover-your-ass antics. Struggling to control his anger, he approached Chandler with a deliberate, menacing stride. The commo's expression became more fearful as he watched Jerry approach; it was as if he saw flames shooting from Jerry's icy blue eyes.

"Wrong answer, mister," growled Jerry; his tone was almost guttural. Chandler gulped audibly. "You are going to draft that message as ordered, with or without Chief Morrison's aid. In nine minutes, you will bring the draft to me. If you are one second late, I will personally put you on report the moment you walk through the wardroom door. DO I MAKE MYSELF ABSOLUTELY CRYSTAL CLEAR!?"

The on-duty ITs cringed and looked about for a convenient place to hide. No one had ever seen the navigator this mad before. In fact, no one in the department had ever heard him yell before. For the patient, professional

Mr. Mitchell to blow his relief valve, the offender would have to have screwed up really, really badly.

Chandler started to shake visibily; beads of sweat lined his brow. "Please, Jerry, I *have* to write it all down." He sounded fearful and desperate, almost pleading. And he'd used Jerry's name.

Completely surprised by Chandler's pitiful-sounding response, Jerry was instantly snapped out of his rage. There was none of the usual bravado, and the smug arrogant attitude was also absent.

Matt Chandler had manned one of the fire-control consoles during General Quarters, and he'd been there when they collided with *Severodvinsk*. It was as good a place as any to watch what was going on, but he hadn't given any orders, made any decisions. Why the fanatical drive to write down his impressions?

Confused as to what was happening, Jerry asked, "I don't understand why you feel this is so urgent. Did you see something, Matt—something important?"

"Important?! Migod, Jerry, we collided with another submarine. Rountree's dead, and we almost lost the boat! We *all* nearly died!"

Jerry looked carefully at his communications officer. Chandler was excited—wide-eyed, even a little breathless. This couldn't be an act. He was actually terrified. Sensing that Chandler was on the verge of losing it, Jerry pushed a little. "How long have you been working on this write-up?"

"I went straight to our stateroom right after we started for Scotland and just started writing. It was like I couldn't stop. I didn't want to stop. I wrote down everything I could think of, before I forgot any of it, I didn't want to miss anything. But I don't know if I can ever forget any of it."

"You've been at it that long? What about your duties? Your men?"

"They don't matter. None of this matters. I just have to write it all down. I have to do it now, if I'm going to finish in time."

Jerry was still confused. "In time for what?"

"For us getting back to port. There's so much to write down. I can remember every detail like it happened only a moment ago, and it takes so long to explain things clearly . . ."

Jerry cut him off. "Matt, why do you have to write it all down right now?"

"Because we could have all died. Not just Rountree, all of us. I really understand now how dangerous submarines are. I knew we had to be careful, follow procedures, but I always thought it was like crossing the street. You never think you're going to be the one in an accident."

"Matt, you can't focus on . . ."

"On what? The danger?" Chandler held his hands out, encompassing the space. "We're surrounded by it. We can't escape it, it's with us every minute of every day!" He paused for a moment, and then said flatly, "I . . . I shouldn't be here. This is a mistake. Why in the world am I working my ass off for a promotion I'm never going to live to see?"

Jerry hardly knew what to do, or what to say. Chandler was obviously on the edge, maybe over it. He'd stared his own mortality in the face, and didn't like what he'd seen. Jerry was not a priest or a psychologist, and he felt completely at a loss. Part of him had always wanted to slap Chandler around, but that only worked in the movies.

"Matt, I need you to get past this." Jerry grabbed Chandler by the shoulders and spoke calmly but firmly. "It's been a shock, but we're still here. And you've got an important job to do. You managed to get the radioes working earlier, so you know you can fulfill your duties even with this monkey on your back. Forget the report for now. There will be a time and place when it will be needed, but right now I need you to get that message drafted."

Chandler looked exhausted, but he listened quietly, passively. Jerry wondered if he'd already given up, but the comms officer nodded slowly. "I'll take care of it right away."

Jerry felt relieved by Chandler's answer. "Good. I'll be in the wardroom when you're ready, Matt."

Still confused and a bit drained, Jerry literally stumbled through the wardroom door ten feet down the passageway. Whatever conversation had been going on had stopped the moment he threw open the door.

"Personnel issues, Mr. Mitchell?" asked Shimko with his trademarked pixieish grin.

Embarrassed and uncertain if he should say anything about Chandler, Jerry dropped forcefully into his chair and replied, "You heard?"

"Nav, I think the Russians heard you!" joked the XO. Everyone else in the wardroom laughed, and even Jerry had to crack a smile.

"Look, I know Chandler is a pain in the ass, but he is a very efficient pain in the ass. So please, try not to kill him." The XO winked as he spoke; letting Jerry know he was on solid ground as far as he was concerned.

"Yes, sir. I will try," Jerry replied wearily, relieved that the XO had been referring to his lost temper and not Chandler's meltdown.

"Okay gents, back to our *leetle* problem. How the hell do we help the Russians with their CO_2 levels?"

Silence and blank stares greeted Shimko's question. "Well, don't all talk at once now."

Still nothing.

Sighing, Shimko stood up, grabbed a black marker and threw a piece of butcher-block paper on the wardroom table. "Let's start listing all the options and their feasibility."

"Rescuing the Russians ourselves," offered Lavoie. "Not an option. We have no way to transfer the crew."

"What about using our high-pressure air to blow their remaining ballast tanks," suggested Ensign Miller.

"It's a nice idea, Tim," remarked Todd Williams, *Seawolf*'s damage-control assistant. "But not feasible. We have no way to hook up our main ballast tank blow system to theirs. Besides, with three compartments flooded and a number of their ballast tanks violated, we couldn't generate enough buoyancy to get them off the bottom."

"All right then. Direct rescue is not a practical option. Agreed?" Shimko asked. All present nodded their heads yes. "So, removing carbon dioxide is the next option. Suggestions?"

"Well, we probably don't have any equipment that's compatible with their systems," said Constantino.

"But we do have CO_2 curtains with the lithium hydroxide canisters," Williams replied.

"Yeah, but how do we get our gear to the Russians?" asked Lavoie pointedly.

"Won't the Russian fleet have the ability to resupply them?" asked Wolfe.

"Maybe," answered Williams. "The problem is that when CO_2 gets over three percent, people get a bit loopy and judgment goes to hell; not to mention a person gets fatigued by merely moving. If the Russians aren't here by tomorrow evening, those guys in *Severodvinsk* will be in the hurt locker."

"Besides, how do we know if the Russian fleet is enroute," injected Constantino. "If you remember, the weather has been pretty shitty as of late and they may not even have left port."

All the qualified deck officers present silently glared at the supply officer with significant annoyance. He had never stood a watch on the bridge during the storm; they had, and they were all well aware of just how bad the weather had been.

Constantino quickly realized that he had "opened mouth and inserted foot" and tried to backpedal. "Hey, it's not my fault I'm not allowed to stand bridge watches."

At that moment the wardroom door opened and mercifully diverted attention from the chop's faux pas. Chandler and Palmer walked in; Palmer squeezed by the engineer and the weapons officer and sat down at the end of the table. Chandler remained standing; he looked pale and exhausted. He slowly approached Jerry, offered him a folder and said, "Sir, the draft message for your review."

Shimko said nothing, and with a raised eyebrow, watched as Jerry took the folder. Jerry ignored the XO's questioning look, quickly read the draft, made some minor changes, initialed it, and handed it back to the communications officer. Chandler then silently offered the folder to the XO. Shimko took the folder, read the message, initialed it, and returned it to Chandler. "Take this to the Skipper for his approval, Matt."

"Yes, sir," responded Chandler barely audibly, and then left.

"All right now, where were we?" remarked Shimko thoughtfully. "Oh yes, we were about to lynch the supply officer." This time Jerry laughed along with the rest.

"Ahh, excuse me, sir," stammered Palmer. Not quite sure what he had just walked into.

"Yes, Jeff. What is it?"

"Sir, LaVerne has completed her photographic survey of *Severodvinsk* and is in the process of being recovered. I should have copies of the sonar images and the pictures within two, maybe three hours."

"Excellent, Jeff," praised Shimko as he gave the young officer the thumbs-up. "Please, join us. The Chop here was just about to tell us his plan to save the Russians."

"Ah come on, XO," pleaded Constantino. "I don't have a frickin' clue, honest."

"But you're 'the Ferengi,' aren't you?" taunted the XO. "You always seem to be able to get us what we need, anytime, anywhere." Shimko's reference to Constantino's nickname on the waterfront went beyond the supply officer's drastically receding hairline and large ears. He had an uncanny knack of getting anything *Seawolf*'s crew needed. He had never failed to fill a requisition.

"XO, you know damn well that I have a good network that enables me to find stuff we need. But I can't get a FedEx or DHL delivery truck to drop the stuff off at our doorstep out here," Constantino protested.

At the mention of the words "delivery truck," Jerry eyes flew wide open and he looked at Palmer, who was staring right back at him with the same eyes. Almost in unison they both cried, "The UUVs!"

Shimko's gaze bounced back and forth between Jerry and Palmer. "What?" he exclaimed.

"We can use the UUVs as a delivery truck," stated Jerry.

"Yes! We can strip them of most of their recon gear, and probably gut an expended energy module to make space and weight available for emergency supplies," Palmer added enthusiastically.

"Absolutely. We could easily get several hundred pounds' worth of atmosphere control chemicals, medical supplies, battle lanterns, whatever, just as long as it physically fits in the vehicle," continued Jerry.

"WHOA, WHOA, WHOA," shouted Shimko. "Let me get this straight. We gut one of our UUVs, fill it with emergency supplies, launch it, and then drive it . . ."

"Into one of *Severodvinsk*'s exposed torpedo tubes," said Jerry as he finished the sentence.

"The idea is feasible," concluded Wolfe. Lavoie also agreed.

"How long would it take you to prepare a UUV, Jeff?" Shimko queried intently.

"I . . . I don't know, XO; maybe ten or twelve hours. We have to remove a lot of stuff then plug the holes so that the cargo space is watertight. And then there are half a dozen interlocks we'll have bypass so we can fly the vehicle into the *Severodvinsk*'s tube. I can get you a better estimate after I talk to Chief Johnson."

"Not to be a pessimist here, but this plan depends on *Severodvinsk*'s torpedo tubes being functional," Wolfe pointed out.

"True enough, Greg," replied Jerry. "We'll have to ask Captain Petrov if his starboard tube doors still work."

"That's good enough for me," beamed Shimko. "Well done, gentlemen." He then reached over for the sound powered phone handset, selected the CO's stateroom, and cranked on the growler.

"Captain, XO here. Skipper, we have a plan."

Old Executive Office Building, Washington, DC

Jeffrey Wright ran the meeting himself, this time. He didn't have a choice anymore. The media had zeroed in on the incident as their next big newsmaker. It had mystery, high tech, and human tragedy—everything needed to keep viewers glued for the next breaking bulletin.

And they were just as happy reporting Russian accusations as they were press releases from Admiral Sloan's office. How long had that lasted? A few hours? Sloan had gladly turned the job over to the CNO, and now the Department of Defense had replaced the Navy.

Wright waited for the CNO to sit, but just barely. "I apologize for the last-minute summons, but Commander Rudel's latest phone report will be all over the media in less than an hour. Have you all seen it?"

All three of the Navy admirals nodded. They'd shown

up quickly. The traffic was light at two o'clock in the afternoon, and they'd all been at the watch center at the Pentagon. The State Department official, the same European Affairs rep that had been present at the first meeting, was the only one to speak. "I read it on the way over. The information is explosive. Isn't there any way of containing it?" He sounded desperate, almost pleading.

The CIA deputy director, a large, well-dressed man named Vincent, looked irritated with the question. "All of Rudel's transmissions have been intercepted, reported, and posted on the web. News organizations, even some private individuals, have the ability to intercept satellite phone signals. It's too easy, and the messages from *Seawolf* are the hottest news in the world." He paused for a moment, and then stated flatly, "No, they can't be contained." He shook his head, as much in frustration as to accent his negative answer.

Wright glanced at his notes. "We have two questions to answer. First, now that we know there are men alive aboard *Severodvinsk,* and that they may not survive until help arrives, is there any more help we can give?" He looked first at the three admirals, but then made sure to look directly at the other side of the table: State, CIA, even Jacob Hoffman, counsel to the president.

After a moment's pause, the State Department rep, Abrams, remarked, "We're passing *Seawolf*'s information on to the Russians, of course. Beyond that, I don't see what we can do but stand by. Given the possibility of misunderstandings with the Russians . . ."

Wright cut in again. "*Seawolf* is going to attempt to pass emergency atmosphere supplies of some sort to the Russian sub, using one of the UUVs. Should we order Rudel to stop? The UUV contains classified technology, doesn't it? What will be the effects of it falling into the Russians' possession?"

Rear Admiral Keller, the senior submariner, gave a small shrug. "It has high-frequency imaging sonars and a powerful microprocessor, but most of the hardware and software technology is available off the shelf. The battery technology is pretty exotic, but again, it's commercially available. I'd have to talk to ONR or the manufacturer's reps to see if there's anything that is controlled or whether there's anything the Russians couldn't buy or make themselves. The only real classified information is the bathymetric data that the UUVs have collected. Rudel has said that information will be removed before they send the vehicle over."

"It doesn't matter, Mr. Wright." Hoffman's tone was final. "Now that Rudel's informed us of his plans to attempt the transfer, and if it has any chance of success, we are legally bound to follow through with it. And, as we've discussed, the whole world will know he's trying it."

"I agree with Mr. Hoffman, although not because of any legal constraints. The political benefits from any constructive efforts to save the men on board *Severodvinsk* outweigh the potential of a minor loss of classified technology," remarked Abrams.

Wright looked frustrated. "So there are really no decisions to make? Which necessarily implies we have no control over events as they unfold."

"We've got *Seawolf* on station, and *Churchill* is en route," the CNO replied.

There was nothing more to say.

18

FIRST AIR

8 October 2008
0730/7:30 AM
USS *Seawolf*

"No pressure," Jerry kept muttering to himself. "We can do this." He'd finally taken off his watch to keep from looking at it. It had been over eleven hours since they started, and they still had a lot of work yet to do.

They'd opened up LaVerne, so Jerry could work out the loading arrangement while Palmer and his torpedomen modified Patty.

Petty Officer Allen came clattering down the ladder holding a battle lantern. "Here's the first one. The chief wanted to make sure this is what you wanted, sir."

A Navy battle lantern was a large waterproof flashlight, a box about six inches on a side. They were placed throughout the ship and designed to turn on automatically if power failed. They could also be detached and used like a standard battery-powered lantern.

The plan was to put three into the UUV, because the Russians' own lanterns were just about shot. Jerry had asked Clausen, the chief auxiliaryman, to remove the mounting bracket on the back and the handle on top. That saved three inches in one direction and five in the other, important for packing them into a small space.

"This is perfect, MM2," Jerry replied. "Tell the chief I need the others the same way, and about six additional batteries. And he should double-check the seals, to make sure they're still watertight."

"We're on it," Allen replied excitedly as he almost raced out of the space.

Jerry handed the lantern to QM1 Peters, who weighed the device on a scale they'd borrowed from the galley.

While Peters entered the data on a laptop, Jerry studied the accumulating pile. The Russians needed lots of help: medical supplies, battle lanterns and batteries, and especially the carbon dioxide absorption chemicals.

Everything had to fit in the space normally occupied by some of the mission payload and most of Patty's batteries. One piece of luck: The UUV's lithium-thionyl-chloride batteries were removable. They had to be replaced after each sortie. Each energy module was made up of three batteries and occupied a space four feet in length and exactly nineteen and three-quarter inches in diameter. Altogether, Jerry had a little over seven feet of Patty's twenty-foot, eight-inch length to work with.

Chief Johnson worked with several of the nuke electricians to rig up a much smaller battery that would give Patty about an hour of juice; more than enough for her to make the short trip to *Severodvinsk.* They'd given Jerry the rough dimensions of the new battery, and it was Jerry's task to fill the remaining space with as many supplies as could fit.

He knew they couldn't exceed the weight of the batteries they'd removed, or it would make Patty too heavy to swim. But weight wasn't the issue. His problem was volume. The supplies he was planning to load didn't come close to the density of the batteries, so he was trying to cram as much as he could to just get close to the original weight. And that weight had to be properly arranged, or Patty wouldn't be able to maintain trim, and that would make her very difficult to steer.

All he had to do was simultaneously solve several multiple-variable equations, and hope he'd get it right. And the only way to test their answer was to launch Patty and hope she didn't drive herself into the bottom. And he kept thinking about the Russian sailors, who would die without these supplies. No pressure at all.

The XO came down the ladder and glanced at Patty, lying gutted on the storage rack, but he barely stopped on his way to where Jerry and Peters were working.

"The Skipper wants to know if there's room for some food. He was just reviewing the list with Petrov and he mentioned that they are running out of food."

Jerry sighed. "Food isn't as heavy as batteries, but it takes up about the same amount of space. Still, it weighs something. Where does it rank on the list? After the CO_2 chemicals, but ahead of light? What about the medicine?"

Shimko almost pleaded. "These guys are getting hungry and they're wasting a lot of body energy just trying to stay warm. We need to be concerned about hypothermia, too."

Jerry threw up his hands, but tried to work it through. "So what are we talking about? Granola bars?"

"I've got the Ferengi going through our stores. Yeah. Granola bars, candy bars, fruit, cheese. Anything prepackaged."

"We'll have to throw in a knife if we send over cheese," Jerry muttered sarcastically. He suddenly felt like he was planning a picnic. "Please have the chop bring me candy bars, preferably with nuts in them, and anything that is small, compact, and as dense as possible. Small hard candies would be good too. But XO, whatever I squeeze in won't be enough for sixty-some-odd guys."

The XO looked relieved. "Great. It's something. I'll tell the Captain."

As Shimko turned to leave, Wolfe and Palmer came down the ladder. They didn't look happy. "We've got a problem with one of the interlocks."

Shimko looked surprised. "I thought you'd bypassed all the interlocks."

"Only on the batteries, XO," Palmer answered. "We've managed to fool the computer into thinking that six charged batteries will be in place when we launch Patty. That was easy. We found the sensors and wired them to a single feed that will . . ."

"What's the new problem?" Shimko demanded impatiently.

"It's the collision-avoidance turn-away circuit, sir," Wolfe responded.

"We disabled that," Jerry said. "It's just a software switch on the control panel." He sounded surprised, almost incredulous.

"There's more than one," Palmer explained.

"Damn."

Palmer explained. "The one on the console commands a turn-away from any object at a preset distance. Drive toward a solid wall, get too close, and it automatically makes a one-eighty. We got rid of that one by setting the turn-away distance to zero.

"But this other one's hard-coded into the navigation processor. It's a simple test. If the range to an object is less than four yards, and it's not getting a homing signal, it executes a turn to avoid a collision. It's a safety check, really."

Jerry replied, "And the Russian can't send out the homing signal."

Patty and the other UUVs were designed to home in on a very-high-frequency sonar signal sent out from a transponder mounted on the recovery arm. The plan, however, was to have the vehicle swim into one of the Russians' tubes without the aid of an arm or a homing signal. Of course, Patty would have to be guided in manually, which explained Palmer's worried expression.

Shimko processed the implications. "So, just before it reaches the Russian sub, she'll turn away and head in the opposite direction."

"Exactly." Palmer looked embarrassed. "I'm sorry, I should have found this much earlier."

Wolfe added, "I missed it, too. The only place it's mentioned is in a safety checklist. In the back of the manual, I might add."

"What's the fix?" asked Jerry.

"We can't reprogram the nav computer. We're just not set up for that. The only solution is to feed a false signal to the ranging logic, so it thinks it's still a safe distance away from *Severodvinsk*."

"But that means we won't have range data as we approach the Russian," Shimko protested.

"We've spent the last half hour looking for another solution," Wolfe argued. "We can't fiddle with the pumpjet's directional controls. We need those to function normally. If we try to feed in a fake homing signal, the seeker will drive Patty into a spin trying to follow it."

"How long will it take to rig?"

"Half an hour or so. Chief Morrison and some of the sonar techs are working on it now."

"The forward looking sonar will still give us a clear picture," Palmer said hopefully. "There's just no depth perception, but if we take it slow, we should be all right."

"Not too slow," Shimko cautioned. "I saw Johnson's endurance estimates on the substitute battery, but I'm still a little skeptical. We're making a lot of changes to this beast, and we can't make a dry run; once we start, we are committed. I don't want us putting a lot of stock into our assumption of how much time we'll have. I'll brief the Captain on our status. He wants us to be ready in two hours."

Jerry looked at the jumble of supplies next to LaVerne.

"Sir, Captain Petrov said their carbon dioxide levels shouldn't reach three percent until this evening. More time to prep would be good."

"The skipper wants to try and keep their CO_2 below three percent, if at all possible. Once the carbon dioxide gets that high the Russian crew's breathing rate will double and things will get worse fast. It's a slippery slope that the Captain wants to stay away from. So he's pushing us a little."

Jerry gave off a weary sigh. Like many of the crew, he hadn't slept since they had conceived of the plan to resupply the Russians. They were all driven by the urgency of the rescue mission and their intense loyalty to Captain Rudel, who seemed particularly determined. "Okay, XO, I sure as hell don't want to disappoint the Skipper. If he wants to launch in two hours, we launch in two hours."

USS *Winston S. Churchill*, 150 miles northwest of Vardø, Norway

"Dr. Patterson?" The male voice startled her out of a fitful, unhappy sleep. An enlisted man stood a foot away, calling her name. The unfamiliar surroundings, including a moving deck and bed, combined with the fragments of her dream, made for a less than restful slumber.

Jane Mastui snapped on the reading lamp over her bunk. In the artificial twilight, Patterson could see a young man in dungarees. He was offering her a folder with a handful of messages. "The Captain thought you should see these, ma'am."

As she became coherent she looked at the clock, it read 0746. Matsui's head popped into view from the top bunk. "Should I take them?"

Finally awake, Patterson answered, "No, Jane, I've got

them." She took the messages, thanking the petty officer, and sat up.

"Breakfast is available in the wardroom, ma'am. Captain Baker invited you to join him in half an hour."

Her stomach debated the pro and cons of breakfast as the enlisted man left and she reviewed the message traffic. Jane Matsui hopped down from the upper bunk and used the washstand. Across the berthing space, just a few feet away, Joyce Parker stirred and mumbled in the lower bunk; the upper bunk belonged to a Lieutenant Sandy Miller, who was the ship's gunnery officer and apparently up already.

The first message was from SUBGRU Two to her. It repeated the information about *Severodvinsk*'s status and *Seawolf*'s improvised resupply plan, which she'd received late last night. It asked for frequent updates. A message from Wright's office also repeated the information on the Russian boat. It added a doctor's evaluation of how long the submariners could last in those conditions, with no surprises, and ended by asking for frequent updates.

President Huber's office had also sent a message. It included his personal best wishes and his confidence in her abilities. He was interested in her expert opinion on the environmental effects if the submarine couldn't be raised. Then he asked for frequent updates.

Other messages gave her information on weather and the status of *Mystic*'s loading in New London. The last message was the important one. The Russian Northern Fleet had sailed, most of the larger combatants, anyway, with *Mikhail Rudnitskiy* as the guest of honor. Intelligence didn't say how they knew, but it listed several of the ships known to have left. They'd sailed, and in strength.

Churchill's wardroom was roomier than a submarine's. It would have accommodated a sub's entire wardroom at once, but *Burke*-class destroyers had twice as many officers as a nuclear submarine, twenty-three, and three times as many enlisted men, over three hundred. Patterson's eleven visitors had added to those numbers.

Surface ships also had doors that opened out onto fresh air. Patterson took a moment on her way to the wardroom to get a personal look at the weather. Glossy gray waves looked unfriendly, almost dangerous, but at least there weren't any huge swells this morning. They raced by. Patterson couldn't guess their exact speed, but *Churchill* was moving fast. A slate-gray overcast matched the water's color, but the air was definitely clearer. Cold air curled into the open passageway, and after a moment, she closed the door and latched it.

Captain Baker and the other officers were all standing when Patterson entered the wardroom. Others from her team were also there. They'd waited for her, and as she entered the wardroom, everyone stood behind their seats. They'd left a spot open at the head of the long table, on Baker's right, and she gratefully took it. The moment she reached her place, the captain said "Seats" softly and fifteen chairs were pulled back as one.

Baker was solidly built, with thinning sandy hair and a round face that seemed stern, even when he smiled. "We're not normally this formal at breakfast, but I wanted to officially welcome you aboard and introduce you to all my senior officers."

Only *Churchill*'s department heads and the XO were present. Even with only some of Patterson's group eating, there was no room for the rest. Not all of her team had made it to breakfast. The word was that Manning and Bover were suffering severe motion sickness. Tech Sergeant Hayes would eat with the crew in the galley, and Parker and the reporter Adams were gratefully absent.

As sailors in crackerjacks served breakfast, starting with Patterson, introductions ran around the table, down one side and up the other, ending with *Churchill*'s XO, a wiry-looking man with a crew cut named Hampton.

"Everyone on *Churchill* understands that this is a rescue mission. They'll help you with anything you ask, Doctor."

"Your crew's already been very generous, Captain. I'm still amazed that you found places for us all to sleep last night."

Baker smiled, but he didn't look happy. "The XO will refine the sleeping arrangements today. We were fine with four extra riders. Eight was a stretch, but we were ready—we thought. But eleven! Doctor, we simply don't have that many spare bunks."

Lieutenant Commander Hampton added, "We'll be rigging hammocks later this morning."

Patterson waited for him to smile, and realized he was serious.

Hampton saw her expression. "Really. They're good for your back. We've got some volunteers already."

"The XO has also added your people to our watch, quarter and station bill." Baker explained, "It says where each of you should go for different situations or emergencies. For example, when we're at General Quarters, I assume you and Commander Silas will want to be with me in the combat information center."

Patterson nodded silently, and Baker continued, "And for Abandon Ship stations, you and Miss Matsui and Miss Parker will be with me and the command team in the whaleboat."

"God forbid," Patterson answered.

"And you're welcome to hear eight o'clock reports with me every morning and evening while you're aboard. It will keep you apprised of our material condition and planned evolutions. For instance, we will practice abandon-ship drill along with several others this afternoon. And we will be running surface tracking and antimissile problems in CIC from now until we get closer to the Russians."

"We aren't going into battle, Captain." Patterson said it automatically, and then realized he could see it as a criticism. She quickly added, "Can you tell me why you think that's necessary?"

"I'm uncomfortable, Doctor. I can be honest about it. We're one ship, not a formation. We're going further north than most Navy surface ships ever get, and I don't know anyone on this ship who's been north of the Norwegian Sea, including me. There's the weather." He leaned forward a little. "And a Russian battle group reportedly just left port, heading for the same spot we're going."

Patterson remembered something in the message she'd read. "Why is it important that the Russians aren't emitting any electronic signals?"

Baker was eating, and motioned to Hampton. "Because if they're transmitting, we can locate them. The type of signal they're radiating can help us identify the exact type of vessel as well," the XO explained.

The captain added, "And if I was leaving port in formation in heavy weather, I'd sure as hell have my navigation radar on. He's using something we call EMCON—emission control. The Russian commander is deliberately taking a serious risk to deny us information about his movements and composition. He's on a wartime footing."

Baker sat back in his chair. "I know what my rules of engagement are, but until I see his, we'll run drills."

"When will we see them?" Patterson asked. "Will we reach the collision site before they do?"

"I don't know, Doctor. We don't know their precise location. The site of the collision is about three hundred and thirty nautical miles to the northeast from their base. The slowest ship in the formation is *Mikhail Rudnitskiy*. She can make what, fifteen knots?" Baker looked at Hampton.

The XO shrugged. "Downhill, maybe."

"All right, we'll assume a fourteen-knot base speed. Under normal conditions, they'd reach the spot in about twenty-four hours. Since the storm is still clearing along the northern Russian coast, that will slow them down a little. So add another hour, maybe two until they're out from under it."

He paused for a moment, then answered Patterson's unspoken question. "We're twenty-four to twenty-six hours away at our present speed of twenty knots. I'll speed up when the weather's clear, but in these seas, twenty-five knots is the best I can do, and we've got five hundred miles to cover."

Patterson felt like she'd already lost the first move. "What will they do?"

Russo spoke from further down the table. "Declare an exclusion zone. It's SOP for any rescue operation. Unfortunately, they can use it to keep us out, and *Seawolf,* too, if they find her."

Hampton followed Russo's logic. "Chase away *Seawolf* and they're screwing themselves."

Silas added, "*Seawolf* has already found *Severodvinsk* and is attempting to provide them with supplies. I'd say they've done their bit. If the Russians want her to leave, that's their problem."

Russo shook his head. "It's never that easy. Having that sub and her UUVs on the scene would be very useful. The data they can provide the rescue force may be the main thing that saves *Severodvinsk*'s crew."

Silas wasn't convinced. "Ma'am, Rudel will surface and report after he's resupplied *Severodvinsk.* I recommend that if he's successful, you order him out of there. His boat is badly damaged, and the Russians already blame him, and us, for the accident in the first place. Limit our involvement and our risk."

"I can't talk to him, not yet. He'll report to SUBGRU Two," Patterson replied.

"Then have Admiral Sloan give the order. He'll follow your lead."

"Rudel is the on-scene search-and-rescue commander," Russo argued. "He can't leave until he hands over control to the Russians."

"He'll have to surface to do that," Silas pointed out. "They'll be able to see the damage to *Seawolf*."

"That's not a bad thing," Patterson said. "*Seawolf*'s damage supports her side of the story." She turned to Baker. "And this is a rescue operation, during peacetime. Run your drills, Captain, but the Russians aren't fools. They won't shoot at anyone. There's no reason to."

"I can't make that assumption."

"Agreed, but we can take steps to make it less likely. We are going to broadcast our position, in the clear, every half hour, explicitly state our actions, and Rudel's as well. In fact, we are going to generate a constant stream of messages to the Russians, to the Norwegians, to everyone who will listen."

"My intention was to use EMCON ourselves, Doctor." Baker didn't look happy. "I'd like to keep the Russians in the dark as long as we possibly can." He paused. "It gives us more freedom of action, and limits theirs—it creates uncertainty in their plans."

"Which in this particular instance is bad," Patterson replied. "We don't want any uncertainties in a rescue mission."

Russo supported her argument. "If we tell the world exactly what we're doing, we can actually limit the Russians' political options. We also reduce the chance that they will blame us for anything by being totally open about our actions."

Bt this time, they'd nearly finished breakfast, and others

were waiting to eat, including Parker and Britt Adams from Skynews. As Patterson got up, she headed over to Joyce Parker, who at first tried to avoid her until she realized that Patterson intended to speak to her. The doctor even had a pleasant expression. "Miss Parker, after you and Mr. Adams have finished your breakfast, please see me in our cabin. There's some important work you can do for me."

USS *Seawolf*

With the supply loadout finalized, allocated, and triple-checked for total weight and trim, the torpedomen transferred the payload from the deck next to LaVerne into Patty. It would be the UUV's last mission. The Russians would pull her inside to unload her, but there was no way for them to launch her again.

Without warning, Captain Rudel came down the ladder. Both Jerry and Palmer stood and faced their CO, but the fast-approaching deadline dictated that those working continue. Rudel handed Palmer a thick envelope, double-wrapped in plastic.

"I hope there is still room. These are hard copy images from LaVerne's survey of *Severodvinsk*. Petrov won't be happy." Rudel looked unhappy as well, largely because he was sending some really bad news. "But at least he'll know the score. I'd want to know." He paused, looking at the work in progress. "How much longer?"

Jerry fought the urge to answer. This was Palmer's show. The jaygee said, "Twenty minutes, sir. We're almost done with the loading, then sealing the case and getting her ready for launch is the same as any other mission."

Rudel checked his watch. "Then we'll set UUV stations

at 0940. I brought this down myself because I wanted to wish you luck, Jeff. I know you'll get the job done."

Rudel left, and Palmer handed the package to Chief Johnson, who added it to the nearly-bursting UUV. While the torpedo division finished loading Patty, Palmer stepped back, motioning Jerry to follow.

Speaking softly, Palmer said, "Nav, I want you to make the run."

Jerry was surprised. "What? You're the UUV operator. You went to school on these things."

"Yes, but we've all heard about your fancy Manta flying on *Memphis*. This run will be in full manual control. I did that once, on the school simulator, for about ten minutes." Palmer pointed back toward the ladder. "You saw what just happened. The Captain came down here to wish me luck!"

"That's because you're the guy doing the job. If I was doing it, he'd wish me luck." Jerry lowered his voice to almost a whisper. "Look, the Captain's pretty tense about this. Is he making the right decision by letting us try this? Is he missing anything that would give it a better chance of success? And you have to admit this plan is pretty wild. Is there anything, anything at all that he can do if it doesn't work?"

"This isn't making me feel better," Palmer gloomily observed.

"So if he didn't think you were the best man for the job, would he let you do it? He'd pull you in a heartbeat if he thought someone else could do it better."

"All those men depend on me doing this right."

"Correction, they depend on all of us, and we're not going to let them down."

Jerry got out of the torpedo room before he yielded and agreed to Palmer's request. He wanted to do it, and part of him believed he was the best man to do it, but not enough of him to take it away from Palmer. It was torpedo division business, and Jerry was the navigator. Palmer had run plenty of sorties, all without a bobble. He'd be fine.

JERRY TOOK his station in control. There wasn't much navigating involved, but *Seawolf* was going to move around to *Severodvinsk*'s starboard side. Since the Russian was listing to port, only the starboard torpedo tubes were accessible. Rudel would position his sub just two hundred yards from where *Severodvinsk* lay, shortening the distance Patty would have to cross with her brainwashed navigation system.

Jerry had prepared for the move by studying the sonar survey of the area. At the same time that LaVerne had imaged *Severodvinsk,* she had mapped the bottom around the crippled sub for two nautical miles in every direction. QM1 Peters was still updating their charts, but Jerry knew to the foot what the depths were, and where the rocks and hollows were. He'd picked a likely spot astern of the Russian sub, a hundred feet off the bottom. There was nothing but smooth seabed between Patty and her goal.

"Control, torpedo room. Maxine is away." Chandler acknowledged the report. As part of his belt and suspenders policy, Rudel had ordered Maxine positioned so they could watch Patty's progress with her sonar suite. Properly positioned, she could give Palmer some of the depth perception he'd lost when they'd bypassed Patty's forward sonar ranging circuits.

The repeater set in control changed from black to blue as Maxine's sonar activated. In map mode, it showed an overhead view of *Seawolf, Severodvinsk,* and Maxine's location.

It took only a few minutes to cover the few hundred yards to the spot they'd decided on, and Maxine swung around. The Russian's hull filled one side. Jerry knew

Palmer would enter commands telling the vehicle to remain in that spot, pointed in that direction, and its own computer would keep it there. He'd be busy enough.

Palmer didn't wait for an order from control. "Control, torpedo room. Patty is away." After Chandler acknowledged that report, Rudel picked up the microphone for the underwater telephone. "*Severodvinsk, Seawolf.* We have launched the vehicle."

The answer, distorted but brief, was "Understood. Good luck." It sounded like Petrov's voice. Passage through seawater had removed any emotion, and Jerry didn't know what had been there. Desperation? Encouragement?

The bridge display shifted to Patty's sonar image, showing the sonar picture from the vehicle's point of view. Palmer brought Patty tight along *Seawolf*'s side after launch. The image shifted, wobbling up and down and left to right, and Jerry saw the difference between the stabilized automatic and the manual mode.

At first, the UUV seemed almost out of control. Wild pitch-downs were followed by equally wild pitch-ups. A zig to the left toward *Seawolf* almost rammed the UUV into her side, but then the hull disappeared entirely as Patty swung almost straight away from the sub.

Jerry realized what was happening. Quickly, he picked up the sound-powered phone handset and connected himself to the UUV circuit. "Torpedo room, control. Jeff, allow for the delay in your commands. Remember everything moves at the speed of sound in water. The time delay will increase the farther Patty is from us. You've got to get ahead of Patty, anticipate her movements more."

Chief Johnson answered. "Mr. Palmer's nodding," came over the handset. The image steadied, swung back toward *Seawolf,* but then steadied again. Steering a slow, less sinuous path, Patty headed aft. *Seawolf*'s stern and propulsor passed, then disappeared off the right edge.

"Control, torpedo room. Patty is running with a slight up angle. Compensating with the thruster." Palmer's voice sounded calm, but clearly stressed.

Rudel nodded approvingly, "Not bad, Nav. You and your team did a good job of balancing the UUV out with just a scale, tape measure, and an Excel spreadsheet."

"Thank you, sir, I'll be sure to pass your compliments on to all concerned," replied Jerry, pleased with the results.

Severodvinsk appeared, a little off to the right, but visible. The image swung left, away from the sub, and for an instant, Jerry was afraid Palmer was overcontrolling. Then he saw Palmer was opening the distance, to line up on *Severodvinsk*'s starboard torpedo tubes.

It took a few minutes, but the Russian swung back into view with her forward hull filling the screen. The open tube was a yellow dot down on the dull-colored hull, even with the forward edge of the sail.

Palmer had Patty advance slowly; he had to make a picture-perfect straight-in approach. This wasn't going to be easy, as *Severodvinsk*'s torpedo tubes were angled out from the hull, like *Seawolf*'s. Complicating the matters was the Russian's list to port and downward pitch. Thus, the tube pointed down as well as out. While the open tube was visible, there was nothing to line up on. They'd estimated what the proper azimuth and elevation angles should be graphically, but they were only approximate values. Patty would have to line up exactly on the tube's axis, perfectly centered on the opening if she was going to make it inside.

Numbers danced at the top and bottom edges of the display. Elevation, azimuth, depth, speed, motor rpm, only range never changed, pinned at "999." Even without range, Jerry could see the side of *Severodvinsk* grow. The false-color image was deep green, and the screen became a solid wall of the color.

It was impossible to see inside the opening, to see whether Patty was aligned with the *Severodvinsk*'s tube. He found himself watching the elevation and azimuth numbers, subconsciously trying to nudge them. The less they changed, the steadier the image, the better Jerry liked it.

The opening grew steadily, but slowly. Three knots was a slow walk, and Jerry began to eye the charge meter. Luckily, it gave an accurate reading, but it had started out in the red, showing only less than an hour where a full set of batteries was good for fifty-plus hours.

The opening kept drifting right, and while Palmer kept correcting, it meant the angle was constantly changing. More and more of *Severodvinsk*'s hull became visible with each correction, and the UUV's angle numbers went past the limits they'd calculated. Finally Palmer turned Patty to the left and circled. It was a small circle, and this time Jerry noticed Patty's speed was a little higher. The image was steadier, and grew quickly, then shuddered and flickered.

"*Seawolf,* we felt a vibration." The underwater telephone still mutated any voice, but Jerry imagined the Russians waiting, hoping. A vibration?

"It missed. Patty must have bounced off the edge of the tube." Shimko's voice couldn't hide his disappointment.

Rudel passed the news to *Severodvinsk*. "Our first attempt failed. We're positioning to try again."

Palmer was already circling for another pass. It was a tight circle this time, but he made his approach at a bare crawl. It looked good, but at the last moment, the display flashed with bright yellow pixels, then froze. A moment later, Patty's computer rebooted, showing the vehicle lying alongside *Severodvinsk*'s hull.

"We can't do that again." Rudel said what everyone was thinking. "Get Mr. Palmer up here."

Palmer set Patty to hover, with her forward-looking

sonar shut off to save power, and then headed for control. The CO, XO, and others were all clustered around the now-dark UUV display, discussing what had gone wrong, when Palmer entered almost throwing his hands up in frustration. "It's the cross-current, sir. It's strong enough to throw Patty out of alignment just before we reach the tube. I don't have enough time to react to the change before she hits the boat."

"Patty can't take another bump like that." Shimko was stating the obvious, but it was meant more as a question.

"I know I'm close, sir. Did you see the bright yellow flash, just before she hit the second time? That was the sonar beam reverberating off the inside of the tube. The rest of the hull has anechoic coating, but the tube is bare metal. We were that close, then the current pushed me out of line."

"So we use a crosswind landing," Jerry announced. Ignoring their expressions, he continued his explanation with Palmer: "The water's pushing you to the right as you try to enter the tube, right? Well, we often had to land on a runway that wasn't exactly downwind."

Jerry held out one hand, moving it in one direction, but angled it slightly to the left. "We called it 'crabbing,' just a little sideway angle that compensates for the crosswind. At the last minute, as we touched down, we'd add a little rudder to bring us into line with the runway."

Palmer nodded slowly. "We are 'landing' the UUV," he agreed.

Shimko said, "We don't know the speed of the cross-current."

Palmer answered that. "Maxine can provide ranges, and we can measure the current from her data."

"Then get back down there and get set for another pass. We'll figure the current's vector and pass it to you." Shimko pointed to the screen. Even though the sonar display was dark, the readouts still showed their numbers. "Even if the sonar can survive another hard bounce, we're running low on juice. The single battery is having trouble meeting all the power demands and we're depleting it faster than expected. We're on borrowed time already."

"Mr. Palmer," spoke Rudel, more as a coach than a commanding officer. "I know you can do this. Stay calm and follow your training. Now go."

Palmer quickly disappeared, and Rudel went back to the Gertrude to update Petrov and tell him they were getting ready to make yet another attempt. By the time Jerry and Shimko finished the math, Palmer was already pointed toward *Severodvinsk*. "It's just a small correction," Shimko explained over the handset. "Add two degrees of azimuth to the left at three and a half knots."

Johnson acknowledged for Palmer, and Jerry added, "It will look like you're off to the left, but it keeps Patty aligned with the tube. You'll know the angle's right if the bearing to the tubes doesn't change."

The chief acknowledged for Palmer again, and Jerry hung up the handset. "This all assumes Jeff's hand is steady," Shimko remarked softly. He was silent for moment, then asked, "Shouldn't you be down there? This is your idea."

Jerry wasn't sure whether the XO meant the crabbed approach or the UUV transfer itself. He wanted to be close to the action, and he wanted to provide moral support. But the skipper told Jeff Palmer that he could do this. Showing up at a critical moment might say the opposite and distract him.

"Jeff's on top of this, XO. He knows what to do. He'll make it this time."

"Lives are at stake." The XO's eyes were fixed on the display, and Jerry realized how wrong it must look to him.

But to Jerry's aviator's eyes, imagining himself landing a jet, Palmer was right in the groove.

Jerry didn't say anything more, but watched the bearing and bearing rate numbers on the display. They held almost rock steady, and Jerry saw the approach from Maxine's point of view; the UUV was just a few yards away from the Russian's hull.

The image flashed bright yellow again, and Jerry tried to guess when Jeff would straighten out his approach. In an aircraft, the friction of the wheels on the runway helped straighten out a plane. The temptation was to do it too early, or overcontrol and make too large a correction. And then there was the time delay. Don't do it too late . . .

Jerry thought Palmer had waited too long, then he saw the image shift and realized Palmer must have sent the signal a few moments ago. The tube opening moved toward the center of the screen and suddenly a bright, sustained flash of yellow filled the display. Then it went dark.

"Control, torpedo room. I'm revving the motor," Palmer nearly shouted over the intercom. "Full rpm!"

"*Seawolf,* this is Petrov. We can hear something in the tube! There is the whine of a motor."

Rudel answered. "*Severodvinsk,* we think it's in."

"Control, torpedo room." Palmer's excited voice blared over the loudspeaker. "Executing command shut down!"

A long moment passed as the sound traveled to *Severodvinsk* and Petrov's reply came back. "*Seawolf,* the whining has stopped. We are closing the outer door."

"Control, torpedo room. I've lost all contact with Patty." Palmer's hopeful tone contrasted with what would normally be very bad news. Moments later, he was in control, waiting for word from the Russians.

Once the outer door was closed, the water would have to be removed from the tube. Normally it would be blown down with air, but with most of the high-pressure air already spent, the Russians could afford to use only the slightest burst to get the tube to start draining into the water round the torpedo tank. If Patty was filling most of the tube, there wouldn't be much seawater to drain. Then the inner door would have to be opened. Again, that normally used hydraulics. But it could be done manually, by cold, exhausted men breathing poor air. Finally, the vehicle would have to be pulled from the tube on a boat with a significant list, and it weighed nearly twenty-eight hundred pounds.

Jerry had been torpedo officer on *Memphis.* He knew how he would have done it on that boat, or even *Seawolf.* How did the Russian mechanisms differ? Whatever the difference, he was going to have to wait a few minutes to find out if they were successful. Considering how long the Russians had waited, he couldn't complain.

Severodvinsk

Petrov leaned heavily against the bulkhead, the microphone in his hand temporarily forgotten in relief and sudden fatigue. They'd done it, he told himself. The Americans had just saved their lives. He hoped.

Rodionov's excited voice came over the intercom. "Request permission to open the breech door."

"Granted," Petrov replied.

"Door's open and the vehicle is inside the tube. My men are rigging a block and tackle. Without power and with this pitch and list, we'll be hauling the damn thing uphill, the wrong way out."

"Understood. I'll have the Starpom send down more men to help with the work." With all of them tired and cold, hauling out the heavy vehicle would be exhausting work.

Kalinin overheard the conversation, and barked orders, sending a half-dozen uninjured men to the starboard torpedo bay. They almost hurried, and he saw several smiling. It was understandable, Petrov realized. There was now a chance they would not die.

He remembered the microphone, and knew Rudel was still waiting for word from him. There was nothing to say until he got word from the torpedo officer. If Rodionov and his people couldn't get that thing out of the tube, they were still dead men. But the American had done his part. Petrov owed him an update. He picked up the microphone and reported, "*Seawolf,* this is Petrov. We have the vehicle. My men are working to remove it from the torpedo tube. This will take a few minutes."

Rudel's voice answered. "*Seawolf* is standing by."

Petrov stood by as well, for about twenty seconds. He'd planned to wait for word from Rodionov. There was nothing he could contribute, and he didn't want to jiggle Rodionov's elbow, but he had to see.

It seemed like more than half a dozen men had arrived to help the torpedomen retrieve the American device, but they made a passage for Petrov as soon as he entered. The senior torpedo michman was organizing the detail around a block and tackle while another examined the front of the American device.

There was no clearance between the American remote and the sides of the tube. It had never been designed to be hauled out nose-first. The smooth, flat nose was slightly rounded near the edges, but there were no attachment points or access panels. They hadn't expected any.

The michman looked at Rodionov, then Petrov, and shrugged. Petrov nodded wordlessly, then added, "Go ahead."

Using a wrench, the torpedoman tapped different parts of the nose. "There's a sonar transducer here, but the metal below it might be part of the frame." He picked up a drill and made several exploratory holes. Two seemed to mark a bar that supported the transducer. The michman widened the holes, then tapped them for a pair of lifting eyes.

Petrov watched the surgery with mixed feelings. It offended him to have to ruin this expensive device, but it would keep his men alive. For all their complexity and cost, all machines—his submarine, the American remote—served men's purposes.

Rodionov had them pull gently at first, but it moved smoothly, and they took a strain, pulling uphill against the port list and bow-down pitch. With only a few more pulls it was almost halfway out.

Now a loading tray was jury-rigged under it, manually, and by the time that was done, some of the men were clearly winded and had to be replaced. Eager volunteers stepped in and picked up the lines, but when they pulled, it only moved a few inches.

They shrugged, then tried again. It would not move. At Rodionov's direction, they pushed it back, then pulled again. It stuck at the same place.

There was no way to see where the thing was stuck. Ten feet of the vehicle was hidden, and the clearance was too narrow for flashlights to reveal the obstruction.

The inside of the tube was not completely smooth. Low rails held and guided a weapon, ports let water and air in or helped them escape. Others locked a weapon in place in case of sudden maneuvers by the boat . . .

"Rotate the thing," Petrov ordered. "The obstruction is probably small, and the only things it can catch on are a centimeter across. Turn it and it might not get hung up."

Rodionov nodded and they paid out the lines slightly, letting it fall back into the tube a few inches. Then, with three or four men on a side, they embraced the vehicle, twenty-one inches in diameter, and tried to roll it in place.

It weighed hundreds of kilograms. It was wet, and cold, and didn't want to turn.

"Try the other way," Rodionov ordered, and the exhausted men shifted their stance. Coughing, trying to find strength in the stale air, they gripped and pulled. This time it moved, a little, and Rodionov urged them on until they'd turned the vehicle almost ninety degrees.

Rodionov stopped them, and exhausted, they dropped to their knees. Panting, gasping, they waited while the other team took a strain on the line and began pulling.

It moved, and they all cheered when it came out farther, almost three-quarters of the way. Then it stopped, hung up on another protrusion. "Switch the groups," Petrov ordered, and the pullers changed places with the turners. Now they knew what was needed, and moved the vehicle back a fraction and began twisting it in the tube.

They repeated the process twice more before the American vehicle finally slid clear. More men had to be brought down to help with the work, and others had to take over the job of actually opening the thing up. What had started with just the torpedo crew turned into an all-hands evolution.

Rudel had told them how to quickly open the vehicle, and the men set to work. Petrov watched them, more than aware of the irony. He'd done his best to take this thing away from the Americans. Its later recovery would have been a minor win for the Russian Navy and personal triumph for his new command.

Now, at great effort, the Americans had deliberately given him one of the remotes, and it would mean a different kind of victory. It wasn't lost on him, either, that the vehicle had no tether. He could have done loops around the damn thing for a week, and it wouldn't have made a bit of difference.

His mistake, his false assumption, had been a factor in

this tragedy—possibly the primary factor. Every commanding officer has to live with the consequences of his mistakes. What grieved Petrov was that others were paying for them as well.

The side panel opened, and like everyone else, Petrov crowded in to see. Unlike everyone else, the men gave him plenty of room. Rodionov turned as the captain approached. "It's all here, sir. The air chemicals, medicines, even some food." He held up a candy bar with a bite missing. The captain-lieutenant's grin was infectious, and Petrov could hear the men talking excitedly, almost shouting. It was time to get organized.

Petrov's voice cut through the hubbub. "All right, the vehicle has been recovered. Anyone who is not part of the torpedo crew, return to your posts." He pointed to one of the michman. "You. Collect all the medicine and *all* the food. Turn it over to Dr. Balanov." He took in the entire group with a stern look. "We're going to give the food to the injured first."

There were several audible sighs as candy bars and other items were turned over. Petrov told the michman, "Pick men for a detail."

Fonarin, in charge of life support, was already present to take charge of the air chemicals. With great curiosity, he examined the six-foot-by-three-foot plastic curtains littered with small pockets. He then picked up a can of lithium hydroxide granules and started to understand. Beneath the first curtain, he found an envelope with the Russian word "Instructions."

"How considerate of them," Fonarin remarked gratefully. "They've even provided instructions on their equipment in Russian. I will get these curtains distributed and hung immediately, sir."

"Excellent, Igor."

"Captain," spoke the torpedomen michman. "This says

it is for you." He came over to Petrov with a plastic-wrapped package. Lettering on the front in Cyrillic and English said it was intended for the Captain of *Severodvinsk.*

That made him think of Rudel, and he turned to the intercom. "Central post, this is Petrov. Pass to *Seawolf,* 'Thank you. We have the supplies.' "

The reply came back a minute later. "Captain, your message was passed. We heard cheering over their microphone." Petrov felt almost like cheering himself as he cracked the seal. They had more time for the fleet to arrive, food, badly needed medicine, and now what had to be information. Curiosity filled him.

Then he saw the first photo. Although in false colors, the image showed his wonderful *Severodvinsk,* listing on the seabed, bow and aft sections scarred. Grief and anger brought tears to his eyes, and he quickly shoved the picture back into the envelope. He hurried out of the compartment, barely noticing the men that quickly jumped out of his way.

His cabin was in the first compartment, flooded and inaccessible. He wanted to examine the contents of the package alone, but that was impossible. Instead, he stood in the tilted passageway, out of the way of the men already bringing up vital supplies, and gathered himself.

In the central post, he called over Kalinin, Lyachin, and the other battle department commanders. They would share the first viewing with him. Several of the officers almost wept when he passed around the first image. The next was a detailed photo of the ragged bow, then worse, the bladeless stub of the propeller shaft. Those three images signed *Severodvinsk*'s death certificate.

"Oh my God," rasped Kalinin as he picked up the next photo. Everyone present either gasped or groaned. The picture showed *Severodvinsk*'s V-600 emergency buoy lying on the ocean floor, a huge puncture in its tiny metal hull. It had never made it to the surface.

"No wonder we haven't heard from the fleet," Lyachin stated in awe. "They had no idea where to look!"

"Our debt to this Rudel fellow continues to grow," responded Kalinin. There was no disagreement from those present.

After that came a detailed bow-to-stern series of photographs, both port and starboard, and annotated maps of the area, large and small-scale. One was marked with the location of debris from *Severodvinsk* and *Seawolf,* torn or broken off during the collision. Petrov was impressed with both the Americans' thoroughness and the capabilities of their underwater vehicles. But it was a lot to take in. It was almost an hour later when he finally gave the package to Kalinin.

He tried to focus on the basics. Some of his crew had been lost, but the rest were alive, and thanks to the Americans, he didn't have to pretend they had a chance of survival. But it was time to accept the bitter fact that *Severodvinsk* was lost. Horribly crippled, in deep water, she would never leave this place. A great sadness came upon him. He didn't think it would ever go away.

19

HEAVY TRAFFIC

8 October 2008
1300/1:00 PM
USS *Winston S. Churchill*

Patterson found Captain Baker on the bridge. "I just got a message from SUBGRU Two. They did it." Patterson handed him the hard copy.

Baker smiled as he read the news. "Three days' worth of breathable air, medical supplies—Rudel's done it." *Churchill*'s captain sounded like a proud sibling. "The Russians ought to give him a medal for this."

"I don't know about the Russians, but we might," Patterson agreed. "It gives them time."

"Not much," Baker countered. "If the Russian ships arrive on scene tomorrow morning, they've got forty-eight hours to come up with and execute a rescue plan."

"I asked them for their ETA," Patterson said.

Baker was surprised. "The Russians?"

She nodded. "Through the State Department. I thought it was time to say hello, especially since we're supposed to be supporting the on-scene search-and-rescue commander." She shrugged. "Actually, I've been trying since we came on board. State says they're passing the requests on to the Russian embassy, as well as our ambassador in Moscow, but so far there's been no response."

"We can try ship-to-ship when they get closer," Baker suggested. "They haven't come up on the search-and-rescue radio net. There's a UN agency called the International Maritime Organization. They have established procedures and radio frequencies everyone's supposed to use for rescue coordination, but so far *Churchill* is the only ship using them." Baker shrugged. "Of course *Seawolf* can't, but the Russians should be all over the net."

Patterson frowned. "Please be careful about communicating with the Russians by radio. As long as it's coordination, ship movements and such, that's fine. Anything else is supposed to go through the State Department."

"Don't you have a State Department rep on board?"

"Yes, but State wants all our communications to go through the Washington-based staff."

"Which sounds very clumsy and slow."

"You're right. It is," conceded Patterson.

BAKER WALKED over to the chart table. Both *Churchill*'s projected course and their best guess at the Russians' path converged on the collision site. "I've scheduled a helicopter launch for 0715 hours tomorrow morning." He saw her expression and the unasked question. He reassured her, "It is the earliest possible minute we can launch. Lieutenant Ross is a good pilot, but he's never done a personnel transfer with a submarine before and I want him doing this in daylight. The helicopter will also be carrying a lot of cargo, and we'll be bringing back several of *Seawolf*'s injured, which means Doc Spiegel has to ride as well."

Picking up a pair of dividers, Baker measured the flight distance off the chart for Patterson.

"We'll be approximately here, one hundred and fifty miles away, by 0700 tomorrow. Once airborne, we expect the helo to reach *Seawolf* about an hour later, and we're allowing half an hour overhead to send the parts down and bring the injured aboard. The winds are subsiding, but they'll still be a major factor. And this type of evolution is never easy. The XO is working on a message telling *Seawolf* when to surface. He'll run it by you before we send it."

Patterson was grateful for the courtesy. "At least we can talk to her."

International News Network

"Reports of a successful attempt by USS *Seawolf* to transfer atmosphere control chemicals and other supplies to the crippled *Severodvinsk* have been confirmed by the U.S. Navy. Although in communication with the downed sub, *Seawolf* has not provided a list of the dead or injured Russian sailors. Inquiries by International News Network as to the reason for this have not been answered.

"Requests for comment by the Russian Federation government have been referred to the Russian ambassador to the United Nations, Madame Elisaveta Yansanov. A spokesman for the ambassador said that the report of the American submarine's activities could not be verified. She also said that she has no data on the location or activities of Russian forces, but that the rescue of the sailors aboard *Severodvinsk* is proceeding according to plan."

The White House

Jeffrey Wright went in first, followed by the Chairman of the Joint Chiefs, the Chief of Naval Operations, and then Rear Admiral Sloan. As National Security Advisor, Wright had been in the Oval Office many times, but was always impressed, and thought carefully before speaking. This was the driver's seat.

The current occupant, President Nathan Huber, looked

up from his desk as Wright and his group were ushered in. An aide was collecting documents as Huber hurriedly signed them. "I'll finish these later," he told the aide, and came around from behind the desk.

He greeted Wright, General Hodge, and Admiral Forrester; then Forrester introduced Rear Admiral Sloan.

"This is Commander of Submarine Group Two, sir. *Seawolf* is one of his boats. We thought his expertise would be useful." Sloan stood at near-attention.

Huber warmly shook Sloan's hand. "Welcome, Admiral." He turned a little to the left, smiling, and automatically, Sloan turned in the same direction. A bright flash filled his eyes, and he heard Huber say, "Thanks, Ray. We'll take some more a little later." Huber introduced a young man standing to the right of his desk. "You all know Ed Rain, my press secretary."

Wright and the other three took seats across from the president, while aides arranged themselves inconspicuously behind the principals. Rain took a seat nearby and began scribbling furiously.

Forrester began his report. "Mr. President, *Seawolf*'s resupply was successful. Captain Rudel reports *Severodvinsk* has an additional three days of breathable air. They also gave the Russians medical supplies, lanterns, batteries, and a little food. Our best intelligence on the Russian task group says they will arrive on the scene by tomorrow morning, local time."

Wright added, "And we've forwarded Rudel's report on to the State Department. They've passed it to Moscow and to the Russian ambassador. No official response."

Rain looked up from his notepad, frowning. "The Russians probably got Rudel's report the same time that we did. It's a commercial satellite phone. Every national intelligence service and even some media organizations can listen in whenever he calls us."

Wright responded, "There's no need for secrecy. The more open our actions, the less the Russians can accuse us of. Look at what Rudel's done. That's great press. He's bought time for *Severodvinsk*'s crew, and brilliantly at that."

"What about this underwater vehicle they used to carry the supplies?" Huber asked. "I won't quibble about cost in the middle of a rescue operation, but didn't we just hand them classified technology?"

Wright and Forrester both looked at Sloan, who shrugged. "They may be able to remove some of the components. The computer and sonar are first-rate technology, but none of the hardware is classified and all of it is commercially available. Of course, the pieces would have to be portable enough to take with them when they are rescued."

General Hodges concluded, "The most they can get are parts of a state-of-the-art UUV. Possibly of some use for their own designers."

"An unintended consequence of Commander Rudel's ingenuity," Rain commented.

"An unavoidable consequence," corrected Sloan.

Rain made a note. "I like that. 'Unavoidable' is good. He simply had no choice."

"That's good, Jeffrey." Huber seemed distracted. "When do we expect the Norwegians to reach the area?"

"The day after tomorrow, the tenth, and *Mystic* two days after that," Forrester answered. "If the Russians can't get their men out, the Norwegians should arrive before their air gets too foul."

"Barely," Sloan added, and Hodges nodded agreement.

"And when the Russians arrive, Rudel can pass control to them and leave, correct?" Huber sounded hopeful.

"Unless the Russians ask *Seawolf* to stay and assist," Sloan answered. "She still has two UUVs. They would be very useful."

Huber looked over at his press secretary. Rain observed, "That could be good and bad. Their asking makes us one of the good guys, part of the rescue effort. But if it fails, we're to blame as well, especially since the collision was our fault to begin with."

Wright, Hodges, Forrester, and Sloan all looked as if they were going to speak, but Huber quickly beat them to it. "According to the reports, Ed, Rudel did his best to avoid a collision."

Rain shook his head. "Undestood, sir. And that's the line we've taken, but the Russians say it's our fault, and until an investigation clears Rudel, a lot of people will believe it's our fault. Our best course of action is whatever gets *Seawolf* out of the area and out of the news before anything else bad happens."

"We don't have a lot of options," Huber mused. "At least until the Russians take over."

"Which is why we have to limit our actions, so as to limit our risks." Rain turned to the officers. "For instance, this something-or-other sulfur chloride they dumped overboard to make room for supplies, this action has already cost us some political capital. I've had calls from several environmental organizations complaining about this flagrant violation of international accords. Do you know how toxic that stuff is? We're talking about alienating some of the President's core supporters!"

Sloan argued, "It had to be done. If . . ."

"Yes, I understand the necessity, but it won't stop some people with an agenda from second-guessing, and that can do more damage than actual events. There's no leverage for us in this crisis. We gain nothing, even if *Severodvinsk*'s crew is rescued."

Huber stood and paced. "I know we're working to save lives, but the best we can expect at the end of the day is to break even." He started ticking off items on his fingers.

"First, attention's been drawn to a classified operation. Second, lives have been lost and a submarine's been badly damaged in a collision. That means an investigation, and possibly a court-martial. More bad press. Third, relations with Russia are going to suffer, even if *Severodvinsk*'s crew is rescued."

Wright broke in. "One other matter, sir. Dr. Patterson is asking permission to contact the Russian government directly, without passing her messages through the State Department here in Washington. She does have someone from the Moscow embassy with her on *Churchill*."

Huber looked a little puzzled. "Why would Joanna want to cut State out of the loop?"

"She says it's interfering with the timely passing of communications. She still hasn't been able to talk to anyone on the Russian side."

"That's probably more the Russians' fault than State's," Rain observed.

Huber shook his head. "I'm glad one of my people is out there, but we've got precious little control over events. I'm not ready to give that up. I want to know what Joanna is saying to the Russians before the Russians do."

Wright looked ready to discuss it further, but Huber cut him off. "Tell her we'll keep State honest—and Jeff, you tell me the moment they're not."

After a moment's pause, he added, "And tell her to get *Seawolf* out of there as soon as we legally can."

Northern Fleet Headquarters

Vice Admiral Kokurin read through the intelligence report, looking for anything he didn't already know. He'd gotten copies of Rudel's conversation with his commanders from the Navy Ministry, the Foreign Ministry, and he'd seen news reports about it on the television as well. Now his intelligence specialists sent him the same thing, copied almost verbatim, with "probably" and "possibly" added here and there to cover their bureaucratic behinds. Stamp something SECRET and they think they own it.

Direction finders had also confirmed the Americans' location during his last transmission. He was sitting right on top of *Severodvinsk*'s supposed location.

The Foreign Ministry had received communications from the U.S. government asking for the movements of the rescue ships and for details of *Severodvinsk*'s construction. The latter request was supposedly on behalf of the Norwegians, but they were still two days away. And why was the request coming from an American warship?

The Foreign Ministry had asked the Main Navy Staff, and they had asked him. Why were they asking these questions? How should they be answered?

Kokurin could imagine many reasons for wanting to know *Petr Velikiy*'s movements. Some of them were reasonable, others were not. As long as it was the Americans asking, he had to assume the worst. As for details of *Severodvinsk*'s hatches and emergency equipment, that information could be sent to the Norwegians, when it became absolutely necessary.

Both ministries had also asked for his estimate of the destroyer's intentions. Intelligence said an American front-line Flight IIA *Burke*-class destroyer was heading north at high speed, loaded with parts to repair *Seawolf*'s radios and civilian experts as passengers.

They were probably telling the truth about the radio parts. Kokurin smiled. Having to surface and use that idiot satellite phone was probably making the submarine captain and half the U.S. Navy insane. Getting his radios repaired would indeed be a high priority. But after that?

Having a surface ship in the area able to observe and

communicate freely would give the American government a big advantage. *Seawolf*'s sensors and her remote vehicles gave her a good picture of what was happening underwater, but even an undamaged submarine was severely limited in what it could see above the surface.

Seawolf was damaged. Would she go home when the destroyer arrived? He didn't think so. She'd stayed there so far, and together they made a powerful team. Kokurin didn't like the idea of the two of them observing and recording.

But if the reports were true, the Americans had bought three days of life for *Severodvinsk*'s crew. The U.S. submarine captain was resourceful. It was possible they would need the Americans' help to rescue Petrov and his crew.

The thought was bitter in his mind. The Navy had already lost its newest submarine and eighteen lives. They might still lose the whole crew. But the thought of outsiders being involved in any way almost revolted him. Even if they could help, that help would disgrace them all.

Interfax Press Release

"The Russian Naval Ministry has declared a maritime exclusion zone, effective at 1500 hours Greenwich Mean Time (1800 Moscow Daylight Savings Time) today. Centered on Latitude 73° 10' North and Longitude 047° 50' East, it is a circular area fifty nautical miles in diameter. All aircraft and vessels are required to remain clear of this area so that units of the Russian Navy can conduct submarine rescue operations. The ministry said that the zone will remain in effect until further notice.

"Ministry spokesman Captain Second Rank Aleksandr Perchov was asked about the presence of foreign naval units in the exclusion area. Will they be asked to join the rescue? He stated that foreign naval units would be asked to leave, since they would be unfamiliar with Russian rescue procedures.

"All vessels and aircraft are required to obtain permission from the Naval Ministry before moving through the exclusion area, and the ministry has already stated that permission will only be granted in cases of demonstrated need."

USS *Winston S. Churchill*

Parker had been after Patterson for an interview, and this seemed like the perfect opportunity. Public media could be an unreliable channel, but this time she knew the Russians would get her message.

They'd decided to use the wardroom as the venue. Her stateroom looked more like a college dorm room, and with Baker pushing *Churchill* at twenty knots, the wind made the weather decks impossible.

Adams had his own small video rig. The small light next to the camera cast an unusual glow over her, but she focused her attention on the reporter, almost shadowed in comparison. She fought the impression that he was an inquisitor. She wanted her story to be told.

"Dr. Patterson, what effect will the Russians' exclusion zone have on U.S. operations?"

"USS *Churchill* will of course remain outside the zone. We still intend to launch our helicopter tomorrow morning, which will be picking up injured men from USS *Seawolf.* We have notified the Russian Naval Ministry, through official channels, of our intentions." She smiled, carefully, just a little, trying to think friendly thoughts. "We are sure they won't object to a mission of mercy."

"What about *Seawolf* herself? She's right in the center of the exclusion zone. The Russians said she must leave."

"We disagree. *Seawolf has* to remain there. According to international convention, the first vessel arriving at a maritime incident is the on-scene commander. International law, as well as common sense, requires that *Seawolf* remain with *Severodvinsk* until Captain Rudel can transfer command of the rescue to another, more capable vessel."

That was a long speech. Patterson was sure none of it would be in the sound byte on the evening news. But she also knew a full transcript would be on the web within hours. She waited for Adams's next, obvious question.

"What will *Seawolf* do once Commander Rudel does turn over command? Will she go home? Will there be an investigation?"

Patterson ignored the last question, and focused on her message. "*Seawolf* was carrying three, now two, advanced unmanned underwater vehicles. They have obviously been very useful. Besides transferring carbon-dioxide-absorbing chemicals to help keep the Russian sailors alive, they have made a detailed survey of *Severodvinsk*'s damage and position on the seabed. This information would be invaluable to any rescue effort. *Seawolf* needs to give this information to the Russians."

"Why haven't they sent it already?" asked Adams.

Patterson smiled. "Remember? All their radios were damaged and don't work. The data will have to be hand-delivered to the Russian commander."

Adams concluded. "So someone from *Seawolf* has to meet with the Russians personally."

"Exactly."

Adams shut off his camera and grinned. He didn't say anything to Patterson, but she knew he had his sound byte.

Petr Velikiy

The admirals' plot was a space designed to manage a three-dimensional naval battle. Most of the displays were dark now. They weren't at general quarters, and aside from a few helicopters aloft, everything was quiet. In spite of an airtight ASW search, they hadn't found any western submarines, in their path or trailing them.

Admirals Vidchenko and Kurganov ostensibly took turns watching the task group's progress, but often both were present, planning, refining, and discussing scenarios with each other.

The messenger had found them both there, with another question from Moscow. He had two copies.

Vidchenko spoke first. "Tell Moscow there's nothing we can do about the helicopter."

Kurganov nodded his agreement, but after the messenger left, he told Vidchenko, "You know, that's not exactly correct."

The submarine admiral looked surprised. "None of our weapons or sensors will be in range of *Churchill* or *Seawolf* by the scheduled flight time tomorrow."

"We will have a Ka-31 radar helicopter up tomorrow morning. Its radar will cover the entire exclusion zone and more."

"True, so we can track their flight. That's useful information, admiral, but a radar helicopter can't stop them."

Kurganov knew Vidchenko well enough by now to risk a small criticism. "You're still thinking like a submariner. We could request a pair of Mi-28s from the Army. They could fly out to *Petr* tonight and refuel. In the morning they would be vectored by the Kamov to an intercept. They could force the American to turn around."

Vidchenko nodded his understanding. The Mi-28 Havoc was a heavily armed attack helicopter. They wouldn't even need to carry antitank missiles. Their 30mm cannon would convince a Seahawk pilot to turn around.

Kurganov continued. "We could also request interceptors from the Air Force. They could be guided by the Ka-31 as well, although they wouldn't have as much time on station as the Army helicopters, and their options would be limited, but . . ."

He didn't have to continue. A helicopter, any helicopter, would stand no chance at all against two jet fighters. If it came to that.

"Good. Request the fighters, and make sure they are armed, but make it clear they will only make an overflight. They will not be interfering with the flight in any way. It will be good training for both the Kamov and the fighters. And it will let the Americans know what we could have done if we had wanted to."

"Why?" Kurganov asked.

Vidchenko patted the map, right over *Severodvinsk*'s plotted position. "Because I believe them when they say they transferred air regeneration chemicals to Petrov's boat. It's too outrageous a lie to make up. It would have been so much easier for the Americans to just leave. So, since they helped our people, I will let them fix their radios and evacuate their wounded."

Kurganov looked surprised. Every plan they'd drawn up hinged on finding the American boat and driving her off. This was not a trivial task. Most tactics were designed to kill a sub once it had been detected and localized. Playing underwater keep-away was much harder.

Vidchenko reassured him. "I don't hate the Americans, but they have no business in the Barents. I know the strategic reasons why they send their boats into these waters, but they are intrusions nonetheless. If *Seawolf* had kept out, eighteen Russians and one American would still be alive.

"We will make sure the Americans don't create any more mischief."

Olga Sadilenko's Apartment, Severomorsk, Russia

They'd settled on Olga's apartment. It was closer to the train station, and only two floors up.

Most of the activity was in the living room. Some of her furniture had been pushed aside, or moved into the bedroom. That was Olga's headquarters, a constant stream of women entering with questions and leaving with wisdom.

The bedroom was small, but like many Russians, she'd filled it with vivid color. She loved tropical fish, and visitors joked about her bedroom looking like the inside of a fishbowl.

Now the bright tropical quilt on her bed was covered with boxes and papers. Someone had moved in the big comfortable chair from her living room. There was just enough space with the bed pushed hard against the far wall. It was a good chair, battered, but it fit her shape. She'd slept in it last night, too tired to move all the clutter off her bed.

In fact, the days had blended together. Word of her meeting with Kokurin and her work afterward had spread. She hadn't believed her tiny apartment could hold so many people.

Irina Ivanova Rodionov had completely taken over one side of the living room, showing up early in the morning with her computer, scanner, and printer. Since she shared her apartment with her invalid mother, Irina had to move into Olga's living room to work on updating the website. Once Yelena showed up with a fancy American laptop, the living room looked more like a computer center. Maria, whose son worked with Irina's Anatoliy, hustled about organizing the flood of photos and papers that had been arriving since last night into neat files.

After Irina scanned the photographs, Maria had started pinning them to the bedroom walls, covering the tropical fish prints and the seaweed wallpaper. Two walls were covered and a third was half filled with the photos of their loved ones. Women would walk in and touch one of the photos. Some prayed. Like a church, the room alternated between a place of hope and a memorial.

Other women had taken over answering the phone, and one of them, somehow, had arranged for a second phone line to be installed. Someone else had brought chairs, and a long plank had turned two of them into a worktable.

Two older women, less savvy with modern technology, took over the kitchen, and there was always something to eat: stew and bread, or pickles or smoked fish.

Irina walked into Olga's room, carrying a plate full of food. "Olga, you really should eat something. We had a nice lunch, but you were busy with that reporter."

"That idiot, you mean," Olga grumbled, sitting up a little straighter. "He was a hack from Interfax, if he was a reporter at all."

Irina looked alarmed. "Do you think he was from the FSB?"

The older woman shrugged and reached for the plate. "It's possible. He seemed more interested in where we got our information than our men."

"There will be others. Yelena says our website is getting more hits by the minute."

"Hits? It's being attacked?" Olga asked alarmed.

Irina smiled. "No, darling. Each 'hit' is a different person looking at our web page, visiting it in cyberspace. Counting the hits measures how many people have seen our web page." She patted Olga's hand. "It's a good thing, and Yelena says it's been doubling about every two hours. Lots of people are reading our message."

"I'm grateful to you and Yelena. All of us are. Without you to help, we'd just be a mob of angry women. Easy for the government to ignore."

As they talked, Olga ate. "This is a feast, but I can't eat it all right now. We have to talk."

She set the plate aside and reached for a stack of papers. "I was reading these American accounts of the collision. Did you know that an American sailor was killed? That they have wounded aboard their submarine?"

Irina nodded. "Yes, but I've been looking at the computer screen for hours and hours updating our story. I haven't been keeping up with the news."

"I've been so worried about my Yakov, and the rest of our men on *Severodvinsk.* The American government has said, officially, that *Seawolf* suffered one dead and several injured. And the families were all told within hours!"

"But the American captain could talk to them, with that satellite phone."

"And that same American captain can talk to *Severodvinsk,* too!" Olga stormed. "What do they know? Who's hurt? Who's dead?"

Irina sighed. "Our Navy doesn't trust the Americans."

Olga quickly retorted, "I don't care. I'd talk to the devil himself if he could tell me how Yakov is. Are those bloated toads afraid of lies from the Americans? They're so full of lies themselves, a few more shouldn't bother them."

Irina leafed through the printouts. "There is another American ship in the area. They are sending a helicopter to their submarine to get the injured sailors."

"Which means they can talk to *Seawolf,*" Olga concluded. "I wish we could give the submarine captain our phone number. He could just call me with that satellite phone of his. Or the ship. It's probably against the law, but I wish we had a radio. I want to talk to that ship."

Irina smiled. "We have something better than radio, Olga—email."

Twenty-fourth Independent Long Range ASW Regiment, Severomorsk-1 Air Base, Russia

Four Il-38s made up the first wave. With the weather finally clearing, it was time for the Russian Navy to show they were making an all-out effort. Interfax news crews invited by the Navy filmed the big four-engine patrol planes as they thundered down the runway.

Positioned at the end of the runway, the film crews got dramatic footage of the planes climbing against a backdrop of ragged overcast.

The Navy spokesman, a pilot himself, gave the interviewer a detailed description of the plane's antisubmarine sensors and its weapons load. He made a point of mentioning that because the search area was relatively close, the planes would be carrying their maximum load of antisubmarine sensors and ordnance. They would be over the collision site in less than an hour.

20

RESCUE FORCE

9 October 2008
0730/7:30 AM
USS *Winston S. Churchill,* 145 nm bearing 078° from USS *Seawolf*

It had cleared overnight. A few high, thin clouds couldn't interfere with the bright daylight. The light held no warmth, though, and with *Churchill* still racing east-northeast at twenty-five knots, the chilly air turned into a frigid blast.

Captain Baker had allowed Patterson and others from her party to watch the helicopter launch. They huddled in a safe spot just behind the after exhaust stack, escorted by *Churchill*'s XO.

It was a strange and exciting place, full of motion: the sea, the deck, the wind, and the whirling helicopter blades made her hold on to a fitting for some feeling of solidity.

She was also surrounded by reminders of *Churchill*'s true purpose. In front of them, between the helicopter pad and the exhaust stack, was the "after VLS magazine." The size of a tennis court, it was covered with sixty-four two-foot-square hatches. Lieutenant Commander Hampton had explained that an antiaircraft missile was housed under each one. Two stories above on the superstructure behind her, she could see a pair of circular missile illuminators. They would guide those missiles to targets a hundred miles away.

Right beside her, a Phalanx gun mount partially blocked the wind as it whipped by. Hampton had described it as a "killer robot," armed with a radar-directed 20mm gatling gun. She wondered if he wasn't sensationalizing things a little, and reminded herself to look up the Phalanx on the Internet.

And then there was the helicopter, turbines spooling up. Patterson was grateful for the wind, because it carried part of the sound aft, away from them. What was left still made conversation impossible.

The Seahawk could carry missiles or torpedoes, but this time it carried tanks with extra fuel. She'd seen helicopters before, even ridden in them occasionally, but not like this one. They seemed small and vulnerable by comparison, like insects in their complexity and fragility. This beast was two or three times larger, vibrating with power as the pilot tested the engines, straining at the leash.

Lieutenant Commander Hampton proudly explained the evolution as the helicopter was brought out of the portside hangar and prepared for flight. It all happened quickly as the machine was moved out, the blades unfolded, and the engines started. An enlisted phone talker stood near the group and provided updates on the launch.

The talker tapped Hampton on the shoulder, and the XO leaned close and listened to the enlisted man's report. Hampton turned and signaled to the group. Shouting over the wind and the engine noise, he said, "The Captain's going to slow us down now. The helicopter's ready, so we have to slow to reduce the air turbulence near the ship."

Patterson and the others nodded, and within a minute the force of the wind lessened. The helicopter suddenly rose and turned to port, falling aft as the ship moved ahead. The Seahawk then banked and headed east-northeast, paralleling and preceding *Churchill* along that course.

Hampton nodded to the petty officer, who unscrewed his phone cord from a jack in the bulkhead. The XO ushered the group toward a watertight door, and they began filing inside. Patterson hung back, letting the others go first, and Hampton remarked, "They'll be tracked by Russian radar soon. We've detected aircraft to the north, both a land-based patrol plane and a radar helicopter."

He saw her look of alarm, and quickly reassured her. "Both types can't harm a helicopter, and there is no indication that anyone will interfere with the helicopter's mission."

Then he paused. "But as long as the Russians are treating this as a tactical situation, we're going to be on guard." He looked to the northeast. The Seahawk helicopter was just visible. "None of us will relax until they're back aboard."

Rider 02, on course 078°

The Seahawk helicopter cruised at one hundred knots. He could go faster, up to a hundred and fifty, but he'd burn fuel too quickly. The pilot held the craft in a slow climb. Like all aviators, he liked distance from the unforgiving ocean, and it expanded his horizon. The increased altitude helped *Churchill*'s radar to keep tracking him, and his own sensors could see farther.

And his own radar was definitely on. They'd seen the Russian radars operating before he'd even taken off, so there was no point in trying to be electronically quiet. Besides, his APS–147 radar was an excellent sensor. As he rode over an empty sea, with home falling away behind, those sensors guided him, and gave him the knowledge he needed to get his job done and find his way home.

The flight proved to be smoother than they had originally thought, and they had a great tailwind. After only forty-three minutes in the air, they got their first glimpse of the injured submarine. "Contact at five eight miles, bearing zero seven niner," the sensor operator reported.

The pilot acknowledged the message, then ordered, "Tell *Seawolf* we have them on radar."

USS *Seawolf*

The XO poked his head into the crew's mess. "They're about thirty minutes out," he said hurriedly, and disappeared. Just aft of the midships escape trunk, Chief Gallant had staged the three crewmen who were to be evacuated. EN2 Brann had been heavily dosed with painkillers, and his broken leg had been padded with blankets. Along with MM1 Heiser, he sat quietly. ET1 Troy Kearney fidgeted, and occasionally looked at the chief like he wanted to speak, but Gallant glared him down.

Several other crewmen were there as well, either to help or say good-bye. Gallant reminded them, "Remember, everyone has an escort up the ladder to the escape trunk. Escorts, don't hurry them, but we need to move quickly."

The captain came into the mess. Everyone except Brann and Heiser started to stand, but Rudel quickly waved everyone back into their seats. "It looks like we're ready here, Doc. Any problems?"

Chief Gallant shook his head, smiling. "Just Kearney's constant complaining."

As if prompted, ET1 Kearney stood and held out his splinted wrist. "It feels great, sir," he said while trying to suppress his wincing. "The doc took care of it and I'm good, sir. You can't send me off the boat with those parts coming aboard. You'll need me, Skipper!"

Rudel shook his head. "You need to get a cast on that break, ET1. A splint isn't good enough. Without one, you could cause permanent damage to that hand. You don't want to end up like Mr. Mitchell. You might never fly jet fighters again." Everyone smiled. "Besides, Petty Officer Kearney, I need you to do something for me."

"Anything, sir."

Rudel handed the petty officer a brightly wrapped package, the size of a large book. "This is the information on the Russian sub's condition, on our latest situation report, letters to Rountree's folks, and some other stuff that's none of your business."

The XO appeared again, and announced, "Sir, the helicopter's in sight. Four, maybe five minutes."

Rudel acknowledged the report, and Shimko added, "I'm on my way to the freezer. They'll start bringing Rountree up."

Somber, Rudel replied, "I'll be on the bridge."

"Yessir." After a short pause, Shimko added, "Chief Hudson is down there, and Mr. Mitchell has everyone organized."

"Understood, XO. Thanks."

Rudel seemed to remember the package in his hand. Turning back to Kearney, he said, "I'm entrusting you with this package. Give it only to *Churchill*'s captain or XO."

Kearney looked at the package carefully, as if it might explode. He asked, "What about Heiser, sir? He's got two good hands."

Chief Gallant said, "Not with his concussion. I've got him full of painkillers. And Brann's got enough to worry about with his leg."

Kearny nodded and took the package with his good hand. "I'll take good care of it, sir."

"If it falls in the water, it will float. Dive in after it."

Kearney grinned. "Yessir, I understand."

Rudel patted Kearny on the shoulder. "We'll be thinking of you while you're gone." He stepped back and looked at all three men, silent for a moment, reluctant to leave. Finally, he said, "Take care of yourselves, and good luck."

Rudel left and Gallant walked over to Kearney. As the chief opened the immersion suit and helped Kearney secure the package inside, the young petty officer remarked, "Sometimes I can't tell when the Skipper is joking or not."

"This goes in the water and nobody's laughing," Gallant answered. "Keep a good hold of it and you won't have to find out."

JERRY MITCHELL wanted to be in several places at once. He was in charge of organizing the men that would pass the repair parts for the radios from the escape trunk to the wardroom, just forward of the opening. He wanted to be with Troy Kearney, one of his men who was about to leave the ship, and most of all, he wanted to be down in stores, with Rountree.

He really didn't need to be in any of those places. Chief Gallant had everything under control in the crew's mess, Master Chief Hess had a working party organized to handle the radio parts, and Chief Hudson and all the off-duty ETs were ready to move Denny Rountree.

Captain Rudel had agreed to let Rountree's division bring him out of the freezer. Once the helicopter was in sight, Rountree's remains had to be moved as quickly as dignity allowed down one passageway, up a ladder, down another short passageway, and then up the vertical escape trunk. It would be rough treatment, and it would be best if it was done by his own people.

But Jerry knew he had to be there when they brought Rountree out, for himself if for no other reason. Quickly, he made his way to the freezer on the third deck. There was little room in the cold storage area, and the ETs struggled with Rountree's frozen form, wrapped in a plastic body bag. "Wish we could have thawed him," Robinson muttered softly. "Idiot," Hudson replied, slightly annoyed. "The whole idea was to keep him cold as long as possible." As they shifted their grip on the slippery plastic, Lamberth and the others apologized to the body.

Jerry kept well clear, but wanted to gauge their progress, or at least that was a credible excuse for being there. Hudson saw him at the base of the first ladder. "We're okay, sir," he reported, and Jerry reluctantly climbed back up. They had some time. Rountree would go up last, after his three injured shipmates.

The 1MC announced, "ATTENTION ALL HANDS, THE HELICOPTER IS OVERHEAD, ALL PERSONNEL GOING TOPSIDE CHECK YOUR SAFETY GEAR."

Jerry stopped briefly in the passageway outside the wardroom. The midships escape trunk hatch was open, and a fresh chill wind whistled down the ladder.

Enlisted crewmen shivered as they waited to pass the supplies forward from the escape trunk to the wardroom. Two others aft of the trunk supported Brann, ready to help him up the ladder, while Chief Gallant watched from the messroom door. Everyone present had a job to do, and there just wasn't any space left for Jerry in the passageway. They didn't need him here, either.

Jerry went to control, but only looked briefly at the chart. *Seawolf* was still steaming into the wind at five knots. They'd hardly moved since he'd checked it ten minutes ago. With the helicopter transfer planned to take no more than thirty minutes, the boat would move two and a half miles toward the northwest. The nearest land was Novaya Zemlya, ninety miles away. In the other direction.

Shimko came down the ladder from the bridge, chilled from the cold air but gratefully dry. After checking with Al Constantino, the on duty contact coordinator, the XO turned to Jerry. "How are they doing below?"

"Everyone's on station. Brann, Heiser, and Kearney are ready to go. My guys are moving Rountree, and Hudson says they're all right."

"Good, and thanks. The pilot's lowering the first batch of supplies now." Shimko dithered for a minute, then said, "I need to be back up on the bridge. Check everything below and report back to me."

"Aye, aye, sir."

The activity made it hard to get close to the midships escape trunk. Until the slingload of supplies was moved out of the way, Brann couldn't go up the ladder. The working party finished quickly, then flattened against the passageway bulkhead to let Jerry pass. He saw Brann, a line passed through his safety harness, being hauled up through the open hatch.

Gallant was at the bottom of the ladder supervising the operation, squinting as he looked up into the cold wind. The sound of the helicopter overhead poured down the hatch along with the wind. "Watkins and Kahanek are up on deck doing the hauling."

Jerry grinned. "Good choices." MM1 Watkins lifted weights. MM3 Kahanek didn't need to.

Heiser was moved into position as soon as Brann had cleared the hatch.

Looking down the passageway, Jerry saw that Hudson and the ETs had Rountree's remains almost at the head of the ladder. Hudson and Lamberth were on top, pulling. Nobody said more than a single word as they worked, and that rarely. The chief saw Jerry and nodded, finally adding, "We're okay." His tone was a little off, as was his expression. Jerry watched them a moment longer, but could see no problems.

Back in control, he used the intercom to report to Shimko. The captain's voice answered. "Thank you, Mr. Mitchell. Please personally supervise the evolution at the midships escape trunk. They're sending down the last of the supplies now."

Jerry answered "Aye, sir" and headed aft one more time. Threading his way past the working party, he managed to get to the crew's mess. Chief Gallant was waiting with Kearney, last of the three injured, and Jerry joked, "Remember your toothbrush?"

Kearney opened his mouth to speak, probably to protest, Jerry predicted, but the 1MC cut though the conversation. "MR. MITCHELL TO THE BRIDGE! ON THE DOUBLE!"

In the half a heartbeat it took Jerry to understand the order and start moving, everyone near the door flattened against the bulkhead or got out of the way. It wasn't until he was clear of the wardroom that he wondered what the problem was.

A rating was waiting in control with a foul-weather jacket, and Jerry threw it on as he climbed up the ladder to the first deck and the access trunk to the bridge. As he exited the hatch, someone was climbing out of the cockpit to make room for him, and in two seconds he was blinking in the cold sunshine.

It was crowded, with the skipper and the XO there, as well as Will Hayes, the OOD. Hayes faced forward, keeping watch ahead of the boat, but both senior officers had their binoculars up and were staring intently to port.

He heard the tail end of a transmission on the bridge-to-bridge radio. ". . . not locked on. Repeat, no lock-on." It was the helicopter pilot. He sounded concerned, even scared, but he was maintaining.

By now Jerry was all the way up, and Shimko turned, handing him his binoculars. Shouting over the noise of the hovering helicopter, he pointed to the port quarter. "There, low. About twenty degrees above the horizon. Company."

Hayes made room along the coaming, and Jerry leaned

against it and turned to the port side. He followed the captain's line of sight. He scanned left to right just above the horizon. Nothing.

Shimko nudged him farther to the left, pointing. "There, and up a bit."

Jerry moved the glasses and two arrowhead shapes appeared in his field of view, passing quickly to the left. Old reflexes flashed through his body, but he wasn't sitting in a fighter cockpit.

"Fighters," Jerry said automatically. "Su-27 Flankers." Excitement filled him. In spite of two years of flight training, he'd never seen a real Russian combat aircraft anywhere, much less in flight; and especially not this close to Mother Russia.

"The helicopter reported detecting their radars about a minute ago. We didn't see anything at first, then these two made a high-speed pass a few miles away."

As Shimko explained, the planes' aspect changed, becoming narrower. They were turning toward *Seawolf*.

Rudel asked Jerry, "Could the Russians have started running interceptor patrols out here?"

"No sir, these guys weren't patrolling or their radars would have been on much earlier." The two arrowheads expanded and became more recognizable as the twin-tailed Sukhoi interceptor. The planes passed down their starboard side. Jerry estimated the distance as a mile. They were keeping well clear of the hovering helicopter. "They were vectored—directed to our location."

"They're armed," Shimko remarked tensely.

The binoculars let Jerry see drop tanks and both versions of AA-10 air-to-air missiles under their wings. "They're loaded for bear. I can see heat-seekers and radar-guided antiair missiles. But no bombs or rockets."

"So they're no threat to us," declared Rudel. The fighters were well ahead of them now.

"They could strafe us, sir, but that's about it. The helicopter's their meat." Jerry checked the Seahawk. Kearney was safely aboard, and they were sending down the sling again; empty this time. All the spare parts were safely aboard. Watkins and Kahanek reached down to bring up Rountree.

Rudel added, "And if they wanted it dead, they could have done it from twenty miles out. Not subtle, but we get the message."

The Flankers, dots several miles ahead, made a tight turn and split up. It looked like they were going to make a pass down each side of the sub this time.

Rudel noticed them attaching Rountree to the hoist. His attention had been focused completely on the fighters. Jerry saw emotions cross the captain's face as he fought for control. The radio announced "Hoisting" and the cable became taut.

Rudel told Hayes, "Pass the word that Electronics Technician Third Class Dennis Rountree is leaving the ship." Rudel saluted, and everyone else on the bridge did as well, holding it for the twenty seconds or so that it took to bring Rountree's body up to the aircraft.

Once the body was aboard, the skipper dropped his hand. Everyone else on the bridge followed and immediately started looking for the Flankers again, but Rudel continued to stare at the helicopter. "Twenty-three years in the Navy and I've never lost a man. Not until now." Tears streamed down his face. "I'd rather it was me in the body bag."

Jerry looked at Rudel. There were times when he felt exactly the same way. He didn't dare speak. Jerry, Rudel, Shimko, and most of the division had written letters to Rountree's folks. At the time, it had helped, a little. But now Jerry felt powerless, sorrowful, and guilty.

The Seahawk's cabin door closed, and the bridge-to-bridge radio carried the pilot's voice. "We're done here,

Seawolf. Godspeed." The helicopter was already applying power and moving forward, leaving hover.

Shimko picked up the mike. "Understood, Rider Zero Two. Have a safe trip back. Please take care of our people."

"We will, *Seawolf.* If those fighters follow us, please notify our next of kin."

Crowded as the bridge was, none of the officers moved. They watched the helicopter climb and head westward. After ten minutes it was just a dot on the horizon. The two Russian fighters had carefully made their passes on the port side of the boat, to the east, until the helicopter was out of sight.

Now, well to the north, the Flankers joined up again. Jerry watched the two planes descend until they were skimming the surface. They were speeding up, too, and he could imagine the grins on the two pilots' faces. He knew what was coming.

Jerry shouted "Brace yourselves and cover your ears!" and pointed aft. As he raised his own hands, the two fighters suddenly changed from dots to toy planes to aircraft fifty feet across, seventy feet long and at arms' length overhead.

A shattering BOOM almost knocked Jerry to the deck. Half a moment later, a shock wave strong enough to rock the boat did make the bridge crew stumble. One man on the hull was literally pushed off his feet and tumbled toward the water. Saved by his lifeline, he hung dangling along *Seawolf*'s flank. The other members of the crew scrambled to his aid. Jerry had been expecting it, but everyone else, especially Rudel, looked alarmed. "They broke the sound barrier right above us!" Jerry shouted.

Clear of the sub, both fighters pulled up until they were vertical. They zoomed upward, spinning slowly, drilling through the air until they were only specks. Along with the rest of the bridge crew, Jerry tracked them with his glasses until they leveled out at high altitude. He noted their direction—to the southwest and back to base. "Show-offs," he muttered enviously.

"I'm glad we didn't have any masts up," Shimko remarked.

"They almost got a sample of our paint," Hayes answered.

"Mr. Mitchell, before our rude guests showed up, Rider Zero Two told us they'd spotted a group of Russian surface ships headed this way." Shimko glanced at his watch. "As of twenty-three minutes ago, they bore two two five degrees at ninety miles. They also said they've got radar intercepts from other aircraft. We passed the information on to Mr. Constantino below."

Jerry checked his own watch and nodded. "I'll give you a visual ETA as soon as I'm down in control."

Rudel, who had been listening, said, "Since the Russians are close, I intend to remain on the surface." He paused for a moment, looking to the southeast. "I've got another data package made up, this time for the Russian surface ships. We may spot a helicopter from the task force anytime now. They seem to know where we are."

"Understood, sir. And as soon as I'm done with that ETA, I'll check on the techs' progress." Suddenly Jerry felt good—even happy. That SH-60 had been their first physical contact with the outside world since the collision. They finally had the parts to get the comm gear working, and within hours the Russians could begin rescue operations, thanks to *Seawolf*'s prep work.

Down in control, QM2 Dunn had the watch, and had already plotted the Russian ships' course and speed, and projected the time to intercept. Even with the storm cleared, the Russian ships wouldn't be visible until they were about fifteen miles away from *Seawolf*. According to

Rider 02, they'd had a speed of twelve knots, which meant another six hours before they came over the horizon.

He passed the times up to the bridge, and Rudel's voice acknowleged over the intercom. A moment later, the XO came into control, smiling broadly. Giving his foul-weather coat to a rating, he said, "I'll go up with you to electronics equipment space. I don't think I could wait for your report."

As they left control, Shimko was still smiling, and actually clapped Jerry on the back. "It's almost over. We pass the data on *Severodvinsk* to the Russians, let them mark our location, and then it's done. If the Russians are aggressive with the helicopters, we could have one overhead by lunch. They grab the hard copy, and we head for Faslane."

They'd climbed the ladder to the electronics spaces, with Shimko, of course, going first. As Jerry got to the top of the ladder, he turned to go forward, but the XO stopped him, and spoke softly. "I want you to know that I'm grateful for all your hard work since the collision. You've done a lot for both us and the Russians over there. They don't know it, and the Skipper isn't really aware, but I am, and . . ." He paused for a moment, then added, "It's been very hard, with the Captain unengaged. He could almost qualify as one of the injured, after the collision."

Jerry was a little surprised by the XO's outburst. He'd never heard him talk about the captain like this. Under normal circumstances, it just wasn't done. At a loss, he finally answered, "I'm glad I was able to help, sir." It sounded weak, but Shimko didn't seem to notice.

"It's part of why we have executive officers, Jerry, to back up a captain. I've always thought I was, but trying to fill Captain Rudel's shoes is hard work." There was strain in Shimko's voice. "And it's been hard seeing the Skipper so shattered by this."

Jerry shrugged. "He cares about his crew—maybe too

much." It was judgmental, and Jerry felt uncomfortable saying it, but it was true.

"He's a good officer, and somehow he's got to get through this, with our help." Shimko said it firmly. He wanted it to be true. Jerry did, too, because he could not imagine the alternative.

The XO smiled, just a little. "Remember this when you're a captain, and be kind to your executive officer." He turned and walked the few steps to the electronics equipment space door. Shimko carefully peered in.

Chief Hudson, Lamberth, and Blocker were all in the space, quietly, even happily working. Jerry looked for Kearney, then sadly remembered he was on his way to the *Churchill*. Hudson was now short two men.

The chief spotted Shimko, then Jerry. "Progressing well here, sirs. No surprises so far. We'll have one HF transmitter up tonight."

The 1MC called them both this time. "XO AND MR. MITCHELL TO THE BRIDGE."

"What now?" Shimko wondered aloud.

They both hurried back to the bridge, climbing back into the cold wind a few minutes after the call.

Rudel pointed to the southwest. "I thought it was the jets coming back, but it's only one plane, and it's larger."

Jerry took a pair of binoculars and inspected the plane, little more than an irregular speck. "Slow mover, and a big one. ASW patrol plane, but not a Bear. Probably an Il-38 May."

"I concur," Rudel answered. "Mr. Mitchell, will those fighters escort him?"

"No, sir. They don't need to, since we don't have anything up here to threaten the patrol plane."

"Can he hear our bridge-to-bridge radio?"

"Yessir, he should be able to. He has the UHF gear aboard. The Russians know our radios are down, and they just heard us use the bridge-to-bridge set to communicate with our helicopter. He'll be listening on our frequency."

The aircraft was closer now. Jerry could see the long, straight wing, four turboprop engines, and that wart of a radar dome below the cockpit. Definitely an Il-38 May. The Russians used them for ASW patrol. It carried radar, sonobuoys, magnetic detection gear, and a bomb bay full of torpedoes and depth charges.

Subs like *Seawolf* were this plane's natural prey, and Jerry felt totally exposed. They were surfaced, crawling at slow speed, in a damaged boat. He forced himself to remember that it was peacetime, that there was no reason for the Russians to attack.

Rudel asked the XO, "Marcus, do you want to try?"

"I'd rather use one of the CTs, sir. My Russian's a little weak for this."

"All right, get one up here," Rudel agreed.

Shimko ordered Hayes, "Have CT1 Sayers report to the bridge."

In the few minutes it took for the CT to arrive, the patrol plane approached, and passed down their starboard side at low altitude and at a respectful distance. It began circling them.

After one circuit, the bridge-to-bridge radio came to life. "American submarine. You are in restricted place. Leave at once." The words were heavily accented, with pauses between every few words.

"Well, that's handy. He speaks English, sort of." Shimko added with a touch of sarcasm, "That's probably what my Russian would sound like to them." He looked at the captain. "With your permission, sir."

Rudel nodded, and Shimko keyed the mike. "Russian aircraft, this is USS *Seawolf.* We have *Severodvinsk*'s location. We have information on her condition." Shimko spoke slowly, watching Rudel the entire time, who nodded approvingly at the end of each sentence. When he released the mike switch, they all listened, straining to hear the Russian's reply.

"American submarine. You are in restricted place. Leave at once."

"Well, this is not promising," Shimko observed.

CT1 Sayers appeared from the hatchway, and somehow they made room for the petty officer. Shimko was trying again. "Russian aircraft, we have important information for you. Please respond."

"American submarine. You are in restricted place. Leave at once."

"He's getting better with practice." The absurdity of the situation almost made Jerry laugh. "We finally contact the Russians, and all they can do is repeat a message to leave. I'll bet it's written down for him."

Shimko handed Sayers the mike. "See if you can establish some useful comms with this guy."

Sayers nodded and keyed the switch. He spoke smoothly in Russian for a minute, then released the button. Jerry recognized the words "*Seawolf*" and "*Severodvinsk*" as the CT spoke. "I said we were guarding *Severodvinsk*'s location," Sayers reported.

Rudel nodded. "That's fine."

The plane made almost a complete circle before responding. "American submarine. You are in restricted place. Leave at once." This time it was followed by a medium-length string of Russian.

Sayers keyed the mike, spoke two words, then turned to Rudel and the XO. "They repeated the same message in Russian, and added, 'This is our last warning.' "

Jerry put himself in the pilot's place. "He's probably been ordered not to discuss anything with us, just deliver the message."

"I don't care what his orders are. Make the SOB listen,"

Rudel ordered. "We have to guide them to *Severodvinsk*'s location. Tell them."

As the captain spoke, the patrol plane had continued its circle until it was dead ahead, then tightened its turn. Even without the binoculars, they could all see doors opening up under the plane's belly. The Il-38 carried its weapons internally.

As Sayers spoke a string of rapid phrases, the Ilyushin headed straight for them, descending. Jerry thought, They wouldn't dare. Professionally, he wondered what ordnance aboard the patrol plane would be appropriate to use against a surfaced sub. Then Jerry saw it was too close to drop anything.

Whatever Sayers was saying over the radio was drowned out by the plane as it passed overhead. All four engines were at maximum throttle, and the massive aircraft blocked the sun for a moment. It was almost twice as long as a Flanker, with three times the wingspan. Jerry tried to study the open bomb bay as the plane passed overhead. It was visible for only a moment, but he could see dark shapes inside.

Then it was past, and Jerry and the others all found themselves blinking, looking at each other. "I could see 'Made in Minsk' on the depth charges," Shimko joked. Rudel smiled weakly.

Jerry tried to reply in kind. "And I left my camera at the hotel."

The patrol plane did not turn, but was climbing. "He won't leave," Jerry predicted. "He'll climb to medium altitude and watch us with his radar."

"And we've been reminded again we're not welcome." Rudel added. "But I won't be driven off. Thank you, Petty Officer Sayers. Let's go below and give Mr. Hayes and his lookout some elbow room."

In control, Rudel gave his coat to a petty officer and asked for the 1MC microphone. Jerry saw him think for a moment, then draw a breath, gathering himself.

"This is the Captain. We've had some visitors, Russian aircraft passing close overhead. We've tried to talk to them, and although I'm sure they heard us, they've only responded by repeatedly asking us to leave, and they've been pretty rude about it. But I am not abandoning the men aboard *Severodvinsk* until I'm satisfied the Russians are on station. Thank you for your hard work and continued dedication to this rescue mission."

Rudel hung up the mike and turned to Jerry. "Nav, make sure we don't get more than two miles from *Severodvinsk*'s position." Grabbing his jacket once again, Rudel snatched the vital satellite phone from its charger near the chart table. "I'm going to report to SUBGRU Two."

Petr Velikiy

Vidchenko and Kurganov waited for the reports. Kurganov was still speaking to the Ilyushin's pilot when the messenger appeared. The rating handed a slip of paper to Admiral Vidchenko. "Intercept reports the American is using his satellite phone."

Kurganov hung up the secure phone and took the slip from Vidchenko. He read the report quickly. "He's reporting in, as he should."

Vidchenko asked, "Still no sign of him moving away from the datum?"

"It's been less than ten minutes. He may be asking for orders. Their radio receivers still don't work, after all."

Vidchenko shook his head. "Not an American submarine captain. They have more autonomy. He may be telling his commander what he will do, but he won't ask." The admiral looked at the clock, then his counterpart and surface group commander. "I say give him another fifteen minutes. If he hasn't left by then, he's not going to."

Kurganov asked, "Is that an order, Admiral? Or are you asking my opinion?"

Vidchenko smiled. "I value your opinion greatly, Ivan Aleksandrovich."

"You know I have two Kamovs on alert plus fifteen. I think we've given the American more time than they deserve."

"Then give the order. And increase the formation's speed to twenty-five knots. We don't have to steer evasively, either, since we know the American submarine's location. Leave one escort with that tub *Rudnitskiy,* but tell her we want maximum speed."

Kurganov responded brightly, "Aye, aye, sir! That will cut our time to datum in half. If *Rudnitskiy* is on the ball, we might get one sortie out of AS-34 before dark."

USS *Churchill*

A radioman knocked on the door to Captain Baker's day cabin. The enlisted man handed hard copies to Baker and Patterson. "Flash traffic, sir," he explained. Silas and Lindstrom watched the others quickly scan the page.

"Rudel's phoned in to SUBGRU Two. He'll have a transmitter up this evening, and he reports being buzzed by Russian aircraft."

"That's old news," Silas commented. "The Seahawk pilot's been back an hour, and he's still twitching from seeing those Flankers."

Baker shook his head. "No, Commander. According to Rudel, after the fighters left, a May patrol aircraft showed up and buzzed them at very low altitude—with an open weapons bay."

Concern flashed through Patterson, and she saw it in the others' expressions. "They wouldn't dare."

"They've violated the incidents at sea agreement," Baker observed. "I wonder what else they'd be willing to do."

"This is the first time an American sub has operated openly that far north. As touchy as they are, *Seawolf*'s mere presence would anger them. Imagine how they must feel after the collision with *Severodvinsk*. And as far as they are concerned *we* sank their submarine. And even though it was an accident, they're bound to be more paranoid than usual."

Patterson studied her copy. "Washington's asking for my recommendations." She sounded a little amused.

Baker replied, "You are the mission commander, ma'am." He smiled, but his tone was serious. "You don't make 'recommendations.' "

"My feelings exactly, Captain. Please take *Churchill* into the exclusion zone and rendezvous with *Seawolf*. So far the Russians have threatened an unarmed helicopter and a damaged submarine. Let's even up the odds and see if that improves their behavior."

Baker stood and started to leave, but stopped at the door. "Speed, ma'am?"

"As fast as you can get us there."

"Aye, aye, ma'am." He was smiling as he left.

Silas looked worried, but Patterson didn't give him a chance to speak. "Get our team in the wardroom right away. We're going to need to put together messages to State, SUBGRU Two, Wright, *Seawolf*, and especially the Russians."

The deck surged forward as *Churchill* increased her speed; they felt the deck vibration as all four gas turbines slammed their power into the two shafts.

"They may not want to talk to *Seawolf,* but we'll make them talk to us."

She looked at Lindstrom. "Besides, you're supposed to be the advance man for Marine Diving and Salvage. You can't do any good fifty miles from *Severodvinsk.*"

21

TURN-AWAY

9 October 2008
1030/10:30 AM
USS *Seawolf*

Jerry and Shimko were both in control when they received the message. Captain Rudel was still topside, so Jerry volunteered to take it up to him. The fresh air helped settle his queasy stomach.

The bridge was roomier with only Hayes, the lookout, and the captain. "Message from USS *Churchill,* Skipper. They're coming to join us."

Rudel smiled broadly. "It will be nice to see a friendly face." The message stated *Churchill*'s intentions and ETA, in a little over two and a half hours.

"They're going to ignore the Russians' exclusion zone," Jerry observed.

"I'll still be glad for the company. Particularly given the Russians' behavior as of late," Rudel answered. There was a hint of relief in his tone.

The lookout called down, "Sir, air contact to the southwest, just above the horizon."

Hayes and Rudel instantly turned their glasses in that direction. Jerry had to wait, then borrowed the pair that Hayes was using. He'd anticipated more fighters, but this was worse: two Kamov antisubmarine helicopters.

"Ka-27 Helixes," Rudel announced as Jerry got his first look, and of course he was right. These helicopters carried their ordnance externally, but they were still too far away for Jerry to see whether or not they were armed.

Rudel didn't wait to find out. "Sound General Quarters." Hayes passed the order below, and soon thereafter the *BONG, BONG, BONG* of the general alarm reverberated from the access trunk. As Jerry handed him back his binoculars and stepped toward the open hatch, Rudel told him, "Tell the XO I'm staying up here."

"Aye, sir." Jerry couldn't see the point in the captain staying topside, but there was little precedent for where the captain of a surfaced nuclear sub should be during General Quarters.

Jerry ran into the organized chaos of the control room and passed the captain's message on. The XO nodded, although he didn't look comfortable with Rudel's decision. Wordlessly, he pointed to the plotting table by the fire-control displays, Jerry's GQ station.

Shimko took station near the useless periscopes. These helicopters were harbingers of the approaching Russian surface task force, a group that contained some pretty significant firepower. Their radar was down, as was the ESM system, and all the bow arrays were useless. They could still use the wide-aperture array on flanks, but they had to steer a beam manually. That was it. They were almost blind.

Jerry tried to imagine what *Seawolf* could see or do. She could fire a torpedo while surfaced, since the tubes were still functional, but you couldn't torpedo a helicopter. Besides, they didn't want to shoot at anybody. This was supposed to be a rescue mission, not a wartime patrol.

Rudel's voice came over the intercom a moment later. "Control, bridge. This is the Captain. I have the deck and the conn." The watch section acknowledged the relinquishing of command from Mr. Hayes to the captain, but not without an odd look. A couple of minutes later, both Hayes and the lookout came in to control and repeated Rudel's intention to stay topside. Confused, Will Hayes shrugged his shoulders. Shimko nodded silently. Jerry could see the XO was even less of a happy camper now. Hayes then sat at one of the blank fire-control consoles, his General Quarters station.

"Control, bridge. Both Helixes are armed." Rudel's voice described their movements. "One's coming straight in. The other's pacing us a hundred yards to port."

Jerry and the others could only wait. *Seawolf* was out of her natural element, and defenseless. Without her electronic sensors, the watchstanders in control had to rely on Rudel's running commentary of the events up on deck.

"The first is passing directly over us. They're loaded with four depth charges." That was bad. Russian air-dropped antisubmarine torpedoes only work against submerged subs, but a Helix could set a depth charge to detonate at shallow depth, say thirty feet. Dropped at close range, it would shatter *Seawolf*'s hull.

"They're not responding to my hails on the bridge-to-bridge radio." Rudel then added, "The helicopter to port is lowering its dipping sonar."

Most antisubmarine helicopters either carried a small sonar at the end of a cable or dropped expendable sonobuoys. Ka-27 Helix helicopters could carry sonobuoys along with the dipping sonar, but only at the expense of ordnance. To hunt for a sub, a Helix driver would be directed to a likely spot where the crew would then lower the sonar "ball" into the water, and listen. If they didn't hear the sub, they could actively search, or ping, for it by transmitting an intense burst of acoustic energy and then listen for the echo. The main advantage of a dipping sonar was that it could change its search depth by raising or lowering the array. This negated a submarine's ability to hide from a shallow sensor by ducking below the thermocline.

While nuclear subs are fast and maneuverable compared to other warships, helicopters can run rings around them. They needed a cue from some other sensor on where to start looking, but if they found you, it was hell to get away.

"Conn, sonar, Lamb Tail sonar on the WLR-9, bearing zero four seven. Signal strength is off the scale." The intercept repeater in control beeped away angrily, alerting the occupants to the presence of a threat emitter.

"Well of course," Jerry muttered cynically. "It's three hundred feet off our port beam." "Lamb Tail" was the NATO designation for the dipping sonar on the Ka-27 Helix. The Russian name for it was "VGS-3, Ros-V," which was probably easier to say in Russian.

Unlike *Severodvinsk*'s brutal lashing, the helicopter's sonar set operated at a higher frequency, but was still within the range of human hearing. The eerily tinny pings hammered away, providing the Helix with precise range and bearing information. But they knew exactly where *Seawolf* was, unless they were blind *and* stupid. Why lower the ball and ping?

Alberto Constantino, still functioning as the contact coordinator, passed the bearing data up to Rudel. The captain answered with "Control, bridge. Concur, bearing matches. The other one's doing lazy eights half a mile out in front of us."

Jerry stared at the meager plot before him, as if it could reveal the Russians' intentions. One to the front, one to the side, using its dipping sonar.

"Conn, sonar. The pinging's stopped."

Constantino acknowledged sonar's report and passed it up to the bridge, then looked around, unhappy at the enforced idleness. There was nothing they could do. They were surfaced, running at five knots, steering a box pattern around a downed Russian sub. And there were Russian ASW helicopters overhead, with unknown intentions.

Rudel reported, "It looks like the dipper's shifting positions. He's moving to keep position off our port beam."

Jerry fidgeted with a pencil over the mostly blank sheet of paper laid over the plotting table. This game was completely one-sided. Not only did the Russians own the ball, they owned the ballpark as well.

"Two minutes to the next turn, new course will be to the left to zero four five." QM2 Dunn's report was routine. *Seawolf*'s track was a square centered on *Severodvinsk*. Three miles on a side, it was designed to keep *Seawolf* close to the downed sub.

"Control, bridge. The helicopter's dipping again," Rudel reported. "Same relative position, to the northeast."

"And directly in our path," Jerry added. Constantino looked at the plot and nodded his understanding. "They've been watching us. They know where our next turn should be."

"The helicopter in front of us just dropped something in the water, about one thousand yards away!"

The end of Rudel's report was punctuated by a BOOM that came right through the hull, muffled but definite.

"That *was not* a signaling charge," Constantino observed. Aircraft that operated near submarines often carried small explosive charges, the size of a hand grenade, designed to attract the attention of a submerged sub. They could also be used to simulate an attack.

This was no simulation. But they could have put it right next to *Seawolf,* if they'd wanted to. Jerry looked at Shimko and Hayes. Nobody in control said anything for a moment; then Constantino asked, "Where are they going to put the next one?"

The XO asked Jerry, "How far was that charge from *Severodvinsk*?"

Jerry barely glanced at the chart. "We're at the corner of the box, so it's a little over two miles." Laying a ruler across their course, he reported, "The charge was fifty-five hundred yards, two and three quarters miles from *Severodvinsk*."

"Time for the turn, sir," Dunn reminded Jerry.

"Belay the turn," Shimko ordered sharply. "I'm going up. This isn't working. And the Skipper's up there all by himself." The XO was on the ladder to the first deck before he'd even finished his sentence.

Shimko had barely cleared the last step when another BOOM came through the hull. Jerry tried to convince himself that his imagination made it seem closer, but Rudel's voice on the intercom confirmed it. "Control, bridge. That one was only five hundred yards away, dead ahead! Hard right rudder! Come right to one eight zero!"

The helmsman acknowledged the command over the intercom as he threw the rudder yoke over all the way to the right. A moment later, Rudel ordered, "Continue coming right to three one five." That put them back along their last leg, but in the opposite direction.

Jerry looked around control, with Rudel and the XO topside, and the engineer back in maneuvering, he was the senior officer present. The younger junior officers, Santana, Miller, and Norris, all looked at him with a mixture of shock, fear, and confusion. He tried to reassure them with a tight smile, but he knew this setup was all wrong.

Suddenly, the XO's voice boomed from the intercom loudspeaker. "Navigator, lay to the bridge, on the double. And bring the satellite phone!" Dunn grabbed the phone and semi-threw it to Jerry as he rushed up the ladder well.

He didn't even bother to put on a parka as he started climbing up the access trunk as fast as he possibly could.

Uncharacteristically, Shimko had left the upper access hatch open. The only reason he'd do that was if his intention was to immediately bring the captain below. Jerry was near the top of the access trunk when he clearly heard Rudel's voice. Given the circumstances, he seemed remarkably calm. "They're still not responding on the radio, Marcus, but they know why we're here. They can only go so far."

"That last charge was only a quarter mile in front of us, Captain. What if they halve it again? And again?"

"They have their rules of engagement, just like we do."

"What if they make a mistake? Did they take into account our stressed pressure hull? One miscalculation by a Russian caused this whole situation. We can't rule out another."

"I have to push this, XO." Rudel's voice was determined, stoic, almost obstinate. "I want them to look us right in the eye, and then blink. Petrov and his men are depending on us."

"With all due respect, sir, the men on this boat are also depending on you." Shimko's intensity matched Rudel's. He was respectful, but Jerry would never dream of talking to the skipper like that. "They're using live ammunition, Captain. And they've made it clear they don't want to talk to us. You've done everything that you can. We have to leave, sir."

Uncomfortably aware that he was eavesdropping, Jerry shouted, "Permission to come up to the bridge."

"Granted," responded Rudel crisply. "Where's the satellite phone?"

"Here, sir." Jerry handed it to his captain, who passed it on to Shimko.

"XO, time to call the boss and issue a formal complaint."

Jerry thought phoning home sounded like an excellent

idea. But Shimko was far from convinced. "Sir, we don't have time for this. They'll drop another charge any minute now!"

As if on cue, Jerry watched as the Helix released another cylindrical object into the water. The explosion was closer and louder than the last one. He could feel the shock wave as it hit *Seawolf*'s hull.

"Damn it, XO! Make the call! That's an order!" shouted Rudel.

Shimko was fuming, but did as he was told and started punching the buttons vigorously. Rudel then looked at Jerry and seemed surprised that he was still there. "Get below, mister!" he commanded.

"Aye, aye, sir," replied Jerry.

As he dropped down into the hatch well, Jerry could hear the XO almost pleading with Rudel. "Captain, they are not going to stop this. We have to turn away and head west!"

"We're responsible for *Severodvinsk*! I'm responsible for *Severodvinsk*!" shrieked Rudel. His voice trembled with pain, as if abandoning Petrov and his men was the same as betraying a close friend.

"And the Russians aren't going to let you do anything about it. Sir, we have to change course to the west now, before they drop another charge." The captain didn't respond before Shimko added, "Group Two is on the line, sir."

Jerry heard Rudel begin his report to SUBGRU Two; then the XO suddenly called down the trunk. "They're dropping another charge close by. All hands brace!"

Rudel's voice came over the intercom. "Hard left rudder! Course two seven zero."

Jerry grabbed onto the ladder as he heard the chief of the watch pass the warning on the 1MC. The KA-BOOM and vibration that followed wasn't as bad as he'd dreaded, but it filled his mind with images of the shoring giving way, of the forward compartment filling with seawater. Had the last-second turn-away helped to deflect the shock?

The slam of a hatch and an urgent "Down ladder!" caused Jerry to slide down the rest of the access trunk ladder, followed immediately by the XO and the captain. Shimko bolted for the ladder down to control and shouted, "Submerge the boat, take us to three hundred feet, steady on course two seven zero, speed seven knots."

The watchstanders hesitated, confused as to who should be giving the orders, who they were supposed to listen to. The last they knew, the captain had the deck and the conn. Lieutenant Wolfe saw the confusion and jumped up to the conning station. "You heard the XO. Chief of the Watch, over the 1MC 'Dive, Dive.' Diving officer, make your depth three hundred feet. Helmsman, all ahead one third."

Jolted out of their inaction by Wolfe's forceful presence, the men acknowledged their orders and began to follow through on the procedure to take *Seawolf* down.

As Shimko entered control he quickly pointed to Wolfe and announced, "The XO has the conn, Mr. Wolfe has the deck." Without waiting for the control room watchstanders to respond, he twirled around and pointed at the damage control assistant. "Mr. Williams, check the hull and the shoring for the slightest sign of new damage. Report back here as soon as you've completed the inspection."

A flurry of "Aye, aye, sir" echoed throughout control. Williams disappeared up the ladder, nearly running over a passive, despondent Rudel, who appeared to be muttering to himself.

With a pained and frustrated expression, Shimko looked over to Master Chief Hess, the battle stations diving officer. "COB, get the Skipper to his stateroom." Then, pointing toward Constantino by the command displays, "Al, you're my diving officer."

"Yes, sir," replied both men simultaneously as they exchanged places. Hess then gently grabbed Rudel and threw his arm over his shoulders. The captain seemed confused, dejected, weak. "C'mon, Skipper," coaxed the COB. "You need a little rest."

Once Hess had escorted Rudel out of control, Shimko turn to the chief of the watch and ordered, "Have Chief Gallant report to the CO's stateroom on the double."

"Aye, aye, sir," said Chief McCord, as he picked up the phone and dialed sickbay.

Shimko paused a moment and took stock of the situation in control, allowing himself a deep breath or two. Satisfied that things were well in hand, he pressed the intercom switch. "Sonar, conn. Hear anything from our friends?"

"Conn, sonar. No, sir. If they're dipping, they're doing it passively."

"I'm sure they are. They'll have no trouble following us." Shimko sounded resigned, but not discouraged.

"Jerry, what's the endurance of a Ka-27 Helix?"

Pulling out an ONI reference sheet, Jerry ran his finger down a table. "Two, maybe two and a half hours, at cruise speed, fully loaded."

"If the Russian ships are now about seventy miles away. When will they have to turn for home?"

Jerry checked his watch and did the math. "Half an hour, forty-five minutes tops, XO."

"Good. Then we'll turn in forty-five minutes to rendezvous with *Churchill*. Give me your recommendation for an intercept course."

Severodvinsk, K-329

Petrov, Kalinin, and the other senior officers made their way to the central post after they heard the active sonar transmissions. It took a little longer than usual, as they had to dodge all those plastic curtains that seemed to be hanging everywhere. The first explosion caught them all off guard. By the second, they were standing around the underwater communications station wondering what the hell was going on. "*Seawolf,* this is Petrov. Do you hear me? What is happening?"

There was no response, only the reverberating echo from the explosions crackled over the loud speaker.

"Those aren't signaling charges," Kalinin stated. "The explosions are far too loud for that."

Petrov shook his head wearily, a look of disappointment on his face. "I fear one of our helicopters is trying to persuade Commander Rudel to leave."

"With live ordnance!?! What kind of moron would authorize dropping depth bombs on a badly damaged submarine!?!" Kalinin's outraged expression was shared by several of the others. "Don't they realize what Rudel and his crew has done for us?"

"Calm yourself, Vasiliy. I agree with you that it is an unwise action, but I'm sure the pilot is not dropping the depth bombs too close."

A third explosion was heard. This one was not as loud, farther away.

"Comrade Captain, I do not share your confidence in the abilities of our airmen. Those are the same idiots that displayed horrible tactical proficiency during our acceptance trials. They couldn't find their ass with either hand! They are just incompetent enough to misjudge the distance and actually lay a depth bomb alongside *Seawolf*'s hull!"

Petrov had to struggle not to laugh. Kalinin's backhanded compliment was as damning as it was accurate. He appreciated his starpom's strong concern for the crew of *Seawolf.* Indeed, he shared it. But this was to be expected.

"Vasiliy, we knew this would happen. It's standard procedure to establish an exclusion zone around a rescue site, and then drive off any foreign vessels. I had hoped that our superiors would see the logic of allowing *Seawolf* to remain. But the fact is they are doing what they think is best."

A fourth louder explosion, even farther away, caused Petrov to wince. "All we can do is hope and pray that our overzealous countrymen didn't inflict any more damage on *Seawolf*."

Skynews editorial office, London, England

Befuddled by sleep, Ed Fellowes answered his stapler and his electric shaver before finally locating his cell phone. He hurriedly flipped it open. "This is Fellowes."

"This is Nicholas Hertz, Mr. Fellowes."

"Nicholas, I've asked you call me 'Ed.' "

"Thanks, Mr. Fellowes . . . Ed. I forgot. I'm still so excited with the new equipment you ordered for me, it's so expensive, but it works great! No more analog displays, and the direct link to my laptop . . ."

Nicholas Hertz bubbled with excitement, like any teen with a new toy. In Nick's case, the "toy" was a signal analyzer that could dismantle a radio transmission almost to its component electrons. And he knew how to use it.

"What have you got for me, Nick?" Shaking off fatigue, Fellowes sat up straighter and woke up his laptop. He'd just sent off a piece on the last intercept to his bosses, and that followed a very long night covering the *Seawolf* collision. Sleeping at his desk wasn't a choice, it was inevitable.

"Another satellite phone call, transmitted 0844 our time, and lasting three and a half minutes. It was Rudel, like always. I'm sending you the sound file now. Ed, I think he was under attack. He said the Russians were dropping depth charges on *Seawolf*!"

"What?" Fellowes had heard Hertz clearly, but he had trouble comprehending his words. Had the Russians actually fired on the American submarine?

"And the conversation just stopped, in midsentence, while he was reporting to the admiral's staff. There may even be the sound of an explosion in the file."

Hertz had been listening in on *Seawolf*'s satellite phone calls from the beginning, using his home-built electronic listening setup. He'd mentioned it to a neighbor, who'd mentioned it to a relative, who knew Ed Fellowes was covering the incident. Skynews had immediately put the young electronics hobbyist on retainer.

The teen hadn't slept much in the past two days, although it was easier on him than Fellowes. Now Hertz sounded genuinely worried. "What if they've sprung a leak in that damaged pressure hull? If they're submerged, they can't call for help, and *Churchill*'s still a couple of hours away to the southwest."

Fellowes checked his watch. It was 0901, less than twenty minutes since the call was made. "Let me listen to the file, Nick. Maybe they weren't actually under attack. Can you do something to the file and confirm whether or not there was an explosion?"

Hertz didn't say anything for a moment. Fellowes fought to suppress his impatience. Let the lad think, he reminded himself. "I've got some software that might be able to isolate the sound. I can sample . . ."

"That's great, Nick, please get on that, as fast as you can. Call me back in fifteen minutes, will you? Good lad. Cheers."

Hertz was still talking when Fellowes hung up. Checking his email, he found the message with the file attached, and opened it. He forced himself to listen to the entire file. Rudel's words were clear, although there was a desperate tone to his voice.

Fellowes didn't understand everything Rudel said. They had a retired Royal Navy officer on retainer who could translate; he'd be listening to the file, along with several other people. He didn't have to be a naval officer, though, to know what "using warshots" meant.

As the file finished, suddenly and in midsentence, he punched a number on his cell, simultaneously forwarding the sound file to a select list of people within Skynews. One of them was the editor-in-chief. The subject line for the email was "Skyrocket," the internal code word for a hot story.

Fellowes waited eagerly, running his fingers through his hair, as the phone rang four times before being answered. A dispassionate voice announced, "Mr. Heath's office."

"Mary, it's Ed Fellowes. I just sent the boss a skyrocket. Tell him the Russians have attacked *Seawolf*."

Mikhail Rudnitskiy

Captain Gradev had lived on the bridge since they'd left port, eating, getting what little sleep he could, and haranguing the engineers. Between his ship's worn-out engines and the cranky minisubmarine, he'd had plenty to deal with.

Alex Radimov, Gradev's starpom, appeared, shaking his head. "The engines are at maximum, Captain. Unless we can scrape the barnacles off her hull, fourteen and a half knots is the best they can do. Still, this is a minor miracle and we should buy the chief engineer an entire case of spirits when we get back."

"Very well, Alex. I'm convinced the engineers are giving us their best."

"I toured the sub hangar as well. Everything is proceeding well. AS-34 will be ready to launch the instant we reach the site."

"I'll send Rear Admiral Vidchenko another message, *re*confirming our readiness."

Radinov looked excited, and Gradev shared it. AS-34 would launch in a few hours. By dinnertime, they would finally know for themselves what had happened to *Severodvinsk.*

USS *Churchill*

The first sign of trouble was when Patterson's laptop died, or rather, her connection to the Internet died. She'd been proud of keeping up on her email, and monitoring Parker's progress with their publicity campaign. Their correspondence with the Russian Wives and Mothers website had proved useful and educational.

Now the site she'd been reading froze. She was still trying to solve the problem when the General Quarters klaxon rang.

Patterson's heart leapt in her throat. General Quarters was only sounded for battle or a dire emergency, like a fire aboard the ship. As she hurried to CIC, she didn't know which one to hope for.

Baker saw her come in CIC. In fact, he must have been watching for her, letting his XO supervise the ship's preparations. *Churchill*'s CIC had chairs for the captain and an embarked admiral, and Baker invited her to sit in the admiral's place. Three large screens faced them. The center one showed a map of the area overlaid with what she assumed were tactical symbols.

As soon as she sat, Baker quietly, almost too calmly, reported, "*Seawolf* reports that she's being driven from the area by ASW helicopters. They're dropping live depth charges."

Patterson tried to match Baker's calm demeanor, and said nothing for some time while her mind flashbacked to her own depth-charging experience. Shivering, she forced herself to focus on the current situation. At once, a number of questions bubbled up. She answered several of her most obvious ones herself, then asked, "Was *Seawolf* damaged?"

"Not as far as we know." He handed her a message slip. "But SUBGRU Two reports the conversation was cut off, and according to them Rudel says some of the charges were getting close."

Baker gestured to the activity in CIC. "As soon as GQ is set, I'll place the ship in Condition Two. Condition One is General Quarters, but you can't do that for very long before the crew gets tired. In Condition Two, all our weapons and sensors are manned, but some of the crew is allowed to rest or do essential work. We'll stay at Condition Two, extended General Quarters, until this ship and *Seawolf* are both out of the Russian exclusion zone."

Patterson absorbed Baker's explanation, and tried to imagine how it changed the situation. "I'm uncomfortable with how this will look to the Russians, Captain."

"I don't care how it looks, Doctor. The Russians have dropped weapons near an American submarine, a *damaged* American submarine. It was a very deliberate act, not an accident."

"They didn't attack her directly. They were trying to drive her from the area."

"With live ordnance! This is unheard of, and unacceptable. They know she's damaged, and that she is responding to maritime emergency. I don't know how many international accords they have just violated. Until I know which side of the line they're staying on, I'm not taking any chances."

He was right, of course. Patterson studied the message, trying to glean clues to the Russians' behavior from the transcript of Rudel's last phone call.

"Your orders, ma'am?"

Patterson shook her head. "No change. We find *Seawolf* and make sure she's all right. Then we figure out how to make these sons of Russia talk to us."

"Understood," Baker replied. A phone buzzed near him, and he diverted his attention to ship's business.

Patterson sat there and stewed; the whole situation was spiraling completely out of control. The Russians' belligerent behavior and outright refusal to communicate irritated her to no end. They seemed hell-bent on a crusade to embarrass and humiliate the United States over this incident. What did her loving husband call it? Ah yes, "chest thumping."

She also saw that this spiral could become a vicious circle unless she somehow penetrated the communications barrier. But how? You can't make someone pick up the phone when you call them. Or can you?

Baker hung up the phone. "Sorry, Doctor Patterson, I had to confer with my XO. We'll be setting Condition Two momentarily."

Patterson didn't respond; she seemed lost in thought. A slight grin on her face.

"Doctor Patterson?"

"Yes? Oh, excuse me, Captain. You were saying?"

"I said that we'll be setting Condition Two momentarily."

"Excellent, Captain. Thank you. Will you please have Ms. Parker and Mr. Adams meet me in the wardroom? We have another press announcement to make."

"Certainly. May I ask what you have in mind?" inquired Baker.

"There is an old proverb that says if you can't bring Muhammad to the mountain, then you bring the mountain to Muhammad. Well, I intend to try that with the Russians."

Baker looked on as she left CIC, more confused by her answer than before.

Olga Sadilenko's apartment, Severomorsk, Russia

Olga heard the commotion in the other room before Irina burst in. "They dropped depth bombs on the American submarine!"

The older woman was puzzled. "But isn't it near *Severodvinsk*? The Americans said they were going to guide our ships to the right spot."

"Not anymore. It's all over the Internet that *Seawolf* was attacked by our Navy's helicopters. She may have been damaged."

Others had crowded into Olga's bedroom now to hear the conversation. They all nodded as Irina read several articles from the news sites. She saw several women pull out tissues. With the strain they were all under, tears came quickly.

"So they dropped depth bombs on the American submarine, with our men trapped underneath." Olga's expression mixed anger with disbelief.

"But there's more news," Irina announced. I just got an email from Joyce Parker aboard *Churchill*. It's a press release. They are going into the exclusion zone, and she says Rear Admiral Vidchenko has agreed to meet with them aboard *Petr Velikiy*. The Americans have vital information they wish to give our Navy, and they will also deliver that Norwegian to our ships."

One of the women behind Irina snorted. "Right. Use a warship to deliver one person. If he's even on board at all."

"He is on board," another young woman insisted. "The Norwegian company says he is aboard an American destroyer, and they sent him ahead to prepare for their rescue ship."

Olga absorbed it all as quickly as Irina could tell her. "And our Navy has said nothing, of course," she predicted.

Everyone nodded knowingly.

Irina answered, "Well, if the Navy will talk to the Americans, then perhaps we should talk to the Americans as well. Do they have that list of our men?"

"Yes, I sent it to them earlier today."

"And our list of questions for Commander Rudel?"

"Assembled and ready for your final review."

"Whatever they say, post their response to our questions on the website as soon as you get them."

Northern Fleet Headquarters

The phone call was from the Ministry of Foreign Affairs. They weren't in his chain of command, but reminding them of that hadn't stopped their incessant questioning.

Vice Admiral Kokurin listened politely, but finally said, "Deputy Minister, I can only accept instructions from the Main Naval Staff. They're in Moscow, the same as you . . ."

He paused to listen, but his body language made it clear he didn't like what he was hearing. "I'm sure the ministry's expertise will benefit us in this situation, but you have to speak to Admiral Pucharin. His office can answer all your questions, as well."

After another pause, he said politely, "I'm not authorized to discuss the rescue operation over an open line."

Kokurin listened for a moment, then hung up. His deputy, Vice Admiral Baybarin, had sat patiently, if curiously, while his superior deflected the Foreign Ministry's questions and suggestions.

"Boris, this is going to get messier. The deputy minister said the Americans have formally protested the 'attack' on their submarine, and at the same time they're meeting with Vidchenko aboard *Petr Velikiy.*" He held up his hands, pleading. "Does this make sense to you?"

Baybarin laughed. "No. There was no attack. Did the Foreign Ministry agree to the meeting?"

Kokurin shook his head. "No, nobody will admit to it."

"They do have Lindstrom," his deputy pointed out.

"He could be transferred by helicopter while they stayed outside the exclusion zone. Instead, *Churchill* will rendezvous with our ships at the collision site, and there will be a meeting—aboard one of our ships!"

"What does Vidchenko say?"

Kokurin made a sour face. "I haven't asked him. He has his orders. He will follow them."

Baybarin waited for Kokurin to say something more, but when he didn't, he asked, "What will you tell him to do about the American destroyer and the meeting?"

The fleet commander thought for a moment, pacing, then asked, "So you think I should instruct him?"

"We have information he doesn't—about the American's reaction to the depth bombs."

"A distraction. I won't let a rescue operation be influenced by diplomatic maneuvers."

Babyarin offered, "They say they have vital information for us."

"Whatever they have, AS-34 is there now, and their data is moot. With any luck, we will know all there is to know about *Severodvinsk* after his first sortie."

"So you don't think Vidchenko should meet with the Americans?"

Kokurin shrugged. "Only if it suits his purpose, and that's his decision to make. I've given him the only order he'll get from me: Find and rescue the crew of *Severodvinsk*."

•

The White House, Washington, DC

The Oval Office was almost bursting, with the Secretaries of State and Defense, the Chairman of the Joint Chiefs of Staff, the Chief of Naval Operations, the Director of National Intelligence, Vice President Clemson, and Dr. Wright, the National Security Advisor. Most of their staffs had to wait outside.

Patterson would have been pleased with the attention *Seawolf* was getting now. The entire National Security Council was present. By rights, they should have met in the secure conference room. Huber had decided to have it in the White House to avoid making it an official NSC meeting, and perhaps because the Oval Office symbolized the authority of the president. That authority had been challenged, at least indirectly.

"Dr. Wright, please tell everyone in this room about your conversation with Dr. Patterson." Huber's tone wasn't hostile, but it was formal, and very different from the easygoing air he usually affected.

Trying not to feel defensive, the national security advisor simply stated, "I've just been on the secure phone with Joanna Patterson. She issued the press release you've all seen to force the Russians' hand."

"Without any communications from them, or us." That was from the Secretary of State. His tone was hostile.

"That's the point, Mr. Secretary. They weren't communicating at all. Has your department received any response to her messages?"

"None," the secretary admitted. "But what if the Russians called her a liar, which would mean calling us all liars?"

Wright countered, "They've already accused us of far worse."

The president asked, "But what is her goal? Why is she doing this? The Russians have made it pretty clear they don't want us up there."

"The sooner they start working with us, instead of depth-charging *Seawolf*, the sooner they'll get their people back. Our obligation isn't to the government of the Russian Federation, it's to the men in that submarine."

"Our first obligation is to *Seawolf*," injected Admiral Forrester, the senior officer in the Navy. It made sense that he'd think of his boat and the men aboard her.

"Then we have two goals. And they're not mutually exclusive." Wright felt uncomfortable defending Patterson, but he was really defending their role in *Severodvinsk*'s rescue.

State was not convinced. "Mr. President, I'm not sure that Dr. Patterson will be able to make this work. She has no foreign policy experience, and no background in crisis management. The quickest end to this mess is for you to order *Seawolf* and *Churchill* out of the area. No more friction with the Russians. We'll just be abiding by their wishes. Any information we want to send to the Russians can be delivered to their embassy."

"That won't work anymore, Mr. Secretary. We're involved, and if this turns out badly, people will ask why we didn't stay and help. Even if the crew is rescued, the Russians will have been rewarded for bullying one of our subs."

"She's cutting us out of the loop," Huber complained. Everyone in the room nodded in agreement, which to Wright only reinforced the correctness of her actions.

Wright threw it in their laps. "What do you want to happen? What do you want her to do?"

"She has to keep us informed, give us a chance to comment on what she proposes to tell or say to the Russians." That was the secretary of state again, but defense and the DNI both nodded as well. "We're running our own operations here, and working at cross-purposes could damage more than just our reputation."

"This is a fast-moving situation, and waiting for Washington's 'guidance' could have a high cost." Wright looked to Huber, who slowly nodded his agreement.

The Chief of Naval Operations seemed more cooperative. "I'm willing to 'conform to her movements,' so to speak, but *Seawolf* is damaged, and the Russians aren't respecting her, or international law. Depth charging an undamaged boat would be an incident. Doing it to *Seawolf* verges on the criminal."

Huber stood up and paced. Wright knew the president liked to walk while he thought, or maybe he was just tired of sitting. Everyone waited.

"If Dr. Patterson is successful in opening talks with the Russians, the risk to *Seawolf* disappears. And the chance of the crew getting off that stricken Russian sub alive goes up." He looked at the secretary of state. "That's got to help our international standing."

Before anyone could respond, Huber added, "She's making things happen, and she's taking all the risks. As long as she keeps us informed—" He gave Wright a hard look. "—she has my authorization to act freely."

Petr Velikiy

Kurganov, Vidchenko, and most of *Petr*'s wardroom had gathered in the central command post. The sonar officer had calculated the range of their underwater telephone as three miles. Racing ahead of *Mikhail Rudnitskiy* at thirty knots, and having reached that three-mile distance from "Point *Severodvinsk,*" the formation had slowed to a bare creep.

While the big cruiser continued to move slowly and silently toward the location provided by *Seawolf,* her escorts fanned out, spacing themselves in a ten-mile-diameter circle around the site. They didn't use their active sonars, but they did listen passively. If a submarine was detected, Vidchenko had issued orders to drive it away.

At five knots, it would take a while to cover the last three miles, but that time didn't matter. *Rudnitskiy* was still two hours behind the warships. They had to slow if they wanted to hear the sub.

The sonar officer spoke into a microphone, sending *Severodvinsk*'s pendant number over and over. "K-329, this is Hull 099, over." He paused for a moment, then repeated the call. "K-329, this is Hull 099, respond."

After five minutes, and checking the navigational plot for the distance, the sonar officer began again. Between each call, he paused for sixty seconds. In spite of the crowded room, nobody wanted to make the slightest noise. Vidchenko could hear the small cooling fans inside the electronic equipment, the click every time the sonar officer pressed the microphone.

It took fifteen minutes and 2500 yards before they heard a response. It was Petrov's voice, clear and recognizable. "This is *Severodvinsk,* we are glad to hear you."

The cheer almost deafened him. They were in a metal-walled compartment, after all. Both admirals glared and the sound stopped instantly, and they heard the end of a sentence: ". . . our families."

The sonar officer managed to say, "Please repeat your last," before Vidchenko took the microphone.

"This is Rear Admiral Vidchenko. What is your situation? Over."

"We are resting on the bottom at a depth of one hundred ninety-seven meters. We have a thirty-four-degree port list and a nine-degree downward pitch. Compartments one, seven, and eight are completely flooded; compartment six is partially flooded. Over."

Vidchenko marveled at Petrov's coolness and the neat summary, even as he digested the information. The forwardmost compartment, which held mostly berthing, was flooded. That meant a hole in the pressure hull forward. That was bad enough.

Worse was the news aft. There must have been a second hull breach near the stern, or perhaps the stern tube ruptured. Compartment eight held the auxiliary mechanisms, such as rudder and stern plane actuators and the emergency propulsion motor. Compartment six and seven had the main propulsion turbines, electrical generation turbines, and machinery that supported the reactor. With that one sentence, Petrov had marked the end of his first command, and the newest submarine in the Russian Navy.

A burst of sadness and grief filled him, and the admiral asked, "Casualties?"

"Sixty-seven survivors, nineteen have serious injuries, but are currently stable." Petrov paused, then reported, "Eighteen dead, sixteen during the collision, and two shortly after from their injuries."

"Understood," Vidchenko answered. "We'll get names shortly. *Mikhail Rudnitskiy* will arrive in just under two hours and will immediately launch AS-34."

"They won't be able to evacuate us, not with compartment eight flooded."

"Agreed," Vidchenko replied. "Based on your report, we'll have it survey the bottom and then we'll determine what is needed to bring the boat level. Is your rescue chamber intact?"

"Yes!" Petrov's frustration came though clearly. "If we can right the boat we will be able to bring everyone to the surface. Why are you surveying the bottom again? *Seawolf* has already performed one. Don't you have it? They gave a copy to me when they sent us the carbon dioxide chemicals and medical supplies. It was very complete."

Vidchenko ignored the question. "What about your atmosphere?"

"Oxygen is at sixteen percent, carbon dioxide at two point five percent. We have forty-four hours of chemicals remaining, thanks to *Seawolf.* We'd be near death by now if she hadn't transferred her own emergency CO_2 absorption curtains to us."

"We will have you righted and out of there by tomorrow, I promise." It was surreal, speaking so easily to someone trapped on the ocean floor. Petrov and his men were in mortal danger, but he might as well have been telephoning his wife.

"Admiral Kuganov will take over now. He can get the details of your dead and injured. I must go see to *Rudnitskiy* and the submersible."

"Thank you, Admiral, we are sure you will save us. And please thank Commander Rudel and the men aboard *Seawolf,* sir. Not only did they find us, they kept us alive until you could get here."

Vidchenko didn't answer.

22

RENDEZVOUS

9 October 2008
1915/7:15 PM
USS *Seawolf*

They surfaced five miles off *Churchill*'s port beam. Normally, when *Seawolf* joined on a surface vessel, she did so by announcing her presence with a green flare, a thousand yards astern, in perfect firing position. This time, instead of "bang you're dead," a yellow flare broke the surface, indicating that a submarine was coming to periscope depth. But without a periscope or most of her sonars, *Seawolf* had poor situational awareness of the surface above, and couldn't safely come up near another ship. Once *Churchill*'s bridge crew saw the yellow flare, they maneuvered away to give *Seawolf* all the room she needed. While a little excessive, nobody disagreed with Rudel's caution.

Once on the roof, *Seawolf* began to close on the now fully illuminated destroyer. Jerry was well aware of *Seawolf*'s limitations, and he swore at times that he could physically feel them, but this surfacing bruised his already tender submariner's ego. It was just plain wrong to meekly surface and then hobble over and take station astern of a surface combatant. Just thinking about it made him wince. And it was doubtful that Doc Gallant had anything, other than his cheery bedside manner, to treat it with.

Even though the weather had improved considerably, *Seawolf* was still very much restricted in her ability to maneuver on the surface. At anything more than five knots, the large gentle swells caused the heavily damaged bow to vibrate and make some very unpleasant noises. Instead of racing northeast at thirty-plus knots, *Churchill* would be limited to *Seawolf*'s glacial pace.

As the boat rolled slowly from side to side, Jerry was starting to get used to being on the surface. His stomach still complained, and he was sure he was losing weight from missed meals, but he was learning to cope with the nausea. It was amazing how much the weather could change in just over a day. The evening sky topside was magnificent, with a colorful twilight having faded away under clear skies. The main act, however, was the aurora borealis, or northern lights, which put on a spectacular display. The chief of the watch had no problems getting volunteers to man the two lookout positions on the bridge. Despite his doubling the number of lookouts, there were so many who wanted to go up that he'd shortened each watch to just an hour.

The captain and the XO slowly walked down the ladder into control, having just come down from the bridge, and handed their parkas to the messenger of the watch. Rudel looked much better, having gotten some rest after the depth-charging incident earlier. He still looked depressed over having to retreat from *Severodvinsk*'s position, but the XO assured Jerry that the captain was finally on the mend. Apparently, being forced to leave was the straw that broke the captain's resolve and all the emotional baggage he had been holding on to since the collision was thrown overboard all at once. Jerry hoped the XO was right. He'd hate to see a leader like Rudel suffer over the collision. There had been enough casualties already.

Both of them came over to the chart table, Shimko actually looked like he was in a good mood. "Nice job on the rendezvous, Nav. I particularly liked that little Kabuki dance at the end."

"Thanks, XO. I think." Jerry smiled; he knew Shimko was jerking his chain over the delay in meeting up with

Churchill. "It's not my fault that no one told me that *Churchill* went to afterburner and roared right by us," he complained defensively. Between their escape course and *Churchill*'s increase in speed, the two ships had failed to link up as expected, and *Churchill* had to backtrack to rendezvous with *Seawolf.* Jerry had taken a little good-natured ribbing once they had realized the destroyer had passed CPA and was opening. "Still, it's nice to finally operate with a ship from *our* Navy."

"I think we all like having a friendly face in the neighborhood," said Rudel.

"Hear, hear!" Shimko exclaimed. "I'd love to see those helos try a repeat of their antics with an Aegis destroyer around."

"Listen, Jerry. I want to thank you for all you've done to help the XO hold this boat together over the last couple days. I guess I let myself get a little too preoccupied with *Severodvinsk,*" Rudel admitted quietly.

Jerry, surprised by Rudel's confession, took a moment to react, and then another when he realized he didn't know how to respond. Shimko covered for him.

"Skipper, wise man says, 'Strong feelings precede great movements.' We all want to help the Russian."

"Perhaps, Marcus. But I think I need to keep better track of my responsibilities. I just didn't see the forest fire for the flaming trees. And now that the Russian fleet is finally on station, they are better equipped than we are to rescue Petrov and his crew."

Rudel studied the nav plot for a moment, then said, "It's too dark to do anything more tonight, but in the morning some experts on *Churchill* are going to come aboard to inspect our damage. Then when they leave, I'm going with them to a meeting on board the Russian flagship, *Peter the Great.*"

Jerry absorbed the news. Visitors at sea, the captain leaving the ship . . .

"And it turns out you know one of them," Shimko added. "There's a Dr. Patterson aboard. She's billed as our SAR coordinator. Apparently, the president's national security advisor appointed her to the position and she's calling the shots." He studied Jerry for a moment, gauging his expression. "She says you and her are old shipmates, which means she must have been with you on *Memphis*."

Jerry searched for a moment, then replied simply, "That's right . . ." and after another pause, "She's a scientist, and she rode with us on our spec op. Since her trip on *Memphis* she's become a big fan of submariners. She even married one."

"She's Lowell Hardy's wife?" Rudel asked a little surprised.

"Yes, sir."

"So ah, do you two keep in touch?" pushed Shimko.

"With her and Captain Hardy? Christmas cards, mostly. I visited them the last time I was in Washington." Jerry was uncomfortable with Shimko's interest and tried to move the conversation on: "XO, what time will they be coming aboard?"

"Oh seven hundred, they'll be guests for breakfast. A woman on a submarine, eh? I'd love to hear some of her sea stories. Yep, I'm definitely looking forward to meeting an old shipmate of yours, Jerry."

As Rudel and the XO both headed aft, Jerry forced his shoulders to unclench. Joanna Patterson. He would be glad to see her, even after, or maybe because of, everything that had happened aboard *Memphis*. He was pretty sure she wouldn't talk to Shimko about *Memphis*'s last mission, but that wouldn't stop the XO from trying.

10 October 2008
0630/6:30 AM
Mikhail Rudnitskiy

Someone was shaking his shoulder. "Admiral, sir, they'll be ready to launch in half an hour." Light flooded into his brain, and Vidchenko stirred. He shook his head, and then blinked several times.

A senior-lieutenant, one of *Rudnitskiy*'s engineers, had stepped back, and was offering him a mug of hot tea. The admiral waved it off, saying, "No, thank you. I'll be there soon."

The officer left, and Vidchenko rolled out of the bunk and stood carefully. He stretched briefly to work out some of the stiffness in his joints, then dressed and washed. Someone had left him a pair of submarine coveralls, more appropriate for AS-34 than the working uniform he'd worn over. They'd even put his name on them, along with the proper rank insignia.

He'd used the captain's cabin, and its unfamiliar layout slowed him a little. Gradev had a large family. The photo over his desk showed a gray-haired woman surrounded by seven children, probably taken by Gradev himself. Other shots scattered around the cabin showed the captain with the children at sporting events. The largest photo was of Gradev in some sort of tropical setting, standing next to an incredibly large fish. He was wearing a Hawaiian shirt.

A petty officer was waiting outside the cabin, and he snapped to attention as the door opened. "Would you like to have some breakfast, sir? There's still time. They've just started . . ."

"No. I'll go to the sub."

"Yessir. Please follow me."

The petty officer led him down a brightly lit passageway, then down two ladders to the main deck level, and out through a watertight door to the dark weather decks. The cold wind pulled at his coat, but the admiral hardly felt it. He was already absorbed in the dive.

A separate set of ladders took them down to the deck of the hold, now open to the air as they rigged lifting lines to the minisub.

Gradev came running over. "Good morning, sir!"

"How long until we launch, Captain?"

"We will disconnect the charging cables in another five minutes. The instant they are gone, you and the crew will board and we will put AS-34 over the side."

"Disconnect the cables now. Petrov and his men are on borrowed time. Those final five minutes won't make any difference."

"Immediately, Admiral." Gradev ran to give the orders, and Vidchenko studied the toylike submersible. It would have fit on the deck of his first command, a nuclear sub, and that boat was half the tonnage of *Severodvinsk*.

Two middle-aged officers in coveralls came up and saluted. "Captain Third Rank Bakhorin, Admiral. I am the officer in charge and pilot. This is Captain Third Rank Umansky, my systems engineer and navigator."

Bakhorin hadn't referred to himself as "Captain" because AS-34 was not a commissioned naval vessel. He wore a submariner's insignia, as did Umansky, and Vidchenko wondered whether it was by choice or circumstance that two middle-grade officers had decided to crew this clumsy craft.

"There's a jump seat just aft of the conning station, sir. There's very little room to shift positions with three of us in there, so you'll have to board first."

"Will I be able to see out any of the ports?" That was the whole reason Vidchenko was going. The photos taken on the first dive had been so poor that it was hard to visualize *Severodvinsk*'s situation. He had to see for himself if that was the best they could do, and at the same time find out what he could of *Severodvinsk*'s plight.

"Yes, comrade Admiral," Bakhorin replied. "Although the viewports are not very big. Your field of view will be limited. Come, let's get on board."

Bakhorin motioned to Vidchenko, pointing to a ladder. "This way, sir." The three walked over to the ladder that provided access to the submersible's deck, with crewmen along the way wishing them luck. Some saluted, others clapped them on the back, some even gave obscene encouragements. AS-34 *Priz* was the reason *Rudnitskiy* was there—the reason for the entire task force. There was a lot of hope riding on something that looked like a bath toy.

Vidchenko turned to start climbing the boarding ladder, but Bakhorin stopped him. "Your coat, sir. I'm afraid there's no room for it inside." The admiral handed it to a petty officer, and then started up the ladder. Vidchenko struggled to keep his feet in the rungs as the ladder flexed and the ship rolled, but found himself quickly and was soon on top. "Just go straight in!" Bakhorin instructed, as he held the ladder extension so the admiral could step straight down into the interior of the minisub.

Stepping onto the hatch rim, Vidchenko grabbed the extension and slowly descended into the opening. It was lit, thank goodness, and he gingerly picked his way into the cluttered interior.

The access trunk was only a meter long, and led into a cylindrical compartment about two meters in length. It was an irregular cylinder, with equipment and consoles invading the space without regard for movement or human convenience. It was impossible to stand fully upright. Behind him, through a hatchway, was another larger cylinder with seating for twenty passengers.

Vidchenko was still surveying the interior when there was a clatter on the hatch rim over his head and a pair of feet appeared in the opening. They were moving quickly, and the admiral shifted aft to give them space.

Bakhorin came down next and took the chair in the bow. After closing and dogging the hatch, Umansky took his seat, just a little forward of the entrance. A loud clang signaled the closing of the hatch.

An air horn sounded and the lines to AS-34 went taut. It sounded again and she came off the cradle, while crewmen with lines steadied her. Vidchenko felt a sudden jerk and then could see that they were being lifted clear of *Rudnitskiy's* hull.

Lights followed the white-and-orange-striped vehicle as the crane swung it out of the hold and lowered it into the water. Vidchenko was too busy holding on to notice that they were in the water. AS-34 was now afloat on *Rudnitskiy*'s lee side, with only a bow and stern line connecting it to the mother ship.

Three measured raps echoed inside the sub. "They've released the mooring lines," Bakhorin announced. "Flooding all tanks."

"Best course is two four seven, distance twelve hundred meters," recommended Umansky.

Bakhorin was his own helmsman as well as diving officer. "Course is two four seven." He turned back to Vidchenko. "We won't use the motors right now, to save battery charge—we'll use a 'gliding' descent to cover a lot of that distance."

"Why do you not power your way down?" asked Vidchenko impatiently.

"We do not have sufficient battery power, comrade

Admiral," responded Bakhorin frankly. "The batteries on this submersible are all beyond their service lives and we have only two hours or so of power. We can save energy by just sinking down naturally."

"How long will this take?" Vidchenko grumbled. It was all about time.

"To one hundred ninety-seven meters? It took us thirty minutes yesterday, but we were proceeding cautiously. Now we are sure there are no obstructions, and know the exact location of the sub. We should be alongside *Severodvinsk* in twenty minutes."

"We're going to survey the starboard side this time, yes?"

Watching the gauges, Bakhorin sighed. "Correct, sir. We did one complete pass around *Severodvinsk,* but we only had sufficient time to do a thorough examination of the port side on the last dive."

"And you'll have just enough time to examine the other side on this one," Vidchenko concluded. "Plus any time you save on the dive."

"Yes sir."

"We have to make enough time to go back to the port side." He tapped a sheaf of papers he'd brought. "These photos are fuzzy, at best. They hardly show the shape of the bottom, much less its composition. If we are going to plant charges to right *Severodvinsk,* it will have to be on the next dive."

"I wish we had more time, sir. I'd skip surveying this side, but if . . ."

Vidchenko waved him off impatiently. The steps they had to take were obvious and mandatory. Even when you cut corners, there were things that couldn't be skipped.

"Sonar contact." Umansky's report came only twelve minutes into the dive. "Four hundred meters, ten degrees to port."

Vidchenko automatically bent over to look out through

one of the ports, it was pitch black; he could see nothing. Umansky saw him look and said, "Our lights aren't on yet, sir, to conserve power. But even with them on, we will only have a visual range of five to ten meters, and that's only when the water is clear. The longer we stay in one place, the more silt we will stir up."

He pointed to the photos Vidchenko held. "These are all the first shots, the best images, of each feature. The second ones were worse, and we didn't bother with a third."

Vidchenko asked, "Where are the cameras mounted?"

Umansky smiled sheepishly and held up an old Canon digital camera. "This is it, sir. We take pictures through the front port, which is optically flat, but we have to maneuver the sub to properly face the subject."

Vidchenko was beginning to write off the chance of getting any decent images. The only worthwhile examination would be his personal observations. He wished he'd brought a demolitions expert on this dive, and chided himself for not being more aware of AS-34's capabilities and limitations.

"Don't bother with the photographs," ordered Vidchenko. "Make one pro forma pass down the port side. Then proceed over to the starboard side."

"Understood, sir. We'll be approaching from the bow."

Bakhorin started the motors, both to slow their downward descent and start them toward the bottomed sub. Umansky reported, "Course is good, two hundred meters. Bottom is in sight, thirty meters."

"We'll go down to seven meters off the bottom," Bakhorin explained. "Any closer and we stir up too much silt, any farther away and the lights won't illuminate properly."

"One hundred fifty meters. Recommend we slow."

"Slowing to two knots, Mother," Bakhorin teased.

Umansky coached them into position, and they made room for Vidchenko to crouch near one of the forward-facing viewports. They'd closed inside fifty meters, and Bakhorin had slowed to a bare crawl, with nothing but inky blackness in front of them. Vidchenko fought the urge to check his watch. Time could be measured in air or battery charge, and there was precious little of either.

Suddenly, a dull greenish black wall rushed at them, but Bakhorin was ready and backed sharply. He cut the motors after one short astern burst, and AS-34 drifted to a stop surrounded by a cloud of yellow and gray silt.

There was almost no curvature to the hull, and Vidchenko realized they could see only a few square meters of it through the port. It would take at least a dozen dives to thoroughly inspect the submarine and the surrounding area.

Bakhorin was already turning AS-34 to pass close alongside the sub's hull. Even at a fast walk, it took a while to cover the one hundred and twenty meters. *Severodvinsk* listed in their direction, so the massive hull crowded over them. All three officers studied the bottom, looking for anything that would interfere with the boat righting itself if the obstructions were removed. Luckily, there was little to see, just an uneven layer of mud with the underlying rock sometimes showing through.

"We're coming up on the stern, Admiral," announced Umansky.

Vidchenko continued to watch, although Bakhorin had pulled the minisub up and away from the bottom. He hadn't stopped moving aft, and one of the stern planes appeared and then passed aft, only a meter from the viewports. As large as the side of a house, Vidchenko remembered seeing them not that long ago, standing on the floor of a drydock before she was launched. Now she'd never leave this place.

"I'll turn to port, sir." Bakhorin turned AS-34 tightly. Vidchenko knew what to expect, but was still shocked when he saw the stern. There at the end of the shaft, distorted and bent upward, was the plus-sign-shaped end cap, but not a single propeller blade was on the hub. Only torn, jagged ridges where the scimitar-shaped blades once were. Vidchenko tried to imagine the shaft bending, flexing with the impact of each blade as it struck the American's hull, the turbines instantly freed from their massive load, water pouring in from the shaft seals . . .

"Have you found the collision debris field?"

Umansky answered. "It wasn't on any of our sonar sweeps. *Severodvinsk* had some way on at the time of the collision. She would have gone some distance, especially since she appeared to be descending when she struck this hillside. There's a scar in the bottom on the other side. With a little time . . ."

"Which we don't have," Vidchenko interrupted. "We'll leave the investigation of the bottom to a proper survey vessel, and hopefully Petrov and his men will be able to personally assist in reconstructing the collision."

"This is where we'd have to plant the first charge, Admiral."

Bokharin had move the mini-sub around to the starboard side and maneuvered it to an irregular rocky mound next to *Severodvinsk*'s hull. It had to be removed so that the sub could roll to starboard and right itself. The lights from AS-34 actually cast shadows, showing an empty space on at least one side of the obstruction.

Mud covered most of the underlying rock. But what kind of rock were they dealing with? Solid bedrock or just a small outcropping? How big a charge would they need to break it up?

"Can you use the motors to clear some of the silt? We need to get a sample of that rock."

Umansky answered again. "We can do better than that, sir, we've got a water jet forward, like a fire hose. If Captain Bakhorin can position us . . ."

"Already in progress," Bakhorin answered. The pilot

gently maneuvered them closer, and Umansky busied himself with the controls. Vidchenko couldn't see the results, and impatiently asked, "How's the battery charge?"

"Over fifty percent, sir, although with all this work you can almost see the indicator needle move."

"I've got a sample!" Umansky exclaimed. "Hah! It's in the basket."

"Good work, Captain." Vidchenko was sparing with praise, but these two men deserved it. But was their hard work going to be worth anything in the end?

"Sir, I recommend taking photos, but we will have to wait for the water to clear."

"Then let's move down to the next obstruction."

"Aye, sir."

They managed to examine four masses of rock altogether. They had to use the waterjet once more to get a feel for the extent of the formation. Whatever material they were made of, it easily resisted the high-pressure water shot at them. Finally, as the low battery charge alarm rang, they headed back to the surface.

Vidchenko was not a demolitions expert, but he was an engineer. The AS-34 crew had planted charges before, although never under such circumstances. The three of them talked all the way up. How much explosive could AS-34 carry? Could they plant all of them in a single dive? What types of work could the mechnical arm perform? Even as they rose, Vidchenko was already thinking ahead to the next dive, the most important dive. Hopefully, the last dive.

USS *Seawolf*

The helicopter crew chief was attempting to give her important instructions. She tried to listen, but even over the interphone, she could only make out half of what he said.

Hovering over *Seawolf,* the rotor wash tugging at her clothes and chilling any exposed skin, Joanna Patterson focused on the crew chief's face. Truth be told, she was terrified. Flying was fine, even in something as improbably aerodynamic as a helicopter. But the thought of dangling over empty space, hung by a thread . . .

The crew chief finished speaking, and Patterson nodded vigorously. He waited for a moment, and it looked like he expected her to do something, but when she didn't move, he took her gently by the shoulders and turned her to face the open cabin door.

He hooked the sling to the attachment points in her exposure suit, disconnected the lead for the interphone, and motioned for her to sit on the cabin floor. It took a moment for her legs to obey, and then he motioned for her to swing her legs over the edge.

She was still watching his face, and he pointed to his eyes and then the hoist in front of her. He repeated the motion, and she nodded, this time understanding. Eyes on the hoist.

He nodded and saluted, then pressed a control. The line went taut, and the suit tugged in uncomfortable places, and she was off the cabin floor and hanging in space. She heard a new sound, in spite of the engines. It was the whine of the hoist motor, and she felt herself slowly descend.

The temptation to look down was overwhelming. She wanted to know how far she had to go, even though she'd seen it from the helicopter and the pilot had told them it would be about fifty feet. Rather than look down, she looked up, at the helicopter's fuselage receding, and the dark disk of the rotor blades. The cold rotor wash buffeted her face, and she welcomed it.

She kept her head titled back until she could hear voices below her, and she looked down to see she was almost there, only fifteen, then ten feet off the deck. One sailor had a long pole that looked like a shepherd's staff, reaching out for her.

Sailors in safety harnesses stood by to steady her, but she kept her feet. They quickly unbuckled her, then guided her toward a hatch behind the sail. Another sailor inside, at the foot of the ladder, greeted her and led her to the crew's mess. As sailors helped her out of her exposure suit, her two companions, Ken Bover and Arne Lindstrom, were escorted in.

Lindstrom efficiently peeled off his suit with almost no help, but Bover seemed unable to work the fastenings. He bubbled with excitement as *Seawolf*'s crewmen helped. "I can't believe we just did that! I wish someone had taken a photo! Why didn't someone have a camera? My daughter will never believe me."

A lieutenant commander appeared and introduced himself as "Marcus Shimko, *Seawolf*'s XO." After introductions, he said, "Don't worry, Mr. Bover, we'll testify on your behalf. By the way, you're all out of uniform." Handing each of them a dark blue ball cap inscribed with *Seawolf*'s name and crest, he asked, "Please follow me. We've got breakfast waiting in the wardroom."

Patterson followed the XO, with her two companions behind, up to the wardroom. It appeared that almost all of *Seawolf*'s officers were gathered to welcome them, and Shimko began the introductions. Captain Rudel, Lieutenant Commander Lavoie, and . . .

"Jerry!" she shouted, and found herself hugging him, surrounded by a crowd of attentive, very curious, but silent officers. Seeing her old shipmate sent emotions cascading through her. There was relief, but then concern, no, more than concern. "I was worried, and I'm so sorry, and it's so good to see you after everything . . ."

She paused, and then let Shimko complete the introductions. When he finished, about half the officers turned to leave, to make room for the rest, but she spoke up.

"Please wait." When they had all turned back to face her, Patterson said, "I have a message from the President. He is deeply sorry for Petty Officer Rountree's death and the injuries to your crew. Captain Rudel, he wants you to know that he believes you and your crew have acted in the best interests of the United States and Russia since the collision. You have his full support."

She hated to rush through what had obviously been planned as a formal meal. Fresh-baked cinnamon buns beckoned, but she settled for fruit. It was best to eat lightly. This would be a long day.

It was a working breakfast, with different officers assisting each of Patterson's group. Ken Bover would be working with Chandler on the repairs to the sub's radios and other systems, Lindstrom would talk to Wolfe and Palmer about the UUVs and what they had seen, and she would brief Rudel.

But first, they all wanted to see the forward bulkhead. She'd already inspected the photos that Rudel had sent back on the helicopter, both of the external damage and the interior.

The reality was so different, she wondered if she'd looked at the right photographs. The charring and the scars from the welds to support the shoring were the last thing she'd wanted to see aboard a nuclear sub.

It was crowded with four people in the small compartment. Only Jerry, responsible for the electronics equipment space, had accompanied them inside. She turned to make sure Bover and Lindstrom could both see clearly. Evidently they could, Bover was pale, almost ashen, his eyes as wide as saucer plates. Lindstrom looked better, but was muttering softly in Norwegian. It could have been a prayer or a curse, but he wasn't pleased by what he saw.

Jerry answered a few questions, but Patterson asked them more to break the quiet than anything else.

JERRY HAD been surprised and more than a little embarrassed by Patterson's sudden affection, but he was glad to see her. She was not only an old friend, but represented the help they desperately needed, both for their own sake, as well as Petrov's crew.

He was glad to leave the electronics equipment space. Chandler's men needed to get back to work. Back in the wardroom, the group was supposed to split up. Lindstrom did leave with Wolfe, headed for the torpedo room, but Bover asked to speak with both Patterson and Captain Rudel immediately. Jerry, Chandler, Shimko, and the others all listened.

"Captain Rudel, Dr. Patterson, this sub has to head for the nearest port immediately. I do not understand how you're still afloat, but *Seawolf* is not seaworthy. She should head south immediately, on the surface." Bover was intense, agitated. Jerry thought he was frightened as well.

Chandler started to speak, and looked like he was going to agree with Bover, but Rudel answered first. "*Seawolf* is tougher than she looks, Mr. Bover. We've submerged, weathered a storm, and we're not done with what we have to do here." There was firmness in the last phrase, more than Jerry had heard from the captain since the collision.

"Captain, it may be your boat, but I repair ships and subs for a living. Your pressure hull has sustained significant damage. I don't know of any boat that has taken damage like this that wasn't immediately put into a drydock. *Seawolf* needs emergency repairs at the nearest port."

The tension in the wardroom grew as Rudel and Bover argued over *Seawolf*'s condition. Patterson looked at both men. Bover was shaking and upset, resolute in his professional assessment. Rudel seemed calm, confident, and just as determined. She was about to say something to defuse the situation, when out of the blue Shimko quipped, "It's just a flesh wound."

Jerry and the other officers struggled to not burst out laughing. A couple did cough to release the built-up pressure. Rudel and Patterson were dumbfounded, caught completely off guard by Shimko's off-the-wall remark. Rudel shook his head and gave his XO an exasperated look. Patterson laughed.

"XO, that's not helping," Rudel scolded.

"Sorry, sir," mumbled Shimko apologetically. The twinkle in his eye said he really wasn't.

"Captain! This is no laughing matter! I implore you to get this boat to a safe port." Bover's voice was becoming shrill.

"No, Mr. Bover," Rudel answered sternly. "*Seawolf* has capabilities the Russians will need before this is over. The only reason Petrov and his men are alive is because of us."

"And the only reason they're on the bottom is because of you." Bover's retort might have been meant to undermine Rudel, maybe deflate him, but the immediate result was to make Jerry want to throttle the man. Judging by the looks of some of the other officers present, he'd have lots of help.

Patterson intervened quickly and said, "That's enough, Mr. Bover. You've got work to do with Lieutenant Chandler. I suggest you get to it." She checked her watch. "And we have to leave in twenty minutes."

Rudel waited until Bover and Chandler left, then asked, "Dr. Patterson, is that why you're here, to order me home?" Patterson quickly shook her head, denying the accusation, but she also glanced at Jerry. He did his best to think positive thoughts.

After a moment, she answered, "If you were a different

captain, perhaps, but remember President Huber's message. He read your service record, and spoke with Rear Admiral Sloan before deciding to back your actions."

"And I didn't even vote for the guy," said Rudel, visibly relieved.

"Lowell sends his best."

Rudel smiled. "Thanks. I need all the friends I can get, right now. And he's in Congress?"

Twenty minutes later, *Churchill*'s helicopter reappeared and quickly winched up *Seawolf*'s three visitors. Last off was Commander Rudel, and Jerry heard the 1MC signal the departure of the ship's commanding officer. "*SEAWOLF,* DEPARTING." It was commonplace enough in port, but more than rare at sea.

Shimko would be in command while Rudel was off the boat. That was the XO's job, and he was more than capable of doing it. But Jerry could sense that *Seawolf* knew that something was missing. QM3 Gosnell, standing watch at the navigation plot, said it clearly, "It doesn't feel right for the Skipper to be gone."

Jerry thought that was a good thing.

Petr Velikiy

Rear Admiral Vidchenko waited in the flag mess with Rear Admiral Kurganov and Captain Chicherin. There had been some debate as to who should meet the Americans. Kurganov had offered to meet with the visitors. Technically, Chicherin didn't need to be there either.

This was their idea, Kurganov had argued. They had bullied their way aboard. They were obviously here to gather information. He could meet them briefly, listen to what they had to say, and then get them off the ship before they'd warmed their chairs.

But Vidchenko could not pass up the chance to see them for himself. They'd sent over a list of names this morning. It included Rudel, *Seawolf*'s captain, and Vidchenko wanted to be there. What was Rudel's purpose? To apologize? Did he think that would help? Would he try to blame Petrov? The man couldn't be that stupid.

Vidchenko had brought the photos from the second dive to look at while they waited for the visitors to arrive. The new batch was no better than the first. Vidchenko had expected as much, and his personal observations, along with the AS-34's crew, had been far more useful to the demolitions experts. While the batteries in AS-34 charged, the technicians were rigging the explosive charges. They would make the dive, plant the charges, and clear the area. With careful planning and a little luck, Petrov's crew would be eating lunch aboard *Petya*.

So Vidchenko regarded this visit as a useless, but potentially informative, distraction. The Americans couldn't know the progress of their efforts, and Vidchenko was more than willing to lead them along. He'd have the meeting, and then get back to work.

THEY WERE almost on time, the Seahawk helicopter landing only three minutes late. A video image of the flight deck let Vidchenko and the others watch the five visitors arrive. Two naval officers, two government officials, and the Norwegian. He wondered which was Rudel, and realized that was his main reason for allowing them aboard. He wanted to meet an American submariner, on ground of his choosing. *Seawolf* was one of their most capable submarines. Rudel should be one of their best.

It took them a few minutes to reach the flag mess after disappearing off the video screen. The woman came in first, followed by two commanders. Deciphering their nametags, the first one was Rudel. He was the right age for a submarine commander, but nothing remarkable. Vidchenko was a little disappointed, although he hadn't known what he expected.

Petr Velikiy had been built as a flagship, and had separate places for the admiral and his staff to work and eat. The flag mess was appropriately furnished, since admirals' behinds needed more padding than the lower ranks. Paintings of Peter the Great as tzar and at the Battle of Poltava were matched on opposite bulkheads by photo portraits of the Russian Federation President, the Commander in Chief of the Russian Federation Navy, and Vice Admiral Kokurin, Commander of the Northern Fleet. To enhance the effect, Chicherin had moved in flags and a plaque that normally graced the bridge.

Vidchenko spoke only a little English, Kurganov was fluent, and Chicherin not at all. Introductions were conducted by the U.S. State Department official, Mr. Manning, and monitored by a senior-lieutenant from the weapons battle department who'd studied in Chicago.

"Dr. Patterson, on behalf of President Huber, wishes to convey her personal gratitude for allowing this meeting to take place. She hopes it will be constructive, and that the rescue of the crew of the Russian Federation submarine *Severodvinsk* can be quickly brought to a successful conclusion." Manning's Russian was flawless, and his greeting appropriately dressed with diplomatic overtones.

Vidchenko was impressed, and a little concerned. The Americans were really pushing this. But why? How guilty was this Rudel?

"Tell the lady we are here to listen to what she has to say."

Manning's translation was more polite, but it did relay the gist of Vidchenko's remark. The senior-lieutenant smiled at how Manning phrased the message, but nodded his agreement to his superiors.

Rudel began to speak, looking directly at the Russian

admirals. Manning indicated that the senior-lieutenant was to interpret the American captain's comments. "He speaks about the collision. He is sorry for the dead and injured aboard *Severodvinsk.* He wishes to do everything he can to help."

Kurganov muttered, "So he's apologizing. Fine. He's done enough," but Vidchenko was genuinely curious. "How does he think he can help?"

In response to the interpreter's question, Rudel placed a colored image of a torpedo-shaped device on the table. "He says they have two of these unmanned robotic vehicles on board his submarine. They used one like it to send emergency supplies over to *Severodvinsk.*"

Rudel spoke again, and the interpreter translated, "The vehicle is equipped with high-precision sonar and photographic systems, which they have used to survey *Severodvinsk* and the surrounding area. He has a copy of the material for you."

Vidchenko saw a fat envelope in Rudel's hand, extended toward him. He looked at Kurganov. His face was hard, made of the same steel as the ship.

"Tell them thank you, but that information has been overtaken by events. I personally surveyed *Severodvinsk* early this morning, and we are now preparing to free Petrov and his crew."

Manning looked surprised and provided the American party with Vidchenko's reason for declining the package. The visitors stirred at this news. The Americans spoke with each other in excited tones. The Norwegian, Lindstrom, turned and asked a question, a one-word question, which the interpreter relayed. "Explosives?"

Vidchenko nodded. "Yes. We will clear some obstructions that prevent *Severodvinsk* from sitting level on the sea floor. When those are gone, the crew will use the escape capsule."

Suddenly, the door to the flag mess burst open and Chicherin's executive officer hurried in. Vidchenko felt a flash of irritation, then curiosity. They'd posted a guard outside to prevent interruptions, but from the look of concern on the starpom's face, the matter was serious.

Chicherin started to reach for the message, but the starpom took it straight to Vidchenko. As he pressed the paper into the admiral's hand, he turned his face away from the visitors, and bent down to speak softly to Vidchenko.

"Sir, this is from the Main Intelligence Directorate. It was just decoded."

Patterson and the others waited while Vidchenko read the message. His face darkened, and he handed the message to the other admiral, Kurganov, as he stood. He looked hard at Commander Silas and spoke in rapid-fire Russian. His voice had an edge to it. Silas and Manning both paled and Manning began to protest.

Patterson began to ask what had just happened, and the interpreter said, "Admiral Vidchenko says you must all leave right away. We have identified one of your party as a CIA agent."

He turned and spoke in Russian to Vidchenko, who was stepping away from the table. Vidchenko answered, then started to leave the room. "Mr. Lindstrom is welcome to stay, but the rest must leave, now."

Manning called to Vidchenko in Russian, he spoke rapidly and intently. Vidchenko, still angry but surprised, turned to listen but obviously was unmoved. Patterson watched the exchange without understanding, but finally Manning shrugged. He leaned close to Patterson, and said softly, "There's nothing more we can do here. I've said everything that could be said. We should leave. I'll explain on the way back."

Confused and reluctant, Patterson followed the others back to the helicopter.

23

REVELATION

USS *Churchill*

The twenty-five-minute flight back to *Churchill* gave Dwight Manning time to explain what had happened aboard the Russian flagship. The truth had not set Patterson free, or removed the incredible sense of failure that weighed her down.

All the work and chances she'd taken to open communications with the Russians, for the benefit of Russian sailors, had been undone by more Cold War mistrust.

Manning reprised his entire conversation with Vidchenko for her, but at the end, she had to admit there was nothing else she could have added or changed to what was said.

AS THEY landed aboard *Churchill,* Patterson rejected the first three things she thought of saying, and finally told Silas, "Please report to me in my stateroom in five minutes."

She had time to dump her coat and laptop before she heard a quiet knock. Commander John Silas stood at the open door silently, his expression impassive.

Seeing him again fanned her anger, and she badly wanted to shout at him. Controlling her first impulse, she stuck to the script. "I assume you understood the Russians' objections to you aboard their ship. Mr. Manning says you speak Russian fluently." Patterson's tone was cold, almost harsh.

"Yes, Doctor, I did." He looked like he was going to say something else, but instead he stopped himself, waiting.

Seeing his self-control strengthened hers, and she asked, "Did you wonder why I didn't take Dr. Russo with us? He's a submarine rescue expert and a former submariner. He has some Russian-language skills. He would have been perfect for this meeting, except for one small problem. He works at the CIA!"

She paused for a moment. Patterson had felt her voice rising. "I knew the Russians would be security-conscious to the point of paranoia. I deliberately left him behind because I wanted them to trust us. I haven't heard you deny their accusations."

Silas sighed. "They're true. I am assigned to the CIA as a senior analyst. I'm their expert on the Russian naval operations. I've been studying and writing on the Russian Navy for most of my naval career. You can see why the Navy thought I'd be perfect for this assignment. I've . . ."

"How long have you been there?"

"Two-plus years. I'm retiring in two more and they've promised to hire me as a civilian."

"And you just hoped the Russians didn't know about your assignment to CIA." She threw up her hands. "Once they hear those three letters, that's it."

"Ma'am, my only goal was to support you. I planned to listen and observe. They might have revealed vital clues about their intentions."

She almost threw something at him. "We already know their intentions! This is a rescue operation! The Cold War ended while you were in college, but you're still thinking that way, and so are the Russians."

"Ma'am, I'm not supposed to discuss my CIA affiliation. It's need-to-know only."

"Which I obviously did!" She fought to keep her temper from rising any further. "That's the problem with need-to-know. The people who need to know aren't the ones who make the decision about what they get to know. Too many secrets."

Silas had no immediate response, but his expression had changed as they talked, the lines in his face sliding slowly downward. He looked profoundly unhappy.

"Dr. Patterson, I'm very sorry that my poor judgment has caused this problem. I understand that you want to help rescue those Russians, and I've messed that up." He spoke carefully, almost formally. "Tell me what I can do."

"There isn't anything," she answered. "That's the worst part of it all. We've missed our chance. I pulled that one opportunity out of thin air and I don't know where the next one will come from."

There was nothing else either of them could say. She dismissed Silas. "Go on, you've got a trip report to write for your bosses at Langley."

PATTERSON FOUND Rudel in *Churchill*'s wardroom, saying his good-byes. Captain Baker had loaded the helicopter with fresh supplies and other items for *Seawolf*'s crew. Baker was wishing the submarine captain luck, but Ken Bover was still trying to convince him that it was time to head for port, with no effect.

Rudel shook Patterson's hand slowly, with a grim expression. "I'm sorry I couldn't be of more help," he apologized. "Do you have a Plan B?"

"Not yet. I'm still trying to pick up the pieces of Plan A."

"You know, I tried to 'forget' that envelope on the table. A Russian officer followed me and gave it back. He treated it like pornography."

She laughed in spite of her mood. "It could have been. They'll never know."

Rudel shrugged. "Maybe they'll get lucky and the charges will work. AS-34 will start its dive in about four hours."

"I really hope it does. But they'd have a better chance if they'd used your survey," Patterson grumbled. "They have to see it."

"Only if you can trick them into looking. You'd have better luck if it really was pornography," Rudel said suggestively.

She smiled knowingly. "And where do you find pornography these days?"

Skynews Report

"Stunning images of the mortally wounded Russian submarine *Severodvinsk* have been obtained by Britt Adams, one of our Skynews correspondents. They show the crippled vessel lying on the seabed, tilted to the left so far that the crew inside are unable to escape.

"These pictures were taken by robotic underwater vehicles launched from the submarine USS *Seawolf,* which was also involved in the collision with *Severodvinsk.* Although the hull looks relatively intact, detailed digital photographs show heavy damage, piercing the pressure hull and flooding several sections of the submarine's interior.

"Russian Federation Navy spokesmen have refused to respond to questions about the images, and U.S. Navy spokesmen will only say that the images were not released through their office, so they cannot comment on their accuracy or authenticity. They emphasize that USS *Churchill* and USS *Seawolf* are both standing by to render whatever assistance the Russians may require.

"Adams also reports that the Russians are in the final stages of preparations and may be ready to attempt a rescue very soon."

AS-34

Captain Bakhorin said, "Start," as he hit the valves, and Umansky clicked his stopwatch. AS-34 began her descent, and as they dropped, Bakhorin fed his navigator depths and descent rates.

Umansky divided his time between the nav display and his hand-drawn graph. Marking their downward speed on the graph, he reported, "Within tolerances."

AS-34 dropped faster and faster. They needed to reach the bottom quickly, to avoid wasting time and precious battery power. But they needed the motors to slow their descent. Using them too soon wasted time, using them too late would be disaster for them and *Severodvinsk*.

"Time for the sonar," Umansky announced. To save energy, he'd left even that vital sensor off. Turning it on now held some risk. A fault could only be corrected on the surface. If it didn't work properly, their dive was wasted.

But it did work, and showed their goal within easy reach. "Recommend course two three one to bring us to their starboard side, three hundred meters."

Bakhorin nursed the horizontal thrusters while he watched depth gauge unwind. Normally, by now he'd be braking, but it was better to wait. One short, powerful burst from the motors took less time and less power than a slow descent. Still, Bakhorin wished he'd checked the figures one more time. They could only do this once.

"Begin braking in five, four, three, two . . . now." Umansky's calm tone held no urgency, but Bakhorin was tense enough for both of them. They'd allowed for the uneven bottom in their calculations. He hoped it was enough.

Bakhorin dumped ballast and hit the motors. He tried to forget about the several hundred kilos of fused explosives that hung in baskets just under his nose.

Umansky had also calculated how long the motors would be needed to stop their descent. He called out the seconds while Bakhorin watched the depth gauge, his hand hovering over the controls.

Umansky called out as the depth gauge nudged one hundred and ninety meters. AS-34 came to a stop with seven meters under the keel and *Severodvinsk*'s port bow thirteen meters dead ahead.

"Let's hope the rest of this mission goes as smoothly," Bakhorin prayed. He then turned the minisub toward the first rock outcropping.

Olga Sadilenko's apartment

Olga Sadilenko hardly knew what to think when she looked at the first image. The colors were all wrong, like a misadjusted television. The shapes were jagged at the edges, but the center shape could only be a submarine. It looked like the photographs she'd seen of *Severodvinsk,* although they were of a surfaced sub at a pier, with smiling sailors lining her deck. Some of the other images looked more reasonable, but they covered only small sections of the submarine. A number of the photos showed the true extent of the damage.

"The Americans sent us these pictures?"

"A Skynews reporter," Irina replied. "He's British, but he's aboard *Churchill.* I'm sure he must have received them from the Americans. They gave him a lot of information. There are maps of the bottom where the sub is located and images taken from many different angles.

"Some are sonar photographs taken by an underwater robot and printed out by a computer. The different colors on the maps show what the underlying substance is: rock, mud, or sand. The contour lines show the depth in three-meter increments. The others are high-definition digital photography."

Irina flipped a few pages over, moving further down the stack. "Look at these pictures. They show the damage to the hull."

Olga took one of the pictures from Irina. In spite of the small field of view, she could clearly see how the metal of *Severodvinsk*'s bow was ripped and dished in. She thought of her little Yakov and struggled not to cry.

The Americans had finally responded to their pleas for information on casualties, and her son was listed as one of the injured. No specific details, just that his injuries weren't considered life-threatening. Praise God! Unfortunately, eighteen families had received the worst possible news—their menfolk were dead. Many tears had been showered upon Olga's floor. Many lives had been forever ruined, including several young girls with small children or a child not yet born. She felt powerless and frustrated that she could not relieve them of their sorrow and pain. She remembered her own grief when her husband fell overboard during a storm and was lost at sea. Yakov was only three then.

And yet, there still had been no word from the Russian Navy. Nothing but silent indifference.

She almost hugged the page, then wanted to hug the Americans; may God bless them. "But why did they do this?" she asked.

Irina answered, "The reporter didn't say why. In the email, he just said it was 'useful information, describing *Severodvinsk*'s exact status.' He said it's not secret. The Americans want to give it to our Navy, to help in the rescue."

Olga Sadilenko smiled. "And that's why they gave them to us. Our Navy hasn't seen these images."

Irina shrugged. "Maybe they don't need them."

"Maybe they don't, maybe they do. I believe they

haven't seen them because they don't want to. It would mean giving the Americans some credit for helping."

"Olga, do you believe our admirals would do that? That they would intentionally ignore foreign help just because it would make them look bad?" Irina's shocked expression showed her naïveté.

Chuckling cynically, Olga took hold of the young woman's hand and said, "Oh yes, child, I do. Are you willing to wager our men's lives on the judgment of those pompous toads in headquarters?" Olga paused, considering. "Can these pictures be added to your web page? Will they fit?"

"Yes," Irina smiled. "We have plenty of room."

"And can we make more copies of these?" She held up the photos.

Irina nodded.

"Then make many copies. Send them to everyone we know, including all those news organizations."

"I've already done that, electronically, and two of our women are working on the website right now. They'll be done in less than an hour."

"Can you send email back to this reporter?"

"Of course."

"Then I have some questions for him—or his friends."

Vice Admiral Kokurin's office, Northern Fleet Headquarters, Severomorsk

"We can't shut them down, Admiral. The server hosting their site is located in Germany. And we can't cut the phone lines to a hundred families . . . and their friends . . . and every public telephone in Severomorsk."

Admiral Babyarin was trying to calm the Northern Fleet commander. Kokurin had exploded when the latest addition to the Wives and Mothers website had crossed his desk.

Kokurin stared at the images. "Could these images be faked, a clever deception?"

"Our experts are examining them right now. They are consistent with what Admiral Vidchenko has told us, and are consistent with what a good imaging sonar and underwater cameras can produce."

"So, how did those civilians obtain this data? From the Americans?"

"According to the website, from a reporter connected to the Americans, but yes, it had to be leaked by them."

"Are they doing this to taunt us? It's like looking at a corpse." Kokurin's heart turned to lead when he looked at the images. Their newest, their best atomic submarine was lost, now a tomb for eighteen sailors and a prison for sixty-seven more.

Babyarin shrugged. "They may be trying to set up some sort of defense for their actions. With Vidchenko so close to rescuing the crew, they want to get these images into the media. They may not have been faked, but they could still have been altered."

Kokurin sat quietly. Babyarin didn't like his expression, and finally asked, "What does Vidchenko say?"

"I haven't asked him. He's too busy rescuing our men to distract him with this business."

"But has he seen the images?" Babyarin pressed.

"It doesn't matter. Petrov and his men could be on the surface in an hour."

Petr Velikiy

Vidchenko stood on the port bridge wing, binoculars fixed on an empty piece of water. It was pointless. A hundred other men watched that small spot of ocean as well, waiting for AS-34 to surface. In fact, it was redundant in the extreme, since the other watchers would all feel duty-bound to report a fact that the admiral had observed himself. Luckily, Kurganov received reports before he did, and filtered out the drivel.

A small splash and a bobbing orange and white shape were all that marked AS-34's return to the surface. A whaleboat standing by started its engine and hurried toward the craft, which had appeared several hundred meters off *Rudnitskiy*'s port side.

While the boat approached, Vidchenko saw a hatch open and someone appeared in the opening, waves lapping less than a meter below the opening.

The bridge-to-bridge radio crackled to life. "This is Bakhorin. The charges have been planted and tested. Everything is ready."

Petr Velikiy's captain, Chicherin, picked up the microphone to acknowledge the transmission, but Vidchenko suddenly walked over and held out his hand. Chicherin gave up the microphone and stepped back.

"This is Vidchenko. Well done, Captain Bakhorin. What is your battery charge?" Curiosity had overcome him, and he didn't want to wait for their report.

"Four percent, sir. We opened the hatch because we needed some light inside."

"Very well done. Join us in hoping now."

Vidchenko hung up the microphone and turned to the underwater communications set.

Severodvinsk

The underwater communications station suddenly came to life. "*Severodvinsk*, this is Rear Admiral Vidchenko. Please respond."

Kalinin reached the underwater telephone first. He acknowledged the transmission. "This is Captain Second Rank Kalinin, sir. Captain Petrov is with the injured men." He waved frantically to a michman and gestured for him to hurry aft, toward the third compartment, where the casualties were being cared for. "He will be here soon."

"Tell your Captain that we are ready to detonate explosive charges that will bring your submarine to an even keel. You must move everyone to the escape capsule immediately."

"Sir, could you please repeat your last transmission?" Vidchenko patiently repeated his message almost verbatim. The admiral then added, a little impatiently, "Tell us the moment you are ready."

"We will begin evacuation procedures immediately, sir. But it will take some time. We have wounded that must be carefully moved. We've had no warning, no time to prepare for this."

Petrov came running into the central post in time to hear Vidchenko answer, "We did not want to give the Americans warning. We know they can monitor these communications. We will do our best to keep them from interfering with the rescue."

Kalinin reported to his captain, "They are ready to free us. The Admiral says we must move everyone to the escape chamber immediately."

Surprised, almost stunned, Petrov blinked at the news, paused a moment, then shrugged. He was puzzled by Vidchenko's remark about the Americans, but that would keep. "Then let's get moving, Starpom." He turned to the rest of the men in the central post. "You heard the Admiral. Let's go home." He smiled, and it reflected off the faces of the men as they scrambled to their feet.

Kalinin started shouting orders. "Get the wounded in

here, but move them gently." He turned to a michman. "Get some rope to rig slings for them."

Petrov picked up the microphone. "This is Captain Petrov, sir. We will move as quickly as possible. It will take some time, possibly over half an hour." He hated to make that admission. The training standard was twenty minutes, but that was with a healthy crew.

Behind him, he heard men laughing, joking. They were going home! It was a surprise, but what a wonderful surprise to get. Kalinin pulled out a checklist from alongside the command console. Being good submariners, they'd planned what to do if the opportunity came to use the escape chamber. He handed the crew roster to his starshini michman, Senior Warrant Officer Zubov, who started crossing off names as men climbed the ladder from the central post into the chamber.

Petrov looked around the room, trying to run his own mental roster, when he realized that the chief engineer was missing. "Where's Lyachin?" he asked, first to the starpom, then to the group. Nobody had an answer. The chief engineer was the next senior officer after Petrov and Kalinin. There were things he was responsible for and should already be here. It was impossible that he hadn't heard the news. Where was he?

Petrov grabbed the shoulder of the nearest enlisted man. "Find the chief engineer and tell him to come here immediately. I don't care what he's doing." He saw the expression on the man's face, and reassured him. "Don't worry, we won't leave without you—or Lyachin." The man hurried off.

Supervised by Dr. Balanov, the wounded started to arrive. A few were ambulatory, with broken arms or wrists, but many had leg injuries and had to be carefully carried through the narrow hatch between the third and second compartment. Their complaints and cries of pain were met with reassurances: "You'll be in the hospital very soon."

Petrov tried to keep clear of the confusion, but found himself organizing the transfer of the injured to the escape chamber. He'd managed to get several aboard when the starpom pulled him aside. Kalinin's expression showed concern, even alarm, and beyond him, Petrov could see the sailor he'd sent looking for the engineer. He had the same expression.

"Sir, Captain Second Rank Lyachin is in the reactor compartment." It was almost a formal report, and Petrov felt confused. There was nothing to do there. The reactor had been shut down immediately after the collision. It was as dead and safe as they could make it.

The enlisted man took a step forward. "Sir, I think you should go see him."

"What? Now? He needs to get his ass up here!"

"Captain, please, I'll take you to him." The rating's pleading only deepened Petrov's concern, but carrying one of the American lanterns, he let himself be led past the confusion in the emptying third compartment, back through the fourth, the missile compartment, then through another hatch into the reactor spaces.

"He's aft, sir, at the hatch into the auxiliary machinery spaces." The man pointed down the dark passageway.

"What's he doing there?" Petrov asked, half to himself, but the enlisted man left without saying another word.

The captain of *Severodvinsk* hurried down the dark passage, searching for his chief engineer. Walking quickly down the empty passageway, he finally found Lyachin right next to the watertight bulkhead, sitting on the deck, leaning against the hatch that led into compartment six. That compartment was now almost completely flooded, and automatically Petrov looked for signs of a leak. Is that what had drawn the engineer here, right now? There. In the lantern's beam, he did see a few droplets of water glistening on the deck.

Lyachin didn't acknowledge his commanding officer's presence, and for a moment Petrov wondered if he was concentrating, absorbed in some task. But time was pressing. If there was a leak, it would be moot the moment they left the boat. "Sergey Vladimirovich, we are leaving. You are needed forward."

"I'm needed here, too, sir. Captain, there are nine of my men back there. Four more in the port torpedo bay. I can't abandon them."

Petrov, astonished, was almost overcome by the depth of Lyachin's grief. Out of courtesy, he hadn't shone the lantern on the engineer's face, but he could see now that Lyachin was freely weeping, tears falling onto the deck.

Suddenly weary, Petrov sat down next to Lyachin as loss and shame washed over him. He'd controlled his own feelings, more or less, but those dead men were in his charge as well. The question leapt up from a dark place in his mind. If Lyachin felt like this, why didn't he as well?

But the grief passed without disappearing. Duty to those still alive took pride of place. "Not all your men are gone, Sergey. There are others who still need you." As do I, he added, to himself.

"Sir, I won't leave them all alone."

"You can't do anything more for them," Petrov responded. He didn't even think of just ordering Lyachin forward. He was beyond simple discipline.

"I can share their fate," Lyachin responded, almost eagerly.

"Which will accomplish nothing but add more tragedy." Petrov shook his head and stood, holding out his hand to the engineer. "And we are not free yet. I am responsible, and guilty for every casualty on this boat. Please, help me save the rest of my crew."

Patting the hard metal of the hatch one last time, Lyachin stood and wiped his face.

Petr Velikiy

Vidchenko had become more impatient as time passed well beyond half an hour. After an hour and twelve minutes, and many updates, Petrov's voice on the underwater communications system finally reported, "Give me three minutes, then trigger the charges, sir."

"Three minutes. Starting now." The admiral watched the second hand crawl around the dial three times.

Vidchenko nodded to Kurganov, who stood by the bridge-to-bridge radio. "*Rudnitskiy,* this is Kurganov. Trigger the charges." As he hung up the microphone, he pressed a button on the intercom. "Central post, bridge. Make sure sonar is alert."

Rudnitskiy would detonate the charges with a high-frequency sonar pulse. It was coded, so ordinary sonar transmissions would not affect the detonators. *Petya*'s passive sonar might or might not hear the trigger signal, but it would definitely hear the explosions.

If they ever happened. Vidchenko waited, and then counted to ten. Assuming there was some difficulty, he was reaching for the radio microphone when the intercom finally barked, "Multiple explosions." After a short pause, the operator reported, "Nothing else."

Sonar would probably hear the escape capsule leave the hull. It would take less than three minutes for it to break the surface. After ten minutes, he called sonar. They'd heard nothing from the sub. After twenty, he called on the underwater telephone. He received no answer, but they might still be in the escape chamber, out of touch. After half an hour, he asked how soon AS-34 could launch to examine the sub. They answered that it would be several hours.

Petrov finally called in after forty minutes. There had been no change in the sub's list, he reported. "We are moving everyone out of the escape chamber."

24

STRIKE ONE

10 October 2008
1835/6:35 PM
Skynews Report

"Although the Russians have made no official announcement, their attempt to rescue the crew of *Severodvinsk* appears to have failed.

"Approximately forty-five minutes ago, at 1448 Greenwich Mean Time, sonars near the scene of the rescue detected a series of small explosions. It is believed these were from charges intended to clear obstructions preventing the release of the submarine's rescue capsule. According to submarine rescue experts, if the charges had worked, the crew would have been able to ascend to the surface in the capsule almost immediately.

"It is believed that the men aboard *Severodvinsk* are running short of the U.S.-supplied chemicals needed to remove the deadly carbon dioxide from their atmosphere. Medical experts are also concerned that they may be suffering from hypothermia, as the crew have been subjected to near-freezing temperatures for several days now. Hypothermia would cause the survivors' bodies to increase their oxygen consumption, in an attempt to preserve body heat, thus complicating the carbon dioxide problem.

"While the Russian Navy has not provided any information on the condition of the men trapped inside, information on the status of the crew has appeared on the Wives and Mothers of *Severodvinsk* website, now one of the most popular websites in the world. Late yesterday, the 'portrait pages' were updated. Several crew-member photographs were modified to include a Russian Orthodox cross, while others had a red cross added.

"Having recently finished her last dive, the *Priz* minisub will now have to recharge its batteries. This will take at least six hours, which means it will be tomorrow morning before the Russians can even hope to make another attempt. What form this could take is not known.

"The Norwegian marine salvage vessel *Halsfjord* is also due to arrive this evening. Whether they will be able to act before the submariners run out of time is impossible to say.

"This is Britt Adams, for Skynews."

Severodvinsk

"Be careful, watch out for the hatch coaming!" commanded Petrov. "Slowly, slowly. There, I have him." Wrapping both arms around the injured man's abdomen, Petrov held him steady while Zubov removed the rope suspending him from the escape chamber. Once free of the sling, the two laid their shipmate on to a stretcher. It was young Sadilenko.

"Nikolay, Nikolay," he moaned deliriously.

"Yes, Yakov, I know," replied Balanov gently. "Let's get you back to bed. Careful now," he said to the stretcher-bearers as they lifted him and proceeded back to the third compartment.

"That's everyone, Captain," reported Mitrov, still up in the chamber.

"Very well. Thank you, Vladimir. Make sure you turn off the emergency lights before you secure the hatch."

"Pavel is doing that now, sir."

"Good, good."

The flickering of a light from the rear of the central post caught his attention and he walked over toward the source. Kalinin and Lyachin appeared slowly from the ladder well. Both were breathing heavily.

"There doesn't appear to be any additional damage from the explosive charges, Captain," reported Kalinin as he leaned against the bulkhead.

"I'm glad to hear that, Vasiliy. That was a most unpleasant experience."

"It wouldn't have been quite so bad if it had worked," he replied as he wiggled a finger in his right ear. "Well, at least now we know what it's like to be inside a kettledrum."

Lyachin and Petrov chuckled at the starpom's apt analogy. The doctor had said the ringing in their ears would take a little time to subside. The smile on Lyachin's face, however, lasted for only an instant, and was replaced by the same forlorn, haunted expression he'd shown earlier. Straightening himself, he turned toward Petrov and asked, "Sir, if I may be excused, I would like to check on my men."

"Certainly, Sergey."

As the chief engineer walked away, Kalinin pointed in his direction and said, "He seems to be doing better."

"Unlike some of us," countered Petrov, remembering the dazed Sadilenko, his voice heavy with fatigue and dejection.

"You need some rest, sir."

"No, Starpom. What I need is some fresh air."

"As do we all," said Kalinin, conceding the argument. For a moment the two leaders stood there in silence, both were tired, cold, and emotionally drained. After about a minute, Kalinin finally brought up the topic they had both been avoiding.

"That failed evolution was rather depressing."

"Yes, it was. I could see it on the men's faces. I should have been more guarded with my optimism."

"What are we going to do now, Captain?"

"I wish to God I knew, Vasiliy. We've done everything we possibly can."

"There's still that option the doctor and I talked about," suggested the starpom.

"What? Oh yes, I suppose we should give it more consideration. It may buy us a little more time," Petrov replied. "I guess we should go find the good doctor."

At that moment, Balanov entered the central post and walked up to them. He looked worn out, but his movements suggested he was agitated.

"Ah, Doctor, we were just about to come visit you," said Kalinin jovially.

"Captain, Starpom," Balanov greeted them formally. "Captain, I wish to report that there are complications developing with some of the injured."

"Complications?" Petrov echoed with a mixture of confusion and worry. "What sort of complications?"

"Sir, a number of the injured have started showing symptoms of mild hypothermia. I've taken the temperature of several of them, and their core temperatures are at or just below thirty-five degrees Celsius. There are some indications that several of the other crew members are starting to show symptoms as well."

"Doctor, we've given you as many survival suits as you

require and most of the bedding," exclaimed Kalinin defensively.

"Starpom, you don't understand! The suits and blankets only slow the rate at which heat is lost! It's taken several days, but with such low ambient temperatures, hypothermia is inevitable."

"All right, Doctor, what are the short-term implications?" Petrov asked. He was well aware that death was the ultimate result.

"At this stage, the patient will start to shiver uncontrollably. It's the body's attempt to generate heat through muscle activity. This means that his blood pressure, heart rate, *and breathing rate* all increase. If enough members of the crew start suffering from hypothermia, our carbon dioxide problem will get considerably worse."

Pained expressions showed on both their faces, as the impact of the doctor's explanation struck them. Ravaged by the seemingly never-ending string of bad news, Petrov fell against the bulkhead for support and rubbed his face with both hands.

"Captain, we must find a way to generate some heat before things get worse," implored Balanov.

"And just how do you suggest I do that!?!" snapped Petrov angrily. Immediately, he regretted lashing out at the doctor. He wasn't the cause of this latest problem; he was just the messenger.

Sighing, Petrov reached out and placed his hand on the doctor's shoulder. "I'm sorry, Viktor, you are merely doing your duty. Thank you, for your report. I will . . . I will try and think of something. In the meantime, I want you to prepare to issue sleeping drugs to as many of the crew as you can. I know, I know it buys us only a little time. But right now I'll take every minute I can get."

Balanov nodded and wearily withdrew.

"Now what?" asked Kalinin bluntly, as he watched Petrov push himself upright.

"I think it's time I have a chat with Vidchenko and inform him of this new problem, then find out what they are going to do next."

USS *Seawolf*

Seawolf and *Churchill* were running parallel racetracks, long, slow patterns designed to let ships move without actually going anywhere. At five knots, it took over an hour and a half for them to cover one side of the eight-mile leg. They'd turn a full 180 degrees, then countermarch back along the same line.

The two ships were separated by three miles, more than enough distance between a surface ship and a submerged submarine. With two of her transmitters and one multimission mast repaired, *Seawolf* could now transmit and receive from periscope depth, letting her stay in her natural, and preferred, environment.

With both ships at creep speed, it also maximized their passive sonar detection. Even though they were about fifty miles away, *Seawolf* heard the rather noisy AS-34 on her TB-29 towed array, both ships heard the charges detonate. Then nothing.

Jerry had wanted the Russian plan to work. He'd prayed and waited, knowing that the Russians weren't stupid. The minisub had made two earlier dives. They could see what needed to be done. They'd overengineered the job with charges that might actually cause more damage to the sub, but were surely big enough to clear whatever was holding *Severodvinsk* in that port list.

Seawolf and Patty had bought *Severodvinsk* some time.

He was proud of that unorthodox resupply effort, but now it looked like it wouldn't be enough. The Russians had wasted that chance, missed their best, and perhaps only, shot. They could have planted charges on their first dive, and done a better job of it, if they had used the information Rudel had tried to give them.

Jerry felt somehow responsible for the Russians' mistrust. He knew it was stupid to think so, and ran though every action, every decision he'd made since the collision, and then since they'd entered the Barents. He could think of nothing that would have affected the Russians' refusal, but the feeling wouldn't go away. His stomach knotted, and with *Seawolf* riding smooth at two hundred feet, he knew it wasn't seasickness.

Were Petrov and his men doomed? After hearing the Russian's voice over the underwater telephone, Jerry thought of him as a person. He could imagine the man, like any good captain, doing his best to take care of his crew until help arrived. It was easy to imagine himself on that boat, in Petrov's place, or more properly as one of his officers. Rudel could imagine himself in Petrov's position. And he probably did, in his nightmares.

Jerry was touring the boat before visiting control. He didn't need to, but it was constructive, and he didn't have the heart for paperwork right now.

As he passed the crew's mess, the Wolf's Den, he saw a new email had been posted. It had been sent by Britt Adams, a reporter on *Churchill,* but the original sender had been a Russian woman, Olga Sadilenko. She had sent questions to Adams, who passed them to Rudel. Rudel apparently answered them and then responded back through Adams. It probably violated several regulations, but Joanna Patterson knew about it and approved. That was enough for Jerry, and also Rudel. The woman deserved answers.

Dear Captain Rudel,

Thank you for the answers Mr. Adams has sent us. Although I thank him as well, I know that they came from you. It must have been hard to give us such bad news, but we have been waiting for any word for a very long time. Knowing who has died and who is hurt is very hard, but the knowing is better. My Yakov is hurt and still in danger, but he has his shipmates and captain to take care of him, and that is a comfort.

All of us are grateful for everything you have done to help our men. Our Navy said that the collision was your fault, but you should know that we do not always believe what our Navy says. Since the collision, you have saved their lives once, maybe twice. You and your men will be in our prayers, along with ours.

Jerry read it twice. He wondered how many times Rudel had read it.

10 October 2008
1855/6:55 PM
Severomorsk

The Seaman's Memorial Church had never closed its doors, even at the height of Communist power. Built when the town was still called Vayenga, it had seen many tragedies. Whatever its name, Severomorsk had always been a port, and sailors didn't always return.

Right now the church was filled with the families and friends of the men of *Severodvinsk*. The mayor and most of the city government had come. It was both a memorial for those known to have died, and a prayer service for those injured and still in peril. With definite news, the wives and mothers had decided not to wait for the crew's rescue.

Olga Sadilenko, along with the other family members, was near the front, so the messenger had to search for a few minutes, whispering questions, before he could find her. Olga recognized him. Sasha was the teenage brother of Irina's Anatoliy. He would have been at the service, but had been drafted to look after the younger children. Was there a problem with one of them?

He didn't speak, but pressed a slip of paper into her hand. It read simply, "There is important news. Please come outside."

Curious, she left as quietly as she could. Outside, Sasha pointed toward an older man she didn't recognize, waiting at the bottom of the steps. He was stooped over, with a face so worn it was almost battered, and he held one arm at an angle. "My name is Dyalov. I used to work at the naval base. I'm a friend of Galina Gudkov's family. She sent me to tell you they tried to raise the sub with explosives late this afternoon. If it had worked, the crew would be out and on the surface by now."

"If it had worked . . ." Olga had repeated the words automatically, attempting to understand. She found she had understood, but her mind didn't want to accept the idea.

"Why did they need explosives? What happened? Did the explosives cause more damage? Why didn't they work?"

Dyalov shook his head. "I'm sorry. I do not know these things. Galina says the article appeared just a short time ago. It comes from the Americans."

Olga's world spun. She took one step to lean against the church's stone wall. "Will they try again?"

"I do not know," Dyalov apologized. "I live down the hall. Galina called me and asked me to deliver the news.

She read the article to me. They heard explosions on their hydroacoustic system, but after that nothing more. Here is a translation she gave me." He pressed a folded paper into her hand.

Her shoulder was cold where she leaned against the church. The stone under her was hard, unmoving. She stood for a moment, shaking, as the carefully restrained fear for her son escaped, draining her strength, her reason. She'd used purpose and hope to keep it locked up, but now it was loose, and she had no way to fight it. She was crying, almost silently, the tears pouring down her face.

Dyalov stood uncomfortably, silent. She realized he was waiting for her answer, but she had none. Finally, she said "Thank you for your kindness." She turned and impulsively hugged him, pecking him on the cheek. Dyalov smiled and limped off.

She had never met Dyalov before, but the old man had taken pity and helped, simply because he knew one of the families. Severomorsk, like most of the towns in the Kola Region, was a navy town. Because of this, the church was filled to capacity and then some. Family and friends had converged here because it was centrally located, and because it was the home of the Northern Fleet Headquarters. Some of the *Severodvinsk* families had come from Gadzhiyevo, near the Sayda Guba submarine base; some lived in Murmansk, a short distance to the south; many lived in Severomorsk itself. But wherever they lived, they were here now, in the church, praying for a miracle and supporting each other.

That human contact had helped her regain her reason, but not her strength. Suddenly frail, she leaned back against the wall of the church again. Olga would never admit it to anyone, but she needed its strength, and the strength of those inside.

She unfolded the paper and read the article, just a few

paragraphs, and much of it addressed what the author didn't know. Crumbs for the starving.

Reentering the church, she saw that the service was almost over. She stood quietly in the back rather than disturb anyone, but those in the rear had seen her come back in, just as they had seen the messenger enter. Now they saw her blotting her eyes, her face red and puffy. There'd been more than a few tears in the church that afternoon, but a murmur ran through the back of the church, then moved its way forward.

A woman she didn't recognize, her young son on her hip, came back and whispered, "Are you all right? Is there news?" Her eyes, her face pleaded for answers, but the last part of her question held more dread than curiosity. After all, Olga had been crying.

"Yes," Olga answered, but when she saw the woman's face fall, she quickly added, "They're still alive."

The young mother stifled her gasp and smiled, a little forced but genuine. She went back to her place as the priest finished the service, but many eyes were on her and Olga.

After the last prayer ended, everyone remained in their places. A low buzz of conversation built, then faded away. The priest spoke softly with someone in front, then took his place again. "Mrs. Sadilenko. Please, if there is news, tell us all."

Olga walked down the center aisle, embarrassed in spite of the priest's polite request. Reaching the front, she turned and faced families and friends of the families. It made sense. *Severodvinsk*'s heart was in that church.

She unfolded the paper and read the news article. The first line announcing the failed rescue attempt brought gasps and cries. She skipped the paragraph about their website, although Olga was sure everyone would hear about it later. The last two paragraphs spoke of the *Priz* minisub and the Norwegians without giving the slightest clue about the Navy's plans.

Finishing, she folded the paper and pushed it back into the pocket of her dress. She was still facing the crowd, full of concern for her Yakov, and anger and frustration at the Navy. She found those emotions becoming words.

"I should stand here and praise our Navy for their efforts to rescue our men. That is what they want me to do, but I cannot, because I do not know if our Navy really is trying to save them!"

She gestured to the church's congregation. "Why are there no uniforms in this church? Are they ashamed?" She paused, and put her hands on her hips. "Has anyone in this room received any information from our Navy about our men?" She waited, then added, "They have never even admitted that *Severodvinsk* is actually missing!

"Are they afraid of what we might discover? Why do they ignore even the simplest of questions?"

The mayor looked distinctly uncomfortable. He was an old-school politician, and while open criticism of the Navy might not get someone arrested these days, it certainly wasn't the norm. But the crowd was responding to her questions. Some were crying. Many more looked angry.

"The only thing the Navy has done is to blame the Americans for this disaster. But the only information we have gotten, information we know is true, has come from the Americans."

Her voice had been rising, not to a shout, but loud and strong. "We have nothing but questions for the Navy, and they have nothing but contempt for us. They have ignored us. They have even lied to us!

"We have the right to know whether everything possible is being done to rescue our loved ones. We have given them our sons, our husbands. They expect us to sit quietly at home and be grateful for our sacrifice.

"But our men don't need us at home! They need us to keep the Navy honest, to make sure that they have missed nothing. We must sit on the Navy's doorstep until we know they have done their job."

Applause filled the church, and without thinking, Olga turned and marched to the front door of the church. The Northern Fleet Headquarters complex lay six blocks away down one of the main streets of the city. The old walrus had turned them away once. He wouldn't do it this time.

She could hear the congregation following her, and briefly wondered what the mayor would do.

11 October 2008
0800/8:00 AM
Petr Velikiy

Rear Admirals Vidchenko and Kurganov stood together near *Petr Velikiy*'s twin-barreled 130mm gun, while Captain Chicherin fussed and the sideboys checked their dress uniforms. The after end of the superstructure loomed above and behind them, with the glassed-in helicopter control station two stories up. A phone talker next to Captain Chicherin gave him constant updates in the helicopter's distance.

"It's down to fifteen kilometers, sir. Bearing is Red one two zero."

Chicherin was the only one with glasses, and swung around to that bearing. "Sideboys, stand by."

The group waiting with the officers took their places while a petty officer hurried them along, then called them to attention.

Vidchenko spotted the Mi-14 helicopter as the phone talker called "Ten kilometers." It was a big land-based machine, usually used for coastal ASW, but in this case, as a

VIP transport. It passed aft of the ship, lining up on the wake, then slowly overtook them.

When it reached the fantail, the helicopter settled onto the pad as gently as thistle down. Vidchenko was willing to put money down that the best helicopter pilot in the regiment was at the controls.

The instant the wheels touched, the captain gestured, and the petty officer screamed commands over the sound of the engines. The sideboys quickly ran aft to places marked on the deck, forming two lines facing each other.

A fading whine replaced the engine roar and the door swung open. First out was a crewman with a small step-ladder. He attached it to the lower edge of the door, and then scrambled down to the deck one and a half meters below.

As soon as he signaled it was safe, Vice Admiral Sergey Kokurin, commander of the Northern Fleet, appeared, followed by Vice Admiral Borisov, commander of the Twelfth Submarine Eskadra. Behind him was a clutch of aides and assistants.

Kokurin hurried down the steps and across the flight deck. He climbed the ladder to the main deck, and paused just long enough to receive the sideboys' salute before heading toward where Vidchenko and the others waited. The supporting cast hurried to catch up as Vidchenko, Kurganov, and Chicherin all braced and saluted.

Kokurin returned their salutes as he approached, and asked peremptorily, "Is the Norwegian ready?"

"Mr. Lindstrom is ready to brief us in the flag mess, sir."

"Then let's get up there. Petrov and his men don't have much time."

Lindstrom was waiting, along with Kurt Nakken, captain of the salvage and rescue ship *Halsfjord*. In a sea of dark blue and gold braid, their civilian clothes seemed almost sloppy, although their manner was professional. They were already set up, and waited patiently as Kokurin and the others took their places and tea was served.

Although *Petr Velikiy* was Chicherin's ship, and Vidchenko commanded the rescue effort, this was Kokurin's meeting. Before Chicherin could begin his welcoming statement, Kokurin pulled a thick sheaf of papers out of his briefcase and plopped them onto the table.

"My staff printed all this material off the Internet. The names of *Severodvinsk*'s crew, the ships in the rescue force, weather conditions, our progress, are all available to anyone in the world. And they are watching with considerable interest. Web pages like the Wives and Mothers of *Severodvinsk* website are receiving literally millions of visitors each day. Word of the failure to rescue *Severodvinsk*'s crew yesterday afternoon was posted within an hour."

He paused for a moment, letting that sink in. The Russian Navy believed in secrecy, a shield that hid both strengths and weaknesses. Seeing their operations exposed, discussed, and criticized was anathema.

Kokurin completed his thought. "We cannot afford another failure. Losing Petrov and his men would be tragedy, but we would also do it in front of the world." Kokurin managed to include the entire room in his gaze, but finished by looking at Chicherin. "Whenever you are ready, Captain."

Chicherin wisely skipped his opening remarks and immediately began by reviewing *Severodvinsk*'s status. Atmosphere quality was the primary concern. A little less than six hours remained before the CO_2 chemicals provided by *Seawolf* were depleted. The injured crewmen were stable, although the cold was now a major concern as well since it was intimately linked with the carbon dioxide situation. Battery power, food, and water were also becoming significant issues. After a week on the bottom, the crew of *Severodvinsk* was running out of everything.

Captain Bakhorin briefed Kokurin on AS-34's material condition. The batteries were still being charged after their latest dive, although he noted that it was taking longer each time to reach a full charge, and that the charge was lasting less each time.

"So AS-34 is almost crippled," Kokurin acknowledged. "Can you get me one more dive?"

"Yes, Admiral," Bakhorin answered eagerly. "At least one more."

Lindstrom was last. He spoke passable Russian, and after introducing *Halsfjord*'s captain, pressed a key on his laptop, which was already connected to the flat-panel display mounted on the bulkhead.

A false-color image of *Severodvinsk* appeared, lying on the seabed. Contour lines and depths were combined with detailed data on the bottom's makeup. Lines led from *Severodvinsk* upward, and lettering in Roman and Cyrillic labeled different parts of the diagram.

Vidchenko was puzzled. The image was very detailed, and even showed the damage to *Severodvinsk*'s bow and engineering section. *Halsfjord* had only arrived last evening. They certainly hadn't had the time to survey the bottom. Was this the work of a computer artist?

The admiral asked that question, but Kokurin cut in before Lindstrom could answer. "I have seen this image before. It is from the American underwater robots."

Lindstrom added, "Yes, that is correct. We thought it would be the quickest way to diagram out our rescue plan."

"But that information hasn't been validated!" Alarm crept into Vidchenko's voice. "It may have been altered, and even if it hasn't, we know nothing about the accuracy of their sensors."

Kokurin's concern showed in his questions. "Did you

find evidence of tampering? How closely does it match your information?"

Vidchenko shook his head. "I do not know, sir. None of us have seen it."

Now the fleet commander seemed confused. "Has anyone on your staff examined the data?"

Uneasy, but unsure why, Vidchenko quickly answered, "No sir. We didn't feel we could trust the data."

Kokurin sat for a moment in thought, then asked the Norwegian, "Have you had any problems with the Americans' information?"

Lindstrom had stood silently, listening, during the exchange. "No, Admiral. I was provided with a copy when it arrived aboard *Churchill* and I've worked extensively with it since then. It is consistent with the data I've seen collected from similar craft."

"How does it compare with the information we have?"

"Much more complete and detailed." Lindstrom pressed a key several times and images flashed. "Here is an enlargement of *Severodvinsk*'s starboard side. Based on Captain Bakhorin's description, I've shown the location of the charges you planted. I'd planned to include this later in the brief, but it shows the rock formations that you mined, and others here and here," he gestured to screen, "that remained, preventing the sub from righting itself."

"When did you receive this information?" Kokurin demanded.

"Approximately two days ago, Admiral."

Kokurin followed the logic. "And if we had seen this data two days ago, AS-34's first dive would have been able to place charges on those formations as well, freeing the sub." He shot a hard look at Vidchenko, who sat impassively. Kurganov looked uncomfortable.

Lindstrom shook his head. "No, sir, I'm sorry to say

that it probably wouldn't have worked. The underlying rock where *Severodvinsk* rests is part of the Fennoscandian crystalline shield and is made up of very strong and hard granite, not the much softer marine shale that is typical in the South Barents Basin."

He keyed a new page. A series of irregular but roughly parallel lines were highlighted in bright colors. They lay on either side of the crippled sub. Beneath the bright lines was a near uniform return from something very large and solid.

"*Severodvinsk* sits between two of these ridges, with the one to starboard holding her in that port list. You'd have to remove this entire ridge to free her. If you look closely, you will also see that ridge is part of this much larger segment that is tens of meters thick. For all intents and purposes, it is impenetrable."

Vidchenko stared at the data, almost uncomprehending. The American submarine had gathered data that was superior, far superior to theirs. But it wouldn't have made any difference. *Severodvinsk* was held tight in the jaws of an indestructible rock formation.

Lindstrom brought up another image, a simple line diagram. It showed the sub in cross-section lying on an uneven surface. Arrows showed forces acting on the hull.

"To right the sub, the hull must be rotated in place, which means overcoming friction. Not only is *Severodvinsk*'s weight being borne by these two ridges, but by this time it has begun settling into the mud that covers the underlying rock. Both of these work to hold the submarine where it is.

"The best solution would be to use water jets to clear the length of the hull of mud and silt where it rests on the rock. At the same time underwater robots would weld padeyes to the starboard side of the hull. These would be attached to towlines running to dedicated salvage tugs. We would literally pull *Severodvinsk* to an upright position."

Vidchenko was impressed. It sounded like it would work. "But how long to do the work?"

Lindstrom answered, "Too long. Four days." It was a death sentence. Vidchenko couldn't accept that, having come this far.

He was still searching for words when Kokurin asked, "Is that our only option?"

Lindstrom shrugged. "We can measure the forces involved, the strength of the materials. We can even estimate the suction effects of the silt from other work we have done. This will work, with a probability of success in the ninety-percent range.

"Looking for ways to speed the process, we came up with this alternative approach." He keyed a new diagram. It showed a row of small explosive charges along the two sides of the sub, and the towlines went to the deck now.

"Instead of welding padeyes, we use the existing deck fittings. They are not as strong, and even using the maximum number of towlines, we will not have the same lifting force. Instead of using waterjets to clear the silt, we propose running small charges the length of the hull, right where it touches the bottom. Hopefully, they will break the suction when they detonate. Additionally, Captain Petrov will have to put every bit of compressed air he has left into the port main ballast tanks, while simultaneously flooding the starboard main ballast tanks. This will generate a momentum that wants to roll the boat to starboard, which should help tremendously to overcome inertia."

"And leave him no reserve air at all," Vidchenko added.

Lindstrom nodded. "It is the only way to make up the shortfall in lifting power. We have to make the sub want to roll to starboard."

Kokurin asked, "How quickly can this plan be put into action?"

Captain Nakken spoke for the first time. "My crew has already started. We expect to have two robots over the side," he glanced at his watch, "in forty-five minutes. With your approval," he added.

Kokurin smiled, the first time Vidchenko had seen the admiral pleased since he came aboard. He felt it, too. There was another option. There was still hope.

"Understand that our estimates are less certain with this concept. We give this plan only a sixty to seventy percent chance of success."

Vidchenko could feel the tension ease. A good plan now was better than a perfect plan too late. "When will you be able to make the attempt?"

"Laying the charges and rigging the lines, with everyone working at best efficiency, will take two days."

"What?" Almost every Russian was on his feet, shouting, asking questions. Lindstrom seemed to expect it, and stood calmly until Kokurin could make himself heard. "I assume you have a way of keeping the crew alive until then."

"They need more air regeneration canisters. *Rudnitskiy* has ample supplies aboard. The Americans can send more over to *Severodvinsk* using one of their underwater vehicles. That will give Petrov and his men enough time—barely."

"That is unacceptable," Vidchenko responded automatically. "The Americans caused this disaster."

"Do you have another suggestion?" Kokurin demanded sternly.

"Use one of the Norwegian's robots."

Lindstrom replied, "No, that will not work. We need them to prepare for the rescue. If we lose one we wouldn't be ready in time. Besides, they are not shaped properly. They couldn't enter *Severodvinsk*'s tubes the way the American vehicle can. I've already spoken to Dr. Patterson and Captain Rudel. They are willing to make the attempt."

The very thought of allowing the Americans near *Severodvinsk* again appalled Vidchenko. "There has to be another way."

Lindstrom didn't respond immediately, and when no one else spoke, Vice Admiral Kokurin stood and said, "We will use Mr. Lindstrom's plan as he has explained it. Mr. Lindstrom, Captain Nakken, thank you for your expertise. I am sure that with your help we will rescue Petrov and his men. Dismissed."

As the meeting broke up, Kokurin left first, but his aide intercepted Vidchenko. "The Admiral asks you to join him on the fantail."

Vidchenko hurried aft. The admiral wanted a word in private. He thought that was wise. Involving the Americans in the rescue could only lead to more trouble. He was still rehearsing his arguments when he reached the fantail.

The Mil helicopter that had brought Kokurin's group filled the helicopter pad. It had been tied down and serviced, awaiting its passengers' departure. Approaching the helicopter from the port side, Vidchenko didn't see the fleet commander until he was almost at the aft railing. Kokurin stood near the jackstaff, the helicopter bulking over him. He'd chosen a very private place to talk.

"Reporting as ordered, comrade Vice Admiral."

Kokurin had been looking aft, at *Petya*'s massive wake. Now he turned to face Vidchenko. "I am concerned for our men, Vasiliy."

"Yes, sir." Vidchenko stood quietly. He could wait for the admiral to make his point.

"Others are concerned as well. There was a near-riot in

Severomorsk yesterday evening when word of the first attempt's failure reached the families. I had several hundred people marching on Northern Fleet Headquarters!"

Vidchenko was puzzled. "How did they find out? We said nothing."

"But others did. As I said, we are being watched. The world is watching us, comrade Rear Admiral. The President called and urged me to use every asset, *any* resource we could to bring our men back safely."

"Yes, sir. Of course."

"But, I just heard you say that you ignored information that the Americans had. You didn't think it was 'trustworthy.'"

"Yes, sir."

"And I just heard you reject the idea of the American submarine sending more air-regeneration canisters to *Severodvinsk,* even though this has worked in the past. In fact, it's the only reason Petrov and his men are still alive."

"Sir, I believe the Americans caused this disaster, possibly deliberately, but even if it were by accident, all they are doing is attempting to expunge their guilt. You can't shoot a man, then wipe away the crime by giving him first aid."

"And if the victim will die without that aid?"

Vidchenko didn't have a ready answer. He was aware of the conflict, but trusted to Russian ingenuity. There were always other options. Finally struggling for words, he could only say, "I thought it was better to keep the Americans as far away as possible."

"A month ago, even a week ago, I might have agreed with you. But they have already helped, and now we need them." Kokurin paused for a moment, then repeated, "Petrov needs them. And I need someone who is willing to work with them, who won't automatically reject their assistance."

Vidchenko suddenly realized what was happening. He had been so focused on the rescue . . .

"Vice Admiral Borisov will take over the operation. My chief of staff will inform Kurganov. I'd like you to come back with me to Severomorsk immediately. You can write your report."

Vidchenko felt drained, a little lost. "My staff?"

"They can follow later. I'd like them to stay behind and help Borisov's people."

"Of course, sir, whatever you want." Vidchenko's words were flat, almost hollow-sounding.

"I am sorry, Vasiliy. You've done your best. You've started the job. Borisov will have to finish it."

25

COORDINATION

11 October 2008
0945/9:45 AM
Churchill's SH-60 Seahawk en route *Petr Velikiy*

It was a much shorter helicopter ride this time, just under twenty minutes, flight deck to flight deck. Patterson barely had time to read the hastily written notes thrust into her hand by Silas as they'd boarded the helicopter regarding Vice Admiral Pavel Dimitriyevich Borisov, Commander of the Twelfth Submarine Eskadra, or squadron, which consisted of all nuclear-powered general-purpose submarines in the Northern Fleet.

He was in his early fifties, came from Belarus, held numerous commands in attack submarines, was married, and had a son at the Frunze Higher Naval School in Saint Petersburg. Solid reputation as a submariner, reasonable admin skills, and most importantly, a close friend of the Northern Fleet commander.

Obviously the Russian Navy wasn't happy with the failed attempt. Parker was almost giddy when she showed Patterson the news coverage of the demonstrations in Severomorsk. So this Borisov was the new commander of the rescue force. She wouldn't miss Vidchenko.

The almost-familiar stern of *Peter the Great* filled the pilot's windscreen, and then they were down on the landing pad. An officer met their party, and in carefully rehearsed English asked them to come to the flag mess.

This time a smaller group met them, just Borisov, Kurganov, and their aides, along with Lindstrom. Bringing a lot of people to a meeting implied insecurity, or a desire to impress the other side. Did this smaller group imply the opposite?

Patterson had of course left Silas and Russo behind, but she'd brought Dwight Manning, the State Department liaison, and Captain Baker from *Churchill.*

Introductions and tea took only a minute. Borisov was shorter than Vidchenko, with a broad face and blond hair. He smiled more, too. Kurganov wasn't smiling, and neither were their aides.

They'd barely sat down before he dove in. "We must discuss the transfer of the air regeneration cassettes and supplies from *Mikhail Rudnitskiy* to *Seawolf.* One of our helicopters can pick up the cassettes and supplies, but we need to know how to pass signals from our helicopter to your submarine."

Glad she'd brought at least one naval officer along, she

let Captain Baker brief them on U.S. Navy communications procedures. Borisov's English was good, with Manning's rapid-fire Russian used only once or twice to clarify technical details.

Borisov passed the information to his aide, who hurried from the room, and referred to what seemed to be a checklist. "Captain Baker, when will your ship and *Seawolf* join the rescue force?"

"Sir, *Churchill* will arrive within the hour. *Seawolf,* unfortunately, won't arrive for another four hours. Her speed is limited because of the damage to her bow."

"I understand. I will assign the southwest sector to *Churchill* and *Seawolf.* Can the transfer be conducted from this position?" Borisov pointed to a chart with the locations of all the ships listed in both Russian and English. *Seawolf*'s assigned location was two kilometers from *Severodvinsk.*

"Yes, Admiral, Captain Rudel and I spoke about this. He will be able to control the underwater vehicles from that position. However, he would like to launch the vehicle from one thousand meters to maximize the cargo payload."

"That is good. That will let me keep *Halsfjord* and *Rudnitskiy* working near *Severodvinsk.* How much time will *Seawolf* need to effect the transfer?"

Halsfjord had already launched her two remote operating vehicles. They were clearing the silt away, getting ready to lay the explosives along *Severodvinsk*'s hull. Demolition experts on both ships were assembling the line charges and detonators. Borisov's question resulted in a long discussion about timing the Russian rescue preparations so they would not delay *Seawolf*'s vital resupply mission.

It was a very technical discussion, and while Patterson remained involved, she also allowed her attention to wander a little and observe the Russians. There was no confrontation this time. They were matter-of-fact, and open with information about their status and their needs. Part of the worry she'd brought aboard disappeared.

The admiral marched down a reasonably long and thorough checklist. After making sure their schedules meshed, and that everyone knew their part for the upcoming second attempt, Borisov asked about ship-to-ship communications, deconflicting the ships' radar transmissions, and even asked about medical facilities on board *Churchill*. "We may ask you to take some of the submarine's crew if our sick bay becomes overloaded. Many of the crew are now suffering from hypothermia and may require immediate care," Borisov explained.

"I'll run a casualty drill this afternoon," Baker replied. "We'll be ready."

"I am glad that we have been able to agree on so much this morning, for the sake of relations between our countries as well as the welfare of *Severodvinsk*'s crew," stated Borisov. Patterson could tell a well-rehearsed speech when she heard one. But it didn't feel like he was winding up the meeting.

"I hope that same openness will be extended to our investigation of the collision itself. Captain Rudel's assistance since the collision will be taken into account when his actions are judged."

Patterson started to protest, but she felt Dwight Manning's hand gently squeeze her arm. She refrained, and let Manning do the talking. His statement was carefully worded, "I am concerned, Admiral, that you have already decided the collision was Rudel's fault."

Borisov shrugged. "*Seawolf* has bow damage, while *Severodvinsk* was holed both fore and aft. I doubt that Captain Petrov rammed the American submarine with his engineering section. There is also the question of *Seawolf*'s presence in these waters. We believe he had motive to avoid detection."

"These are international waters, ninety miles away from the nearest Russian coastline."

"And his purpose here?"

"He was performing a hydrological survey, as allowed by international convention. Perhaps you can explain why Captain Petrov so strenuously objected to his presence."

"We have no evidence that Captain Petrov behaved incorrectly," responded Borisov defensively.

"He made several high-speed passes dangerously close to *Seawolf.* Captain Rudel did his best to avoid a collision with *Severodvinsk* by attempting to turn away."

"Captain Petrov has not reported any of this to me," Borisov stated, with such finality that Manning didn't answer immediately. Patterson tried to think of a response that didn't call Petrov a liar.

"Admiral, we can provide logs and other evidence to support Rudel's account," Manning countered.

Borisov still wasn't convinced. "Will that evidence be consistent with *Seawolf*'s damaged bow?"

Now he was hinting that the Americans were liars. Patterson had heard enough and spoke up. "Our analysis shows that *Seawolf*'s bow damage came from an impact with *Severodvinsk*'s screw. The damage to the other areas of *Seawolf*'s hull and sail supports the conclusion that *Severodvinsk* struck *Seawolf.*"

"I don't see how that could possibly happen." Borisov's reply lacked Vidchenko's belligerence, but he was still Russian and he just couldn't accept their explanation.

Fine. If he wanted proof, she'd give it to him. "Admiral, would you care to inspect *Seawolf*'s damage yourself?"

Patterson's offer surprised Borisov. He paused, as if looking for a hidden trap. Then she looked at Manning and Baker. They both looked just as surprised as Borisov. In fact, Baker seemed alarmed, and she suddenly felt very nervous. Had she missed something? Was she giving something important away?

"Your offer is most generous, Doctor. I accept. Given our schedule, sooner would be better than later."

11 October 2008
1300/1:00 PM
USS *Seawolf*

"She did what?" Shimko was surprised by the intensity of Rudel's reaction. It was the most energy he'd seen in the skipper since the collision. On the other hand, this obviously hit a nerve.

"They'll be here in half an hour. She wants us to show Borisov the damage to the boat. Right now he's convinced you rammed *Severodvinsk*."

Shimko could tell that hurt, and was immediately sorry he'd said it. But Rudel seemed galvanized by the accusation. "Fine," he announced sharply. "We'll bring the Russian aboard and let him look wherever he wants. Have Jerry make copies of the timeline and all the other material he collected after the collision. We'll give that sumbitch so much data he chokes on it."

"Or on what it shows," Shimko added.

"Get us on the roof, Marcus. And use the low-pressure blower to get the bow as high out of the water as possible. We can all get a good look at the damage. Warn the crew it will be a rough ride. And prepare the ship for an official visitor."

"Aye, aye, sir. Surface the ship, prepare for an official visitor, and I'll tell Jerry to double up on his seasick meds."

THE KA-27 Helix appeared overhead precisely on time. By this time, *Seawolf*'s crew was well-drilled in getting visitors safely on deck and then down the escape trunk. There was no room for sideboys or a boatswain topside or in the passageway below, but as Borisov came down the after escape trunk, the 1MC rang with six bells, then, "TWELFTH SUBMARINE SQUADRON, NORTHERN FLEET, ARRIVING."

The chief of the boat was waiting, and saluted, then asked Borisov to follow him. Borisov's aide, Patterson, and Manning followed the admiral to the wardroom.

Rudel and his department heads were waiting, and the wardroom table was covered with documents, neatly organized and labeled by Shimko. A detailed chart showed the tracks of the two subs and the UUV, surrounded on one side by log pages and on the other by photographs of the damage, both inside and outside the ship. A plate of warm chocolate chip cookies and a carafe of hot coffee were off to the side.

"Nice touch, Al," complimented Shimko, pointing to the refreshments. "That should help put our guests into the proper frame of mind."

"A wise cook once said, 'An empty stomach is not a good political adviser.'" Constantino chortled as he finished, clearly very pleased with himself.

Shimko initially looked shocked, then menacing. "You trying to horn in on my territory, Chop?"

"Quiet, you two," scolded Rudel as he saw the mess steward signal him from the pantry. Seconds later, the door to the wardroom opened and Borisov walked in.

Rudel was the only one who spoke. "Welcome aboard *Seawolf,* Admiral. We've laid out this material for your inspection. You may take all of it with you when you leave, if you desire. My executive officer and department heads are ready to answer any immediate questions you may have, then we will tour the damaged areas of the ship." As Rudel spoke, a mess steward poured Borisov a cup of coffee. He took it wordlessly, distracted by the wealth of information laid out before him. Shimko had even included a blank note-pad and pen.

"While you're reviewing this material, I'd like to speak with Dr. Patterson privately, just for a few moments." Borisov nodded, already examining the track chart, and the captain took Patterson by one elbow, guiding her forward to his cabin. Jerry Mitchell followed, then took station in the passageway, to make sure they weren't overheard.

Rudel closed the door to his stateroom, then spoke softly, but intently. "Doctor, are you aware of the regulations and procedures that have to be followed when you invite a foreign visitor aboard a nuclear submarine?"

Patterson wasn't intimidated. "You don't approve of me bringing Admiral Borisov aboard." It was a flat statement, but she included understanding, even sympathy in her tone. "I'm sorry for springing this on you, but I believe it's the best way—the only way—to convince Borisov that the collision was not your fault. Improving your standing with the Russians will help us in many ways."

Rudel looked angry, barely under control. "Letting a Russian on board *Seawolf* goes against everything I've been taught. And he's not just any Russian. He's a submariner, and a senior officer! I don't see how this can turn out well.

"It's not the documents. He would get copies of those anyway," Rudel continued. "But we could just as easily have briefed him aboard his ship."

Patterson shook her head, disagreeing. "He needs to see your damage for himself. There is a small risk of a security breach," she acknowledged, and he nodded agreement, "but the payoff is winning over Borisov, and with him the commander of the Northern Fleet and potentially, the Russian government."

Rudel didn't look entirely convinced, but didn't reply, instead motioning toward the door. They left, and with Jerry following, returned to the wardroom.

While Rudel's officers came to attention when he entered, Borisov appeared absorbed in the documents. Patterson assumed his English was good enough to read the material, and that he wasn't just posing.

Shimko leaned over and whispered, "Not a word since you left. But I think he likes the Chop's cookies." He pointed toward the now half-full plate.

A few moments after they entered, the admiral stood. Without a word about the documents in front of him, he said, "I would like to see the damage to the outside hull, please."

That meant a trip through control, and Patterson followed the others from the wardroom. Once they reached the bridge access trunk, Rudel turned to the contingent and said, "There isn't as much room on our bridge as on one of your submarines, sir. You, Dr. Patterson, and I will go up. The rest will have to wait here."

"Very well, Captain. Proceed."

Both Borisov and Rudel insisted Patterson go first. Borisov followed, then Rudel.

Seawolf was running with the wind, the following sea lapping over her stern. Ballasted aft, the sub had lifted more of her crushed bow out of the water than Patterson had seen, even in other photos of the damage. Slate-gray waves barely reached up the sides, and Patterson studied the bow, along with the two officers. Lieutenant Chandler, on watch as conning officer, did his best to stay invisible.

Rudel pointed back, to a long scar on *Seawolf*'s aft deck. "We believe this is where *Severodvinsk* struck us first, then here," he pointed to the battered sail. "Finally, her screw struck us on the bow, nearly slicing our pressure hull open."

Chandler handed Patterson his glasses and she studied the bow. Rudel explained to his visitors, "See those parallel slash marks on the casing? They were caused by *Severodvinsk*'s screw as it struck our hull. If you do the math, the distance between the scars matches the blade rate we heard on sonar and her speed at the time of impact. The softer bronze blades broke up on impact with the hull and our forward momentum bent the propeller shaft upward."

Patterson handed her glasses back to Chandler, and watched Borisov. This was all for his benefit.

Borisov studied the bow for another moment, then lowered his glasses. "I see different-colored metal embedded in the casing," he said solemnly.

"Those are pieces of bronze from *Severodvinsk*'s propeller. We recovered some fragments, and will give you some to take with you."

Rudel pulled out a close up photograph of *Severodvinsk*'s propeller hub. "Here's a digital image of the propeller shaft and hub. You can see the ragged remnants where the blades blended into the hub." The bladeless, distorted shaft almost filled the frame. Borisov's stoic expression was worthy of a professional poker player.

Rudel produced a second piece of paper, a smaller version of the same track chart showing the two submarines as they maneuvered that Borisov had seen below. A small colored square lay along the Russian sub's path between the estimated point of impact and its current location. "That's where one of the unmanned vehicles found the impact debris. We believe additional pieces of the blades can be found there."

Rudel let the Russian admiral study the image for a moment, then spoke carefully. "I know you believe that *Seawolf* rammed your submarine. But we have three different damage patterns spaced out along our upper hull. How could we have done this and still managed to tear off *Severodvinsk*'s propeller blades?"

Borisov sighed, but didn't answer. "Could I see the damage to the bow from inside? You said that you had reinforced that part of the hull."

It only took a few moments to go back down to ladder, take off their cold-weather gear, then over to the electronics equipment space. Chandler had alerted the chief of the watch to clear the technicians out of the space.

Since it was Jerry's space, Rudel signaled for him to follow. Rudel led them into electronics space, showing Patterson and Borisov the wooden shorings that supported the pressure hull. Once they'd carefully stepped around the bracing, Rudel pointed out the damage. "Our pressure hull is deformed here and here. The seals around several of the masts started to ship water. We used wood, and later steel reinforcing plates, to seal the leaks."

"How much water came in?" asked Borisov.

"Approximately two metric tons." The actual amount meant little to Patterson, but Borisov looked alarmed. Rudel motioned to the scorched bulkheads and equipment racks. "The salt water obviously ruined all the equipment in here. There was a major fire."

As Rudel spoke, Borisov studied the damaged compartment. In one corner, an open equipment rack held a photograph of a smiling young sailor. It was surrounded with small items—a pair of silver dolphins, a *Seawolf* ball cap with a third-class crow pin in it, and a pile of notes. A sign that said PLEASE CHEER ME UP hung over the photo.

"This was where your crewman died."

"Yes, Admiral."

"Is there anything else you wish me to see?"

"No, sir."

"Then let us go back to your wardroom."

They were gathering and packaging the documents, photos, and metal fragments when the party entered. Borisov sat down heavily at the table and asked, "Coffee, please."

Jerry poured for the admiral, who sipped the cup thoughtfully, then cradled it, as if warming his hands. "It is good coffee," he finally remarked.

The chief of the boat was waiting in the corner, and caught Rudel's eye, who nodded. Walking over to the admiral, he said, "Sir, I am Master Chief Hess. I'm the chief of the boat, the senior enlisted man aboard. We'd like to thank you for coming aboard, and we'd like you to have these, to remember your visit."

He handed Borisov a ball cap and a framed photo of *Seawolf*. They were traditional gifts for visiting VIPs, but Jerry felt the strangeness of giving them to a Russian.

But Borisov smiled broadly and thanked Hess. "These are excellent." Then the smile went away. "You have been much better hosts than me." Slowly, deliberately he stood, and turned to face the American crew. "I now believe that *Seawolf* did not ram *Severodvinsk*, deliberately or accidentally. For now, that is all we can say. We must wait for the investigation to tell all of the story of what happened."

After a short pause, he added, "I cannot speak for my government, or even for my Navy, but for myself, I am very sad that two fine crews have suffered injured and dead. We must work much harder to make sure this never happens again."

Patterson waited a moment, making sure Borisov was finished speaking. As he handed the gifts to the enlisted man to put in the package, she said, "There are a lot of press reports from your Navy. They accuse *Seawolf* of many things, and they're simply not true. Can you speak to your Navy, ask them to stop making such accusations?"

The Russian didn't answer immediately, but finally said, "You are right. Those stories are not helpful, but now anyone in Russia can speak to the newspapers."

"Many of the stories are coming from sources in your Navy," Patterson insisted.

Borisov nodded. "I will stop any false stories."

Patterson smiled. "The newspapers need to print something. You could provide them with better stories—accurate ones."

"I will consider it."

National security advisor's office, Old Executive Office Building, Washington, DC

"She did what?" Wright's exclamation echoed out of the office and down the hall.

Admiral Forrester's voice mixed anger and frustration. "It's all in the message. She *informed* Admiral Sloan that she invited Vice Admiral Pavel Borisov, a Russian submarine officer, to visit *Seawolf* and inspect her damage for himself."

Wright skimmed the printout. "Operational precedence, but she must have sent it right before the meeting. By now Borisov has come and gone." He set the paper down carefully on his desk, as if it would bite.

"This is not good," Admiral Forrester insisted. "She's making her own deals. We are out of the loop."

"That doesn't mean she's made a bad decision."

"What? How could letting a Russian admiral aboard one of our best submarines be a good idea?"

"He didn't inspect the submarine. He was there to see the damage."

"So he got a good look at a modern attack boat, *and* her vulnerabilities."

Wright was calming down, but Forrester still seemed very upset. He'd never seen a chief of naval operations this emotional. "So you would have rejected her request?"

"Absolutely," Forrester replied forcefully.

"Which is why she informed us, instead of asking our permission."

"You have to get her out of there. Better still, get everyone out of there."

"That's not my call," Wright replied. "I picked her, but the president approved her selection."

"Then we need to take this to him."

USS *Churchill*

She'd had about fifteen minutes' warning, barely enough time to leave her dinner and get up to *Churchill*'s CIC. Captain Baker and Lieutenant Commander Hampton had come as well, to make sure the video link was functioning properly, and Dwight Manning, her State Department liaison and de facto second-in-command, was there as well, off-camera but available.

The command position in *Churchill*'s CIC was dominated by three large flat-panel computer displays. Normally they displayed maps or status boards, but the center one now held a widescreen image of several men seated, facing the camera. The background behind them was dark and functional-looking. She guessed they were in the White House situation room. It certainly wasn't the Oval Office.

Patterson had been seated and ready when the link was activated. President Huber was flanked by the secretaries of state and defense. She was relieved to see Jeffrey Wright present, and she had the impression that many others were in the room as well. She felt a little alone.

Her image must have appeared there at the same time, because President Huber looked off to the right, then announced, "I'm taking fifteen minutes out of a very busy day, Joanna."

"Yes, sir. Thank you."

"Don't thank me yet, Doctor. Tell me why you invited a Russian admiral aboard *Seawolf* without getting approval from the Navy or DoD."

"Vice Admiral Borisov has replaced Rear Admiral Vidchenko, the admiral who threw us off their flagship. I had to convince him beyond any reasonable doubt that *Seawolf* did not cause this incident, or that we had any motives beyond helping to rescue their trapped crewmen."

"And this was worth cutting the Navy out of the loop." That statement came from Hicks, the Secretary of Defense. His calm tone didn't match his expression. The benefit of video teleconferencing was seeing as well as hearing.

"Time was short," she answered. "The visit had to take place before rescue operations took up all his time."

Huber answered again. "You had enough time for a phone call to clear this with Rear Admiral Sloan. You know that the submarine community is sensitive to such visits. No Russian has ever been aboard a *Seawolf*-class sub."

She hadn't expected them to buy it. "True enough. All right. I set up the visit on my own because it's vital that we build some trust—not just for the sake of international relations, but for those trapped crewmen.

"I was there. Captain Rudel implemented his visit ship procedures. Displays were covered, sensitive material was stowed, and the Russian admiral showed absolutely no interest in *Seawolf*'s hardware. It was clear from his words that he was convinced, even moved, by what he saw."

"The Russians will say anything," Hicks answered sharply. "Doctor, I think you've been set up."

"And I think you're about twenty years out of date," Patterson fired back. "Mistrust has already cost lives. We either learn to work with the Russians or we could lose more. And I don't need to tell you how bad we'll look in the eyes of the world if we walk away now because of a cold war mindset."

"At any cost?" Summers asked.

"At almost no cost . . . except maybe to the Navy's pride." Patterson immediately regretted the retort, and quickly added, "To save their crew, the Russians are being forced to reveal information about their newest, most advanced submarine. We'd think they'd be foolish to withhold it. Our situation is no different."

Both secretaries started to speak, but Huber stopped them. "All right, Doctor. I'm endorsing your decision—after the fact." He paused for a moment, and then added, "I can't remove you. That wouldn't look good to the Russians or the media. But be very careful, Doctor. We need the situation simplified, not complicated."

11 October 2008
1600/4:00 PM
Severodvinsk

Captain Third Rank Fonarin swept the light from the battle lantern around the central post, looking for his captain and starpom. Although he was tired and cold, he moved about quickly, his breathing labored, a notebook clutched in his left hand. As chief of the chemical services, Fonarin had just completed his latest test on the atmosphere's quality; the news wasn't good. It was times like this that he wished he had a different job on board *Severodvinsk*. After a quick look by the engineer's post, he found Petrov and

Kalinin huddled up on the deck aft, by the underwater communications station.

"Captain, sir, the latest report on the atmosphere," panted Fonarin as he handed the notebook to Petrov.

"Just give me the bad news, Igor," he said, as he accepted the pad.

"Yes, sir. Unfortunately, my suspicions have been confirmed. The American chemicals are fully depleted. Carbon dioxide has increased to two point seven percent."

Petrov nodded wearily. He was physically unable to get upset any longer. "How long do we have?"

"Even with many of the men asleep, the carbon dioxide levels will rise to three percent within six hours. After that, things will get worse quickly. I estimate that no more than twenty hours later we'll be at lethal concentrations; over five percent."

"So, essentially we have one more day," Petrov summarized.

"Yes, sir. I'm sorry."

Petrov looked up at the junior officer and gave him a slight smile. "You have nothing to be sorry for, Igor. It is I who must apologize, to you, to the whole crew. Now go and get some rest."

"Aye, sir."

Kalinin watched as Fonarin shuffled slowly away, his shoulders hunched over in defeat. "He's a good lad. But he shouldn't take his responsibilities quite so personally."

Petrov chuckled a little. "I think the pot just called the kettle black."

"Perhaps," admitted Kalinin with a shrug. "So what do you think our good squadron commander is up to?"

"I don't know," replied Petrov with some irritation. "You heard what he said a few hours ago. Help was coming but it would take a little time."

"Hmmm, you'd think he'd realize that we don't have much time to spare."

"One would think."

Petrov leaned back against the bulkhead, physically exhausted and emotionally spent. He was out of ideas, and almost out of time. A part of him wished that death would stop toying with them and just get it over with.

Without warning, the loudspeaker on the underwater communications system crackled to life, and a familiar voice filled the central post.

"*Severodvinsk,* this is *Seawolf.* Captain Petrov, please respond."

Petrov snapped out from his brooding and looked over at Kalinin, who was equally surprised. They both struggled to their feet and Petrov grabbed the microphone.

"*Seawolf,* this is Petrov. Captain Rudel, it is good to hear your voice."

"Likewise, my friend. Please have your crew prepare to receive more supplies."

"Thank you, Captain. Give us some time to open the tube's outer door."

"Understood. *Seawolf* is standing by."

"A remarkable fellow, this Rudel," Kalinin observed nonchalantly, although his face radiated relief.

Petrov didn't answer. He couldn't. It required all his strength to simply hold back the tears brought on by this latest emotional roller coaster. But, for the first time since the failed rescue attempt, Petrov dared to hope.

26

TEAM EFFORT

11 October 2008
1645/4:45 PM
Severodvinsk

The recovery of the second supply vehicle from *Seawolf* was welcomed, but Petrov had forbidden any spectators. Unnecessary movement consumed more oxygen, producing even more carbon dioxide. There was enough poison in the air already; they didn't need to make more simply to satisfy someone's curiosity.

Captain-Lieutenant Rodionov checked the sight glass to make sure the torpedo tube had drained. Once satisfied that most of the water was in the tanks, he ordered his men to manually open the breech door. It still seemed very wrong to open a tube's inner door and see the front of something that looked a lot like a torpedo staring back at you. After a quick inspection, Rodionov moved aside to make room for his torpedo specialists to prepare the vehicle for extraction. And this time they were ready. Hauling the first UUV, "Patty," out of the tube had been a nightmare.

This time the tube had been prepared. Duct tape covered every obstruction, and having studied the vehicle's construction, they knew which tools would be most effective for drawing it from the tube. Some would damage the exterior casing, but it was the last trip for it anyway, just as they would never bother removing the duct tape lining the tube. *Severodvinsk* would never move from her resting place, either.

As with all things in submarines, preparation made all the difference. Beaded with water, the dark green cylinder rolled smoothly onto the tray. The torpedomen moved it to an empty rack and began working on it like they'd done it their whole lives.

This time, the load was mostly V-64 air regeneration cassettes. "I count eighteen, Captain," Rodionov reported. "They've also sent several batteries for our own lanterns and some boxes wrapped in plastic. There are also some more candy bars stuffed around the cassettes, but ours fit much better than those American curtains," he said proudly.

"So Russian cassettes fit better in a jury-rigged American vehicle than the American equivalents."

Rodionov shrugged. "Well, if you put it that way . . ."

"Look at this!" One of the torpedomen held up a fat envelope, labeled "For the crew of *Severodvinsk*" in crisp Russian. He started to tear open the flap, but stopped himself, then handed it sheepishly to Petrov.

The captain didn't wait to satisfy his curiosity. Inside was a thick sheaf of papers. The top sheet was a handwritten note from Admiral Borisov. He had taken command of the rescue operation, and was using every available resource to save them, etc., etc. . . .

He'd read it later. The second sheet was from his father, in the city of Severodvinsk. Automatically, he started to read it, then stopped himself and turned to the next page. It was also for him, from his sister Nadya in Moscow. The next one was addressed to Kalinin, and then to Lyachin, and one to Mitrov, and so on. There was at least one letter for every surviving member of the crew!

"What are these?" interrupted one of the torpedomen holding two bags with numerous wrapped objects. "Is this food?"

Petrov took one of the bags, punched a hole in it, and pulled out one of the objects. Raising it up into the light, he read the label and chuckled. "No, I don't think you'd want to eat this. I believe it's poisonous." He then opened the wrapper and removed a plastic tube about ten centimeters in length. Grasping the tube with both hands, he bent it until it made a crunching sound. He shook the tube vigorously, and it began to glow brightly. "Those clever Americans knew we would need some light to read our letters from home."

Taking the top three pages, he thrust the rest of the papers and the glow sticks toward Rodionov. "Take these to the Starpom, and have him pass them out to the crew."

"At once, Captain," responded Rodionov eagerly.

Petrov only half-watched as the torpedomen collected the cassettes, batteries and food. There were two other unidentified wrapped boxes for Dr. Balanov. Medicines, thought Petrov as he shifted his position slightly. There were only two lanterns left in the torpedo bay, Rodionov having just taken the third one when he left. One was placed over the torpedomen as they worked on the American vehicle. The other provided general illumination, and Petrov positioned himself so the paper could catch as much of the light as possible.

Dear Aleksey,

The Navy says they will give this to you, but what should I say to a son who is trapped at the bottom of the sea? It is hard knowing you are in danger, but I try to remember that you are an officer in the Navy. This is part of your service.

The television is full of news about you and your crew. All of Russia, and many people around the world know about Severodvinsk. Everyone I know has asked me to tell you how sorry they are about the men you have lost, and that they are praying for your safe return.

Nadya says she will write to you as well. You know how she worries, but she is being very brave. The Navy should give her a medal.

All of your sub's families have formed a "Wives and Mothers" group. They are taking care of the families of those who died, and pressing the Navy for information about your rescue. Olga Sadilenko is in charge, and the group is so successful that other navy families are joining, from other submarines and ships. They are thinking of making it a permanent organization.

In all my years of building submarines I never had to face what you are facing now. No matter what happens, I know you will always act for the good of your crew, the Navy and your country. I am proud of you, and I love you, my son.

Petrov finished the letter, then the one from Nadya, then his father's letter again. It was still cold, and the air was still foul, but for the moment, it didn't matter so much.

AS-34

Umansky nervously tapped the gauge that measured the battery discharge rate. It never helped, but he did it anyway. Just in case. This was the eighth dive for AS-34 on *Severodvinsk,* and the discharge rate increased almost every time. They weren't drawing any more power, but the batteries were losing their charge more quickly. He'd tried to troubleshoot the problem back on *Rudnitskiy,* during charging cycles, but the increased loss was probably internal, inside each battery.

He checked his watch, then noted the rate, time, and remaining charge on the neatly columned pad. Detailed records might lead to understanding, and like every good submariner, Bakhorin wasn't happy until he knew exactly how much trouble he was headed for.

Luckily, the trip down was short now, almost familiar. One of *Halsfjord*'s remotes had planted a sonar beacon near *Severodvinsk*'s bow. It was simple to home in on it, and they also didn't need to use their active sonar. That meant more power saved.

This trip, the biggest drain would be the motors. AS-34 was carrying a cable, one of six that would be attached to *Severodvinsk*. Topside, they would be connected to two salvage tugs that were enroute from Severomorsk. *Pamir* and *Altay* were due to arrive early tomorrow, but it took time to attach the cables to the sub's hull. For the time being, the upper end of each cable was fastened to a lighted buoy, which also served to mark *Severodvinsk*'s position.

AS-34 held the lower end in one of her handling arms, which had to be strengthened to accommodate the heavy wire cable. The wire rope was over an inch in diameter. A loop spliced onto the end would be attached to the hull where the sub's mooring lines were usually placed.

When the word was given, *Severodvinsk* would blow her port tanks, flood her starboard tanks, the charges lining her hull would be fired, and the two tugs would pull on the cables for all they were worth. At some point, the cable would snap, or the mooring points might be ripped from the casing, but by the ghost of Admiral Makaroff, they would right *Severodvinsk*.

"Fifty meters." Bakhorin's depth report was routine, and Umansky checked the passive sonar display, as if his partner would stray off course. They were moving slowly, which seemed strange because the weight of the cable should make them descend more quickly. But three hundred meters of cable had considerable drag, and much of it was still on *Rudnitskiy*'s deck. It wouldn't be completely paid out and attached to the buoy until AS-34 did their part of the job.

"Seventy-five meters." Bakhorin was still on track, and Umanksy took another set of battery readings.

Discharge rate was more than doubled. He could almost watch the charge meter go down. "We're down to eighty percent," he warned.

"What?" Bakhorin's immediate response was to look for some errant piece of gear that was drawing power. There was none, of course. Umansky was busy with his tables and a calculator. Bakhorin wanted to let him finish his calculations, but the answer was obvious. "Are the batteries failing?"

Umansky nodded, a look of frustration on his face. "The only question is how much power do we have left. I have to assume the discharge rate will increase, instead of staying constant." Finally, he tossed the calculator into a corner with disgust. "Twenty minutes at most, maybe as little as ten. I'd like to plot the change in the discharge rate. It may be an exponential function."

"You don't need mathematics like that to know we can't make it back to the surface in time."

"We can still make it to *Severodvinsk*."

"With barely enough time to attach the cable," Bakhorin confirmed. "But this is the second one. I know what needs to be done."

"Then we proceed," Umanksy answered.

By the time they'd reached *Severodvinsk*, the battery charge was down to thirty-four percent. It should have read in the seventies, because it took more power to ascend than descend.

The first cable had been attached forward, so they headed aft. In spite of his haste, Bakhorin was careful to steer clear of the bow. There was no telling exactly where the dark-colored cable was, and running into it could damage both AS-34 and the cable.

Neither Russian was terribly worried about their minisub at this point. They knew it was her last dive. With the batteries shot, and no replacements or any way to fix them, she was finished.

The mooring point was under a retractable plate. It was designed by Russians, to work when the deck was caked with ice and snow, and it worked underwater as well.

Using one claw, Bakhorin uncovered the mooring point, and as carefully as a watchmaker, slipped the eye of the loop over the cleat. Once it was settled into place, he released the claw and announced, "I'm clear."

Umanksy gave him a thumbs up and said, "Good. Move us away from the submarine."

"Understood. I'm heading to the northeast."

"Away from the buoy and the ships. I concur."

As Bakhorin guided them to their new location, Umansky checked the discharge rate again. It had increased slightly. Whatever was going on inside those batteries, it was only getting worse. They only had ten percent of a full charge now. It would be impossible to make the surface with the motors. In fact, Bakhorin hoped they would be able to get at least half a kilometer away from *Severodvinsk*.

Twenty seconds later, the display panel lights began flickering and the motors started losing thrust. "That's far enough. Releasing yellow flare." Bakhorin pressed a lever, releasing a smoke float. They were not coming up where they were supposed to, so it was only polite to mark their current location.

The minisub drifted to a stop, and Umansky reached over to cut the switches to the motors, the passive sonar, and the exterior lights. The gauge read less than five percent charge. The batteries were essentially flat. Bakhorin laughed. "Well, that's it for me. I'm just a passenger now."

"You always were the lazy one," Umansky shot back. "I think it's time to quickly shed some unnecessary weight."

"Make sure that panel still has some power," Bakhorin joked.

"We have a green board," Umansky replied. "Dropping ballast."

A dull BANG reverberated through the hull and they felt a sudden jolt.

Umansky pressed a second button, and another BANG sounded as explosive bolts detached the mechanical arms from the bottom of the minisub. Between the ballast and arms, nearly a thousand kilograms of dead metal landed on the seabed, just a few meters below them.

They were rising, but there was no point in taking their time. "Initiating gas generators." The last button fired four chemical containers located in the minisub's ballast tanks. Each was fitted with a small hydrazine charge that would fill the tanks rapidly with gas; emptying them of water. The sound was smaller, but they could still feel the vibration, and better still, the depth meter started spiraling upward. They'd be on the surface in moments.

"Now comes the hard part," said Bakhorin ruefully, "breaking the news to the Admiral."

Skynews Network
Russian Submariners Risk Lives to Continue Rescue Effort

Preparations to rescue the crew of trapped submarine *Severodvinsk* received a setback today, when the overage batteries on the rescue submersible AS-34 failed during a dive.

The Russian submersible, over fifteen years old, has suffered from battery problems since the rescue began, but until now they have only limited the number of dives the submersible could make, and their duration.

On the last dive, the batteries suddenly began to lose their charge, and the operators, Captains Third Rank Bakhorin and Umansky, faced a difficult choice. If they aborted the dive, the rescue would be delayed, but if they continued and attached the cable, they would not have enough power to return to the surface.

The two submariners took the dangerous course, and successfully attached the rescue cable. With barely enough electrical power remaining to move away from the downed submarine, they performed a risky emergency surfacing, which succeeded.

AS-34 is one of three underwater vehicles working on the rescue. The other two are remote operating vehicles operated by the Norwegian salvage and rescue vessel *Halsfjord,* and according to Mr. Arne Lindstrom, are in "excellent mechanical condition." He estimates that the loss of AS-34 will cost "about six hours."

In an interview with Skynews reporter Britt Adams, Vice Admiral Pavel Borisov, commanding the rescue operation, called Bakhorin and Umansky "heroes upholding the best traditions of the Russian naval service," and said that such men were "common throughout the fleet."

Preparations are now expected to be complete at one o'clock tomorrow afternoon local time. If they are successful in righting the submarine, the survivors will be on the surface within minutes.

Navy Wives and Mothers Organization, Gorshkov Prospekt, Severomorsk

The walls were stained in one corner, the pattern had worn off the linoleum in many places, and Mariska and her husband had left in search of a proper lock for the front door.

But a sign painter was at work on the front window, and secondhand furniture was streaming in from half a dozen places. And most importantly, Irina had her Internet access.

Olga had appropriated the small office in the back. She was supervising a couple of the new girls as they organized the furniture when Galina found her. "There's another reporter here." She smiled broadly.

Olga was curious. "What's so funny?"

"Nothing's funny, Olga. I'm pleased. He's from the base newspaper." The base newspaper was run by the Navy, and only printed articles approved by the headquarters.

"I was expecting him. Thank you, Galina. Show him in."

He'd phoned ahead, which was polite, and Olga had insisted he come over straightaway. In all the bustle she'd forgotten to tell Galina, but no matter. She chased the other women out of her half-finished office, satisfied that there was a battered desk for her to sit behind, and a chair for her guest.

She was still sitting down when she heard Galina say, "Go right in." The tone of Galina's voice was the first warning. The young man that entered looked like he was still in university, younger even than her son Yakov. She felt like fixing him lunch.

But he was here for an interview, and his age really didn't matter. They all seemed so young to Olga.

"Mrs, Sadilenko, thank you for seeing me." The young man fiddled with a notepad and tape recorder.

"I'm flattered that the paper is interested in our new organization, Mr. Borzin."

"I'm hoping that the story will run on the front page, Mrs. Sadilenko."

"Please, call me Olga." She fought the maternal urge to straighten his tie.

"Thank you, Olga, and I am Ivan Pavelovich." He referred to his notepad for a moment, then asked, "What is the goal of your new organization?"

Borzin spent about fifteen minutes quizzing Olga about the Navy Wives and Mothers group. How many members did it have, what were the requirements for membership, how did they operate?

"With much confusion," Olga joked. "We are still sorting ourselves out into some sort of structure. Irina talked about a 'wiring diagram' and I thought she meant the insides of her computer."

"But your organization is doing much work." He referred to his notepad. "I asked for this story because I heard about the phone call you arranged between Captains Bakhorin and Umansky and their families."

Olga smiled. "That was Galina's idea, but it was a good one. The Navy praised these men, but they had to risk death to become heroes. Their loved ones are proud, of course, but even after the fact, they were worried about the risks their men were taking. Hearing each other's voices for just a few minutes gave heart and strength to both the naval officers and their families back home."

"Has the Navy ever allowed that before—letting men aboard a ship speak to their families ashore?"

"Oh, no." Olga smiled. "They were quite surprised when we suggested it."

"But wouldn't it be a distraction to the men?"

"Their experiences are the distraction," Olga countered. "Hearing from their loved ones helps them get back on an even keel."

"And what did the Navy say when you suggested this?"

Olga waved her hands about. "They worried about the precedent it would set. They worried that it would reveal state secrets. But Vice Admiral Kokurin graciously allowed it this time as a trial. We want to show the Navy we can be an asset, that the fleet will be stronger with us."

"What other activities have you performed?"

"Of course, we are helping those families who lost loved ones aboard *Severodvinsk.* This includes helping them obtain all the survivor's benefits the Navy is supposed to provide. In the past, some people have had problems with this. From now on we will be there for them."

Borzin closed his notepad. "I'm going to ask for an interview with Vice Admiral Kokurin. I understand you've met with him a few times."

"That's true." Olga didn't smile, and fought the urge to say something unwise. She finally said, "I'm sure you will find it worthwhile."

USS *Churchill*

The messenger found her in wardroom. "Doctor, Captain Baker sends his compliments, and asks if you would join him in CIC."

They really did talk like that, she marveled. Contacts abaft the beam, marlinspikes, and piping people on and off the ship. Secretly, she loved it.

Baker was smiling when she saw him sitting in his command chair, an unusual smile in the middle of a life-and-death submarine rescue. "The Russians have reported a surface contact to the southwest. It's entered the maritime exclusion zone."

He gestured to the contact display in the center screen. The six-by-six display showed not only the ships in the rescue force, but a large circle marking the fifty-mile exclusion zone. Baker had shown her how to read the symbols. The symbology was easy to interpret once you knew the system, and she could see a surface ship just across the arc marking the exclusion zone. It was headed straight toward their position.

"This is why you're smiling?"

"The Russians sent a helicopter and visually identified it as a Norwegian-flagged fishing vessel. The aircraft challenged it by radio but the boat won't answer."

"What would they like us to do?"

Their helicopter will be out of fuel in about half an hour. They'd like one of our birds to relieve it. They also want *Churchill* to back it up, in case they refuse to change course."

"Intercept them?" she asked.

"With your permission, ma'am."

"Borisov is the SAR commander, after all. Did this boat ask them for permission before entering the exclusion zone?"

"I asked the Russians that question and they said it did not."

"Then there's no guarantee they'll behave themselves. Yes, Captain, permission granted."

Baker's hand was already resting on the phone. "Bridge, launch the alert bird, bring the other helo up to plus thirty readiness. After it's gone, change course to intercept Track zero three four seven, speed twenty-five knots."

Baker listened for a moment to the reply, then hung up. "They were ready for my word. We'll launch our helicopter in about five minutes. We should intercept in about an hour, a little after sunset. Our helicopter will be there in twenty minutes."

Motor Vessel *Stavanger*

Captain Jonson didn't look happy, even when the Russian helicopter left. Brewer had persuaded Jonson to not answer the helicopter's radio calls, even when they switched from Russian to passable English.

Truth be told, Brewer had been a little nervous himself, at least until he satisfied himself that the helicopter was unarmed. He smiled as it flew off to the northeast. It couldn't do a thing to stop them.

Jonson didn't smile when the helicopter left, but he hadn't turned his boat around, either. At the time, promising him triple the normal charter rate had seemed a little excessive. Now Brewer thought it was money well spent.

Jonson had been willing enough to take them out. The fishing season was over. He'd been slow putting his boat up for the winter because of needed repairs. Brewer's fee had not only paid for the repairs, it more than made up for the fishing Jonson had missed.

Brewer was willing to spend. The *Severodvinsk* story was big news, but almost every piece was secondhand, from either Norwegian or Russian or U.S. official sources. The media couldn't even interview families of *Severodvinsk*'s crew. Severomorsk was a closed city, barred to foreigners, much less Western reporters.

So Harry Brewer, INN news producer, had flown from the U.S. to Norway. Heading north from Oslo in a chartered plane, he and his crew had found Jonson and his men on the northern coast, in the fishing town of Ålesund.

Stavanger was a sturdy-looking craft, not big, but big enough for Brewer, his assistant, a cameraman and a soundman. Jonson's crew of five spoke at least passable English, and the cook had proven to be very good, although Brewer was getting a little tired of fish.

There was no question about where to go. The Internet was full of maps and diagrams showing the location of the rescue site. And as for the exclusion zone, Brewer dismissed the prohibition. The only good stories were on the far side of the police tape. Working as a journalist, he'd climbed dozens of fences. Sometimes they shooed him away, sometimes he got the goods. On something like this, with worldwide play, he was ready to do whatever it took. To tell the truth, he'd enjoyed the adrenaline rush when the Russian helicopter had appeared, and watching it disappear had been even sweeter. His cameraman had gotten plenty of footage.

Brewer checked their progress on the chart, although he already knew what it would show. They were on course, on schedule, chugging away at *Stavanger*'s best speed of twelve knots. Most of Jonson's repairs had been to her two diesel engines, and now he was running them almost flat out.

It was vital that *Stavanger* reach the rescue site by dawn tomorrow. Most of the activity would take place in the morning, and he needed daylight to position himself properly. Footage of the Russian rescue capsule would be flashed around the world within minutes of it breaking the surface, and it would be his crew that got it. Definitely Pulitzer Prize material.

A shout in Norwegian pulled him back to the bridge windows. Jonson quickly raised his glasses, and searched to the north. The first mate, manning the helm, translated for Brewer. "The lookout says he can see a helicopter."

"The same one?" Brewer asked.

The mate shrugged. "It's coming from the same direction."

Brewer wanted to borrow the captain's binoculars, but he wouldn't know what he was looking at. It only took a few minutes to confirm that the aircraft was approaching them again, but from dead on, they could tell nothing about it.

Finally, it grew from a speck to a shape, and Jonson announced, "It's not the same kind. I think it's American."

"What?" Brewer was surprised at the idea of an American aircraft in these waters. But an American destroyer was part of the rescue group. It could have come from that ship. What did they want?

Jonson maintained course and speed, and the helicopter circled them twice, first from a distance, then closer in, only a few hundred yards away. As it circled, Brewer studied the craft, wondering if this one was armed. Jonson had the same thought, and reported, "No weapons. Those pods on each side are drop tanks."

Finally, it came up on their port side, only a hundred feet up and not much farther away. The radio came to life. "Norwegian fishing vessel, this is a U.S. Navy helicopter. You are inside a maritime exclusion zone established during a rescue operation. Turn around immediately and head southwest."

Jonson looked at Brewer who shook his head violently. "Do not answer. As long as we don't answer, they can't say we received their transmission. This is just like the other one. It's unarmed."

The helicopter repeated its message, and when it didn't receive a reply, it changed position, dropping aft and closing. Brewer knew they were looking for the vessel's name on the stern, but he'd had the captain cover it with a fender. He hadn't been able to talk Jonson into taking down the Norwegian flag.

"Norwegian fishing vessel, you are violating international law. You are approaching an area where rescue operations are underway. If you do not come about, you will be arrested on your return and fined."

Brewer quickly said, "INN will pay the fines and any other expenses."

Johnson looked unconvinced. He scratched his blond beard thoughtfully. "What if I lose my license?"

Brewer answered lightly, "If they're going to arrest us when we go back, let's go back with the story. INN will be more interested in backing you up if you help us."

The fisherman looked dubious, but Brewer said, "Look, you're working for me. I'll take the heat, and all they ever do to a journalist is kick us out. I'm trying to do my job."

Jonson looked over at the first mate, who said nothing for a long moment. Finally, he gave a slight nod, and Jonson said, "All right. I will not pay any fines. Your bosses will pay them."

They pressed on. The helicopter climbed and took station behind the fishing boat; steering large, slow figure eights to stay in position. Every ten minutes the aircraft would call them, but never received a response. Brewer wondered how long the aircraft's fuel would last.

At sunset, the helicopter was still in position, its navigation lights marking its position long after its shape had blended with the night sky. Brewer knew the helicopter could track them with radar. They'd used radar to find *Stavanger* in the first place. There was no way to evade detection or slip in. He was just going to call their bluff.

They were having an early dinner when the lookout's excited call brought Brewer and the captain up to the bridge. The third mate pointed to the radar, mounted in front of the ship's wheel. "Twenty kilometers," Jonson commented, "about eleven miles."

The second mate was standing in the companionway, and Johnson barked orders in Norwegian. The second took the helm, while the third fastened his cold-weather gear and picked up a pair of binoculars.

Jonson studied the scope for a minute, then took a second range reading. "He's coming fast," the captain remarked. "About thirty knots."

"Could it be a commercial ship?" Brewer asked.

Jonson snorted. "In these waters? At this time of year? At that speed? No, mister reporter, that is a warship." Several emotions quickly played across the captain's face—frustration, disappointment, then resignation.

Brewer went through a different set of emotions. He would have thought they had more important things to do than chase a harmless fishing boat, but he was ready for them.

The position of the lights didn't change, but the shape they marked grew steadily larger. With only a quarter moon and a partly cloudy sky, it was virtually invisible, even with Brewer knowing where to look.

Then, at one mile's distance, the ship suddenly flashed into visibility. They'd turned on their exterior lights. In the pitch darkness it almost floated somewhere between the dark sky and the darker sea.

"Norwegian fishing vessel, this is a U.S. Navy destroyer USS *Churchill*. Identify yourself." The voice sounded like a Brit.

Confused, Brewer shook his head again, and half-reached out as Jonson walked toward the radio. The captain ignored him, and instead handed Brewer the glasses, pointing toward the ship as he picked up the microphone.

Brewer looked though the binoculars at the warship. He recognized it as an Aegis destroyer. He'd bought several books in the U.S. and studied them on the flight. It was a gray thing, all angles and shapes. It looked huge, even a mile away.

"This is motor vessel *Stavanger*, out of Ålesund."

Brewer studied the ship. It was exciting, seeing a warship like this, in its element. He wasn't worried, even when he saw the gun on the bow pointed in their direction. This was an American ship.

"*Stavanger*, what is your business?"

"Tell them we have been chartered by Marine Salvage. We are bringing supplies to *Halsfjord*."

Jonson gave Brewer a strange look, but shrugged and repeated the claim, in English.

Churchill rogered for the explanation, then said nothing

more. She slowed and took position a mile off their port side. Above and behind *Stavanger,* the helicopter continued to fly lazy eights.

As the minutes passed, Brewer began to believe the explanation had worked. After all, the Russians had declared the exclusion zone. The U.S. hadn't honored it earlier. Now, here they were headed northeast with an American destroyer alongside.

"*Stavanger,* this is *Churchill.* Marine Diving and Salvage and *Halsfjord* both deny any knowledge of your charter. *Halsfjord* expects no vessels. Heave to immediately and stand by to be boarded. If you do not cut your engines, we will fire."

"They can't mean it," Brewer protested.

Jonson reached for the throttles. "They mean it. No bluff."

Stavanger slowed quickly, the boat rolling unevenly as it drifted and turned to face the wind. Brewer watched *Churchill* slow as well, and take position upwind a hundred yards away. Her forward gun stayed trained on them, and Brewer could see sailors manning other weapons on her decks.

The destroyer lowered a boat on her lee side and it bounced through the waves to *Stavanger*'s side. Brewer could see men in the boat. Several of them were armed. At Jonson's orders, a boarding ladder was waiting for them. The first man over the side was not armed, but the second and third were, and took covering positions on the deck while the rest of the group climbed aboard. Jonson and his first mate stood quietly until the leader introduced himself.

"I am Leftenant Keith Figg, Royal Navy. Who is master aboard?"

"I am. Captain Jonson."

"Captain, what is your business in these waters?" Brewer

noticed that as Figg asked his questions, another sailor was videotaping the proceedings—making a legal record.

"I am under charter by INN to carry a reporter and his men to the rescue location."

"Were you aware that you entered an internationally recognized exclusion zone?"

Jonson didn't answer immediately, and Figg said, "All mariners are required to know of any exclusion zones." After a moment, he added, "And the Russians haven't kept this one a secret."

Finally Jonson nodded. He'd rather admit to a violation than ignorance. "Yes, I was aware of the exclusion zone."

"Where are your charters?"

"Here," Brewer replied. "Harry Brewer, INN." Reflexively, he offered Figg a business card, then realized the absurdity of the act, standing on a heaving deck in the middle of the night to men with guns pointed at him. "May I ask why a British officer is on a U.S. warship?"

Figg ignored the question and took the card, but didn't look at it. "Did Captain Jonson inform you of the exclusion zone?"

"Actually, I informed him. I didn't want to deceive him about where we were going."

"And you deliberately entered the exclusion zone."

"As I said, I'm with INN. We're here to cover the rescue of *Severodvinsk*'s crew. I've got equipment that will let us send the images worldwide, in real time."

Figg shook his head. "I'm afraid that's not going to happen. Captain Jonson, what is your best speed?"

"Twelve knots."

Figg spoke into a handheld radio, then turned back to the two men. "Captain Jonson, Mr. Brewer, you are in violation of Article Twenty-five of the UN Convention on the Law of the Sea. We are confiscating all recording devices aboard—cameras, tape recorders, cell phones, all of it." Brewer started to protest, but Figg cut him off. "It will all be logged and carefully handled. After your case is disposed, if the Russians choose, they can return your equipment to you."

"The Russians?" A shocked Brewer started to ask a question, but Figg's radio barked and he listened for a moment.

"Captain Jonson, you will steer course one nine seven for Severomorsk harbor, where your boat will be impounded by the Russian authorities. At a speed of twelve knots, you are expected to arrive by 1830 tomorrow evening. Senior-Lieutenant Andreyev and Warrant Officer Babochkin of the Russian Federation Navy will remain aboard as liaisons."

Brewer exploded. "You can't turn us over to the Russians!"

Figg answered, "This is a legally declared military exclusion zone to effect the rescue of a Russian submarine. You've knowingly violated an official announcement by the Russian Federation government, with a senior Russian naval officer in command of the operation. You're trespassing on their estate. Who did you think you'd be dealing with?"

Figg ordered his team, "Search the boat." Jonson motioned for his first mate to go with them as Brewer looked on in complete amazement. A pile quickly developed on the aft deck, although it took almost half an hour to find not only the INN video equipment, but also personal cell phones and even a crewman's personal camera.

While the contraband was loaded into *Churchill*'s whaleboat, Figg warned Jonson, "If you do not reach Severomorsk by 1830 tomorrow evening, your boat will be confiscated. You will be tracked by aviation assets and from shore until you arrive. If you have difficulties, we will be monitoring the standard international distress frequencies."

Jonson nodded silently.

Brewer made one last plea. "This is insane. Nobody was hurt. Why can't we just turn around? We'll go back to Ålesund."

"You ignored warnings from two different aircraft, and lied to us about your business here. Be grateful it was an American vessel that intercepted you. And by the by, there is a formal billet for a Royal Navy officer on board USS *Churchill* as a tribute to Sir Winston. Have a good day, sir."

27

SECOND TRY

12 October 2008
0815/8:15 AM
Rescue site, Barents Sea

Borisov and Lindstrom had agreed to wait until it was light to move the cables from the buoys to the tugs. In spite of the urgency, there was no rush to perform this step. The limiting factor, especially after the loss of AS-34 *Priz*, was still the number of dives needed to lay the line charges and attach the last cables to *Severodvinsk*. The two Norwegian ROVs had held up so far, which meant they were still on schedule for the second attempt early that afternoon.

Halsfjord's two vehicles would keep working during the transfer, both laying the charges that would break the

Russian sub free of the bottom. On the surface, the salvage tug *Altay* backed carefully until it was only meters from one of two buoys, each a checkered orange and white sphere almost ten meters in diameter. Cables from *Severodvinsk* curved up out of the water to huge padeyes on the sides of the buoy. Those cables would be transferred from each buoy to one of the tugs.

A workboat passed close alongside *Altay*. A crewman on the back of the tug tossed a "monkey fist" to the men in the boat. Nothing more than a ball wrapped with cord, it trailed a thin line. The men on the boat started pulling on the line while the men on the tug payed it out. After a dozen meters, the line became cord, then after another interval rope, then after a longer span, a nylon hawser over an inch in diameter.

Motoring over to the buoy, the workboat's crew attached the line to the cable, passing it through the six-inch loop on the end. It was difficult work, with the boat and buoy moving in the swells, sometimes banging into each other hard enough to break bones, if anyone was careless enough to get in the way.

The final step was to unscrew the heavy padeye, allowing the cable end with the hawser attached to drop free. As it hit the water, a winch on *Altay* started up, pulling the hawser in toward the tug's stern. Once the hawser had pulled the cable aboard, it was slipped over a bollard at the stern. With the cable safely attached to the tug, the workboat went back to get the next cable.

Each tug would pull three cables, going to *Severodvinsk*'s bow, midsection, and stern. It was important to have the tugs doubling up. With each tug pulling on *Severodvinsk*'s bow, middle, and stern, there would be fewer problems in synchronizing their pulling power. It also provided a safeguard against a cable parting, or, God forbid, an engine failing on one of the tugs.

But it meant that the cables had to be different lengths, carefully calculated and cut, and once the tugs took the cables aboard, they were stuck to that one spot in the ocean where their three cables came together.

Five were already laid out to *Severodvinsk,* and with the arrival of the tugs, the last one would be attached directly to *Pamir.*

MEANWHILE, ON the seabed, *Halsfjord*'s two remotes worked carefully, laying fifteen-kilogram charges as far under the hull as possible. It was a time-consuming process because the mud and silt had to be cleared away before each charge was emplaced. In fact, the charges were being placed where the mud was thickest, as much as two meters. The explosions had a much better chance of freeing the sub if they went off inside the mud, next to the underlying rock, instead of just resting on top.

Another complication was that the charges would be detonated by electrical signals over wire, instead of by an acoustic signal, as they were the first time. The speed of sound in water was slow enough that a fraction of a second would pass between the nearest charges getting the signal and the ones farther away. Instead, the detonation signal would be sent over wires carefully cut to an exact length so that they went off in a staggered sequence, a ripple effect from stem to stern.

The web of detonation wires and cables required the remote vehicles to steer a careful path each time they approached the downed submarine, and as they ascended. It all took time.

AFTER CONNECTING the last cable to *Severodvinsk*'s hull from *Pamir,* the ROV did not immediately ascend to the surface. Instead, it rose just a little and turned to "face" the sub. Powerful lights illuminated the hull as it glided above the hull toward the bow. It slowed to almost a crawl, then followed the streamlined curve of the sail. Finally, embedded in the middle of the sail, the grayish outline of the rescue chamber's panels came into sight.

The operator, sitting in *Halsfjord,* brought the ROV to a stop. "There it is," announced Lindstrom. He told the operator, "Get as close as you can, then circle it."

A Russian observer aboard *Halsfjord,* a qualified submariner, studied the image closely. The picture was also broadcast to *Petr Velikiy, Rudnitskiy,* and to *Churchill.*

USS *Churchill*

Aboard *Churchill,* a TV monitor in CIC displayed the underwater image sent by *Halsfjord.* Patterson, Russo, and Baker had the front-row seats, while the rest of her group and many of the crew clustered behind as closely as rank would permit. The grayish boundary of the escape chamber stood out clearly from the black anechoic coating.

One of *Churchill*'s officers, on watch, asked, "Isn't it a little late in the game to be checking the escape chamber?"

Russo shook his head. "This isn't the first inspection, it's the last. We examined the chamber's exterior panels on the very first dive from *Halsfjord.* This is a final check to make sure that we haven't created an obstruction. We have to make sure the cables won't snag the chamber when it detaches, or that some piece of debris hasn't jammed it in place."

Patterson and some of the others watched over his shoulder, but after the allotted twenty minutes, two complete circuits around the sail showed no obstruction. Everything looked like it was falling into place, adhering to Lindstrom's intricate plan.

USS *Seawolf*

Jeff Palmer found Jerry in his rack, relaxing with a trashy paperback he'd borrowed from Chief Hudson. Boredom wasn't usually a problem for Jerry, but with *Seawolf* simply waiting and watching, he had even managed to get caught up with all his paperwork.

He looked up at the knock, then put down the book and rolled onto his side when he saw Palmer's expression. "What's going on?"

"Nothing right now, thankfully," Palmer answered, "but I've been doing the math again. *Severodvinsk* will have used up most of the chemicals we delivered yesterday and that will leave them hanging if this attempt fails. Shouldn't we start preparing Maxine for another supply run?"

Jerry immediately shook his head. "We can't. We need her to watch when they try to raise *Severodvinsk*. She has sensors that the Norwegian ROVs don't."

Palmer nodded quickly, but pushed his point. "Of course, but there are things we could do to prepare—bring over more cassettes from *Rudnitskiy*, for instance. And my guys think they can even precut some of the packing material. It would shorten the time we need to get more supplies over to them—just in case."

Jerry thought about Palmer's suggestion and seriously wondered if it was a good or a bad idea. There was a downside to making the preparations. The Russians might see it as a negative attitude. And while everybody acknowledged the possibility of failure, nobody wanted to think about it. Jerry certainly didn't.

"So you think we should expend our last UUV getting more atmosphere control chemicals to them?"

The torpedo officer shrugged and looked uneasy. "I don't like it, but it's that or wait for them to suffocate . . ."

"And what happens once we've sent them more cassettes?" Palmer didn't answer right away, and Jerry continued. "Everyone is already doing everything that can be done."

Jerry forced the words out. "If this second try fails, and I was Petrov, I don't know if I'd want more chemicals."

Palmer shuddered. "You might be right. But choosing to end it, just giving up . . ."

"The extra time would just give them more opportunity to think about what's coming."

"Unless someone can come up with something else."

Jerry joked, "Sure, the Jolly Green Giant with a big-ass fishing net," but neither he nor Palmer smiled.

"But it's an option," Palmer countered.

Jerry made a face. "All right, make up a checklist and a timeline. I'll make sure the XO and the Skipper know we're ready."

"For the unthinkable," Palmer added.

"For the unfixable," Jerry replied.

Severodvinsk

Petrov kept them out of the escape chamber for as long as possible, but even huddled under their blankets, dozing and coughing in the foul air, he could feel the energy. He had skipped the last round of sleeping pills, and the crew was rousing, starting to feel restless. They wanted to move, but he told them to stay put, stay quiet. Save your strength.

He tried to rationalize it. It was colder in the escape chamber. All the food and medical supplies had been removed days ago. The wounded were more comfortable where they were. The rescue force wouldn't be ready on time, or there would be some last-minute snag.

There. That was it. He couldn't bear the thought of them going up into the chamber and then climbing back out of it again. They'd done it once already, and while most of his men had kept up a brave front, some had broken down, given up.

The arrival of the Norwegians had given them new hope, sustained by the letters from their families and the supplies from *Seawolf*. With tangible support from three nations, they'd found the strength to endure, but Petrov knew how fragile that endurance was.

Besides, his men had waited for so long. He would enjoy making everyone else wait for them for a change.

Petr Velikiy

Borisov watched from his command chair as they ran down the checklist. He fought the urge to ask questions. The timing was calculated almost to the second, and he'd checked their calculations over and over. He even had a copy in front of him.

The real question was, what else should be on that list? Like a traveler leaving the house, the question nagged at him. What had they forgotten?

Halsfjord was positioning its remote vehicles now. The American remote, "Maxine," was already in place, while *Seawolf* herself had withdrawn to three kilometers, close enough to maintain acoustic communication, but clear of the three small underwater vehicles or anything that might go over the side.

The three unmanned vehicles, two Norwegian and one American, were spaced equally around a circle three hundred meters in diameter. If the rescue went well, they'd be able to record the process. If there was a problem, there was a small chance they would be able to correct it.

He scanned the monitors that filled every spare corner of the flag command post. Most displayed status reports:

helicopter fuel, weather, equipment breakdowns. One showed a video image of someone in an impossibly bright blue parka, standing on the fantail of one of the tugs. A crawl across the bottom in alternating Russian and English identified him as Britt Adams, a reporter for Skynews aboard the tug *Pamir.* Thankfully, the audio was off.

Patterson had convinced the admiral that the tug was the best place for a reporter to be. He was going to report anyway, she argued, and Borisov had conceded that point. And he certainly wouldn't find any state secrets aboard a tugboat. The admiral had agreed with that as well. And what better way to show the Russian effort to save their crew than a live feed of *Pamir* straining at the cables?

Borisov had given his permission, and Adams had been helicoptered over to *Pamir* at dawn. A condition of his presence was that his video signal was relayed from *Pamir* to the flagship, and then to a satellite. Borisov could cut this transmission at any time—rather, the English-speaking captain-lieutenant who'd been ordered to watch Adams's broadcast could.

The tugs and *Halsfjord* were all in position. In fact, they couldn't move out of position, and that was beginning to make him impatient. The rest of the task force had assumed stations one mile away from *Severodvinsk,* and every ship had at least one boat out with a crew standing by. *Legkiy*'s boat was already in the water, standing by with a line she'd attach to the escape chamber.

Every ship with a helicopter had it fueled and ready. Every sickbay, including *Petr Velikiy*'s extensive medical facilities, was on alert. Everything that could be thought of had been done.

Borisov would not give the order. As far as that went, he'd already given the order, back when he took over the rescue. Lindstrom had control of the detonators and a Russian liaison on *Halsfjord* would tell the two tugs when to start pulling. And Lindstrom would give the signal only when Petrov said he was ready.

Severodvinsk

"It's time," Petrov announced softly. Kalinin stood slowly, favoring his sprain, ready to direct the evacuation, but everything had been thoroughly planned. Even if they hadn't held evacuation drills before the collision, they'd dreamed of little else since. Petrov had even calculated and recalculated how long it would take them to reach the surface. From their current depth, he figured one minute and forty-nine seconds. That was all it would take.

Now, with few words, and not as quickly as he would have liked, men pulled themselves up, taking care to stay wrapped against the cold.

Senior-Lieutenant Shubin did show some energy as he opened the access hatch, hopefully for the last time, Petrov thought, and then climbed up into the chamber. A moment later, he poked his head out and looked towards Kalinin. After reporting that everything was in order, a weary smile appeared on his tired face. "Why am I looking forward to going somewhere even colder than this place?"

Senior-Lieutenant Kozyrev, waiting for his turn to climb, answered, "I'd take up with a polar bear and live on the ice to get away from your breath." Several crewmen laughed. Nobody had been able to brush their teeth for several days, and there were worse odors.

"Yours is no better," Shubin countered. "You can use yours to stun a bear. I now know why it is so hard for you to find dates." That made everyone laugh, and the pace increased a little.

Once a dozen able-bodied men had climbed into the escape chamber, it was time to send up the wounded. The sixteen injured crewmen all had injuries that prevented them from climbing the ladder into the chamber: sprains, broken bones, wrenched backs. Kalinin was the first to go up. He would supervise the men in the chamber, and he wanted the men to practice with him.

It was a slow process. In drills they'd held before the collision, they'd gotten eighty-five men into the escape chamber in seventeen minutes, beating the navy requirement by three minutes. Now, even with fewer men to load, Petrov guessed it would take an hour.

One by one, the injured were gently lifted and carried to the base of the ladder. Some could stand, but many had to be held upright while a line was passed under their shoulders. Then the men above gently, carefully, brought their disabled shipmate up into the chamber and belted them in place. The exertion made the men on the ropes cough, and it took five or six to do what would normally be the work of two men.

The escape chamber was a cylinder two decks high. Each deck was a circular space with seats lining the bulkhead. The upper deck was open in the middle, and little more than a wide ring, allowing the men to move to and from their seats. It was not the best of accommodations. The injured were all strapped in on the lower deck, with healthy men on either side. Sadilenko was a special case. Dr. Balanov had insisted on keeping him completely sedated, and in a straitjacket as well. He was sent up last, after the injured men, limp as wet paper. A rope harness added to the seat held him upright.

Maybe it was the thought of escape, or the increased activity. Certinly the coughing and moans of the wounded hadn't helped, but Petrov felt a wave of claustrophobia wash through him. Suddenly he couldn't draw a full breath. The cold air filled his lungs and refused to sustain him.

The last of the men were climbing now. Lyachin, the

senior officer after the starpom, reported to Petrov, "Codes and classified material have been passed up, sir." He held up the logbook. "I was going to take this up myself. We are the last two."

The engineer's report pulled Petrov out of his funk, and he instinctively looked around the command post, as if to make sure nothing had been left behind. Lyachin saw him look, and said, "We've had two people count, and they matched. Sixty-five men are in the chamber, comrade Captain. You and I will make it sixty-seven."

Petrov nodded and walked over to the underwater communications station. "*Halsfjord*, this is *Severodvinsk*. Everyone is in the rescue chamber." He looked at his watch for a moment, then said, "We will flood the starboard ballast tanks in one minute . . . mark!"

"Understood, *Severodvinsk*. Good luck to you."

Petrov hung up the mike and reflexively switched off the set, smiling as he realized how ridiculous that was. Tracking the second hand on his watch, he hurried over to join Lyachin at the engineer's post.

Thirty-five seconds. Petrov looked around the central post again. He tried to take it all in, fixing it in his memory. His first, and very likely last command. Regardless, he'd never be back here again.

Fifteen seconds. "On my count," Petrov ordered.

Lyachin nodded silently, his hands hovering over the switches but not touching them.

Ten seconds. It was foolish to time things to the second, but Lindstrom was watching his own clock on the surface. Petrov wouldn't be the one to mess up the timing.

He watched the second hand, and called "Five seconds," resting his hands on the controls. He counted down the last few seconds, and at "Zero," both he and Lyachin pushed the valve controls opening the vents on the starboard main ballast tanks. Suddenly, there was a loud roar coming from *Severodvinsk*'s starboard side as the air in the ballast tanks surged their way to the surface. By putting all their reserve air into the port ballast tanks, and flooding the starboard ones, the engineers hoped to create a torque on the submarine's hull; a torque that would help rotate *Severodvinsk* upright.

Petrov waited for the few seconds it took for the indicators to change, then told Lyachin, "Go."

Halsfjord

The passive sonar on the Norwegian ship wasn't nearly as sensitive as a military suite, but they were sitting almost directly over the bottomed submarine. The operator reported, "I can hear mechanical noises, and air moving."

Lindstrom nodded and said "Good," never taking his eyes from the second hand. He'd conferred with the Russians about how long it would take the water to fill *Severodvinsk*'s ballast tanks, how long it would take for thousands of tons of steel to start to move. Some of her port tanks were ruptured, though, and some of that air would be lost. The next step was timed, hopefully, to coincide when the sub began to twist.

He turned to the Russian officer. "Tell the tugs to go. Full power." It would take them some time to come up to full power as well.

"Thirty seconds."

Severodvinsk

In spite of his haste, Petrov took extra time to double-check the hatch, then carefully climbed to the seat reserved for him next to the starpom. Kalinin was staring at his watch. Petrov looked again at the inclinometer. It showed thirty-six degrees of port list. They had to get within ten to fifteen degrees of an even keel.

According to the briefings he'd received, the escape chamber should not be released if the submarine was moving too much. He hoped a sideways roll wouldn't be a problem, because the instant they showed less than twelve degrees, he was pulling the release.

"Ten seconds," Kalinin announced.

Petrov called out "All hands brace! Remember, I can't pull on the release until we roll vertical, so stay braced after the explosion. I don't know how long it will . . ."

The shock and noise were as violent as anything he'd ever imagined, almost as bad as the collision itself. A Russian PLAB-250 depth charge held sixty kilograms of high explosive. Dropped close enough to an enemy submarine, it could crack the pressure hull and shake equipment off its mountings. Now, dozens of charges were exploding in a ripple fashion, not a hundred meters away, or fifty, or ten, but directly against the hull. Two rows of gas bubbles abruptly appeared, shoving the water and mud away from the sub's hull, then collapsed in on themselves.

Like driving fast over a washboard road, or a hailstorm of hammers, Petrov felt each blast, or imagined he could. The seat he was strapped to carried the shock wave right into his body, jarring his spine and giving him an instant headache. The sound seemed to come from the water outside the chamber, from the hull below them, and from inside the chamber itself. Many of the crew yelled in surprise, and the injured men cried out from the pain. It was rough treatment, and Petrov felt their pain, helpless to avoid or forestall it.

In spite of the violent motion of water and gas under the hull, the list remained. He waited for them to roll, or at least shift position, but the inclinometer stayed frozen at thirty-six degrees.

The force of the explosions lasted for only a fraction of a second, but Petrov continued to feel, or imagine that he could feel, the wham-wham-wham vibration they had caused. Then the feeling became a real sensation, and Kalinin remarked on it as well. Still half-deafened by the explosions, Petrov couldn't distinguish any sound, so he placed his palm against the metal bulkhead of the chamber, listening with his hand.

There was a vibration, low and jumbled. He tried to visualize it, but nothing in the submarine was working, so . . .

"It's the tugs," Petrov announced. Others mimicked his actions, feeling the rumble of the tugs' engines carried through the cables to the hull.

Petr Velikiy

Borisov found himself watching Adams's transmission, even ordering the sound turned up. Maybe he was attracted to the video image. Adams's camera was trained on *Pamir*'s fantail, wreathed in white froth. Three thick black lines led in a tight fan from her fantail into the water.

"I'm standing on the topdeck of the Russian salvage tug *Pamir.* Those cables you see lead to the crippled submarine *Severodvinsk,* its half-frozen crew critically short of breathable air." The camera swung to show the Norwegian ship, perhaps half a kilometer away. "Moments ago *Halsfjord* detonated thirty-two explosive charges on both sides of the stranded submarine's hull. These are supposed to free her from the bottom suction and jar her loose of the rock ledges. Now the tugs are straining to pull the twelve-thousand-ton submarine upright."

The camera shifted again to show *Pamir*'s sister *Altay,* just a hundred meters to port. With her white superstructure and a dark gray hull, she made an impressive picture as she strained at the cables. "Although a fraction of *Severodvinsk*'s size, each tug's engines produce nine thousand horsepower. Their combined . . ."

The image tilted suddenly, then shuddered and spun. It stopped to show a portion of *Pamir*'s deck and handrail. Voices in Russian and one in English shouted, but the words were drowned out by an angry howl from the tug's diesels. The engine noise quickly stopped, and someone, probably Adams, picked up the camera. There was an "I've got it" in English and the image steadied again, to show *Altay* heeling over to starboard, sliding sideways across the water toward *Pamir.*

A shout in Russian made Adams swing the camera to *Pamir*'s fantail. Two of the cables were no longer taut, and the third draped over her stern and was visibly moving to port, increasing the angle between it and the other two.

It had taken moments for Adams's video to show the disaster. By the time his camera steadied on the limp cables, Borisov was on his feet, shouting orders. "Call the tugs! Talk to both of them, find out their status! Call the Norwegians. I want to speak to Lindstrom! Kurganov, call *Severodvinsk.*"

"I can't," the admiral replied, "they'll still be in the escape chamber."

Borisov paused. "You're right, of course. Then call *Seawolf.* See what their remote vehicle saw."

"I've got Lindstrom on the radiophone," a lieutenant announced. Borisov hurried over and took the handset. "Borisov here. What happened?"

Lindstrom's voice showed his confusion. "I don't know what's happened. Both tugs suddenly veered to starboard. It looks like the cables to the sub's bow are slack on both tugs."

Nicherin, one of Borisov's staff, interrupted, "Admiral, I've got reports from both *Pamir* and *Altay*. No casualties, but each has lost the cable to *Severodvinsk*'s bow."

"That still gives them two cables each. Tell them full power!" Nicherin nodded quickly and hurried off.

Borisov returned his attention to the handset. Lindstrom was speaking, and Borisov asked him to repeat. "We're moving the ROVs in to get a closer look at the cables."

The sailor in Borisov thought about the forces, the way they were applied. "Concentrate on the bow section. The cables must have come loose somehow."

"I agree. The chance of two breaking at the same moment is incredibly small."

"How long until you can see?" Borisov asked.

"There's a lot of silt from the charges," Lindstrom answered. "We'll have to get in very close, almost on top of the submarine. With the tugs still pulling, there is a risk we could lose one."

"I understand," Borisov answered. "Go ahead."

"We are already sending one of the ROVs in. It will take three, maybe four minutes."

"If they've simply come loose, be ready to reattach them."

"Understood. We can do that."

USS *Seawolf*

Jerry and most of the wardroom were in control, with as many of the crew that could fit down in the torpedo room, watching the displays. Maxine had been running slow, angled racetracks, her sonar optimized for short range, high-resolution images.

They'd heard the explosion through the hull, a little

alarming in spite of being right on time. Sonar also reported the tug's engines running flat out. Maxine's sonar showed most of *Severodvinsk,* lying angled to port. They all longed for her to slowly roll to starboard, and then for the escape chamber to appear above the sail. The UUV would be able to see it, even through the murk from the explosions.

Rumor was, the cooks were putting together a big party, with a Russian menu. Blinis, something called piroshki. They might even invite Borisov back. Seemed like a nice enough guy.

Sonar then reported the engines slowing, followed by a revving up again to full power.

But *Severodvinsk* never moved. Kurganov's call over the underwater telephone confirmed the bad news.

USS *Churchill*

They'd moved from CIC to the bridge, as if actually seeing the vessels would tell them something new. The radiomen piped the circuits over the bridge loudspeakers, and they listened to Borisov's questions and his order to maintain power.

After about five minutes, Lindstrom came back on the circuit. "We have a clear view of the bow from the first ROV. The mooring point is gone! It's been torn off of the casing!"

He was reporting to Borisov, who responded in English. "I do not understand."

"The fitting that the cables were attached to has been ripped from the submarine's deck."

"Impossible. Those mooring points are designed to withstand tremendous forces."

Lindstrom patiently answered, "We will be sending the

photos to you in a few moments. The foundations are cracked, and the metal of the casing is torn. The fitting itself is missing entirely. The cables did not come loose, they pulled it off the deck."

Borisov's voice, even over the radio, was incredulous. "How could this happen?" He was asking himself as much as Lindstrom.

"*Severodvinsk* suffered a lot of damage to her bow. The hull's structure must have been weakened."

There was a long pause, and everyone on the bridge could imagine the Russian searching for some solution. "Can the cables be reattached to the bow some other way? It must be done quickly," he added.

"No, Admiral. There's nothing left to attach them to. And the tugs would have to stop while we did the work."

After another pause, Borisov answered, "Very well. I intend to continue with the remaining two lines."

Lindstrom's answer was simple. "Good luck. Out."

Joanna Patterson, Captain Baker, and the others stood listening to the conversation. After the Norwegian had signed off, they stood silently, absorbing and understanding. Silas cursed, Russo walked out to the bridge wing, and Patterson saw him pounding his fist on the rail.

She was surprised when Joyce Parker pulled out a Kleenex and offered it to her. She hadn't felt the tears until then.

They watched as the tugs strained, working to move *Severodvinsk*. Borisov had them alternate, then angle left and right. All the while, *Seawolf* and *Halsfjord* watched their vehicles, eager to report any movement. Finally, after half an hour with nothing to show, the admiral had each tug cast off one of its cables, so that *Pamir* had the midships while *Altay* pulled on the stern. He ordered them to pull in opposite directions, hoping that the twisting motion might somehow help.

Severodvinsk

Petrov waited, holding his hand against the metal bulkhead of the capsule. It was a lousy way to monitor the rescue efforts, but the capsule had no sensors. He held his hand there, feeling the vibration, knowing the tugs were working, but the inclinometer never moved.

Soon after the explosions, he'd felt a jar that had passed through the deck, but the vibration had resumed quickly. It stayed constant, and he could only wait and hope and watch the needle as it hovered at thirty-six degrees.

After ten minutes, he pulled his hand away, but others took up his watch. He visualized the tugs, tried to calculate the forces, but his thinking kept trailing off into worries about his men, and what was taking so long.

After fifteen minutes, he started to look for reasons why the hull hadn't shifted yet, but would. After another ten minutes, he confirmed that the vibrations were still there, but according to the inclinometer, they were not having any effect. Were the vibrations something else? If not the tugs, what? He decided he didn't want to know.

The excitement of moving into the chamber and the explosions had passed. The crew waited patiently, and silently. There was no point in wasting air by asking questions. They knew as much as their captain. Most of the injured appeared to be asleep, or at least passed into a quiet state brought on by exhaustion and stress.

Petrov promised he'd wait until forty minutes had gone by, and then found himself looking for reasons to keep waiting. Waiting meant there might still be a chance. When he stopped waiting, and opened the lower hatch, it meant that yet another rescue attempt had failed.

He knew Borisov and Rudel and Lindstrom were probably calling on the underwater telephone. But they knew he and his men would be waiting here in the chamber, out of touch but ready to ascend the instant the sub rolled far enough to starboard.

Fifty-two minutes after the explosive charges had been detonated, the vibration stopped. He waited a full five minutes for it to resume, or for anything else to happen. Feeling like a failure, he unsnapped his seat belt and stood.

His action, final as a jail door slamming shut, brought moans and cries from his crew. A few wept as he walked to the hatch and unsealed it. Before descending, he turned to Kalinin and ordered, "Keep them here for a few more minutes while I call *Petr Velikiy.*" The starpom nodded sadly, even though it was just delaying the inevitable.

Petrov left the escape chamber, heading for the underwater communications station and bad news.

28

FINAL PUSH

12 October 2008
1433/2:33 PM
Petr Velikiy

It took only a few sentences for Borisov to tell Petrov what the unmanned vehicles had revealed. No explanations were needed. They both understood exactly what it meant.

"What is your CO_2 level?"

Petrov reported, "Fonarin did an analysis just before we boarded the capsule. It was three point two percent, and he says the chemicals, the cassettes, everything is exhausted.

The physical activity of climbing in and out of the escape capsule has also produced more of the gas. We've all had headaches for some time now, but many of my crew are starting to complain of dizziness and seeing spots before their eyes. With all the regeneration cassettes depleted, there really isn't much we can do. Dr. Balanov is attempting to administer another round of sedatives, but some of the men are refusing to take them."

Borisov could understand men not wanting to end their lives in a drugged trance. "I understand. The Americans have another unmanned vehicle. They've offered to send you more cassettes."

"No. Absolutely not." At first, the strength of Petrov's answer surprised Borisov, but then he realized it shouldn't. One or two more days of lingering cold misery, and for what? To sit around and contemplate a fate that could not be changed? It would be his choice, if he were down there.

"My apologies, Admiral. I appreciate Rudel's offer, but it wouldn't matter. My Chief Engineer reports that we are almost out of reserve battery power. We can't operate the air-regeneration system anymore, even if we had cassettes. I'm afraid we are just running out of time." Petrov's voice was remarkably frank, almost mechanical, as he made his report.

"We are not yet ready to concede, Captain. I must go now, to speak with Lindstrom and the others. Everything will be considered. We will speak again afterwards."

"Thank you, sir. But, I fear it will be a short meeting." Borisov couldn't tell if Petrov was joking or not.

USS *Churchill*

Captain Baker told his crew after the Russians tugs stopped pulling. Most of them already knew. When the tugs had whipsawed, and the escape chamber hadn't appeared, it was obvious they'd failed. But Baker waited, like everyone else, hoping and praying for a miracle.

Patterson was with him, on the bridge, when he spoke on the 1MC. If the expressions of the bridge watchstanders were typical, the crew took it pretty hard. She tried to understand why the crew of *Churchill* would care so much about the Russians. They'd even printed pictures of the crew from the Wives and Mothers website and posted them in the mess. Perhaps her husband had best summed it up when he said, "It was a sailor's thing."

A short time later, they watched while workboats transferred the cables from the tugs' sterns back to the buoys, freeing them to maneuver. Saving the cables was pointless, really, but nobody wanted to abandon that physical link to *Severodvinsk.*

More by mutual agreement than design, many of Patterson's group had congregated in the wardroom, along with several of *Churchill*'s officers. It had the feeling of a wake, or a deathwatch. Nobody used either of those words, but they gathered and talked quietly, or simply shared each other's company. When they did talk, they searched for any alternative, however absurd, that might have been overlooked or dismissed as being too risky.

Some talked of stretching the crew's breathable air somehow. Others wanted to move the sub. Commander Silas actually suggested detonating a small nuclear weapon on the seabed. "It's simple physics. Figure out how much force we want to apply to the hull, account for the transmission through the rock formation, and then drop the device far enough away. Boom. The sub rolls upright and up they come."

Unfortunately, the general consensus was that the resulting blast would still crush what was left of *Severod-*

vinsk like a dented beer can, and besides, there wasn't enough time to do all the necessary calculations to figure out if it were truly feasible. Sometimes, physics isn't quite so simple.

Each scheme, no matter how harebrained, was inspected, measured, and eventually found wanting, either time or technical reasons, sometimes both. It was pointless, but there was nothing else to do while they waited.

USS *Seawolf*

They listened to the conversation between Petrov and Admiral Borisov over the underwater telephone. Rudel didn't have anything to add; besides, he wasn't part of the Russian chain of command. There'd be opportunities to talk later, when Petrov might need it more.

Most of *Seawolf*'s officers had also gathered in their wardroom. They weren't as shy as *Churchill*'s or Patterson's people. Shimko had called it a "deathwatch" from the start. Men like them, men they could easily have been, were slipping off the edge of existence. Jerry, Shimko, Lavoie, and others sat and talked about what should happen next, or what should have happened.

"The big mistake was getting too cocky," Shimko declared. "We got complacent and assumed nobody was in the area, so we got sloppy in our searching when we were recovering the UUVs. We could have placed one in a position to cover our blind spot aft, to make sure we weren't caught unawares."

Jerry shook his head. "That would have meant less survey time for the UUVs on each sortie, and we have a limited number of sorties. We would have been out here longer, which would have increased our risk of discovery.

No, all I had to do was realize that the Russian, Petrov, was trying to cut a tether that Patty didn't have. If we had sent Patty straight away at max speed, Petrov would have seen his mistake."

Lavoie disagreed this time. "That only explains the first two passes. By the third pass, he had doped it out. On the third pass he was trying to corral *Seawolf*."

"And once he'd made that decision, the result was inevitable." Rudel's voice surprised them, and they started to rise, but he motioned for them to sit. He poured himself a cup of coffee, then sat down wearily. "I don't like my stateroom right now." He paused for a moment, contemplating, searching for the right words. "There's no rule that says there has to be a solution for every problem. Sometimes you're just going to be on the receiving end, no matter what you do."

"How do you handle those situations, sir?" Will Hayes asked, frustrated and perplexed.

"Many times, Will, there are answers," Rudel replied, "but that's not when you earn your pay. You get paid the big bucks for situations like this—when all the outcomes are bad. Having to choose between rival goods, or worse, rival evils, is when one truly understands the burden of command."

He paused again; nobody spoke, or even moved. Rudel continued, "Recovering from a complicated, dangerous situation, with no outcomes but lousy choices, requires more than skill. Beating yourselves up over the road not taken is worse than a distraction. It may lead you to believe that you're no longer able to make a good decision. Learning from the past is the mark of a good officer, but don't *ever* think it has all the right answers."

Rudel leaned back, seeming to sit straighter than before. Looking around the wardroom table, he noticed Lieutenant (j.g.) Williams. As the damage-control assistant, he was responsible for life support on *Seawolf* and was the resident expert on a sub's atmosphere. "Todd, what's your estimate?"

"Based on Petrov's last report, carbon dioxide is probably near three point four or three point five percent now. It will build up very quickly once it's over four percent." He seemed reluctant to give any details, but finally concluded, "I don't think anyone's going to be conscious in twelve hours."

Rudel nodded. "Thanks, Todd. That matches my own estimate."

"What about ballons? Flotation bags? We could put them in the damaged ballast tanks, or have the Norwegians weld attachment points right to the hull." Ensign Santana looked excited, hopeful. "There's room for dozens of lines to be rigged, and it could be done quickly."

Rudel answered, "No, they thought of that on day one. Putting the bags inside is a good solution, but the ballast tanks would have to be opened up even more to get the bags inside. It would have taken too long, about a week. Now we've got less than a day. And just attaching bags to the hull? *Severodvinsk* displaces some twelve *thousand* tons submerged, and then add the water in three or four flooded compartments. She probably displaces close to fifteen thousand tons. How many bags would we need to shift her?"

Lavoie added, "That's more right than you know, sir. I just spoke with *Halsfjord*'s chief engineer. Lindstrom and the rest of his team are kicking themselves. They're still trying to figure out why their plan didn't work. He wanted to run over some of the figures. So many tons from the tugs, so many from flooding the starboard tanks, and so on."

The engineer explained, "Their problem wasn't that the mooring point pulled loose from the sub's hull. At that time, the tugs were at full power, and *Severodvinsk* hadn't shifted a single degree! She should have shown some sort of movement. Their bet is that if the fitting hadn't come off one of the cables would have parted."

Rudel sighed. "In other words, they just couldn't couple enough force to *Severodvinsk*'s hull to do the job."

Lavoie said, "The only thing they could have changed was to push *Severodvinsk* from the side with AS-34, but that only increased the total force on her hull by a few percent. And that's before *Priz*'s batteries failed. She was never really an option."

Jerry's eyes widened a little bit. In that quiet gathering, several people noticed his hopeful expression. "What is it?" asked Shimko.

"What if we did the pushing?" The idea, half-formed, took shape as he spoke. "We don't ram *Severodvinsk.* Ease in. We can use Maxine to guide us. Make contact at a slow creep, and then carefully increase power in stages. And unlike tow cables, we apply the force directly, hull-to-hull contact."

Nobody responded immediately, although from their expressions it was clear they had heard him. "Brute force," he explained. "*Seawolf* can generate nearly three times the push of both those tugs."

Lavoie was the first to respond. "But our bow . . ."

Then Chandler said, "They'll never agree . . ."

And Wolfe replied, "Hell, we're going in the yards anyway."

Shimko started to speak, then paused, and stated flatly, "The forward pressure hull is not at full strength. It might not hold. If it goes, we'll be in the hurt locker."

Jerry answered, "Once we start pushing, it will only take a few minutes to do the job. We'll be ready for it, and do an emergency blow the moment the escape chamber separates."

Lavoie speculated, "We'd have to cut away some of the

debris forward to make a smoother contact surface. The supporting structure for the forward arrays is like a spear. It would slice right through *Severodvinsk*."

"Skipper, we can do this," Jerry pleaded. Captain Rudel had sat silently through the exchange, listening. Like every other officer in the room, Jerry could see him calculating. *Seawolf* added almost forty-six thousand shaft horsepower to the equation.

Rudel stood suddenly and headed for the wardroom door. "We'll meet back here with department heads and chief of the boat in fifteen minutes . . ." He paused, since two-thirds of his wardroom was already there, and added, "Others may also attend. Have a rough draft of the procedure and a timeline ready for me."

He turned to leave, but then looked back. "Mr. Lavoie, calculate how long we can handle flooding forward before we can't surface from an emergency blow."

Rudel disappeared, and Jerry helped Shimko summon the few missing officers and chiefs to the wardroom.

USS *Churchill*

"It's *Seawolf,* ma'am, Commander Rudel is on the scrambler phone." Everyone in the wardroom mirrored Patterson's puzzled look. All other ship-to-ship communications had been in the clear.

"He says it's urgent, ma'am. Captain Baker is already in CIC."

Patterson knew the way well enough by now that the messenger let her set the pace while he followed. In CIC, Baker stood, holding the handset. "All he'd say is that he has to tell you first."

"Tell me what?" Patterson asked as she took the handset. "This is Dr. Patterson," she said cautiously.

"We've got a plan to save *Severodvinsk*." His explanation followed so quickly and was so fantastic that she had him repeat it—twice.

By the time he'd finished, Baker had guessed enough from her side of the conversation to understand Rudel's plan, and he wondered if his expression matched hers.

"And you're just *informing* me? Not asking my permission?"

She heard Rudel sigh. "If I ask your permission, you might say no. If you say yes, you could be buying yourself some serious trouble. I don't want to take anybody else down with me."

"Forget that, Captain. Are you sure *Seawolf* will come out of this intact?"

"I wouldn't suggest it otherwise."

Rudel sounded defensive, and she quickly said, "I'm sorry, Captain, but I had to ask that question. You not only have my official permission, but my cooperation. What can we do?"

"I'll know that after my officers tell me. Can you please call Admiral Borisov and Arne Lindstrom? Set up a conference call for thirty minutes from now?"

"When will you be ready?" she asked.

"They're going to tell me that, too." After a short pause, he added, "We will be ready in time."

"Then I will speak with you again in half an hour, Captain, and God bless you."

"I hope so. We'll need all the help we can get."

Petr Velikiy

When he heard the topic, Admiral Borisov had followed Patterson's advice and cleared the flag plot of everyone but Kurganov and their two deputies. He didn't know what would be worse: Hearing some bizarre scheme that was doomed to fail, or having to hope again.

Lindstróm was on the screen five minutes early, fidgeting in front of the TV camera, then Patterson and Baker sitting together, and finally Rudel, looking hurried, almost breathless. His watchstanders had reported *Seawolf* surfacing ten minutes earlier.

"Admiral, Doctor, Captain, Mr. Lindstrom, thank you for agreeing to listen to me. My officers and I have a plan that has a good chance of working. But we will need help to make it work, and I'm open to any suggestions that will improve it."

Borisov spoke first. "Petrov and his men will not be able to move into the chamber for much longer. Even if they move in now, they will not be able to release it if they are unconscious."

Rudel asked, "What is your best estimate of their CO_2 level?"

"They could start losing consciousness in as little as eight hours. Some perhaps as long as fifteen."

"Then we need every welder and engineer in the rescue force. It would be best if we tied up alongside *Halsfjord*. Is that acceptable, Mr. Lindstrom?"

Lindstrom looked off-camera and spoke in Norwegian briefly. "Yes, port side. Bow-to-bow?"

Rudel shook his head. "No sir, bow-to-stern. We need your aft fifty-ton crane to lift out the damaged forward array structure once it is detached. Perhaps *Pamir* and *Altay* can moor outboard of us. Detaching the forward arrays and cleaning up the surface will take the most time, and anything we can do to speed that up will help."

Kurganov added, "*Rudnitskiy* will join you as well. She has divers for the underwater work."

"What about cushioning the impact?" Lindstrom asked. "We could construct a framework of timbers that would fit over your bow. My men could fabricate it on deck while others are cutting away the arrays and their mountings."

"How long?" Rudel asked.

"No longer than it takes to remove the sonar structure," Lindstrom answered. He looked to the side and spoke in Norwegian. "And we've just started."

The two Russians spoke briefly, then Borisov said, "We assume you will also be reinforcing your pressure hull."

Rudel shrugged. "We will do what we can, but space is limited."

Borisov spoke again, smiling. "I noticed during my visit to *Seawolf* that the shoring in your electronics space was wooden, with brackets spot-welded in place."

"That's correct."

"Russian damage-control shoring is steel, in prefabricated sections, with threaded brackets on the end to ensure a snug fit. Would they be of use to you?"

Rudel smiled. "I'd gratefully accept them, gentlemen."

"Can this be done in time?" Kurganov asked. "On our boats the main hydroacoustic array and its mounting weigh over ten tons."

Rudel answered, "Things come apart a lot faster than they go together." He smiled. "And we don't have to worry about being neat."

Severodvinsk

Petrov hadn't expected a call from Borisov so soon. It had been only an hour or so since the last conversation. The final good-byes would come later, so he assumed the admiral wanted to ask about the carbon dioxide levels. Useless, really, but there was nothing else to do.

"Captain Petrov, prepare to get your men back into the escape chamber."

"What? I just finished getting my men out of it. They will be much more comfortable in the hull."

"Rudel has a plan to right your boat." Borisov started describing it, but Petrov grasped it almost immediately, and cut off the admiral. "Is he insane? Have you all lost your minds? We don't need another boat next to us."

"He is convinced this will work, and he has convinced all of us as well: Lindstrom, Patterson, everyone. Work has already started."

"Can I speak to him?" Petrov asked.

"*Seawolf* is already surrounded by other vessels. With all the noise, I doubt if her underwater telephone would even function. You should see it, Aleksey. It would amaze you. Foreign vessels, including a Russian salvage and rescue ship, surround an American nuclear submarine preparing it for this effort. Workers from three countries cover the bow like ants. And there are over half a dozen divers underwater right now with their cutting torches blazing, a dozen more standing by."

Borisov's description fired his imagination. Petrov's first surprise had worn off, and his mind had begun to consider the plan more dispassionately. Would it work? The problem with believing in that plan was that Petrov and his men had already begun to accept their fate. He didn't know if they could hope again, or withstand the fear that came with it.

The admiral described Rudel's plan in more detail, and explained, "You must move up into the chamber as soon as you can, while your men still have the strength to do so."

Petrov answered, "Some of them have taken sedatives. I'll have to see what Balanov can do to rouse them. And the extra activity will drive the carbon dioxide levels even higher."

"We've factored that into our calculations. And we'll need hourly updates, to check those figures."

"You'll have them, Admiral. And tell Rudel to make a careful job of it. No rushed work. That's when accidents happen."

The White House

President Huber didn't mind the budget meeting being interrupted, but he had a vital meeting with an industry group in fifteen minutes that he couldn't ignore. Wright had insisted the call was extremely urgent.

"Sir, I've just spoken with Dr. Patterson. There's to be another attempt to save the Russian sub."

"What?" Huber's voice showed more confusion than was expected from a chief executive. "You told me not half an hour ago that there was nothing more to be done. My people are working on a statement of condolence now."

"They still need two statements. They are making hurried preparations now, and should be ready in about six or seven hours. Petrov and his men could begin to lose consciousness in as little as eight."

"That's cutting it a little close," Huber observed.

"It's a last-minute thing, Mr. President." He described how Rudel would use *Seawolf* to push *Severodvinsk* upright. "And the Russians are completely on board. There is some risk, sir, but Dr. Patterson says she's been reassured by Rudel and other qualified engineers that everything will be done to reduce it. And no, she doesn't have a number."

"I asked her to keep me informed," Huber grumbled.

"And she's doing so, sir."

"And like before, the only control I have is to order her to stop."

"You could give that order, sir. You took control of the situation by sending good people."

"And they'll try in six hours?"

"That's the estimate as of now, sir. If this works, it will be successful immediately."

"Keep me informed."

Halsfjord

Rudel and Shimko stood on the aft deckhouse, looking down at the fantail. The Norwegian rescue ship had enough room aft to land a large helicopter. Now the flood-lit surface was cluttered with men and a gridwork of timbers. The heavy lengths of wood were carried aboard the rescue ship for just such a circumstance. A strong framework could be quickly assembled to reinforce a damaged ship, or construct a cofferdam.

Rudel could see that the box-frame-like structure was well along. Lindstrom explained how it would be attached to the hull. "The welders will attach plates at the front edge of the hull. Stubs on the edge of the framework will be attached with simple pins to those plates. After you're done it will be simple to detach whatever's left and cut off the attachment plates."

"After we're done," Rudel muttered. "I like the sound of that."

"We've based it on the blueprints you provided. We will lower it into place and attach it literally in minutes."

"And it will be ready in time." Shimko didn't ask a question, but Lindstrom reassured him. "My chief engineer says they will be finished cutting in two, maybe three more hours. There is a lot of very tough metal to cut through. The framework is actually almost done. Until we need to lift it over to *Seawolf,* we will reinforce it and improve the design.

"The work on your forward ballast tanks is also proceeding, and will be done in time."

Rudel answered, "Keeping any air in those tanks at all will be a tremendous help."

Lindstrom shrugged. "Removing the antisonar coating around the holes is taking time, but as each section is cleared, we start patching it. The patches won't be completely airtight, of course, but they should help."

"We're very grateful," Rudel said.

Lindstrom grinned. "Don't thank me. I'm adding all this work to the Russians' bill." A shout in Norwegian attracted his attention, and he excused himself, saying "Please, stay as long as you like. I'll send a messenger when the Russians are ready."

The two Americans watched the frantic work on *Halsfjord*'s fantail, then walked over to the port side and looked down at *Seawolf.* Even though she was lit up by dozens of lights, they could still easily see welding flames and sparks almost covering the bow. The water in front of her glowed with the cutting torches from divers working on the structure underneath, and even more men were at work in the electronics equipment space. Only the Norwegians and Americans were being allowed inside the sub, but there were plenty to do the work.

"They're working damn fast, XO," commented Rudel approvingly. "Pretty soon we'll see if this semi-crazy idea of ours really works."

"Ah, Skipper? Sir, there's one thing. That order you gave about nonessential personnel?" There was concern in Shimko's voice.

"What about it, XO?"

"Nobody will leave, sir. The officers and chiefs say everyone is essential, and when I tell the men individually, they respectfully refuse to carry out my order. All of them."

"Dammit, XO, I made it an order because I knew nobody would leave voluntarily. It's no disgrace. We drop them off just before we make the dive, and pick them up as soon as it's done. They'll wait on *Halsfjord* for what? An hour? Fewer lives at risk."

"'Fewer men to help' was the universal response," Shimko reported.

Rudel sighed heavily, leaning on the deckhouse rail. "This could go south in a dozen different ways we can't imagine."

"True, sir, so it may be hard to say who's 'essential' and who isn't."

"So you disagree with my order as well?" Rudel sounded surprised.

"Disagree, maybe, sir, but never disobey." Shimko continued, "I think they all appreciated the thought, Skipper, but nobody wants to be left out, so to speak."

"I think the appropriate word describing this is 'mutiny,' Mr. Shimko," Rudel grumbled.

"Other captains would kill to have a crew this undisciplined," countered Shimko with a wide grin.

"Then belay my last."

THE "RUSSIANS" Lindstrom had referred to were Vice Admiral Borisov and Rear Admiral Oleg Antonovich Smelkov, chief of the Technical Directorate of the Northern Fleet. Both joined by teleconference, Borisov from *Petya* and Smelkov from his office ashore. Patterson and her group aboard *Churchill* were also electronically present.

Smelkov didn't look like an admiral. A harried bank clerk, maybe. Or possibly a university professor during exam week. His uniform coat was off, and he sat at his desk, surrounded by computer printouts. Two voices spoke quickly offscreen.

They had gathered to hear Smelkov answer the big question: Where to push? Smelkov was not only a naval constructor, he had helped describe the fleet's requirement for *Severodvinsk,* and then supervised her construction.

Smelkov was pale, with hair so blond that at first glance it seemed white. His thin face added to the first impression of an elderly man, almost frail. Then he spoke, and twenty years disappeared.

He didn't waste time. "I will hope my English is acceptable. The answer to your first question is no. Not only is it too close to the escape chamber, but the sail's structure was never designed to withstand that much side force. It would most likely rip clear of the hull.

"So, if you must push on the hull itself, I say here." He typed for a moment, and the image changed to show a cross-section of *Severodvinsk.* A heavy black line just inside the outer hull showed the pressure hull, divided into compartments by similar lines.

A circle marked a spot on the lower hull, just aft of the sail. "This is in the center of the third compartment. You must set your depth so you are below the hull's centerline. It will overhang your bow. When you push, also blow your forwardmost tanks to lift as well. Is this clear?"

"Yes," Rudel answered simply. "Have you calculated how much force we will need?"

Smelkov shook his head. "There is no way to know. Mr. Lindstrom's first figures were very reasonable, and his preparations very thorough. It should have worked. The only conclusion I can make is that *Severodvinsk*'s lower hull has been caught on the uneven surface she lies on."

"Snagged on the rocks," Rudel suggested.

"Yes," Smelkov answered.

"That is our theory as well," Lindstrom added.

"When you first start to push, the outer hull will give way. This is acceptable. It may even form a 'pocket,' or recess that will prevent your bow from sliding to the left or right."

"When will *Severodvinsk*'s pressure hull give way?"

Smelkov threw up his hands. "I estimate near two-thirds of your full power, Captain Rudel. The hull is designed to resist the steady pressure of the sea and sudden shocks from torpedoes and depth bombs. This will be localized, like a depth-bomb attack, but longer, and harder. The hull will deform before it fails."

"Which Petrov and his men won't be able to see, because he will be in the escape chamber," Rudel concluded.

"Given Petrov's situation, the additional danger is irrelevant," Borisov added. "No, Captain, before Petrov would start moving his men into the escape chamber again, he said he was not climbing out, no matter what happened.

"Also, I have a message from Olga Sadilenko. Do you know her?" Rudel nodded and Borisov read from a sheet of paper. "She says they are praying for the crews of both submarines, and that you and your men are very brave, as brave as her son's crew. I will add my own prayers to hers."

"Thank you, Admiral, and thank Mrs. Sadilenko for us."

"Good luck to us all."

Severodvinsk

It had taken almost two hours to move the men. Everyone was weak. Some refused to make the climb and had to be bullied, almost dragged to the ladder. As desperate as they were for light, warmth, life itself, they dreaded the thought of climbing into the escape chamber.

This time, he'd sent Lyachin up right away to supervise the loading inside the cylindrical capsule. Kalinin remained at the base of the ladder, cajoling and hectoring the men into climbing faster, or even climbing at all.

Finally, the injured had been moved, the logbooks and classified material stowed, and Petrov reported to the surface. "Comrade Admiral, *Severodvinsk* is ready."

"Very good, Captain. What is your CO_2 level?"

"Fonarin just took a new reading. It's three point seven percent."

Borisov didn't reply immediately, and Petrov added, "We're still breathing, Admiral."

"Good. They are getting ready to fit the wooden framework over *Seawolf*'s bow. Then they will get under way and submerge. It should be no more than half an hour."

"I would prefer to remain in contact until the Americans are ready. Is that acceptable?"

"As long as you can get into the escape chamber in good order, that will be fine."

"Yes, sir. We will stand by for your call."

Petrov hung up the microphone and sat down wearily. It took all his concentration to manage a simple conversation. The constant headache made thought almost impossible. Still, he had to keep thinking.

Only four officers were left in the central post: Petrov, Kalinin, Fonarin, and Mitrov. There was nothing left to do.

"One collision put us here, another will save us."

"*Will,* comrade Captain?"

"I believe in having a positive attitude, comrade Starpom." He smiled. "Besides, the surface holds its own hazards. The fresh air may finish me off."

Fonarin chimed in. "I'm willing to risk it, sir."

"You're a brave man, Igor Mikhailovich." Kalinin grinned. "Such sacrifice."

"And I'll risk the real food," Mitrov said.

"And warmth," Kalinin added.

"As long as they have enough painkillers for our headaches," Petrov commented, and they all agreed.

"What will you do after we get home, sir?"

"Fill out a great many forms, I fear." They laughed for a moment at his joke, but it was dark humor. "There must be a lot of paperwork involved with the loss of a submarine—and people."

"It wasn't entirely your fault, sir," Kalinin said.

"Whether or not I was completely or partially at fault is irrelevant, Vasiliy, the safety of this ship and crew is ultimately my responsibility, and mine alone. In any case, there's a shortage of boats in the fleet. I doubt if I'll get another command right away." Petrov saw their expressions, and smiled. "Do not worry, shipmates, I now have a new standard for what to call a 'bad day.' "

They ran through the checklist again, slowly, just to burn up time, and then speculated about what Admiral Borisov would say in his welcome-aboard speech. He was, after all, an admiral, so there would have to be a speech.

Rudel's voice jolted them out of the desultory conversation. As Petrov grabbed the microphone, the American reported, "*Seawolf* to *Severodvinsk,* we are ready."

"*Seawolf,* this is Petrov. Nobody's ever ready for this. For the record, I still think you're insane."

"It will take us about ten minutes to get in position. How long do you need to board the escape chamber?"

"Give us five minutes, starting now, my friend, then give it your best. *Severodvinsk* out."

USS *Seawolf*

Rudel had sounded General Quarters as soon as they'd left *Halsfjord.* Palmer had Maxine in the water a few minutes later heading for her preprogrammed observation point. The instant she was clear, Jerry said, "Recommend course three two seven to the initial point at ten knots, time to initial point four and one half minutes."

"I'm going to keep her at five knots, Jerry. No sense

stressing the framework," replied Rudel. For this evolution, the captain had the deck and the conn.

"Understood, sir." Jerry watched QM1 Peters update the chart and the log.

"Chief of the watch, how are the ballast tanks holding?"

"Better than before, sir," Chief McCord said cautiously. "One alpha and one bravo were still bleeding a little when we tested them with the low-pressure blower, but I think they will give us enough buoyancy."

Rudel ordered, "Save the high-pressure air for the right moment, Chief. I don't mind being heavy by the bow when we start pushing. Once we've started, then keep number-one main ballast tank as full as you can."

"Keep it full when we push aye, sir," McCord responded automatically.

Jerry updated their position. "Five minutes to initial point. Recommend keel depth of six hundred and forty feet. Recommend port turn at that time to approach course of two seven four."

"Diving officer, make our depth six hundred and forty feet. Jerry, does that approach course allow for the cross-current?"

"I've factored in a two-knot southerly current sir."

"Very good."

"No vibration at five knots," Rudel observed. "The Norwegians did a good job."

"The pitlog reads four point three knots with turns ordered for five," Shimko observed. "We may slow down faster than we'd planned."

Jerry nodded. "We knew there'd be drag, but not this much. I'll work on it." He added, "Peters, time the turn, please." The QM1 nodded.

"Torpedo room, conn. Report on Maxine's status."

Palmer's voice answered immediately. "Conn, torpedo

room. In position, in line with both subs. *Severodvinsk* is one hundred and twenty-three feet in front of her."

"Excellent," Rudel answered. "Start feeding us ranges as soon as we make the turn."

"Conn, torpedo room aye."

"One minute to turn—mark!" Peters reported. "Recommend slowing to three knots at the time of the turn." Jerry was still working furiously, calculating *Seawolf*'s new drag factor.

Rudel divided his gaze between the displays and the clock. "Stand by . . . Left standard rudder, steady on course two seven four, speed three knots."

The helmsman repeated the order, and as the bow swung over, Palmer's voice reported, "Conn, torpedo room. Range one thousand twenty yards." Chief McCord acknowledged his report.

"Jerry, what's the drag figure?"

The navigator didn't reply immediately, but Peters, watching him work, looked up to the XO and nodded reassuringly. Ten seconds later, Jerry announced, "Recommend stopping engines one hundred and forty yards from *Severodvinsk*."

"That's pretty close," Rudel observed, "just over a boat length."

"With a smooth bow from three knots, it's four hundred. We'd figured two fifty, but the drag is greater—much greater than we originally thought."

"Then we'll stop at one forty," Rudel concluded.

"Range is eight hundred yards, bearing of *Seawolf* from Maxine shows slight left drift."

"Change your course to two seven six," Rudel ordered. "Sonar, conn. Watch the bearing to Maxine's sonar. We need it to be steady."

"Conn, sonar, aye. Current bearing is two seven five."

"Depth is six hundred forty feet, sir," reported Hess.

"Range is six hundred yards," relayed McCord.

"Casualty-assistance team, report status of the electronics equipment space," barked Rudel.

The IC man on the phones spoke briefly. Jerry's people were supposed to be standing by next to the electronics room. With all the extra shoring that had been added, there was barely room for a man to stand. The switchboards were wrapped with several layers of plastic, techs stood by with parts and tools at the ready. Additional personnel were staged just inside the crew's quarters.

"Seaman Blocker reports they're ready. Chief Hudson is watching both the packing glands and the reinforcing frames."

"Very well," Rudel acknowledged. Mentally, Jerry crossed his fingers.

"Four hundred yards."

"Sonar, conn. What's the bearing to Maxine?"

"Steady at two seven five."

Rudel picked up the 1MC. "All hands, this is the Captain. We are about five minutes from contact. Be ready to brace for impact, and after that, be ready for anything." Then he keyed the intercom. "Torpedo room, conn. Give me a mark at one hundred forty yards."

"Conn, torpedo room. Understood. Stand by . . . Stand by . . . Mark!"

"Helm, all stop!" It was the only time Jerry heard Rudel speak in louder than conversational tones. "Chief, watch your air. Save enough for the final blow."

"Save enough for the final blow, aye," McCord responded.

"Sound the collision alarm!" McCord pulled the lever and *SCREE, SCREE, SCREE* echoed. In spite of all their careful preparations, Jerry's chest tightened. His mouth felt like it was filled with sand. Intentionally running into another submarine? This just wasn't natural.

They waited, while Jerry counted down the carefully calculated two and a third minutes it would take for *Seawolf* to drift to a dead stop. In a perfect world, that would leave her modified bow just touching *Severodvinsk*'s hull.

Jerry's nightmare was that he'd overestimated the drag, that *Seawolf* would drift to a stop short of her goal, hanging in the water helpless to cover the last ten or thirty yards without using the screws. That meant a low-speed collision, but even walking speed times nine thousand-some-odd tons . . .

It wasn't a sound as much as a vibration, a grinding sensation that seemed to push the bow down slightly as they slowed. There was an uneven crackling mixed in—the wooden framework.

Shimko grinned. "Bow down. That means we're under her—right where we're supposed to be."

Rudel fired orders. "Status in the electronic equipment space." Over the intercom, "Torpedo room, conn. Reposition Maxine." Then he turned to the control room crew. "But we're not waiting. All ahead dead slow."

The talker waited for the helmsman's echoed reply before reporting, "Electronics equipment space is dry."

Rudel grinned. "This is a good start." He held one palm flat against a metal surface, feeling the boat's engines as well as her contact with the Russian's hull. Jerry did the same. As the normal-sounding thrum of the screw increased, the grinding, crunching sensation decreased, the relatively light pressure holding the bow in place, preventing further movement.

"Helm, all ahead slow. Torpedo room, conn. Is Maxine in position yet?"

"Conn, torpedo room. She's moving now, sir. In position in less than a minute."

"Understood, Mr. Palmer. You know what we're looking for."

"I'll report any rotation of the hull."

Jerry felt the hull shudder a little as the screw increased its turns from "dead slow" to "slow." Although it seemed like a small change, at those RPMs the screw had enough power to push nine thousand tons of submarine through the water at three knots.

Severodvinsk

There'd been no warning before the gentle crunch of *Seawolf*'s bow contacting the hull. Strapped in, Petrov pictured wood and metal being compressed, breaking, bending. The wood structure would press against the rubberized coating . . .

There. Rudel had added some power, just a little. Petrov was surprised at how clearly he could feel the screw's effects. That meant a good contact between the two vessels, and an efficient transfer of engine power.

He looked at the inclinometer. It hadn't moved, but it was early yet. He was optimistic.

USS *Seawolf*

"Helm, all ahead one-third."

Rudel's voice was firm, firmer than Jerry thought his might be giving that order. Real power was beginning to run through the ship's structure, and the shuddering sped up into a strong vibration. Jerry imagined the boat on hard rubber wheels, rolling over the rumble strips on a highway.

But it was just a vibration, steadily increasing. The electronic equipment space was still dry. When he heard the report, Shimko said, "We need to buy those Norwegians a drink."

"More than one," Rudel answered. He keyed the intercom again. "Topedo room, conn. Report."

"Conn, torpedo room. We're in position, sir. The image has a lot of static near our bow. That's probably air bubbles from main ballast tanks one alpha and one bravo." Palmer sighed, then added, "*Severodvinsk* has not moved yet."

"We're not done yet, Mr. Palmer . . ." Rudel was interrupted by a piercing groan, a sound of metal being stressed. It was loud enough to make conversation impossible, and it went on for several moments.

Shimko tried to give an order to the phone talker, but couldn't make himself understood. He was repeating himself when the groan, becoming almost a howl, suddenly stopped. ". . . report! All compartments report any damage."

The phone talker, eyes as wide as everyone else's, passed the word, and immediately reported, "There's a seawater leak in the electronic equipment space! Chief Hudson says it's from a packing gland around number two periscope. They're handling it."

Rudel seemed artificially calm as he acknowledged the report, then spoke to Shimko. "What do you think, XO? Stresses on the hull adjusting themselves?"

The XO made a face. "Yes, but where? At the bow? Near the mast's penetrations? Somewhere else? We weren't designed to push. This may void the warranty."

"Casualty-assistance team reports they're having problems slowing the flow of water."

"Very well. Helm, all ahead two-thirds."

"What?" Shimko was alarmed. "Skipper, shouldn't we control the leak first?"

Rudel shook his head. "If we're doing this, let's do it quickly." The deck shuddered again, and for the first time, there was a small sideways lurch. "Chief, how's main ballast tank one holding?"

McCord replied, "I'm bleeding air in slowly to maintain pressure. We can do this for a little longer—maybe four, five minutes."

"Level us if you can, Chief. I want our stern no higher than our bow, so we're pushing up."

"Pumping water from forward trim to after trim."

Several of the displays in control suddenly went dark. As Rudel and Shimko turned to the phone talker, he reported, "They're securing power to the electronic equipment space! The leak's become a spray." After a pause, he added, "The gravity drains are handling it, so far."

The displays went dark again, and stayed that way. Immediately the helmsman reported, "Sir, the rudder has shifted to emergency hydraulic control."

Severodvinsk

Seawolf must be putting some real power into their engines now. Sitting at the top of the sail, Petrov could feel a back-and-forth vibration, as if the American submarine was straining against some great weight. He was encouraged that the motion was side to side, although now he was worried that when they did finally move, they might roll too far, to end up trapped lying on their starboard side.

To guard against that chance, Petrov kept his hand resting on the red-and-yellow-striped handle that would release the chamber from the sail. It was a simple mechanical release. Normally one wouldn't rest one's hand on any control, to prevent it being accidentally triggered. He smiled at the thought of that happening.

It was hardest on the injured. The vibrations were strong enough to cause them real pain, and Balanov had unstrapped himself and was doing his best to cushion their hurts, and administering more painkillers. Petrov watched him, but didn't caution the doctor about moving around. He had his work, and besides, what was one more risk?

Petrov stared at the inclinometer, willing it to change.

USS *Seawolf*

"Skipper, I'm losing pressure in main ballast tank one alpha. It's almost gone." Chief McCord added, "The Norwegians' patch must have given way. The other tank is still all right."

"All engines ahead standard."

"Electronic equipment space, report."

"Chief Hudson says there is a half-inch solid stream from the number two scope's packing. The backup team is on the scene and they are trying to plug it somehow, but there's a lot of pressure. Robinson got caught in the stream and got pretty banged up. He's on his way to sickbay."

"Very well. Tell Hudson to just contain the flooding and watch those frames."

The phone talker relayed Rudel's order. The flooding was bad enough. Water would accumulate and weigh down the bow. But they'd told Jerry about Smelkov's estimate. At two-thirds power, *Seawolf* would begin to deform *Severodvinsk*'s pressure hull. But when would *Seawolf*'s start to go?

Seawolf's hull was already stressed, and weaker as a result of the collision. If the frames started to bend, there would be no more time, no warning.

"All ahead full." The captain's voice was calm, but he couldn't hide his anxiety.

"I'm losing pressure in one bravo," McCord reported. Rudel nodded acknowledgment. Jerry could see him trying to visualize the two hulls, feeling how they were fitting together. What would make the Russian move?

The vibration was audible now, and so uneven that the control room crew either strapped themselves in or braced themselves as best they could. The deck shifted from side to side, and occasionally pitched up or down, as if the entire sub was fishtailing as it struggled to shift *Severodvinsk*'s hull.

"All ahead flank. Maneuvering, make maximum turns!" Rudel shouted.

Rudel's final engine order started to have an effect. Racing through the water at full power, Jerry remembered how *Seawolf*'s hull seemed almost alive with energy. Now her struggles grew more violent.

An upward jolt almost knocked Jerry from his feet, and some of the watch cried out in surprise. Another followed, and another.

"Control room, torpedo. The sail's moving!"

Palmer's report pulled Rudel over to the intercom. "How much?"

"Five degrees, maybe more. Those shocks we just felt were the start. Definitely more, approaching eight degrees now."

"Captain!" shouted the phone talker. "Chief Hudson reports there are now multiple leaks in the overhead in the electronics equipment space."

Severodvinsk

When the motion came, Petrov only knew it because of the inclinometer. The vibrations were so strong that he had become almost numb. It was impossible to tell whether they moved him to the left or right or backward.

But his vision had been fixed on the inclinometer, and it had changed. He called out "Thirty degrees!" Then came another shock, hard enough to make some of the uninjured men cry out in alarm, but Petrov called, "Twenty-four degrees!"

He heard cheers and prayers, and encouragements to the Americans to keep pushing. Petrov kept his eyes fixed on the inclinometer. His left hand squeezed the release handle so hard it hurt.

USS *Seawolf*

A series of sideways jolts made the hull creak, then a sharp downward bump seemed to allow *Seawolf* to slide forward. Shimko asked nervously, "What are we doing, tunneling under the Russian?"

"A little scared, XO?"

"Sir, a wise man said that fear is just excitement in need of an attitude adjustment!"

Rudel shook his head. His executive officer was a certified loon, for that matter so was the rest of this crew.

Looking over at the chief of the watch, he shouted, "We have to get her bow up. Fill after trim to the mark and blow a little air into main ballast tank two." As heavy as the bow was, they had to make the stern heavier. Jerry remembered an old submariner initiation. "Skipper, send the crew aft."

Rudel nodded and grabbed the 1MC microphone. "All hands not on duty, to the shaft alley on the double." There was no way to tell if it was enough, or if it mattered at all, but it was the best they could do.

"We're using the boat like a giant crowbar," Rudel muttered. "A nuclear-powered crowbar. This can't be good for the hull." But they all felt another sharp jolt, and it was a welcome sensation.

"That's doing it!" Palmer's report on the intercom was encouraging, if nonregulation. But was it enough?

"What about the escape chamber?" Rudel demanded.

"It's still in place," Palmer reported. "It looks like the angle is less than twenty degrees. They should have released the capsule. Are they all unconscious?"

"We are not stopping until the chamber is released!"

"Chief Hudson reports leaks from all mast penetrations. He can also see the hull frames starting to bend. He says it's small, but it's definite."

"Sir, I recommend we put her on the roof, *now*!" Shimko's request was soft, but urgent.

"Not until that escape chamber leaves," Rudel insisted.

Their conversation was punctuated by more jolts and another long groan. Suddenly, ET2 Lamberth appeared at the forward door to control. He was soaked to the skin, shivering and breathless, a cut on his arm. "Captain, Chief Hudson reports that some of the shoring arms are starting to buckle. He says to tell you we are officially on borrowed time!"

Severodvinsk

Petrov pulled the release almost before he understood the numbers. First, the inclinometer had jumped from twenty-three to seventeen, then back to twenty-five before he could move his arm. He cursed, afraid he'd missed his chance, when the numbers began to crawl down again, each short jerk counting the angle down a little more each time. Finally, it stayed below fifteen and they were free.

They never heard or felt the clamps release, not with all the other noise and vibration, but to Petrov it felt as if they'd been thrown upward toward the surface. The deck, canted for so long, suddenly felt properly level, and he could sense the upward acceleration as they rose.

The submariner in him wanted to time the ascent, to double-check his calculation of one minute forty-nine seconds, but instead, Petrov started to laugh, almost uncontrollably. Relief flooded through him, and he felt weak, still in a state of astonishment.

It took all his strength to lift his head and look at the men around him. They were mirrors of himself, many laughing or cheering if they weren't weeping or simply screaming at the top of their lungs. Nobody was cold, or had a headache, or was hungry any longer. They were rising from the dead.

USS *Seawolf*

"Conn!" screamed Palmer. "I can see the chamber. It's clear!"

"Helm, all back full!" Jerry heard Palmer's report, and some part of him was glad, but now it was time to focus on their own immediate concerns.

"All pumps to maximum! Chief, get as much water out of the bow as you can."

"Working it, Skipper." McCord's hand flew over the ballast-control panel, trying to purge the ship of the weight they'd just desperately needed.

Jerry felt the vibrations beneath the deck become weaker, then start again. Lavoie and his engineers had stopped the shaft, and now it was turning in the other direction. Before they could rise, they had to clear *Severodvinsk*'s hull. It wouldn't take much, but it would be a good thing if they hurried.

The vibration grew, and for a moment Jerry thought they might be entangled somehow, but the screw bit and he felt the deck shift as they backed away from the Russian's hull.

Rudel keyed the intercom. "Torpedo room, conn. Report! Are we clear?"

"Conn, torpedo room. We're clearing the hull, sir. We had almost half our bow under the Russian. I can see sternway on." Jerry was grateful for Palmer's report, and Maxine's ability to track their progress, because right now they were blind. While backing down, the pitlog was worthless. In fact, submarines were pigs with sternway on. Jerry could see the compass heading swing to port and starboard. It was a short trip, but it would have been even shorter if they could have kept the stern pointed in one direction.

"Conn, torpedo room. We are clear of *Severodvinsk*."

"Emergency surface! Left full rudder, all ahead flank! Dive, how's our trim?"

As McCord hit the chicken switches, Hess shook his head. "We're very heavy forward, with all that water in the bow."

"Well, for God's sake don't let our stern get too light."

"What we can't get over the side, we're moving aft, and the stern planes are starting to bite."

"Mr. Mitchell, give me a course," Rudel ordered.

"We can continue this port turn to two two five. That will keep us clear of the rest of the formation."

"Helm, steady on two two five."

"We are rising," Shimko announced, "we're coming up!"

Jerry felt his own spirits rise, and he studied the rest of the watch. He saw relief, excitement, fatigue, but no fear. They were done.

"All tanks blown, sir." McCord grinned, an infectious expression.

"Very well." Rudel answered with his own smile as well.

THEY SURFACED into five-foot swells and a high overcast. *Seawolf* shot out of the water like a drunken walrus, seesawing back and forth before she settled on the surface, seriously down by the bow. By the time they'd set the bridge watch, Rudel had turned them back toward the rest of the formation, a mile and a half distant.

Jerry and the other officers took turns coming up to the bridge to watch the rescue. He could see the black tile-covered escape chamber, bobbing like a child's ball. *Pamir* and *Altay* were standing by on each side, and the tug's sailors were helping the crewmen out and over to their two ships. Helicopters were taking turns lifting the injured from their fantails.

The bridge-to-bridge radio crackled to life while Jerry watched the two tugs go by. "USS *Seawolf,* this is *Petr Velikiy.* Please take station one thousand yards to starboard of my position. We wish to see if you have suffered any additional damage."

He passed the message to control, and Rudel approved the request. Jerry guided *Seawolf* toward the massive warship. It lay near the center of the Russian formation. Looking aft, he could see USS *Churchill* falling in trail, half a mile behind them.

Jerry studied the Russian vessel as they approached. It loomed over them, even from nearly a mile away. Being so low to the water didn't help either. The formation was only steaming at five knots, so they were overtaking slowly . . .

A shrill whistle blast cut through the air, coming from the battle cruiser's forecastle. Jerry saw men pouring out of the weather deck hatches. What was going on? Were they sounding General Quarters? Then he saw the crew arranging themselves along the edge of each deck, from the main deck up through the many stories of the superstructure.

They were manning the rails. Jerry hit the intercom. "Captain and XO, lay to the bridge."

The lookout tapped his shoulder and pointed to a destroyer on their starboard side. Jerry turned and saw its crew taking places along the railings as well. He quickly made a survey of the rest of the ships, and other than the two tugs, every ship in the Russian formation had its crew on deck.

They were only a few hundred yards short of their assigned station. Jerry called "Captain to the bridge!" with more urgency, and seconds later, Rudel appeared, followed by the XO. Both officers looked around frantically, searching. "What's wrong, Jerry? Is it the bow?"

They relaxed a little when they saw his calm expression, but then Jerry pointed to port, toward *Petr Velikiy*'s starboard bridge wing, two hundred yards ahead and a hundred feet above them. It was filled with blue and gold uniforms, all at attention and facing to starboard.

Rudel took Jerry's glasses and studied the group. "Migod. That's Borisov, and Kurganov, and Chicherin, and all their cousins and uncles." He keyed the intercom. "Chief, send up the XO's and my combo covers, and do it now!"

Rudel opened the hatch and tossed down his foul-weather coat. The XO followed suit. By that time, the chief had climbed up the ladder holding their uniform covers. They quickly replaced their ball caps.

They turned and faced to port just as *Seawolf* came abreast of the Russian flagship. Even at half a mile, they heard the shouts. An earsplitting blast from *Petr Velikiy*'s whistle carried across the water, and was echoed by the other ships in the task force. Led by Vice Admiral Borisov, every sailor in the task force saluted.

Standing stiffly at attention, Captain Rudel and his officers returned the Northern Fleet's salute.

EPILOGUE

Olga Sadilenko sat nervously on Ludmilla Tatiana's flower-print couch. She'd arrived early, and the two women tried to chat as the minute hand slowly crawled toward ten o'clock. They'd wanted this to be low-key, so Olga had arranged to meet them here, at her friend Ludmilla's apartment, instead of at her own apartment or the Wives and Mothers Organization's office.

Precisely at ten, they heard a knock, and Ludmilla had to force herself to pause for a moment before opening the door.

She'd seen photos of Rudel, taken from the Internet, but here he was, in a foreign-looking uniform. He was younger than she expected, and looked more like a college professor. Jerry Mitchell could have been one of his assistants, younger still, shorter and more athletic. Both smiled warmly, but they were nervous. She could tell.

"Mrs. Tatiana, I am pleased to meet you." Rudel had obviously been practicing the phrase, and Ludmilla drew them inside, smiling. A young Russian sailor, serving as driver and interpreter, stood outside until he was ushered in as well.

Olga stood, and Rudel walked over, taking her hands in his. "Mrs. Sadilenko, I am pleased to meet you." She almost laughed at Rudel's rote speech, but managed to turn it into a warm smile. They just stood, silently, for a moment, then she reached over to take one of Jerry's hands, welcoming him as well.

Ludmilla waited, then spoke to Rudel's driver. "Ask them if they will sit, and take tea."

Both men smiled and nodded, then sat while their hostess poured two steaming cups from her good tea set. With her guests served, Ludmilla urged one on the embarrassed driver as well.

"How is your son?" Rudel asked through the driver.

Olga answered, "I will see him again, later today. They say he is doing well, that soon he will learn to live with his grief." It was easier to speak of her Yakov, now that there was hope for him.

"He saved many lives," Jerry offered respectfully.

Olga sighed. "By killing his closest friend. It was a high price for both of them to pay."

Rudel paused for moment, struggling for words. Finally, he said, "I want to say how sorry I am, how sorry all my men are, for what . . ."

She held up a hand, stopping him. "Please, Captain." She laid a hand on his arm. "Nobody thinks this was your fault, or Captain Petrov's. These things are tragedies—something we can learn from, but that cannot be anticipated or prevented."

Then she reassured him, "You risked your own lives to save our men on *Severodvinsk*. That is what we will always remember."

Ludmilla came over with a plate of tea cakes, speaking softly. The driver explained to Rudel, "She says it is good you came, that friends can share grief, and make it hurt less."

A knock at the door called Ludmilla out of the conversation. It was Irina, holding a covered plate. "I brought some cake. Oh, am I too late? Are they already here?" A man in his late twenties, in a michman's uniform, stood behind her.

"As if you couldn't tell time, Irina Ivanova Rodionov!" Olga said sharply, but smiling at the same time. She then escorted the younger woman over and introduced her to the Americans, explaining, "She is our *webmaster*," using the English term. The michman saluted, and the three men shook hands, smiling.

Irina greeted them each with a hug. In English, she said, "I had to thank you myself." She looked over at her escort. "This is Michman Maksim Yerasov. He is the senior rating who works for my Anatoliy. He begged to come and meet you; to meet the men who saved them."

RUDEL AND Jerry were becoming rather uncomfortable with all the gratitude that was being heaped upon them. Clearing his throat, Jerry tried to change the subject. "Your husband isn't here?"

"No, Anatoliy is already at the inquest. Since he is the torpedo and mine battle department commander, he has been very busy."

After a moment of awkward silence, Rudel made another attempt at small talk. "So you are the one who constructed that amazing website?"

"Yes, yes, I did, with much help from Olga and the others. When Anatoliy was trapped, I had the computer to keep my mind busy, to help me not to worry so much, but whenever I stopped working . . ." She started to tear up, and Olga came over, squeezing her shoulder reassuringly.

"They wanted to apologize to us. Can you imagine such a thing?" Olga remarked brightly.

There was another knock on the door. This time it was Nadya. She held a bottle, and she was barely inside before another woman arrived.

It turned into quite a party, in spite of their planning. Jerry and Rudel had both wanted a quiet visit, and a chance to talk. But word had leaked out. Over a dozen couples, parents, and families came to see the men whose submarine had saved their loved ones. It wasn't raucous, but it was lively, an impromptu celebration of their survival, with Rudel and Jerry as the honored guests.

Finally, after almost two hours, and pleading a previous engagement, they managed to make their good-byes. Irina had given them email addresses for *Seawolf*'s webmaster to post, and every woman there hugged them both at least once. Ludmilla tried to send them away with food, but there was no way to bring any of it back.

Olga followed them outside, away from the noise of the party, and kissed them good-bye on the cheek, embracing the two like her own Yakov. "I am glad we met, even if I am sorry for the reason."

The driver translated, and Rudel answered, "I'm glad I came, too."

Jerry added, "Tell Mrs. Tatiana we're sorry for the mess. She is a very good host."

The driver spoke urgently in English, and Rudel apologized, "I'm sorry to leave so soon, but we have another appointment."

Olga nodded. "I know, and thank you for that as well. Will we see you at the memorial service? I double-checked. Dennis Rountree's name will be read with the rest."

Both nodded. "Thank you. We'll be there by six," Rudel promised as he climbed into the car. He nodded toward the driver. "Pavel says he knows the way to the church."

Olga watched the car drive away, then went back to the party.

DWIGHT MANNING and a knot of Russian officers were waiting on the steps when they pulled up outside. Manning almost pulled Rudel from the car. "This is cutting it just a little too close."

"There was traffic," Rudel apologized.

Manning turned to face the waiting Russians. "Captain First Rank Aleksey Igorevich Petrov, may I present Commander Thomas Rudel."

Rudel and Jerry and saluted Petrov, the senior in rank; then Rudel offered his hand. Jerry studied them both, but their faces were masks, at first.

Petrov took Rudel's hand, grasping it firmly. He said, "I am pleased to finally meet you," in a formal voice. He didn't smile, but Russians don't automatically smile just to be pleasant.

Rudel did smile. "It's good to meet you face-to-face. You sound different than you did over the underwater telephone."

Petrov asked curiously. "How so?"

"Drier," Rudel replied.

Surprised, Petrov burst into laughter, and clapped Rudel on the shoulder. "And you sound different, too, my friend. Not like a wobbly fish."

"Gentlemen, we have two minutes," fussed Manning.

Both captains nodded. "Later, we will talk," promised Petrov.

"I would like that very much," Rudel answered.

The rest of the group was quickly introduced. Jerry waited for his turn to shake Petrov's hand, and to greet the Starpom Kalinin and Chief Engineer Lyachin. The last few words were exchanged as Manning urged them up the granite steps. The sentry in front braced and saluted as the group hurried past.

Inside, they slowed to a fast walk, and made one turn to face an oak door, marked by a flag on a stand. "We made it," Manning announced with a glare, "with one minute to go." He brushed a few cake crumbs off Jerry's uniform.

Another guard, a junior officer this time, saluted. He opened the door for them, then stepped aside.

The far side of the room was lined with leaded-glass

windows. The walls were columned marble, adorned with paintings of great naval battles. A long green table sat in front of the windows, one side half filled with high-ranking officers, facing them. Jerry recognized Borisov, and Kurganov, and Vidchenko.

Chairs filled the room, with most of them occupied by naval officers, with the occasional civilian mixed in.

Petrov pointed to three empty chairs one row back as they hurried up the center aisle. They had slips of paper taped to them with "Rudel," "Mitchell," and "Manning" spelled in Cyrillic, and below in English. Petrov, Kalinin, and Lyachin joined the rest of *Severodvinsk*'s wardroom, already seated in the front row.

They'd barely sat down when a shouted command brought everyone in the room to attention. Jerry rose with the rest, and watched as a party of senior officers entered from a side door. "The one in front is Vice Admiral Kokurin, commander of the Northern Fleet," Manning explained in a whisper, "then Vice Admiral Baybarin, his deputy. Vice Admiral Radetskiy is his chief of staff . . ."

The group reached their seats at the table, and stood for a moment before turning to face the Russian flag, displayed at one end of the table. The recorded strains of the Russian national anthem played; then, at another command, everyone sat.

Kokurin spoke first, and Manning translated. "We meet here to investigate the loss of the Russian Federation submarine *Severodvinsk* and the death and injuries suffered by its crew. We thank those who have come far to testify. There is much to learn from this tragedy. May we all grow in wisdom."

AFTERWORD

Authors choose names to provide clues to a character's personality, to help make them easier to remember, or sometimes to say hello to an old friend. In this case, the names of the crews aboard *Severodvinsk* and *Seawolf* were taken, with some minor exceptions, from the rosters of USS *Thresher* (SSN-593), USS *Scorpion* (SSN-589), and the Russian Project 949A SSGN *Kursk*.

All we used were their last names. The characters' physical descriptions, their personalities, their actions, and their words are entirely our own. We wanted to use these names so that they would be heard once more, and not pass from memory.

All three crews perished in peacetime accidents. Considering the number of miles steamed by submarines and how long they have been doing it, submarines have a very low accident rate, but going to sea in a ship designed to submerge beneath the waves will always involve a higher degree of risk.

Those who sail on submarines accept this risk as a part of their service, which is also demanding and difficult. Thousands of men, and some women, are serving right now, and we honor their service with this story.